MONTANA SKIES

*The Legacy of Faith and Love
Continues in Four Complete Novels*

Ann Bell

BARBOUR
PUBLISHING

ISBN 1-58660-508-9

Cover by Michael Melford/The Image Bank

Published by Barbour Publishing, Inc., P.O. Box 719, Uhrichsville, Ohio 44683, www.barbourbooks.com.

 Member of the
Evangelical Christian
Publishers Association

Printed in the United States of America.
5 4

ANN BELL

Ann is a librarian by profession and lives in Iowa with her husband, Jim, who is her biggest supporter. Ann has worked as a librarian and teacher in Iowa, Oregon, Guam, and Montana. She has been honored in the top three picks of **Heartsong Presents** members' favorite authors. Her eight **Heartsong** books all center around a fictional town in Montana called Rocky Bluff. She has also written numerous articles for Christian magazines and a book titled *Proving Yourself: A Study of James.*

Healing Love

*Dedicated to the caring people of Montana
who have devoted their lives to comforting victims of violent crime.*

Chapter 1

Angie, can you hear me?" Serafina Cruz gasped as she knelt beside her friend's motionless body.

Angie didn't respond. A trickle of blood oozed from a cut on the side of her head.

Serafina's face blanched as she surveyed the darkened campus. In the distance a familiar figure emerged from the library. "Steve, hurry. Angie's hurt."

Steve Salas raced across the lawn of Guam Community College. "Oh, no. What happened? She looks terrible." He leaned closer and shook the injured woman's shoulder. "Angie, can you hear me?"

Angela Quinata moaned and turned her head. The look of terror in her eyes softened as she recognized her classmates. "Help me," she whispered. "I can't move." Steve turned and raced toward the phone in the entryway of the library.

Serafina brushed Angela's blood-soaked dark hair away from her eyes. "Just relax. Steve's calling an ambulance. Everything'll be okay."

Angela closed her eyes, seemingly unaware of her friend kneeling beside her. Tears filled Serafina's eyes as she straightened Angela's rumpled skirt. "Please, God. . . Please help us. Angie's hurt, and I don't know what to do."

Serafina studied her friend's battered body. Her eyes settled on the scratches and bruises on Angie's legs. She pulled back in horror. "Please, God, don't let her have been raped. She's the most innocent girl I know. . . . Please help her."

Through the darkness, Serafina caught sight of Steve racing across the freshly mown lawn. "The ambulance is on its way," Steve shouted as he neared his classmates.

The minutes ticked by slowly as Serafina continued holding Angie's hand, while Steve paced nervously beside them. A warm trade breeze rustled through the palm trees. Their tense nerves jerked as a coconut hit the sidewalk and rolled onto the soggy grass. Angie's five-foot two-inch frame resembled a broken Barbie doll as she moaned and turned her head. She never responded to her friend's encouraging words.

Sirens pierced the tropical night air as red flashing lights reflected against the encircling palm trees. The ambulance screeched to a stop in the nearby

7

parking lot, and three attendants jumped out. Two of them raced to the back, flung open the door of the ambulance, and pulled out a gurney, while the driver grabbed a large black kit.

Serafina released her classmate's hand as the Emergency Medical Team approached. The driver knelt beside the injured woman as Serafina stepped aside.

"What happened?"

"I don't know. I found her lying here covered with blood."

The driver wrapped a blood pressure tunic around Angela's arm and squeezed the ball as he stared at the gauge. He took a pen from his pocket and recorded his findings on a clipboard. "Both her pulse and blood pressure are a little low." He gently lifted her head. "It looks like she took a mighty powerful blow on the head, and she's lost a lot of blood."

The tall, graying attendant knelt beside the driver. "Do you see any other injuries?"

The driver shone his flashlight up and down her body. The light settled on Angie's trim legs. "Oh, no," he gasped. "I don't like the way her legs are bruised. We better admit her to the hospital as a possible rape victim."

The driver rose to his feet and moved the gurney as close to Angie as possible, while the other attendants positioned themselves at the victim's head and feet. They moved smoothly and methodically, so as not to cause additional pain to their patient. Angie moaned as the medical team lifted her gently to the stretcher. "Mama? Mama, where are you?"

Serafina's knees trembled as she again took her friend's hand. "Don't worry, Angie. Steve and I will follow the ambulance to the hospital. I'll contact your mother from the emergency room. Just relax. . . You're in good hands now."

Angie's eyes opened, and the corner of her mouth turned up slightly. Her mother's face flashed before her as she imagined her mother holding her in her arms as she did when she hurt herself as child. Gradually her eyes began to fade as her forehead creased once more. "Where's Mama?" she muttered, then closed her eyes.

❖

Mitzi Quinata reread the letter she had just completed to a former colleague at Guam Christian Academy. Rarely had she made such a close friendship with a teacher from the mainland who stayed on Guam for only two years, just long enough to complete a teacher's contract, but Rebecca Sutherland Hatfield was different. She didn't carry the distant, aloof mannerism that many of the statesiders did. Rebecca appeared genuinely concerned for the Guamanians as people. She'd started several peer support groups for those in crisis and spent many hours before and after school counseling students.

Mitzi pictured her matronly friend as she was bidding her farewell at the Won Pat International Airport exactly one year before. Rebecca was aglow with the excitement of returning to Montana and her upcoming marriage. She had agreed to teach in Guam for two years after retiring from Rocky Bluff High School. Rebecca had walked to her plane anticipating a relaxing retirement, but her letters to Mitzi the last few months reflected a busy, productive life. Married life had been exhilarating for her. She described the beauty of the Montana mountains and the peacefulness of the small lake nearby. She talked about the friendliness of the people and their enjoyment of the outdoor sports available in that area.

I wish I could visit Rebecca in Montana, Mitzi smiled. *The way she describes it, Rocky Bluff is next to heaven on earth. Nothing could possibly be that perfect.*

The ringing of the telephone interrupted Mitzi's thoughts. She laid her pen and paper on the kitchen table and hurried to the phone. "Hello."

"Hello, Mrs. Quinata?"

Wrinkles deepened on Mitzi's forehead as a knot built in her stomach. "Yes."

"Are you Angela's mother?"

"Yes, I am. Is something wrong?"

"I'm afraid so." Taking a deep breath, the young woman continued. "This is Serafina Cruz. I'm a classmate of Angie's. She was attacked on the GCC campus and taken to the hospital in an ambulance."

Mitzi's bronze face turned ashen. "What happened?"

"Steve Salas and I found her in the bushes between the administration building and the library. She was covered with blood. We called an ambulance and followed it to the hospital. Angie keeps asking for you."

"Tell her I'll be right there," Mitzi gasped as she flung the phone into its cradle.

She grabbed her purse and raced toward her car. A gentle rain soaked her flowered blouse and blended with the tears on her cheeks. *Please, God, help Angie. Don't let anything happen to her.*

The drive to Guam Memorial Hospital normally would have taken Mitzi twenty minutes, but the traffic was light, and fifteen minutes after Serafina's phone call, Mitzi raced through the emergency room door.

"Mrs. Quinata?" Serafina said as the plump, graying woman stepped into the entryway.

Mitzi forced a smile and extended her hand. "You must be Serafina. Thank you for coming to the hospital with Angie. I'm so glad she has friends like you. How is she?"

"She's in X-ray right now." Serafina's words tumbled from her lips in rapid succession, while her voice became high and tense. "The nurse said that she's beginning to regain consciousness, and there are other positive signs. However, they can't be sure until all the tests are completed."

Mitzi's eyes roamed the corridors. "I've got to see her." She paced around the lobby looking for someone in charge. Her hands were clutched as the perspiration dripped from her forehead. "Where is everyone? There should be someone at the desk."

"There usually is," Steve replied, "but when they admitted Angie, they said they were short of staff tonight. I understand that several of the nurses are in Honolulu for a training session."

Mitzi continued to pace. "I can't understand how anything like this could happen. Angie's always so careful when she's out at night by herself."

Moments later, a nurse dressed in a white pants suit with blood stains on her smock hurried toward the concerned three. "Are you Angela Quinata's mother?"

"Yes, I'm Mitzi Quinata. How's Angie?"

"She received a severe blow to the head and has lost a lot of blood, but the X-rays didn't show any fracture to the skull. It took twenty-five stitches to close the wound. We'd like to keep her overnight for observation."

Mitzi studied the deep furrows on the nurse's face. "Do you think there'll be permanent damage?"

The nurse shrugged her shoulders. "The physical injuries will heal, but she's been sexually assaulted and is terribly upset. The emotional injuries are often the hardest to heal."

"Does anyone know who did it?"

"The police are on their way to interview Angie. I'd think it'd be best if you were present when they arrive. She needs a lot of moral support."

"I'll do everything I can," Mitzi choked, while her eyes filled with tears as she noticed the reddish stains on the nurse's uniform. "Where is she?"

"Examining Room Four. Follow me."

Serefina waved good-bye as Mitzi obeyed the nurse. "I'll check with you tomorrow to see how she's doing."

Mitzi's knees trembled as she hurried down the hallway. She took a deep breath as the nurse pushed open the door to Examining Room Number Four. She stifled a gasp as she recognized her daughter. Angie was lying on the bed quietly sobbing. Both her eyes were blackened and swollen. The left side of her long black hair had been shaved and replaced by an enormous gauze bandage. "Hi, Darling," Mitzi whispered as she leaned over to kiss her daughter's forehead. "How are you?"

Angie clutched her mother's hand. "Mom, you're finally here."

"I came just as soon as I heard what happened."

Angie's sobs increased. "It was awful. I could withstand the beating, but a stranger stole what I was saving for my husband. I feel so dirty."

Mitzi bit her lip and tried to force a smile. "Angie, you're a brave girl. It's over now. Just relax and think about the bright future ahead of you. . . Graduation. . .a new career. . .romance."

"My future's over."

"No, Honey. You have your whole life before you. You'll feel better tomorrow. Saturday night is graduation, and you'll be receiving one of the highest honors in your class. Everyone is so proud of you."

"No, Mother. You don't understand. I can't attend my graduation. I won't be able to bear having people whispering about what happened."

"Of course no one will blame you. People will understand. You'll be surprised how compassionate people can be."

"That doesn't change the facts of what happened. My future's over. No man will ever want a spoiled woman, especially not the good ones like Jay."

Mitzi swallowed hard and wiped a tear from Angie's cheek. "Jay loves you. He'll accept you just the way you are."

"He deserves better. Besides, I can't let him see me now. Look how ugly I am. I'm covered with bruises, and part of my head is shaved."

"Angie, you'll be able to hide most of the bruises under makeup and get a wig to hide the bandages."

The pain of watching her bright, vivacious daughter in such depths of despair was almost more than Mitzi could bear. Her words seemed trite compared to the magnitude of Angie's pain. "Your hair will grow back, and your bruises will heal. They're just surface injuries," she persisted as she wiped away the tears from Angie's cheek.

Angie's eyes became distant. She continued to cry for several minutes, while her mother stood helplessly beside her bed. "What did I do to deserve this? Why is God punishing me? Ever since I was a kid, I tried my hardest to please Him. Why did He let this happen?"

Mitzi studied her daughter's troubled face. "Darling, God isn't punishing you," she said as she squeezed her daughter's hand. "As long as there's evil in this world, bad things are going to happen. You just happened to be in the wrong place at the wrong time."

Angie shook her head. "I should have been more careful. I knew better than to stay so late, then walk across campus alone. God's punishing me for my stupidity."

"Angie, God doesn't work that way. Right now you're hurt and upset. After a night's rest, you'll feel better. As you close your eyes tonight, visualize yourself wrapped in God's loving arms."

"Mother, it's not all that easy. You don't understand. You've never been raped."

Mitzi bit her lip. *I would lay down my life for her. Why doesn't she understand that I don't have to be raped to share her pain?*

Slowly, the examining room door opened, and the nurse entered, followed by two police officers.

"How are you doing, Angie?" the nurse asked as she approached the distraught patient.

Angie tried to gain her composure. "I don't think I'll ever be able to stop crying."

"You'll feel a little stronger tomorrow," the nurse assured her, then motioned to the two police officers. "I'd like you to meet Officers Irene Santos and Vincente Muñoz. They'd like to talk with you about what happened tonight."

Angie forced a smile as she surveyed the trim woman officer and her male partner standing rigid and businesslike. "Hello," she murmured.

"Hello, Angie," Officer Santos greeted as she reached for the young woman's hand and shook it gently. "Do you mind if we ask you a few questions?"

A lump built in Angie's throat. The thought of rehashing the events of the last few hours terrified her. "I don't remember much of what happened," she murmured.

"We'll try to make this as easy as possible. We know the trauma you've been through," Officer Santos said. Officer Muñoz carried two chairs from the waiting room and placed them on the left side of Angie's bed, while Mitzi remained seated on the right, unwilling to leave her daughter's side.

Officer Muñoz took a tape recorder from his pocket and placed it on the table beside the bed. "I hope you don't mind if we record this. We don't want to miss any details. We need all the help you can give us to find the person who hurt you before he hurts someone else."

Angie shrugged her shoulders with resignation.

"Angie, will you tell us exactly what happened tonight?" Officer Santos asked gently.

"I told you that I don't remember anything." Angie clutched her fists under the sheet. She just wanted everyone to leave her alone. Each question became more and more difficult.

"Let's take it step-by-step," Officer Santos replied gently. "I've worked with a number of women who were assaulted. The first time a victim talks about the attack is the hardest, and it occasionally takes awhile before they remember the details."

"I'll try my best," Angie whispered without commitment.

"What was the last building you were in?"

"I took the final exam for my customer relations class in the main class-room building."

"What time was that?"

Angie hesitated. A look of puzzlement covered her face. Gradually a light of recognition appeared in her eyes. "I finished my test about eight-thirty, but I stayed after class to talk with the instructor. It must've been getting close to nine o'clock when I actually left the building."

"Did you see anyone else as you left?"

"No, the campus was deserted by then."

"Who was the instructor you met with?"

"Leon Paplos. He's an excellent teacher and is helping me get a job."

Angie did not notice Officer Muñoz stiffen at the name of the head of the cosmetology department at the community college, but Mitzi directed a puzzled glance at him which he ignored.

"Did Mr. Paplos leave at the same time you did?"

"No. He said he was going to work late and try to get most of the tests graded before he went home."

"As you crossed the campus did you see anyone else?" Officer Santos continued.

Angie's stomach tightened. "No one," she choked. "That's why I thought I'd cut across the lawn in front of the administration building to get to the parking lot."

"Then what happened?"

Angie remained silent for a couple moments, then began to sob uncontrollably. Mitzi leaned over the bed and cradled her daughter against her breast. "It's okay, Darling," she whispered, stroking her daughter's hair. "It's over now. You're safe with us."

Hearing Angie's hysterical cries, the nurse hurried back to the emergency room. She went to a cupboard in the corner of the room and unlocked the case. Meticulously, she filled a syringe as Mitzi continued to hold and comfort her daughter. "I think we'd better give her something to calm her. Being this upset is not good for her head injury."

Within seconds, the relaxing fluid entered Angie's bloodstream, and she lay back on her pillow and closed her eyes.

Mitzi tucked the blanket under her daughter's chin and returned to her chair beside the bed. "Poor dear, she's been through so much. I wish I could take her pain away."

"As much as you'd like to ease her pain, in the end, the victim is the only one who can bring about healing," Officer Santos replied. "Healing comes in time, but the more that society victimizes the victim with its attitudes, the longer the healing takes."

"I hope Angie's strong religious background will help her conquer this, but so far it seems her training is more of a handicap than a help. Somehow she blames herself for what happened."

Officer Santos nodded with understanding. "Religious people often suffer the most emotional pain after a rape because they falsely blame themselves."

"What can I do to help her?" Mitzi begged as her eyes settled on her battered daughter.

"Only a proper understanding of the love of God can heal her pain," Officer Santos replied. "I wish I had an easy answer for you."

After the nurse disposed of the syringe, she turned to the police officers. "She's not going to be able to talk for awhile. Would you mind coming back tomorrow morning? We'll be moving her to a private room in a few minutes."

"We'll be back first thing in the morning. I hope she'll be able to talk then. We can't let the perpetrator get too far ahead of us."

Officer Muñoz picked up his tape recorder and placed it in his pocket. "We need to go by the campus and see if we can get any information. We'd like to have the attacker in custody as soon as possible."

Within minutes, two orderlies arrived and moved Angie to a private room on the third floor. Mitzi remained by her sleeping daughter's side until the wee hours of the morning. Finally, overwhelmed by mental and physical exhaustion, she scribbled her telephone number on a slip of paper and handed it to the ward nurse on her way out of the building. "Call me if Angie awakens and needs me. I better get some sleep tonight, or I won't be of much help to her tomorrow."

"We'll let you know if there's any change," the nurse assured her. "The best thing for you is to get some sleep. It's been quite an ordeal for both of you. We'll take good care of your daughter."

Mitzi left the hospital parking lot and turned onto Marine Drive. She scarcely recognized the well-traveled street. What was familiar to her in the daylight looked so different at night. In the daytime normal, middle-class people went about their lives, earning a living, shopping, and visiting friends. Now the streets were full of prostitutes, pimps, and drug addicts. *I never knew this kind of lifestyle was present on Guam. I've always felt safe on our little island getaway.*

As the lights of Agana disappeared into the background, Mitzi's mind drifted back to her sleeping daughter lying sedated in the island hospital. *I wonder what tomorrow will bring for her? Angie has to accept what has happened to her and go on with her life. She kept saying, "Jay will never want a spoiled woman."*

But I've found that Jay is the most understanding young man I've ever met. I'm sure he'll be the key to her recovery.

As Mitzi turned onto the Cross Island Road, she pictured the tall, dark-haired airman from Andersen Air Force Base at the northern end of the island. Ever since Rebecca Sutherland introduced Angie to the young man from her hometown, Angie and Jay Harkness had been inseparable. Usually, Mitzi had ignored the large military population on the island, but somehow Jay was different. Like his former teacher and librarian, Jay took a special interest in the local people and their customs. He escorted Angie to as many of the fiestas and local celebrations as he could. However, it was obvious that Rocky Bluff was never far from his heart. As much as he was involved in island affairs, his heart was always in Montana. During the months that Angie had been dating Jay, Mitzi noticed the same interest in getting to know other peoples and cultures develop in her own daughter. *Would their love survive such a difference in backgrounds? Would this tragedy destroy or strengthen their relationship? Could Jay be able to restore her daughter's zest for living?*

When she got home, Mitzi stumbled toward her front door, unlocked it, and headed straight for the bedroom. Without removing her clothes, she fell across her bed. Every cell in her body was crying for sleep. For three hours she scarcely moved, but when the first rays of morning sun streamed through the east window, Mitzi bolted upright. *I have to talk to Jay before he goes to work. I don't want him to read about Angie's assault in the* Pacific Daily News.

Mitzi fumbled through the drawer under the phone and found her list of special phone numbers. She punched the numbers on the handset and waited for what seemed like an eternity.

"Hello," a sleepy voice greeted.

"Hello, is this Jay Harkness?"

"Yes, it is," the airman replied as he wiped the sleep from his eyes.

"This is Mitzi Quinata, Angie's mother." Mitzi took a deep breath as she tried to choose her words carefully. "I'm calling to let you know that Angie was admitted to the hospital last night."

Jay bolted upright in bed. "What happened?"

"Last night she was assaulted and raped as she was walking across the campus. She was knocked unconscious, and it took twenty-five stitches in her head to close the wound. They kept her in the hospital overnight for observation." Mitzi's voice trembled as she retold the details.

Jay was immediately on his feet. "Is she going to be all right?"

"I hope so," she sighed. "The nurse doesn't think there'll be any lasting physical damage, but Angie's extremely despondent. They had to give her a sedative. Hopefully, she'll be better today."

"That's terrible," Jay gasped. "I'll call my first sergeant right away and see if I can take the day off to be with her."

"Before you see her, I must warn you that she feels she's been ruined for life and that no man would ever want her again."

Jay sighed as he buried his face in his hands. A new tone of determination entered his voice. "She's not a spoiled woman to me. In the sixteen months that I've known her, she's become very precious to me. I'll just have to prove to her that God's love and my love are stronger than her own fears and false guilt."

Chapter 2

An antiseptic smell permeated the corridors of Guam Island Hospital as Jay Harkness paused at the third-floor nurses' station. He was tall and imposing in his dress uniform. He had dreamed of being an airman since he was a child, and now he wore the United States Air Force blues with pride.

"May I help you?" the ward clerk asked as she removed her computer glasses and laid them on the counter beside her.

"Where may I find Angela Quinata?"

The clerk frowned as she surveyed the handsome, young airman. "She's in Room 314, but she won't be able to have visitors now. The police are with her, and it could be some time before they're finished. You can wait in the cafeteria if you'd like."

"Thanks, but if it's all right with you, I'd rather wait at the end of the hall. I want to be as close to her as possible."

"Suit yourself, but the waiting area on this floor is rather limited." Jay turned the corner and strolled down the corridor. He paused in front of Room 314. The door was closed. He took a deep breath. The girl he loved was behind that door, yet he could not go in. Glancing around he noticed a sofa under the window at the end of the hall. Dejectedly he slumped onto the lumpy cushions. *This is the time Angie needs me the most, and I'm not able to be with her. I bet she's scared to death.*

Jay stared at the hands of the hall clock for what seemed like hours. Only the second hand appeared to move. While growing up, he had spent a great deal of time visiting in hospitals during his grandparents' long illnesses, but that was nothing compared to the desperation he felt waiting to see his best friend and sweetheart. The young airman surveyed his drab surroundings. Everything was scrubbed clean, but the paint on the walls was faded, and the fixtures were antique compared to the modern community hospital in Rocky Bluff. *If only I could take Angie back to Montana where she'd get personalized care with the latest technology and professionals.*

The large hand on the hall clock inched its way to the bottom of the case. Jay watched the hospital personnel go about their routine tasks. The hustle

17

and bustle of Montana hospitals was strangely missing. Activity was relaxed and slow, yet the work seemed to get done quietly and efficiently. At long last, two police officers emerged from Room 314 and closed the door gently behind them.

"She'll probably never recover from this," the woman officer whispered to her partner. "In all my years of rape investigation, I've never dealt with a victim who felt it was so important to save herself for her future husband. With her self-imposed guilt I wonder if she'll ever marry."

The male policeman shook his head. "I thought that attitude went out with the sexual revolution of the sixties."

"With all the sexually transmitted diseases going around today, I wish more young people had Angie's values. It would make our job a lot easier."

As soon as the officers turned the corner at the nurses' station, Jay knocked softly on the door.

"Come in." It was Mitzi's voice.

Jay gasped as he scarcely recognized Angie who was sobbing into her pillow. Mitzi was sitting on the side of her daughter's bed, rubbing her back gently.

"Hello, Jay. I'm glad you could come. Did you have to wait long?" Mitzi queried.

"Too long," Jay replied as he hurried to Angie's bedside. "I've been here about a half hour." He put his hand on Angie's shoulder and spoke softly. "Angie, how are you doing?"

She rolled over and shook her head vigorously. "Talking with the police was absolutely awful," she cried. "They expected me to remember every detail that happened. . . . But it was dark and I couldn't see anything. . . . I tried to fight, but the man was too strong. Then he hit me over the head."

"Whoever did this to you should be behind bars," Jay snarled, then tried to soften his approach as Angie grimaced. "It sounds like the police don't have a good description to go on."

"I'm afraid not. There was something distinctive about him, but I can't put my finger on it," she sighed. "Maybe someday it'll come to me. But now I don't want to remember what happened. . . . It's too ugly."

Jay stroked her forehead. "It's over, Sweetheart. We can go on with our lives and forget all this. . . . When will you be able to go home?"

Angie wiped the tears from her eyes and set her jaw firmly in place. "I'll never be able to forget this." She pounded her fist into the mattress, then paused. She took a deep breath and tried to force a smile. "The doctor said I can go home by noon. . .which is none to soon for me. I just want to get to my own apartment. . .away from this maddening world."

"Hospitals have never been my favorite place, either," Jay agreed sympathetically. "I'll drive you home when you're released. I've taken the entire day off work so I'll be able to stay with you for awhile."

"Jay, I'd appreciate you staying with Angie for a few hours. I don't want her to be alone in her condition," Mitzi whispered, unable to mask her fatigue. "I'd rather have her come home with me for a few days, but she insists on being in her own apartment. Knowing she's in good hands, I can go home and rest without worrying. I'll call you later in the evening."

Angie's eyes danced. "You don't have to fuss over me," she protested. "I'm able to take care of myself. I don't need to be pampered."

Jay took her hand and pressed it to his lips. "Angie, we love you and want to help you."

Tears again gathered in Angie's eyes as she pulled her hand away from his. "Jay, our relationship is over. I vowed I would keep myself pure for my future husband, and now I'm ruined." She fumbled with the friendship ring on her finger and placed it in Jay's palm. "Take your ring back. I'm never going to have anything to do with men again."

Mitzi watched as the pain built in Jay's eyes. They exchanged panicky glances. Each hoped the other had the magic words to calm her, but neither did. Jay clutched Angie's hand next to his cheek. "Sweetheart, you're still the same beautiful woman you were yesterday at this time. Your body and spirit may have been wounded, but God's in the healing business. I'll keep this ring in my pocket, and when you're feeling better, I'll be honored to place it back on your finger. I still love you, and God still loves you."

"That may be so, but I don't feel God's love. . . I feel He's abandoned me. Why did He let this happen?" Angie surveyed Jay's worried face as she continued to bombard him. "Can you answer my question? Why did this have to happen to me?"

"Angie, don't torture yourself with all these questions. You were simply in the wrong place at the wrong time," Jay said, holding her hand as he sat on the edge of the bed. "As long as there's evil in the world, bad things are going to happen to good people. But God still loves you regardless of what happens. He gives us strength to get through the rough times."

Angie shrugged her shoulders in disbelief. "That's what Mom said," she retorted, "but when I look at my bruised body and remember what I lost last night, how can I possibly feel God's love?"

"Fortunately, God's love is not based on our feelings. It's present even when we're least aware of it. Your Christian friends will support and uphold you with love and prayers until you can feel God's love again."

"I wish I could believe you," Angie sighed, "but I'll never be the same again."

"Of course you won't be the same. In the end you'll be a much stronger person, able to help others going through similar situations."

The door creaked open. A doctor and a floor nurse entered the room. Angie immediately pasted a phony smile on her face.

"How are you doing today?" Dr. Cruz asked brightly. "Are you ready to go home?"

Angie smiled. "You better believe it," she replied, trying to act equally as bright. However, her words could not mask her inner turmoil. *If the doctor knew how I really am, he'd never let me out of here.*

The doctor glanced at Jay and Mitzi, then turned back to his patient. "Angie, if your guests will step outside the room, I'll do a quick examination. If everything checks out, you can be on your way."

"I can hardly wait," she said, sitting upright in her hospital bed.

"I wish I could leave as well," the doctor chuckled. "It's a beautiful day outside. The sun's shining, and there's a slight trade breeze."

As Dr. Cruz took out his stethoscope, Mitzi and Jay walked into the hallway. The worried mother smiled at the young airman as they approached the sofa at the end of the corridor. "I'm glad you came. I could talk and talk but never get Angie to accept the fact that she's still the same person she was yesterday. You're the best one to get through to her."

Jay shook his head and sighed. "I'm not doing a very good job of it right now."

"You're doing a lot better than I am. Angie needs your love now more than ever."

Jay shook his head and wrung his hands. "I feel so helpless," he confessed as he watched a ship sail from nearby Apra Harbor. *If only my family were here to help me. I need more wisdom now than I ever have in my life,* he thought as he pictured his mother's and grandmother's faces.

He turned back to Mitzi. "With God's strength I'll do my best to help her," he sighed. "I never realized how much I loved her until I saw her there, bruised and hurting. She's a woman worth waiting for."

Angie's mother nodded knowingly. "I feel equally helpless. I wish I could suffer this pain in her place," she sighed. "Watching her suffer is breaking my heart."

The pair sat in silence for several minutes. Words could not express their grief. Finally Mitzi spoke. "After I take a nap, I'm going to get a letter off to Rebecca Hatfield asking her to pray. While she was librarian at my school, she seemed to have a direct pipeline to heaven. I don't know anything about Rocky Bluff, Montana, but I've met two dynamic Christian people from there."

Jay's face flushed as a slight grin covered his lips. "That's nothing; you should meet my grandmother," he replied with marked pride. "Her body may be wearing out, but she's a tremendous prayer warrior. She may not be able to get out as much as she used to, but we all know we have Grandma's prayers supporting us. As soon as I can, I'm going to call Mother and ask her to call Grandma. When Grandma prays, things happen."

Mitzi stared out the window at the parking lot lined with palm trees. *So much has happened in the last twenty-four hours. Will we ever be able to restore our lives to normal again?* They sat in silence as the clock ticked softly beside them. Mitzi became pensive. "I wish I had your grandma's kind of faith, but I become too impatient when my prayers aren't answered right away. . . . To be honest, this is the first time my faith has really been put to the test. Sure, little things have happened, but never anything like this."

"Grandma's been through a lot in her life, and instead of giving up and becoming bitter, she drew closer to the Lord. Everyone in town looks up to her. They even named the new wing of the high school after her."

"What an inspiration. I'd like to go to Rocky Bluff someday, if she's an example of the kind of people who live there. Guam has become such a melting pot of nationalities that we've lost our own identity. No one seems to care much about anyone else anymore. It's not what it used to be."

"Don't get the wrong idea. Rocky Bluff isn't heaven on earth, regardless of what Rebecca led you to believe," Jay tried to explain. "We've more than our share of problems and crime, but we always hang together during a crisis."

Now it was Jay's turn to become pensive. He pictured the small lake just outside of town with the Rocky Mountains providing a protective tower. He remembered the Easter sunrise service held on the banks of its glistening waters. He thought of his favorite Scripture, *"I lift up my eyes to the hills—where does my help come from? My help comes from the Lord, the Maker of heaven and earth."* He ran his hands across the knees of his uniform and stared down the hallway. "In a way Rebecca is right. Rocky Bluff is a special place. When I graduated from high school, I couldn't wait to get away from there, but regardless of how much I love Guam now, I'm counting the months until I can get back."

Mitzi nodded and placed her hand on the airman's shoulder. "That's so common around the world. Many of our graduating seniors hurry to the mainland, but one by one they return. There's something in each of us which yearns for the place of our upbringing. Some people can move home again, but others only return in their hearts."

Just then the door of Room 314 opened. The nurse turned toward the nurses' station, while the doctor headed toward the anxious pair waiting on the sofa.

Jay and Mitzi rose as he approached. "Angie's doing fine. With a little rest and a lot of tender loving care, she'll be back to normal in a couple days. However, she needs to see me in my office in five days to have the stitches taken out of her head and to do more tests."

Mitzi extended her hand to the doctor. "Doctor, thanks for all you've done. I feel that Angie has the best care available anywhere."

"Thank you, Mrs. Quinata. You have a lovely daughter," he replied as he shook her hand. "One other thing," he continued cautiously. "Keep an eye on her mental state. Her faked cheerfulness doesn't fool anyone. She's in a deep state of depression. Hopefully, it will lift in a few days; otherwise I'd suggest seeking outside counseling."

"We'll keep a close eye on her. She has a lot of friends and family to help her through this."

"Tender loving care and time are the greatest healers in the world," the doctor said as he turned to leave.

Mitzi and Jay returned to Angie's room where she was sitting on the edge of the bed trying to comb what little hair she had left.

"Are you ready to go home?" Jay teased.

Angie grinned. "The sooner the better."

"Good. I'll bring the car to the front entrance while your mother helps you dress. Just remember you're going to be stepping into a different and brighter world. You can now be categorized as a survivor. You can have the confidence that with God's help you are able to conquer anything."

"I may be a survivor, but I don't have the confidence to face the outside world," Angie retorted. Jay leaned over and kissed her gently on her lips, muffling her protests.

As Jay left the room, a sense of determination overwhelmed him. He would do his best not to let Angie dwell on the negative, but it was going to be difficult to put any type of positive spin on Angie's tragedy.

Jay parked his car near the emergency room door and met Angie and Mitzi at the doorway. Mitzi hugged her daughter, then said good-bye to Jay. She walked to her car in the distant parking lot, while Jay helped Angie to his car parked in the loading zone.

As they entered the hospital courtyard, Angie blinked against the tropical sun. *What right does the sun have to keep shining when my world has fallen apart? I'd feel much better if a torrential rain were falling.*

Sensing her uneasiness, Jay put his arm around her shoulder. "Are you all right?"

Angie shrugged her shoulders. "I wish I had a hat," she said as Jay opened the car door for her. "I don't want anyone to see my shaved head and bandages."

"After you're settled into your apartment, I'll run to the mall for you," Jay promised. "Let me know if there's anything else you'll need. My time is your time for the rest of the day."

Angie heaved a sigh of frustration. "I'm embarrassed to say this, but I'll need a pair of heavy-duty sunglasses. I don't want anyone to see my black eyes."

Jay slid behind the wheel, fastened his seat belt, and started the engine. "No problem at all," he assured her. "But first let's stop for some hamburgers. I'm famished, aren't you?"

"Not really, but I guess it is getting close to noon."

Angie sat rigidly in her seat as Jay drove the familiar streets of Agana. *I wonder if the driver of that car is the one?* she thought every time they passed a car driven by a male. *This is ridiculous,* she scolded herself. *I've got to get hold of myself.* Angie tried to focus on her immediate surroundings as Jay neared their favorite fast-food restaurant.

They ordered drinks, fries, and cheeseburgers at the drive-thru window. The aroma of the French fries activated Angie's sense of hunger. She unwrapped the sack and popped a couple of fries in her mouth as Jay drove toward her apartment. She could hardly wait for the comforts of her simple home. Arriving at Angie's complex, Jay parked in the vacant slot beside Angie's red Honda and helped her inside.

Angie stopped at her mailbox in the front of the building. "I suppose I better check my mail," she said as she fumbled in her purse for her keys. "I usually don't get anything but advertisements, but I keep hoping that today will be my lucky day, and I'll receive good news through the mail. . . . Yesterday definitely was not a lucky day."

She unlocked her box and fumbled through the "Current Occupant" brochures. A white business envelope was last in the pile. With trembling hands she tore it open as Jay waited silently beside her. She silently read the small print, then let out a scream of delight and threw her arms around Jay.

"I got it. I got it!"

"Got what?"

"I got the job at Coiffure and Manicure Beauty Salon in the Agana Mall. That's the best salon on the island. They want me to start a week from Monday."

"Fantastic," Jay exclaimed as he embraced her. They were both momentarily caught up in the joy of the news. "Let's go upstairs and eat these cheeseburgers to celebrate."

As they entered Angie's modest, one-bedroom apartment, Angie's mood shifted dramatically. "I can't start work in ten days. Look at me. My hair won't be grown out, and I'm covered with bruises."

"Your bruises should be pretty well healed in a week," Jay reminded her.

"With your knowledge of makeup, I'm sure you'll be able to mask the remaining discoloration. Tell you what, when the stitches come out, I'll buy you a nice blond wig," he teased.

Angie giggled through her frustrations. "Now wouldn't I look great as a blond with my dark complexion and dark eyes?"

"You'd look good even if you were bald. Now let's eat our food before it gets cold," Jay quipped.

Jay and Angie spread their food bags around the kitchen table. Momentarily Angie forgot the trauma of the night before. "Coiffure and Manicure is the most prestigious salon on the island. Everyone tries to be hired by them, but they only take the very best. That's why I didn't expect to be selected."

"You are the best," Jay reminded her. "You're graduating with honors."

Angie took another bite from her hamburger. "I think my instructor, Leon Paplos, had something to do with me getting the job. He's a good friend of the owner."

"What else do you know about the salon?"

Angie's eyes reflected a momentary twinkle of her old self. "I've heard the owner is one of the most eligible bachelors on the island."

"Are you saying I'm going to have competition?" Jay teased.

Angie grinned, then became suddenly serious. "Of course not. He's definitely not my type. . . . I've heard a lot of rumors about his nightlife, but I'm sure it's just idle gossip."

Jay took Angie's hands in his and gazed into her eyes. "I just want you to know how much I love you, and I want to share the rest of my life with you."

"Jay, don't. . . . Please. . .I'm no longer the innocent, pure young woman that you deserve."

"Angie, how can I convince you that no matter whatever happened to your body, your soul and spirit are still pure."

Tears welled up in her eyes as she bit her lip to choke back sobs. "If only I could go back to what I was before I left class last night."

"Darling, how many times must I remind you that you are the same person I fell in love with and want to marry?"

Jay painfully watched Angie shrug her shoulders and take another sip of her Coke. *What am I doing wrong in trying to convince her of my love? Does my love appear that shallow?*

After finishing her lunch, Angie rose from the table and yawned. "Jay, I hate to leave you with nothing to do, but I've got to take a nap. I'm so tired I can hardly keep my eyes open."

"That's the best thing for you. I'll be here if you need anything. In fact I may take a quick nap on the sofa myself."

Angie disappeared into her bedroom, while Jay thumbed through the travel magazines on her coffee table. After Angie had been sleeping for half an hour, Jay reached into his wallet and took out his telephone calling card. He took the phone from its cradle and punched in a series of familiar numbers. The clicks of connections being made amazed him as he envisioned the telephone signal bouncing up to the satellite and finally coming to rest in his parents' home in Montana.

"Hello," a sleepy voice mumbled.

"Hello, Mom. Did I wake you?"

"I should be getting up anyway," Nancy Harkness yawned. "I've got a lot to get done today. How are you?"

"I'm fine, but it's not me I'm concerned about. I'm calling to ask for prayers for Angie Quinata."

Nancy sat up straight in bed. "What happened?" she asked as she swung her legs over the side of the bed.

"She was attacked and raped while she was walking across campus last night." Jay took a deep breath and glanced toward the closed bedroom door behind which Angie was sleeping. "She now has twenty-five stitches in her head and is an emotional wreck. She thinks she's ruined for life and that no man will ever want her, especially me."

"How awful," Nancy gasped. "We'll be sure and remember both of you. I'll call your grandmother right away and ask her to pray as well."

"I'd appreciate that. Angie needs all the prayer support she can get. Would you also call Rebecca Hatfield, as well? If it wasn't for her, I never would have met Angie."

"I'm going to be seeing Rebecca this afternoon at the community bazaar. I'll tell her about Angie," the attractive, middle-aged woman promised as she reached for her fleece robe. "She's another one who's become a real prayer warrior."

"Thanks, Mom. I appreciate all your help. You and Grandma have always been my greatest sources of encouragement." Jay's voice nearly broke as he ended the conversation. "I love you all, and I miss everyone in Rocky Bluff. I can hardly wait to get back."

"I love you too, Son. Good-bye for now. We'll all be praying for both Angie and you."

"Good-bye, Mom."

❖

That afternoon as Nancy Harkness was admiring a collection of embroidered wall hangings, she spotted Rebecca Hatfield browsing through a nearby booth. "Rebecca, how are you?" she greeted. "I haven't seen you in ages."

"I've been extremely busy lately. Working four hours a day at the florist's, plus my volunteer work at the historical library, I haven't been out and about much," Rebecca replied. "We have a lot of catching up to do. Let's go over to the food booth, and I'll treat you to a piece of pie and a cup of coffee."

"Sounds good. However, I was planning to invite you. I have something I need to talk with you about."

The two longtime friends headed toward the northwest corner of the community center where the Rocky Bluff Garden Club was holding a food fair. After selecting their favorite piece of pie and pouring themselves a cup of coffee, Nancy and Rebecca found an empty table in the back of the booth.

"You look upset. What's wrong?" Rebecca asked.

Nancy shook her head. "I didn't know it was that obvious," she replied softly, "but I'm worried about Jay and his friend, Angie Quinata."

"What happened?"

"Jay called this morning and asked us to pray for Angie. He said she was raped last night as she was leaving class. He said it took twenty-five stitches to close a wound in her head, but he was more concerned about her mental state."

"Poor Angie. She's such a sweet girl. This could traumatize her for life. I know what she's going through. Something similar happened to me when I was her age."

Nancy could not hide her shock. "I'm sorry," she said as she reached for Rebecca's hand. "You've never told me this before. You've always seemed so well-adjusted."

Rebecca lowered her eyes. "It's something I don't like to talk about, but if I can use my pain to help bring healing for someone else, it's well worth speaking out. I wish I could bring Angie here to spend several weeks with me. I'd try to love her out of her misery."

"That'd be nice," Nancy agreed, "but the chances of Angie ever coming to Montana are almost nil. Jay says their relationship hangs in the balance unless she comes to grips with what happened. He seemed terribly discouraged."

"Nothing's impossible. Prayer and love were able to restore my life, and I'm confident they'll also restore Angie's."

Chapter 3

Angie stood in front of the full-length mirror and adjusted her new shoulder-length wig. She scowled as she wrapped a strand of hair behind her ear.

"Angie, you look terrific," Jay encouraged. "You'll be a hit at your graduation tonight."

"The wig might look okay, but it hurts," she fumed. "I don't think I'll be able to wear it until the stitches come out. Even if I wanted to, I won't be able to go tonight."

Jay shook his head in frustration. Nothing he said seemed to make any difference. "I wish you weren't so self-conscious about your appearance. People will understand you've been through a lot in the last few days."

"But I don't want their sympathy. I don't want anyone to say, 'Oh, she's the poor thing who's been damaged for life.' "

Jay pulled her close. Angie's lips trembled as she buried her face against his shirt. "You're not damaged goods. You're beautiful. I'd be proud to escort you to your graduation or anyplace else. Do you have a scarf you could wear?"

"Let me check." Angie went to her dresser and rummaged through the bottom drawer. "I do have this black-and-gold scarf. Maybe I can tie it so it looks like a fashion statement and not just something to hide my shaved head."

Angie returned to her mirror and folded her scarf in a modified triangle. With a few added folds she was able to make a turban. She pulled out a few locks of hair around her face.

Jay stepped back and cocked his head. "Hmm. Not bad. You're definitely making a fashion statement with that. You'll be the hit of the ceremony."

"I wish I could put my head in a bag, but I guess this'll be okay," Angie stated dejectedly. "At least I won't be letting everyone down by not attending."

"Great. Let's call your mother and see if she wants to join us for dinner at the Garden Plaza. After the ceremony we can all go to the reception at the Commons."

Angie remained unconvinced but gave in to Jay's persistence. She was split between her old rational self and her current mental turmoil. *Will anyone ever understand what I'm going through?*

Angie shrugged her shoulders. "Yeah, I guess," she sighed. "I've already paid the rent for my cap and gown." She reached for the phone. Her fingers touched the familiar sequence of numbers without hesitation.

"Hello."

"Hello, Mom. How are you?"

"I had a good night's rest, and I'm doing fine. More importantly, how are you?"

"I guess I'm okay," Angie replied, unable to hide her frustrations, "but I won't be able to wear my new wig. It looks all right, but it hurts where the stitches are."

"Would you like me to bring some of my scarves along? Maybe one of them will be the right size and color."

"Thanks for the offer, Mom, but I think I'll wear my black-and-gold one. It's not the best, but it's passable," Angie replied. She searched for encouragement from Jay. He grinned and winked at her. The tension faded slightly from Angie's face. "Mom, I was wondering if you'd like to join Jay and me for dinner at the Plaza Gardens? Jay insists on making a big celebration out of my graduation."

"Angie, don't sound so dejected. This is a time for celebration," Mitzi persisted gently. "I can hardly wait. Would you like me to drive?"

"No, Jay's going to drive. Meet us here at five-fifteen, and we'll go together."

Early that evening the threesome gathered in a corner booth at the finest restaurant on the island. Each ordered Steak Albert, the entree which had made Plaza Gardens famous in Guam. When the steaks arrived, Jay and Mitzi were overcome by the delicious aroma; they ate heartily, while Angie merely picked at her food. To her the entree held no flavor.

"Honey, what's wrong? You've hardly touched your dinner," Mitzi said as she took another sip of her coffee.

Angie stared blankly out the window at the sun setting behind the distant beach. "Oh, nothing. I'm just not hungry."

"Are you nervous about the ceremony?"

"The ceremony's no big deal," Angie shrugged. "I haven't missed a college graduation ceremony in three years. I've watched all my friends graduate." She hesitated and took a deep breath. "It's just that I don't want to go back to the campus."

Jay put his arm around Angie's shoulder and pulled her closer to him. "You won't be alone. Your mother and I will be in the audience, and you'll be surrounded by your friends."

"It's not that. . . It's. . .it's the memories."

Mitzi's eyes studied her daughter's black-and-gold turban and the heavy makeup that hid her fading bruises. "Angie, you'll make new memories tonight. You'll walk across that stage the third-highest-ranking student in your class. That's a memory you'll cherish forever."

Angie's lip began to tremble. "Do you think anyone will notice the award? They'll all look at the scarf and say, 'She's the poor girl who was raped leaving class the other night.'"

Jay continued to hold her next to himself. "Angie, God will give you strength to face your fears. If you hide from them now, they'll keep getting bigger and bigger. Do your best to confront them, please. Your mother and I will be there to cheer you on."

A waitress in a black-and-white uniform stopped at their table and inquired about the food. After receiving two affirmative nods, she left the bill on the corner of the table and slipped away, conscious of the fact that something extremely personal was happening and her customers needed their privacy.

The trio finished eating in relative silence, each lost in their own thoughts of helplessness. Jay reached for the bill, and the three walked silently to the front. He handed the hostess his credit card, waited for the receipt, and signed his name. Their celebration dinner had been a dinner of dismal formality and unresolved pain.

Tension filled the car as the three rode to the campus of Guam Community College. Jay and Mitzi exhausted every combination of words trying to console Angie who sat in sheer terror, but to no avail. Angie sat stiffly in the front seat beside Jay.

Upon arriving at the campus, Jay parked his car in the lot behind the baseball field. He opened the car door for Angie and her mother, then reached into the backseat for the box containing Angie's graduation gown and mortar board. He tucked the box under his left arm and offered his right arm to Angie. He could feel her arm trembling as it encircled his. "You're doing great," he whispered. "You'll be able to face your fears and conquer them."

"I'll do my best, but I can't guarantee anything." Angie sighed. "I feel so weak and inadequate."

Mitzi strolled beside the young couple, caught up in the excitement of the evening she had long been anticipating. "Look at the moon," she commented, unaware of the continued tension beside her. "I've never seen it this full and bright before. The campus is so peaceful tonight with the breeze rustling through the palm trees. It's a perfect night for an outdoor ceremony."

Jay and Angie did not respond to Mitzi's words but slowly walked toward the stadium where the graduates were assembling. Angie clutched his arm tighter with each step. As they neared the library, Angie's trembling became more apparent. She bravely took a deep breath, but when she saw the bushes where she had been raped, Angie screamed, "Take me home. Take me home."

"Angie, this is your big night," Mitzi insisted. "You've got to go on."

"I can't. I can't do it. Jay, please take me home."

Angie collapsed against Jay's chest. He wrapped his arm around her to support her weight. She stood there trembling and sobbing several minutes. Mitzi tried to encourage her to go on, but to no avail. Finally, Jay took Angie's face in his hands. "Everything's going to be all right. I'll take you home."

The sidewalk was now crowded with cheerful graduates and their families heading toward the stadium as the trio wove their way back to the parking lot. "Isn't that Angela Quinata?" a girl whispered to her friend.

"Yeah, I think so," her friend whispered back. "She looks terrible."

Angie's knees weakened under her, and she collapsed onto the sidewalk. Jay scooped her into his arms and carried her to his car. Mitzi opened the door for him as he laid the stricken graduate gently on the backseat. Mitzi squeezed into a corner of the seat beside her daughter, while Jay opened the front door and started the car.

Jay headed toward Angie's apartment. Her sobs subsided as they neared her familiar street. Parking his car in front of the complex, Jay opened the back door so Mitzi could alight. He took Angie's hand in his. "Do you think you'll be able to walk?"

"As long as I have your arm to hold onto, I'll be fine," she whispered as she slid from the backseat and wrapped her arm in his. "I'm sorry I'm such a bother and disappointment. I know how much you and Mother wanted to see me graduate."

"We're proud of you for making such a brave effort. Anyone else in your position wouldn't even try to set foot on the campus."

Mitzi hurried ahead and unlocked the door to Angie's apartment. Once inside Angie collapsed on her bed. Mitzi pulled the sheet over her daughter and tiptoed from the room. She smiled at Jay, trying to conceal her intense concern.

"I think she was asleep as soon as she hit the bed. She's emotionally exhausted. It will be no problem for me to spend the weekend with her. She's been through so much." Mitzi went to the kitchen and opened the refrigerator. "Jay, would you like a soft drink?"

"That sounds good," he replied, pulling up a chair to the kitchen table. "I only wish there were something I could do to help her."

Mitzi handed Jay a cold can of soda pop. "A good night's rest will be the best thing for her."

Mitzi slipped into a chair opposite Jay. Her face appeared ten years older than it did the week before. They sat in silence for a few moments, each enjoying their cold refreshment.

"I hope she'll be able to sleep the whole night through. I doubt if she's slept more than four hours in a row since the attack," Jay said as he studied Mitzi's wrinkled brow. "I wish I could stay tonight, but I have to be at work at midnight. My first sergeant has been more than understanding about letting me have time off, but the work is piling up."

"I appreciate all you've done for her. I don't know what we'd do without your help. I just hope Angie will be ready to start her new job."

Jay took the last sip from his can of pop, dropped it in the recycling bin, and walked toward the door. "She has ten days to go before she has to report to work. Hopefully, she'll be over this trauma by then. She's a strong lady." Jay hesitated as his large physique filled the door frame. "I'll call you tomorrow and see how she's doing."

❀

Angie slept for most of the weekend. She would awaken for a few hours, her mother would fix her a warm, home-cooked meal, then she'd lie on the sofa to watch a little TV, only to fall asleep again. By Monday morning she was able to laugh at her own clumsiness when she dropped an egg on the kitchen floor while preparing breakfast.

"Mom, would you mind coming to the doctor's with me this morning? I still don't feel like driving."

"I'd be glad to. Afterwards, if you're feeling up to it, we could go by the college and get your diploma."

"As long as it's light outside, I think I'll be able to go back." Angie smiled as she finished her cheese omelet and carried her plate to the sink. "After all my hard work, I'd like to see that piece of paper. Maybe we could then go by the mall and get a frame for it. I want to have something positive to look at instead of my bruises and shaven head."

Mitzi gave her daughter a hug. "That's my old strong-willed daughter talking. Together we'll be able to conquer this."

"I'm tired of being miserable," Angie sighed. "I want to go back to what life was before the attack, but I know I can't. I don't understand why Jay keeps hanging around. He knows I'm damaged goods."

"Jay loves you for who you are. You have a very sweet spirit, and that is what attracts him. He knows that, regardless of what happened to your body, nobody can rape your soul."

"But, Mother, that man did rape my soul. I'm an emotional wreck. I've never cried so much in my entire life as I have these last few days."

"Your tears are a sign of your healing. They're a good thing, not a bad sign."

❀

Promptly at eleven-fifteen, Angie and Mitzi were ushered into the doctor's examining room. The nurse weighed Angie, took her pulse and blood pressure, and removed the bandage from her head. "Looks like your wound is healing well," she said. "The doctor will probably remove the stitches today."

"I hope so. They're beginning to itch."

After the nurse left the room, Angie turned to her mother. "I don't even remember what the doctor looks likes. That night in the hospital was such a blur."

"He's a graying Filipino. I thought he showed a great deal of professionalism and compassion."

Angie studied the degrees on the wall. "I'd feel a lot more comfortable if I had a female doctor."

"I wish we had a female gynecologist on Guam, but there just aren't enough women doctors who want to come here," her mother replied. "I've just accepted the fact that my doctor is going to be male. They're all well trained, but sometimes they don't have enough empathy for what a woman has to go through."

Suddenly, the door of the examining room opened, and Dr. Cruz entered, followed by his nurse. "Angie, how are you doing?" he said as he extended his hand.

"I guess I'm as good as can be expected." Angie shuffled and gazed out the window. How could she possibly tell a strange man her innermost thoughts?

Sensing his patient's discomfort, Dr. Cruz turned his attention to her mother. "Hello, Mrs. Quinata. How have you been doing?"

"It's been extremely difficult for both of us. I'm concerned about Angie. She's unduly upset and doesn't seem to be bouncing back like I'd hoped."

"Oh, Mom," Angie sighed. "Just because I wasn't able to go to my graduation doesn't mean I'm a basket case. I'm going to be okay; I'm just tired."

"I know, Honey. I just can't bear to see you so unhappy."

A stern look crossed the doctor's face as he frowned at Mitzi. "Often it takes a lot longer for the inner pain and fears to heal than the physical. I can take care of the physical problems now. We can deal with the other later."

Mitzi nodded with resignation. *If only he understood a mother's heart. Many doctors are always too matter-of-fact and seldom hear our real pain.*

"Angie, let's take a look at your stitches. Hopefully, I'll be able to take them out today."

"I hope so," Angie replied as she removed her flowered scarf.

Dr. Cruz took her head in his hands. "Hmm. Looks like the stitches are ready to come out." He looked over his shoulder to his nurse who was already getting supplies from the cupboard. "Gloria, would you prepare a suture removal kit for me?"

Dr. Cruz's hands moved swiftly and confidently as one by one he snipped each of the twenty-five stitches in Angie's head. In a few moments he stepped back and beamed. "In a few days the cut will be completely healed. Of course with a wound that size, there will be a slight scar, but when your hair grows back, no one will ever know."

Angie smiled shyly. "Thank you, Doctor. I appreciate all you've done for me."

"You've been a brave patient, but before you go I'd like to take another blood test."

"I thought I'd been put through the entire gamut of tests while I was in the hospital."

"You were, but we had to wait a few days before we could perform this particular one."

"And what is it?" Angie asked softly.

"HIV."

Horror smothered Angie and Mitzi as they exchanged panicky glances. Neither one could speak for several minutes. Finally Mitzi gasped, "I never even thought about AIDS."

"I did," Angie whispered as tears filled her eyes, "but I was afraid to say anything. I was hoping that since they didn't take an HIV test at the hospital that I wasn't at risk. Jay would never get close to me again if he thought I had AIDS."

"There's such a small number of AIDS cases on Guam, the chances are good you were not infected. But let's not take any chances. It's best to be sure."

Mitzi's face remained ashen, while she watched the nurse draw blood from her daughter's arm. "I heard that tests sometimes don't turn up positive for months or even years after contact."

"That's true," the doctor replied. "That's why Angie should be tested every two or three months for the next couple years, or until the perpetrator can be found and tested for HIV."

"But the police don't have many clues to go on. The chances of finding him is practically nil. He probably caught the next plane out of here," Angie cried.

The doctor handed his patient a tissue from the nearby counter and waited while she dried her eyes and regained her composure. "Angie, I wish I could talk with more certainty now, but I don't want you to take any risks. Until more research is done, the medical community cannot cure AIDS."

"So what should I do? Avoid other people?" Angie asked bitterly. "If anyone thought I had AIDS, they would avoid me, wouldn't they?"

Mitzi put her arms around Angie and drew her close. "It'll be okay," she whispered as she brushed Angie's hair away from her cheek. "God hasn't let us down before, and He won't let us down now."

Angie appeared not to have heard her mother, but the words sunk deep into her soul where they collided with a mass of anger, rage, and guilt. "I can't go on. I can't bear the thought of AIDS."

The doctor watched the mother-daughter exchange with concern. When both of them paused for lack of words, the doctor put his hand on his patient's shoulder. "Angie, I have a doctor friend who specializes in helping victims of rape. May I give him a call and set up an appointment?"

"Are you saying I'm crazy?" Angie's eyes blazed through her tears. "I don't need a psychiatrist. All I need is the assurance that I didn't contract the HIV virus."

"Would you consider talking with him at least once?" the doctor persisted.

"I don't want to see any psychiatrists. If I thought I needed help I'd see my minister."

The doctor stroked his beard. "That might be one solution," he replied. "I don't know your particular minister. However, I do know that some are exceptionally well trained as counselors and others cause more harm than good. I hope yours is one of the well trained."

Angie took a deep breath and forced a smile. "I'll consider it," she murmured.

Dr. Cruz reached into a drawer beside him and took out a business card. "If you change your mind about seeing a professional, here's my friend's name and telephone number. He has an answering service so feel free to contact him day or night. He's always willing to help."

Angie studied the letters and numbers on the card, then tucked it into a corner pocket of her purse. *This is the last person on earth I'd call,* she told herself as she wrapped her scarf around her half-shaved head and rose to leave.

Mitzi and Angie drove the streets of Agana in silence. A coconut fell from the palm tree directly beside their car, yet neither reacted. Their senses remained numb with shock. When Mitzi turned her car down the street to her daughter's apartment in Magnolia, Angie spotted Jay's car parked by the curb. "Mom, if you don't mind, I'd rather be alone when I tell Jay about the HIV test."

Mitzi's face softened as she stopped her car behind Jay's. "Of course, Dear. You two need to be alone. If you need anything, be sure and call me tonight."

"Mom, don't make such a fuss over me. I'll be fine."

"I know you will. I just want to help take your pain away."

"I know," Angie said as she opened the car door and spotted Jay hurrying toward her. "I'll talk to you later. Thanks for taking me, Mom."

"Hi," Jay greeted as he reached for his friend's hand. "What kind of good report did the doctor give you?"

Angie forced a smile and tried to add a tone of gaiety. "The stitches came out so now maybe I can wear my new wig. I'm getting tired of this silly scarf."

"That's my girl. I'm glad to see the old Angie back."

Angie unlocked the door to her apartment and motioned for Jay to follow her. "Can I get you a glass of iced tea?"

"I'd love it," he replied, leaning over to kiss her.

Angie jumped back in terror. "You can't do that," she shouted. Seeing the pain in Jay's eyes, she immediately regretted her reaction.

"What's wrong? I've always greeted you with a kiss. Have I done something?"

"I'm sorry. . . . I don't know if I'll ever be able to kiss you or anyone else again."

The grooves on Jay's forehead deepened. "Why's that?"

Angie felt a lump building in her throat. She had to be brave and not let Jay know how upset she actually was. "They tested me for the HIV virus this morning," she replied, trying to make her voice sound matter of fact.

Jay wrapped both his arms around her. "I'm sure it will come back negative."

"But maybe the tests don't show anything for months or even years after contact. I don't want to risk spreading the virus. I hope you understand." Angie's eyes pled for patience.

Jay again wrapped his arms around her and pulled her close. "Angie, you can't get AIDS from a simple kiss. It can only be spread by sexual contact, dirty needles, or tainted blood."

Angie shook her head vigorously. "Jay, I think too much of you to take any risks. Besides, I heard that you could get AIDS by any exchange of body fluids."

"Angie, there are so many rumors and false notions about AIDS floating around that you could live in total fear and isolation. As long as we have no proof, let's go on with our lives as if this had never happened. Hopefully, they'll find the attacker soon, and we will know for sure if he's infected or not."

Angie relaxed as she squeezed Jay's hand. "I'll do my best. Now how about the iced tea I promised you?"

Chapter 4

Angie adjusted her new hairpiece. *Not bad for a cheap wig,* she sighed. *Maybe I'll be able to hide my scars for a few months until my hair grows out. I'm going to wear this and try to forget that anything ever happened. Hopefully, no one saw the article in the paper. After all, it was hidden on the third page.*

She glanced at her clock radio. *Seven o'clock.* She paced nervously around the room. *I don't have to be at work until nine. I'd better recheck my supplies. It'd be embarrassing not to have everything I need. I don't want to appear like a novice, even if I am one.* For the next hour Angie counted her curlers, then arranged and rearranged her cosmetic box. She took out her class notes and compared her supplies with the recommended list. Everything had to be perfect.

Ten minutes before nine Angie walked into the Coiffure and Manicure Beauty Salon at the Agana Mall. She hesitated as she gazed around the mirror-lined walls. Angie had been in this salon several times as a customer when she was in high school, but now she was to be the one standing above the chair with scissors and curling iron in her hand.

As she stood there in awe, a dark-haired man emerged from the back room. "Hello, you must be Angie. I'm Yan Chung, the owner. I'm glad you could join our little family. You'll add a touch of class."

"Thank you." Angie blushed as she lowered her eyes. "I'm glad to meet you. Mr. Paplos, my teacher at the college, spoke very highly of both you and your salon."

"He's a great guy. That's why I take his best students, no questions asked."

He paused, his penetrating eyes drifted up and down Angie's trim body. "All my friends call me Yan. Here, let me take your box, and I'll show you around."

Yan carried Angie's box of supplies to the back of the salon and set it on the counter in front of a beauty chair. "I'll start you out here in the corner across from my office so I can help you whenever you need it. When you build up your clientele, I'll see that you move closer to the front windows. Your pay will go up in proportion to how well you produce."

Angie studied the area: sink, mirror, outlets, drawers, and carts. "Looks like I have more space than I could possibly use," she smiled. "I'll take a few minutes and unpack my things."

"There's plenty of time for that. Let me show you the beauticians' lounge." Yan put his hand on her shoulder and steered her toward the back door. Angie muffled a gasp as she stepped onto an Oriental rug in the posh lounge.

"My girls work hard so I try to give them the very best. You're free to keep whatever you'd like in the refrigerator and use the microwave. Of course, there's continual disagreement as to what to watch on the TV during the slow times."

"It's beautiful." Angie smiled. "Hopefully, I'll have enough business that I won't have much time to watch TV. I'm sure there'll be plenty of laundry and cleaning to do in my free moments." Angie surveyed the room. "Where does the background work take place? The cleaning supplies and the laundry?"

"You're a practical one." Yan snickered. "I told you I take good care of my girls. You won't have to worry about the menial tasks. I've hired a young immigrant for that. Her English is broken, but she's learning fast."

Suddenly, the bells on the door tingled, and Yan stuck his head out the door. "Hi, Sweetie. Come back and meet our latest addition. She's likely to double our business."

A beautiful Chamorro woman walked into the lounge. "Hi. I'm Tracy Ada. We're glad to have you here, but I hope you don't believe half of Yan's stories." She grinned as she winked at her boss.

Angie wrinkled her forehead with puzzlement, then smiled. "I'm glad to be here," she replied. "My name's Angela Quinata."

"It's nice meeting you. We need a new face around here. Life's getting a little boring."

"I've got some work to do so I'll leave you two to get acquainted," Yan said as he patted Tracy on the shoulder as he left the room.

"You've got to take him with a grain of salt," Tracy grinned. "He's all talk and little action."

"He does have a pretty strong come-on," Angie replied as she shrugged her shoulders and smiled. "But I met guys a lot worse while I was in college."

Angie and Tracy spent the next few minutes comparing their training background. One by one, four other beauticians joined them as the salon became busy with customers. Several beauticians were overbooked and were more than happy to schedule customers with Angie. On several occasions she spotted Yan in her mirror watching her work from his glassed office. *I wonder if he doesn't trust my work,* she mused. *Does he check up on all his new beauticians this way?*

At lunch time Angie had only a few minutes to eat a quick sandwich in the lounge before returning to her next haircut. The looks of pleasure on her customers' faces when they surveyed their finished hairstyles increased Angie's self-confidence.

She worked for several hours before the thoughts of her attack slipped into her consciousness. *If I discipline my mind and keep busy, maybe I'll be able to get over what happened on the campus,* she told herself during the moments when memories rose to torment her.

"Angie, you don't have to do a week's work on your first day." Yan grinned as he came out of his office and paused next to her chair. "It's after five; you won't be any good at all tomorrow if you don't go home and get some beauty rest. I bet you have someone special waiting for you."

Angie shrugged her shoulder and reached into the bottom drawer of her station for her purse. How should she answer? She'd given Jay back his ring, but regardless of how cruel she'd been to him, he was always there helping her as if she only had a case of the flu instead of having been ruined for life.

"I have a lot of special people in my life," she replied cautiously. "Have a good evening."

Angie gathered her things and turned to the other beauticians. "I guess I'll call it a day as well. I'll see you tomorrow."

"See ya," they responded in chorus as Angie left the air-conditioned salon.

The hot tropical wind slapped Angie in the face as she left the mall. She hurried across the parking lot. A tall, athletic man was walking toward his car in the next row. Angie ran to her car, slid behind the wheel, and locked the door. She laid her head on the steering wheel as her heart raced and her hands trembled. *Could he be the one?* Minutes passed as she watched the man climb into his car and drive away. Breathing a sigh of relief, she started her engine and headed toward her apartment in Magnolia. Her nearly perfect first day of work ended with an unwarranted scare.

Angie finished eating two hamburgers, potato chips, and reached for a chocolate bar. *Mother would be infuriated with me if she knew I was indulging in such junk foods,* she justified, *but after all I've been through, I deserve it. The added stress is probably burning up most of the calories so it won't add to my weight.*

As she stuffed the last bite of the chocolate morsel into her mouth, the doorbell sounded. She hurried to the door and paused. Her voice trembled, "Who's there?"

"Relax, Angie. It's just me," Jay shouted through the door. "I came to see how your first day of work went."

Angie flung open the door. "I'm sorry. Under the circumstances I just can't be too careful."

"Aren't you going to invite me in?" Jay teased.

"Of course. Come on in. Have you eaten yet?"

"I ate before I left the base. I'm not in the habit of turning up hungry on someone else's doorstep." Jay pulled out a chair at the kitchen table. He smiled and automatically reached into the bag of potato chips. "Now, tell me about your first day of work."

"I loved it. After all my months of training, I got a real adrenaline high from seeing the expressions on the ladies' faces when they saw how I changed their straight, disheveled hair."

"Women are so vain." Jay chuckled.

"Ah, come on. I was merely helping their self-esteem," Angie retorted lightly.

"How many did you do today?"

"I did one perm, three wash and sets, and I can't remember how many cuts. The other girls were all overbooked, so I was busy all day. It was great."

Jay reached for Angie's hand. "It's good to see you happy again. I knew you could do it."

Angie's joy was short-lived. She wrinkled her forehead. "The day wasn't entirely perfect," she sighed. "Yan, the owner, gives me the creeps. I can't quite put my finger on it, but there's something about him that bothers me."

"You're probably just gun-shy about all men. After all, it's only been less than two weeks since your attack."

Angie nodded her head. "I suppose you're right." The tone of her voice did not reflect the confidence in his voice. "He does seem to take good care of his employees. He has the fanciest beauticians' lounge I've ever seen. He's even hired a maid to launder the towels and clean up after us. It's nothing like what our textbook described."

"Don't knock a good thing when it happens." Jay chuckled. He glanced around the small apartment. "How about going to a movie to celebrate your successful day?"

"I'm not leaving this apartment when it's dark outside, even if I'm with you."

"Then how about me running to the video store and renting a couple of videos for the evening? I'll make sure they're comedies."

"That I can handle," Angie replied as Jay rose to leave. "If you want to get some snacks along the way, I could handle that too."

The pair spent the evening nestled on the sofa laughing at the latest antics from Hollywood. Angie was proud of how well she was able to suppress her pain and act as if everything was back to normal. Maybe if she masked her pain and anger, it would go away.

❧

Four other beauticians were gathered in the lounge of Coiffure and Manicure the next morning when Angie arrived.

"Hi, Angie," Tracy greeted. "Have you seen the morning paper yet?"

"No. I've been running a little slow this morning."

"Another woman was raped at the college last night. The article said it was the sixth one in the last three months. I'd be scared to death to go near that place until that crazy has been caught."

Angie turned pale and slumped into a chair. Her heart pounded while her hands trembled.

"Angie, are you okay?" Tracy asked. "You look like you've seen a ghost."

Angie took a deep breath and scolded herself. *I've got to get control of myself. I don't want to blow it on my second day of work.* She forced a smile. "I'm all right. I live in that neighborhood, and I get extremely upset whenever that happens."

"I don't know why the cops can't figure out who it is," the blond beautician on the other side of Tracy said as she arranged her curlers in their tray. "I wonder if they really care about the plight of women."

Just then Yan appeared in the doorway. "I see you girls have seen the morning paper about the mad rapist. I'll tell you why the cops can't figure out who did it," he said with a strange gleam in his eye. "They're stupid." With that he turned and walked away.

The beauticians exchanged puzzled glances, shrugged their shoulders, and went to their individual stations to prepare for their day's customers. Angie shook her head as the others seemed to accept his attitude as a normal, off-the-cuff comment.

Angie could scarcely keep her composure as the latest rape was the chosen topic of conversation of nearly every woman who came into the salon that day. At three o'clock Grandma Santos entered the salon. Mrs. Santos lived just two blocks from the mall and frequently treated herself to a new dye job to hide her nearly gray head of hair. Everyone else was busy, and she was sent to Angie's station.

Angie helped her select an appropriate color and had just begun the process when Grandma Santos asked, "Young lady, did you read about the rapes in the paper?"

"Uh-uh," Angie mumbled. "It's pretty terrible."

"Well, if young girls today wouldn't run around half naked, they wouldn't be attacked. They ask for it every time they dress that way."

Angie's face reddened. "No one deserves to be raped. It's a violent crime against all women."

"If the truth were known, I bet some of those girls actually enjoyed it. That's why they choose to dress the way they do."

Angie slammed the dye bottle onto the counter, grabbed her purse, and ran from the salon.

"What got into her?" Mrs. Santos asked Tracy, who was putting the finishing touches on a perm at the next station. "You'd think I personally attacked her or something."

"I don't know what's wrong," Tracy replied. "She's been acting strangely ever since she came to work today. Give me a few minutes, and I'll finish doing your hair."

"I hope Yan doesn't hear about this. He's always been fussy about who he picks to work here, but it looks like he picked a neurotic one this time. I guess it goes to show that you can't tell a book by its cover."

Tracy shook her head. "She's totally different today than she was yesterday. I don't know what got into her. The way she's been acting you'd think she was the one who was raped."

❖

Angie ran to her car. She could scarcely see through her tears as she drove the familiar streets to her apartment. Her heart raced, and the blood vessels in her head pounded under her wig. *Oh, God, where are You?* she pleaded. *I can't take any more. Isn't there someplace I can go to get away from this?*

Parking her car, she breathed a sigh of relief when she recognized her mother's car in the visitor's spot. She hurried to her apartment. "Mom, how come you're here? How'd you know I needed you?"

Mitzi grinned as she hugged her daughter. "Mother's intuition. When I read the article in the paper today, I knew it was going to be tough for you. I didn't know how long you'd be able to last at work so I thought I should be here when you got home. I'm glad you gave me a key."

"Mom, it was awful. Everyone is either scared to death, or they think it would never happen to them. One of my customers thought it was the woman's fault. She got obnoxious, and I just couldn't handle it. I broke down and ran out of the shop leaving her in the middle of a dye job. I'll probably lose my job over it."

"Was your boss there at the time?"

"No, but I'm sure she'll tell him. Grandma Santos is not someone to reckon with. She'll go right to the top."

"If your boss asks you about why you left, why don't you simply tell him the truth? I'm sure he'll be sympathetic."

"Mother, you don't understand. I can't talk about it with anyone except you and Jay. And I don't understand how Jay can keep hanging around. Doesn't he realize I'm ruined for life?"

"If Jay can understand and stand behind you, I'm sure your boss will also understand once he knows what happened."

Angie sunk onto the sofa and reached for the box of chocolates she had left on the end table. She sighed as she took a bite from the candy. "If I'm going to lose my job, I might as well go out fighting."

"That's the spirit," Mitzi replied as she patted her daughter on the knee. "You'll see. Everything's going to work out. Just be patient."

❖

The next day Angie walked into the Coiffure and Manicure Beauty Salon exactly at the appointed time. Yan had not yet arrived, and the other beauticians were already busy at their stations. "Hi, Angie. Are you feeling better today?" Tracy greeted.

"Much better, thank you," she replied as she put her purse in the bottom drawer. "I'm sorry I ran out yesterday. I just couldn't take any more of Mrs. Santos's comments. I assume she was pretty upset with me."

Tracy giggled. "She'll get over it. I finished her dye job. Fortunately, Yan wasn't here when she left so she didn't have an opportunity to tell him her side of what happened."

Tracy studied Angie's face. "I know I haven't known you for long, but is something wrong? Ever since you saw that article in the paper you completely changed."

"Tracy, have you ever been raped?"

"No."

"Then you'd never understand."

Their conversation was interrupted by the ringing of the phone. Tracy hurried to the front desk. She reached for the master schedule and recorded the caller's name and request, thanked her, and hung up. Angie busied herself by straightening her already immaculate work area.

"Angie, this customer specifically requested you," Tracy said as she handed a slip of paper to her. "She said you did her friend's hair, and she just loved it and wanted you to fix hers as well. For only having been here two days, I'd say you're off to a great start. They're already asking for you by name."

Angie worked all morning as if nothing had happened the day before. Yan came to the salon at eleven o'clock and went directly to his office without saying a word. Several times Angie noticed him watching her through his office windows, but he made no effort to contact her. *Maybe he doesn't know about what happened yesterday,* she mused as she again observed him in her mirror. *Leaving work was a dumb thing for me to do, but I just couldn't control myself.*

Angie was just saying good-bye to a customer when Yan approached her station. "Can I see you in my office for a few minutes?" he asked as he put his hand on her shoulder.

Angie's heart sank. *It's all over. . . . I'm being fired. . . . But if he were going to fire me, why didn't he do it when he first came in this morning?*

Yan closed the door behind them, then motioned for her to be seated. "I understand you had a little problem here yesterday."

Angie's eyes fell to the floor as blood rushed to her face. "I'm sorry. I won't let it happen again."

"What did Grandma Santos say that upset you so badly? She's been a customer of ours since we opened." Yan tried to project an air of concern, but a hollowness reverberated in Angie's ears.

"She was making a lot of unkind remarks about the rapes that have been taking place around the college. I just couldn't handle it. I'm afraid I lost control of myself."

"But the other girls heard them, and they didn't run out the door," Yan said as his dark eyes pierced deep into her soul.

Angie's palms began to sweat, and her voice trembled. "B–b–but they've never been raped."

"And you have?"

"Yes," Angie mumbled as her eyes stared on the sparkling tile at her feet.

Yan scrutinized the quaking young woman before him. His silence unnerved her even more. "Do you know who did it?"

"It was dark, and he knocked me unconscious first."

"It's over. You should just forget it and go on with your life. I know a perfect cure. I'll pick you up at seven o'clock; we'll go out to dinner, then have a little fun afterwards."

Tears filled her eyes. *Doesn't anyone understand what I'm going through? Going out is the last thing I want to do, especially with Yan.*

"I'm sorry, but I'm just not up to it tonight," she responded cautiously.

"It'll be good for you," Yan retorted. "You can't stay home and sulk about it. I'll show you what a good time is."

"Please, I'd prefer not."

"You like working here, don't you?"

"Yes."

"Then we need to get better acquainted," Yan whispered.

Angie took a deep breath. "I prefer to keep my career separate from my personal life."

Yan shook his head with disgust. "If that's the way you want it. Just remember your career could expand a lot faster if you made the right connections. This is a very competitive business."

"I'll remember that," Angie replied as she rose to leave, "but I prefer to make it in the hairdressing business strictly on my styling talents." She glanced nervously out the window and breathed a sigh of relief. "If you'd excuse me, my next customer just arrived."

"Customers do come first." Yan grinned. "But ten years from now you could still be working at the same station for the same pay if you don't begin to make social contacts."

Angie closed the office door, took a deep breath, pasted on a phony smile, and greeted her customer. She began to style her hair just the way she requested even though she personally thought the style was not suitable for her square face. Fortunately, the middle-aged woman carried on a monologue about her family, and Angie merely had to nod at the appropriate time.

When Angie finished, the woman admired herself in the mirror. "This is the best hairstyle I've ever had. I'm going to be back next week for you to do the same thing. Here's an extra ten dollars. You're worth every cent of it."

After the satisfied customer left, Tracy turned to her neighbor. "Angie, you're really starting off with a bang."

"She was rather generous, wasn't she?"

"No, I mean with Yan," Tracy replied. "Did he ask you out?"

"Yes. How'd you know?"

"He takes everyone who works here out. Usually he spends time sizing up his new employees and waits for at least a month to ask. He asked you the third day on the job."

"He said it would further my career, but I'd rather keep my personal life separate from my job."

"You're still a naive, fresh graduate. You'll soon learn Yan holds a key to big money." Tracy broke off her conversation as her next customer walked in.

Mystified, Angie checked the master schedule and noted she had no one else scheduled for the day. She took her purse from the bottom drawer in her station and slipped out the door. She still had her job, but something strange was happening that she didn't understand.

Angie stopped at the mall grocery store and bought a large frozen pizza, a six-pack of soda pop, and another box of chocolates. If the world was spinning out of control around her, she could at least treat herself to the foods she liked.

She hurried home, put the pizza in the oven, and sank onto the sofa, too depressed to even cry. *The first day Jay came to see how my day went. Yesterday mother was here, but tonight I'm on my own. . .me and the four walls.*

The buzzer on the oven timer broke her depressing fantasies. Angie took her pizza to the table. Within minutes she'd devoured the entire pizza, then reached for a chocolate for dessert. *I'd like to talk to Jay, but it's not fair to him. He deserves someone better than me. I returned his ring for a reason, but he still keeps coming around. He'd have fits if he knew Yan asked me out tonight.* She popped another piece of chocolate in her mouth. *I've already lost my purity and the best man on earth. Maybe I should find out what Tracy was talking about when she said*

Yan was the ticket to big money. If I made a lot of money, I could make a sizable donation to the church building fund. Making money couldn't be all bad. My life has already been destroyed.

Angie went to bed early that night, but sleep escaped her. Life had been so good up until three weeks ago. She was graduating with honors, she had a mother who doted over her, she thought she had a faith in God that was unshakable, and the most desirable man on the island was interested in only her. Now she had a sterile diploma, a mother who couldn't understand her turmoil, a God that she was convinced had abandoned her, and a boyfriend she did not deserve. Life was scarcely worth living.

Chapter 5

Rebecca Hatfield's eyes surveyed the majestic Rocky Mountains that surrounded her town of Rocky Bluff. The inspiration of the rugged mountains and glimmering lakes of Montana had helped maintain her during her two years on Guam as a librarian. Now she was home for good with only her fond memories of the tropical island. A blanket of snow still glistened from its peak even though it was nearly the middle of the summer. *Nothing is more beautiful than the mountains of Montana,* she mused as she opened the door to the Looking Glass Beauty Salon.

Barbara Old Tail emerged from the back room as the bells on the door tingled. Her face broke into a broad grin. "Hi, Rebecca. It's good to see you again. It's been a long while."

"I've been working part-time at the florist shop, then I agreed to set up the county historical library. I didn't realize it would be such a task when I consented to do it, but I'm sure it'll be well worth my time when we're finished."

"I heard about your work from one of my clients, and I'm extremely excited about the Native American collection. It's something our community has needed for a long time," Barb said as she motioned for Rebecca to be seated in the stylist's chair.

"We should be done in a few weeks," Rebecca replied as she scowled in the mirror and fingered through her hair. "It looks like it's perm time again, doesn't it?" she chuckled.

"It has been several months since you've been in," Barb replied with a twinkle in her eyes. "I suppose your new husband has been filling up all your spare moments. How is Andy anyway?"

"He's doing great. They just broke ground for the new addition to the fire station, so he's been busy with the contractor and not home as much as when we were first married."

Barb tilted the chair backwards and rested Rebecca's neck over the sink and began running warm water over her hair. She added a palm of shampoo and began sudsing Rebecca's hair. "Andy's the best fire chief Rocky Bluff has ever had. He's had to take command of more than his share of crises. People are still talking about the hardware store fire and the night the Reed home burned. His fire prevention program is the best in the state," Barb said. "You must be very proud of him."

"I've been extremely proud of his accomplishments. I think supervising the addition will be his last major project before retiring. He's talking more and more about retiring to the golf course."

"I can't imagine Andy limiting himself strictly to the golf course. Are you sure you won't be taking another adventure to Guam or some other distant port?"

Rebecca shook her head vigorously. "I loved my two years on Guam, but that was enough adventure for me to last a lifetime."

For the next hour as Barb washed her patron's hair and wrapped it onto pink rollers, the pair discussed the people, climate, and education of Guam. Outside of a few vacations to the coast, Barbara had not been out of Montana, and she was fascinated with the tales of the Chamorro people. Being part Native American, Barbara Old Tail readily identified with a people who, although American, nevertheless struggled to maintain their culture's unique identity. Her mind drifted back to her aging mother on the Blackfoot Reservation near Browning.

"When Mother was in better health, she had trouble reconciling being both American and Indian. Now it's a case of struggling from day to day," Barb said as her voice faded into a whisper.

Rebecca studied the beautician's strained face. Her features portrayed only a faint hint of her mixed ancestry. "Has your mother been ill?"

Barb continued mechanically unrolling the curlers. She rarely shared her personal concerns with her patrons, but Rebecca Hatfield was different. She had compassion and wisdom rarely seen in a beauty salon. "Physically, Mom's been doing quite well for being nearly eighty years old. She's one of the oldest living members of the tribe, but our family has been living with a painful secret for the last few years."

"How lonely," Rebecca responded, not wanting to pry but, sensing the desperation in Barb's voice, wanting to do what she could to help. "Is there anything I can do to help?"

"I wish there were." Barb sighed. "We can't hide the fact any longer that mother was diagnosed with Alzheimer's disease three years ago. She refused to leave her home, so my brother has been driving thirty miles each day to check on her. This past year she has deteriorated so much that it'll be dangerous for her to stay by herself any longer. I'd like to bring her to Rocky Bluff to live with me, but she'd be by herself all day while I worked," Barb hesitated as she finished rinsing Rebecca's hair.

Rebecca waited in silence for her beautician to continue. "I wish there was some way I could turn this shop into a partnership so I could be more flexible, but it's just too small."

"Have you checked other possibilities?"

"The cost of renting space in the mall would be prohibitive, and I can't afford to build a place of my own so I kind of gave up hope."

Rebecca was never one to give up easily. Two years in another culture had sensitized her problem-solving skills. "I stopped at the café next door for dinner last night, and someone was saying that the gift shop on the other side of you might go out of business. If that's the case, maybe you could knock out part of the wall and combine the two areas."

Barb's face brightened. "If that's true, it could be an ideal situation. I'll go over and talk to Renee when I finish my last appointment today."

"Be sure and let me know what you find out," Rebecca responded. "I'm really interested in your growth potential. Rocky Bluff's short on good beauticians, plus I'd hate to have your mother living by herself much longer."

Barb finished styling Rebecca's hair just as her next customer walked in with her three-year-old child. Rebecca complimented Barb's work, wrote her a check, and hurried from the shop. She still had several errands to run, and she wanted to get home early so she could prepare an extraspecial dinner before Andy returned. Ever since they started construction, he was near exhaustion when he returned at night.

❖

After devouring a rib steak, carrots, a baked potato, salad, and two pieces of cake, Andy gave Rebecca an appreciative kiss and collapsed into his recliner. He leaned back, took the remote, and began channel surfing. He soon settled on a football game but was asleep within minutes in spite of the intensity of the game.

Rebecca loaded the dishwasher, poured herself a glass of iced tea, took her favorite mystery book, and curled up on the sofa. Time stood still as she immersed herself in clues and deceitful antagonists. Just as a vital clue was being revealed, the ringing of the phone intruded into her world.

"Hello."

"Hello, Rebecca. This is Barb. You're a real genius."

The retired librarian shook her head and tried to shift mental gears from her novel. "How so?" she chuckled.

"I visited with Renee after work today, and she said they were closing down the end of the month. I immediately called the owner of the building, and he's coming by tomorrow morning to talk specifics."

"That's terrific," Rebecca nearly shouted, then lowered her voice as she noticed Andy stirring in his recliner. "I hope things can be worked out for you to expand."

"So far it looks good. Hopefully, I'll be able to remodel, but I'm afraid I won't have the time to do it and still keep my business going."

"I'd love to help you," Rebecca replied. "It would be a welcome change of pace from my work at the museum."

"You're an angel. I don't know how you find the time to do all you do."

Rebecca looked around her living room, remembering how horrified people were when she first bought the neglected, rambling house. After a lot of creativity and a little money, it was now one of the showplaces in Rocky Bluff. She was energized just thinking about the possibility of redecorating a cold, sterile building. "Just tell me when to begin, and I'll be there," she laughed.

"If this goes through, it would probably take most of the rest of the summer to remodel. Hopefully, I'll be ready to hire another beautician by fall," Barb planned out loud. Her mind began to race. The longer she talked the faster her speech became. "I could then move Mother into my spare room before the snow flies."

"Sounds like you have everything all mapped out," Rebecca said as she brushed her graying hair from her forehead. "I certainly admire your forethought. I'm sure everything will turn out okay."

Barb took a deep sigh. "The remodeling will be the easy part," she said. "The hardest part will be to find a beautician who is pleasant, easy to work with, and won't demand a lot of money."

"You're right." Rebecca nodded. "Most new beauty school graduates expect a lot of money the first year on the job and want no part of small towns. It would take a unique young person to come here and be happy without the excitement of city life."

Barb hesitated. With all the problems she was facing, it was hard for her to keep her confidence high. Yet, somehow when she was pressed to the limits, she tapped an unknown resource. "The Lord hasn't let me down yet. So I'm sure the right person is out there someplace just waiting to be asked."

❧

Angela Quinata screamed and bolted upright. Her sheets were soaked with perspiration. The impression of a man with deep penetrating eyes continued peering through the darkness at her. A coiled snake had reflected off the dark-haired stranger's right shoulder. She lay back on her pillow and sobbed. A dog began barking beneath her window. She ran to the kitchen, grabbed a chair, and propped it against the already double-bolted door.

Returning to her bedroom, she peered into the darkness. The dog was barking at a cat he had chased up the banana plant just outside her window. Normally she would have laughed at her own fears, but tonight was different. She returned to her bed, flopped across the sheets, and sobbed hysterically.

Daylight seemed to never come.

When the first glimmer of sunlight slid between Angela's blinds, she staggered to the kitchen, fixed herself a cup of instant coffee, and took three bonbons from their box. Slumping into a chair at the kitchen table, she buried her face in her hands. She had to manufacture enough courage to go to work, but that was still three hours away. Her mind drifted back to the evil stranger with a tattoo. The tattoo seemed permanently imprinted in her mind.

Angie reached for the envelope from Dr. Cruz that was lying on the counter. She unfolded the wrinkled page. Her hands trembled as she reread its frightening message.

> HIV TEST — NEGATIVE.
> PLEASE RETURN IN TWO MONTHS FOR ANOTHER
> HIV TEST SINCE THESE TESTS ARE NOT VALID FOR
> SEVERAL MONTHS AFTER EXPOSURE TO THE VIRUS.

Maybe I have the HIV virus. Maybe everything I touch will be contaminated. Maybe I shouldn't even go to work. Angela paced around her apartment like a caged lion. Her eyes fell upon her Bible on the end table. She picked it up and clutched it to her breast. Somewhere there had to be a sense of peace. She sunk onto the sofa and began thumbing the pages. She read a few familiar passages here and there. Finally she received enough internal strength to shower and dress for work. She took extra care with her makeup as she had to conceal the dark circles beneath her eyes.

❖

"Good morning," Tracy greeted as Angie walked into the salon at five minutes after nine. "I hope you had a good night's rest. You were so stressed out when you left yesterday."

"I'm fine," Angie replied as she nervously rearranged her station. "I have a pretty full schedule today."

Angie mechanically got through the day. Her styling was flawless, and she was able to make appropriate small talk with each of her clients. Her movements became robot-like without feeling or emotion. At five o'clock she left the salon, picked up a TV dinner, chips, and a soft drink, and headed home. Food had become her only source of consolation.

After eating her TV dinner and snack foods, Angie flopped onto her sofa, grabbed her TV remote, and began mindlessly surfing the channels. Nothing attracted her interest. Just as she clicked off the remote, the phone rang. Angie jumped with fear even though nothing was there to frighten her, then relaxed as she reached for the phone.

"Hello."

"Hello, Angie. How are you doing?" Jay asked.

"I'm fine. How are you?" Angie's voice was dull and monotone.

"Angie, you don't sound well. Is something wrong?"

"No. I'm just tired."

"I'm sorry. I was hoping to come and see you tonight," Jay replied sadly.

"I'd love to have you come, but I plan to turn in early tonight. I was having nightmares last night and didn't get much sleep. What frightens me is that it was all so real."

"I wish there was something I could do for you. Would it help to talk about it?"

"I don't know," Angie sighed. "I relived the entire rape. In my dream I could see a snake tattooed on the attacker's right arm. Do you think seeing the tattoo in a dream is important?"

"It could be you're now recalling a repressed memory, or it could be just your mind playing tricks," Jay said cautiously. "However, I'd suggest you call Officer Santos and tell her about your dream. It won't be enough to convict anyone, but they need any clues they can get."

"I'd hate to call her. I don't like talking about it."

"I can understand why you'd feel that way, but I do think they need to know. Doesn't Officer Santos work the evening shift?"

"I think so. Maybe if I get my courage up, I'll call her before I go to bed."

"Good girl." Jay smiled. "I'm really proud of you. I know it won't be easy for you, but you have a lot of inner strength. How about going swimming with me at Tarague Beach Friday afternoon?"

"I'd love to," Angie replied.

"Good. I'll pick you up at about two."

The two visited for a few more minutes, then agreed to get together the next evening. Angie hung up the phone and took a deep breath. Did she really have the courage to call the police station?

Basking in Jay's encouragement, she reached for the telephone book. She found the non-emergency number and dialed it. The phone was answered after the second ring by a male voice. Angie's voice trembled as she asked for Officer Santos.

"Officer Santos," a female voice greeted.

"Hello, this is Angela Quinata. I think I remember something more about my attacker, but I'm not sure."

"Any little bit of information will be helpful. We still don't have a lot to go on," Officer Santos replied.

Angie described her dream and the vividness of the snake tattoo. She explained she wasn't sure where her dream ended and reality began. At that point she felt silly and wished she hadn't called.

"Angela, I'm glad you called. As you know, that's not enough to convict anyone, but we'll keep our eyes open for men with tattoos. So far, outside of him having dark hair, that's all we have to go on. If you think of anything else, be sure and call me."

❖

The days passed with marked similarities for Angie. The customers continued to be pleased with her work. Yan kept watching her from behind his glass office window, and she kept having nightmares about a dark-haired man with a snake tattoo.

On Friday Yan did not appear at work at his normal time, and by noon Angie became curious. Between customers she turned to Tracy. "Where's Yan today? Is he ill?"

Tracy wrinkled her forehead. "Angie, you're so naive. You'll have to learn that you don't ask questions about what goes on at Coiffure and Manicure. Yan does his own thing. If you want to get ahead in the business, you have to go along with what he says without questioning. He sets his own hours."

Blood rushed to Angie's face as she shrunk into herself. "Sorry," she muttered. "I didn't realize."

Just then Yan walked into the salon and went directly to his office without speaking to anyone. Angie stood frozen in horror. Yan was wearing a beige tank top with plaid shorts. On his right shoulder was the tattoo of a coiled snake.

Yan's dark eyes pierced her haze as it settled on Angie's trembling body. She grabbed her purse and ran from the shop. A red Toyota screeched to a stop as she darted between the rows of cars.

Not knowing what to do, Angie started her car and turned down Marine Drive toward the police station. Perhaps Officer Santos could help her. Tears filled her eyes as she maneuvered through the traffic. If only Jay wasn't busy with his job until Saturday afternoon.

Angie parked her car in front of the Guam police station and raced up the steps.

Her heart pounded wildly.

"May I help you," a stern face asked as she entered the building.

"I need to see Officer Santos," Angie's voice trembled.

"I'm sorry; she doesn't come on duty until seven o'clock. Can someone else help you?"

"I–I–I don't know. I just have some more information about the rapist near the community college. Maybe I should come back later."

"No, don't do that," the brisk officer replied as he rose from his desk. "I'll take you to someone else in that division."

He motioned for her to follow him down a dark hall into a back office. Another stern male officer was hunched over his desk. "Officer Aguigui, this young lady claims to have more information about the rapes." The officer then turned and disappeared down the same dark hallway.

"Please be seated, Miss," Officer Aguigui said as he reached into his desk and took out a tape recorder. "Do you mind if I record this?"

Angie took a deep breath. She had been through this before, but never with someone as expressionless as Officer Aguigui. "No problem," she answered.

Angie then proceeded to recount what she remembered about the night of her rape and her nightmares about the dark-haired man with a coiled snake tattoo. Then she added about how she had seen that same tattoo on her boss. Her voice trembled with each sentence. Officer Aguigui took notes while the tape continued to turn.

When Angie finished, he looked over his dark-rimmed glasses. "Is there anything else you'd like to tell me?"

"No."

"Thank you for coming. I'll pass this information on to Officer Santos. We will certainly take a hard look at Mr. Yan Chung—but we can't arrest someone because of what you saw in a dream."

"I understand," Angie muttered as she rose to leave. Her shoulders slumped as she hurried toward her car. *What if Yan followed me from the mall?*

She drove home through the side streets and alleys, always looking over her shoulder. Children played in the yards as chickens wandered free around the tin-roofed houses. Her love for the diversity of Guam battled the fear of Yan and the lack of police protection. She wanted to call her mother, but she knew what her response would be. . .move back home with her. Angie was determined to be her own person and solve her own problems, regardless of how difficult they might be.

Angie hurried into her apartment and double-bolted her door. Breathing a sigh of relief, she hurried to her refrigerator. She took out a bowl of leftover Chinese noodles and popped it into the microwave. Within minutes she was relaxing in front of the TV, consoling herself with food. She vowed she would not let the events of the day haunt her until she talked with Jay. Her entire career as a beautician was on the line.

An hour before Jay was scheduled to arrive, Angie reached into her drawer for her swimming suit. The thought of spending an afternoon at Tarague Beach with Jay thrilled her. Tarague Beach was the nicest one on the island. Located on Andersen Air Force Base, only military personnel and their guests were allowed to use it.

She pulled on her aqua-and-blue-striped swimsuit and examined herself in the mirror. A look of horror spread across her face. Extra rolls of fat padded her normally petite five-foot two-inch frame. She threw herself across her bed and sobbed. Her mother's warning kept flashing through her mind. *Honey, you're not tall enough to add even a few extra pounds. You better watch your diet. You're eating more junk foods now than ever before in your life.* She lay on her bed and berated herself for gaining so much weight.

In the midst of her grief, the doorbell rang. She hurriedly tied her swimsuit wrap around her waist, dried her eyes with a tissue, and ran to the door. "Is that you, Jay?" she shouted through the bolted door.

"Who are you expecting?" he teased.

Angie opened the door and motioned for him to enter. "Hi, Jay. I'm glad you came, but I'm afraid I can't go to the beach with you."

Jay studied Angie's red, puffy eyes. "Why not? We've been planning this for days."

Tears again filled Angie's eyes. "I–I–I just can't. I look terrible."

"You look lovely," Jay assured her. "Your scarf looks like what all the other women are wearing at the beach."

"It's not my hair," Angie protested. "It's my new fat. I can't let anyone see me this way."

Try as he might, Jay could not convince her to wear a bathing suit to the beach. He finally convinced her to wear a pair of slacks and just enjoy the warm trade breeze while they watched the setting sun together."

Angie relaxed in the seat next to Jay as they drove toward the gate of Andersen Air Force Base. Maybe she was silly about being so upset over a few extra pounds. After all, if she exercised and watched her diet again, she could lose those pounds in a few weeks. She reached for the radio dial in Jay's car and settled on a local, popular station. Her spirits lifted slightly as her favorite love song echoed through the car. As the song ended, an excited announcer came on the air.

"And now for some late-breaking news," the announcer shouted. "The Guam rapist was apprehended as he attacked his thirteenth victim in the vicinity of Guam Community College. Officials will hold a press conference in the police station conference room at six o'clock. Please stay tuned for more details."

Chapter 6

Angie Quinata took a deep breath as Jay opened the front door of the Guam Police Station for her. Her desire to learn the truth of the Guam rapist was only slightly stronger than the fear of having to relive that horrible night.

"Angie, I'm glad you came," Officer Santos greeted as the young couple entered the reception area. "I've been trying to get ahold of you all afternoon. I need to talk with you before the press conference."

Angie shuddered, then forced a smile. "Why do you need to see me? I told Officer Aguigui all I knew."

Officer Santos patted Angie on the shoulder. "Relax. Everything's going to be all right."

"I'm sorry," Angie stammered. "I'm scared."

The police officer smiled and put them both at ease. "Come with me, and I'll fill you in on the details. Your friend may come too, if he'd like."

Angie looked at Jay for reassurance. He nodded his head and smiled. "Soon this will all be over for you."

The trio entered a small, glassed-in room with a large wooden desk, an upholstered executive chair, and three smaller chairs. Officer Santos arranged the guest chairs in a semi-circle and gestured for them to be seated. "I'm sorry I wasn't here when you came in yesterday. I listened to the tape of your interview with Officer Aguigui. It must have been a grueling experience for you."

"He was so harsh. I didn't think he understood what I was trying to tell him."

Officer Santos gave an understanding nod. "Men aren't often very sensitive about emotional issues."

"That's an understatement," Angie sighed.

"He understood a lot more than you realized. He got right to work on your lead just as soon as you left the police station. He had an immediate surveillance put on Yan Chung. Fortunately, we were there when he snuck up behind his next victim and tried to drag her into the bushes."

Those words calmed Angie's fears. She gradually unclutched her fists, and the wrinkles on her forehead faded.

Officer Santos studied the faces of the handsome couple across from her.

They've been through so much together. I wonder if this will be the end of their friendship? Few relationships survive such ordeals.

Angie breathed a sigh of relief and took Jay's hand. "So I wasn't wrong after all. I was afraid the snake tattoo was just a dream and that I might be ruining an innocent person's life with my neurotic fears."

"Angie, don't be so hard on yourself. Repressed memories often surface in the form of a dream," the police officer explained. "That's why we were willing to take a chance and follow your lead."

"Do you think Yan has AIDS?" Angie blurted. "I have to have HIV tests for years to come, and I'm afraid to get close to anyone."

"We did some preliminary testing on Yan today, and one was the HIV test. We should have the results back in a few days."

Jay squeezed Angie's hand. "As soon as those tests are back, your fears will be over."

"It's not all that easy," Angie protested. "Even if I don't have HIV, I'm still a spoiled woman."

The hard, professional look faded from Officer Santos's face. "You remind me of my own daughter. She had a gentle spirit much like yours. She always put the needs of others over herself. We lost her in a diving accident a couple years ago." Silence enveloped the room as tears welled in the police officer's eyes. "Angie, I know it doesn't feel like it right now, but you're not a spoiled woman. You may have been physically harmed, but no one can damage your spirit."

"That's what I've been trying to tell her ever since this happened, but she doesn't and won't listen to me. I feel so helpless," Jay said.

"Jay, I know you want to protect her and make everything right for her, but this is a very individual experience for a woman. Those who have been violated respond best to other women who have been through the same thing. The emotions involved are hard to explain unless you've experienced it yourself. Rape is not something you can recover from overnight."

"Thank you," Angie whispered as she continued staring at the floor. "I'm glad someone understands what I'm going through."

Just as quickly as it had vanished, the professional side of Officer Santos reappeared. She glanced nervously at the clock over the young couple's heads and jumped to her feet. "It's almost time for the news conference; perhaps we can talk more after it's over."

The conference room was crowded with cameras, microphones, and reporters with tape recorders when Angie and Jay found a seat in the back row. Angie scanned the room nervously. *I hope no one recognizes me. What if they ask me questions? I could never speak in front of all these people.* She fidgeted in her chair as the Guam police chief walked to the podium.

"Welcome to this impromptu press conference," the chief said as he scanned the room. "It is with mixed emotions that I address you at this time. Fear has engulfed all the women on the island since the rapes began near the community college this past spring. Thirteen cases have been reported to the police department, and probably more than that have not. Many women are afraid to report such crimes and live the rest of their lives in fear and shame."

If I hadn't been beaten and taken to the hospital, I don't think I'd have had the courage to report the attack, Angie told herself. *It's all too embarrassing.*

The police chief's eyes settled on Angie's trembling lips. "Thanks to a tip from a brave young victim, we were able to locate the suspect and apprehend him just as he was attacking another woman. We have arrested Mr. Yan Chung, owner of the Coiffure and Manicure Beauty Salon, and charged him with thirteen counts of rape. We are also investigating allegations that he ran a drug and prostitution ring from his salon. We expect to announce further arrests in the near future. I can't divulge details that would impede our ongoing investigation, but I'm willing to entertain any questions at this time."

A flood of hands flew up around the room. The police chief pointed to a reporter from a local TV station who had raised his hand. "Who was the woman who provided you the tip which led to the arrest of Yan Chung? What kind of information did you have to go on?"

Angie took a deep breath. *Please, God, don't let him say my name. I want to get as far away from Guam as possible. I don't want to be the subject of island gossip.*

The chief glanced at Angie's closed eyes and wrinkled forehead. He hesitated, then turned his attention back to the reporter. "I'm sorry, but that information is confidential. We must respect the privacy of the victims."

The maze of questions that followed were a blur to Angie. It was all she could do to keep from running from the room. Her entire life lay in ashes around her. She was a spoiled woman, her place of employment was being investigated as a center for drugs and prostitution, and her reputation was ruined.

When the press conference was over, Angie and Jay merged with the crowd noisily rushing toward the front door. The last rays of the soft pink sun were setting over the Philippine Sea. The palm trees were still in the oppressive tropical heat. Angie was unaware of people scattering to their cars in the parking lot. She felt numb from head to toe. *I must be having a dream. This can't possibly be happening to me. Soon I'm going to wake up and be back in college planning for my graduation and applying for jobs.*

Angie sat quietly as Jay drove the familiar streets of Agana and turned toward Magnolia. There seemed to be no escape. Tears streamed down her cheeks as they neared her apartment. She took out a tissue and wiped her eyes.

Jay reached over and took her hand. "Honey, what's wrong? You should be happy; it's over."

"It will never be over for me," Angie snapped. "My reputation's shot. Even if the public never knows about the rape, everyone knows I worked for Coiffure and Manicure. I wish I could get as far away from Guam as possible. If I had relatives on the mainland, I'd be on the next plane out of here."

"You have a lot of friends in Montana," Jay replied. "Let me make a few calls tonight, and I'll get back to you tomorrow. You might begin mentally packing your bags. I'm confident I can work something out for you."

"No one will want an unemployed, penniless misfit," Angie objected bitterly. "Why should they care about my problems? They don't even know me."

"Rebecca Hatfield thinks the world of you. She's been writing almost twice a week asking how you're doing. I'll call her tonight and explain what has happened. There is plenty of healing love in Rocky Bluff."

❖

Barbara Old Tail laid down her brush and wiped the perspiration from her forehead with the sleeve of her paint-splattered shirt. "I'll be glad when this heat wave breaks. If I thought it'd do any good, I'd get a bigger air-conditioner now, but there's just not enough summer left to make it worth my while."

"We're just about finished," Rebecca Hatfield said as she reached for her glass of iced tea. "You can be mighty proud of this extension. Hopefully, you'll be ready for customers by the first of September."

"I may have all the structural changes made by then, but I don't know where I'll find someone to help. I called the beauty schools in both Great Falls and Billings, and none of the graduates were interested in coming to Rocky Bluff. I'm getting plenty discouraged."

"There must be someone out there who's just right for your salon. God wouldn't have brought you this far to let you down now," Rebecca reminded her.

Barb shrugged her shoulders and grinned. "I know you're right. I guess I get discouraged too easily." Barb stepped back and surveyed the room that was once the Genteel Gift Shop. "I think I need to trim this with floral wallpaper. Would you like to go to Great Falls with me tomorrow and help me select wallpaper and mirrors?"

"I'd love to," Rebecca replied lightheartedly. "Andy is so busy with the addition at the fire station I doubt if he'll even miss me."

"Now that's talking like a true married woman," Barb chuckled. "How about if I pick you up around nine o'clock in the morning?"

Rebecca readily agreed, and the two women turned their attention back to the task before them. They added the final touches of paint to the room, then hurriedly cleaned their brushes. They were both eager to get home to prepare dinner for their spouses.

While Rebecca and Andy were relaxing over a bowl of sherbet after dinner that evening, their telephone rang. "Oh, no," Andy groaned. "I hope I don't have to go back to the station tonight. I was looking forward to a quiet evening at home with my bride."

Rebecca patted him on the shoulder as she hurried to the phone. "Hello," she said as she pushed her graying hair away from her ear.

"Hello, Rebecca," a deep male voice greeted. "How are you doing?"

"I'm doing great," she replied with a look of puzzlement. Suddenly her face brightened. "Is this Jay Harkness?"

"I knew you could never forget me," he teased. A wave of Montana homesickness swept over him, followed by a vision of Angie's troubled face. "How's life in Rocky Bluff?"

"Busy," Rebecca replied. "Andy's been putting in long hours at the fire station, and I've been busy helping Barb Old Tail remodel and expand her beauty salon. The physical plant is almost complete, but she's having trouble finding a beautician who's willing to come to Rocky Bluff to work for her."

Jay's heart began to pound. "Rebecca, could this be providence in action? Angie's begging to leave Guam, but she doesn't have any relatives on the mainland. She's been sheltered all her life. She doesn't know how to apply for a job, much less get set up on her own in a strange place. Do you think Barb would be interested in hiring Angie?"

Rebecca squealed with delight. "Angie would be perfect for her. I'm going to Great Falls with Barb tomorrow, and we'll discuss it then. I'll also talk with Andy about her staying here with us. We've remodeled the basement so she'd have her own private bedroom, bath, and sitting room. Why is Angie so anxious to leave Guam? She never seemed like the adventuresome type to me."

Jay shook his head with frustration. "Rebecca, it's the most unbelievable story. I'd have trouble believing it myself if I wasn't living it right along with her. Yesterday they arrested her boss for at least thirteen rapes in the vicinity of the community college. If that's not enough, they believe the place where she worked was the center of a prostitution and drug ring. She's in a deep state of depression."

"How terrible," Rebecca gasped. "That's reason enough for her to come to Rocky Bluff. I'd like nothing better than to take her under my wing and love her out of this. Give me twenty-four hours, and I'll see what I can work out. Will you be home tomorrow at this time so that I can call you back?"

"I'll be waiting anxiously for your call," Jay sighed. "Thanks so much. The people of Rocky Bluff have never let me down."

Rebecca hung up the phone and joined her husband in the living room.

Even though they had been married just a little over a year, she was confident he would welcome a long-term houseguest. She and Andy talked late into the night. Andy had met Angie briefly on his visit to Guam before he and Rebecca were married. He remembered her merely as a shy Chamorro girl with an infectious giggle ready to burst forth at any time. The newlyweds planned how they would rearrange the basement so Angie could have privacy and comfort. As a confirmed bachelor for many years, Andy now looked forward to having a home bursting with the life and enthusiasm of a young person. He did not know, though, how deeply disturbed Angie really was.

Promptly at nine o'clock the next morning, Barb Old Tail stopped her black Mercury in front of the Hatfield residence. Rebecca grabbed her sweater, kissed Andy good-bye, and hurried to the waiting car.

"All ready?" Barb greeted.

"Couldn't be more so," Rebecca chuckled as she slid into the passenger seat and fastened her seat belt. "And do I have news for you."

"What's that?"

"Jay Harkness called last night and said his Guamanian girlfriend would like to come to Rocky Bluff to live for awhile."

"That's nice," Barb replied politely. "I suppose she'll stay with Bob and Nancy?"

"No, we both agreed that it would be better if she stayed with Andy and me," Rebecca could scarcely hold back her enthusiasm as her words began to fall over each other. "The best part is that Angie is a trained beautician right out of the School of Cosmetology at Guam Community College."

"She's a what?" Barb exclaimed as a rush of adrenalin shot through her body.

"A beautician. . .just what you've been praying for these last few weeks. And you were ready to give up hope," Rebecca exclaimed.

Barb's hands tightened around the steering wheel. "I can't believe it," she gasped. "I honestly thought I wasn't going to be able to get anyone. How soon is she going to come?"

"I have to call Jay back tonight with an answer. Are you certain you want to hire her? You know she does come from a slightly different background."

"Don't be silly," Barb chided. "Of course I do. In fact, it'll be fun having her. I'll start making plans for her to get her Montana Beautician's License right away. It shouldn't be too difficult since she graduated from an accredited cosmetology school."

"Then it's settled," Rebecca said. "I'll call Jay and tell him to buy the plane ticket. She'll probably come in a couple weeks since you usually get the cheapest fare with a fourteen-day notice."

The day flew by for the two friends from Rocky Bluff. They excitedly went from store to store looking for the perfect wallpaper for the salon. Knowing that she would soon have help added even more enthusiasm to Barb's shopping spree. God was answering her prayers far better than she had ever anticipated. Instead of preparing a Montana girl to come to Rocky Bluff, the long arm of the Lord had reached half the world away.

❁

In that place half the world away, Jay could no longer stand the suspense of waiting for Rebecca's call. He dialed Rebecca from Angie's apartment. After he and Rebecca talked for a few minutes, he handed the phone to Angie. "Rebecca, how can I ever thank you?" she said with tears running down her face. "I hate to leave Guam. It's the only place I've ever known, but I can't stay here," she sobbed. "I'll never be able to get another job. Being employed at Coiffure and Manicure is fatal to have on my resume. Everyone knows about the charges against them. But I don't want to impose on you and Andy."

"Don't be silly," Rebecca protested. "We're looking forward to having you. You'll love Rocky Bluff and all the people here."

"I've heard so many good things about it," Angie replied as she wiped the tears from her eyes and began to calm herself. "I'm anxious to meet all of Jay's family, especially his grandmother. She's sounds like quite a lady."

"She's one of a kind. She's the matriarch and mentor of nearly the entire community. She has a way of taking everyone under her wing and erasing the pain, regardless of how deep it might be."

Angie's eyes became distant as she gazed through the living room window at the palm trees below. "I need someone to erase the pain," she murmured.

❁

Jay spent as much time as possible with Angie before she was to leave. He tried to describe the rolling plains and the nearby majestic snowy mountains. Nothing could ever replace his love for Montana.

"Angie, I wish I could be with you to experience the changing of the seasons. It's something words cannot describe. One day the leaves on a tree are solid green, and nearly overnight they become vibrant with oranges, yellows, and reds."

"It sounds beautiful," Angie replied as she slid closer to him on the sofa. "I stopped at the library this afternoon and thumbed through the travel books and magazines about Montana. It's so different from the cowboys and Indians that I pictured from the old westerns on TV. I can hardly believe that a week from today I'll actually be there."

Jay continued describing his hometown, then made a list of all his family and friends that he wanted Angie to be sure and meet. She watched in awe as one name after another was added to the list.

"You can't possibly expect me to remember all these people," she protested good-naturedly.

"It won't take you long," Jay assured her. "Rocky Bluff is a close-knit, friendly community."

The ringing of the phone interrupted their lively conversation. Angie grudgingly picked up the receiver. "Hello."

"Hello, Angie?" a business-like woman's voice greeted. "This is Officer Santos."

Angie's face blanched. *I thought all of this was over and I'd never have to talk with the police again.* "Hello, Officer Santos," she answered politely. "What can I do for you today?"

A warm chuckle echoed over the phone wires. "Angie, relax. I just called to give you some good news."

The young woman breathed a sigh of relief. "And what is that?"

"Yan Chung's blood tests just came back. You'll be glad to know that he tested HIV negative." Officer Santos hesitated and waited for a response from the other end of the phone lines. Hearing none she continued, "You no longer have to worry about having AIDS."

Angie exploded with excitement. "Thank you. Thank you," she shouted. "I can go to Montana without fear of carrying AIDS. Thanks so much for calling."

"Good-bye and good luck," Officer Santos replied as Angie hung up the phone and turned to the handsome airman standing beside her.

"Now you'll no longer have an excuse not to kiss me," he chuckled as he took her in his arms, and their lips touched with sheer relief.

❁

The last few days Angie and Mitzi tearfully sorted through Angie's things. It was difficult deciding what to ship to Montana and what to store at her mother's. Each article of clothing or household knickknack held a special memory.

"Are you sure I can't convince you to move back home?" Mitzi persisted as she taped shut still another box of clothing. "You're too young to be going halfway around the world by yourself."

Angie's eyes blazed. "I'm not a child anymore. Besides, I'm going where I'll have friends."

"That's the only redeeming part of this whole deal," Mitzi sighed sadly. "I know Rebecca will take good care of you, but it's so far away. If you'd only wait a few months, everyone will forget about the arrests at Coiffure and Manicure. Any salon on the island would love to have a beautician with your talent."

"Oh, Mother. You're just prejudiced," Angie protested meekly. "There's nothing special about my talents. I just do what I was trained to do."

"You are a very special person," Mitzi persisted, "and I'm going to miss you."

Angie's face softened as she studied her mother's countenance. She noticed a few extra gray hairs and added wrinkles in her forehead. "I'll miss you too," she said as she leaned over to give her mother a hug. "I hope you'll be able to come and visit me. You've always said you'd like to visit Montana sometime."

"As soon as your plane lifts off from the airport, I'm going to begin saving my pennies to go. I've never seen snow before, so maybe I'll try to come during Christmas vacation. Just remember my love and prayers will always be with you wherever you may be."

"Thanks, Mom," Angie replied. "I need all the prayer support I can get. I'm really scared, but this is something I know I have to do. I hope you'll understand why I must leave Guam. It's not that I don't love you and don't want to share my life with you."

"As much as I'll miss you, you'll go to Montana with my blessing and all my love," Mitzi said as she hugged her only daughter, while tears streamed down her face.

Chapter 7

Rebecca Hatfield was overjoyed to spend a few hours with Edith Dutton. She hadn't seen her dearest and best friend for several weeks, and it was good to bask in her warmth again. She relaxed on Edith's sofa and told her of the recent telephone conversation she had with Jay Harkness and of the trauma that had befallen his girlfriend. She also told Edith of her friendship with Mitzi Quinata, the girl's mother, during her years in Guam. The former librarian vividly related the details that led up to her introducing Mitzi's daughter to the young airman from her hometown in Montana and the pleasure in watching their friendship develop.

Finally, Rebecca became even more intent in the conversation. "Edith, would you like to ride to Great Falls with me Wednesday to meet Angie's plane? It's a long drive to make alone."

"I'd love to," Edith Dutton replied excitedly. "I can hardly wait to meet her, but I'm afraid I won't be able to keep up with you. Maybe you should find someone else to go with you."

"I plan to make this a relaxing trip with a lot of stops in the rest areas. We have a lot of catching up to do." Rebecca answered. "I've been so busy helping Barb Old Tail expand her salon that I haven't had time to stop for my regular cup of coffee with you."

"I'd be lying if I said I didn't miss our coffee times together. I was having my hair done at the Looking Glass yesterday, and I have to congratulate you and Barb for a job well done." Edith smiled. "The entire Harkness family is extremely grateful for all you're doing to help Jay's friend. If I were ten years younger, I'd love to take her under my wing myself."

"You took more than your share of troubled young people under your wing," Rebecca replied with a twinkle in her eye. "It's time to let the rest of us do our part."

"It's hard for me to slide into the background," Edith chuckled. "Nancy and I would like to host a buffet dinner Sunday afternoon. That way everyone can meet Angie."

"That's extremely thoughtful of both of you, but Angie is such a shy person I'm afraid it might be overwhelming for her."

"I've considered that," Edith replied. "That's why I thought I'd invite

Dawn and some of her friends to have lunch with Angie on Saturday. I suggested that they pick out a comedy video to watch that afternoon to help break the ice. That way Angie could meet Jay's sister and several young people her own age in a more relaxed setting."

"I hope our good intentions aren't too much for her. I keep forgetting she's just been through an extremely traumatic experience. But, hopefully, if she's busy the first few days she's here, she'll be off to a good start of putting her past well into the past. Angie's a delightful girl," Rebecca replied, "but judging by Jay's description, she's pretty well traumatized. It may take us quite awhile to love her out of this."

"If there's one thing Rocky Bluff has plenty of," Edith chuckled, "it's love."

Rebecca leaned back in her chair and stretched. "I imagine Angie's going to be exhausted by the time she gets in. Why don't we make motel reservations in Great Falls, then show her some of the local sights before we drive home."

"Sounds great," Edith nodded. "In fact, it might be a good idea for us to do some serious wardrobe shopping with her. Winter's going to be upon us in a few weeks, and all she'll have will be clothes for eighty-five-degree weather. Since you'll be providing a place for her to stay, the least I can do is provide a winter wardrobe."

"Things are falling into place much easier than I first expected. If Angie only knew what she was coming into, she wouldn't be nearly as fearful as Jay says she is." Rebecca glanced at the clock over the kitchen sink. "I suppose I better be heading home in a few minutes. I still have a lot of housework to do. Tomorrow I'm going to go to Browning with Barbara and help move her mother to Rocky Bluff."

"How is her mother doing?" Edith asked.

Rebecca shook her head sadly. "Alzheimer's disease is ravaging her life along with those who love her. She's fortunate that she has a family that can nurse her during her failing years. Many Alzheimer's patients end up facing a confusing world alone and neglected."

"I'm fortunate that Alzheimer's is one disease that has passed me by," Edith said. "Even though my heart condition has been very frustrating at times, at least my mind keeps functioning."

"I hope scientists come up with a cure for that disease soon," Rebecca said as she stood to leave. "It's a shame people who've lived vibrant, wholesome lives have to spend their last years in a state of mental deterioration. No wonder depression is so common among its victims."

Edith nodded her head knowingly and walked her friend to the door. They bade each other good-bye, and Rebecca hurried home to finish preparing Angie's room. She and Andy, along with Edith Dutton, shared a common conviction that with the combined efforts of the entire community of Rocky Bluff, Angie could be restored to her former self.

❖

Angela Quinata bit her lip as she hugged her mother and Jay. She tried her hardest not to show how frightened she was as she headed toward the ramp of the Hawaiian Airlines 747. She had been to the airport many times before as she waited for friends who were arriving or leaving the island, but she had never flown herself. The passengers around her pushed confidently toward the doorway as their boarding section was called. Angie was swept along with the crowd into an unknown future.

"Welcome aboard," the trim, dark-haired flight attendant greeted.

Angie surveyed the rows of seats. She had seen scores of airplanes on TV, but being on one was totally different. Everyone seemed to know exactly where to go and what to do. "Hi," Angie said timidly. "I've never flown before. Where do I sit?"

"Let me see your ticket," the attendant replied kindly.

Angie handed her the ticket. The attendant studied the ticket, then looked down the aisle. "You have seat twelve A. Do you see the lady in the flowered dress?"

Angie nodded. The attendant smiled as she continued. "You'll be beside her, next to the window."

The frightened young girl clutched her bag and inched her way down the aisle. She stuffed her bag into an empty bin above her seat and turned to the lady in the flowered dress. "Excuse me. I think that's my seat by the window," Angie said as she stepped in front of the woman.

Her neighbor watched Angie nervously become familiar with her surroundings. "Is this your first trip off the island?" the older woman queried.

"Yes, it is," Angie murmured.

"I remember how frightened I was the first time I left the island. That was more than thirty years ago. Now I've been back and forth to the mainland at least once a year, so it's getting to be a rather boring routine."

Angie became entranced watching the ground crew go about their normal preflight duties. She even thought she spotted her new set of luggage on the baggage cart which had just parked under her window. Her excitement soon faded as her eyes drifted to the reflective glass of the terminal. Behind those windows were the two major loves of her life, her mother and her boyfriend. Tears filled her eyes. *Will I ever see them again? Will I ever be able to return to Guam?*

Angie watched the island of Guam become smaller and smaller until it was a mere speck surrounded by miles of water. The screen rolled down in the aisle, and a dated thriller appeared. In sheer boredom, Angie reclined her seat, closed her eyes, and dozed off. Sleep was a welcomed release from her fears of flying into the unknown.

The eight-hour flight to Honolulu seemed endless; the movies and airline meals did little to make the miles pass quickly. Only conversation with the lady in the flowered dress beside her made the trip bearable.

"Where are you going?" the woman asked kindly.

"I'm landing in Great Falls, Montana; then a friend is driving me to Rocky Bluff," Angie replied. "I have to change planes in Honolulu, then Seattle. My boyfriend tried to explain how to find out which gate my next plane leaves from, but I'm afraid I'll get on the wrong plane or get lost in the terminal and miss my flight."

Her neighbor smiled. "Don't worry about a thing. I'm on my way to Seattle myself. I'll make sure you get on the right plane to Great Falls."

"I'd appreciate that, but I can't expect a total stranger to take that much time in helping me," Angie protested.

The lady in the flowered dress burst into a lusty laugh. "My name's Rose Chargalauf. I'm a professor at the University of Guam during the school year; then I teach classes at the University of Washington during the summer. We'll be sharing a limited amount of space for at least eleven hours, so we'll no longer be strangers when we get there. I'd be glad to help you through the terminal."

Angie giggled, then introduced herself, but when Rose asked her what she was going to be doing in Rocky Bluff, Montana, Angie blanched. *What can I say? I can't tell her I'm trying to get as far away from Guam as possible because I'd been raped and my place of employment is under investigation for drug and prostitution violations.*

Angie's mind raced. Words tumbled out on top of each other. "I was offered a job in a salon in Rocky Bluff, Montana. I don't know how long I'll stay."

Rose wrinkled her face. "Why did you choose Montana of all places? I heard that it gets real cold there."

"My high school librarian lives there, and she was able to find a job for me," Angie murmured. "I thought it'd be fun to live around snow. Maybe I can even learn to ski."

"That sounds like quite an adventure for a single girl," Rose noted. "I admire young women who aren't afraid to follow their dreams."

Angie nodded and looked out the window. *If she only knew how fearful I really am. I'm not following my dreams; I'm running from a mess.* She leaned back in her seat, closed her eyes, and pretended to sleep. She didn't want to have to explain her tumultuous life any further.

Sensing Angie's tension, Rose spent most of the trip preparing for her summer classes, while Angie dozed or stared blankly out the window. Having worked with young people all her adult life, she understood the need for quiet contemplation during troubled times.

At long last a faint speck of Oahu came into view and gradually became larger and larger. All the passengers leaned toward the windows as the details of the island began to take shape. "To the right is the famous Punchbowl Memorial Cemetery," Rose said as she pointed to a dome-shaped structure on a grassy knoll. "Many of our war heroes are buried there."

The plane bounced onto the runway and taxied toward the terminal. "We have a two-hour layover before our plane leaves for Seattle. I know of a real cute restaurant not far from the gate we'll be leaving from. Let me treat you to dinner."

"Okay. . .sure," Angie smiled. "That's very generous of you."

The excitement of the landing, disembarking, and the hustle and bustle of the terminal distracted Angie from her inner turmoil. Even though Guam was becoming a melting pot of races, until she met Jay, she had stayed primarily with her own Chamorro people. The Honolulu airport was filled with nearly every nationality on earth. Some were dressed in eastern garb, others in western wear, and many in island wear. Tour groups from Japan and the mainland were greeted by hostesses with a lei for each of the vacationers.

The two-hour layover passed quickly as the two acquaintances browsed the gift shops and dined in a Chinese restaurant. The college professor's enthusiasm for life was contagious, and Angie's fears did not resurface until she was on the plane again heading for Seattle. She again tried to watch another boring movie and sleep, but her fears consumed her. *I wonder if the people of Rocky Bluff will like me, especially Jay's family. What if I can't get used to the cold weather? What if I'm not able to earn enough to support myself?* Angie's thoughts became consumed with "what ifs," and she fought to choke back her tears.

When the Hawaiian airliner landed in Seattle, Rose walked her to the gate where the Northwest flight to Great Falls would depart. They arrived just as the other passengers were beginning to board. Angie hurriedly thanked Rose for her help and presented her boarding pass to the agent at the door. She silently thanked God for giving her Rose to guide her through the crowded terminals. More than ever before, Angie's frightening world closed in around her. She surveyed the male passengers on the plane. *Are any of them capable of rape?* she pondered. The better groomed they were the more frightened she became of them.

❁

The drive from Rocky Bluff to Great Falls was uneventful for Rebecca

Hatfield and Edith Dutton. The bright red harvesters provided a vivid contrast to the fields of ripened wheat surrounding the highway. The last days of summer always provided a flurry of activities in Montana. Rebecca and Edith discussed the sights and events they'd like to share with their new guest. If there was time the next morning, they hoped to visit the Charlie Russell Museum and Art Gallery, then Giant Springs Park before leaving Great Falls. With the young people's luncheon, the Sunday buffet, and the Little Big Horn County Fair the next week, there was a myriad of events to enjoy. There was always something new and exciting to do in the Treasure State.

Upon arriving in Great Falls, Rebecca and Edith checked into the Holiday Inn. They enjoyed a relaxing dinner in the hotel dining room, then headed for the Great Falls International Airport an hour before Angie's plane was scheduled to arrive. Both were beside themselves with anticipation. Rebecca would again have a link to her beloved Guam, while Edith hoped for another link to her beloved grandson.

Rebecca mechanically stopped her car at the red light at the corner of Tenth Avenue South and Fifteenth Street. *Great Falls has got to be one of the most orderly cities in the country,* she thought as she patiently waited for the light to change. She was halfway across the intersection after the light turned green when she screamed.

A red pickup truck coming from the right slammed into the rear panel of her Chrysler Fifth Avenue. "Dear Jesus, help us," Edith gasped as the car spun around and blocked traffic in both directions.

When the car finally jerked to a stop, Rebecca looked over at her friend. "Are you okay?"

"I think so," Edith gasped. "I'm just thankful to still be alive."

The next hour was a blur of events. Rebecca and the driver of the pickup were able to move their vehicles to the side street, away from the flow of traffic. The Great Falls police were on the scene within minutes. Rebecca was prepared for the usual presenting of driver's licenses and insurance companies; much to her chagrin the other driver was uninsured. The police did not waste time before writing tickets for speeding, failure to stop at a red light, and failure to have proper insurance. The young man dressed in a cowboy hat and boots did his best to soften his role in the mishap, but to no avail. The police were more determined than ever to charge him with the traffic violations.

In the background a wail of sirens drew closer. An ambulance pulled to a stop behind Rebecca's car, and two attendants jumped out. "Is anyone hurt?" the driver asked as he hurried toward the officer.

"Check the passenger in the car," he replied as he nodded toward Edith who had her head laid back on the seat, relaxing. "I understand that she has a heart condition."

The two emergency medical technicians hurried to the side of the car and opened the car. "Are you all right, Ma'am?"

"I think I'm just shaken a little," Edith replied cautiously.

"Let me check your pulse and blood pressure," the paramedic continued as he reached into his bag for a stethoscope. Within minutes he was recording the data on his sheet.

"How is it?" she asked.

"Both your pulse and blood pressure are high, but not unreasonable for someone who has just been in a car accident. I'd suggest you go home and relax. If you have any problems, be sure and get in touch with your family physician right away."

"I'm from Rocky Bluff," Edith explained. "We're on our way to the airport to pick up my grandson's friend." She glanced nervously at her watch. "In fact, the plane would have landed fifteen minutes ago."

Edith fidgeted, while Rebecca finished talking with the police. Her eyes scanned the skies for incoming flights. Much to her chagrin, lights were rising skyward from the bluff on which the airport was located. With so few planes in and out of the Great Falls airport, it was obvious that this was Angie's plane departing.

Rebecca took a deep breath as she slid behind the wheel of her damaged car. "I hope Angie doesn't arrive before we get there. Can you imagine how frightening it would be to be in a strange place, not knowing a soul and not knowing what to do?"

"I think she's already there," Edith sighed as the car turned back onto Tenth Avenue South and headed for the airport. "It looked like her plane taking off a few minutes ago."

Rebecca stopped her car in the ten-minute parking area. Only airport personnel were in the nearly vacant terminal. She wanted to run up the escalator to find her young friend, but she knew Edith was not capable of keeping up with her. The pair hurried through security and went to the desolate gate where the plane from Seattle landed. An attendant at a nearby gate confirmed their worst fear. That plane had landed more than a half hour before.

Rebecca and Edith next headed toward the baggage claim area. There in a corner sat a frightened Pacific Island girl surrounded by suitcases, sobbing hysterically. The look of terror in her eyes cut deep into Edith's and Rebecca's hearts. The last half hour must have been one of the longest in her short lifetime. It would take a major miracle to restore that broken spirit, but did they have the capacity to reach into the inner crevices of her soul?

Chapter 8

"Angie," Rebecca shouted as she ran toward the sobbing young woman. Angie collapsed into Rebecca's arms and continued sobbing as the older woman embraced her. "You came," Angie choked. "I thought you didn't want me to come and weren't able to get ahold of me."

"Oh, Angie, we're excited about you coming. Please forgive me for being late. It must have been terrible for you. We had an accident an hour ago, and I couldn't get away."

"I'm sorry. I couldn't imagine that you would let me down, but I was so scared," Angie replied as she reached for a tissue to dry her eyes.

"Angie, I'd like you to meet Jay's grandmother, Edith Dutton. Edith, this is Angie Quinata."

Edith stepped forward and hugged Angie as if she were an old friend. "Welcome to Montana. I'm so happy to meet you at last. Jay has told me so much about you in his letters."

"Edith, it's so nice to finally meet you. Jay told me you were praying for us daily. It's been so terrible, I don't know what I'd have done without knowing I had prayer support from all parts of the world."

Rebecca surveyed the desolate terminal. "I don't see anyone to help us with the baggage, but there's a row of carts down the way. I'm parked in the loading zone so I'm sure we can handle them ourselves."

Edith followed as Rebecca and Angie loaded the cart and headed for the Hatfields' Chrysler. Much to Rebecca's dismay the trunk was too bent to open. She tried to open the back door, but it too was bent and would not budge. With frustration, Rebecca pushed the cart to the left side of the car and began loading Angie's luggage. "I'm sorry, but it looks like you'll have to ride in front with us," Rebecca noted. "I can't make enough room back in the backseat."

"That's okay. I just hope I don't crowd the two of you," Angie replied timidly.

"That's one advantage of larger cars," Rebecca chuckled as she motioned for Angie to slide into the middle of the seat. "Space is no problem."

Angie's eyes danced as she saw the lights of the city spread for miles as Rebecca turned onto I-15 from the Great Falls airport. On Guam the island is so flat and the vegetation so thick that drivers can only see for a few yards

71

at any given point. As Angie began to relax in the warmth and friendship of Rebecca and Edith, fatigue overtook her. "What time is it here?"

"Ten o'clock," Edith replied.

"It seems strange to have spent more than eighteen hours in the air or in terminals, and it's only four hours later than when I left."

"Our bodies get so confused when we cross the International Date Line," Rebecca agreed. "It usually took me at least three days to get over my jet lag when I flew back and forth from Guam."

"Now I understand why Guam is known as "Where America's Day Begins," Angie laughed as she laid her head against the seat.

"Are you hungry?" Edith queried. "It's probably been quite awhile since you ate."

"I'm sorry, but I'm just too tired to sit in a restaurant," Angie sighed. "I could take a nap in the car if you want to stop."

Rebecca glanced at her young friend in her rearview window. "We'll do nothing of the sort," she scolded gently. "We'll call room service when we get back to the hotel."

"I think I'm too tired to even eat, but it's been awhile so I suppose I should before I fall asleep," Angie replied as she closed her eyes in exhaustion.

Arriving at the hotel, Rebecca parked her car near the doorway closest to their room. She turned off the engine and slid from behind the wheel. "Angie, what suitcases will you need for the night?"

Angie followed Edith out the passenger side door. "Everything I need is in my shoulder bag."

"Good, it's right on top," Rebecca replied as she took the bag from the backseat.

As soon as Angie saw the bed, she collapsed lengthwise across it. It seemed like forever since she had slept in a bed. "I could use a small bowl of rice and a glass of milk before I go to sleep."

Edith and Rebecca exchanged glances. "Sorry," Edith replied. "Rice isn't on the hotel menu. Montana is beef and potatoes country. Would you like to see the menu?"

Angie glanced through the menu. "I guess I'll have a lot to get used to. . . a club sandwich with a soda will be fine."

Edith and Rebecca also decided on sandwiches and pop. While Rebecca was on the phone to room service, Edith looked over at Angie who was sobbing softly into the pillow. Edith sat on the bed beside her. "What's wrong, Dear?"

Angie turned her face toward her new friend. "I can't explain it," she sobbed. "It's just too much. Everything is happening too fast, and I'm so confused."

"I know it's hard having gone through the most traumatic experience in your life and now to be halfway around the world," Edith said softly as she brushed Angie's dark hair away from her eyes. "When my husband was in a nursing home, one of the nurses taught me how to give a back massage to help him relax before going to sleep. I may be a little rusty, but would you like a massage?"

"It sounds great," Angie replied. "The muscles in my neck and shoulders feel like they're tied in knots."

While Edith massaged Angie's tight muscles, she shared some of the antics of Jay's growing-up years and how he used to play airplane pilot with his friend, Ryan Reynolds. The bond between the two was instantaneous and based on something deeper than their common love for Jay Harkness. There seemed to be more healing in Edith's hands than the mere massaging of sore muscles.

"Angie, Sunday afternoon I'm planning a welcoming brunch for you to give you a chance to meet all the Harkness clan and many of our close friends."

"How thoughtful," Angie replied.

"Saturday, if it's all right with you, I've invited Dawn, Jay's sister, and some of her friends for pizza and a video. I thought it would be nice if you got to meet some of the young people of Rocky Bluff."

"That is very kind of you," Angie yawned.

While Edith massaged Angie's back and neck, Rebecca called Andy to tell him about the accident. She didn't want to shock him when she drove into the drive with a damaged car.

When their sandwiches arrived, Angie quietly ate, then prepared for bed. Within minutes she was fast asleep. A look of peaceful relaxation covered the young girl's face as she lay sleeping in a hotel half the world away from her home. Instead of leaving everyone she loved behind, she again was immersed in love and acceptance.

❖

Angie's arrival in Rocky Bluff was not fully understood and supported by the younger generation. Rumors abounded as to the nature of the Pacific Islander.

"Mom, do I have to take my friends over to Grandma's Saturday?" Dawn Harkness protested. "It'll be embarrassing explaining to them that my brother, the most handsome guy in his graduating class, fell in love with a foreigner."

Nancy Harkness looked at her daughter and shook her head with disbelief. "Dawn, I'm surprised that you feel that way. Guamanians are American citizens the same as you are. Their culture may be slightly different from yours, but so what? You've lived around Native Americans all your life, and some have become your close friends. Please give Angie a chance. Your grandmother would be heartbroken if she heard you say that."

Dawn hung her head. "I suppose. I don't want to hurt Grandma's feelings." Dawn then forced a smile. "Besides, Jay will be furious with me if I don't treat his girlfriend right. I'll talk to the girls about what video to get, and we can order a couple pizzas to go with it. I know Sarah's going to be hurt meeting Angie. Ever since she was in junior high, she's had a crush on Jay. After all, he and Ryan were the stars of both the football and the basketball teams."

"I knew I could depend on you," Nancy replied. "Just remember what you would feel like if what happened to Angie had happened to you. Think how scared she must feel never having been off the island of Guam before and suddenly to be in the wide open spaces of Montana. She needs all the love and support the people of Rocky Bluff can give her. Being sized up by a bunch of critical teens will only make it harder for her."

Dawn was proud of her brother, but as she grew into her teens, she felt more and more pushed into the background as her teachers, fellow students, and the community members compared her with her brother's athletic ability. The comparison didn't hold up. Dawn excelled in music and could care less about sports.

Several of her friends were looking forward to Jay returning to Rocky Bluff after his discharge from the Air Force. Now Jay was sending a Chamorro girl to Rocky Bluff ahead of him. Even though he claimed they were not engaged, that was the only conclusion Dawn's friends could make. The most eligible guy in town was now taken by an outsider.

❖

Edith Dutton and Rebecca Hatfield awoke around seven o'clock. They bathed and dressed, while Angie's sleep was so deep that she scarcely moved the entire night. The older women curled up with favorite books to avoid waking the weary traveler. By eight-thirty Rebecca whispered, "Edith, we're going to be needing breakfast pretty soon, but I'd hate to awaken Angie. Let's call room service for breakfast. We don't have to check out until eleven."

"Sounds good. I am getting a little hungry," Edith agreed. "Let me take another look at their room service menu."

"I'll load our luggage in the car while we wait for room service," Rebecca whispered as she finished closing her suitcase.

The rest of the morning, Rebecca and Edith quietly enjoyed their breakfast, then propped themselves on their beds and enjoyed their leisure reading. Every few minutes they glanced at the beautiful young girl peacefully sleeping in the next bed. At ten-thirty Edith became concerned. "If we have to be out of here by eleven, don't you think we ought to wake Angie so she has time to get ready?"

"I hate to do so, but we really don't have a choice," Rebecca replied. "Maybe we'll have a little time to stop at the mall before we head back to Rocky Buff."

Edith bent over Angie's bed and shook her shoulder gently. "Angie, Angie. I hate to wake you, but we're going to have to check out in a few minutes."

Angie's muscles tightened as she sat up with a start. A shrill scream filled the room. A look of terror was in her eyes.

"Angie, it's okay," Edith assured her as she stroked her shoulder. "You're in Montana with friends."

The young woman rubbed her eyes and looked around the room. "I'm sorry. I don't know why I wake up screaming. It's happened a lot to me lately."

"You're probably suffering from Post Traumatic Stress Syndrome," Edith explained as Angie gradually stopped trembling. "It's a very common malady. Hopefully, it will go away as you become more secure in your new environment."

"Before we leave town, would you like to stop at the mall and find some winter clothes?" Edith asked as Angie reached for her robe.

"I don't think I'll have enough money to do any serious shopping until after I've worked for a few weeks," Angie replied meekly.

"I'd like to help you with that," Edith replied. "I received a little extra money from Roy's life insurance policy, and I'm certain helping you get reestablished would be exactly what he would have chosen himself."

"But I've never worn winter clothes before. I don't know what to look for."

"We'll help you," Rebecca inserted. "All you'll need to do is tell us which style out of many you like the best."

"But this is August. Do they have coats in the stores now?"

"The back-to-school sales are starting, and they always have a good supply of winter wear then. It should be a lot of fun." Edith smiled.

The remainder of the day was a blur of activities for Angie. First there was lunch in the mall restaurant, then there was the flurry of trying on clothes— a lightweight jacket, then a heavy winter coat, a scarf, gloves, boots, three sweaters, dress slacks, jeans, and a couple of wool suits. At the cash register, Angie was afraid to look at the total as Edith reached for her credit card. *Why would someone I just met yesterday be willing to do all this for me?* Angie asked herself.

The clerk helped the women load their parcels into a shopping cart. "Thank you," Edith said. "You've been most helpful."

Rebecca pushed the cart to her Chrysler and unloaded the packages in the backseat on top of Angie's suitcases. The wind tossed their hair in all directions. This is the kind of wind we get on Guam before a typhoon," Angie said matter-of-factly.

"Great Falls is one of the windiest cities in the United States," Rebecca chuckled, "but the natives are used to it. They go about their business without even noticing it."

As Rebecca headed east toward the city limits, Angie marveled at Highwood Mountains to the left and the Little Belt Mountains in the far distant right. "The mountains are more beautiful in real life than in any picture or TV program. There's such a sense of peace and tranquillity about them."

"I know," Edith replied. "When Roy and I were able to drive, after we'd have a particularly frustrating day, we'd get in the car and drive into the mountains. We had a special spot where we liked to park and sit on a log and gaze at the vast plains below. Somehow that seemed to make our problems seem so small."

Angie smiled as she responded eagerly to her friend. "I hope you'll show me that spot. I love to meditate in peaceful surroundings."

"I'm sure we can find someone to drive us there. It's the most beautiful sight at sunset," Edith promised.

The three women rode in silence for several miles. Angie's eyes sparkled as she surveyed the rolling fields of golden wheat with harvesters busy at work. Never before had she been able to see for scores of miles at a time. Her gaze then drifted to the dashboard. . .sixty-five miles per hour. . . . "I've never been in a car going this fast," she giggled. "The roads are so crowded on Guam that the speed limit is thirty-five miles per hour."

Before long, fatigue again overtook Angie. She laid her head back on the seat and closed her eyes. It was completely dark when Rebecca stopped in front of Edith Dutton's home. Rebecca retrieved Edith's overnight bag from the backseat and carried it to Edith's front door. "Thanks for riding with me," Rebecca said as she set the suitcase inside the front door. "I'll be sure that Angie has a ride to your house Saturday noon; then I'll see you Sunday at her welcoming buffet."

Angie was just awakening as Rebecca returned to her car. "Edith has a nice home. I'm looking forward to having lunch there Saturday."

"Jay's sister, Dawn, and some of her friends are going to be there as well. I hope you like pizza."

"I love it. I hope Dawn is like her brother."

"I'm sure you'll enjoy yourself," Rebecca replied as she parked her car in her driveway on Rimrock Road. Andy soon appeared at the front door. He greeted Angie and Rebecca warmly and began carrying Angie's bags to her basement suite. Within half an hour, Angie was again fast asleep in bed. The combination of emotional and physical exhaustion had taken its toll on her petite body.

The next day, Angie had a leisurely breakfast with Rebecca and Andy. She was immediately impressed with Andy's devotion to his new bride. For someone who had lived the confirmed bachelor lifestyle for nearly all his adult life,

Andy seemed to have a sensitivity of how two shall become one. *I wish I could someday have the kind of marriage the Hatfields have, but after what has happened, I'll never be able to be a pure, true bride.*

Later Rebecca took Angie sightseeing. She drove the streets of Rocky Bluff and pointed out historic landmarks. Everything seemed new and strange to Angie. She pictured Jay as a young boy riding his bicycle down the wide, tree-lined streets. No wonder he never stopped talking about his home in Montana, she thought.

Rebecca turned off Main Street and parked her car in front of the Looking Glass Salon. "This is where you're going to be working. I want you to meet Barbara Old Tail. I'm sure you'll like her. She's very proud of her Native American ancestry and has just moved her mother from the reservation to live with her."

Barb was polishing the mirrors in the new addition to her salon when Rebecca and Angie entered. After Rebecca did the formal introduction, Barb and Angie began speaking beauticians' talk as if they were old cosmetology school classmates. Rebecca was amazed at how the two were so well matched for each other. *Maybe Angie's adjustment to Rocky Bluff won't be so difficult after all,* she told herself.

Chapter 9

Girls, I'll leave you alone to watch the video," Edith Dutton said. "I'm going to take a quick nap. Wake me when it's over. Besides, I've already read the book, and I don't want to spoil it with the movie," she chuckled.

Dawn, Angie, and Dawn's friends, Tara Wolf, Linda Wright, and Marsha Harris, made themselves comfortable in Edith's living room. Tara stretched out on the floor while Dawn, Linda, and Marsha curled up on the sofa, and Angie sat in a reclining chair.

"Angie, the name of the movie we selected is *A River Runs Through It*," Dawn Harkness explained as she took the video out of the box. "It's getting kind of old, but it was filmed here in Montana, and I thought you might enjoy it."

Angie's eyes brightened as she leaned back in the recliner nearest the television. The chair had been Roy's favorite before he went to the nursing home. "That was kind of you. I've been fascinated by this state ever since I met Jay."

"Rumor has it that you and Jay are engaged. Are you planning to get married soon?" Marsha asked as she flipped her long blond hair over her shoulder.

"I don't know how that rumor ever got started." Angie grimaced. "I doubt if I'll ever marry."

"See, Marsha, there might still be hope for you after all," Dawn teased. "Jay'll be coming home for good in June. He'll be surprised that you're no longer a skinny high school freshman but a beautiful college coed."

"After I get to the university, I may not be interested in Jay anymore," Marsha retorted. "I'll have to size up all the fraternity guys before I make a decision."

The group howled with laughter as a look of confusion spread over Angie's face. She had never been in a group before where trapping a guy was treated as a game. Angie tried to ignore the conversation going on around her and became enthralled with the photography of the majestic mountains and the art of fly fishing. She had lived around deep-sea fishing all her life, and this was an entirely new concept to her. The others watched the video with polite boredom for awhile, but gradually their conversations became more animated. Angie tried to ignore the whispering going on around her and focused on the movie. Little by little she began to catch bits and fragments of their conversation.

"When are you leaving for college?". . . . "What party did you go to last week?". . . . "Who was there?". . . . "What were they drinking?". . . . "How much?". . . . "What were they smoking?". . . . "Who ended the night in a motel with whom?"

The beauty of the movie faded into the background as Angie became more and more troubled by the conversation going on around her. *Are all state-side teenagers like this? Jay would be shocked if he knew his sister ran with such a crowd. After being associated with what went on at Coiffures and Manicures, I don't want to have anything to do with these girls, but Jay will be crushed if I don't make friends with his sister.*

Toward the end of the video, Edith returned to the living room. "How's the movie?"

"Fascinating," Angie replied. "I hope someday I'll be able to see some of those places it showed."

"I'm sure someone will be able to take you to western Montana. It's totally different from the central and eastern part of the state," Edith said.

Within minutes, the credits began to roll, and Dawn stood to turn off the recorder. "I have some things I need to get done this afternoon. Angie, would you like me to drop you off at Rebecca's on the way?"

"I'd appreciate that," Angie replied, then turned her attention back to Edith. "I want to thank you for lunch and for a pleasant afternoon."

"I'm glad you could come," the older woman replied. "I'm looking forward to introducing you to the rest of the family tomorrow at the buffet."

Angie nodded in agreement and followed the others to Dawn's car. All five of them crowded into the small vehicle, and Dawn sped toward Rimrock Road. Everyone in the car appeared happy and carefree except Angie. The cloud of alienation and frustration hung heavy over her. *Why did I ever come to Montana? I just don't fit in.*

Rebecca was bursting with news when Angie walked in the front door. "Welcome back," she greeted. "How was your afternoon?"

"The video was great. They played *A River Runs Through It,* and the scenery was beautiful."

"I dearly loved that video and watched it three times," Rebecca replied. "You received a phone call while you were gone."

"Who was it?"

"Jay. He said he'd call back tomorrow evening."

Angie spent the remainder of the day relaxing. Life in Rocky Bluff was so different from Guam. Rebecca, Edith, and Barb Old Tail had accepted her with warmth and understanding, but the younger people seemed to keep her at a distance.

The next morning, Angie attended church with Rebecca and Andy. She enjoyed the music, and Pastor Rhodes's sermon about forgiveness and salvation through Jesus Christ was like salve on the open sore of her heart. *If only I could keep this feeling forever,* Angie thought as she sang the closing hymn.

As Angie followed Rebecca down the side aisle, an attractive, middle-aged woman approached her. "Hi, you must be Angie Quinata," she greeted. "My name is Teresa Lennon. Welcome to Rocky Bluff. I'm so glad you could come and help Barb Old Tail in her salon."

"It's nice to meet you, Mrs. Lennon," Angie replied. "I'm looking forward to working with Barb. It was nice of her to offer me a job when I was halfway around the world."

"Please call me Teresa," she insisted. "I'm sure we'll be seeing a lot of each other during the next few months. In fact, I was planning to attend your welcome-to-Montana buffet at Edith's this afternoon."

Angie was impressed with the warmth Teresa had for her even though they had never met. When she joined her host family in the parking lot, she couldn't help but ask, "Rebecca, tell me about Teresa Lennon. She's especially sweet and understanding."

"She's had lots of experience dealing with women who have been traumatized," Rebecca explained. "She's the director of the Spouse Abuse Center. She's dealt with all kinds of domestic and violent situations."

"Has she ever dealt with rape victims?" Angie queried.

"I can't say for sure, but as far as I know, there's never been a rape in Rocky Bluff."

Angie's eyes fell to the ground as a faint smile spread across her face. *What a lucky place,* she thought.

Andy opened the doors of the newly-repaired Chrysler for the women. "We have time to go home and take a quick nap before we go to Edith's. You'll need all the rest you can get," Andy chuckled. "The Harkness clan is a mighty big family to meet all at once."

"I am a little nervous," Angie admitted, "but I did promise Edith I'd be there."

"She's a perfect hostess. You'll feel right at home," Rebecca assured her.

❖

Two hours later, the Hatfields and Angie arrived at Edith's home. Edith welcomed them with a warm hug. A dark-haired, distinguished-looking couple emerged from the kitchen. "Angie, I'd like you to meet Jay's parents, Nancy and Bob Harkness."

Angie extended her right hand to greet them, but Nancy embraced her. "Angie, we've heard so much about you. I feel like I've known you all my life."

"Thank you," Angie murmured. "You have a very nice son."

Bob took Angie's hand in both of his. "Welcome to Rocky Bluff. I hope you'll come to love the community as much as we do."

Before Angie could respond, the doorbell rang, and Edith hurried to answer it. An athletic young man of Angie's own age entered the room. Finally, Edith turned back to the guest of honor. "Angie, I'd like you to meet Ryan Reynolds. He's Jay's closest friend. He's now attending Montana A&M in Butte. Ryan, this is Angie Quinata."

Ryan extended his right hand. "It's nice meeting you, Angie."

Angie flushed under her copper skin. "Hi, Ryan. Jay has told me a lot about you and of your love of sports."

"Good for him," Ryan laughed. His laugh was infectious, and soon Jay's parents and grandmother were caught up in the conversation about incidents Ryan and Jay had shared from Little League baseball through high school.

The talk flew happily and freely as Angie's reservations about Dawn subsided. Within minutes, Jay's aunt and uncle, Jean and Jim Thompson, and their two little girls arrived from Running Butte. Close behind came Ryan's older brother, Larry, his wife, Libby, and their two children.

Bob Harkness took some folding chairs out of the closet for the additional guests. The doorbell rang again, and Teresa Lennon greeted Angie. Then Pastor Rhodes and his wife, Thelma, arrived, and Dawn came with Marsha and Tara. The doorbell kept ringing, and guest after guest filled the living room, dining area, and kitchen. Edith's home echoed with love and laughter. *No wonder Jay loves Rocky Bluff and can hardly wait to return,* Angie sighed.

Angie's eyes often drifted to the corner where the three teenage girls sat, immersed in their own conversation of how soon they would be leaving Rocky Bluff and going to college. *What is it that concerns me so much about them?* she asked herself. *They act like Rocky Bluff is the last place on earth they want to be, and yet Dawn has such a delightful family.*

Everyone filled their plates from the abundance of food loaded on the dining room table and the nearby counters and scattered throughout the house and backyard. Even though laughter and warmth echoed throughout the crowd, Angie was overwhelmed by the sea of faces. She had always been comfortable with two or three people at a time, but this loud and friendly crowd was so foreign to her. She withdrew from it more and more and finally sat on the corner of the patio by herself. Visions of tropical palm trees replaced the pine trees in Edith Dutton's backyard. Instead of Edith, Rebecca, Teresa, or Nancy, she was seeing her mother's face. Tears filled her eyes, and she choked back a sob.

"All these people getting too much for you?" Edith whispered as she put her arm around Angie and sat on the step beside her.

"I was just thinking about home and the people there," Angie admitted. "I guess I'm not used to being the center of attention."

The late summer sun glistened off Edith's silver-gray hair. "I felt much the same way when my first husband introduced his family to me here in Rocky Bluff. They were a bunch who worked hard, played hard, and laughed easily, but I would rather have curled up quietly in a corner with a good book. However, through the years I've become a lot like them."

"You have a wonderful family," Angie replied. "Now I understand why Jay is so much fun to be with."

"You've been such a good sport putting up with all of us," Edith said. "Would you like to go back to Rebecca's now?"

Angie nodded as she looked up and smiled into Edith's warm, affirming face. In only a few words, Jay's grandmother was able to articulate the feelings stirring within her.

"I'll go get Rebecca, and you can slip out the side, if you'd like. I'll explain to everyone that you're tired and still suffering from jet lag and need to get some rest."

Angie could not refrain from embracing Edith. "Thank you for your understanding. You have a wonderful family, and I'm looking forward to getting to know each one of them individually, but I'm just brain-dead today."

"Don't try to explain. Everyone will understand," Edith said as she stood to find Rebecca and Andy.

Within minutes, Angie was relaxing with one of Andy's Western novels in the solitude of her sitting room in Rebecca's basement. She had never been interested in Western novels or movies before, but now that she had seen Montana, she could relate to the vastness of the land and the frontier spirit of its people. She was lost in the world of frontier life when a shout echoed down the steps. "Angie, Jay's on the telephone."

Angie raced up the stairs and grabbed the phone lying on the counter. "Hello," she panted.

"Angie, how are you?" Jay greeted, excited to finally hear her familiar voice.

"I'm fine," Angie assured him. "I'm beginning to get over my jet lag. How are you doing?"

"Guam isn't the same without you," Jay replied. "I've already started my planning calendar until June when I'll be able to come back to Rocky Bluff. Every evening I mark off another day."

"June seems so far away. I can't even think past next week."

"What all's happening? Rebecca said you met my entire family this afternoon."

"Your grandmother went to a lot of work to throw a welcoming buffet for me, but I made such a fool out of myself."

Jay burst into his infectious laugh. "What could you have possibly done to make a fool out of yourself?"

"Jay, it's not funny," Angie protested. "Everyone was being so kind to me; then I got homesick for Guam and started crying. Rebecca and Andy had to bring me home."

"I'll admit my family can become overly exuberant and overwhelming at times."

"They were absolutely delightful," Angie retorted. "I'm used to small, relaxed groups and occasionally some fussing from relatives. Your family genuinely enjoys being with one another. I can understand why you're so anxious to get back and see everyone."

"How was Dawn?" Jay queried.

Angie gulped. She didn't want to hide anything from Jay, but she didn't want to cause hard feelings in the family. "Your grandmother invited her and some of her friends for pizza and videos yesterday."

"So how was Dawn doing?" Jay persisted.

"I liked Dawn a lot."

"She is a sweet girl," Jay continued, "but she's not writing anymore, and she's never home when I call."

"She's busy working and getting ready to go to college. She's planning to join a sorority as soon as she gets there. I think she already has one picked out. I met a friend of hers who's trying to get Dawn to join her sorority."

"Do you remember the name of that friend?"

"Tara Wolf, I think."

There was a long pause on the line. "Oh no, not Tara. She's one of the biggest party girls that Rocky Bluff has produced in recent years. I've heard rumors that her sorority is one of the wildest on campus. I hope Dawn doesn't get involved with them."

"I'm sorry I told you something to concern you. Maybe it won't be as bad as you think."

"I hope not," Jay sighed. "At least Dawn has had a good upbringing, and underneath everything she knows right from wrong."

"I'm sure she'll get direction to her life soon," Angie tried to assure him. "She has such a sweet personality underneath all that frivolous facade."

"Thanks," Jay replied. "I needed to hear that. Now let's get back to you. When do you start work?"

"I officially start the first of September. I hope my box of beauty supplies gets here by then."

"Didn't you take them with you?"

"No. I was over the luggage limit so Mother had to mail them to me. Hopefully, they'll be here next week; otherwise I won't be able to start."

"If it doesn't arrive on time, it will give you a few more days to see Montana."

"The county fair is next week, and Rebecca and some of her friends want me to go. There's a rodeo at night which I'm really excited about seeing. I've never seen anything like that before."

"It's good to see a rodeo at least once," Jay replied, "but prepare yourself. Sometimes the crowd can become extremely rowdy."

Tears began to build in Angie's eyes. "How's Mother?"

"I'm sorry, I've been awfully busy at work. I haven't seen her since we left the airport. I'll try to give her a call when I get off the phone and let her know you are doing well."

Angie's tears turned to sobs. "Please tell Mom that I love her and I miss her very much."

Chapter 10

Angie Quinata unpacked her beauty supplies in her station at the Looking Glass Beauty Salon in Rocky Bluff, Montana, one week later than expected. She checked the post office every day until the parcel from Guam finally arrived. Rebecca drove Angie home with her treasured box. Angie hurried inside and reached for the phone book. She dialed the number and waited.

"Looking Glass Beauty Salon," Barbara Old Tail greeted.

"Hello, Barbara. This is Angie. My supplies from Guam finally arrived."

"Great. When would you like to begin work?"

"Right away," Angie replied eagerly.

"Would you be able to come to the salon now so I can run home and check on Mother?"

"I'd be glad to. See you in fifteen minutes."

Angie's heart pounded as Rebecca drove her downtown. After three months of confusion, she was finally having an opportunity to start over in the profession she loved. Six weeks ago she was sure all her hard work at Guam Community College had been in vain.

Angie was all smiles as she walked into the Looking Glass Salon. The shop sparkled with cleanliness, and the decor was simple, warm, and homey, much different from the plush interior of Coiffure and Manicure in Agana, Guam.

"Welcome," Barb greeted. "You came at a good time. It's been kind of quiet this morning so I'll have time to show you around."

She motioned for Angie to follow her. "This station will be yours. Set your box here."

"You've decorated this beautifully," Angie noted.

"Rebecca helped me with the remodeling. You wouldn't believe how small this was before."

"I must say you both have good taste," Angie said as she surveyed the mauve-flowered wallpaper trim.

"Thank you," Barb replied as she led the way to the back room. "This is nothing fancy. Just the usual washer and dryer, supply cabinets, microwave, refrigerator, and chairs." Barb laughed as she pointed to the side wall. "My next project is to replace that old sofa."

"It looks comfortable," Angie replied as she observed the threadbare green couch.

"It is," Barb chuckled. "That's why I've never wanted to part with it. Maybe I'll just have it reupholstered instead."

Barb led Angie back to the front counter. "This is our schedule book. We'll just divide the columns in half; yours on the right and mine on the left. My home number is in the automatic dial on the phone in case you have any questions."

"Thanks." Angie smiled. "Don't worry about a thing. I hope your mother is doing okay."

"She just gets lonely and confused if someone's not around. I never know what to expect from one minute to the next. I won't be gone long."

Barb reached for her sweater and hurried into the brisk fall breeze. Angie turned her attention back to her cherished box and her station. She painstakingly arranged and rearranged her curlers, curling irons, and bottles. *This area is not as large as what I had at Coiffure and Manicure, but the layout is much better,* Angie told herself.

Angie turned on the radio on the front counter. Country western music filled the salon. She spun the dial. . .more country western music. She moved the dial another notch. . .still more country western music. *You always know you're in the real West when that's all you can find on the radio,* she chuckled.

Angie's amusement was interrupted by the ringing of the phone. "Looking Glass Beauty Salon."

"Hello, Barbara?" the voice greeted.

"I'm sorry, but Barb is out of the salon now. This is Angie Quinata; I just started as her assistant. Is there anything I can help you with?"

"Well, hi, Angie. This is Teresa Lennon. I met you at church, then at Edith Dutton's house right after you arrived in Rocky Bluff."

"Oh yes, I remember you," Angie replied. "You're the director of the Spouse Abuse Center."

"That's right. . .and that's part of my problem. I just found out I have state inspectors coming from Helena in the morning, and my hair is a mess. Do you think you'd have time to give me a perm this afternoon?"

"Just set your time. You'll be my first Rocky Bluff customer."

That afternoon as Angie rolled Teresa's hair, the young beautician was fascinated by the services the Spouse Abuse Center provided. "That sounds like such a worthwhile program," Angie noted. "I heard of several cases of spouse abuse on Guam, but if they didn't have family to turn to, they were just out of luck. If Guam had a Spouse Abuse Center, I wasn't aware of it."

"Emergency social services vary from location to location. Rocky Bluff is fortunate to have both a Crisis Line and a Spouse Abuse Center. They both work closely with each other and with the police department. For a community of this size to have both speaks well of the people here."

"In the two and a half weeks I've been here, I can't believe the personal support I've gotten," Angie said as she squeezed the curling solution into each roll of hair. "Not to be prying, but what happened to some of the women who've used your services? Were they able to get on their feet again?"

"We have a track record to be proud of," Teresa replied. "One of our clients went to the local community college for training, then became a successful paralegal. In the meantime, her husband was able to get his life straightened out, and they were later reconciled. A couple of other women who had suffered abuse became volunteers at the center during their transition period and later began a successful day care center. The list can go on and on. I'm pleased with each one of them."

As Angie rinsed the solution out of her customer's hair, her mind raced. *Outside of Rebecca and Edith I've never told anyone in Rocky Bluff about my attack. I wonder if they'd accept me if they knew the real reason why I came to Rocky Bluff.*

"Do you have a psychiatrist who works with the abused women?" Angie asked cautiously.

"I have a master's degree in psychology, and I counsel both individuals and small groups."

"Do you ever counsel women who have not suffered spousal abuse?"

Teresa studied Angie's face and body language. It was obvious she was trying to communicate something much deeper than her words. "Occasionally. Adjusting to a new environment can be extremely difficult, but a beauty shop is not a place to discuss personal matters. Can you come to the center Thursday morning?"

Angie's eyes brightened. "Thank you. My doctor suggested I seek counseling on Guam, but I was afraid to go. I heard that some psychiatrists made fun of Christianity, and I needed someone who'd understand how important my faith is to me. I don't know how I'd get through tough times without looking to God for strength."

Just then Barb Old Tail returned. A smile spread across her face as she saw Angie already working on a customer. "I'm sorry it took so long. Mother was having a real confusing time, and I just couldn't get away. I see I left the shop in good hands."

"She's doing a mighty fine job," Teresa replied. "Angie's definitely an answer to your prayers."

The next few days flew by for Angie. The relaxed, casual mood of the clients and her employer helped the tension lines fade from her forehead. When Thursday morning arrived, she awoke early, dressed, ate breakfast, and hurried to the Spouse Abuse Center. Teresa was waiting for her.

She led Angie into a comfortable sitting room. "You're not going to ask me to lie down while you sit at the desk?" Angie asked.

Teresa burst into gales of laughter. "You've been watching too much television. We're sitting here as equals. You have training as a beautician, and I have training as a counselor."

Angie blushed with embarrassment. "I'm sorry. I've never been to a counselor before. I just got started working here, so I don't have much money to pay for your services."

"If that's the case, then let's make a deal. . . . Your counseling sessions for a wash and set twice a month, and haircuts and perms as needed."

"That sounds like the old-fashioned barter system," Angie giggled, "but it's a great idea."

For the rest of the hour, Angie poured out her anger and guilt over being raped and violated. Feelings that she never knew existed came tumbling out. There was much more she wanted to say, but it was time to go to work. She scheduled another meeting, then nearly skipped to the Looking Glass. Maybe there was hope for her yet.

❦

When Angie returned home after work that evening, Rebecca was bursting with excitement. "Angie, do you have plans for Saturday afternoon?"

"No, why?"

"An old friend of mine is returning to Rocky Bluff this weekend. She and her family will be staying with Edith, and she's invited us over for lunch. I'm sure you'll like them."

"Sounds like fun. I'll try to be more relaxed than I was the last time I was at Edith's."

"You had every reason in the world to be upset that day. We all deluged upon you at the same time," Rebecca apologized. "From now on only small groups at a time will be allowed."

"Don't worry about me. I'm beginning to get adjusted now," Angie said as she got a soft drink from the refrigerator. "What's your friend like?"

"Her name is Beth Blair. Her story is a testimony to Edith Dutton and the Crisis Center. She came to town as a scared, pregnant sixteen-year-old runaway and left town seven years later with an education, an upstanding husband, a growing family, and the desire to finish her college degree. She worked as a clerk in the Rocky Bluff High School library when I was the librarian there. She now wants to become a librarian herself."

"I'd love to meet her. I can't imagine a community doing that much for an outsider. On Guam we always looked out for our own, but off-island people were on their own."

❖

On Saturday Angie immediately fell in love with Beth Blair, her husband, Dan, seven-year-old Jeffey, and baby Edith. Conversation in the group flew easily and lightly. Much of it centered around the Crisis Center in Missoula, Montana, that Dan was managing while Beth was finishing her degree at the university. Dan had directed the Rocky Bluff Crisis Center and had received most of his training from Roy Dutton, Edith's second husband. They reminisced about old times and how the entire community pulled together when Jeffey was kidnapped from the day care center by his biological father and taken to Canada.

Later in the afternoon, Angie joined Beth in the bedroom where she was nursing Edith. "Beth, you've been through so much, and yet you seem so happy," Angie began as she sat on the corner of the bed. "How did you do it?"

"I didn't do anything but live my life the best I could," Beth replied. "It was the grace of God, all these good people in Rocky Bluff, and, of course, Dan who made the difference. I tried to do everything on my own and was completely upset and frustrated. That's when I called the Crisis Center and met Edith. She taught me to rely on God's strength and the encouragement of others. I'd never have survived the kidnapping without the support I received from Edith and her family."

"But didn't people criticize you because you were pregnant out of wedlock?"

"A few did behind my back. In fact, I got one terrible letter from a stranger during Jeffey's kidnapping saying I wasn't fit to be a mother, but the people that mattered knew that Christ died for my sins as well as theirs. They did everything in their power to build me up and help me start a new life."

"What about Dan? Didn't he have reservations about marrying someone who wasn't a. . .virgin?"

"When I ran away from home, my parents made me feel so guilty; I was sure I was spoiled for life and no one would ever want to marry me, but the people of Rocky Bluff taught me about true love and forgiveness. Dan stood by me through good times and bad and kept reassuring me that he loved me for what I was today, not what I used to be."

Tears built in Angie's eyes, and she began sobbing. Beth creased her forehead as she put her hand on her new friend's shoulder. "Angie, what's wrong?"

Angie tried to choke back her tears. "That's where I am today. Jay Harkness and I were extremely close friends, and we were talking about getting married as soon as he got out of the service. I had vowed I was going to remain pure until my wedding night, even though a lot of my friends thought I was old-fashioned and ridiculous. On my last day of college, I was raped on my way to the parking lot. The one thing I was saving for my husband is gone. I feel I am spoiled for life and can never marry."

"Jay must still love you; otherwise he wouldn't have sent you here to be with his family and friends," Beth reminded her.

"Jay has been a jewel even when I've been cruel and unkind to him. He even kept coming to take care of me after I gave him his friendship ring back. I just don't understand why."

"Sometimes it seems like there are few good men left," Beth replied gently, "but Dan and Jay have the integrity and compassion to love someone for what they are inside, not what has happened to them. Hang on to Jay; he's a man worth having."

Angie took out a tissue and dried her eyes. "I'm finding that out. Meeting the people who shaped his life is beginning to change my mind about never marrying anyone. Rocky Bluff is a unique place."

"That it is," Beth agreed, "but there are kind, compassionate people wherever you go. You just have to know where to look for them."

Just then Jeffey ran into the room. "Mommy, can you come watch a video with us? Granny Edith picked out a real funny one."

Beth looked at Angie who nodded her head, then turned back to her son. "Sure, let's go," she said as she slid off the bed and motioned for Angie to follow.

❖

The next few weeks Angie had her first experience with the changing of the seasons. The beauty of the foliage in the fall was exactly as Jay had described it, only better. On Saturdays she helped Andy rake and bag the leaves that had fallen or blown into their yard. The crispness in the air made her feel invigorated and alert. She was thankful Rebecca and Edith had taken her shopping for fall clothes before they left Great Falls the day after she arrived. She would have had no idea how to select functional winter clothing.

The first snowfall of the winter came early. The day before Halloween, Angie stood at the front window of the Looking Glass Salon and watched with fascination as the large flakes drifted gently to the ground. She had waited for years to see snow, and now she was finding it even more beautiful than she had expected. Business in the salon was light that morning so she took a chair near the window and wrote her mother.

Dear Mom,

 I'm sorry I've been so negligent in my writing. There have been so many people to meet and things to do I feel as if I'm living in a whirlwind. I've appreciated all our phone conversations and all your letters. Before I left Guam, you said you were going to start saving your pennies so you could come to Rocky Bluff for Christmas to see me and the snow.

 The first snow is falling today, and words can't express its beauty and intrigue. I can hardly wait to learn to ski.

 How is your penny jar coming? Will you be able to come for Christmas?

Love,
Angie

Barbara Old Tail finished the haircut on her last client and looked nervously out the window. "If you wouldn't mind tending the shop by yourself, I think I better run home and check on Mother. She often gets confused when something different happens. She used to love the snow, but I don't know how she'll react to it this time."

"I'd be glad to," Angie replied. "If no one calls or stops in, I'll just sit here and watch the snow fall."

❖

A feeling of apprehension engulfed Barb as she drove home. She put the key in the lock and was surprised to see that it was already unlocked. *I was sure I locked this door before I left this morning,* she thought. She turned the knob and walked inside. "Mother. . . Mother, I'm home."

Only her own voice echoed throughout the house. She ran from room to room. . . . No one. She opened the back door and surveyed the yard. . . . No one. Barb went to the coat closet and flung the door open. Sure enough, her mother's winter coat was gone.

When she reopened the front door, even her own footprints were covered with snow. There was no hope in following her mother's tracks.

Dear God, she prayed. *Please help me find her. Let her be okay.* Barb ran back to her car and drove around the block. All she saw were people standing in their windows watching the snow fall. She hurried back home to see if her mother had returned. The house was empty. Again she rushed to her car and drove for several more blocks without results. Returning home for the third time, Barb began calling her neighbors. Either no one was home or they had not seen an older woman walking in the snow.

She took a deep breath and dialed 9-1-1.

"Emergency services."

"This is Barbara Old Tail. I'd like to report a missing person. She suffers from Alzheimer's, and I'm afraid she's in danger if she's wandering in this snow."

The dispatcher got a complete description of Barb's mother and the pattern of her behavior and assured her she would send as many police as possible to the streets to search for her.

Barb then called Edith Dutton. "Hello, Edith, this is Barb Old Tail. Are you still chairing the church prayer chain?" she queried as soon as the gray-haired matriarch of the church answered the phone.

"Yes, I am. Is something wrong?"

"Very. I came home from the salon to check on Mother, but she's wandered away. I've driven through the neighborhood and called all the neighbors, and no one has seen her. I just asked the police to search for her. Would you ask the prayer chain to pray that we find her before she gets too cold?"

"How dreadful," Edith sighed. "We'll get the prayer chain started immediately. Hang in there. I'm sure the police will find her shortly. We have an outstanding force in Rocky Bluff."

"Thanks," Barb replied. "I'll let you know just as soon as we have any word on her whereabouts."

Barb hung up the phone, then dialed the Looking Glass. "Hello, Angie. You're on your own at the salon," she said, choking back the sobs that were beginning to overwhelm her. "Mother has wandered away in the snow. I've called the police to look for her. I'm afraid if they don't find her soon she'll freeze to death."

Angie's facial muscles tightened. "Don't worry about the salon; I'll take care of everything here. Let me know as soon as you find her."

Angie hung up the phone and walked to the window. *It's hard to imagine something this beautiful could possibly be deadly.*

Chapter 11

Jay Harkness sat at his desk in the Enlisted Men's Dormitory at Andersen Air Force Base, Guam. A picture of Angie Quinata was on the left, and his planning calendar was on the right. June fifteenth seemed so far away. He opened the worn envelope with the familiar postmark, Rocky Bluff, Montana, and reread the words. By now he could quote the letter line by line, but it was more comforting to see it on paper.

> Dear Jay,
>
> I'm sorry I haven't written for awhile. Taking classes while I'm working part-time is consuming all my time. I was back in Rocky Bluff this past weekend and learned that John Paterson will be leaving his position as Computer Systems manager at Rocky Bluff Community College. He's going to be attending the university for advanced training this fall and wanted to train his replacement over the summer.
>
> Also, this past summer there was a change of administration at the college. President Oaks retired, and our high school principal, Grady Walker, was selected in his place.
>
> If you're interested in the position, I'm sure he'll look favorably on his old basketball star.
>
> Keep in touch,
> Ryan

This is too good to be true, Jay told himself. *I thought I'd have to go to one of the larger cities in Montana to get a job in computers. I can hardly wait to let Angie know.* Jay sat at his desk in silence for a few minutes. *Maybe I better write to the college and apply for the job before I tell anyone. I don't want to have everyone disappointed if I don't get it.*

The remainder of the evening, Jay wrote and rewrote his resume. This was the first time he had applied for a job in his life. When he was a teenager, he worked after school, weekends, and summers at the family hardware store. After joining the military, his life had been dictated to him. After nearly three years, civilian life was looking more and more appealing, but he was finding he would have to take the initiative in job hunting himself. No one would do it for him.

93

Finishing his resume, Jay reached for the phone and dialed Angie's mother.

"Hello," Mitzi greeted.

"Hello, Mitzi. This is Jay. How are you doing?"

"I'm doing fine, except I miss that child of mine."

"I know. I didn't know it would be so lonesome without her. I can hardly wait to get there in June."

"Jay, I'm glad you called. I was just getting ready to call you," Mitzi Quinata said. "There are some airfare wars going on, and I was able to get a fairly inexpensive ticket to Great Falls for Christmas."

"How exciting. I wish I were going with you."

"While I'm there, I'm going to try to talk Angie into coming home with me. She sounds likes she's gotten over the shock of the attack so there's no reason for her to stay in Montana."

"She does appear to be healing emotionally," Jay agreed, "but I also get the feeling that she's falling in love with Rocky Bluff."

Mitzi ignored what Jay had said and immediately changed the subject to Angie's reactions to some of the uniqueness of Montana, especially the rodeos. It was good to talk with someone who also knew and loved Angie. They both chuckled and bade each other farewell.

A frown crossed Jay's face as he hung up the phone. He realized that Angie would again be faced with another decision between cultures, lifestyles, and romance.

❖

Capt. Philip Mooney and Sgt. Scott Packwood took separate patrol cars and began systematically cruising the streets and alleys of Rocky Bluff looking for Maude Old Tail. After two hours they had covered all the streets in Rocky Bluff and returned to Barb's home.

With long faces they rang her doorbell. "Did you find her?" Barb asked anxiously.

"I covered all the streets and alleys east of here, and Scott cruised the streets and alleys to the west, but to no avail," Phil explained. "Is there any place she might have stopped to get warm?"

"The only places she's been to in Rocky Bluff is Dr. Brewer's office, the grocery store, and the church," Barb replied anxiously. "I'm sure they would have let me know if she turned up at any of them."

"Scott and I will check with businesses downtown and see if anyone has seen her. If he takes everything north of Main Street and I take the businesses on the south, we can probably check them all in an hour," Phil said. "The important thing is that we find her before dark."

While Barb waited and prayed, her phone kept ringing with calls from concerned friends. Remembering how terrifying it was for Beth to be alone when her four year old was missing, Rebecca drove to Barb's home. "Barb, do you have anyone staying with you while you wait for word about your mother? I know minutes can seem like hours," Rebecca said as Barb greeted her at the door.

Tears filled Barb's eyes as Rebecca wrapped her arms around her friend. "Thank you for coming. I'm losing my mind with worry."

"Edith has the prayer chain working so I'm sure we'll get some good news soon," Rebecca said as the two women walked into the living room.

Barb had just poured Rebecca a cup of coffee when the phone rang for the twentieth time that afternoon. "Rebecca, would you mind answering that? I don't think I can answer any more questions."

"I'd be glad to," Rebecca said as she reached for the phone. "Hello."

"Hello, Barb?"

"No, this is Rebecca Hatfield. May I help you?"

"Hi, Rebecca, this is Coach Watson. Has Mrs. Old Tail been found yet?"

"I'm afraid not. It's been nearly six hours now."

"We're getting ready to begin basketball practice, and everyday the team has to run at least two miles before we work on drills. I thought we could send the entire team out to run in different directions to look for Mrs. Old Tail."

"Todd, how ingenious. That's a great idea. I'll be sure and tell Barb."

Two cups of coffee later, there was still no word as to the whereabouts of Mrs. Old Tail. Phil Mooney and Scott Packwood returned with another unsuccessful report. All anyone could do was wait and pray.

Rebecca and Barb dozed all night and would awaken only to pace back and forth. At the first ray of sunlight, Barb made another pot of coffee and fixed toast for herself and Rebecca. Promptly at eight o'clock the doorbell rang. Fearing the worst, Barbara ran to the front door. She felt her heart drop to her feet as she saw Pastor Rhodes through the peephole. She solemnly opened the door.

"Mother!" Barb shouted as she embraced her aging parent. "Are you all right?"

"I'm fine," Maude Old Tail's eyes were blank and unresponsive. "What's for breakfast? I'm hungry."

"Pastor Rhodes, where did you find her?" Barb asked as tears of joy flowed unashamedly down her cheeks.

"I was going into the sanctuary of the church early this morning to change the banner before the Sunday service and found her sleeping in a pew. Someone must have inadvertently left the side door unlocked."

"Thank God for that," Barb gasped. "Her guardian angel must have really been looking out for her. It's amazing how God uses someone's mistake to save someone else's life. Thank you so much for bringing her home."

Pastor Rhodes smiled as he turned to leave. "It was my pleasure. I'm thankful everything turned out well for everyone."

Rebecca fixed a large breakfast of bacon, eggs, toast, and juice while Barb helped her mother bathe and dress. She relished the task since a few hours before she thought she would never have the opportunity of showing her love to her mother again. While her mother ate, Barb dialed Edith Dutton's number.

"Edith, our prayers have been answered," Barb nearly shouted in the phone. "Pastor Rhodes found Mother sleeping in one of the pews in the church this morning."

"Thank the good Lord," Edith replied calmly. "I knew He wouldn't let us down. I'll let the others on the prayer chain know that their prayers were answered and your mother is safe."

"I know one thing," Barb stated matter-of-factly. "I'll never be able to leave Mother home alone again, but I don't know how I'll be able to even work part-time. I've never heard of adult day care services in Rocky Bluff."

"Until something opens up for you, why don't you bring your mother over here while you go to work?" Edith suggested. "I won't be able to do much except to fix a salad or sandwich for lunch, but I could give you a call if she becomes disoriented and insists on going outside."

"Edith, I can't ask you to do that. You've spent your entire life helping others," the concerned daughter replied.

"That's why I want to do it," the older woman protested. "I don't want to feel set on the shelf and passed over. I want to continue living life and helping others just as long as I can."

Barb and Edith continued making detailed plans, and Barb agreed to bring her mother the next morning at ten. By the time they finished their conversation, Rebecca had finished the morning dishes, and Mrs. Old Tail was comfortable in her favorite chair watching her favorite game show. Rebecca said good-bye to her friend, and Barb sank into the cushions of the sofa with exhaustion. Rocky Bluff had survived another crisis by pulling together and helping one another.

❖

Nancy Harkness had prepared a large Thanksgiving dinner for her husband, Bob, her mother-in-law, Edith, and her daughter, Dawn. After nearly three months at Montana State University, Dawn had returned for the holidays just the day before. Dinner-table conversation centered around Dawn's college activities. Every time they asked about her social life, she changed the subject to her classes and midterm tests.

Sensing her discomfort about talking about her social life at college, Edith queried, "How are you going to spend your vacation in Rocky Bluff?"

"Tomorrow Tara and I plan to get up early and go skiing. With the early snowfall this year they say there's a good snowpack on the slopes."

Edith looked thoughtful for a moment. "Honey, would you do me a favor? Would you mind asking Angie to go with you? She keeps talking about wanting to learn to ski, but she doesn't know anyone who does."

Dawn rolled her eyes and took a deep breath. "I suppose we could give her a ride, but she'll have to stay on the bunny run until she learns how. We want to do some serious skiing. Maybe we could get the lodge's ski pro to give her lessons while we go to the slopes."

"Thanks, Dawn. I'll give you enough money for gas, everyone's ski lift tickets, and rental money for Angie's skis." Edith paused, then chuckled. "I wonder if Angie will be interested in skiing after her first trip to the slopes. I'll never forget how appalled she was after she went to the rodeo last summer."

At six o'clock the next morning, the three young women headed toward the ski lodge in Dawn's minisized car. Angie marveled at the picturesque beauty of the snow lacing the pine trees. The magnificence of the rising sun reflected across glistening snow. Her dream of learning to snow ski was finally coming true.

Arriving at the ski lodge, Dawn immediately found the ski pro. "Duke, we brought a friend along who's fresh off the boat from Guam. She's really anxious to learn to ski so she'll have something to write home about. Will you have time to give her lessons today?"

Duke surveyed the petite dark-haired woman standing with Tara Wolf. "Just leave her to me," he chuckled. "She'll be in good hands."

"Thanks; you're a dear," Dawn replied and hurried out the door. Approaching her friends, Dawn shouted, "Angie, you're in luck. The ski pro said he'd stay with you until you can ski on your own. Tara, let's hit the slopes."

Angie watched her two companions hurry toward the ski lift as advanced skiers whisked down the slopes. *Why did I even come? What makes me think I can learn to do that? I would probably break my leg the first trip down.*

"Hello. You must be Angie," a deep voice behind her said.

She whirled. A tall, thin, bearded man smiled down at her. "Yes, and you must be the ski instructor."

"Duke Harrington in person. In a few short hours I'll have you whisking down those slopes with the best of them."

Angie shuddered as a fresh blast of cold air hit her cheeks. "I'm a pretty slow learner."

"First things first, let's go inside and fit you with skis," Duke directed as he put his hand on her shoulder. "What size shoes do you wear?"

"Five and a half," Angie responded as she felt her freezing cheeks blush.

The next half hour the ski instructor explained the variations in skis and the type of bindings she'd need. He then took her outside where he helped her put on her skis, then slipped into his own. He demonstrated how to push off, stop, and steer to the right and left. Angie clumsily copied his movements.

"Let's have some hot chocolate before we hit the bunny run," he said as he motioned to the small coffee shop at the corner of the lodge. "I'll be right with you. I need to check in with my office."

"Sure," Angie replied as she headed for the lodge. "I could use a break."

As Angie sipped her hot chocolate, she watched Duke's tall physique in the distance. Even with heavy clothing she could see his firm muscles bulging under his coat. The beard was a novelty. Only on TV and in the movies had she seen beards. *That beard is so distinguishing. It's just too hot to wear them on Guam. I wonder how his wife likes it?* Angie silently giggled. *I wonder how much trouble he has eating?*

Duke returned to Angie's table. "Can I order you a bowl of chili?"

"I'd love it," Angie replied and then blushed. "This is my first winter on the mainland so I've never had chili before."

"Try it; you'll like it."

After Duke placed their order, he told how during the summer he was a forest-fire fighter and when snow began to fly, he returned to being a skiing instructor. Angie was fascinated with his rugged lifestyle, so different from what she had grown up with. *It's interesting that Montana could turn out sophisticated, well-groomed men like Jay Harkness along with rugged, outdoorsmen like Duke Harrington. No wonder they say that Montana is a land of contrasts.*

The remainder of the afternoon, Angie spent conquering the bunny slope. Occasionally she would wave when she saw Dawn and Tara skiing down the advanced slopes. Duke was never far away. . .always cheering her on. Guam seemed a long way away. The crispness of the air rejuvenated her troubled spirit and relaxed her tense nerves.

At four o'clock Dawn and Tara skied to the base of the bunny slope. "Having fun, Angie?" Dawn asked as she began unbuckling her boots.

"This is great," Angie replied, her face aglow from exhilaration.

"I hate to call it quits, but it's going to be getting dark before long," Dawn apologized.

Angie looked over at her ski instructor. "I've got to come back and do this next weekend. I don't want to forget everything I've learned today."

"For someone who's never been around snow before, you learn faster than most of the natives. You'll be ready for the intermediate slopes by then," Duke replied. "I'll be waiting to see you next Saturday."

Angie took off her rented skis and handed them to Duke, while Dawn and Tara removed their skis and hooked them on top of the car. Duke put his arm around Angie. "I'll see you next Saturday," he whispered.

As the trio drove away from the ski lodge, Tara looked over her shoulder at Angie. "Duke sure is interested in you. Not every student gets that kind of personal attention."

"He won't spend that kind of time with me next week," Angie protested. "Duke was just trying to get me off to a good start."

"Angie, don't be so naive," Dawn teased. "Duke was definitely trying to make time with you."

Angie's face flushed. *What if Dawn writes to Jay and tells him that someone else is interested in me? I'm sure everyone's going to be talking about Duke and me when nothing happened. He merely taught me to ski.*

❖

Neither Rebecca nor Andy were home when Angie returned. The warmth of the house relaxed her. She went to the kitchen and fixed herself a cup of hot chocolate and found a couple of chocolate chip cookies to go with it. She sat at the kitchen table to enjoy her treat. There on the table was a letter in her mother's familiar handwriting. She hurriedly tore it open.

Dear Angie,

I took advantage of the recent price wars and bought a round-trip plane ticket to Great Falls. I'll be arriving December 15th and leaving January 5th. I can hardly wait to see you and have you show me Rocky Bluff.

I have some good news for you. Another beauty salon called the Hair Corner has taken over the space of Coiffure and Manicure. In just two months they have already built a good reputation. Yesterday I took the liberty of talking with the owner, and she was interested in you coming back and working for them.

I was so excited I could hardly stand it. I went directly to the travel agent. Since this was the last day of the cheap airfares, I purchased you a one-way ticket home. Things are working out too good to be true. I'm looking forward to your return. If you'd like to have your old room back, I'd love to have you, but if you'd rather have your own apartment, I'll try to find one for you.

I'm looking forward to seeing you the 15th.

Love,
Mom

Angie read and reread the letter. *I don't know if I want to go back to Guam. I can't leave Barbara now when she needs me the most. If I went back to Guam, I'd never be able to perfect my skiing skills. I wonder what Jay will want me to do?*

Chapter 12

Andy, Rebecca, and Angie dined leisurely in the Great Falls International Airport cafeteria. They made sure they were at the airport long before Mitzi's plane was due to arrive. They did not want Mitzi to repeat Angie's experience, alone in a strange land with no one to meet her.

Angie folded, unfolded, and refolded her napkin nervously. "Rebecca, what will I tell Mother? She bought a return airline ticket for me, but I don't want to use it. I'm not ready to return to Guam. But I don't want to hurt her feelings."

"Angie, if you don't want to return to Guam now, tell your mother that. Of course she'll be disappointed, but she'll understand."

"Maybe when she meets Edith, Nancy, Bob, and all my other friends in Rocky Bluff, she'll understand why I feel the way I do," Angie replied.

"Take her skiing, and maybe she'll love it so much, she'll decide to stay here," Andy teased.

"I'll admit skiing has become my life. Ever since Dawn first took me, I've been skiing every weekend," Angie laughed, then became serious. "But there's something more involved here than skiing. I made a commitment to Barb. She needs my help, and I'm beginning to build up a clientele."

"And your clientele is extremely well pleased with your work," Rebecca replied. Rebecca thought for a moment before she spoke again, and she tried to pick her words carefully. "Angie, before you make your decision, think about where you would be in five years if you went back to Guam. . . . And, if you decide to stay in Rocky Bluff, where would you be?"

"I love Rocky Bluff, and I'm looking forward to seeing Jay again," Angie replied. "I really miss him, but if I leave my job and go back to Guam now, the chances of us developing a permanent relationship when he gets out of the service will be slim or none."

"Explain that to your mother," Rebecca urged. "I'm sure she'll understand."

"She'll be heartbroken. I'm an only child, and she has centered her entire life around me. It's been hard for her to let me grow up."

"After she sees what you've accomplished in Rocky Bluff, she'll accept the fact that you're an adult now."

Andy glanced at his watch and reminded the others of the time. He paid the bill, and the trio hurried to the gate where Mitzi would deplane.

Angie eagerly scanned the passengers as they emerged from the ramp. She began to wonder if her mother had missed connections. When she finally spotted her weary mother, she was shocked how much grayer her mother's hair had become in the four months since she had last seen her. Angie ran into her mother's arms and cried unashamedly.

"Mom, how are you? I've missed you so."

"I've missed you too. Guam just hasn't been the same since you left."

Angie ignored her comment and stepped aside so Rebecca and Andy could greet her. Rebecca handed Mitzi one of her winter coats. "What's this?" Mitzi queried.

"You'll need this as soon as you step outdoors. It's five degrees below zero today."

"That's hard to believe," Mitzi replied as her eyes widened. "You mean you came out in that kind of weather? I'd think no one would leave their homes with temperatures like that."

"This is nothing," Andy chuckled. "Montanans only stay indoors during major blizzards, and those only happen every few years. We're prepared to live with snow and cold, so nothing slows us down."

Angie took her mother's arm, and they walked toward the baggage claim. She would tell her mother of her decision later, but right now she wanted to bask in the pleasure of her presence.

During the return trip to Rocky Bluff, Mitzi's eyes sparkled as she scrutinized the banks of snow beside the highway. She eagerly shared some of her adventures in flying, but gradually jet lag began to overtake her. She leaned her head on the back of the seat and fell asleep. Angie smiled with amused understanding. *I felt exactly the same way when I arrived. Everyone wanted to talk, and all I wanted to do was sleep.*

Arriving at the Hatfields' home, Mitzi went right to bed and slept for twelve hours straight. Everyone tiptoed around the house in order not to awaken her. Finally, Mitzi emerged from her bedroom rested and eager to see Rocky Bluff. Rebecca suggested their first stop should be the Burr and Saddle Cafe. Its Western motif and Montana hospitality projected the true spirit of relaxed Rocky Bluff.

Mitzi glanced through the menu. "Almost everything here is beef."

"Enjoy it," Rebecca laughed. "You're in cattle country now."

"I guess I'm used to a diet of pork, seafood, and rice, but this won't be hard at all to get used to."

While they were eating, Duke Harrington entered the cafe, spotted Angie, and walked straight to her table. "How's my favorite skiing student?" he chuckled.

"I'm fine," Angie replied as she turned to the others. "I'd like you to meet my mother, Mitzi Quinata, and my Rocky Bluff hostess, Rebecca Hatfield. This is Duke Harrington."

"How do you do?" Duke said with overdone politeness. "Mrs. Quinata, you have a lovely daughter."

Mitzi glanced at Angie's flushed face, then back to Duke. "Thank you. I couldn't agree with you more."

Duke then turned to Rebecca. "Would you be any relation to Andy Hatfield?"

"Yes. He's my husband. Do you know him?"

"Every year he teaches classes in firefighting to our new recruits in the forest service. He's quite a guy."

Mitzi's eyes widened. "You mean you fight forest fires besides giving ski lessons?"

"In summer I fight forest fires and in winter I work at the ski lodge, so I'm never unemployed."

"How exciting," Mitzi gasped.

Duke turned to leave. "It's nice meeting you folks. I hope you'll be coming to the mountain soon. The ski lessons will be on me."

As Duke joined a friend in the far booth, Mitzi turned to her daughter. "He's a very nice young man. I think he really likes you."

"I'm just another one of his many ski students," Angie protested.

"For such a polite man, he looks awfully shaggy with hair all over his face," Mitzi noted.

"He says it keeps him warm up on the ski lift."

"I guess that makes sense," Mitzi said as she turned back to her Salisbury steak. She silently chuckled as the local men entered the restaurant wearing cowboy hats and boots. *This is even better than the old-fashioned Westerns on TV,* she told herself.

Angie enjoyed the company of her mother after a separation of nearly six months, but a wall remained between them, and the conversation was superficial. *How will I ever tell her I'm not returning to Guam with her? Will she be so upset with me that we can't enjoy our time together? Should I wait for her to bring up the subject, or should I?*

During the entire lunch, Mitzi studied her daughter and listened to her trivial chatter. *Has Angie changed? She used to be open and honest with me and often ridiculed idle chatter. Has six months made this much difference?*

After finishing lunch, Rebecca drove the Quinatas to the Looking Glass Salon. Angie proudly showed her workplace to her mother and introduced her to Barb Old Tail. "Mrs. Quinata, it's so nice to meet you. I can't tell you how happy I am to have Angie with me. She's an answer to my prayers. I don't know what I'd do without her. I'm afraid I'd either have to put my mother in a nursing home or quit work all together."

Mitzi gulped. *What will poor Barb do when Angie returns to Guam?* she pondered. "I'm glad Angie could help you. She's always dreamed of becoming a beautician."

"She's been a real jewel," Barb replied as her next customer walked into the salon.

Rebecca glanced at her watch and turned to Mitzi. "I told Edith Dutton, Jay's grandmother, that we'd stop by for coffee this afternoon. Jay's mother is also going to be there putting up Christmas decorations."

"I'm anxious to meet them," Mitzi smiled. "I heard so much about them. Jay has presented them as super women."

"They are extra special people, just like Jay has said," Angie said as they walked through the snow toward Rebecca's car.

A half hour later, Rebecca, Mitzi, and Angie made themselves comfortable in Edith Dutton's living room. Mitzi admired the string of lights Nancy Harkness had hung around the window. She had decorated the tree in the corner with white lights and red bows. Mitzi was more than happy to relate as many antidotes about Jay as she could remember. "I haven't told Jay yet, but I was able to get an inexpensive one-way ticket so Angie can return to Guam with me. There's even a salon interested in hiring her when she gets back."

Edith examined the young woman sitting nervously across the room. "Angie, you didn't tell us you were leaving so soon."

Angie looked at her mother, then at the floor. "I'm not. I love it here, and I don't want to hurt Mother, but I can't return now. Barb needs me. Besides I want to be here when Jay gets out of the service this summer."

Tears filled Mitzi's eyes. "You mean I wasted my money on that ticket? I thought for sure you'd want to come home. Every Guamanian who leaves the island gets homesick and returns within a few months. I thought you loved Guam and your family. You have aunts, uncles, and cousins in nearly every village."

Angie joined her mother in tears. "Mother, I do love you and all of my other relatives there, but I just can't return now. I hoped you'd understand. For once in my life I have to do what I think is right, whether anyone agrees with me or not."

"I love you and have missed you so much since you went away," Mitzi sobbed. "I suppose I should have asked you before I bought that ticket. I just wanted to surprise you. I didn't realize that you'd begun an entirely new life here. I was foolish to have wasted my money."

Rebecca, Edith, and Nancy watched the mother-daughter encounter with deep compassion and understanding. Both Edith and Nancy had experienced the struggles of letting their own children grow up. Nancy especially remembered the pain she and Bob had known when Jay decided to enlist in the Air Force rather than go to college.

"Maybe it's not all wasted," Nancy said. "I haven't told anyone, but I've been setting money aside every month so I could go to Guam and see Jay before he comes home. I could buy your ticket to Guam, then buy the return ticket from a local travel agent."

Mitzi looked up and dried her eyes. "I don't want you to feel obligated. I should have checked with Angie first."

"I'm not doing this out of obligation. I'm doing this because I want to visit Jay while he's still on Guam," Nancy protested.

Mitzi broke into a broad grin. "If you'd be going anyway, that's a good idea. I know Jay will be anxious to see you. I'd love to have you stay with me while you're there. Who knows, someday we may be sharing grandchildren."

Angie flushed. "Please don't rush things. We're not even officially engaged yet."

❖

As the days flew by, Angie and Mitzi enjoyed each other's company more than ever before. They had both learned to relate to each other as woman-to-woman. Angie loved showing her mother the community and introducing her to friends. While Angie was working, Mitzi spent time with Rebecca and Edith. She'd always known family togetherness on her island home, but never before had she felt such community togetherness as she did in Rocky Bluff. *If Angie stays here and marries Jay, maybe I'll retire to Montana instead of staying on Guam. It may be cold here, but the personal warmth of the people negates the weather.*

Early Saturday morning, Rebecca, Mitzi, and Angie headed for the ski slopes fifty miles north of town. Duke met them at the pro shop. "Hello. Are you ready to try your hand at skiing?"

Rebecca and Mitzi looked at each other. "I'm game if you are," Mitzi giggled. "If we both break our legs, Angie's here to drive us home."

Duke helped them select rental skis and boots. Angie picked out her favorite set and had them on within minutes. "I'll leave you two at the bunny slope for your lessons. I'm going to try to conquer the intermediate. If I'm successful, maybe I'll even take on the advanced slope today."

Mitzi wrinkled her forehead. "Are you sure you're up to the advanced slope? You've only been skiing less than a month."

"Normally I'd agree with you," Duke replied with pride, "but she's an amazingly fast learner."

Both Mitzi and Rebecca ended up facedown in the snow several times. Age had helped remove much of their self-consciousness. When they fell, both would lay in the snow and laugh at themselves, while Duke looked on with puzzlement. *This is really different trying to teach women over fifty to ski. They'll never learn if they don't quit laughing. They're worse than junior high school students.*

Angie joined them for a late lunch in the coffee shop. "Well, are you ready to hit the slopes again?"

"Every muscle in my body aches, and I'm cold to the bone," her mother moaned.

"Do you want to go home then?"

"Oh, no. Enjoy yourself. We'll just sit in the lodge and sip hot chocolate while we watch you conquer the slopes."

"Thanks, Mom. I'm so glad you came to Rocky Bluff. This is the best Christmas season ever."

Mitzi leaned over and hugged her daughter. "As soon as I get back, I'm going to start saving my pennies again so I can come back next Christmas. What better way to spend the holiday season than to feel the crispness of a snowy Montana breeze!"

On Christmas day Angie, Mitzi, and the Hatfields joined the entire Harkness clan at Nancy and Bob's home. How different it was from Angie's first meeting with the family soon after her arrival in Rocky Bluff. She had lost her shyness and self-consciousness. In their own timing and their own way, each had learned of the tragedy which had befallen her on Guam. Angie was surprised that instead of being critical of her they loved her even more. Through them she had begun to come to accept the fact that she had been temporarily hurt, not damaged for life.

After the meal was over and the gifts opened, the family gathered in the living room to sing Christmas carols. In the midst of the merrymaking, the telephone rang, and Nancy raced to answer it.

"Merry Christmas, Mom," Jay greeted.

"Merry Christmas to you."

"I finally got through," Jay sighed. "All the international phone lines have been busy for the last two hours. I suppose everyone is there enjoying themselves."

"Everyone but you. We all miss you, especially today."

"I miss you too. I can hardly wait to see you all. The next six months will probably go by very slowly."

"There might be a chance you'll be able to see one of us before then,"

Nancy said, trying to hide her excitement.

Jay wrinkled his forehead in puzzlement. "Who's that?"

"Me. That is, if it doesn't conflict with your work."

"I'll always have time to work in my mother," Jay laughed, "but what's up?"

"Did you know that as a Christmas present Mitzi bought a cheap, one-way ticket for Angie to return to Guam?"

"No! Is Angie coming back with her?"

"No, Barb Old Tail can't get along without her, and Angie loves her work and Rocky Bluff. Mitzi was just overeager. She thought she was doing Angie a favor."

Jay shook his head. "It's too bad she wasted her money without first checking with Angie."

"It's not totally wasted. I decided to buy the cheap ticket from her and then get a return ticket from the local travel agent. She even invited me to stay with her while I'm on the island."

Jay beamed. "Great! When are you going to come?"

"If the dates are suitable with you, I'll fly to Guam with Mitzi on January fifth and stay until the twentieth."

"I can hardly wait," Jay replied.

Nancy turned on the speakerphone and the entire family got in on the conversation with Jay. He was most interested in learning how business was going at the hardware store from his father and how the new satellite store in Running Butte was doing from his aunt. They all wished each other a merry Christmas; then Nancy switched off the speakerphone so Angie could have a private conversation from the bedroom extension.

The young couple lovingly greeted each other, and each asked how the other was doing. Finally, Angie could no longer hold back the real issue on her mind. "Jay, I miss you and can hardly wait until we can be together, but I hope you understand why I made the decision to stay in Rocky Bluff."

"I'm glad you did. I'll be home in six months; then we'll spend the rest of our lives together."

Angie paused. *Before the attack those words would have been music to my ears. After the attack I would have said "no way," but now I'm not sure. I love Rocky Bluff and all Jay's relatives, but there's so much I want to experience before I settle down—improving my skiing, learning to ride horseback, sightseeing across the rest of the mainland.*

"I'm looking forward to seeing you again," Angie replied evasively. "We have had so much fun together."

Jay told her that he'd applied for the Computer Systems manager position at the local community college and how much he wanted that position. Angie told Jay about her new love for skiing, but she avoided any mention of Duke Harrington and her skiing lessons. She was sure Duke was merely a passing novelty in her life.

The remaining days of her mother's vacation flew by. A bond deeper than ever before built between them. Mitzi finally accepted the fact that Angie was now an adult and responsible for the decisions in her life, and Angie realized that her mother's overprotectiveness was motivated out of love. Saying good-bye was excruciatingly painful for both of them.

For three days after her mother's departure, Angie remained in a blue mood. To console herself, on Saturday Angie went to the ski slopes. The ski runs were nearly deserted when she arrived. As she was lacing her boots, Duke Harrington appeared. "Mind if I join you on the ski lift?" he greeted.

"Sure. Why not?"

On the way up the lift, Duke chattered about the condition of the snow and the warmth of the weather. Angie watched him with curiosity. Very rarely did he leave his post at the ski lodge before his replacement came.

When the pair arrived at the top, Duke motioned for her to follow him. His eyes gleamed with strange haughtiness. "Let's rest on this boulder before we go down," he suggested.

Angie crouched in the snow, while Duke leaned his back against the rock. "Tell me about your boyfriend back in Guam," he prodded. "I heard he was a local boy."

Angie wrinkled her forehead. "His name is Jay Harkness. His folks run the Harkness Hardware Store in Rocky Bluff."

"I remember him. He was a couple of years ahead of me in school. He was known as a real jock back then," Duke sneered.

"He did tell me that he loved sports and participated in almost all of them," she replied, trying to lighten up the situation. "They said he couldn't try out for girls' basketball," she giggled.

"You've been here a long time without him," Duke said as he scooted in the snow until he was beside her. "I bet you miss a little loving." With that he took Angie in his arms and planted a heavy kiss on her lips. She drew back, instinctively slapped his face, sprang to her feet, and raced down the ski run. Her legs trembled as she approached the lodge. Flashbacks to six months before enveloped her. Quickly unlacing her boots and abandoning the rental skis at the door of the pro shop, Angie jumped into Rebecca's Chrysler and raced toward Rocky Bluff.

Several miles down the road, she began to relax. This was the second time a man had violated her. The first time she had felt guilt, humiliation, shame, and self-condemnation. This time she felt only anger. *If only everyone had the same* concern and respect for the opposite sex as Jay has, she thought. *I really appreciate all the love and advice I received from everyone in Rocky Bluff. As Edith reminded me so many times since I've been here, it's not the exciting men who make the best husbands; it's those who are as comfortable as an old pair of shoes.*

Chapter 13

Angie basked in the warm spring air as she walked the twelve blocks from the Looking Glass Beauty Salon to the Hatfields' home. Spring-time in the Rockies was even more beautiful than Jay had described. She marveled at the return of the robins. Birds had disappeared from Guam many years before when the brown tree snake had taken over the island and devoured them. Tulips were blooming in the yards, and the lilac bushes were on the verge of bursting forth. Some of the neighbors were tilling up a section of their backyards for a garden. *When I get a home of my own, I want to try gardening. It looks so rewarding to watch your food grow from a seed instead of having everything shipped in cans and boxes.*

As Angie opened the front door, Rebecca hurried from the kitchen to greet her. "Angie, Jay just called. He was so disappointed that he'd missed you. He has something exciting to tell you. He'll call back at six o'clock our time."

"Did he give you any idea of what's happening?"

"Jay said it was something very exciting, and he wanted you to be the first one in Rocky Bluff to know."

Angie took off her sweater and hung it in the hall closet. "I can't imagine what it'd be. Jay is usually pretty laid-back and seldom gets excited."

For the next half hour Angie stayed close to the phone. She took a soft drink from the refrigerator and sat in an easy chair to read the *Rocky Bluff Herald*. Every few minutes she glanced at the clock over the TV. Promptly at six o'clock, the telephone rang. "Hello, Hatfield residence."

"Hello, Angie," Jay Harkness greeted. "How are you doing?"

"I'm curious. What's your good news?" Angie replied lightly.

"Remember me telling you about my high school principal, Grady Walker?"

"Yes."

"He's now the president of Rocky Bluff Community College, and he just offered me the job of Computer Systems manager at the college. The present manager leaves September first, but Mr. Walker wants me onboard in July. Isn't that great?"

"Jay, I'm so proud of you. I knew all your hard work at computer school would pay off."

"I'm just glad I can come back to Rocky Bluff. With my specialized training

I expected that I'd have to go to one of the major cities to obtain a job."

"I couldn't imagine any town could be as friendly as you claimed, but it definitely lived up to your description," Angie replied. "I now understand why you're so eager to come home."

"Angie, I hate to hang up, but I need to call my folks and let them know before I go to work. I'll call you again next week."

Angie said good-bye and retreated to her basement room. She flopped across her bed and closed her eyes. *What would life be like with Jay back in Rocky Bluff?* She pictured herself running into his arms at the airport. . .dining out together. . .watching videos together. . .taking long walks together hand in hand. . .talking and laughing together. That was their life together in Guam, but this was Rocky Bluff.

Jay has always assumed our relationship would deepen when he returned, but am I ready for a more permanent relationship? If he should formally ask me to marry him, what should I say? How long should we be engaged before we marry? What if Jay doesn't like what I've become and wants to break off the friendship? Should I immediately return to Guam? I don't want to even consider that possibility.

Angie's anticipation grew with each passing day, causing her to become more and more restless. Her friends sympathized with her apprehension and tried to keep her occupied. Every weekend one of her Rocky Bluff friends took her on a minivacation to see the various sights of Montana: Yellowstone Park, Glacier Park, Virginia City, Helena, Fort Peck Reservoir, Flathead Lake. The vastness and beauty of the state overwhelmed her but could not mask her anticipation.

At long last, June fifteenth finally arrived. Angie made her third trip to the Great Falls International Airport, this time with Bob and Nancy Harkness. The miles seemed to never end as Angie's anticipation mounted. It had been ten months since she had last seen Jay. Fears began to overtake her. *Will he still love me after such a long separation? I treated him so rudely between the time of my assault and when I left the island. Will he have forgotten my cruel words? Will he have changed? Will he think I have changed into someone he's no longer comfortable with?* After several miles of worrying, Angie relaxed and conversed with the Harknesses in the front seat.

The miles faded away, and soon Bob was parking his car in the airport parking lot. They checked Jay's arrival gate on the monitor and hurried to the waiting area. Angie paced back and forth in the viewing area scanning the skies. Finally, she spotted a speck in the west which gradually became larger and larger.

Angie, Bob, and Nancy ran to the end of the loading ramp as the jetliner rolled to a stop. They scanned the deplaning passengers for a familiar face.

Finally, a handsome, dark-haired passenger dressed in his best Air Force blues uniform appeared. Spotting his family, Jay broke into a run. He scooped Angie into his arms and swirled her around as tears ran down her cheeks. All of Angie's fears faded into oblivion. Jay had not changed. Jay embraced his mother, then his father. After being away for three years, Jay Harkness was finally back home in Montana.

"Would you like to stop for something to eat before we head back to Rocky Bluff?" Bob queried as they joined the others heading toward the baggage claim.

"Let's go to the Black Angus Steak House. The meat shipped to the base could not compare with good old Montana beef," Jay replied as he took Angie's hand. "The memory of the taste of a Montana filet mignon kept me going for three years."

Less than an hour later the Harkness family and Angie were gathered in a private booth in the Black Angus Steak House enjoying their steak dinners. "How's Dawn?" Jay asked his mother. "She hasn't written me for months."

Bob and Nancy exchanged nervous glances. "She says she's very busy with her sorority activities. She hasn't been home for several weeks."

"I've been concerned about her ever since I learned what sorority she joined. They have the reputation of being a wild bunch with a lot of drinking and partying. I know some of her friends' reputations," Jay replied, "and their reputations are not good."

"We're also very concerned," Nancy replied. "I hope that you'll be able to get through to her. We've tried, but she only shrugs it off and tells us we're not in tune with her generation."

Driving home, jet lag overtook Jay, and he slept most of the way. Angie sat silently beside him memorizing every curve and angle in his face. He was even more handsome than she had remembered. Once Jay was home, he went straight to bed and slept for two days.

After he was fully rested, he picked up the phone and called Angie at work. "Angie, can I pick you up after work and take you for a ride in the mountains? We can pick up some sandwiches and soft drinks to eat as we watch the sunset. We have a lot of catching up to do."

"I'd love it," Angie replied. "I'll be done by five tonight."

"Great. Grandma and Roy had their favorite spot in the mountains where they often went to watch the sunset. I'd like it to become our special place as well."

By six o'clock Jay and Angie were propped against a rock in the Big Snowy Mountains. "This is beautiful," Angie said as she held Jay's hand. "I can see why your grandparents liked it so well."

"Just to see the majesty of the mountains reflected in the lake has a way of putting one's troubles to rest. We have several more hours before the sun begins to set," Jay replied. "That's when words won't be able to describe the beauty."

"The long days are hard for me to get used to. In Montana there are only six and a half hours of darkness in the summer and only six and a half hours of daylight in the winter. On Guam there's hardly any variation in the length of the days."

Jay reached in his pocket and took out a small box and handed it to Angie.

"What's this?" she asked as she gingerly lifted off the lid, then burst out laughing. "Your friendship ring. I'm sorry that I gave it back to you the way I did that night in the hospital. That was so rude and unkind of me." Angie slipped the ring on her finger.

"I knew what you were going through when you returned it," Jay said as a mischievous twinkle appeared in his eye, "but I'm not going to give it back to you now."

Angie looked shocked. *Don't tell me that after I've waited so long for him to come home he's going to break up with me? Maybe I should have gone home with Mother at Christmas.* She handed the ring to Jay and muttered, "Why's that?"

"Because I have something better for you," Jay replied as he reached into the other pocket of his light jacket. He took out a small black velvet box. He opened the lid to show her the most beautiful marquee diamond she had ever seen.

"Angie, I love you so much and want you to wear this instead. Will you marry me? I promise to love and cherish you for the rest of my life."

Angie threw her arms around Jay. "Of course I'll marry you. We have been through so much together, and all the pain of it has drawn us closer together instead of separating us. I love you so, and I've been dreaming of this moment for months. But why did you have to tease me with the friendship ring?"

Jay's eyes again began to twinkle. "Just so you'd have a story to tell to our grandchildren. When I was little, I always bugged my grandparents about their romance, so I wanted to add a little color to our love story."

The cool mountain breeze refreshed the young lovers as they embraced. "Angie, we've been separated so long; I want to get married as soon as possible. Would the first part of September be too soon for you?"

"That sounds perfect," Angie replied. "I'll at least have a little time to plan a wedding."

"More important than the ceremony, I want to find a cozy bungalow of our own."

"Can we have a backyard big enough for a garden?" Angie queried.

"I'll even build a white picket fence if you'd like," Jay laughed.

Angie and Jay stayed at their special spot until the last ray of sunlight was gone. There was so much to talk about and plan. Jay marveled at the confidence and self-reliance Angie had developed since she had come to Rocky Bluff. Their love was stronger than he could have ever imagined while he was waiting on Guam for this moment.

As they drove down the mountains in the darkness, Angie turned to her fiancé. "The first person I want to tell of our formal engagement is Mother. She's stuck with me through good times and bad."

"Let's call her as soon as we get to town. This is one call she's been waiting for since I gave you the friendship ring a couple of years ago. I'll even offer to buy half of her plane ticket if she will come to our wedding."

Mitzi was thrilled to get Jay and Angie's call. "Just let me know the date, and I'll be there," she nearly shouted into the phone. The next stop was Jay's parents. Angie proudly displayed the diamond ring and shared their tentative wedding plans. Half an hour later they were on their way to Edith Dutton's home. Jay's grandmother had been their strength through the tough times, and they were now overjoyed to share this happy time.

Two weeks later, Jay started his new job at the college and spent many long hours learning the idiosyncrasies of their particular system. One evening while sitting in the Hatfields' backyard, he finally admitted his frustration. "Angie, I'd love to have a more active role in planning the wedding, but if you wait to talk every detail over with me, we'll never get anything done. Teresa Lennon used to plan a lot of weddings. I was at both the Reynolds' remarriage and the Blairs' wedding, and they were beautiful. Teresa masterminded both affairs."

"I'll talk to her," Angie replied. "She sure helped me get over my problems. I wonder why she's never remarried? At times she seems so lonely and tries to hide it by helping others."

Jay hesitated for a moment. "I've never thought about it that way," he replied, "but something traumatic must have happened to her a long time ago. She never talks about her past."

"That must be why she's so understanding about women's problems," she replied as she took another sip of her lemonade. "I'll give her a call tomorrow and see if she'll have time to help us."

Teresa was only too happy to plan for yet another wedding in Rocky Bluff. In the weeks that followed, she and Angie seemed to be everywhere—picking out a silverware pattern at The Bon, Angie's wedding dress and dresses for the bridesmaids at Fashion's by Rachel, and china and crystal at Laura's Jewelry Store. This wedding was fast becoming the social event of the year for Rocky Bluff.

Chapter 14

Amid her wedding preparations, Angie kept hearing the people of Rocky Bluff talk about how dry the weather was. Everyone began irrigating their lawns daily. She noted that the Hatfields' lawn was turning brown and asked Rebecca if she could water it.

"The mayor just ordered water rationing until further notice. Our city water supply is running dangerously low, and we need to have a reserve in case of a major fire," Rebecca replied. "There is to be no watering of lawns and washing of cars until further notice."

"That sounds serious," Angie gasped. "It's so different from Guam where they worry about typhoons with their torrential rainfalls."

"Andy is extremely concerned about the lack of water. He's been in close contact with the fire service in case a forest fire might break out in the area. The Fire Management officer is afraid that if we don't get rain soon we'll burn."

Just as Andy and the Fire Management officer had anticipated, a lightning strike twenty miles from Rocky Bluff erupted into a fire about midnight that night. By morning the fire had already burned twenty acres. Firefighting crews were dispatched from all over the area. They immediately dug a fire line ten miles from Rocky Bluff, confident that it would contain the fire. However, two days later a hot southern wind fanned the flames across the fire line.

That morning, just five days before his wedding, Jay rushed into the Looking Glass Salon.

"Angie, the fire's jumped the fire line and is headed this way. They're calling for volunteers from the community to help dig firebreaks. They need every ablebodied person they can get so I volunteered. I hate being away from you just before our wedding, but if the town goes, there can be no wedding."

Angie's hand trembled. "I don't want anything to happen to you. Are you sure you won't be in danger?"

"I'll be far enough away from the actual fire, but the wind can be fickle, and you can never be too careful. Forest fires are one of the risks of living in Montana," he explained as he kissed her on the forehead and hurried out of the salon.

The fire was the talk of the town, and every client who came to the salon that day had an update from the fire line. Rumors abounded. As Angie walked home that evening, her eyes continually drifted to the red glow and black smoke in the northern skies. Somewhere out there her love might be in serious danger.

For three days Rocky Bluff seemed to be on hold as the fire spread. It jumped several secondary roads, and the main road north was closed to all traffic. Several mountain cabins were destroyed. Businesses closed as more and more people joined the fire crews. Barb closed the beauty shop as no one was interested in having their hair done at a time like this. Pastor Rhodes called for a community-wide prayer vigil. Rocky Bluff was in a fight for its sheer survival.

❖

As soon as Jay got to the fire camp, they immediately assigned him to a crew of twenty and handed him the appropriate equipment for building a fire line. Meals were brought to the site, and Jay did not return to the fire camp until darkness had settled over the mountain. As he was preparing for a few short hours of sleep, the Fire Management officer called to him.

"Jay, I understand that you were recently discharged from the Air Force," he said briskly. The sweat was rolling down his forehead and soaking his green forest service shirt.

"That's right, Sir. I just got back a couple months ago after more than two years on Guam."

"Did the military give you any medical training?"

"Yes, everyone gets first aid training."

"Good. We're short of medics. First thing in the morning, would you report to the medical tent. You'd be of more value to us there than on the fire line."

"I'd be glad to," Jay replied.

Jay was asleep as soon as he hit his bedroll. He hadn't been that tired since basic training. For the next three days, he helped treat blisters, minor burns, and heat exhaustion. Two firefighters had to be emergency evacuated to the hospital in Rocky Bluff. Jay was so busy at the medical tent he barely noticed the airplanes from Missoula flying over and dropping fire retardant on the fire and the helicopters dumping buckets of water. But the fire crept ever closer to Rocky Bluff.

On the fourth day a firefighter was brought in who had been hit by a falling tree. As Jay checked him for possible broken bones, the young man asked, "Aren't you Jay Harkness?"

"Yes, I am," he replied. "You look faintly familiar, but I can't remember your name."

"My name's Duke Harrington. I was three years behind you in high school, but I went to all the basketball games you played."

"That was a long time ago," Jay chuckled. "I just got back after serving in the Air Force in Guam."

"I know," Duke replied dryly. "I met the Guamanian girl you sent home ahead of you. She's a mighty fine catch."

Jay wrinkled his forehead and finished his examination. "Angie is the most loving, compassionate person I've ever met. We're supposed to be married on Saturday."

"That's if the church is still standing," Duke replied sarcastically.

Jay finished examining Duke and applied salve to his burns and assigned him to a cot to recuperate. His wounds were superficial, but his tongue cut deeply into Jay's spirit which longed to be with his beloved.

Andy Hatfield went from street to street with his portable speaker system. "Prepare to evacuate. Prepare to evacuate. The fire is within five miles from town. Prepare to evacuate."

Rebecca knew exactly what to do: load her valuables in the car, hose down the house, and build a firebreak around the house by getting rid of all brush and shrubbery from next to the house.

"But isn't there anything else we can do? We're supposed to be married in two days," Angie nearly sobbed.

"Take the garden hose and soak down the house, especially the roof. If the fire does come this way, hopefully it will be too wet to ignite."

"It's all in God's hands now," Rebecca said and began chopping down her favorite shrubs. "Only a strong gully washer will put out this inferno, and the weather forecast is for more hot and dry temperatures."

As the two women frantically prepared to evacuate, Jay sped into the drive. He jumped from the car sweating and covered with dirt. Angie was immediately in his arms. "You're safe. You're safe."

"Some of us were sent to town to help people evacuate."

"I guess our wedding is off," Angie sobbed. "People in Rocky Bluff will soon lose their homes and everything they own, and there's nothing we can do about it."

"All we can do is pray," Jay said as he wiped the tears from Angie cheeks.

Suddenly, a loud clap of thunder echoed through the valley. All eyes turned westward. There a small storm cloud was beginning to build.

"Please, God, let that cloud bring rain," echoed throughout the community. People kept preparing to evacuate with one eye on that growing cloud in the west.

"Angie, do you feel that?" Jay asked.

"Feel what?"

"The wind is beginning to shift. It will fan the flames away from Rocky Bluff."

As the three exhausted workers stood on the front lawn of the Hatfields' home, the heavens opened and torrential rains poured from the skies. Angie took Jay's hand as the late summer rain immersed them. Slowly the smoke in the north subsided.

Angie thanked God for that rain as she silently told herself, *Just as the rain is quenching that flaming inferno, the healing love of Rocky Bluff has quenched my scorching pain and restored my life so that I can love again. Saturday will be even more special than before. Not only will the people of Rocky Bluff celebrate our healing love, they will also celebrate the healing water that saved their beloved city.*

Compassionate Love

Chapter 1

At midnight, Teresa Lennon closed the door of the Rocky Bluff Spouse Abuse Shelter. She had spent the last few hours comforting a distraught, battered young woman, and Teresa sighed now, exhausted. She had finally calmed the troubled woman, then led her to a bedroom on the second floor of the shelter and stayed with her until the woman was ready to sleep. Now Teresa could at last go home.

Teresa had devoted all her working years to helping women in distress, and each person's pain triggered a sense of personal responsibility inside her. She knew what it was like to be emotionally and physically abused. Years before, others had helped her, and now she was always ready to help someone else in crisis. Still, each session left Teresa emotionally drained, and tonight was no different. She lifted her face to the cool fall wind that whirled around her, then made her way to her car.

When she reached her home, she slipped into a nightgown and fell across her bed. Within minutes, she drifted into a deep sleep. Only two hours later, the sharp ring of the telephone pierced the silence of Teresa's bedroom. She grabbed the phone.

"Teresa. . .Teresa," a panicky voice cried. "Can you help me?"

Teresa jerked upright and threw her legs over the side of the bed. As director of the shelter, she was used to being awakened in the middle of the night, and now she was instantly alert.

"I'll do what I can," Teresa said calmly. "To whom am I talking?"

"This is Dawn. . .Dawn Harkness," the voice sobbed. "I can't get ahold of my parents, and I don't know what to do."

Teresa pictured the beautiful daughter of one of the community's leading citizens; Dawn was also the granddaughter of a dear friend. Teresa had not seen Dawn since the younger woman had left for college several months before, and now Teresa felt a wave of concern.

"Dawn, where are you?"

"I'm in the Chief Joseph County Jail," the young coed sobbed.

"Jail? What are you doing there?" Teresa gasped.

"A bunch of us from the college went to a ranch outside of Nez Percé. . . just to have a good time. The police busted the party, and several of us were

121

arrested for using drugs. They won't let us go until we appear with our parents and an attorney. But I'm not able to contact my parents." Dawn gulped back another sob.

"Do you know where they are?" Teresa tried to speak in a calm, relaxed tone even though her heart was beginning to race.

"They're on vacation in the Caribbean. They're not going to be home for a couple of weeks. My brother Jay and his wife Angie are with them too." Her sobs turned to desperation. "I don't know what to do."

"I know it's tough," Teresa replied calmly. "Since you're not able to go any place, try to get some rest tonight. I'll get in touch with an attorney first thing in the morning, and we'll leave immediately for Nez Percé. In the meantime, I'll be praying."

"Thanks," Dawn murmured. "I knew you wouldn't let me down."

Teresa hung up the phone and lay back on her pillow, but sleep escaped her. She thought about the dramatic string of events that had brought her life together with the attractive coed now sitting in the Chief Joseph County Jail.

After an abusive marriage and a traumatic divorce, Teresa had obtained a master's in psychiatric social work from the University of Montana; she had then taken the job in Rocky Bluff, Montana, as director of the Spouse Abuse Shelter. The last fifteen years had been good to her. She had fulfilled a vital need in the community and had made many long-lasting friends, including Dawn's grandmother, Edith Dutton. Teresa had watched Dawn grow from a blond, giggly toddler to a vivacious teenager who anxiously sought the independence of college life. She was aware of Dawn's excessive partying during her senior year in high school, but she had never suspected it would lead to this.

❖

Though Teresa had had less than four hours of sleep, before seven o'clock she was up, showered, and dressed. She dropped two pieces of bread into the toaster, while she dialed an attorney friend, David Wood.

"Good morning." The male voice sounded sleepy.

"Good morning, Dave," Teresa replied. "I'm sorry to call so early, but a crisis occurred last night, and I need immediate legal help."

"I'll do what I can," the young private attorney replied. "What happened?"

"Dawn Harkness called about two o'clock this morning. It seems that a bunch of college kids went to Nez Percé to party. Before the evening was over, the police came and arrested six of them for using drugs. She's now in the Chief Joseph County Jail until her parents and attorney appear before the court. The problem is the Harknesses are vacationing in the Caribbean and won't be back for a couple of weeks. I told her I'd find her legal counsel and drive to Nez Percé first thing this morning. Would you be willing to come with me?"

David paused a moment as he tried to recall the coming day's appointments. "I have a light agenda today." He reached for his robe. "I'd be glad to go with you. The Harknesses have done a lot to support me throughout the years. It's the least I can do. I'll call my secretary and have her reschedule my clients. Give me an hour, and I'll come by and get you."

"Thanks, Dave. I knew I could count on you."

Teresa hung up the phone and took a deep breath. *As much as I hate to, I think I better call Edith. She'd be crushed if one of her family members was in trouble and she wasn't notified so she could pray. Her health has been so bad lately, prayer is the only thing she can do to help her family and friends.*

Teresa dialed the familiar number and waited six rings. "Hello," a breathy voice greeted.

"Hello, Edith. How are you today?"

Recognizing her friend's voice, Edith smiled. "Hi, Teresa. I'm doing fine. I just wish I could get out of the house more often. I miss helping all my friends and family."

"Your prayer power is the best help you can give," Teresa replied. She took a deep breath before continuing. "Please pray for Dawn today. She needs all the support she can get."

Edith's brow wrinkled as she pictured her vivacious granddaughter. "What happened to my sweetie?"

"I hate to be the bearer of bad news," Teresa said. "Dawn called me last night from the Chief Joseph County Jail."

"What was she doing there?" Edith gasped.

"She'd been at a party. The police came by, and she and several other college kids were arrested for using drugs. They won't release her until her parents and attorney appear before the court."

"But Bob and Nancy won't be back from vacation for two weeks," Edith protested.

"That's why she's so upset," Teresa explained. "Her family has always been there to help her, and now she's on her own. She was begging for help and was totally distraught."

"I can imagine," Edith replied, shaking her head. "The Harkness family has always taken care of their own. The poor thing must be terrified."

"She is. David Wood and I are leaving for Nez Percé at eight o'clock. I'm sure Dave will be able to help her."

"Thanks," Edith replied as she sunk deeper into her chair. "I appreciate all you're doing for her. I'll be praying for her and her friends all day today. Be sure and call me as soon as you get back."

"I'll call as soon as I get back," Teresa replied. "Better yet, I'll have Dawn come see you herself." Teresa said good-bye to her friend and hung up the receiver. She was comforted by the knowledge that Edith Dutton would be praying.

❖

The foothills of the Rocky Mountains were a somber backdrop as Teresa and Dave drove toward Nez Percé. Snow glistened from the distant peaks, but the drab, brown sagebrush and bare trees reflected the bleakness of the cold November morning.

Teresa rode in silence for many miles before she spoke. "Dave, what do you think will be the best way to handle the situation?"

"I've been pondering that myself ever since you called me." Dave hesitated. "Do you think Dawn has become a drug abuser since she went to college?"

"I'm afraid to even consider that possibility," Teresa sighed, "but last summer she was hanging out with some pretty rough kids. When she pledged Alpha Gamma Kappa sorority, her brother had a fit. He'd heard rumors about that particular sorority doing a lot of partying. Jay did everything he could to talk her out of pledging, but to no avail."

"That's not a very encouraging note," Dave said, shaking his head. "However, there's one thing in her favor. If she is using drugs, I don't think she's been using them very long. The less time she's been taking drugs, the better the chances of her getting off them altogether. I'm a firm believer in rehabilitation centers during the early stages of drug abuse."

Teresa's eyes drifted over the landscape. The sight of cattle grazing on the hillside usually lifted her spirit, but today the tranquility of the Montana scene conflicted with her internal struggles. *How can this be happening to a beautiful young woman from a fine Christian home?*

Teresa turned her attention back to her traveling companion. "But there is no rehabilitation center in Rocky Bluff," she protested weakly. "Dawn needs her family and friends now more than ever before in her life."

Dave nodded his head in agreement. "That's true," he replied, "but usually separation from family and friends for a short period of time gives drug users time to examine themselves and set new goals and objectives. . .without outside influence."

"That makes sense, but Dawn seems too young and innocent to be sent out of state," Teresa responded. "It's not like she doesn't have a family who loves and supports her."

"There's a center in Billings that I'm familiar with that might be helpful," Dave replied. "I've made arrangements for several of my clients to receive therapy at the Rimrock Rehabilitation Center. They all have come back to thank me for steering them in the right direction. Several of them had been addicted for a number of years and had a lot of other problems to overcome. If the center could help them, maybe it would be able to help Dawn as well."

For the remainder of the trip, Dave and Teresa discussed the services available at the Rimrock Rehabilitation Center. Both hoped that they would find Dawn a mere victim of being in the wrong place at the wrong time, but they feared the worst. Had she slipped from casual social drinking to heavy drinking to drug use? As they examined the change in her behavior since she had left for college, the case against her seemed overwhelming. Her grades had dropped. She no longer cared about her personal appearance. She avoided the people and places that had once been important in her life. The few times she had returned to Rocky Bluff, her eyes were distant and glazed. Her mother had commented on her increased moodiness.

When they arrived in Nez Percé, they went directly to the Chief Joseph County Jail. The deputy led them to the visitors' room, and shivers crept down Teresa's spine when the barred door of the jail slammed behind them.

Teresa paced nervously around the room until Dawn entered. She was thinner than Teresa had remembered her, and her eyes were red and swollen from crying. She rushed into Teresa's arms, sobbing.

"I'm sorry. . . . I'm such a fool. . . . I've ruined my entire life. . . . I've disgraced the Harkness name."

Teresa held her until her crying subsided. Dave seated Dawn at the small conference table and nodded to Teresa. "Now tell us exactly what happened," the older woman insisted gently but firmly. "We'll do our best to help, but we have to know every detail that happened."

Dawn fidgeted nervously as the words tumbled from her mouth. "One of the fraternity guys invited our sorority to a party at his parents' ranch while they were away." She twisted a lock of her hair around her index finger. "I don't know how the sheriff's department heard about the party, but they turned up around midnight. Nearly everyone was drinking beer, but the police were looking only for drugs. They arrested six of us for using cocaine."

Dave looked at Dawn gravely. "Were you using cocaine?"

Dawn's eyes fell to the floor. Her face flushed. "Yes," she whispered.

"How long have you been using drugs?" Dave persisted.

Dawn did not lift her eyes as she muttered, "I started a year and a half ago when I first went to college."

"What kinds of drugs have you used?"

Dawn choked back her sobs as she stared blankly at the tiled floor. "First it was just drinking, then I tried marijuana. I started sniffing coke about three months ago. I'm not addicted to it or anything like that. It just helps relieve the stress of my classes. Whenever I'm faced with a big test, a little cocaine helps me get through it."

Dave shook his head. "You are faced with a very serious charge," he said softly. "You are charged with possession and use of a controlled substance. The judge may not be very lenient. I suggest you agree to enroll in the Rimrock Rehabilitation Center in Billings. They have an excellent success rate, and the judge will be more inclined to give you a break as a first offender."

"But I'm not addicted," Dawn persisted. "I just wanted to have some fun and relieve my stress."

"Judges don't accept that logic," Dave replied sternly. "They could fine you and send you to jail. If I were the one making the choice, I'd choose rehabilitation over jail."

Dawn's jaw dropped, and her face turned ashen. "You mean it's that serious?"

Dave nodded his head. "It's that serious."

Tears again filled Dawn's eyes. "Do you think I'll have to stay here until my parents get home?"

"I'll talk to the judge if you'll promise to go to the rehab center as soon as there is an opening. This might be your only way to prevent having a criminal record," Dave explained. "If he agrees, I'll ask that you be released to Teresa's custody until you enter rehab."

Dawn thought a moment, then turned to Teresa. "Are you sure you want to do this?"

Teresa took Dawn's hand and looked into the frightened young woman's eyes. "Of course I do. If we all work together, you'll be back in college in no time."

❖

The next few hours were hectic for all three of them. The court released Dawn to Teresa's custody and arranged for Dawn to enter the Rimrock Rehabilitation Center in three days. Teresa signed the necessary papers, and Dawn agreed to avoid all drugs and alcohol.

Late that afternoon, Dave, Teresa, and Dawn drove to Dawn's sorority house and packed her belongings. The next stop was the registrar's office, where Dawn withdrew from college but retained the right to reenroll at a later time.

By five o'clock the three were on their way to Rocky Bluff. After a day of tension and frustration, the sunset's red glow behind the mountains relaxed the trio. Dawn was soon asleep in the backseat. Her blond hair framed her petite face, giving her an air of innocence that belied her recent experiences. She did not awaken until the lights of Rocky Bluff shone through the windows of David Wood's car.

"Can we go see Grandma as soon as we unload the car?" Dawn asked shyly. "I know I've been a lot of trouble to everyone today, but it would mean so much if I could see her. When I was a little girl, I used to crawl up in her lap, and she always seemed to make everything right again."

Teresa turned around in her seat. "Of course," she agreed. "I promised her I'd either call or bring you over just as soon as we got back to town."

Dave parked his car in Teresa's driveway, and the three hurriedly carried suitcases and boxes into Teresa's spare bedroom. As Dave set the last box in the corner, Dawn extended her hand. "Thanks for all your help. I don't know what I'd have done without you," she murmured, her face red. "Rehab will be a lot better than going to jail. But I still don't think I'm an addict."

Dave smiled at her and placed his hand on her shoulder. "I'm looking forward to talking with you next month after you have been through treatment. You'll see drug use in an entirely different light then," he said. "Good luck. I'll be praying for you."

While Dave backed his car down the driveway, Teresa and Dawn hurried to the garage. They were silent as they drove the familiar streets to Edith Dutton's home. Dawn's mind drifted back to the day when her grandmother had moved here from the spacious, two-story family home. She had turned the large house over to her son and grandchildren, and Dawn remembered the joy of unpacking the treasures she had collected in the first seven years of her life in her upstairs bedroom. She pictured her grandmother's wedding with Roy Dutton and the fun she had had with them. A lump built in her throat as she thought about Roy's stroke and the year he had spent in the nursing home before he passed away. Roy had been a welcomed replacement for the grandfather who had died before she was born.

Dawn scarcely waited for Teresa to stop her car in front of the Dutton home before she sprang from the front seat and bounded up the sidewalk. Before she could reach the doorbell, Edith flung open the door and wrapped her frail arms around her granddaughter. "Grandma, Grandma. I'm sorry," Dawn gasped. "I've let everyone down. I've never had such a terrible experience in my life."

Edith motioned for Teresa to close the door behind her, then led the trembling young woman to the sofa. "Dawn, tell me everything that happened," she insisted gently. "There's nothing so bad that God and the Harkness family can't handle together."

For the next two hours, Dawn poured out the details of her guilt and fears. Teresa was amazed at the loving acceptance Edith showed her wayward granddaughter. So often when she had worked with people in trouble, their families would turn their backs on the struggling person until they had regained some level of acceptability. But Edith's love for her granddaughter never wavered.

Edith gently tried to move Dawn from the denial of her addiction to admitting that drugs had taken control of her life, but the beautiful young coed was still not ready to accept the impact that drugs were having on her life.

After she had poured out her heart to her grandmother, Dawn noticed the dark circles gathering under the old woman's eyes. "Grandma, I didn't mean to keep you up so late. I better let you get some rest. I'll come and see you before I leave for Billings." Dawn stood to leave.

"Get a good night's rest," Edith replied as she hugged her granddaughter. "I'll be praying for you."

"Thanks, Grandma." Dawn returned the hug. "There's one other thing. If Mom or Dad call, would you tell them what happened and let them know how sorry I am to disgrace the Harkness name? Don't let them cut their vacation short on my account. They've saved for this trip for years. They deserve every moment of relaxation they can get."

"I'll do the best I can," Edith assured her, "but knowing your parents, they'll probably be on the next plane back to Rocky Bluff."

❖

Dawn slept most of the next day. The security of being home in Rocky Bluff relaxed her tension-filled body. When she awoke, she began pondering drug rehabilitation and bombarded Teresa with questions. Teresa went through her files until she found several brochures, pamphlets, and a book on the subject. Dawn spent the rest of the evening poring over them. She searched for any clue as to what the future might hold for her.

The next morning, Dawn arose early, showered, and was waiting in the living room when Teresa stumbled to the kitchen with her eyes only partially opened.

"Good morning," Dawn greeted as she looked up from the morning paper.

"You're up early for a Sunday morning," Teresa replied. "You look nice today."

"I want to go to church with you," Dawn replied. "I haven't gone since I went to college, and I think I better get back in the habit. Maybe if I hadn't ignored what my parents taught me about walking daily with God, I wouldn't be in this mess."

Teresa smiled and nodded with agreement. "Your family did give you a firm foundation, and Pastor Rhodes has always been available to teach and console those who have needed him."

"He's the only minister I've ever known," Dawn replied. "Every time there was a high point in my life he was always there. Now he's here during the lowest point in my life. I'd like to talk with him before I leave for Billings."

Dawn fixed breakfast, while Teresa dressed. After they had eaten, they drove to Edith's house to give her a ride to church. Since Bob and Nancy were gone, Edith was left without transportation.

The church service that Sunday took on a special meaning for Dawn. She squeezed her grandmother's hand as she recited the Lord's Prayer. *"Forgive us our trespasses as we forgive those who trespass against us."* The hymns, the sermon, and the prayers seemed to have been tailored just for her. After the closing hymn, instead of walking to the back to greet the people, Pastor Rhodes motioned for the congregation to be seated. Everyone exchanged puzzled glances as they quickly obeyed.

"I have some sad but exciting news for you," Pastor Rhodes began. "The first of January, I will be leaving Rocky Bluff to accept the pastorate in Sheridan, Wyoming. I am leaving this congregation with deep regret. We have shared many years of joys and sorrows and have grown together as a family of God. I will miss you greatly, but there comes a time for change. I now feel it is time for me to move on and turn this congregation over to a younger minister. I trust you will receive your new pastor with the same love and acceptance you have shown to me."

Dawn didn't hear any more of Pastor Rhodes's farewell speech. Just when she needed him the most, he would be leaving them. No one would ever be able to fill his place in her life. By the time Dawn completed drug treatment, a new minister would be in the pulpit, and church would never be the same again.

Chapter 2

Dawn Harkness gazed out the window of the Rimrock Rehabilitation Center. Tears filled her eyes as she watched her grandmother and Teresa Lennon leave the parking lot. *I shouldn't be here,* she mused as Teresa's car turned the corner and went out of sight. *I should be back in the sorority house. I'm not a drug addict like the others here. What will my parents think when they get back from the Caribbean? I have humiliated the Harkness name. Grandma was so gracious about helping me, but I could see the pain underneath her smile. She didn't deserve to see me here.*

"It's hard to say good-bye, isn't it?" a voice behind her said as a gentle hand was placed on her shoulder.

Dawn turned to face a tall brunette dressed in a comfortable sweater and jeans. "I shouldn't be here," Dawn protested. "I'm not an addict. I only used drugs at a few parties to relieve the stress of college life, and now I'm an embarrassment to my entire family."

"That's the way I felt when I first came," the other young woman replied. "It looks like we're going to be roommates for several weeks so it's time we became acquainted. Let's go down to the rec room, and I'll buy you a soft drink."

"Thanks," Dawn replied. "I guess I'll have to make the best of a bad situation."

The two young women strolled down the wide corridor to the recreation center. "It's not so bad here once you get used to it," the tall young woman said. "My name's Lori Hauser. I'm from Missoula. What's your name?"

"Dawn. . .Dawn Harkness. I'm from Rocky Bluff, but I went to college at Montana A&M. Being here is ruining one entire semester." Dawn selected her favorite soft drink from the vending machine. She shrugged her shoulders as a can slammed into the bin at the bottom of the machine. "I suppose it doesn't matter. . . . My grades were falling anyway."

Lori led the way to a table for two in the corner. "You sound just like I did when I came here three weeks ago," she chuckled. "The counselors and other residents helped me understand what casual use of drugs was doing to my body and my life. I've had to reexamine my life and attitudes from the very beginning. It was touch and go for awhile. I didn't have a very pretty picture of myself, but I figure it will be worth it in the end. My family's coming next week for family week, and I can hardly wait."

Dawn wrinkled her forehead. "What's family week?"

"After a resident is here about three weeks, they encourage the entire family to come and stay for a week. Drug addiction is not just an individual's problem. It affects the entire family."

"But I wasn't using drugs when I was living at home. My using drugs had nothing to do with my family. It was my own choice. They'll be horrified when they get back and find out where I am." Dawn gazed out the window as a light snow began to fall on the barren tree limbs. "If I hadn't gotten arrested at a party, they would never have known I was using drugs."

Lori looked at her new friend with understanding. "Hiding your drug use from your family is one of the first signs of addiction," she said softly. "Denial is one of the defenses we use to escape accepting the reality of drug addiction. It's the major stumbling block to a cure."

Dawn continued gazing out the window. *Maybe I am an addict. Some people at school have taken drugs a lot longer than I have, and they're still in control of their own lives. But somehow I seemed to lose control right away.* She turned her attention back to her new friend. "Lori, perhaps I was headed toward addiction, but it's not a big deal yet. I could quit any time I wanted. I've only used cocaine at parties. If the cops hadn't gotten word of my last party, no one would have known the difference."

Lori shook her head. "Minimizing is another defense against accepting reality." She laughed and shook her head. "I'm sorry. Three weeks ago I was saying the exact things you are. And here I am now, quoting the counselors word for word. But it's true. Believe me, I know. I was one of those people who say their drug problem's no big deal, even when I had nearly destroyed my life. Admit it. Drugs were destroying your life too, otherwise you wouldn't be here."

Anger danced in Dawn's eyes. "Your experiences were different than mine," she said coldly. "I don't have to sit here and be insulted." She rushed from the rec room in tears.

Others relaxing in the room looked up from the TV corner. "What's wrong with her?" one of them asked.

"She's new. She's having trouble accepting her problems. Give her a couple of days, and she'll be fine," Lori explained as she joined the group watching television. "She doesn't understand that we've all been through the same thing."

Dawn ran to her room and flopped across her bed. Pain vibrated through her, spreading out from her heart, until she curled into a ball and rocked herself back and forth. *If only I had some cocaine. The stress I felt at college is nothing compared to this. Why did Lori assume I'm in a state of denial or that I'm minimizing my problem? She seemed nice until she brought up all the defense mechanisms she thinks*

I'm using. She sounded so sure of herself, like she knew all the answers just because she's been here three weeks. Three weeks couldn't possibly make that much difference. I'll stay here because I don't want to go to jail, but I won't change my mind. They're not going to brainwash me into believing I'm an addict.

Shadows fell across the room as the sun set behind the distant Beartooth Mountains. As Dawn's sobs subsided, she drifted into a deep sleep. She did not hear Lori slip quietly into the room, prepare for bed, and crawl beneath the blankets in the bed across the room.

The room remained quiet until six-thirty the next morning when a loud ringing from down the hall caused Dawn to bolt upright in bed. "What's that?"

"Just our morning wake-up," Lori laughed. "They don't want us to sleep a minute past six-thirty. Then they give us only forty-five minutes to shower, dress, make our beds, and get to breakfast. It takes me that long just to get my makeup on."

Dawn threw back the covers, slipped her feet into her slippers, and trudged to the bathroom. Her movements were robotlike, the emotions of the last few days repressed. Her consciousness could not deal with more pain.

❖

Nancy and Bob Harkness and their son and daughter-in-law, Jay and Angie, stepped off the airplane in Great Falls, Montana, and mingled with the crowd who hurried toward the baggage claim. "I'll go get the car," Jay volunteered. "I hope I won't have any trouble starting it. Leaving it parked for weeks in this cold weather isn't too good on the engine."

"We'll get your luggage and meet you in the loading zone," Bob replied.

A cold blast of winter wind hit Jay in the face as he stepped outside the airport building. He wrapped his light sweater tighter around himself as he jogged across the parking lot. *I'm glad we left our winter coats in the car.* He fumbled with the key, opened the front door, and reached over the seat for his coat. He breathed a sigh of relief as he pulled the fleece-lined suede coat over his shoulders. After three weak shudders, the engine started; he idled it for a few minutes, then drove to the loading zone. Spotting his family waiting behind the entrance windows, he put the engine in neutral, grabbed their coats, and rushed inside.

Within minutes the luggage was loaded into the trunk and the Harkness family was on their way home to Rocky Bluff. Nancy leaned her head back against the seat. "That was the most fantastic vacation we've ever had. It's too bad Dawn wasn't able to go with us."

"If I remember right, we offered to postpone the trip until her semester break, but she said she wasn't interested in going on any yuppie vacation trip," Jay reminded her.

"I know," his mother sighed. "It's just a phase she's going through. It won't be long before she discovers the value of being with her family." Nancy admired her tall, dark-haired son behind the wheel of the car. *God has been so good to our family,* she mused. *Our family has shared a lot of joys and pain, and we've always come out stronger and more unified.* "I remember how anxious you were to get out of Rocky Bluff when you graduated from high school. You joined the Air Force and requested an assignment in Guam, as far away from Montana as you could get," she chided.

"I'm glad he did," Angie giggled. "Otherwise I'd never have met Jay and found out how beautiful Montana is."

Jay nodded his head and smiled. "Just think, Mom, you'll be the only one in Rocky Bluff who'll have half-Guamanian grandchildren," he teased.

Bob, who had appeared to be dozing, instantly straightened his back. "Son, are you trying to tell us something?"

"We're not sure yet," Jay replied, "but Angie went to the drugstore while we were in St. Croix and bought a home pregnancy test, and she passed with flying colors! Please don't tell anyone until she's had time to go to the doctor to have it confirmed. We don't want to get our hopes up, then be disappointed."

Nancy nearly burst with excitement. "I hope you make an appointment first thing in the morning. This is news to be shouted from the housetops of Rocky Bluff."

"I plan to," Angie assured them as she squeezed her husband's hand.

For the rest of the trip, Jay rotated gospel tapes in the car stereo, while his family dozed or idly watched the landscape fly by. The end of a perfect vacation had climaxed with the possibility of another generation of Harknesses.

❀

The next morning, Nancy sat relaxing in her robe over her morning cup of coffee. Bob had left early for the hardware store, and a pile of laundry was beckoning her. Suddenly, her calm was interrupted by the loud ringing of the telephone. She picked up the phone.

"Hello?"

"Hello, Nancy," answered Teresa's voice. "It's good to have you home."

"Hi, Teresa. I'm glad you called. I'm anxious to hear everything that happened in Rocky Bluff while we were gone. There was something wrong with the connection the last time we tried to call Bob's mother, so I'm way behind on the news."

Teresa gulped. The news she had for her dearest friend was not going to be easy to tell. "We have a lot to talk about. How about if I come over in about a half hour?"

"Spending time with my best friend will be a lot more fun than facing

133

a pile of laundry."

After she'd hung up the phone, Nancy hurried to the bedroom and pulled on a pair of blue sweats, then tied her hair back with a bow. When the doorbell rang, she flung the door open and embraced her friend.

"I didn't hurry you, did I?" Teresa asked, trying to hide the tension in her voice. "I figured after a vacation to the Caribbean you'd be sleeping late for a week."

"Oh, no. I was up early. Bob was anxious to get to the store. The Christmas merchandise is beginning to arrive, and he wanted to get everything displayed as soon as possible."

Nancy poured two cups of coffee, while Teresa brought her up to date on the minor happenings of Rocky Bluff. After Nancy was seated at the table, Teresa became serious. "Nancy, Dawn had a major problem while you were gone, and she needs you now more than ever before in her life."

A deep furrow creased Nancy's forehead. "What happened?"

"She was at a party at a ranch outside of Nez Percé, and the sheriff's department arrived and arrested six of them for using illegal drugs. She called me from jail in the middle of the night. She didn't know what to do, and they wouldn't release her unless her parents were there, and she didn't know how to get ahold of you. She was hysterical."

Nancy's face blanched. "What happened? Where is she now?"

"Dave Wood went to Nez Percé with me. He was able to convince the judge to release her into our custody if she would consent to drug treatment at the Rimrock Rehabilitation Center in Billings. Dawn wasn't very pleased with the idea, but she figured it was better than sitting in jail and having a criminal record."

Nancy stared at the floor in silence. Never before had anyone in her family been on the wrong side of the law. She choked back a sob. "Do you think she was actually using drugs?"

"I'm afraid so," Teresa replied. "She admitted that she started using cocaine last summer. Edith rode with me when I drove her to Billings a week ago Sunday. Dawn was certain she had humiliated the Harkness name, but her grandmother did her best to convince her that regardless of what happened, her family would always love her."

"When can I talk to her? She can't go through this alone," Nancy objected.

"I understand she has a pretty heavy schedule of lectures, individual and group therapy, and assignments. I'll give you the name and number of the director of the center, and she'll be able to put you in contact with Dawn."

The muscles in Nancy's neck tightened. "Bob and I will need to go to Billings to see her right away."

"Residents aren't allowed to have guests until family week, which is usually the third week of the treatment. During that week, the families stay at the center and go through therapy with the resident. There's a much greater success rate if the entire family participates."

Nancy rose. Her hand trembled. "I better call Bob and have him come home so you can explain this to him as well. I'll also give Jay a call. I don't think he had to be to work until noon today. It's time for a family meeting, and we need your expertise to help us through this. I don't know what we'd do without friends like you."

❖

Two weeks later, Dawn, Jay, Angie, Nancy, and Bob Harkness gathered in the family therapy room in the Rimrock Rehabilitation Center. Dawn sat tensely as she surveyed the faces of her family. Even though each affirmed their love, Dawn was unconvinced. She felt she had committed an unforgivable sin in defaming the family name.

"Dawn, can you tell us when you began to feel estranged from your family?" the therapist asked.

Dawn stared at the floor. She sat in silence for several long minutes. "Everything changed when I was in junior high school," she murmured. "Everyone was so wrapped up in Jay's basketball and football that no one seemed to care if I was around or not. The entire town seemed to worship basketball and its stars. I felt that if a person wasn't good in sports they weren't worth having around."

"Honey, that's not true. We've always loved you both equally," Nancy protested. "You excelled in music, while Jay excelled in sports."

"Not very many people came to my music concerts," Dawn retorted. "Those who did were there only because their kid was performing. They sat there bored to death during the rest of the performance. But those same people talked about ball games for weeks afterward."

"That may be an accurate observation," Bob noted, "but that doesn't negate your accomplishments."

Dawn continued to pour out real and imagined situations that had upset her, and the family explained their perception of the same events. Dawn told how she felt pushed aside when Angie had come to Rocky Bluff. With that, Angie broke into tears.

"I didn't mean to hurt you," Angie sobbed. "I liked you, and I tried so hard to get you to like me. I wanted so badly to be accepted by you and your friends, but you always excluded me."

With that, Dawn broke down crying as well. "I wanted to be with you, but my friends didn't want a foreigner marrying the handsomest guy in town. They wanted him for themselves." When her sobs subsided, Dawn got up and wrapped her arms around her sister-in-law. "I'm sorry I hurt you. I'm proud to have you married to my brother. I knew you were so much better and kinder than the girls I was hanging around with, but I wanted to feel accepted by that crowd. Look at what it got me. I'd hate to have any of them as a member of the family."

Little by little as the week progressed, the wall Dawn had built around herself crumbled. Everyone accepted responsibility for their role in the situation. They confessed their sins to each other and to God and begged each other's forgiveness. They prayed together in total unity. Never before had the therapist observed the true inner healing that only God can provide.

Before the week was over, the therapist began exploring Dawn's future with the Harkness family.

"I'd like to go back to college next fall," Dawn explained, "but I don't feel strong enough to be separated from my family right now. I'm so emotionally drained and vulnerable. Can I come home and work in the store?"

"Of course you can," Bob replied as he squeezed his daughter's hand. "In fact, it would be a big help to us. Our bookkeeper wants to take some time off to stay home with her family, and I didn't know how I was going to replace her."

"If you returned to Rocky Bluff, you would still need to have some form of aftercare," the therapist reminded Dawn. "As far as I know, Rocky Bluff does not have any facilities for follow-up care."

"Psychological help is very limited in rural Montana," Bob reminded the therapist, "but Teresa Lennon has a master's degree in psychiatric social work. She has helped hundreds of young women at the Spouse Abuse Shelter."

The entire Harkness family nodded their heads simultaneously. Angie was the first to speak. "When I was going through a difficult time in my life, Teresa was the one who helped me get my life back together. It meant so much to have a trained therapist who understood my Christian faith."

The therapist nodded. "Yes," she said thoughtfully, "after seeing your family in action this week, I think I can understand that. Dawn, let me call Teresa Lennon and see if we can work out a plan for your aftercare."

When their last family therapy session was over, the therapist thanked each one of them for participating. "I've never seen this kind of love and support from a family and community for any of our residents before," she admitted. "I'll make arrangements for Dawn to return to Rocky Bluff within the next ten days. Good luck to all of you. It was a pleasure to work with such a concerned, compassionate family."

The family said good-bye to Dawn and prepared for their trip home. Farewells were hard to say, but each knew they were preparing for a new beginning with Dawn back in her rightful place in the family.

Chapter 3

Teresa Lennon leaned back in her chair in the minister's study of the Rocky Bluff Community Church. "Pastor Rhodes, you don't know how much I hate to see you leave," she admitted sadly. "Now that the court has assigned Dawn Harkness's case to me, I need all the support I can get."

"Teresa, I have confidence in your expertise," Pastor Rhodes replied. "You've been in the counseling business for a long while and have handled life-threatening situations. I'm certain you'll be able to handle Dawn's situation as well." The pastor's compassionate, gray eyes surveyed the woman across his desk. Leaving Rocky Bluff after nearly twenty years of ministry was going to hurt. He had seen an entire generation of children grow up, and he had watched people like Teresa climb from the beginning of their career to the peak of their productivity.

"My experience is all with spousal abuse, not drug abuse," Teresa answered. "Up until now, we've had few cases of drug abuse in Rocky Bluff. The situation is even more difficult because I've been a family friend of the Harknesses ever since I moved here."

"Your friendship with the family could be more of an asset than a detriment," Pastor Rhodes said.

Teresa nodded. "I know. It's just. . ." She sighed. "Dawn seems to have a deep sense of guilt. She's going through an intense spiritual struggle. I'm not sure my counseling skills will be enough. I think she's going to need pastoral counseling as well. She's very upset that you're leaving, especially now in the midst of this crisis."

"Remember, all things work together for good in God's kingdom." Pastor Rhodes stroked his chin. "Besides, God's grace does not depend on any one person. Fortunately, the new minister will be here this weekend. I understand he had undergraduate training in alcohol- and drug-abuse counseling."

"He could be a great help." But Teresa was not really convinced. "What's his name?"

"Bryan Olson. He's in his late forties, never married, and totally committed to his profession."

A wry smile spread across Teresa's face. "It's going to be different for our church not to have a pastor's wife. We've come to depend too much on Mrs.

137

Rhodes. She's had to do tasks over and above the call of duty."

"Rest assured," Pastor Rhodes replied, "she enjoyed every minute of it. This congregation has truly become our family."

"At least Rev. Olson is beyond the age of everyone trying to play match-maker for him," Teresa chuckled. "Nothing is more repulsive than overanxious mothers trying to marry their daughters off to the local minister."

Pastor Rhodes's laughter mingled with Teresa's. "I've known of a situation where the competition among the mothers nearly tore a church apart. The funny part about that competition was that not one of the daughters was the least bit interested in the young minister."

"The life of a minister's wife has got to be the most difficult one in a com-munity," Teresa said. "She would always have someone criticizing her, regardless of what she does. Her time would never be her own. That's one role I've never wanted."

"Yes, there is a downside to parsonage life." Pastor Rhodes nodded his head. "However, Emily would not have had it any other way. She loves help-ing people. The hardest part was raising our family in the spotlight. After the children were grown, she found things easier. That's when she truly began to thrive in her role as a pastor's wife."

"Both of your children turned out well in spite of the public scrutiny," Teresa protested. "That speaks well of their home life."

The older minister's eyes grew distant. "We tried our best to maintain a certain amount of family privacy while they were growing up. Few people real-ized the personal struggles we were going through behind closed doors. It wasn't easy. . .but God was faithful."

Teresa watched the gentleness that shone in the pastor's face. She had not realized how fond of him she had become until she faced the reality of his mov-ing. "Hopefully, the new minister will be able to relate to Dawn. I'm not trained to deal with all her problems," she sighed. "When the court assigned her to me, they didn't recognize the difference between spiritual, emotional, and drug-related problems." She glanced at her watch, and her forehead wrinkled. "Oh no. I didn't realize it was getting so late. I need to be at the shelter by three."

Teresa bid the minister farewell, then hurried to her car. As she drove, she wondered if the new minister would be able to help Dawn. *In all my years working with spouse abuse cases, I've never known a confirmed bachelor who could understand a woman's emotional pain well enough to help her. Unmarried men always seem to have textbook answers to personal problems.*

After her meeting, she drove home, looking forward to a relaxing evening at home. She had just changed into comfortable clothes when the telephone rang.

"Hello?"

"Hello, Teresa," said Nancy's voice. "I was wondering if you'd like to come along on Friday when we bring Dawn home."

Teresa glanced at her daily planner. "I'd love to," she replied. "It's about the only day I have free this week. Saturday I'm going to be decorating the fellowship hall for the pastor's farewell dinner."

The two continued to chat about Dawn's homecoming and the community dinner for their pastor. Both avoided the underlying question nagging them. *How will Dawn readjust back into the community after having been through rehabilitation? Will she remain strong enough to resist temptation from her peers?*

❧

On Saturday evening more than two hundred people crowded into the fellowship hall of the Rocky Bluff Community Church. While everyone else gorged themselves with the potluck dinner, Dawn pushed her food back and forth with her fork, a lump in her throat. "Teresa, how am I going to get along without Pastor Rhodes? I need a minister now more than ever."

"The new minister will be at church tomorrow," Teresa whispered. "I'm sure you'll like him. He's a bachelor who comes to us highly recommended."

"If he's never been married, how can he possibly understand what a woman goes through, especially one who's had as many problems as I've had?" Dawn protested.

"Dawn, give him a chance," Teresa persisted. "He may be the answer to our prayers. They say he had a tremendous ministry to alcohol and drug addicts in Boise."

Dawn shook her head. "He might have been able to work with the men, but I doubt if he was able to help even one woman. If a man gets into his late forties and has never been married, something must be wrong with him."

Teresa frowned as she felt the eyes of others at their table waiting for her response. "That's not always true," she replied softly. "Remember all the years our fire chief, Andy Hatfield, was a bachelor before he married Rebecca. He was so committed to his job that he never developed a personal life until Rebecca taught him how to slow down and enjoy life."

Dawn shrugged her shoulders and sneered. "But Andy's different. Most normal men are married before they're thirty."

With those words Teresa flushed, and everyone at their table looked away in embarrassment. The Dawn they had once known had never spoken in such a hard, cold voice. What had happened to the lovely Harkness daughter who had been the pride and joy of the family?

❧

The next morning, Dawn was sitting with her parents in the back of the church when Teresa and Edith Dutton joined them. "Good morning, Dawn," her grandmother whispered as she slid in beside her granddaughter. "You're looking good today."

Just then a hush spread throughout the congregation as Pastor Rhodes entered the sanctuary followed by a handsome, middle-aged man with graying temples. After the usual hymns, Scripture readings, and prayers, Pastor Rhodes introduced the new pastor to the congregation. Then Pastor Rhodes sat down, and Pastor Olson began his sermon on love and forgiveness.

Maybe he won't be so bad after all, Teresa mused. *I hope he'll be able to relate to Dawn.*

❖

Every evening after work, Dawn met with Teresa. Teresa became more and more concerned about her, for during each session she appeared more depressed than the day before. Dawn seemed to be holding something back. Finally, Friday afternoon Dawn entered Teresa's home crying.

Teresa ran to her side and wrapped her arms around the young woman. "Dawn, what's wrong?"

"I've disgraced my family," she sobbed.

"What happened? When you left Billings, you felt you had the most loving, accepting family possible and that all was forgiven."

"I did then, but I was wrong," Dawn replied. "No one else in town understands what happened. They're all talking about the Harkness drug addict. They're wondering what other secrets our family is hiding behind closed doors."

Teresa led the shaking woman to the sofa. "Whatever gave you such an idea?"

"I heard a couple of old ladies talking about me in the restaurant today." Dawn's voice trembled. "You know how tall the dividers between the booths are at the Main Street Grill. They didn't see me sitting there, so they said the cruelest things."

"But who cares what they said?" Teresa questioned. "You know the truth, and what happened is none of their business."

"I know that." Dawn wiped her tears with the back of her hand. "But they said they were going to quit buying at Harkness Hardware because as long as I was working there I could be selling drugs and using the store as a cover."

Teresa's mouth tightened. "That's the most ridiculous thing I've ever heard."

"Don't you see," Dawn shouted, "it's not just me. I've hurt and humiliated the entire family. I wish I were dead."

"Dawn, please don't talk that way. You're a forgiven sinner whom Christ died for. God knows the truth; that's all that counts."

"No," Dawn sobbed. "I've hurt and destroyed the very people I love the most. I've committed the unpardonable sin."

"I don't fully understand what the unpardonable sin is, but the Bible says it is blasphemy against the Holy Spirit. I've never heard you do that," Teresa replied. "You're just extremely hurt by what you heard today."

"No. I've committed the unpardonable sin. Everyone would be better off if I were dead."

Teresa's mind raced. She knew she was being faced with the threat of suicide, but she felt helpless to assist Dawn with her spiritual struggle. How could she, when she didn't even know what the unpardonable sin was herself? Teresa knew she needed expert guidance immediately. "Dawn, I can't answer some of your questions about sin. Would you permit me to call our new pastor? He's been trained to handle such questions."

"But I'd rather talk to Pastor Rhodes," Dawn protested.

"I know," Teresa sighed. "I would too, but we have to accept the fact that he's not here any longer. Wait here while I call Pastor Olson."

Teresa hurriedly pushed the buttons on her phone's keypad. As she listened to the phone ring, she breathed a silent prayer for help.

"Hello, Pastor Olson speaking," a voice finally answered.

"Pastor Olson, this is Teresa Lennon. I met you Sunday in church. I'm the director of the Spouse Abuse Shelter. I have a young woman in my home who is a member of our church. She is going through a very difficult time and is extremely despondent. She is sure she has committed the unpardonable sin. Would you possibly be able to come over and meet with us? I feel we're in a crisis situation right now."

The pleading in Teresa's voice sent a shiver down the pastor's spine. He understood the message she was conveying, for he had worked with potential suicide cases before. This was his first major challenge in Rocky Bluff, and he knew the respect of his congregation might depend on how he handled this crisis.

"Teresa, where are you located?"

Teresa told him.

"I'll be right there," Pastor Olson promised.

Dawn had stretched out on the sofa, her face buried in the cushions. Teresa hung up the phone, then balanced herself on the corner of the sofa and put her hand on Dawn's trembling shoulder. "Dawn, please turn over and talk with me. You can't hide from your problems this way."

Dawn continued sobbing, while Teresa gently rubbed her back. Dawn seemed oblivious to her counselor's presence; all Teresa could do was wait and pray that the new minister would be able to relieve Dawn's distress.

When the doorbell rang, Teresa ran to greet Pastor Bryan Olson. In a soft voice, she quickly explained Dawn's drug abuse problem and her experience at the Rimrock Rehabilitation Center. Pastor Olson nodded and entered Teresa's living room. He pulled his chair close to the sofa where the sobbing young woman lay.

Instead of talking directly to Dawn, he lifted his eyes toward heaven. "Heavenly Father," he prayed, "please shower Your love and mercy down on Dawn. Ease her broken heart and take away her pain. Let her feel Your presence. Give her the assurance of her salvation through the death and resurrection of Jesus Christ."

With each passing word, Dawn's sobs became softer and further apart. When Pastor Olson finished praying, Dawn rolled over and sat up, tucking her feet under her. "Thank you," she murmured.

"How are you doing, Dawn?" he asked kindly.

She looked down at her hands. "I'm a disgrace to God, my family, and the entire community. I don't deserve to live."

"None of us deserves to live," Pastor Olson replied.

A look of shock spread across Dawn's face. "Teresa, my family, and especially my grandmother deserve the very best. They're such good people. I love all of them so much. They're always helping others without thinking about themselves."

"Even the best of people are still sinful in God's eyes," Pastor Olson reminded her. "But because of Christ's death we are covered with a robe of righteousness. When you cling to Christ, you become the same in God's eyes as any saint."

Dawn sat motionless for several minutes. The words of the gospel slowly cut through her bruised emotions. "That's what Grandma always told me," she finally whispered. "I never fully understood what she was telling me until now."

For the next two hours, Dawn poured out her frustrations, while Pastor Olson shared Christ's love and understanding with her. Teresa watched with amazement. *To think I thought that a confirmed bachelor would never understand the emotions and pain of a woman,* she scolded herself. *He seems to have a direct pipeline to heaven and knows the exact words to say to help her. All my years of psychological training never prepared me for this moment.*

Gradually, Dawn began to relax, and finally, she was able to lift her head and look directly at the pastor.

"Dawn, you look awfully tired." Pastor Olson watched the way the young woman sat wilted on the sofa with the back of her head against the cushion.

"I am," she admitted. "The only other time I've ever cried like this was my first night at the rehabilitation center."

"Tears can be God's healing medicine," Pastor Olson replied softly. "Why don't we have Teresa call your mother to give you a ride home? I suggest you stay home tomorrow and rest. I'll check with you later in the day."

Dawn nodded, and Teresa hurried to the phone. She dialed the familiar number, then explained the situation.

When Nancy arrived, she hugged her daughter, who immediately begged for forgiveness. After assuring her daughter that she was forgiven and she was still loved dearly, Nancy turned to the others. "I want to thank you for helping us. I don't know what we'd do without you. I feel so helpless. It seems like I ought to be able to help my own daughter better."

"It's often the hardest to help those we love the most." Pastor Olson placed his hand on Nancy's shoulder and walked them to the door.

Teresa hugged Dawn. "Be sure to call me whenever you're feeling alone and discouraged. That's what I'm here for."

Dawn nodded, and Teresa then turned to Nancy. "You've got a lovely daughter. I'm glad I'm the one allowed to share her difficult moments. With God's help she's going to have a beautiful future." Nancy smiled as she accepted Teresa's words of comfort.

As soon as the door closed behind the Harknesses, Teresa breathed a heavy sigh of relief and turned to the minister. She noticed that he too looked emotionally drained. "Pastor Olson, would you like a cup of coffee before you go?"

The minister collapsed onto the sofa. "I'd appreciate that," he replied with a smile, "but please call me Bryan. I think we're going to be working together a great deal in the next few months."

Chapter 4

"Nancy, do you think we have enough lights on the tree?" Teresa stepped back to admire the twelve-foot-high Christmas tree that adorned the front corner of the church sanctuary. "It looks kind of skimpy toward the top."

Nancy's eyes drifted toward the angel on the top of the tree. The white lights ended nearly two feet from the angel's skirts, and Nancy couldn't mask her amusement. "It does look pretty bad, doesn't it?" she giggled. "I'll run to the hardware store and get more lights, while you finish putting the boughs on the windowsills."

"Greenery is one thing we have plenty of," Teresa noted as she headed toward a huge box of boughs in the corner. "The youth group had a good time going to the woods. It's a wonder none of the kids were hurt with all the chopping they must have been doing."

"Don't worry, I was with them," a voice said from behind them.

Teresa and Nancy wheeled around and found their pastor walking down the aisle toward them.

Bryan chuckled at their startled faces. "I didn't mean to sneak up on you. Incidentally, I worked my way through undergraduate school by fighting forest fires in Idaho, so I've had a lot of experience felling trees."

"I must say you found a tree perfectly shaped for that corner. We didn't have to trim a single limb," Teresa replied.

As Teresa and Bryan began arranging greenery, Nancy excused herself. "I better get the lights so we'll have time to finish up before the choir comes to practice the cantata."

As Bryan put the finishing touches on an arrangement of evergreen boughs, Teresa stared at him in amazement. Never before had she known a man with such a sensitive sense of beauty. "You're a man of many talents," she laughed. "You make greenery arrangements like a pro."

"I almost am one," he laughed. "My parents ran a flower and gift shop before they retired. I had to help them every weekend when I was growing up."

Teresa smiled. "You must miss them a lot now."

"I do," Bryan replied. "My brothers and sisters have scattered so we're able to get together only during our annual family reunion every July. What about you? Are you going to be with family for Christmas?"

"I wish," Teresa sighed, "but the holiday season is the busiest time at the shelter. Money is often tight, and that makes for domestic troubles. Families are expected to spend more time together, whether they want to or not. Alcohol consumption soars, and so does family violence."

Bryan shook his head. "It's too bad the happiest season of the year has to be tarnished like that."

"Yes, and it's the children who suffer the most." Teresa frowned. "This year it looks like we'll have five children from two different families spending Christmas at the shelter. The mothers must stay away from their husbands at all costs, so I'm planning a big Christmas party for them."

"Do you need someone to play Santa Claus?"

Teresa nearly dropped a lightbulb she was placing in the greenery on the windowsill. "You?" she gasped, trying to control a snicker.

"Sure. Why not? I think it'd be a lot of fun."

"The kids would love it. Could you come about eleven in the morning, then stay for dinner?" Teresa's mind began to race with ideas.

"That would be perfect." Bryan smiled. "Christmas morning services will be over by nine-thirty. That would give me plenty of time to greet everyone, then change into my Santa suit."

The back door of the church creaked shut as Nancy returned from the hardware store. "Sorry it took so long," she said. "The store was extra busy, and I ended up having to wait on customers before I could leave." She paused and surveyed the sanctuary. "That's beautiful," she said. "If I'd known you were doing such a good job without me, I would have taken more time."

"We just make a good team," Bryan laughed as he placed a ladder close to the tree. "Nancy, if you'll hand me the lights, I'll string them for you. If anyone is going to fall off the ladder, it'd better be me instead of either one of you."

Within minutes the church was completely decorated. As Teresa trudged through the snow to her car, she thought, *That was a strange comment. I wonder what Bryan meant when he said we make a good team. He could have decorated the church twice as well without my interference.*

❂

On the day before Christmas, the skies were dark by four-thirty, and the wind began to howl off the Big Snowy Mountains. The snow, which began as light, graceful flakes, was soon descending on Rocky Bluff in blankets. Teresa stayed at the shelter late into the evening, making sure the food for the Christmas meals was ready to be popped into the oven the next day.

The two mothers staying at the shelter had trouble getting their children to bed. Even when they had finally resigned themselves to stay in their beds, the little ones only pretended to be sleeping, hoping they could catch a glimpse of Santa.

Teresa said good-bye at last and stepped out into the blizzard. She swept the snow off her car's windshield, then shivered and shook her head. *It's not worth risking my neck to drive home in this,* she thought. *I might as well stay here for the night. I'll just use the shelter's extra toothbrushes and nightclothes.*

"What are you doing back so soon?" Brenda, one of the women staying at the shelter, asked Teresa as she reentered the building.

"I don't think anyone should go any place in this." Teresa stomped the snow from her boots. "I'll just sleep in the blue room tonight and help you fix breakfast in the morning. It'll be fun sharing the excitement of Christmas morning with the children."

Brenda gazed out the window at the heavily falling snow. "I hope they won't be too disappointed." Teresa heard a note of sadness in her voice. "I didn't have much money to buy many presents."

"I was going to keep this as a surprise for everyone." Teresa smiled. "But I'm not going to be able to keep quiet. Tomorrow I've arranged to have Santa come; then he's going to stay and have dinner with us. He took the names and ages of the children so he'll be bringing a bag of goodies with him as well."

Brenda put her arm around the shelter's director. "Teresa, I don't know how to thank you for all you've done. This is the most miserable Christmas in my life, but you're demonstrating what the real meaning of Christmas is all about. The kids just don't understand why they can't go home. I can't even tell them where home will be."

"These difficult weeks will gradually fade into the background as your new life unfolds," Teresa assured her. "Next year at this time, you'll be surprised how far you've come."

"You're so positive." Brenda smiled as the director moved toward the hallway. "Good night, Teresa. Have a good rest."

Teresa slipped into a pair of the shelter's flannel pajamas and crawled under a pile of quilts. Sleep soon enveloped her.

Seven hours later, Teresa's eyes slowly opened as she realized she was in a bed at the shelter and that it was Christmas morning. *I wonder who turned down the thermostat?* she mused. *It's freezing.* She reached through the darkness for the lamp and turned the switch. Nothing. She turned the switch the other direction. Nothing. *Oh, no. The power's out.*

Teresa reached in the nightstand drawer and took out a flashlight. She hurriedly pulled on a sweat suit and her coat. Judging by the temperature of the large, two-story building, she knew the electricity had been off for some time. She hurried downstairs and began searching for candles, flashlights, and matches. In the kitchen, she turned on the faucet to start a steady stream of water to keep the pipes from freezing and bursting. She looked over at the large fireplace at the end of the living room. *I wish I'd followed my instincts and bought several cords of wood for the shelter. It's been several years since Rocky Bluff was without power for an extended period of time, but it was bound to happen sooner or later. These poor children are going to be miserable. It's a terrible way for little ones to start Christmas morning.*

Just then Brenda entered the living room wearing her winter coat. *"Brrr, it's cold. That must have been some storm last night. The drifts in the front yard look like they're over four feet high."*

"I could just kick myself for not having firewood available," Teresa moaned. "I was hoping we'd have a reasonably decent Christmas for the kids, and now we can't even keep them warm. If the snowplows don't clear the streets, I doubt if Santa will be able to get here, either."

Louise, the other mother, joined Teresa and Brenda in the kitchen. Her "Merry Christmas" was muffled and unenthusiastic. Instead of the planned breakfast of ham and Denver omelettes with toast, Teresa served cold rolls, lukewarm orange juice, and bananas. The children seemed to take the lack of power as an adventure, but the adults bemoaned the inconvenience.

After they had finished eating, the oldest boy wandered into the living room to check the size of the snowdrifts from the large picture window. Suddenly, he gave a loud hoot that brought the others running. "Hey, Santa drives a Jeep Cherokee."

Everyone ran to the front window. A man dressed in a Santa suit took a large bag from the back seat and flung it over his shoulder. Seeing the small faces pressed against the window pane, Santa gave a loud "ho-ho-ho" as he trudged toward the front door.

"Santa, why didn't you use the sleigh?" the youngest girl squealed as she flung open the door.

"My reindeer refused to go out in this weather," Santa chuckled, "but fortunately my Jeep was able to start." He leaned over and opened his bag. "I have some presents in my bag with your names on them."

"It's warmer in the kitchen. Maybe the children would like to open their gifts there," Teresa suggested.

Santa handed three gifts to each child and one to each of the mothers. "Where did you get these?" Teresa whispered to Santa.

"The Harknesses helped me pick them out from their store. They were more than happy to donate to the shelter. They have an excess inventory in the hardware store, and these would be going on sale tomorrow anyway," he whispered back.

While the children happily opened their gifts, Santa and Teresa retired to a corner of the kitchen. "Bryan, how could you come so early? I thought Christmas services weren't going to be over until later."

Pastor Olson watched the children play on the floor with their new toys. "Because of the storm only Dawn and Bob Harkness turned up, and they stayed just a few minutes. They were on their way to get their grandmother. Everyone was very concerned about her being without heat, so Bob had started a big fire in their fireplace and was on his way to get Edith. Dawn just happened to mention that the shelter had a large fireplace that had never been used."

"I should have had the forethought to buy at least a cord of wood for emergencies such as this," Teresa lamented.

"Hindsight is always twenty-twenty," Bryan reminded her, "but I brought some firewood with me. It's in the Jeep. I'll get it and start a fire for you."

He went back out into the snow and hoisted the large box of firewood from the back of the Jeep onto his shoulder. Teresa flung open the door as soon as he reached the front step.

"I suppose you learned how to build a fire when you were an Eagle Scout," Teresa teased as Bryan stomped the snow off his Santa boots. "You always seem to have had some past experience that prepares you for whatever life brings."

"Actually, I *was* an Eagle Scout, but I learned to build the family fire before I was eight," the pastor chuckled. He leaned over and arranged newspapers, kindling wood, then logs in the fireplace. Within minutes a roaring fire was heating the living room, and the children moved close to the fire to play with their new toys.

"We all need to thank Santa," Teresa told the children. They gave him a round of applause, and the littlest ones hugged him. The children were even more thrilled when Santa sat on the floor and played with them.

"Don't you have other presents to deliver?" one of the boys asked.

"Nope," Santa chuckled. "This was my last stop, and I'm exhausted. I hope you don't mind my hanging around for awhile."

"We'd love to have you stay for dinner," Teresa said, wondering how Santa could transform back into Pastor Bryan Olson. "But if the power doesn't come on soon, I won't be able to cook the turkey and all the trimmings."

"No problem at all," Santa replied. "We'll just pretend we're on a camping trip. Do you have any hot dogs in the freezer?"

"Sure, we have plenty of those," Teresa replied. "We also have plenty of potato chips, buns, and ketchup."

"Do you have any wire coat hangers?" Santa asked.

"There's some extra ones in the closet in my bedroom," the oldest boy volunteered. He ran to his room to retrieve them.

The women scouted through the kitchen looking for food that could be cooked over an open flame, while Santa entertained the children in the living room. Teresa had envisioned a traditional Christmas meal, and considering other possibilities was hard. The insightful magic of Santa, however, began to fire her imagination. An hour later they had moved the dining room table close to the fireplace and begun arranging their Christmas dinner.

Santa motioned for everyone to join him around the fireplace. He placed the two smallest children on his knees. "Do you know why we celebrate Christmas?" he asked them.

They looked at each other with bewilderment. "It's fun to get presents," one said.

"Do you know what the best present of all is?" Santa asked.

All the children shook their heads. "The best present doesn't come in Santa's sack," Santa said. "The best present was given to us by God. The best present was a baby called Jesus."

All the children listened attentively as Santa told the story of the very first Christmas. When he finished, he made an exaggerated movement of looking at his watch. "Oh, I almost forgot that Mrs. Claus was expecting me home by one o'clock. I'm going to have to be going. I hope you all enjoy your dinner. Merry Christmas to each one of you." With that Santa winked at Teresa, disappeared out the door, and got into his Jeep. Everyone waved as he backed out of the driveway.

"I can hardly wait to tell everyone at kindergarten that Santa stayed and told us the story of the very first Christmas," one of the girls exclaimed as she ran to her mother. "I don't think anyone will believe me."

Just as everyone was voicing their agreement, the doorbell rang. Teresa hurried to answer it. "Pastor Olson, so nice you could come," she greeted as he winked at her. "I hope you'll enjoy our Christmas dinner over the fireplace. That's the best we could do without electricity."

"I wouldn't miss this for anything," Pastor Olson replied as he stomped the snow from his boots and entered the living room.

"Where did you leave your car?" Teresa whispered.

"The Jeep's around the corner. I left my Santa suit on the backseat," he whispered back. "I hope none of the neighbors saw me taking it off. It might disillusion any believing four-year-old child."

Just as they sat down to eat, the power came back on. Everyone cheered, but one of the children looked disappointed. "Does this mean we'll have to stop our camping-out Christmas?"

The adults exchanged amused glances. "I'm not going to give up this hot dog," Teresa laughed. "It's the best one I've ever had."

Pastor Olson stayed and played with the children and their new toys. Then he helped the women carry the leftover food back to the kitchen and returned the table to its proper place. While the others washed dishes, Brenda took the younger children upstairs to bed.

"Mommy, this was the best Christmas ever. I didn't even miss not being in our house," the youngest one said as Brenda leaned over and kissed her good night. "I hope Santa comes and plays with us again next year."

"It was a Christmas we'll remember for a long time," Brenda replied as she tiptoed out of the room.

Downstairs the phone began to ring. Teresa picked up the receiver. "Hello?" A worried expression spread across her face as she listened to the voice on the other end. "What's wrong, Dawn?"

"I think Grandma had another heart attack," Dawn sobbed. "She's having trouble breathing. The ambulance is on its way. I think it was just too much for her to sit in her cold house for several hours, then have to walk in the deep snow from our car to the house."

"Oh, no. I hope it's nothing serious." Teresa looked up and met Bryan's concerned gaze. "Pastor Olson is here right now. We'll meet your family at the hospital. Just remember, God still has everything under control."

"Teresa, what happened?" Bryan asked as she returned the phone to its cradle. "You look like you've lost your best friend."

"Not yet," Teresa replied sadly. "But she's mighty ill. That was Dawn Harkness. She thinks Edith may be having another heart attack. They're waiting for the ambulance to arrive. I told her that you and I would meet them at the hospital."

"Has Edith had heart trouble before?" Pastor Olson asked as he put his arm on Teresa's shoulder.

"She's had chronic heart trouble since she had a massive coronary thirteen years ago. She tried to make the best of a bad situation after her last heart attack, and she married Roy Dutton in spite of her limitations. She's an outstanding woman and has been an inspiration to all of us."

"Get your coat," Bryan said gently. "The Jeep can get through the snowdrifts better than your car. I want to be waiting at the hospital when the ambulance arrives." He sighed. "I know Edith is in God's hands, but this is no way to celebrate Christmas Day."

Chapter 5

The minutes passed slowly for the Harkness family as they paced the halls of the Rocky Bluff Community Hospital. They had totally forgotten that this was Christmas Day.

"Dawn, use the pay phone down the hall and call your aunt Jean. Let her know that your grandmother's in the hospital." Bob rubbed his hand across his face and looked around the ER waiting room. "Tell her not to venture out on these roads. We'll keep her advised on Mother's progress. Oh, and call your brother."

"I wish Aunt Jean could be here," Dawn sighed as she rose to leave. "It's nice having a nurse for an aunt. Remember when she stayed with Grandma after her last heart attack?"

"Where does Jean live?" Pastor Olson asked Bob as Dawn left the room.

"She's the head nurse at the new hospital clinic in Running Butte," Bob explained. "Her husband, Jim, runs the Harkness Two Hardware Store."

Pastor Olson encouraged Bob to talk about his family, trying to help him forget his worry. "Isn't Running Butte on the edge of the Indian reservation?"

"Yes, it's about a hundred miles north of here." Bob watched his daughter drop a quarter into the pay phone down the hall. "Jean helped organize the medical center and spent months cutting through federal regulations. The locals were extremely grateful and made her an honorary member of their tribe."

Pastor Olson leaned forward. "She sounds like a tremendous person."

"She is," Bob replied. "Jean's much like her mother. Always putting others before herself. She's always counseling someone or praying for them."

While the two men talked quietly, Teresa sat close beside Nancy, holding her hand. "The Harkness clan has spent a lot of time at this hospital through the years." Nancy tried to relax in spite of her anxiety about her mother-in-law. "Rural health care has always been a problem for Montana, but Rocky Bluff is fortunate to have this hospital with three doctors. I don't know what we'd do without it."

"I remember when Edith had her first heart attack," Teresa said. "If it hadn't been for the fast action of Dr. Brewer, she would never have survived to become Mrs. Roy Dutton. That was truly a marriage made in heaven." Teresa sighed.

Nancy's smile relaxed the tense lines on her forehead. "Their autumn love was an inspiration to many other couples, both young and old. The Harkness clan was thrilled to include Roy in the family," she said softly. "We were crushed when he had to spend his last year in a nursing home after his stroke. He'd become such an important part of our lives."

Dawn's lower lip trembled when she returned to the waiting room. "Aunt Jean said she and Uncle Jim will drive to Rocky Bluff in the morning. They haven't gotten the roads cleared that far out. But Jay and Angie said they'll be right over. Everyone was shocked that Grandma was sick again. I guess we all got lulled into thinking she was indestructible."

"Edith's faith in God is indestructible," Teresa reminded her, "but her body has gradually gotten weaker and weaker."

"I couldn't stand to have her in a nursing home like Roy," Dawn said with tears in her eyes. "I'd quit work and stay with her twenty-four hours a day."

"I agree," Nancy stated firmly. "After what happened today, your grandmother cannot live by herself any longer. We can always remodel the den and have her move in with us. She'll be right at home since it was originally her home for nearly forty years. It wasn't until after her first heart attack that she decided the house was too big for her to care for any longer. When she and Roy married, they chose to live in his house because it was the smaller of the two houses. But it's time for her to come back home."

The Harkness family and Teresa shared with their new pastor the impact that Edith had had on the family and the entire community. They told of her bravery in disarming a distraught high school student while she was still teaching home economics in Rocky Bluff High School. They told of all the people she had helped while she was a volunteer at the crisis center. They enjoyed telling how she met and fell in love with the director of the center, Roy Dutton. With each passing anecdote, Pastor Olson was amazed that one woman could have accomplished so much in one short lifetime. *Edith sounds like the model virtuous woman the Bible talks about in Proverbs,* Pastor Olson thought.

Just then a cold wind blew across the hospital waiting room. Glancing up, Dawn saw her brother and sister-in-law shaking snow from their boots. "Jay!" she exclaimed as she ran to embrace him. "I'm so glad you came."

"How's Grandma doing?" Jay asked as he hugged his younger sister.

"We haven't had any word," Dawn replied grimly. "She looked terrible when the ambulance brought her here. Her breathing was so shallow."

Jay and Angie turned to greet the others, then found chairs next to Dawn. Their presence seemed to lift the cloud of anxiety that hung over Dawn. "It's going to be all right, Sis," Jay said as he patted her hand. "God has taken good care of Grandma for all these years. He's not going to let her down now."

Dawn's eyes settled on a water spot on the carpeting. "Grandma's always been there every time I've needed prayer support," she murmured. "I don't know what I'd do without her."

"I guess it's time we all start depending on our own faith in God instead of relying solely on Grandma's prayers," Jay replied solemnly.

"That's easy for you to say," Dawn protested. "You've always been strong and in control of your life. Look what a mess I've made of mine."

Jay shot a panicky look at the others. He couldn't think of what he should say. After a long silence, Teresa was the first to respond. "Dawn, I think you're selling yourself short. Strength comes from God. You can't manufacture it yourself."

Pastor Olson marveled at Teresa's theological perception. Rarely had he seen such depth of spiritual understanding, even in the seminary he had attended. Yet here in small-town Montana where the common, ordinary people lived out their lives, Christian faith and wisdom abounded.

Suddenly, Dr. Brewer appeared in the doorway, and everyone jumped to their feet. "How is she?" Bob asked.

"She's stabilized now, and I think she's going to make it," the doctor replied as he motioned for everyone to be seated. He took the chair next to Bob and pulled it a few inches closer to the others. "From all indications her heart has been further weakened, but she seems to be holding her own. We're going to move her to intensive care so we can monitor her tonight, but I expect tomorrow she can be moved to a private room."

A deep furrow creased Nancy's forehead. "What's her long-term prognosis?"

"We can't be sure for a few days, but my guess is she will be much weaker, and walking will become even more difficult for her," Dr. Brewer explained. He had spent many hours with the family through the years, and he knew he could speak openly and frankly with them. "If I were you, I'd invest in a wheelchair for her as soon as she's discharged from the hospital. I also wouldn't recommend her living alone any longer."

"I couldn't bear to have her in a nursing home like Roy was," Jay said.

Dawn nodded her head in agreement. "We discussed that before you got here," she explained. "We're going to remodel the den and put her bed and dresser there."

Jay rubbed his chin. "That's where she had her bedroom after her first heart attack when she could no longer climb stairs. She always loved that room. It's so light and airy."

Dr. Brewer stood to leave. "If you'd like to spend a few minutes with Edith before she's moved to intensive care, you may do so. Just remember, she is still very weak."

The Harkness family, followed by Teresa and Pastor Olson, tiptoed into the emergency room where Edith lay connected to an oxygen tank and several monitors. They each spoke to her, though she scarcely responded. Pastor Olson led the family in a quiet prayer of comfort and healing, and they all went softly from the room. They all had lumps in their throats, and Dawn could not hold back her tears.

The family said good-bye to each other and made plans when each would return to the hospital. Jay and Angie headed across the snowy parking lot to their car; Bob, Nancy, and Dawn went the other direction; and Pastor Olson and Teresa walked to the pastor's Jeep.

"This has definitely been an eventful Christmas," Bryan said as he opened the door for Teresa. "From blizzards, to playing Santa Claus, to preparing dinner without power, to being involved in a crisis with one of the most faith-filled families I have ever met. There never seems to be a dull moment in Rocky Bluff."

Teresa mulled over Bryan's words as he scraped the ice from the windshield of the car. As he slid behind the wheel, she said, "Montana is a land of contrasts. You never know what's going to happen next, but there's one thing you can be assured of: In a crisis, all Montanans pull together."

❖

The next morning, Bob slipped out of bed before the sun was up and headed for the bathroom. Hearing the shower running, Nancy rolled over and looked at the illuminated clock. She waited for her husband to return. "Bob, it's your day off. Why are you up so early?"

"I want to get to the hospital as soon as possible," Bob replied as he reached in the closet for a clean shirt. "The last time Mother was ill, I dumped her on Jean. I figure now it's time for me to do my part."

Nancy nodded in agreement as she remembered how Bob had been determined to put his mother in a nursing home instead of being responsible for her care. Edith's first heart attack had caused Bob to do a great deal of soul searching, and he was now a changed man.

"Even if you're there, I bet Jean will still hover over her mother," Nancy chuckled. "Once a nurse, always a nurse." Nancy got up and wrapped a robe around her slim waist. "I'll fix you a hot breakfast before you go."

"That's not necessary," Bob replied as he finished buttoning his shirt. "I'll get something later. I want to check on how Mom did through the night."

Nancy combed the tangles from her hair. "Call me as soon as you know anything," she replied. "In the meantime, I'll start clearing out the den for her. Jean and Jim and the girls are planning on leaving Running Butte first thing this morning so they should be here by ten o'clock. I'll ride to the hospital with them."

Bob brushed his lips across Nancy's as he hurried out the door. "See you later. Don't work too hard. I'll do the heavy stuff when I get home."

The snowplows had worked most of the night, and the major streets were now passable. Bob did not lose any time driving to the hospital. He went directly to the intensive care wing and greeted the head nurse. "How's my mother doing?"

"She had a good night and is resting comfortably," the nurse replied. "I'm sure the doctor will move her to a private room some time today."

"If she's awake, may I see her?" Bob asked.

"I'm sure she'd like that." The nurse nodded for him to enter the room near the end of the hall. "She should be waking soon."

Bob thanked the nurse and made his way quickly to his mother's room. As he opened the door, Edith turned her head and opened her eyes. "Hi, Bob. What are you doing here so early?"

"I just wanted to check on how you were doing."

"I'm a lot better today. Sorry I messed up your Christmas." She smiled weakly.

"You didn't mess it up as much as the snow and power outage did," Bob chuckled. "It's good to see you looking so chipper. Sounds like you'll be moved to a private room later today."

"I'm glad of that." Edith's face became serious as she hesitated, trying to chose exactly the right words. "I don't think I'll ever be strong enough to live by myself again," she stated matter-of-factly. "Would you check to see if there will be any openings in the nursing home soon?"

Bob's eyes scolded his mother as he took her hand. "We'll do that only as a last resort. Right now Nancy is cleaning the den so you can have it as your room again. She and Dawn will take turns caring for you."

"But I don't want to disrupt your family life," Edith protested. "You all have jobs to tend to and lives to live."

Bob shook his head and smiled. "You know from all the years you and Dad ran the store that winter is the slowest time of year. This will give me a good excuse to cut back Nancy's and Dawn's hours without hurting their feelings."

"Bob, quit teasing," Edith replied as her normal twinkle returned to her eyes. "I know full well what you're trying to do. I appreciate your offer, though."

Edith hesitated. She needed several minutes before she could come to terms with the dramatic change about to occur in her life. A look of resignation spread across her face. "Maybe we could give it a try for a few weeks and see how it works out. Do you think someone could help me move my bed and a few clothes to your den?"

Bob patted his mother's hand. "Believe me, you'll be overwhelmed with help. Jean and Jim are on their way to Rocky Bluff now, and of course Jay and Angie will be happy to help."

Just then the door opened, and a nurse's aide came in carrying a breakfast tray. "Ready to eat, Mrs. Dutton?"

"I'm very hungry," Edith replied. "I missed out on the big Christmas dinner last night."

"Looks pretty good for hospital food," Bob laughed as he turned to leave. "I wonder if they have something similar in the cafeteria for me to eat."

❖

Teresa awoke early and groaned as she looked out the window at the heavy snowdrifts in the front yard. *One disadvantage about being single,* she sighed. *I have to shovel my own snow or wait two days before one of the neighbor boys has time.* She pulled on a pair of sweats and hurried to the kitchen where she ate a breakfast of oatmeal and hot chocolate.

Taking a parka and boots from the hall closet, she bundled herself against the cold elements. When she opened the door, the harsh, subzero temperature numbed her face. She found the snow shovel in the garage and began shoveling the front sidewalk. By the time she was only halfway to the street, tears were running down her cheeks. *I'll never get this finished. And even if I do, then I'll have to go to the shelter and see that it's dug out. I wish I'd contracted for snow removal, but I hated to spend the money. I thought since we had so much snow last year we'd have an open season this winter. That was so stupid of me. Montana weather is totally unpredictable.*

Teresa stuck her shovel in the snow and leaned on it to rest. A familiar Jeep Cherokee stopped in front of the house. "Do you need some help?" Bryan shouted.

"You better believe it," Teresa yelled back. "I'm kicking myself for not having a snow-removal contract."

"Well, how about going inside and putting on a fresh pot of coffee? I'll have this done in no time." Bryan opened the back of the Jeep and took out a snowblower.

Teresa watched from the kitchen window as Bryan not only cleared the snow from the sidewalk but the driveway as well. When he was finished, he turned off the snowblower and headed for the front steps. "Come in and warm yourself," Teresa greeted as she flung open the door. "You must be freezing."

"I am," Bryan replied as he sank into a kitchen chair, "but doing your driveway didn't take nearly as long as doing the driveway and sidewalks at the shelter."

Teresa's eyes widened as she set a piping hot cup of coffee before him. "You mean you've already been over there?"

"Well, of course," he chided. "You don't think I'd stay in bed all morning, do you? Besides, I thought you might like to come with me to check on Edith Dutton. I've known her only a few days, but after last night, I feel like I've known her a lifetime."

"It'll take me a bit to change clothes and freshen up," Teresa replied. "I hope I won't keep you from doing your pastoral duties."

"Oh, no." Bryan chuckled. "I'm sure your presence will be more healing and therapeutic than mine. There's something about a woman's touch when you're sick."

Teresa poured her pastor another cup of coffee. "Thanks for the vote of encouragement." She smiled. "I'll try to hurry."

Within a half hour Teresa and Bryan were pulling into the parking lot of the Rocky Bluff Community Hospital. As they went inside, Dawn came racing toward them.

"Grandma's a lot better today. They've just moved her to a private room," she said breathlessly. "Let me take you to her."

She led the way down the wide hospital corridor. "We're going to move her bed over to our den this afternoon. The doctor says she'll be out of the hospital in a couple of days so I'll have a chance to take care of her. Maybe that way I'll be able to make up for all the terrible things I've done."

Pastor Olson opened his mouth, but before he could speak, Teresa put her arm around Dawn and chided lightly, "Where did you ever get your lousy theology? Regardless of how hard you work, you'll never be able to erase your past mistakes. Just confess them to God and those you've offended; then go on with your life. Jesus has already paid the price for your sins, so you don't have to keep beating yourself with them."

Tears filled Dawn's eyes. "Teresa, you're such a wonderful person. You always know just the right thing to say. You're such an encouragement to me. I don't know what I'd do without you."

"Probably rely on the good Lord a lot more," Teresa chuckled as she gave Dawn a hug.

Pastor Olson fell a few steps behind the two women but stayed close enough to hear their conversation. *The ministry of encouragement is the most neglected ministry in all Christendom, and yet Rocky Bluff is blessed with both Teresa Lennon and Edith Dutton as encouragers. I wonder if they've studied Barnabas's relationship with the Apostle Paul?*

Chapter 6

New Year's Eve was a quiet, uneventful evening but exciting nonetheless for the Harkness family as they gathered in the living room of Bob and Nancy's home. Nancy and Dawn had finished converting the den into a bedroom for Edith. Jean had moved a few of her mother's favorite things from the house Edith had shared with Roy Dutton for nearly ten years, back to the original Harkness family home.

An expression of contentment spread across Edith's face as she relaxed in her wheelchair at the end of the sofa. She watched her two youngest grandchildren lying on the floor, playing with the hand-held computer games they had received for Christmas. Her eyes next drifted to her older grandchildren seated on the sofa. Jay sat tall and handsome, lovingly holding his pregnant wife's hand.

"There couldn't be a better way to usher in the new year than surrounded by my family," Edith sighed. "Not a single one is missing, and the hope for the coming year is extremely bright."

Everyone nodded in agreement except Dawn, who was lost in her own thoughts. *How can Grandma be so optimistic a week after she nearly died? I wish I had her confidence that next year will be better than the last one. I'd like to go back to college, but I'm afraid I'll make a mess of things again. I know I don't have the strength to stand up to the temptations there and to keep my mind on my work.*

Edith's heart twinged as she noted the pained expression on her granddaughter's face. She tried to avoid drawing attention to Dawn's inner turmoil and focused instead on her granddaughter-in-law. "Angie, will your mother be able to come to Rocky Bluff when the baby arrives?"

"I'm due the end of May," Angie replied. "She's already purchased her round-trip ticket from Guam and will be here from the middle of May until after the Fourth of July."

"This is her first grandchild, and she can hardly contain herself," Jay laughed. "I wouldn't be surprised if she moves to Montana after she retires from teaching."

"I couldn't think of a better place to retire," Edith replied with a twinkle in her eyes. "There's a lot to do here, and watching grandchildren grow up is worth a major move."

"Take it from the world's greatest doting grandmother," Jean teased. "When I had my first baby, if you'd listened to Mother, you'd have thought Amy was the first baby born in the great Northwest."

Nancy shook her head. "I doubt that," she laughed. "Long before Amy, she let Bob and me think that Jay was the first and greatest child ever born."

Just then the phone rang, and Bob hurried to answer it. "Hello. Yes, Dawn is here. One moment, and I'll get her."

Hearing her name, Dawn hurried to the phone. "Hello?"

"Dawn, I haven't talked to you since early last fall." Dawn recognized the voice of her friend, Tara Wolf. "How have things been going?"

"Fine," Dawn murmured. "I've been keeping busy."

"I'm home from college, and I wanted to see you and catch up on the latest. We're having a big party at Linda Wright's, and all the old gang will be there. Can you come and join us?"

Dawn hesitated. She thought back to the laughs and good times she used to have with her old friends. She remembered the midnight swimming, the skiing races, and the rodeo parties. *Sure, I'd love to,* almost slipped from her lips, but the cell in the Chief Joseph County Jail flashed before her. "I won't be able to come tonight. My entire family is here now, and I'd hate to leave them on New Year's Eve."

Dawn shuddered as Tara snickered. "That never stopped you before. I've never known you to turn down a party. This isn't a big deal. We're just going to get together, have a few beers, have some fun. Why don't you want to come? What gives?"

"Oh, nothing," Dawn retorted. "Grandma just got out of the hospital today. She's moving in with us."

"You mean you'd choose being with your grandmother over being with us?" Tara taunted.

Blood rushed to Dawn's face, and her voice trembled. "Yes, I would."

"If that's the way you want it, I'll see you around." Tara hung up the phone.

Dawn stared blankly out the kitchen window as she returned the phone to its cradle.

"Is something wrong, Dear?" Edith called from the living room. She watched the stunned expression on her granddaughter's face.

Dawn shook her head and redirected her attention back to her family. "No, I'm fine." She rejoined her brother and sister-in-law on the couch. "That was Tara Wolf. Some of my old friends are having a party at Linda Wright's house tonight, and they wanted me to join them. I turned them down. I'd rather spend New Year's Eve with my family."

Jay beamed and patted his sister on the shoulder. "Atta girl. I'm really proud of you for turning down a party invitation from that crowd. Even when I was in high school, they lived a pretty risky lifestyle. Their parties always seemed to be one step ahead of the law."

"So I found out," Dawn replied, "except it was me who got caught by the law, and not them."

Jay hugged his sister. "You're the lucky one. You're well on the way to normalcy, while they're still wasting the best years of their lives partying."

Dawn sighed and laid her head on her brother's shoulder. "I wish I was as strong as everyone thought. I'd like to return to college for the spring semester, but I don't think I'd make it. I almost said yes to Tara tonight, even surrounded by those who love me. Without your presence, I'm sure I would have gone to that party and probably ended back in rehab."

"You'll make it, Sis. Just hang in there," Jay assured her.

The rest of the evening the family watched videos and ate popcorn. Even though she was weary, Edith was determined to stay awake until after midnight. Ever since her December 31st wedding to Roy Dutton, every New Year's Eve held a sweet specialness for her. The beginning of a new year was like the beginning of a new life. Even though her body was becoming weaker and weaker with each passing year, her spirit was constantly being restored and refurbished. She was able to sit back and watch the ministry of encouragement, which she had tried to demonstrate for so many years, being practiced by her family and friends. She only wished she was still in the center of the activities in Rocky Bluff.

❖

Teresa slept late New Year's Day. Crisis counseling was emotionally draining for her, and her body ached with fatigue. Whenever a holiday gave an excuse for a lot of partying and drinking, the incidents of spousal abuse skyrocketed. She had been busy most of the night, and two new women and their children were now staying at the shelter.

She stumbled into the kitchen and made herself a cup of instant coffee. As she dropped a couple slices of toast into the toaster, the telephone rang.

Who can that be? I thought all of the New Year's Eve crises would be over, she thought as she hurried to the phone.

"Happy New Year, Teresa. This is Bryan Olson."

"What are you doing up and about so early New Year's morning?" Teresa chided.

"I've been at the hospital most of the night," Bryan replied solemnly. "There was a group of young people who were partying last night, and it got totally out of hand. The mixture of bad drugs and alcohol caused the death of one girl, and another is in critical condition. A third is in satisfactory condition."

Teresa's face blanched as her knuckles whitened around the phone. "Who are they? Nobody local, I hope."

"I'm afraid so," Bryan sighed. "A young woman named Tara Wolf died, Linda Wright is in critical condition, and Marsha Harris is recovering and could be discharged later today. The pastors of the parents of Tara and Linda are with their families, but Marsha's parents live in Wyoming. I tried to help her the best I could and contacted her parents for her. They're on their way from Sheridan now."

"How awful," Teresa gasped. "Is there anything I can do?"

"That's why I called. I think Marsha needs a woman's hand to hold until her mother gets here. She's extremely distraught."

"I just woke up. Give me at least forty-five minutes." Teresa glanced in the hall mirror and frowned at her disheveled hair and the bags under her eyes.

"I'll be by to pick you up in about an hour," Bryan replied. "I was sure I could count on you to help me out. There are times when a woman's touch can accomplish more than all my years of seminary training."

❧

Marsha Harris lay sobbing on her hospital bed when Teresa tiptoed into the room. She rolled over when she heard the door open and forced a faint smile. "Hello," she murmured.

"Hi." Teresa approached the bed. "My name is Teresa Lennon. Pastor Olson said you might like some female company until your mother gets here."

"It would beat staring at the ceiling," Marsha sighed as she took a tissue from the box and wiped her eyes. "I feel so alone and scared. Last night was a nightmare."

"What happened?" Teresa pulled up a chair next to the bed.

"It all started as an innocent party, but by midnight things had gotten out of hand. At first we were just enjoying a few drinks; then some guys from Billings turned up with drugs that weren't supposed to have any lasting effects. Now look at us. Tara's dead. . .Linda's in critical condition. . .and my father has told me that if I were ever involved in drugs again he'd completely disown me."

"If you level with your father and go through drug rehabilitation, don't you think he'll forgive you?"

"He's pretty hardheaded," Marsha said, "but underneath he's got a tender heart. It all depends on which side of him prevails."

Teresa took the young woman's hand. "Most fathers are like that. I'm sure he'll come around."

"I know," Marsha sighed. "I only wish I had the strength that Dawn Harkness had. Do you know her?"

A small grin spread across Teresa's face. "I've been a friend of the entire family for years."

"She's lucky," Marsha replied. "She chose to stay home with her family on New Year's Eve instead of going to the party. Tara begged her to come, but Dawn insisted that her family was more important. I wish I had a flawless family like that."

Teresa shook her head and gave a dry smile. "Dawn's family is definitely not problem-free. In fact, at times I wonder how they have withstood all the tragedies they have had, but their faith in God is equal to any hardships they've had to face."

Marsha's eyes began to brighten, but she hesitated for several moments. "I heard rumors that Dawn went through the drug rehab in Billings. Is that true?" she asked shyly.

Teresa paused, not wanting to betray any confidences that Dawn had shared with her. However, she knew how burdened Dawn had become about her friends still using drugs. "She completed treatment right before Christmas. I'm sure she'd be willing to talk with you about it. She's becoming a real crusader for a drug-free society."

"Maybe I'll talk to her later," Marsha replied. "Right now all I want to do is go back to Sheridan and forget I've ever been in Rocky Bluff. Maybe in a few days I'll feel like giving Dawn a call and talk about going to rehab myself. If it did that much for her, maybe it would help me too."

"Rehab is an excellent recovery method," Teresa said as she watched the interest increase in Marsha's eyes. "However, Dawn had something else going for her to give her strength."

"What was that?"

"Dawn turned to God, and she found that He was always there to help." Teresa paused, fearing she might be minimizing the inner struggles Dawn had experienced. "It hasn't always been easy for her, but through this long ordeal Dawn discovered God's forgiveness and love even when she felt alone and rejected. It was extremely liberating for her to find God not only on the mountaintops but in the valleys as well."

Tears began to stream down Marsha's cheeks. "You know, I used to go to Sunday school when I was a kid," she confessed, "but when I got in high school, church seemed so silly and only good for little old ladies who were getting ready to die. I didn't think it would have anything to offer me. Now look at me. I have absolutely nothing, plus one dead friend and another who may not live. I don't have anything."

Teresa handed Marsha another tissue and waited for her to dry her eyes. "That's just where God wants all of us," Teresa explained. "He wants us to quit relying on our own strength and turn to Christ for our strength."

The two were still in deep conversation an hour later when Pastor Olson appeared in the doorway with a smile on his face. "Marsha, how are you feeling?"

"Better, thank you."

"Well, I have some good news for you."

"What's that? I need something good to happen," Marsha murmured.

"They just took Linda out of the intensive care unit and upgraded her condition to stable. She's going to be all right."

Marsha heaved a sigh of relief. "That's wonderful."

❀

At two o'clock that afternoon, Marsha's parents arrived at the Rocky Bluff Community Hospital and signed the necessary release papers. Pastor Olson said good-bye to the family with a prayer and received an assurance from them that they would call if there was anything he could do to help.

After the Harrises disappeared across the parking lot, Bryan turned to Teresa, "I haven't eaten since breakfast. How about joining me for lunch at the Hamburger Shack?"

"Sounds good, but I don't want to stay too long," Teresa replied. "I want to touch base with Dawn and let her know what happened before the gossip gets around town. At one time she was extremely close to the kids at that party."

"Why don't we call Dawn and see if she can join us?" Bryan suggested. "I'm sure we can find a quiet corner this time of day."

"Give me a minute, and I'll call her from the pay phone in the lobby." Teresa reached in her purse for a quarter.

Bryan sunk into an overstuffed chair in the lobby while Teresa made her call. He admired her soft brown hair that she had pulled back with a bow to match her blouse. *Teresa always looks so nice, and she knows how to handle the most sensitive issues. It's going to be interesting to see how she breaks the bad news to Dawn. If it were not for Dawn's family and Teresa's encouragement, I doubt if Dawn would have had the strength to say no to the party. She could be lying in the hospital herself.*

❀

Forty minutes later the threesome huddled in a back booth of the Hamburger Shack with hot chocolate and hamburgers in front of them. Dawn looked from Bryan to Teresa and back again. A wrinkle spread across her forehead as she saw their strained faces. "Judging by your expressions, you didn't invite me to lunch to discuss the weather. What's going on?"

Bryan and Teresa exchanged glances. "Dawn, did you hear what happened at Linda Wright's party last night?"

Dawn's face blanched as she shook her head. "No," she replied. "How'd you know there was a party?"

"We just left the hospital after having been there several hours," Bryan explained sadly. "Tara Wolf, Linda Wright, and Marsha Harris suffered drug overdoses. Marsha was just released. It was touch and go with Linda, but they finally upgraded her condition and removed her from intensive care by noon."

Bryan hesitated as Dawn's eyes widened. "What about Tara?" she begged. "Is she going to be okay?"

Teresa reached out and took her young friend's hand. "I'm sorry. They weren't able to save her. She died early this morning."

"She can't be dead!" Dawn slammed her fist onto the table. "They were only going to do a little drinking. She told me so when she called and invited me to the party."

"Marsha says a couple of young men came from Billings with some bad drugs," Teresa replied. "They told those from Rocky Bluff that the drugs would not have any lasting side effects."

Dawn's face reddened as she again slammed her fist onto the table. "I hate them. They killed my best friend. I hope they rot in jail." Her voice was shaking uncontrollably.

Teresa rubbed Dawn's shoulder. "You have every right to be angry. Giving drugs to others is one of the cruelest forms of inhumanity, but you can't let yourself become consumed with hatred. It will only destroy you and will never work for any good."

For the next ten minutes, Dawn sobbed while Teresa and Bryan sat in understanding silence. Gradually the sobs became further and further apart until they finally ceased. "I almost went to that party. I could easily have been the one lying in the morgue instead of Tara. I'll never go to another wild party as long as I live. A few minutes' high isn't worth dying."

Bryan and Teresa waited for Dawn to sort out her emotions. Finally, a resolute gleam appeared in the young woman's eyes. "God must have spared me for a reason. I'll do whatever I can to convince others not to use drugs."

Chapter 7

Dawn Harkness surveyed the eager faces that filled the auditorium of the Rocky Bluff Middle School. Eight years before, she had been sitting in one of the same seats, listening to returning graduates tell about their college experiences. However, Dawn's message was not about selecting a major, attending college classes, or cramming for finals. Instead, she was talking about the temptations of alcohol and drugs.

"Last week I buried one of my closest friends," Dawn said, and a hush spread over the room. "A group of my friends were partying, thinking only of having fun, without considering the consequences of their behavior. I know, because until a few months ago I would have been partying with them. Oh, we had all heard of people overdosing on drugs, but we never thought it would happen to us." Dawn paused as she noticed a large boy with peach fuzz on his face wiggling uncomfortably in his seat. "Would any of you like to guess why I am standing before you now instead of being in the cemetery with my friend?"

The silence that had settled over the room grew more intense. The students leaned forward in their seats. Finally the boy with the peach fuzz murmured, "You must have been lucky."

"Yes, I was very lucky," Dawn agreed. "A few months ago I got caught using drugs and went to jail. So I wasn't at the party where my friend lost her life."

"That doesn't sound very lucky to me," the boy snickered.

"As strange as it may seem, the night I got busted was the luckiest night in my life. It scared me straight. It forced me to accept the fact that I had a problem and had lost control of my life. Only then was I willing to go through rehabilitation."

With that honest confession, Dawn was able to share the physical and emotional effects that drugs had had on her body. She shared the loneliness of going through the rehabilitation program. She told of the love and support her family and the people of Rocky Bluff had shown her during this difficult period. After her talk, Dawn passed out cards and asked the class to join her and sign their names to a pledge promising to refrain from all forms of substance abuse.

Every pair of eyes was glued to the floor. No one moved. *I've failed,* Dawn moaned silently. *I've poured out my heart to them for nothing. I'll never speak to another group of students again. Teresa said that sharing what happened to me and encouraging others not to go down the same path would strengthen me in my commitment, but it's not true. I'll never do this again as long as I live.*

"Why is everyone just sitting here?" the boy with the peach fuzz exclaimed. "I don't want to end up in jail, rehab, or the cemetery. I'm going to join Dawn and promise to remain drug-free." He hurriedly scribbled his name on the bottom of a pledge card, walked to the front of the room, and handed it to Dawn. One by one, all the others followed his lead.

Tears gathered in Dawn's eyes. *Teresa was right, after all,* she thought. *If I can keep just one other young person from using drugs, the humiliation of retelling my story will make it all worthwhile.*

❖

Teresa Lennon gazed out her office window. The trees were beginning to bud. The winter had been long and hard, with an overabundance of tragedies and heartaches, but the new leaves brought the hope of springtime.

Teresa leisurely flipped through the day's mail. *Just imagine the number of trees that had to die to produce all this junk,* she sighed. The one letter in the pile that caught her eye had the return address of the Drug and Alcohol Abuse Center in Great Falls. She hurriedly tore it open.

> *You are invited to a one-week seminar on identifying and assisting drug abuse victims, sponsored by the United States Department of Health, Education, and Welfare. Please complete the enclosed registration form and return it before March thirtieth.*

Teresa finished reading the enclosed brochure. She recognized the main speaker as a nationally renowned authority in the field. *After all my experiences with Dawn these last six months, I sure could use more training.* She immediately filled out the registration form, wrote a check for the registration fee, and placed them in an envelope.

Just as Teresa licked the envelope, the telephone rang. "Hello, Spouse Abuse Shelter. This is Teresa. May I help you?"

"Hello, Teresa. This is Bryan. I haven't heard from you in several days. I was wondering how things were going."

"Life has been pretty quiet around here lately," Teresa replied as she leaned back in her chair. "I think the death of Tara Wolf had a sobering effect on the entire community."

"It definitely had a sobering effect on me," Bryan admitted. "Ministering to so many people who were directly or indirectly connected to the drug party was mind-boggling to me. I feel that I'm not trained to minister to that kind of social problem. I worked with drug addicts in Boise, but I always felt so inadequate."

"You're being too humble," Teresa encouraged. "I heard many positive comments about how much help you were to them."

Bryan shook his head. "People were very supportive, but in my heart of hearts, I knew that I should have been able to do more."

Teresa shuffled through the papers on her desk. "I just received something in the mail that might be of interest to you. There's a week-long seminar in Great Falls coming up in April on identifying and helping victims of drug abuse. It's put on by the United States Department of Health, Education, and Welfare. They're bringing in some pretty high-powered speakers. I just sealed the envelope with my registration fee."

"Sounds interesting. Mind if I go along?"

"Please do," Teresa replied. "Since Rocky Bluff is no longer immune to drug abuse, the more of us who receive this training the better equipped we'll be to cope with the problems."

After a long pause on the other end of the line, Bryan finally responded. "Do you know if anyone else from Rocky Bluff is going?"

"I don't know of anyone," Teresa replied. "Like I said, it just came in today's mail. Why do you ask?"

"One thing I've learned in my early years of ministry is to avoid even the appearance of impropriety. If it got around that you and I went out of town for a week together, I'm sure it would set tongues to wagging."

Teresa smiled ruefully. "I'm afraid you're right. That's the downside of living in a small town. . .the local gossip mill. As a pastor you're more susceptible to it than the rest of us."

"I am well aware of that," Bryan sighed. "I know several God-fearing ministers whose reputations were tarnished because of idle gossip and misunderstandings."

Teresa thought a moment. "Maybe I could call the guidance counselor at the high school and see if she's interested in going."

"Just don't ask her to go along as a chaperon," Bryan snickered. "I don't want to feel like a sixteen-year-old boy again."

"I'll be discreet," Teresa chided back. "I'll also make a copy of the brochure and the registration form and get back to you later today or tomorrow."

As the two bade each other good-bye, Teresa felt a warm flush spread across her face. *Bryan seems much more interested in me than in his other parishioners.* That moment of ecstasy was soon followed by concern. *I wonder if Bryan would be as interested in me if he knew my background? I so enjoy our times together, but I'm afraid I'll become too attached and will be hurt again if he ever finds out about my past.*

She shook her head sharply as if to erase all bad memories and walked to the kitchen to refill her coffee mug. Too many people with more serious problems were depending on her; she didn't have time to spend considering her own emotional needs. Returning to her desk, she took out the phone book and looked up the number of the Rocky Bluff High School. Moments later the call was transferred to the counseling office.

"Hello. This is Valerie Snyder."

Teresa explained about the seminar, and Valerie was enthusiastic about going along with Teresa and Bryan. "I just have to have my principal approve my leave time and expenses. He's generally pretty agreeable about additional training."

Valerie cleared her throat. "Not to change the subject, but I just spoke with one of the middle school teachers. She said Dawn Harkness spoke to the students earlier this afternoon about how drugs nearly destroyed her life. She was a smashing success, and everyone in the auditorium signed a pledge promising to live a drug-free lifestyle. Dawn has a tremendous message."

Teresa smiled. "Dawn has come a long way. If it hadn't been for her family, I don't know if she could have come through this difficult time of her life."

The conversation drifted to lighter topics, then they said good-bye. Teresa had just hung up the phone when it rang again. "Hello. Spouse Abuse Shelter," she replied mechanically.

"Hi. It's me again," Bryan Olson chuckled. "I was just thinking that a nice juicy steak would sound pretty good for dinner tonight. Would you like to join me at the Steak House?"

Without hesitation Teresa replied, "I'd love to. I'll bring the copy of the seminar brochure with me, and we'll talk about it there."

"Great. I'll pick you up at seven," Bryan agreed.

Something in his voice as he said good-bye made Teresa feel nervous and giddy. Afraid to acknowledge her feelings, she left her desk and began cleaning the already immaculate kitchen. She tried to mentally plan the next meeting with the volunteers, but her mind kept drifting back to the handsome pastor who seemed to be slipping into every facet of her life.

❂

That evening after finishing a filet mignon, Bryan and Teresa leisurely sipped their coffee as they enjoyed their dessert. They discussed the upcoming seminar, and Bryan agreed to drive his car to Great Falls. They discussed current events at the national level and locally. Everything was light and superficial.

Then Bryan became serious. He studied Teresa's deep green eyes. "Teresa, I've known you for five months now, and underneath your deep compassion for others, I sense a hidden story that needs to be shared. How did you happen to get into working with spouse abuse cases?"

A distant gaze settled on Teresa's soft face. The moment she had feared was upon her. Would her background cool their friendship? Teresa took a deep breath. "I once had to take advantage of the services of the spouse abuse shelter in Missoula."

"I'm sorry to hear that." She could see nothing in his face except sympathy. He leaned toward her. "You seem to have turned tragedy into triumph. Would you care to tell me what happened?"

Again Teresa took a deep breath. "I've never talked much about it. Mine is such a strange story. Are you sure you want to hear it?"

"Only if you care to share it." Bryan reached across the table and took her hand.

Teresa flushed as she nervously twisted the corner of her napkin. "My husband was a respected marriage counselor who lived a double life. At home he was totally different than he was in public. Although he was outwardly a Christian, it was all a sham. He was subject to—" She bit her lip, looked quickly at Bryan, then away. "Fits of rage," she finished. "Soon after we were married, he began to verbally abuse me. He soon escalated to physical violence, though he was careful to leave bruises only where they could not be seen."

Her voice was very low now. "When I could no longer take the physical and emotional abuse, I called a spouse abuse shelter. They were extremely helpful and encouraged me to move to the shelter for a few days to get through a crisis. I'll always be grateful for what they did for me."

A furrow deepened on Bryan's forehead. "So what did your husband do when he discovered you were gone?"

Tears filled Teresa's eyes. "I had thought he would be upset and would try to get me back. I thought he would be willing at last to get counseling. But he merely moved in with the woman he had been seeing on the sly. It wasn't until after I had left that I learned the extent of his adulterous relationships."

Bryan squeezed Teresa's hand. "That must have hurt. Rejection like that. . ." He shook his head, and she saw her own pain reflected in his face. Then he grew very still, and though he still held her hand, his grip loosened. He looked down at the table. "Are you still married to him?" he asked hesitantly.

Teresa sighed. "I was raised to believe that divorce was unthinkable, and yet I was faced with a reality I couldn't escape. I knew the Bible said adultery was grounds for divorce, but I had trouble accepting it."

Bryan let go of Teresa's hand and leaned back. He carefully folded his napkin. "I share your feelings about divorce. How were you able to decide what to do?"

Teresa shook her head. "I didn't have to decide anything. I had no say whatsoever in what happened next. He divorced me and married the 'other woman' six months later. They moved to the East, and I picked up the pieces of my life. I felt that in God's eyes I was still married, and so of course I shut myself off from relationships with other men. I felt as though I had reached a dead end in my life. I couldn't see where I was supposed to go next."

Teresa sighed. "Somehow, even though I was the victim, I carried a cloud of guilt around with me for many years. Just admitting that I was a divorcée was more than I could bear. I took very seriously the Scripture that said divorced women should not remarry, and I refused to develop even a friendship with any man."

Bryan looked up at her. "You didn't have any trouble developing a friendship with me." He looked at her questioningly. She could still see the kindness in his gaze, but the warmth was more distant, as though he had put up a wall between himself and her.

Teresa picked up her coffee cup and looked down into it. "My circumstances are different now," she said softly. "You see, I'm a widow now, not a divorcée. Not that that made any difference to me for a long time. I'd been hurt so badly that I just wasn't interested in being close to a man in any way." She looked up at him and smiled shyly. "But you were different. You kind of slipped in through the back door. Circumstances kept throwing us together, and I couldn't resist your friendship."

Bryan let out a long sigh. "Your husband died?"

"That's the tragedy of it all," Teresa replied. "Five years after he left me, he found out he had cancer. His new wife refused to nurse him. I suspect he had abused her also. She moved back to Montana, and he died alone, a broken man. However, before he died, he made peace with God. He wrote me a letter telling me about his illness and his conversion, and he begged me for my forgiveness." She smiled faintly. "It was a very strange experience. In a way, he had died for me years before when I accepted he no longer loved me. And yet I had remained faithful to him, had stayed married to him in my own mind and heart. So I grieved when he died. . .and yet I couldn't share my sorrow with anyone, because no one here knows about my past. I was sorry I never got to see him again. I never even got to tell him that I forgave him gladly. By the time I received the letter, he was already dead."

"At least you have the assurance that he did make his peace with God before he died," Bryan reminded her.

"That's true," Teresa said.

Bryan looked at her face. "Why didn't you remarry then?" he asked gently. "After all, when your husband died, in God's eyes you were free to marry again. I know you'd been hurt, but after all those years God must have brought healing to your heart. Otherwise you wouldn't have been able to minister so effectively to others who were hurting. Someone as caring. . ." He smiled, and added, "and attractive as yourself. I'm surprised no man entered your life in all these years."

Teresa hesitated. "You're right. After my husband died, I did feel free to remarry. But by then I was so busy with my career. I had been single long enough that dating just wasn't part of my lifestyle. I was just too immersed in the lives of those who came through the doors of the shelter. All the people of Rocky Bluff have become my family." She met his eyes. "I never felt the need for anyone else." *Until now*, something whispered inside her.

"Rocky Bluff may be your family," Bryan said, his voice soft, "but if you've never shared your past, then you've kept part of yourself separate and alone. I feel honored that you have shared that part of your life with me."

Teresa leaned forward and smiled at her pastor. "It is rather liberating to be able to talk honestly with someone without feeling that underneath I'm hiding something."

She set down her coffee cup and sighed. "My husband's counseling office was in our church, so when I lost my husband, I also lost the church where I was a member. I couldn't go back there. No one knew the true story, and many blamed me for the breakup of our marriage. It caused an extremely intense spiritual struggle for me. I knew it wasn't God's fault, but I couldn't understand why things had happened the way they did. I had tried so hard to save my marriage, but I hadn't felt God wanted me to stay and be beaten any longer. I still hoped our marriage would be healed, even when I was at the shelter. You see, when I went to the shelter, I never thought I was walking away from my marriage. I just knew I needed help."

She sighed again. "I had loved being active in the church. I always loved working with the children and the women's Bible study groups. But suddenly it was over, and I was out in the cold. I vowed I would never get actively involved in a church again but would remain by myself in the back pew."

She smiled. "Gradually, Edith Dutton was able to get me involved again. Other than you, she's the only one in Rocky Bluff who knows I was once the wife of a church marriage counselor."

"Your secret is safe with me," Bryan assured her. "But I'll bet you were a tremendous counselor's wife. I'm surprised that anyone would have rejected you." He looked into her eyes. "It wasn't your fault, Teresa. You did all you could. Someday maybe you'll not feel ashamed to talk more freely about your past."

Chapter 8

Teresa, Bryan, and Valerie Snyder relaxed over late-night desserts in a diner down the street from their hotel. The conference on drug addiction and intervention had been exhausting; yet no one was ready to retire. They needed time to process the day's load of information.

"That was a provocative session tonight," Valerie noted as she laid her fork on her empty plate. "It was an eye-opener for me that drug abusers have trouble talking about their problem. Most of the kids I work with are pretty open about their situations. They want to talk, and they're just looking for someone to listen. But the people we learned about today—" She broke off and shook her head. "I can't imagine living a life with a hidden secret."

Teresa shifted nervously in the booth. "Sometimes people are afraid of being rejected," she said as her gaze drifted across the restaurant's dark windows. "Life can get so complicated. . . . It's hard for people to understand another person's problems unless they have experienced them themselves. That's why there are support groups for every known problem imaginable."

"From that aspect, I can understand a certain degree of privacy," Valerie agreed. "If a person felt that others were judgmental, he'd be bound to pull into his own shell. It must be dreadfully lonesome to carry a private secret, afraid to share your pain with anyone."

Teresa and Bryan exchanged glances. "It is," Teresa said solemnly. "I can speak from experience."

Valerie studied her friend's face. "Not you?" she gasped, unable to mask her surprise. "You're one of the most all-together people in Rocky Bluff. I can't imagine the Rock of Gibraltar having some hidden past."

"There's a lot about me that people don't know. I've spent years trying to mask my pain," Teresa replied. "I was hoping I was doing a good job."

"Believe me, you did an excellent job of hiding your feelings," Valerie said, "but has it been worth it?"

"At times I wonder." Teresa's eyes moved blankly from the windows to the salt shaker on the center of the table. "It wasn't until I met Bryan that I realized how foolish I'd been. He helped me understand that people accept me for who I am, not for what has happened to me."

Bryan took Teresa's hand and looked into her face. "Teresa, that's the first time I've heard you admit that masking your feelings was not the best way to live."

"You've been a big help," Teresa sighed. "I didn't know how relaxing life could be until you moved to Rocky Bluff and became my pastor." She tightened her jaw to keep back the other words she longed to say.

Valerie smiled at her older friend. "Pastor Olson has been a comfort and guide to many of us in Rocky Bluff. I'm sure nothing in your past would have been a shock to him."

Teresa and Bryan again exchanged glances. "He wasn't shocked," Teresa agreed, "but he had to admit it was highly unusual for a marriage counselor to be traveling the country with his wife, giving marriage seminars while he was having extramarital affairs on the side."

Valerie gulped, trying hard not to react. "You mean you were the wife? That must have torn you to the quick. How did you ever adjust?"

"I don't think I ever did," Teresa replied. "When I learned about Chris's behavior, I was devastated. I had already tried everything possible to try to keep him. I had let him subject me to all kinds of physical and emotional humiliation. I thought I had to live up to our public image." Teresa paused, and a tear glistened in the corner of her eye. "Nothing I tried worked, and he left me for another woman in spite of all my noble attempts."

"He must have been a real jerk," Valerie stated firmly. "How could you have stayed with him as long as you did?"

"Everything I'd been taught since I was a child emphasized the importance of saving a marriage at all costs, especially since we were presenting ourselves as a model couple. Divorce was something that happened to other people, never to me."

"None of us are immune to heartache," Valerie reminded her. "You are so compassionate to the failures of others. . . . Why couldn't you accept divorce for yourself?"

Teresa shrugged her shoulders. "I must have thought I could do superhuman feats on my own strength without relying on God's grace and support," she replied. "That's how foolish I had become."

Valerie turned her attention to the man beside her. "Pastor, isn't adultery considered grounds for divorce?"

Bryan nodded his head. "Yes, in fact it's the *only* biblical grounds for divorce. But human emotions run deep, and every situation is different. Some marriages are healed even after abuse and adultery. We have a God who is able to work miracles of healing when we commit ourselves to doing our part. But when one spouse hardens his heart and leaves, there's not much the other can do."

"I felt that although Chris had remarried I should remain single the rest of my life," Teresa told Valerie. "Just because he had broken his marriage vows didn't mean I couldn't remain faithful to mine. However, three years ago Chris died of cancer. I'm ashamed to say this, but in the midst of my grief I also felt liberated, no longer tied to a dead marriage." A faint smile curled the corners of her lips. "However, I think I've been single too long and am too set in my ways to start over now." She shrugged her shoulders and slumped deeper in the booth.

"After watching the changes in Edith Dutton and Rebecca Hatfield after they remarried in their later years, I'd say autumn love must be sweeter than first love," Valerie noted as she yawned and glanced at her watch. "I think I'd better call it a night and get some shut-eye."

The three paid their bills and walked slowly to Bryan's Jeep. The wind whipped around their heavy coats and tousled their uncovered hair. The late-night desserts had relaxed their bodies and emotions, but a faint uneasiness hung over Teresa. *Will an autumn love be possible for me?*

When they arrived at the hotel, Valerie said good night and turned down the long corridor toward her room. Bryan took Teresa's hand. "You look troubled. How about finding a corner of the coffee shop for a little true confession?"

Teresa blushed. "You mean my feelings are showing?"

"No, I'm just a good mind reader," Bryan chuckled as he led the way to a corner table.

After the waitress served two cups of hot tea, Bryan studied the lines on Teresa's soft face. "I was proud of you tonight. I know it was difficult for you to share the pain of your past."

"In this situation it seemed to come naturally," Teresa replied.

"I think Valerie's opinion of you grew tremendously when she realized the inner strength it took to go through what you did," Bryan replied.

Teresa shook her head. "I don't think I should be admired just because I've been through a lot of pain."

"You didn't let the pain embitter you," Bryan replied. "You drew upon it to develop true character. I just hope you haven't hardened yourself against ever marrying again."

Teresa gave a faint laugh. "I've never given it much thought. I've been too busy trying to help others in crisis situations."

"I think it's about time you think of Teresa Lennon once in awhile. Teresa deserves to love and be loved as much as those who come to the shelter do."

Teresa blushed, then hesitated, trying to choose her words carefully. "If I'm not being too personal, why did you never marry? Did you not want to love and be loved?"

"I asked for that," Bryan chuckled. "I was engaged once. . .back when I was in seminary."

"What happened? Did she leave you for someone else?"

A pained smile spread across Bryan's face. "I think I could have accepted that better," he sighed. "There are a lot of guys out there better looking and with greater personalities. The reason she left me was because she didn't think she'd be able to cope with the pressures of being a minister's wife."

"You mean you had to choose between her and your calling to serve God in the public ministry?"

Bryan nodded his head. "You put it very well," he replied. "I almost dropped out of my last semester of seminary. In fact, I was halfway across the campus toward the registrar's office with my withdrawal form when it hit me. . . . I had to put God first in my life."

"Do you know what happened to her?" Teresa asked.

"The last I heard, Sherry had married a computer engineer and has three children. Since she left me, I've been afraid to ask any woman to live her life under the ministry's close community scrutiny."

"In a little town everyone lives under close scrutiny," Teresa laughed. "Our former pastor's wife seemed to thrive on the opportunity to serve the community. She just laughed if someone hinted she didn't quite fit the stereotype of a proper minister's wife."

"That's one thing you definitely need in this business," Bryan replied with a twinkle in his eyes. "A good sense of humor."

Teresa took another sip of her tea and replaced the cup in its saucer. "How true that is," she replied, "but it's not much different from being the director of a spouse abuse shelter."

"Teresa, I've been encouraging you to take down your barriers for weeks. Now it's my turn to admit the softening of my own shell," Bryan said as he gazed into her eyes. "I do feel lonely and need someone to share my life. After I met you, I began to reveal parts of my life that I'd never shared with anyone. The feelings I have for you are different from what I've felt toward anyone else. It's entirely different from what I experienced with Sherry years ago."

Tears gathered in Teresa's eyes. "The attraction is mutual. Even during the good times of my relationship with Chris, I never shared as much as I have with you. It's like I'm entering into new and uncharted waters. I think I like it, but I'm afraid I'll be hurt again or make a fool of myself."

"Then let's go slowly," Bryan replied gently. "I love you, and I'm looking forward to charting unfamiliar waters with you. We both will need to do a lot of soul-searching to adjust to the smoldering coals within us. My guess is that those embers of attraction are going to ignite into a steady flame. . .something that may warm us for the rest of our lives."

Teresa blinked the tears from her eyes. She felt both frightened and elated at the same time, but she looked away from Bryan's intent gaze, afraid she'd say something she'd regret later. She did not want to either commit herself to more than she was ready for or push him away. "Perhaps," she replied at last, her voice light, "but in the meantime, I think I'd like to get some sleep. The morning session is going to be starting too early."

Bryan wrapped his arm around Teresa's waist as they walked down the corridor to their rooms. When they got to Teresa's door, she took her key from her purse and turned to say good night. Bryan took her firmly in his arms and pressed his lips against hers.

Teresa's pulse began to race. She had long since forgotten the ecstasy of being held and loved. "I love you," he whispered. He let go of her reluctantly. "If I'm not careful, those burning embers I told you about are going to burst into roaring flames." He smiled ruefully.

"The feeling is mutual," Teresa replied, her voice shaking. She turned the knob and slipped into her room.

Valerie was sleeping peacefully in the far bed. Teresa flopped across her own bed with her mind in a whirl. *Is this for real? Am I really falling in love? Is Bryan really falling in love with me? I feel more confused than a teenager.*

When the conference ended at the end of the week, every participant raved about the knowledge they had gained and planned how they would apply this new information to their particular situation. The effects of this conference were going to be felt all across the state, but most particularly in Rocky Bluff, for Bryan Olson and Teresa Lennon had learned something besides techniques for counseling drug abusers. They had learned something about each other, and they had each admitted the growing love between them.

❖

Her first morning home, Teresa leaned back in her kitchen chair and sighed. *I'm just too tired to tackle the mountain of work that has accumulated at the shelter. I'll give Edith a call and see if we can share a cup of coffee.*

Within minutes, Teresa and Edith were seated at the Harkness kitchen table. Nancy, Bob, and Dawn were at work so Edith had the entire house to herself. Her mind was as alert as ever, and she listened with a keen interest as Teresa told her the details of the conference and how they were going to use that information to help those in Rocky Bluff.

Teresa shifted in her seat. "Now, what's happened in Rocky Bluff while we were gone?"

Edith smiled and shook her head. "I guess the most exciting thing is that Bob has a new employee at the hardware store, and the town is really humming.

Gabriel Brown is an Afro-American from South Carolina. He's an expert at repairing farm machinery, but the community definitely didn't put a welcome mat out for him and his family."

"Why not? We have people moving in and out of town all the time."

"But this is the first black family to move to Rocky Bluff." Edith spoke with a new intensity. She shook her head. "I must say I'm both surprised and dismayed by the town's reaction. After all, ten percent of our population is Native American, and Angie Harkness is a Pacific Islander. But we've never had Afro-Americans before." Her lips pressed together. "I'm ashamed that anyone in Rocky Bluff cares what color a person's skin is."

Teresa shook her head. "As much as we'd like to think Montana is an island unto itself, I guess we're not immune from the social problems the rest of the world has to face."

"The part that concerns me the most is that Gabriel and Mandy Brown have an eleven-year-old son named Nathan. Most of the kids at school have accepted him, but several have begun taunting him with racial epithets."

Teresa wrinkled her brow. "Has the school done anything about it?"

"The principal called the entire student body to the gym and told them there would be severe repercussions if anyone is caught using racial slurs or discriminating against someone of another race," Edith explained.

"Do they think it did any good?" Teresa asked.

"It may have stopped it at school, but until you change people's attitudes, the problems will persist," Edith replied. "There's evidence that racial prejudice is not limited to kids on the playground."

"What else is going on?" Teresa queried, not believing that racial prejudice could be in their sleepy town.

Edith shook her head with disgust. "Last night racial threats were spray-painted on the Browns' garage. This is more than a children's prank and will be treated by the police as vandalism and a hate crime."

"Do they know who did it?"

"Police Chief Philip Mooney is working on it, but so far they don't have much to go on. However, the word is around town: Rocky Bluff will not tolerate racism nor permit vandalism. The new motto is: Not in our town."

"I have all kinds of confidence in our police and fire departments," Teresa replied. "After all they've dealt with in this town during the last years, I'm sure they can find and punish these vandals."

"Chances are it's a bunch of kids." Edith sighed wearily. "The school's keeping its ears open."

"Good. Valerie never misses anything that goes on in that school," Teresa replied. "After spending a week with her at the conference, I'm even more impressed with her than I ever was."

Teresa glanced at her watch and noted the slump in Edith's shoulders. Concern mounted each time she visited her older friend, for Edith seemed to be weaker than the time before. Teresa realized how heartbreaking it had been for her to give up her home and move in with her son and his family after all her years of independence. "Edith, before I go, would you like me to fix you a sandwich and a bowl of soup?"

Edith took a heavy breath. "I'd appreciate that," she sighed. "They're so busy at the store lately; I don't think any of them are planning to come home for lunch."

Teresa went to the refrigerator and surveyed its contents. "What would you like me to fix? There's some cheese here in front. Would you like a grilled cheese sandwich?"

Edith nodded her head. "Sounds good. I think there's probably a can of tomato soup in the bottom left-hand cupboard."

Teresa glanced back at her older friend. "Why don't you go lie down while I fix lunch? I'll let you know when it's ready."

"Thanks," Edith replied, her voice hardly above a whisper. Edith then walked cautiously to the living room, holding onto the wall and pieces of furniture as she went. She closed her eyes as soon as she stretched out on the sofa. Teresa had followed her into the living room, and she gently spread an afghan over her. Edith drifted off to sleep.

Twenty minutes later, Teresa had a light lunch arranged on TV trays for Edith and herself. An artificial flower arrangement graced the kitchen table so Teresa gently removed one blossom and placed it on Edith's tray. Going an extra step for such a saintly woman was the least she could do.

As she set a tray beside the sofa, Edith opened her eyes and looked around. "Oh. . .I must have dozed off," she said as she reached for her glasses on the end table. "The tray is beautiful."

Teresa said a short prayer of thanksgiving, and they ate their lunch in relaxed silence. They were used to not only sharing their words but also their quiet times, and they found peace in each other's presence. After they ate, Teresa did the dishes, while Edith stretched out again and was soon fast asleep.

I better get to the shelter and see what's going on, Teresa told herself. *I hope there weren't any crises while I was gone.*

But as soon as she opened the door to the shelter, Mary Evers, one of the volunteers, came bounding toward her. "Teresa, am I glad to see you," she gasped. "Can we go to your office and talk?"

"Sure," Teresa replied as she motioned for her to follow. "What's up?"

Mary dropped into a chair. "The night before last a man living up Hunter

Creek Road went berserk and held his family captive for three hours before the sheriff's deputies could talk him out. He's still in custody, but they brought his wife and the children here."

"I'm glad to hear they're here," Teresa replied. "That's what we're here for. How are they doing? They must be terribly traumatized."

Mary shook her head. "They are. The mother has stayed in her room, crying for twenty-four hours straight. I can scarcely get her to eat. Her name's Michelle Frank. I hope you'll be able to help her."

A deep furrow creased Teresa's forehead. "I'll go and talk with her and see what I can do. What about the children? How are they doing?"

"Richie is ten and Chuck is twelve," Mary said as she sunk deeper into her chair. "They're in school now, but they're absolute monsters when they're here. I don't know how we're going to deal with them. They don't have any relatives to turn to so I feel like we're on our own with a couple of uncontrollables."

"I'll talk with the counselor at the school," Teresa said. "I'm sure we'll be able to do something to help those poor children."

Mary shook her head in disbelief. "It won't be easy."

Chapter 9

Teresa collapsed onto her sofa. She mindlessly reached for the TV remote and flipped through the channels. Nothing caught her attention, and as the phone rang, she flicked the remote's off button.

"Hello," she wearily greeted.

"You sound tired." Bryan Olson's voice was deep with concern. "How are you doing?"

"I'm exhausted," Teresa replied. "The best part of my day was this morning when I visited Edith Dutton, but even that was a little depressing because she's continuing to fail. I wish I could do something for her. She's such a sweet and loving person."

"I agree," Bryan replied. "I don't think we could find a more perceptive and compassionate person in Rocky Bluff. . .unless her name is Teresa Lennon."

Teresa blushed. "I could never live up to her standards," she sighed. "In fact, I've spent the entire afternoon with a family problem that is way over my head."

"Would you like to talk about it?" Bryan asked. "As a pastor you can count on my confidentiality. . .and as a friend you need someone to lean on."

Teresa leaned her head against the back of the sofa. "It would be nice," she sighed, "but I'm sure you're just as tired as I am."

Bryan laughed. "Of course I'm tired, but it's time we put away our superficiality. Let's be tired together. We've got to quit playing super-helper and admit our need for each other's support. I'll be over in half an hour."

After she hung up, a new surge of energy raced through Teresa, and she hurried to the bathroom. She plugged in her curling iron and added fresh makeup while it heated. By the time Bryan arrived, Teresa was dressed in a crisp blue jumpsuit. She looked as fresh as she had at the beginning of her day.

After fifteen minutes of small talk, Bryan took Teresa's hand in his. "Enough chitchat. Now tell me what the real problem is."

A dam seemed to break inside Teresa, and she poured out the feelings of inadequacy she had experienced while dealing with the traumatized Frank family. As the words tumbled out her mouth, the intensity of her feelings surprised her. "I think I was able to communicate with Michelle," she explained, "but I feel completely helpless with the boys. After talking with Valerie about their behavior at school, I found out that things were even worse than I thought.

I don't know what we're going to do. Not only are they defiant at school, but they are completely insubordinate at the shelter. The volunteers are suspicious they are sneaking out after everyone is in bed, but they haven't been able to catch them yet. I can't expect my volunteers to stay up all night guarding the doors."

"Maybe we should talk to Chief Mooney about the situation. I'm sure his police officers don't miss a thing when they're out on night patrol."

"Bryan, why didn't I think of that myself?" Teresa smiled at him. "In the big cities the police are so overworked with murder and mayhem they'd never be able to help with trivial problems. At least in Rocky Bluff, the police have the time to practice preventive crime control."

They agreed on a time to go to the police station; then they changed the subject to a more relaxing topic—the anticipated arrival of Jay and Angie Harkness's baby. Since his bride was a beautiful Chamorro girl from Guam, everyone was anxious to view the most beautiful baby ever to have taken a breath in Rocky Bluff.

But after Bryan left that night, a melancholy mood settled over Teresa as she thought of the arrival of Jay and Angie's baby. Teresa had long ago accepted her life of singleness, but now the thought of having a baby of her own to love and nurture overwhelmed her. If only it were possible. . . . She knew her biological clock was ticking loudly, and to consider having a child after the age of forty was probably unreasonable. *I wonder if Bryan has ever missed having children?* she thought. *He would make an ideal father and role model.*

❄

The next morning at ten o'clock, Bryan and Teresa were seated in Police Chief Philip Mooney's office expressing their concern about the Frank family. Chief Mooney explained the legal status of the father who had been sent to a mental institution for psychological evaluation and treatment.

"I'm concerned about his wife and children," Teresa said. "Michelle is extremely emotional, and the boys seem to be getting themselves in all kinds of trouble. The volunteers are suspicious that the boys might be sneaking out at night. Would it be possible for your night patrol to keep a watch on the shelter for any unusual happenings?"

The police chief leaned back in his chair. "I wonder. . ." He scratched his head. "Those boys just might be the guilty parties we've been looking for. The night before last, the garage of the new African-American family was spray-painted with racial epithets. Last night, Rocky Bluff's Native American families were the spraypaint targets. Judging by the spelling, it has to be children. I wonder if they're taking their frustrations out on the rest of the world. We'll surely keep an eye out for any unusual activities around the shelter."

Bryan and Teresa thanked the police chief for his help, then walked hand in hand back to Bryan's Jeep. As he started the engine, Bryan turned to Teresa, "Would you like me to drop you at your home or at the shelter?"

Teresa hesitated. "That's a tough choice. I have desks piled high with work in both places. Maybe I better clear off my desk at home first."

Arriving at Teresa's home, Bryan walked her to the door. "Hang in there," he said as he took her in his arms. "I'll be praying for you. Don't try to carry the burden of the entire community on yourself. The Lord will see that everything works out for the best."

The warmth and assurance of Bryan's embrace calmed Teresa's nerves, and the tension lines on her face began to fade. "Thanks," she whispered. "Just knowing there's another human being who understands and supports me means so much. I truly understand now what the Bible means about us all being one church, functioning together as a single body." She smiled up at him, her eyes shy. "Thank you. Thank you for showing me that I can depend on someone. . .that it's not just me and the Lord all by ourselves."

Bryan's lips melted over Teresa's, while their souls seemed to entwine. The pressures of the present and the uncertainties of the future faded in that moment of union. They were each finally convinced that they would share the rest of their lives together.

❖

Teresa had just finished booting her computer when the doorbell rang. *Who could that be?* she sighed as she hurried toward the door. *I hope everything's okay at the shelter.*

Her face spread into a broad grin as she opened the door. "Dawn, come in. How are you doing?" Teresa gave the young woman a warm hug.

"I'm doing fine, but things aren't going as well for Angie," Dawn replied.

"Take off your coat and tell me what's going on. Is there a problem with the baby?"

"There could be." The pair seated themselves on opposite ends of the sofa. "She and Jay just got back from the doctor's, and there is a good chance she could go into premature labor. The doctor wants her to remain bedfast for the remaining six weeks of her pregnancy."

"That's going to be hard," Teresa said.

"I know," Dawn replied, "but Angie's determined to do whatever is necessary to give that baby the best chance it can possibly have. But Jay's really concerned about Angie being by herself while he's at work. He asked me to move in with them until the baby comes."

"That's a good solution. I hope everything works out for all of you."

"There's one big problem," Dawn explained with frustration. "Dad's new employee, Gabriel Brown, and his family are very uncomfortable with the racial tension that seems to be developing in Rocky Bluff. If there's one more incident of graffiti, they're planning to move back to South Carolina. If they leave now and I have to be with Angie all day, Dad will be short of help. He's already putting in too many long hours as it is. Do you think the police will find out who's doing all this graffiti and put a stop to it soon?"

Teresa took a deep breath and paused. She wanted to calm Dawn's fears, but she knew the police had no proof, only strong suspicions. "Pastor Olson and I talked with Chief Mooney this morning," she said carefully. "Hopefully they'll have a handle on this in a few days."

"I guess all we can do is take one day at a time." Dawn shook her head with frustration. "I'd hate to have the Browns leave town. I've really enjoyed getting to know them."

The two chatted for another half hour; then Dawn left to pack her clothes to move into Jay and Angie's spare bedroom. Teresa returned to her computer and stared blankly at the screen. *Why do all the crises in Rocky Bluff have to come at the same time? The community has barely calmed down from the dreadful drug party New Year's Eve, and now they're faced with this. It's curious. Whenever something happens in this town, the Harkness family is somehow involved. I guess if you live on the cutting edge like they do, you're going to be impacted by the sins and frailties of others.*

❖

Just as Teresa was leaving for the shelter the next morning, the telephone rang. She hurried back to answer it. "Hello?"

"Teresa, you've got to come right away," a frantic voice cried.

"Dawn, is that you?"

"Yes. Teresa, you've got to come and help me."

"What's wrong?"

"Someone has spray painted the words, 'Go back to your little grass shack,' on the side of Jay and Angie's garage. Angie's hysterical. I'm afraid if she doesn't calm down she'll lose the baby."

"I'll be right there," Teresa promised as she hung up the phone.

She paused, then dialed a familiar number. As soon as she heard Bryan's voice, she explained what had happened.

"Oh, no," Bryan said. "When is this ever going to end? I'll stop by and talk to Chief Mooney, then join you there. I'll be praying the entire way."

"Thanks," Teresa replied. "We all need it."

❖

For the next two hours, Teresa talked with Angie and Dawn. Little by little, Angie's sobbing stopped, and she grew calm. Teresa fixed everyone soothing cups of herbal tea, and the mood of the three turned to levity. However, during Dawn and Angie's string of silly jokes, Teresa became more and more restless. *Where's Bryan?* she wondered. *He said he would be right over. It's not like him to let me down. Fortunately, Angie was able to get ahold of herself before anything serious happened. I don't know what I'd have done if I couldn't calm her. I suppose I would have had to call an ambulance. Isn't that just like a man—make a promise, then not follow through? I suppose something must have come up.*

Just then the doorbell rang, and Dawn went to answer it. "Pastor Olson, Chief Mooney, do come in."

"How's Angie?" Pastor Olson asked as Dawn led them into the living room where the pregnant woman was lying on the sofa.

"I'm doing better," Angie replied. "I feel silly for having come apart the way I did. I think my hormones are all out of balance."

"You needn't apologize," Bryan said as he pulled up a footstool next to the sofa beside her. "Your reaction was perfectly understandable under the circumstances. We have some good news for you." He glanced at Teresa who was sitting in the chair at the end of the sofa. "We solved the mystery and apprehended our graffiti artists."

Teresa leaned forward in her seat. *How could I have possibly questioned Bryan's reliability?* she thought ruefully.

"Who was it?" Angie asked as she propped herself up with the pillows.

"Two brothers ages ten and twelve who are staying at the spouse abuse shelter. They will come by in a few days with a paintbrush and remove their damage." Pastor Olson's words were for Angie, but he kept his eyes on Teresa.

"So it *was* them." Teresa sighed. "How did you figure it out?"

Chief Mooney stepped forward. "While we were driving down the alley behind the shelter, Capt. Packwood spotted a pile of spray-paint cans. We went to the school and talked with the boys. They both had black paint all over their hands. They admitted what they had done pretty readily."

Teresa shook her head in disgust. "What happens to the boys now?" She looked from Bryan to the chief of police.

"We've had a long talk with the boys, their mother, and the school officials," Bryan replied. "I think we've come up with a temporary solution."

"What's going to happen to them?" Angie asked. "The kids must be scared to death."

"The mother is having a lot of emotional problems adjusting to what has happened, so she has agreed to admit herself to the psychiatric ward in the Great Falls hospital. Hopefully, she'll experience a good quick recovery and will be able to return home and care for her family," Pastor Olson explained. His eyes settled on Teresa's concerned face before continuing. "While she's in the hospital, I've agreed to have the boys stay in the parsonage with me. I'll supervise the boys while they repaint all the buildings in Rocky Bluff that they've vandalized. The school counselor will work extensively with the boys while they're at school."

Teresa smiled. "That's so generous of you. You'd make a great father figure."

Bryan shook his head and grinned at Teresa. "I'm headed into uncharted waters again. I'm going to need all kinds of support."

After everyone had finished discussing the ramifications of the latest calamity that had struck Rocky Bluff, Teresa, Pastor Olson, and Chief Mooney excused themselves, leaving Angie to get some rest. As soon as they were outside, Bryan turned to Teresa. "Since I came in the police car, would you mind giving me a ride home?"

"No problem at all," Teresa responded as they turned toward her car.

"I'm famished. How about stopping at the Uptown Restaurant for lunch?"

"Better yet," Teresa said as she started the engine, "would you like to come to my house for lunch? I have a home-cooked casserole in the freezer, and it would take only a few minutes to microwave it."

"I'll take home-cooked meals any time," Bryan laughed. "Besides, we have some personal planning to do. I've never been a father before, and these boys are going to need a substitute mother until their own mother is better."

Chapter 10

Bryan Olson perched himself on the stool at the counter while Teresa prepared lunch. The kitchen's homeyness melted any remaining hesitation he'd felt about surrendering his bachelorhood. *Why have I wasted all these years? I wish I'd met her years ago. My spiritual life did develop when I had no one to share my life with except my Lord, but I need a soul mate now to share my struggles and dreams.*

They sat down, and Bryan said the blessing. They ate in silence, but the quiet was companionable rather than awkward. At last, Bryan laid his fork on his plate and sighed. "Teresa, I don't know if I'm up to what I just committed myself to. I've never been a father before."

Teresa nodded. "Every new parent feels the same way. Everyone wants a child to come with an instruction manual."

Bryan sighed again. "I'm the one who preaches about walking by faith, but when I'm confronted with uncharted waters, I'm the first to panic."

Teresa chuckled as she recognized her own failings in Bryan's words. "I'm willing to panic with you. I haven't had much experience with preadolescent boys myself, but I'm willing to help all I can."

"Okay, then let's plan our strategy." Bryan squared his shoulders. "As soon as the boys move into the parsonage, I'll take them around to all the people they've offended, have them apologize, then set up a time when they can repaint the garages and sheds they defaced."

"Do you know how many buildings are involved?"

"At the last police count, there were fifteen, so they're going to be a couple of busy boys for several months."

"That's the best way to keep them out of trouble," Teresa replied, "but we'll also need to get them involved in long-term activities." She paused thoughtfully. "They've lived in the woods most of their years, and their socialization has been minimal. They rode the bus to school in the morning and went home directly after school, so they never had an opportunity to participate in any of the extracurricular activities the other kids did."

"The Boy Scouts are active here," Bryan suggested. "It might be good to encourage them to join. I think Scott Packwood is the troop leader." His enthusiasm mounted. "Speaking of socialization and moral training, every Wednesday

186

after school we have a group of children meet at the church. They call them-selves the King's Kids. Everyone I've talked to is impressed with the group."

"The King's Kids sounds like a good idea. Also, Little League season will be starting in six weeks," Teresa noted. "I know Jay Harkness coaches one of the teams. Maybe we can get the boys interested in that."

Bryan chuckled. "If all goes as planned, we'll have the boys so busy they won't have time to get into trouble."

"That's the main idea." Teresa laughed. "Every Saturday when the new TV schedule comes out we can sit down with them and plan the programs they'll view for the week. We can even help them decide which videos they want to rent that week. That ought to be a real treat since they didn't have access to a TV while they were living in their cabin in the woods."

Bryan gazed into Teresa's soft green eyes. "We sure make a good team, don't we?"

Teresa flushed. "Sure do. Neither one of us could do this alone." She hes-itated, realizing the magnitude of their undertaking. "When were you plan-ning to take charge of the boys?"

"This Saturday. I'm planning to drive their mother to the hospital in Great Falls. The doctors want to meet with the children at that time. Saturday would also be a good time to take them shopping. It ought to be fun furnish-ing their rooms. We can give them a fair amount of liberty when it comes to decor. Money and good taste would be their only limiting factors." He glanced up at her quickly. "Would you be able to come to Great Falls with us?"

Teresa's eyes brightened. "Sure. It'll be great fun buying the boys new clothes and helping them plan their bedrooms."

Bryan moved his chair closer to Teresa's and took her hand, pressing it to his lips. "While we are in Great Falls, we can also pick out a diamond ring for you."

"A what?" Teresa gulped.

"A diamond ring," Bryan replied calmly. "Teresa, I love you, and I want to share the rest of my years with you. I hope you feel the same about me."

Teresa laid her head against his shoulder. "I love you more than I ever thought possible. I can't imagine spending the rest of my life without you. I've been alone for so many years that I didn't realize how much I was missing until I met you."

"You're not afraid of being a pastor's wife, in spite of all the challenges that accompany it?" Bryan was tormented by the twenty-year-old memory of rejec-tion because of his vocation.

"I once thought a pastor's wife had one of the most difficult jobs anyone could have," Teresa confessed. "But now I've decided that if I could live in the public eye as wife of a prominent marriage counselor, I can easily face the challenges of being a pastor's wife in Rocky Bluff, Montana." She hesitated. Her background too came back to haunt her. "But what if someone questions you about marrying a divorced woman?"

Bryan's face reddened. "After I told them to mind their own business," Bryan paused, recognizing the level of his anger. He took a deep breath. "I would gently explain that your divorce was your ex-husband's idea, not yours, and that since then he has passed away. As a widow, you are free to remarry. I admit that people can be very cruel at times, but when Christians face objections with love and understanding, obstacles can be overcome."

"I've lived in Rocky Bluff a long time now, and I've learned one thing about its people," Teresa replied. "Occasionally they react to a situation without thinking, but in the end, this is probably one of the most supportive communities anyone could find."

Bryan took Teresa in his arms. Silence enveloped the pair as years of unacknowledged loneliness melted. "Then you will marry me?" he pleaded. His voice was hesitant, as though he could barely believe his good fortune.

"Yes," she whispered, tears filling her eyes.

"If we buy the ring Saturday, may I announce the good news to the congregation Sunday?"

"Are you ready to handle a congregation that may faint when they learn that two confirmed singles, who have never shown an interest in the dating game before, now plan to marry?" Teresa chuckled.

Bryan leaned back his head and laughed. "I'll have to deal with that when it happens. I suppose there will be a lot of shocked expressions. I think most people thought we were merely interested in the same public service projects and never noticed our lingering glances."

Teresa's smile widened. Never before had she known the love and assurance she felt when she was in Bryan's presence. "I'll be proud to proclaim our love to the entire world."

❁

The next few days flew by for Teresa. She helped Bryan rearrange the two back bedrooms in the parsonage. She registered Chuck and Richie in the Boy Scouts and checked into the Little League schedule. She helped their mother organize her business affairs for her absence during her hospital stay and spent hours listening to Michelle pour out the pain of years of abuse. Teresa's thoughts of her recent engagement were pushed to the background.

Six o'clock Saturday morning, Bryan picked up Teresa at her house, then drove to the shelter. Michelle had just finished preparing toast and scrambled eggs for the boys and herself. Bryan and Teresa loaded the dishwasher and tidied the kitchen, while Michelle and the boys ate their breakfast.

"Mom, are you sure you have to go away?" Chuck pleaded. "I don't want you to leave us."

"Honey, I don't want to leave you, either, but it has to be done," Michelle replied as she hugged her son. "We can't go on living like this. I have to get better. Pastor Olson will take good care of you, and he promised to bring you to Great Falls every two weeks to see me. Just keep thinking about what we can do when I'm better. I'll be able to get a job and find a home of our own."

"I know, Mom." The young boy choked back his sobs, "but I want to stay with you. I don't want you to be sad anymore."

Michelle's eyes again became distant. Silently, she turned and went to her room. Within minutes she returned, carrying a small suitcase, which she sat in front of the door. She sank onto the sofa and buried her face in her hands. A cloud of gloom hung over the entire family as the boys went to their room to get their coats.

The ride to Great Falls was tense. Michelle stared out the window without saying a word the entire trip. The pain of her depression was more than she could bear, but love for her sons motivated her to keep going and seek professional help. The boys occasionally snapped at each other, while Teresa and Bryan tried to carry on light conversation.

Meanwhile, Bryan was wondering if he would make a good stand-in father. Teresa wondered if she would make a good wife. Richie and Chuck worried about their mother, while Michelle felt frozen and numb. Could she ever escape the depth of her depression?

When they finally arrived at the Great Falls hospital, Teresa helped Michelle complete the admission forms; then Michelle turned to say goodbye to her sons. She took both of them into her arms at the same time and sobbed.

"Maybe the boys would like to come and see the room where you will be staying for the next few weeks," a nurse's aide suggested. "We encourage family togetherness as much as possible. We'd like the boys to see your room and meet the people who will be important to you. If fact, we have an activity room where you can be together and enjoy each other's company for a couple of hours. It will make the transition much easier. We can order lunch trays from the cafeteria for them."

Chuck looked up at Bryan with pleading eyes. "Pastor, can we stay for just a little while?"

Bryan nodded his approval. "Of course you may," he assured them. "Teresa and I have some shopping to do, but we'll be back around two o'clock. Afterward we want to take you to the mall so you can pick out bedspreads and curtains for your new room. We'll even hit the boys' clothing department before we leave."

"Really?" Richie exclaimed. "You'd let us buy brand-new things?"

Pastor Olson bent over and looked both boys directly in the eyes. "A lot of people in Rocky Bluff are very concerned about you. To show their love, they took up a collection to help you get started in your new life."

"Wow, thanks," they chimed in unison.

As Teresa and Bryan left the hospital, the crisp spring air stung their cheeks. "I know Michelle feels as if this is the lowest day of her life," Teresa began as they walked across the parking lot, "but I'm excited for her. I see this as the start of a whole new life for her. She has so much potential."

"How true." Bryan took her hand. "I hope that we'll be able to help the boys reach *their* potential. They both have a long way to go, and I've never been a father before. It's easy to give advice to others, but it's entirely different when you're faced with the same situations."

"I guess you'll have to follow your own advice and pray, expect God to answer those prayers, and live one day at a time," Teresa chided.

Bryan wrapped his arm around her slender waist. "The first thing I want to do as soon as Michelle is out of the hospital and the family is reunited is to make you my wife. It's not fair to expect you to move into the parsonage before then when you'd be acquiring not only a husband but a ready-made family."

Teresa smiled defiantly at him. "Why not? I've been helping care for them while they've been at the shelter."

"You're one of a kind," Bryan replied as he pulled her closer to himself. "If you're sure, let's plan a wedding for the first weekend in June. We'll plan the biggest gala affair Rocky Bluff has seen in years."

"How about asking Pastor Rhodes to come back and perform the ceremony?" Teresa asked. "He has meant so much to me through the years."

"I'll contact him as soon as we get home," he said as he opened the door of the Jeep for Teresa. "Now, off to the jewelry store."

❀

Early the next morning, Teresa rang the door to the parsonage. "I'm glad to see you," Bryan said as he opened the door. "On Sunday mornings I'm used to eating a quick bowl of cereal and hurrying to the church. Today I've got a couple of hungry boys to feed."

"That's why I came." Teresa took off her coat and headed for the kitchen. "I'll fix their breakfast, and we'll be there before church starts. I know I won't have any trouble getting them to wear their new clothes."

"Teresa, you don't know how much I appreciate this," Bryan said as he took her in his arms. He raised her left hand to admire the quarter-karat diamond on her left hand. "That is the most beautiful ring I have ever seen, and you are the most beautiful woman I've ever known. Today is our big day. We can shout our love from the mountaintop. After church today our engagement will become public knowledge."

Just then, Richie entered the kitchen rubbing the sleep from his eyes. "What's for breakfast?" he mumbled.

"How about pancakes?" Teresa replied as she reached for the griddle in the cupboard next to the stove.

Richie's eyes brightened. "I love pancakes."

"Good. Go wake Chuck while I'm getting them ready," Teresa replied. "While you're at it, lay out the clothes you want to wear to church. Then as soon as you finish eating, you can take a quick shower."

Bryan grabbed his suit coat and tie, gave Teresa a quick kiss, and hurried out the door. While she was fixing the pancakes, she could hear the boys' excited voices from their bedrooms. She heard the crackle of cellophane as they hurriedly unwrapped their new clothes and laid them neatly on their beds. For the first time in their lives, they were going to wear brand-new, store-bought clothes.

An hour later Teresa and the two boys slipped quietly into the back pew of the Rocky Bluff Community Church. The boys' eyes became like saucers as they surveyed the stained-glass windows of the simple church and the beautiful altar. They had been inside a church only once before, at their grandfather's funeral.

As the pews filled up, the two boys scanned the congregation, trying to find people they knew from school. Chuck pointed to Valerie Snyder. Richie pointed toward the fifth-grade teacher. They both recognized Bob Harkness who ran the hardware store. They shuddered when they spotted the chief of police, Philip Mooney.

Just as the organ began to play, Nathan Brown walked in with his parents and took the pew two rows in front of them. The boys exchanged puzzled glances. The Browns were the first Afro-American family they had ever seen. They had expected them to not be very bright, but Nathan was the smartest kid in the sixth grade. The Frank boys had felt threatened by all the attention he had gotten at school, and they had vented their feelings by spray painting racial slurs on the Browns' garage. They had heard their father make derogatory remarks about people from other races, but now, to the boys' amazement, the people sitting around them greeted the Browns with genuine warmth. The Browns, the boys realized, were well respected by everyone but themselves.

During the service Chuck and Richie tried to do everything everyone else did. They studied the bulletin, but it made little sense to them. They decided to copy everything Nathan did. When Nathan stood, so did they; they bowed their heads when he did; and Teresa helped them find the hymns and the Scripture readings. They exchanged glances and grinned, glad to be part of the large, happy congregation.

After the sermon and the closing hymn, instead of walking to the back to greet the people, Pastor Olson motioned for the congregation to be seated. Everyone exchanged puzzled looks.

"Friends, I have two announcements to make concerning my personal life. First of all," he began slowly, trying to choose exactly the right words, "I am now the stand-in father for Chuck and Richie Frank while their mother is away receiving treatment. I hope you all will welcome them with open arms into our church family." The boys blushed as everyone gave them a round of applause.

Pastor Olson took a deep breath as his eyes settled on the mature, beautiful woman sitting beside the boys. "An even bigger change in my life will come about the first weekend in June." Every eye widened, and people leaned forward with interest. "Teresa Lennon has agreed to become my wife. . .and Pastor Rhodes has agreed to return to Rocky Bluff to perform the ceremony. You are all invited to the wedding."

A gasp spread through the sanctuary, followed by an even louder round of applause. Tears filled Teresa's eyes as people crowded around her with congratulations, wishing her God's continued blessings. Pastor Olson walked to the back of the church to greet a cheerful congregation that was filled with love and good wishes. The uncharted waters he was entering did not feel near as lonely now; after all, he realized, he and Teresa had their church's love and prayers to support them.

Chapter 11

Dawn Harkness hurried up the sidewalk toward the Rocky Bluff Spouse Abuse Shelter. Today, instead of seeking support, she was bursting with excitement. She rang the doorbell and waited impatiently.

"Guess what?" she said as soon as Teresa opened the door. She stepped through the doorway, and without giving Teresa time to respond, she continued, "I've been accepted into summer school at Montana State University in Bozeman."

A broad smile spread across Teresa's face. Dawn's emotional roller-coaster rides had leveled out, and she was now ready to face life with dignity and purpose. Teresa patted the edge of the sofa. "Sit down and tell me all about it."

"Montana State has accepted my poor grades from Montana A&M and admitted me on academic probation," Dawn stated excitedly. "I'm sure if I stay away from the parties and work hard I can get my grade point up in a semester or two."

"I have all the confidence in the world that you can do it," Teresa replied. "You've come a long way this past year."

"Thanks to you," Dawn answered, unable to mask her love and respect for the woman beside her. "I'm really excited about going to summer school when the schedule is more relaxed. The timing is perfect. Jay and Angie will have had their baby by then, and Angie's mother will be here from Guam to help them. It will also be easier for Dad to hire help in the summer instead of later in the year. In fact, he already has someone in mind whom he'd like to give a chance at the job."

Teresa raised her eyebrows, her interest peaked. "And who's that?"

"Michelle Frank," Dawn replied. "I understand she's progressing better than expected in her treatment, and rumor has it she should be home by the time the boys are out of school for the summer."

Teresa smiled and nodded. "The rumors are true," she replied. "Her love for her sons has really motivated her to get well. I'm thrilled your dad is considering offering her a job when she comes home. That will speed recovery. She felt uncomfortable about having to live on welfare."

The pair then discussed the impact Bryan Olson had had on Michelle's sons. As soon as Bryan's name was mentioned, Dawn noticed the way Teresa glowed. Dawn smiled. "And how are the wedding plans coming?"

"All the details of the ceremony are falling into place," Teresa replied. "I've already ordered my dress, the flowers, and the invitations, and I've made arrangements with a photographer. I'm going to have Chuck and Richie serve as junior groomsmen. My sister is coming from Boise to be my matron of honor. She says she can't imagine me getting married and has to see it with her own eyes."

Dawn shook her head. "I don't understand why people are surprised when people get married later in life. It's a normal occurrence in Rocky Bluff. Grandma seems to have blazed the trail and demonstrated to the community that mature love is often the most satisfying and fulfilling love there is."

"It's certainly a lot different for me," Teresa agreed, then immediately changed the subject. "Dawn, I'm sorry I haven't had a chance to call you, but I was wondering if you would be willing to sit at the guest-book table at our wedding. You have such a sweet, welcoming charm about you. You're good at putting people at ease."

Dawn's eyes widened. "You actually want me to be a part of your wedding, after I've been such a pile of trouble for you?"

"Of course I do," Teresa persisted. Her tone became stern and loving at the same time. "And you have not been a pile of trouble. You've been one strong, brave woman to face your mistakes the way you did and turn your life around. I'm extremely proud of your accomplishments, and I'm sure your family is as well."

Dawn giggled. "Especially Grandma. She took me on as a personal prayer project and loved me through times when I was unlovable. I'm going to really miss her when I go to Bozeman."

After Dawn left the shelter, Teresa returned to her work with renewed vigor. There were so many discouraging moments in her line of work that she cherished the success stories.

She was hoping the Frank family would also become a success story. The boys had already painted over the epithets on many of the town garages. After school today, they were scheduled to repaint Angie and Jay's garage. Under Bryan's careful guidance they had learned to accept responsibility for their actions. Best of all, Nathan Brown was fast becoming one of their closest friends.

The boys had joined the Scouts just in time to be a part of a weekend campout and survival-skills training. Now they could talk about nothing else. The day of the campout was fast approaching.

❖

"Boys, are you ready to go?" Bryan Olson shouted as he loaded their sleeping bags into the back of the Jeep.

"We'll be right there," Chuck shouted back. The boys grabbed their duffel bags and raced toward the car.

"I've never been on a campout before," Richie exclaimed as he slid into the backseat and threw his duffel bag behind the seat.

Bryan started the engine. "This is more than a Boy Scouts' campout. It's a weekend of wilderness survival. Every person growing up in Montana needs survival skills, and Scott Packwood is an expert in that area."

"I know survival skills are important," twelve-year-old Chuck replied with confidence. "I heard some kids at school talking about their father who got lost in the mountains while he was hunting and had to spend the night alone in a shelter he built himself."

Bryan turned the corner and headed toward the parking lot where the Scout troop was gathering. "I hope you boys learn a lot this weekend and have fun too."

"Oh, we will," Richie chimed in. "Nathan is going to be there, and he promised to share a tent with us."

When Bryan parked the car, the boys bounded out and raced toward the group of boys, their leaders, and several fathers. "I'm here," Richie shouted. "When are we going to leave?"

"We're all loaded," Scott Packwood said. "We were waiting for you to get here. Would you boys like to ride in my rig with Nathan?"

"Yeah!" they shouted. Grabbing their sleeping bags and duffel bags, they raced toward Scott Packwood's crew-cab pickup.

Bryan waited as the caravan of vehicles left the parking lot. *This will be a weekend the boys will remember for a long time.* He got back in his Jeep and sighed. This would also be a weekend he could devote entirely to Teresa and his congregation.

❖

The caravan carrying Troop 95 wound up the narrow road to a clearing midway up the mountain. The boys laughed and cheered with each jolt of the vehicle. About fifty miles out of town, the troop reached a wide place in the road where they parked their vehicles. Each of the boys gathered their gear and began hiking up a narrow mountain path. They sang marching songs as they went along.

Although Chuck and Richie had spent most of their growing-up years in the woods, this trip was entirely different from what they had experienced in their cabin. Their father had not let them explore the surrounding terrain. Never before had they followed a path to see where it led or followed a creek around a bend.

When the troop arrived in a clearing, each group of boys began to select a site where they could pitch their tent. Nathan, Chuck, and Richie chose the site farthest to the north. Nearby there was a path that disappeared between the trees toward the summit of the mountain. The boys hurriedly pitched their tent, arranged their things, and gathered with the others in the center of the clearing.

Scoutmaster Packwood was just beginning to give his directions to the group. "Boys, it's getting late and will be dark soon, so we're going to fix basic hot dogs over an open flame for dinner tonight. I know you're all getting hungry after that long hike. Let's hurry and gather wood for our fire, and I'll show you ways to start a fire without matches."

The boys scattered and began picking up twigs. Some took out their pocketknives and cut off small branches. The three tent mates looked at each other. "Everyone else is getting wood nearby," Chuck exclaimed. "Let's get our wood farther down the path near our tent."

"We really don't need to go that far," Nathan protested.

"Sure we do," Chuck retorted. "We might find some wood that burns better than the picked-over stuff the others are getting."

Chuck pushed a branch aside as the three entered the narrow path. The ground was soft and mushy, and a few piles of snow remained in sheltered areas. The fresh breeze of springtime invited them on.

"Most of the wood out here will be too green to burn," Nathan noted as he pulled a lower limb toward him.

"Yeah, this stuff is wet," Richie replied, trying to sound knowledgeable.

Chuck was already several yards ahead of them. "Hey, there's a creek up here. I bet we can find some dry wood upstream."

The boys skipped from stone to stone in the middle of the creek bed. "I'm sure glad Pastor Olson bought us these new sneakers," Chuck exclaimed, "otherwise I'd be sliding into the water."

Nathan looked up through the heavy overhang of pine tree branches. "It's starting to get dark. Don't you think we'd better get our wood and head back?"

The two brothers looked up and shrugged their shoulders. "It's still light," Richie replied. "It's just getting a little cloudy."

Chuck was well ahead of the others and had just turned another bend in the creek. "Nathan, Richie, come see. . . . Here's a beaver dam."

Nathan and Richie hurried around the bend to where Chuck was standing beside a pile of dry sticks in the middle of the creek. Suddenly, Richie lurched sideways, as his foot slipped on a rock. The evening quiet was broken by a large splash followed by a screech of pain.

"Richie, are you okay?" Nathan exclaimed as he knelt over his friend.

Richie remained motionless. He moaned, while his brother raced toward him. "Come on, Richie. Get up. You're going to get soaked lying there," Chuck cried.

Richie moaned again. "I can't. My leg hurts."

"Here, we'll help." Nathan and Chuck each took hold of the injured boy and dragged him out of the stream to a grassy knoll.

"I'll go back and get help," Nathan said as Richie's moaning turned to sobs.

"But it's starting to get dark," Chuck protested. "Did you bring a flashlight?"

"Mine's in my duffel bag back at the campsite," Nathan gasped.

"So's mine," Chuck said as he glanced down at his younger brother. "Look, he's shaking. He's all wet and getting cold. I'm scared. What are we going to do?"

"I guess we're going to have to stay here until it's light again," Nathan replied as he surveyed the sky. "See, there's only a little sliver of a moon tonight. And it's so cloudy there probably won't be any stars."

"My friend's dad who got lost while he was hunting built an overnight shelter for himself," Chuck said as he surveyed the nearby terrain.

Nathan looked around, then pointed to a cluster of trees. "See those two trees with the bush between them? They look like they could make a little cave. Maybe we could get dead branches to build a roof."

Chuck nodded in agreement. "We better work fast while we still have a little light. Let's drag Richie over there, out of the wind."

The two boys pulled Richie under the bush, while he sobbed with pain. They made a pillow for his head from a pile of dry leaves. Then Nathan and Chuck scurried deeper into the woods and grabbed up armloads of sticks.

They raced back to their makeshift shelter and placed the sticks on the bush, making a three-foot-wide overhang. They worked until the sky was completely dark, and they could no longer see their way through the trees.

Nathan and Chuck snuggled into the shelter beside Richie. The hoots of night owls echoed through the trees, mingling with distant coyotes' howls. Richie's moans became softer.

"I hope Richie will be all right," Chuck said between chattering teeth. "I'm scared."

"So am I," Nathan replied as he snuggled even closer to the brothers.

"I want my mommy," Richie sobbed. "Why did she have to go away?"

"Mom's in the hospital, and they're making her better," Chuck replied with tears in his eyes. "We had a lot of fun with her last week when Pastor Olson and Teresa took us to see her. I've never seen her so happy. She's going to be home soon."

Richie continued to sob. "But I want my mommy, *now!*"

Chuck began to cry along with his brother. All the pent-up anguish of years of physical and emotional abuse poured out. Richie's physical pain was intensified by his fear and emotional pain. The brothers held each other and sobbed. After awhile their sobs turned to hiccups, and they began to talk quietly about the fear they had of their father, their loneliness, and their feelings of being misunderstood. They talked about their remorse for spray painting racial graffiti, about their love for their mother, about the day she would be out of the hospital and they could be a family again.

Outside their makeshift shelter, snow began to fall, and the temperature dropped. The ground froze. The boys' footprints in the soggy path and along the creek bed were now hidden under the snow.

Nathan snuggled close and listened to the brothers talk. He thought about his own family. . .his mother and father in Rocky Bluff. . .his grandparents, aunts, uncles, and cousins in South Carolina. *What would they do if they were here?* he pondered, trying to calm his panic. He tried to picture each of them sitting in the shelter with them; then he knew what they would have done. They would have prayed.

"Dear God," Nathan whispered, "I never paid much attention during the times Mama made me go to Sunday school and church, and I'm not sure how to pray, but please help us. Help somebody find us."

Chuck choked back a sob and turned to his friend. "Do you actually believe in God? Do you think He'll answer our prayers?"

"Yeah, I guess so," Nathan replied. "Whenever anything happens in our family, everyone prays, and things seem to work out. I guess there's nothing else we can do so we might as well pray."

"But I don't know how to pray," Chuck admitted cautiously. "Until we moved into the parsonage, I never heard anyone pray before. Praying is Pastor Olson's job. He uses all kinds of big fancy words. I don't know how to talk like that."

"Mama just talks to God like she talks to the rest of the family. She begins by saying, 'Dear Heavenly Father,' and she closes by saying, 'In Jesus' name. Amen.' "

Chuck took a deep breath to regain his composure. "That sounds easy enough. Let's give it a try."

Nathan looked at the brothers. Richie's eyes were closed, and he was breathing heavily, still moaning. "Okay," he said. "I guess we're supposed to bow our heads and fold our hands."

Richie appeared to have slipped into a painful sleep, but the two other boys bowed their heads and closed their eyes. Nathan took a deep breath. "Dear Heavenly Father, I don't know how to pray, but please help us. Richie is hurt real bad, and we don't know how to get him out of here. Help them find us. Don't let anything bad happen to Richie. Don't let us freeze to death. In Jesus' name. Amen."

Chuck opened his eyes, leaned closer to his brother, trying to see his face, then turned back to Nathan. "My friend told me that when his dad was lost in the woods he had to force himself to stay awake. He said that if he went to sleep he would have never woken up again."

"Yeah, I heard that happens when a person gets too cold and goes to sleep," Nathan replied. "Maybe we'd better try to keep Richie awake. There's no way anyone can find us until daylight." He took a deep breath. "Guess it's going to be a pretty long night."

Chapter 12

Scott Packwood surveyed the scout troop crowded around the fire, each boy holding a stick with a hot dog roasting on the end. Darkness was beginning to settle over the mountain, and Scott had the uneasy feeling that something was wrong. He counted bodies. He counted again. His heart pounded as he realized three boys were missing. He began to mentally run down the list of boys. *Where were the Frank boys and Nathan Brown?*

"Hey, guys. Listen up," Scoutmaster Packwood shouted. "Has anyone seen Chuck, Richie, and Nathan?"

The boys exchanged puzzled glances. Everyone shook their head.

"I haven't seen them since they pitched their tent next to ours," a freckle-faced boy replied as he pulled his hot dog away from the flame.

"Which one is their tent?" Scott asked.

"The dark blue one at the far end," the boy replied.

The scoutmaster and Ed Running Tail, one of the fathers, took their flashlights to the distant tent. Scott shone his flashlight inside. "It looks like all their stuff is here," he said grimly, "so if they've wandered away, they don't have any survival gear with them."

Ed flashed his beam on the surrounding ground. As an avid deer hunter he had become an expert at spotting minor disturbances of ground cover. He walked toward the path heading into the trees. He paused. "Scott, come here."

Scott hurried to Ed's side. "Look at this," Ed exclaimed. "We have foot-prints and broken lower branches leading into the woods this direction. Those boys must have gone exploring as soon as they got here."

Scott sucked in a breath, while adrenaline surged through his body. "Let's have the other chaperons get the boys singing around the campfire. You and I will go look for them."

He hurried back to the campfire, explained the situation to the other leaders, and asked them to take responsibility for the troop while he and Ed Running Tail searched for the missing boys. He then followed Ed down the narrow path.

Ed kept the beam of his flashlight focused on the ground in front of him as they walked. When they came to the creek, they leaped across and resumed searching the ground for footprints. After walking scarcely five feet more, Ed stopped.

"I've lost the footprints," Ed sighed. "There just no way we can pick up their trail in the dark."

Scott sighed and shook his head. "Let's go back to camp. I brought a cellular phone so we can call for help."

Arriving at the campsite, Scott raced toward his tent. He took out his duffel bag, rummaged through its contents, and found his cellular phone. He hurriedly pressed the numbers 9-1-1. The scoutmaster explained the details to the police dispatcher. As he broke the connection with the Rocky Bluff Police Department, a sense of helplessness overwhelmed him. All he could do was wait for daylight.

He let the boys sing songs and tell ghost stories far into the night. When their eyes became heavy at last, he urged the boys to retire to their tents. While one by one the whispering in the tents subsided, the adults gathered around the fire and waited.

"I'm really scared about those kids," Scott said as he paced back and forth in front of the flames. "Nathan Brown just moved here from South Carolina. . . . He wouldn't have any survival skills. Although the Frank brothers spent most of their lives in a cabin in the woods, they were never allowed very far from their father's eyes. I was shocked at how ignorant they were about the basics of outdoor life."

As the men planned their strategy for an early morning search party, a light snow began to fall. Little by little the flakes became larger and closer together. The ground was soon glistening with a half inch of snow.

"We're going to have a hard time finding them with their tracks covered by the snow," Ed Running Tail noted, "and with the snow their chances of suffering hypothermia increases."

Scott continued pacing around the fire. "I'll call my wife and have her make arrangements for someone to come and get the other boys first thing in the morning. We'll keep the food here to help feed the search parties. Outside of that, there's nothing we can do until morning. Except pray." The flames reflected off Scott's neon orange hunting jacket as he squatted beside the fire and bowed his head. "Let's take a few minutes of silence and each pray for the boys' safety."

❧

As soon as the Rocky Bluff police dispatcher received Scott Packwood's emergency call, the town of Rocky Bluff sprang into action. The volunteer search and rescue team members began to assemble. The hospital was notified, and an EMT crew along with an off-duty nurse responded. A local pilot volunteered to fly aerial reconnaissance. The K-9 Academy was notified, and three trained tracking dogs and their handlers were dispatched from Great Falls. The police department became the hub of activity.

Police Chief Philip Mooney called Bryan Olson. Pastor Olson was working late in his study when the phone rang, and the police chief quickly told him the bad news. "We're organizing search and rescue teams. The first will be heading out to the mountain in about an hour. Do you think the women of the church could prepare meals for them?"

Bryan took a deep breath, trying to calm the panic that raced through him. "I'll call the president of our women's group, Rebecca Hatfield. Although it's late, I'm sure she and her husband will do anything they can to help. Her husband is experienced at handling crises."

"The Browns have already been contacted, and they're on their way to the campsite. What should we do about notifying the Frank boys' mother?"

"It's too late to get in touch with her tonight," Bryan replied. "Hopefully, by morning we'll have some good news for her. I'd hate to worry her if we don't have to, especially about something she's helpless to do anything about. I'm afraid it could send her back into depression. She's been doing so well lately."

Bryan and Philip finished coordinating their plans and ended their conversation. Bryan hurriedly found the Hatfields' telephone number.

Although she was awakened from a sound sleep, Rebecca readily agreed to plan food and hot drinks for the search and rescue team. She knew that this night, like the night several years before when her neighbors' house had burned, she would have no sleep.

Bryan then dialed Teresa's number. "Hello," a sleepy voice greeted him.

"Hello, Teresa. It's me," he responded. "I hate to bother you so late at night, but the boys and Nathan Brown wandered away from their troop and are lost in the woods. A search and rescue operation is being organized. I'm going to be gathering some gear and heading for the mountain in a few minutes. Do you want to come along?"

"Of course I want to go!" Teresa bolted upright in bed. "I'll make a thermos of coffee and gather some extra blankets."

"Great," Bryan replied. "I called the Hatfields, and they're going to be preparing food and drinks for the search and rescue personnel. I think I've done as much as I can from here. I'll be over to get you in fifteen minutes."

Teresa ran a comb through her tousled hair and pulled on a pair of insulated underwear and sweats. This was definitely not a time to worry about fashion. She filled her coffee percolator and took her thermos from the top cupboard. While the coffee was perking, she went to the hall closet and took out three extra blankets and a sleeping bag. She took her parka, boots, and gloves and laid them on a chair by the door. By the time the coffee was done, the doorbell rang.

Bryan stuck his head in the door. "Teresa, are you about ready?" he shouted.

"Come on in," she called back. "I'm in the kitchen."

Bryan gave Teresa a quick kiss on the cheek as she finished pouring the coffee into the thermos. "I hope you dressed warmly. They say snow is predicted for above five thousand feet. The campsite is halfway up the mountain."

"I have my long johns on," she assured him. She stood on tiptoe to kiss the worried lines that creased his face. "They're in God's hands," she reminded him softly.

"I know." He took a deep breath and squared his shoulders. "I brought a change of clothes for the boys. I'm glad we got them insulated underwear and sweatshirts in Great Falls. I'm feeling sick about what they're wearing now. I'd assumed they would have dressed warmly, but judging by what I found in their rooms they dressed for the weather in Rocky Bluff, not in the mountains. Even their hiking boots were still in their rooms. I could kick myself for not checking them over before they left." He grimaced. "Some stand-in father I am."

Teresa screwed on the lid of the thermos, then took Bryan's hand. "You can't blame yourself. You're just not used to being a father. Besides, no one predicted the weather would change this abruptly."

"Maybe the weatherman didn't predict this, but common sense from living in Montana would," Bryan replied with disgust in his voice. "It's always a lot colder in the mountains. That's one of the survival skills I wanted them to learn this weekend."

I'm sure they've learned it now, but I hope they haven't suffered too much in the meantime, Teresa thought as she put on her coat and boots.

Soon, Teresa and Bryan were bouncing along on the narrow road up the mountain toward the campsite. Several sets of vehicle lights could be spotted on the usually desolate road. Five miles from the turn-off it began to snow. The higher they climbed, the heavier the snow fell. "It's times like this I'm glad I have a four-wheel drive," Bryan said absently, his mind on the missing boys.

As they neared the campsite, they saw a string of vehicles along the roadside. Bryan pulled the Jeep to a stop behind the last parked car, and Teresa reached for the thermos and a bag of Styrofoam cups from the backseat. Together they hiked the last quarter mile to where the others were gathered. An ambulance, two EMTs, and a nurse were already there, along with several volunteers waiting for daybreak.

❖

Through the long night the boys huddled together in their makeshift shelter. Nathan and Chuck had to keep shaking Richie to make sure he stayed awake.

Toward dawn it quit snowing, and the temperature began to drop. "I can't feel my toes," Chuck whispered to Nathan. "You don't think they'll drop off, do you?"

Nathan's eyes widened. "I don't think so, but I don't know. I've never been this cold in my life."

"I wish I'd worn my old hiking boots instead of the new sneakers that Teresa and Pastor Olson bought for me," Chuck moaned.

"Yeah, that was pretty dumb," Nathan replied.

"I don't think God heard us when we prayed. Maybe He's mad at us because of all the bad stuff Richie and I did." Chuck gulped back tears. "What if we freeze to death? Will they just dig a hole and put us in the ground, or will they use a casket?"

"Chuck, quit talking that way," Nathan scolded. "They're going to find us when it gets light. I know they will. My mama always tells me that God loves me even more than she does and that He'll always forgive me if I do something bad, so long as I'm sorry. You and Richie aren't the same as you used to be. God knows you're sorry for what you did." He lifted his chin and said firmly, "He's going to answer our prayer. Just you wait."

"But what if He doesn't? What if no one ever finds us, not until it's too late and we've all frozen to death?"

"As soon as it starts to get light, I'll walk back to camp myself," Nathan stated bravely.

"Do you know how to get back?"

Nathan bit his lip. "I can't remember for sure, and everything will look different when it's covered with snow," he admitted. "While we were running along the creek bank, we passed some other paths. I won't know which one leads back to camp."

"Maybe we'd better stay together." Chuck clung tighter to both his friend and his brother. "I'd be scared without you."

"Do you think anyone has missed us by now?" Nathan's voice wobbled. For all his brave words earlier, he too was scared. "Maybe they won't miss us until it's time to go back home. That won't be until tomorrow."

As a pink glow appeared in the east, Nathan crawled outside their shelter and looked around. Within minutes he was back. "It looks so different covered with snow." He ducked back into the shelter. "There's a clearing across the creek. I'm going to walk over there and write the letters H-E-L-P. Maybe an airplane will fly over and see it. They did that last week on a TV show I saw."

Chuck muffled a sob. "I'd help you, but I can't stand up. My feet hurt too much."

"Just stay here with Richie," Nathan replied. "I can do it myself." He slipped outside and trudged across the creek, then walked down the creek bank until he was at the far left of the clearing. He jumped onto the bank and dragged his feet through the snow until the four letters were formed. A sense of exhilaration filled him as he leaped back across the creek. At least he had done something, something that might help them be found.

"All we can do now is sit back and hope someone sees our signal." Nathan looked down at Richie. The injured boy had a distant, glazed look in his eyes.

"I'm thirsty," he whimpered.

"Should we give him some snow to eat?" Chuck asked.

Nathan shook his head. "I read in a book that people freeze to death faster if they eat snow. I'll go down to the creek and try to get some water. It'll be pretty cold, but at least it'll be warmer than snow. I'll only be able to bring back what I can carry in my bare hands, though."

Richie moved his head from side to side. "Please. . .water."

❖

About fifty men and women had gathered at the scouts' campsite by six o'clock that morning. The Hatfields were there with food, hot chocolate, and coffee. Dawn Harkness was there with three of her friends. Three tracking dogs were ready. The EMTs and the nurse had all the equipment necessary to treat hypothermia. The aircraft had been gassed and was ready to roll. The volunteers were divided into groups of four, each carrying a handheld radio.

When the searchers dispersed, Dawn Harkness turned to one of her friends. "If I were a kid and had just pitched my tent, I'd want to see where this path behind my tent led."

"That's where Ed Running Tail said he saw some footprints before it started to snow," one of her partners agreed, "but there's no guarantee it was their footprints and not someone else's. But without any other clues it's worth a try."

Dawn led her group down the path. Wet branches swatted them in the face as they went. When they got to the creek, Dawn stopped. "Okay, if you were a ten-year-old boy, which way would you go?" she asked the group.

"I've always been fascinated with rivers," one of her companions replied. "I'd have followed the creek."

"Upstream or downstream?" Dawn asked.

"Upstream," he replied. "The challenge is always to climb a mountain, not walk down a mountain."

The snow became deeper, and the pace of the search party slowed. The buzz of a single-engine plane echoed overhead. They watched as the plane seemed to be making smaller and smaller circles ahead of them.

Suddenly, the handheld radio in Dawn's hand squawked. "Attention all searchers. The pilot has spotted what looks like the letters H-E-L-P trampled in the snow in a clearing near the creek, northwest of the campsite. Whoever's in that area, would you please check it out?"

Dawn pushed the speak button. "This is Dawn Harkness. We're heading up the creek bank in that direction."

"Let us know as soon as you find them," a deep voice replied. "Don't try to bring them out yourself. Take careful note of their condition, and the nurse will help us decide what to do."

The foursome trudged on up the creek bank for another hundred yards. As they turned a bend in the creek, one of them shouted, "There's the clearing with the letters! They have to be close by."

"Chuck! . . . Richie! . . . Nathan! . . . Can you hear me?" Dawn shouted.

Nathan ran out of the shelter, and Chuck crawled as close to the opening as he could without standing. "We're here! We're here!" the boys shouted.

The foursome raced toward the makeshift shelter. Nathan clung to the first person who got to them. "You found us. You found us," he cried.

Dawn got down on her hands and knees and crawled into their shelter. She hugged Chuck who immediately burst into tears. "How are you boys doing?" she asked.

"Richie's hurt real bad," Chuck cried. "He can't walk, and he looks really funny. My feet used to hurt, but now I don't feel them at all. I can't walk on them. How are we going to get out of here?"

"There's all kinds of help at the campsite. I have a radio in my jacket. I'll let them know we've found you, and that you and Richie can't walk out."

Sounds of cheers echoed throughout the mountainside as word spread that the boys had been found alive. Bryan's eyes met Teresa's for a long moment. "Thank You, God," he whispered. Within minutes the nurse, EMTs, three stretchers, food, drinks, blankets, and scores of searchers descended on the boys' makeshift shelter.

As the nurse examined the boys, Pastor Olson led the others in a prayer of thanksgiving for caring for the boys through the long, cold night. He asked God that their injuries would heal quickly. Chuck listened, his eyes shining, and when Bryan said "amen," the boy pulled on his jacket sleeve.

"Pastor Olson," he cried, "Nathan and I prayed that somebody would find us. And God heard us. He really did." For the first time in their lives, he and his brother had experienced the power of prayer.

Chapter 13

The ambulance bearing the boys raced down the mountain. The nurse had placed a temporary splint on Richie's leg and had wrapped all three boys in several blankets.

Bryan Olson rode in the front seat of the ambulance and nervously looked over his shoulder as the nurse and EMT treated the boys. *This is all my fault. I should have checked to see what the boys were wearing before they left,* he chastised himself. *I should have warned them not to wander off by themselves. Their mother has enough to worry about just getting herself stabilized. She doesn't need this extra worry. And here I promised her that her boys would be well cared for.*

When the boys arrived at the hospital, the medical team immediately set to work. Nathan was evaluated, then released into the arms of his relieved parents. Chuck was admitted for hypothermia and frostbite. Richie was immediately whisked into X-ray.

Bryan paced back and forth, waiting for word on the boys' condition. Would Chuck lose any of his toes, or possibly both his feet, because of frostbite? How serious was Richie's injury? The questions haunted him, intruding on his prayer. *I know they're in Your hands, Lord. I just feel so guilty for not taking better care of them. Forgive me, Father. Please don't punish them for my mistakes.*

After reading the X-rays and consulting with other staff members, Dr. Brewer approached Pastor Olson. "Who is legally responsible for the boys at this time?"

Bryan shrugged his shoulders and sighed. "I'm responsible for them up to a point. I can approve all routine medical treatment. If there's anything serious, I think their mother needs to be contacted in the Great Falls hospital."

"It's serious," Dr. Brewer replied grimly. "I don't know yet if we'll be able to treat Chuck here in this hospital. It depends on how the circulation returns to his feet. If we have to amputate the little toe, I would be able to do it here. But if he requires more extensive surgery, I'd rather have it done in Great Falls." The doctor hesitated and took a deep breath. "Richie is a different matter."

A deep furrow creased the pastor's forehead. "How bad are his injuries?"

"They need specialized attention," the doctor replied. "Besides suffering from hypothermia and frostbite, he has a compound fracture, and the bone is nearly through the skin. It will take an orthopedic surgeon to set the leg properly. I'd suggest we medevac him to the Great Falls hospital right away."

"If we do that, they might as well take Chuck along and have him treated there as well," Bryan said. "I'll drive to Great Falls and stay with their mother. She's doing well and is scheduled to be released sometime next week."

Dr. Brewer stared out the window, lost in thought. "I'll call and talk to her doctor. I'll have him tell her the condition of her sons and that they will be arriving at the hospital within three hours. That way they'll be able to monitor her anxiety level until they arrive."

Pastor Olson extended his hand. "Thank you, Dr. Brewer. I appreciate all you're doing to help the boys."

As Dr. Brewer turned toward the doctors' lounge, Teresa entered the waiting room. She gave Bryan a hurried embrace. "How are they doing?"

"Richie is going to need surgery to set his leg. Dr. Brewer felt it would be better if it were done in Great Falls. They don't know yet if they'll have to amputate part of Chuck's feet or not, so both boys are going to be medevacked to Great Falls." He studied his fiancée's mud-splattered face. "As soon as I change clothes, I'm going to be leaving for Great Falls. Would you come with me?"

"I wouldn't let you leave me behind," she replied. "I'm sorry it took me so long to get here. After the ambulance left, there were all kinds of traffic problems on the mountain. A bunch of cars got stuck in the snow and mud. Everyone had to take turns pushing them out."

"Did you have any trouble driving the Jeep?"

"It was different," Teresa admitted. "I'd never driven a four-wheel drive before, but I made it."

Bryan wrapped his arm around her waist as they headed for the door. "Better get used to it. It will soon be half yours."

Although neither one had had much sleep that night, within an hour both Bryan and Teresa had showered, changed clothes, and were on their way to Great Falls. "I'm going to have to drive back late tonight so I can get a few hours of sleep before Sunday morning services." Bryan turned onto the main highway outside of Rocky Bluff. "Would you like to come back with me, or would you rather stay in a motel in Great Falls?"

"I'd like to stay there until everyone is released from the hospital. Michelle is going to need all the support she can get," Teresa replied as she leaned her head against the back of the seat. She let her eyes fall shut.

The rolling wheat fields flew by as Bryan prayed silently for Michelle and her sons. Now and then he glanced at Teresa and smiled, glad that she could get some sleep. She awakened just as they merged with the traffic on Tenth

Avenue South. "Are we here already?"

"Sure are."

"I feel a lot better after having slept. But I should have taken the wheel part of the way so you could sleep too." Teresa reached for Bryan's hand. "You must be exhausted."

"I'll be all right. I'm just anxious to get there."

When the pair arrived at the hospital, they went directly to Michelle's floor. The nurse at the station there told them that Richie was in surgery and Michelle was waiting with Chuck in his room on the third floor. Bryan and Teresa hurried back to the elevator, worried about Michelle's anxiety level. Having both sons in the hospital at the same time would be a hard load for any mother, but particularly hard for one who was only just recovering from a major depression. They were both prepared to deal with anything from hysterics to apathetic withdrawal, and outside Chuck's room they each took a deep breath and said a quick prayer for strength and wisdom.

When they had slipped into the room, though, their eyes widened with amazement. Michelle was sitting beside her sleeping son's bed, dressed in an attractive, teal-colored dress. Her hair was styled, and she was wearing make-up she had never worn before. Her face was grave but composed.

Teresa hurried to her side and embraced her. "I'm so sorry this happened," she said. "How are you doing?"

"I'm doing fine." Michelle smiled. "I'm scheduled to be released on Thursday."

Bryan stepped forward and shook Michelle's hand. "How are the boys doing?"

"Richie has been in surgery about an hour," she replied. "The doctors are very optimistic about his recovery. They said his biggest problem probably would be learning how to walk on crutches." Michelle looked over at her older son sleeping beside her. "They're keeping a close eye on Chuck. It appears that the circulation is returning to his feet except for the small toe on the left foot. I hope they don't have to amputate, but I feel he'll be lucky if that's the worst that happens."

Bryan looked seriously into the mother's hazel eyes. He sucked in a breath. "Michelle, I feel terrible about this. I should have noticed what kind of footwear the boys had on. I just assumed they would wear their old hiking boots instead of their new athletic shoes. I guess I wasn't cut out to be a stand-in father." He looked down at Chuck's sleeping face. "I'm so sorry. I wish there was something else I could say."

"There's no way you could have imagined this would happen," Michelle replied. "Before he went to sleep, Chuck was blaming himself for Richie's broken leg. He doesn't even mention his own pain. He claimed it was all his idea to go exploring when they were supposed to be gathering wood." She shook her head. "I'm the one who is to blame."

A puzzled look spread across Teresa's face. "How can you say that? You weren't even there."

"If I had been a better parent, I'd have stood up to their father long ago. If he would have let the boys have some breathing room, they wouldn't have been so tempted to follow the first unknown path they saw." Her voice trembled. "I'm their mother. My first job is to take care of them, to do what's best for them. I got my priorities all mixed up. . .and I failed them." Her eyes filled with tears.

An understanding smile spread across Bryan's face. "I think I understand for the first time a little of what it means to be a parent. What an enormous responsibility." He squared his shoulders, then reached a hand out to Michelle. "None of us is perfect, Michelle, not you, not me. We all make mistakes, even when we have the best intentions. But we have a loving Father Who forgives all our sins and shortcomings. And our children are in His hands. He's the only One Who can truly keep them safe."

He squeezed Michelle's hand. "A lot of prayers went up last night for the boys' safety. God answered those prayers and protected them." The pastor's smile broadened. "What amazes me is that without any survival skills training, they instinctively figured out how to build an ingenious shelter to protect themselves from the elements."

Michelle's eyes became distant. "I've always believed we have guardian angels looking after us," she said softly. Then she smiled. "It must take an entire legion of angels to take care of my two."

There was a rustle of movement outside the door, and a large man in surgical green stepped into the room. "Mrs. Frank?" the doctor queried. He looked back and forth between the two women.

Michelle stepped forward. "I'm Michelle Frank. How's my son?"

"Richie has a mighty nasty break and we had to insert a pin, but I think it will heal without any permanent damage. I'll send his records back to Dr. Brewer in Rocky Bluff so he can monitor its healing. Richie's a very lucky young man." The doctor smiled.

"Thank you, Doctor," Michelle said. "Everyone here has been so good to us. When can I see my son?"

"He's in the recovery room now. The orderlies will bring him up as soon as he comes out of the anesthesia. He should be able to go home Monday. In fact, if your other son continues to improve, he'll also be on his way home at the same time."

The doctor excused himself, and Michelle gazed at the empty bed in the room. "In a few minutes, I'll have both my sons under the same roof as me for the first time in six weeks," she said. "I've been praying for this day. But," she added dryly, "this wasn't quite how I had imagined it."

Bryan put his hand on her shoulder. "After Thursday you'll all be under the same roof in Rocky Bluff."

Just then Chuck stirred in his bed and opened his eyes. "Mom, Pastor, Teresa," he exclaimed. "You're all here. Where's Richie?"

"They just finished surgery on his leg, and he's going to be in this other bed in a few minutes," Michelle replied. "How are you feeling?"

Chuck grinned. "I can wiggle all my toes. See?" He pulled back the sheet and wiggled his toes to prove his point. Michelle couldn't see much movement through the bandages, but Chuck's declaration was enough to give her hope.

A few minutes later, Richie was wheeled into the room with his leg in a cast, suspended from a frame over the bed. Chuck raised his bed as his brother came into the room. "Hi. I bet I can finally run faster than you can."

Through sleepy eyes, Richie's face broke into a broad grin. He looked around at the smiling faces. "Hi, everyone. It's nice and warm in here." He closed his eyes and drifted into a peaceful sleep.

Teresa turned to Michelle. "I plan to stay here in Great Falls and help you until the boys are ready to go home, but I need to check into a motel for the night. Bryan has to get back to Rocky Bluff tonight so he can get ready for Sunday's services. I'll be back later."

Michelle turned to Pastor Olson. "I appreciate all you've done for me and the boys. I don't think I'll ever be able to repay you."

Pastor Olson gave the answer he gave to everyone who told him that they didn't know how to repay him. "Don't repay me. But when you're able, repay the debt to someone else who needs help."

"Thanks," Michelle murmured. "Don't worry. When I get back to Rocky Bluff, I'm going to be first on every volunteer list in town."

"Good," Pastor Olson said as he picked up his jacket to leave. "I'll be back Monday morning to get Teresa and the boys. Meanwhile, I'm going to be looking for a place for you and your family to stay. Bob Harkness said that you can start work as soon as you move back and are settled in Rocky Bluff. With planting season approaching, he says his business is beginning to pick up. He could use you as soon as possible."

❖

After the Sunday service, Pastor Olson told his congregation that the Frank boys and their mother would be released from the hospital this week. "There is a box in the back of the church if anyone would like to contribute to help them set up a household again. They will also be looking for a place to rent," he explained. "Please talk to me if you have any suggestions."

Bob Harkness and his mother held back until everyone had shaken hands with the pastor. Seeing Edith in her wheelchair, Bryan approached them. "Good morning, Edith. I'm glad you could make it out today."

"I hate missing church, but it's getting harder and harder for me to leave the house," she replied. "Being here always rejuvenates me." Edith paused for a moment and moistened her lips. "You said that Michelle Frank and her boys are looking for a place to stay?"

"Yes," Pastor Olson replied. "Do you have any suggestions?"

"I'd be willing to let them live in my house free of charge until they get on their feet. All they would have to do is pay the utilities. We can work out a rent schedule later. It's obvious I'll never be able to live alone again, so someone should make good use of the hard work that Roy Dutton put into building that house. I had many happy years there with Roy, and I hope they'll enjoy it as much as I did."

"Edith, I can imagine how difficult this decision must be for you to make. You're cutting all ties to your old home." Bryan took her hand.

A tear glistened in Edith's eyes. "I've always tried to look forward with hope and never look back with regret. I have a comfortable life with Bob and his family. Lately, my mind has been dwelling on the past—my autumn love with Roy Dutton, and before that, the good life I had with George Harkness. I have much to be grateful for. I want to share what I can with others."

Pastor Olson looked at Bob who was nodding his head in agreement. "Letting the Franks use the house is the most unselfish act I have ever known," Bryan responded. "I'll be going to Great Falls tomorrow to bring the boys home. I'm sure Michelle will be thrilled to know she has a home waiting for her."

"I'm glad to still be useful," Edith replied. "I wanted to be out in the woods looking for them, but I have to accept my limitations."

Pastor Olson watched Bob push his mother's wheelchair out of the church. *Rocky Bluff is full of good people,* he thought, *but few have the strength of character of Edith Dutton.*

❁

On Monday morning when Pastor Olson walked into the Frank boys' hospital room, he found them up and dressed. Richie was sitting in a wheelchair with a set of crutches beside him. Michelle and Teresa looked on lovingly.

"Hi, guys," Bryan greeted. "Are you ready to go home?"

"You bet," Richie replied. "Will they be having another campout? I wish I hadn't missed this one."

Bryan exchanged grins with Michelle and Teresa, then turned back to the boys. "They're planning to reschedule one sometime before school is out."

"One thing's for sure," Richie replied with a laugh. "I won't be able to wander away if I'm on crutches."

Bryan turned his attention to Michelle. "I found a furnished house for you and the boys when you come home Thursday. Until you get settled, all you'll have to pay is the utilities."

Michelle's eyes widened with amazement. "Who would do that for us?" she gasped.

"Edith Dutton," Bryan replied. "She knows she will never be strong enough to live alone again. She hopes that the three of you will be as happy there as she and Roy were."

"She's amazing. I've heard she's done more for Rocky Bluff than anyone else," Michelle replied.

Michelle hugged the boys good-bye, knowing that in three days they would be a family once more. The six weeks of rest and rehabilitation on the psychiatric floor of the Great Falls hospital had restored her zest for life.

The nursing staff helped the Frank boys to Pastor Olson's Jeep, and they left for Rocky Bluff. They had a few more nights to sleep at the parsonage until their mother returned home.

❖

That night after the boys were settled in their beds, Bryan and Teresa relaxed in the living room. This was the first time they had been alone together in over a week. "Now that the Franks' problems are beginning to smooth out, we should spend some time planning for our future," Bryan said as he slid an arm around her shoulders.

"Our wedding plans are coming along," Teresa replied softly. "I mailed the invitations over a week ago. It doesn't seem possible that in less than three weeks I'll be Mrs. Bryan Olson."

"With all the weddings we have both participated in, wedding details are the least of my concern," Bryan said as he pulled his fiancée against his chest. "We have moving plans to make. . .and we haven't even talked about a honeymoon."

"Why don't we take a honeymoon and not worry about moving until we get back," Teresa replied. "I think we both could use a long vacation."

"So where do you want to go on a honeymoon? It's got to be farther away than Billings." Bryan grinned.

"I've always had a secret desire to go to the Cayman Islands." Teresa looked rueful. "But I'm realistic enough not to even consider it."

"And why not? It never hurts to dream. I'm going to check into the Cayman

Islands before we come up with alternate plans B or C. I've been saving for a rainy day for a long time, but the good Lord has protected me, and I haven't had too many rainy days." Bryan pulled her closer, and their lips melted onto each other's.

"Any place alone with you would be a honeymoon," Teresa whispered.

"I just hope we won't have any more crises in Rocky Bluff before or during our honeymoon. I don't want you to start your life as a pastor's wife dealing with someone else's problems."

"Bryan, please don't underestimate me," Teresa begged. "I love you, but I've also dedicated my life to helping the people of Rocky Bluff. We will walk this path together, and that's all I want. Never having any problems, that would be boring. But sharing the problems as they come, knowing that we're together. . ." She looked into his eyes. "You never need apologize to me again for the responsibilities that come with being a pastor's wife. God has work He wants me to do in this town. And I want to do it. . .with you by my side."

Chapter 14

Jay Harkness and Rebecca Hatfield sat in the waiting area of the Great Falls International Airport. They were waiting for the arrival of Mitzi Quinata, Jay's mother-in-law, from Guam. While they waited, Jay and Rebecca reminisced about the time each of them had spent in Guam. Rebecca had worked two years as a librarian for Guam Christian Academy. During her second year as librarian, Jay had arrived on the island as an airman at Andersen Air Force Base.

"I'll never forget the day you introduced me to Angie," Jay said as his eyes remained glued on the runways in the distance. "If it hadn't been for you, I wouldn't be happily married and anxiously awaiting the birth of our first baby."

"That was a very interesting period in our lives," Rebecca replied. "Angie was the model student, and her mother was the best friend I had on the island. Most of the islanders kept their distance from statesiders, but Mitzi welcomed me with open arms and taught me the island ways," Rebecca said. "I'm so thankful we've been able to maintain our friendship through the years since I left Guam."

Jay nodded his head as he nervously watched the western sky. "I didn't expect Mitzi to fall in love with Montana the way she did when she was here for our wedding two years ago. Now that she'll soon have a grandbaby, it wouldn't surprise me if she moved to Montana after she retires from teaching."

"That would be nice," Rebecca agreed, "but people's roots run deep. When I was on Guam, I could hardly wait to get home. I'm sure she'll feel the same way when she's in Montana."

"There's one big difference," Jay teased. "Your true love was still in Montana while you were on Guam. They say true love knows no distance."

"I'll admit it was difficult making wedding plans while we were so far apart."

Simultaneously, they both rose to their feet as a faint speck appeared in the western sky. They stood in silence as the plane became larger, then finally touched down on the far runway. Jay and Rebecca watched as it taxied to the gate and the ramp was rolled out to the newly arrived plane. They waited as one by one the passengers deplaned.

After about a score of people emerged from the ramp, Jay spotted his mother-in-law and immediately ran to embrace her. "Welcome to Montana," he greeted. "How was your flight?"

"Long," Mitzi replied. "I was so afraid I wouldn't get here before the baby arrived that I couldn't sleep. I'll probably sleep all the way back to Rocky Bluff."

Mitzi then turned to Rebecca and hugged her. "Rebecca, I'm so glad you came to the airport with Jay. We have so much catching up to do. Guam Christian Academy just hasn't been the same since you left."

Rebecca grinned. "I hope the library automation system I installed is still working."

"Perfectly. It's the envy of all the other libraries on the island."

Mitzi turned her attention back to her son-in-law. "How's Angie?"

"She's doing great, but her boredom level is about maxed out," he laughed. "It's hard to keep a young, healthy woman flat on her back for over a month."

"I can imagine," Mitzi said with a chuckle as the three walked toward the baggage claim area. "At least she made it, and the baby is big enough now that he or she won't be in any danger from low birth weight. Do you know if it's a boy or girl?"

Jay smiled and shook his head. "Everyone keeps asking us that, but we decided we didn't want to know until the baby is born. We'd rather be surprised."

"If it were me, I'd be dying of curiosity," Mitzi replied, then she shut her eyes and leaned her head back.

True to her word, Mitzi slept most of the way to Rocky Bluff. She awakened a few miles out of town and talked impassionately about her coming grandchild. Mitzi could hardly contain herself with excitement as Jay drove Rebecca to her home first.

As soon as Jay pulled into his driveway, Angie emerged from the front door to greet them. "What are you doing out of bed?" Mitzi scolded as she embraced her daughter.

"It's all right, Mother," Angie giggled. "Yesterday the doctor said I could be up and about. The baby is big enough and could come naturally any time." She heaved a deep sigh. "As far as I'm concerned, the sooner the better."

Angie and Mitzi walked into the house arm in arm, while Jay retrieved his mother-in-law's bags from the trunk of the car. The aroma of homemade bread filled the house. The table was set with their best china, topped off by a beautiful floral centerpiece.

Dawn Harkness appeared in the doorway of the kitchen. "Mitzi, it's so good to see you again," Dawn exclaimed as she hugged their newly arrived guest. "We thought you'd be hungry when you got in, so we fixed a ham with all the trimmings. I wanted to cook an old-fashioned Chamorro meal, but we couldn't find all the ingredients at the local grocery store."

"When I'm on Guam, I'll eat like a Chamorro, but when I'm in Montana, I'll eat like a Montanan," Mitzi laughed. "You shouldn't have gone to all this trouble."

"Yesterday when the doctor said I could be up and about again I just couldn't wait to get into the kitchen," Angie laughed. "Cooking has always been my least favorite thing to do, but when I had to depend on Dawn to do all the cooking, it suddenly became the thing I missed the most. Believe it or not, I've enjoyed spending the day in the kitchen."

"I really appreciate this," Mitzi replied. "Airplane food is so skimpy."

The savory meal was enriched by the delight the family shared in being reunited. They made plans for the homecoming of the baby and shared the changes in Rocky Bluff since Mitzi had last been there two years before. Jay told Mitzi of his concern about his grandmother's health, then described the racial tension that had turned out to be the result of two traumatized boys.

Finally the conversation turned to the talk of the town. "Mom, do you remember Teresa Lennon, the director of the Spouse Abuse Shelter?" Angie asked.

"I didn't spend much time with her, but I was impressed with her compassion for other people. I was so grateful for the wise counsel she gave you," Mitzi said. "What's happening with her?"

"The first of June she's marrying our new pastor, Bryan Olson. The entire community is so excited."

Jay grinned and patted his wife on the shoulder. "The wedding is less than two weeks away, and Angie's afraid she'll be in the hospital and miss it."

"Mom, if I'm in the hospital on the big day, you'll have to go to the wedding in my place," Angie said as she laid her fork on her plate.

After the meal, Mitzi soon retired to the guest room, which Dawn had recently vacated. Mitzi slept the rest of the evening and throughout the entire night. Sleep was the only cure for jet lag.

The next week the Harkness family anxiously awaited the arrival of the baby. Mitzi helped plan the layette and shopped for baby necessities. A holiday atmosphere surrounded the Harkness household.

The evening of May thirty-first, Jay, Angie, and Mitzi were relaxing in the living room watching TV. Angie began to feel sharp abdominal pains. After the third one Mitzi said, "You better start timing those pains. Tonight could be the night."

"But they're not unbearable," Angie replied. "My friends tell me I don't have to worry until they get really bad."

"Trust me and begin timing them," her mother retorted.

The next pain came within five minutes. Jay hurried to the bedroom and grabbed the suitcase Angie had packed two days before. Mitzi wrapped her arm around her daughter as she escorted her to the car. In spite of her pain, Angie managed a shaky laugh. "It looks like I'm going to miss the big wedding after all," she quipped.

❖

Ten o'clock the next morning, Edith was relaxing in the living room when the phone rang. She slowly walked to the kitchen phone. *Lately it takes too much energy to even walk the few feet to the telephone. My heart just doesn't seem to be able to keep enough blood pumping for me,* she thought as she reached for the phone.

"Hello?"

"Hello, Grandma. This is Jay. I have some exciting news for you."

Edith's face broke into a broad grin. "The baby must have arrived."

"How did you know?"

"Jay, I've known you all your life. Nothing would have made you this excited except a new baby. How are Angie and the baby doing? Is it a boy or girl? How much does it weigh? Have you named it yet?"

Jay shook his head. His grandmother had a knack of cutting right to the heart of a matter without mincing words. "To answer your questions in order," Jay laughed, "Angie and the baby are both doing great. It's a girl. And she weighs six pounds, nine ounces. We named her Edith Mae Harkness."

Edith froze, hardly comprehending what she had heard. "You mean you named her after me?" she said at last, her voice trembling. "Rocky Bluff now has a second Edith Harkness to carry on the tradition. I don't deserve such an honor."

"Grandma, we're honored to name her after you."

Edith shook her head in disbelief. "This is the second baby that has been named after me. Four years ago, Beth and Dan Blair named their baby Edith. But when they moved to Missoula, I never had a chance to get to know my little namesake." Edith paused. "But your baby will carry the Harkness name and will grow up right here in Rocky Bluff."

They talked some more about the baby; then Jay changed the subject. "Grandma, are you planning to go to the wedding this afternoon?"

"Oh yes," Edith replied enthusiastically. "I wouldn't miss this wedding for anything."

"Good," Jay replied. "I'll see you there. Angie's disappointed she won't be able to go, but her mother will stand in for her."

"I'm looking forward to seeing that new baby," Edith said as they ended their telephone conversation.

Edith slowly walked the few steps back to the recliner and sunk deep into its cushions. *I have so much to be thankful for,* she mused as she thought back through the years. *I have a family that has been through a lot together and have grown strong in their love for God and each other. I spent many years trying to help the young people of Rocky Bluff, and I saw so many answers to prayer. I have truly been blessed with a full, worthwhile life, and I have lived to see my first great-grandchild. What more could I expect out of life? God has been so good to me.*

❖

Teresa stood in the back of Rocky Bluff Community Church and surveyed the huge crowd that had gathered to help her and Bryan celebrate their wedding. A sweetness filled the church, as familiar hymns of love echoed from the organ. Beside her stood Andy Hatfield who was to escort her down the aisle. Since her own father had died several years before, she had chosen someone who had also experienced a midlife marriage to share these special moments.

As the organ music began to swell, Pastor Rhodes took his position in front of the altar. He was followed by Bryan, Bryan's brother who was best man, and the two Frank boys as junior groomsmen.

When the bridal march began, Teresa kept her eyes focused on Bryan as she walked slowly down the aisle. Her heart soared as she gazed upon her future husband. Bryan stood tall and handsome, dressed in a rented tuxedo. She had never seen him look so happy.

Bryan and Teresa repeated their wedding vows, their eyes fixed on each other. They had both heard the words hundreds of times before; only this time it was different. They were the ones making the pledges before God.

When Pastor Rhodes turned to Teresa and said, "Teresa Lennon, do you take this man, Bryan Olson, to be your lawful wedded husband?" Teresa's mind raced.

I not only take Bryan as my husband, I accept his ministry as well. I will support his service to God in any way I can, whether it is in an active or a passive role.

Somehow Bryan heard the words in Teresa's heart instead of the words on her lips. He whispered a "thank you" so softly that neither Pastor Rhodes nor the congregation heard or understood the intense spiritual commitment that was being made between the two.

Following the ceremony, Bryan and Teresa stood in the receiving line for an hour and a half, greeting well-wishers. When Jay Harkness and Mitzi Quinata came through the line, a puzzled expression, then a smile crossed Teresa's face. "Is Angie in the hospital?"

Jay nearly burst with pride. "Along with Edith Mae Harkness the Second, the most beautiful baby ever born in the Rocky Bluff hospital."

"Congratulations!" Teresa hugged the new father. "What did your grandmother say when you told her you had named the baby after her?"

"That was the first time I've ever heard her speechless," Jay chuckled. "I'd forgotten that Dan and Beth Blair had also named their second child after her.

She couldn't believe that now two babies have been named after her."

Teresa nodded. "She's also had the new wing of the high school named after her. If anyone's life should be immortalized, it's hers."

Dawn Harkness was behind her brother in the receiving line. She too had a warm hug for Teresa. "Teresa, I want to wish you the very best. I'm leaving for college next week with a real purpose and mission. I don't know what I would have done without your compassionate understanding. If it wasn't for you and my family, I'm afraid to think about where I might be today."

Tears filled Teresa's eyes. Truly she felt as committed to ministry as Bryan did, only in a different area of service. Because of her background, she reached out quickly to women in crisis. She glanced across the room at Michelle Frank who was surrounded by new friends. The nights of interrupted sleep and frustrations had been well worth the investment; she could see the changed lives around her.

Next the two Frank boys appeared in the receiving line. "Congratulations, Teresa. I hope you like living with the pastor as much as we did," they teased.

"I'm sure I will," Teresa smiled.

"Where are you going on your honeymoon?" Chuck giggled.

"That's a secret, but it's a long ways away," Teresa teased back.

"Are you going to leave tonight?" Chuck continued.

Teresa leaned over and whispered in his ear. "If you won't tell anyone, we have a honeymoon suite some place close by so we can rest for a couple days; then we're going to be some place no one can find us."

"Will you tell me where?" Chuck begged.

Hearing the young boy's plea, Pastor Olson leaned over. "Not on your life. I don't want to be awakened in the middle of the night." Everyone standing nearby burst into laughter.

The line seemed endless, but Teresa and Bryan enjoyed every minute of it. Teresa stepped out of her high-heeled shoes and hoped no one would notice her feet underneath her long wedding dress. The church had not been so packed in years. Everyone was bound together in a bond of love and well wishes.

At the very end of the reception line were Bob and Nancy Harkness, pushing Bob's mother in a wheelchair. Edith looked tired and worn, yet radiant.

Teresa bent over to give her a hug. "I'm so glad you could come and share this special time with us."

"I just had to be here," Edith replied. "I know how cautious I was in considering marriage later in life. But when I finally took the plunge, I cannot describe the happiness I had with Roy. I just wanted to wish you that same kind of happiness. I fully understand the lines in one of Robert Browning's poems that say, 'Grow old along with me! The best is yet to be.'"

Chapter 15

The day after the wedding of Pastor Olson and Teresa Lennon, the Harkness family slept later than usual. When Nancy and Dawn went to the kitchen to prepare breakfast, Nancy glanced at the clock. "We'd better hurry," she said as she took a skillet out to begin frying eggs. "Pastor Rhodes is going to be preaching today, and we all want to welcome him back. Would you go check on your grandmother and see if she needs any help?"

Dawn smiled in agreement and hurried down the hallway. She knocked on the door. "Grandma? Grandma? Grandma, do you need any help?"

The room remained strangely silent. Dawn opened the door and peeked around the corner. Her grandmother remained perfectly still. She tiptoed toward the bed. "Grandma? Grandma?" There was still no response. Edith Dutton's eyes were closed, and a peaceful expression covered her face. Dawn took her hand. It was still and strangely cold. She turned and ran toward the door. "Mom! Dad! Come here quick! Hurry!"

Bob and Nancy came racing. They had not heard such urgency in their daughter's voice since she was a little girl. Inside his mother's bedroom, Bob instinctively took his mother's arm and felt for a pulse. His eyes widened, and he readjusted his fingers. Nothing. "I think she's gone," he said, his voice shaking. "We'd better call an ambulance."

❦

Pastor Rhodes was immediately notified of the death of Edith Dutton. When he announced it to the congregation, gasps and faint sobs could be heard throughout the church. "Yes, this is a time of mourning. We all grieve the loss of a dear friend and community member," he said softly. Then he added confidently, "Yet this is also a time of rejoicing. Psalm 116, verse fifteen, says, 'Precious in the sight of the Lord is the death of His saints.' Edith was truly one of God's saints, and she is now released from her frail body to join our precious Lord and Savior in heaven. Let us all rejoice in her homegoing."

❦

Word spread quickly of the death of Rocky Bluff's beloved Edith Harkness Dutton. The motels were crowded as friends and relatives gathered from all over Montana and neighboring states. Pastor and Mrs. Bryan Olson postponed their honeymoon to the Cayman Islands until after the funeral.

Pastor and Mrs. Rhodes remained in Rocky Bluff in order to officiate the service. At the request of the Harkness family, the funeral service would not be a time of eulogizing their mother and grandmother, but a time to express praise and thanksgiving to the Lord she served.

After the funeral, Edith Harkness Dutton was laid to rest in the Pine Hills Memorial Cemetery between her two husbands, George Harkness and Roy Dutton. The warm spring breeze whispering through the new leaves and the birds chirping in the trees seemed to say, "Welcome home, My beloved daughter. You have fought the good fight and have finished the race."

After the interment, the huge crowd in the church fellowship hall continued to reflect on the impact one woman's life had had on an entire community. Then one by one the congregation began to scatter to their own homes and motel rooms. The close friends and family were invited to an open house at the Harkness home for a special time of remembering.

The amount of food was overwhelming in the Harkness home during the open house, but few were interested in eating. Larry Reynolds stood to address the group. "I would like to share what a difference Edith Dutton made in my life," he began. "During the darkest day of my life, Edith was willing to risk her own life to prevent me from taking the life of my high school principal. She stood by me, believed in me until I could believe in myself and change my life."

Libby Reynolds, Larry's wife, nodded in agreement. "I found Roy and Edith Dutton's love for each other to be infectious. Through their example, Larry and I were able to rebuild a marriage that we felt was totally destroyed. I can truly say we experienced a type of contagious love."

Libby smiled across the room at Beth Blair who nodded knowingly. Many years ago they had shared troubled times together, and Edith Dutton had been there to act as their mentor. Beth could no longer hold back her words. "I want to emphasize what Libby said about how Roy and Edith Dutton's autumn love affected others. I met Edith when I came to Rocky Bluff as a scared, unwed teenage mother," she explained. "It was Edith's work at the crisis center that gave me the focus and direction I needed to take control of my life. It was Edith who upheld me with her prayers and encouragement during the days that my son Jeffey was kidnapped. It was Roy and Edith's love that inspired Dan and me. We discovered that we too could share a similar love because of the inspiration from the Duttons. Later we named our second daughter after Edith. You might say she was the one who inspired love between us."

Rebecca Hatfield nodded in agreement to Beth's words. "Beth was working with me at the Rocky Bluff High School when Jeffey was kidnapped. I don't know what we would have done without Edith during those dark days," Rebecca said. "When it came time for me to retire, I did not know what to do with myself. I assumed my productive years were over, but when I saw how Edith and Roy dedicated themselves to the crisis center, I realized I still had many productive years left to use my skills. I signed a two-year contract with a school on the island of Guam. I never thought that another chance at love would ever be possible, but because of Edith's example I found that distance could not be a hindrance for love. As soon as I returned from Guam, I followed Roy and Edith's example and began a beautiful marriage with Andy Hatfield. Ours was a distant love that grew into something close and permanent."

Angie Harkness remained seated on the sofa with her five-day-old baby on her lap. "I would like to add my thank you to all of you in this room," she began softly. "It was Rebecca who introduced me to Jay while he was stationed with the Air Force on Guam. When I too faced my darkest hour following a rape, I thought I was ruined for life and no respectable man would ever want to marry me. For me as well, it was Edith Dutton who brought renewal to my life so I could love again and later marry her grandson. Edith helped me find a healing love with Jay."

Bryan and Teresa Olson stood together holding hands. They were aglow with their new love. "I have known Edith for a long time," Teresa began. "We worked closely together when she was a counselor on the crisis line and I was director of the Spouse Abuse Shelter. Her compassionate love always served as a model for me. It was her love and encouragement that helped me accept and share my embarrassing, difficult background, and it was her wisdom and understanding that gave me the courage to follow my heart and marry Bryan Olson."

Bryan kissed his new bride on the forehead. "We will always be grateful for Edith's life. I came to Rocky Bluff as a confirmed bachelor, not knowing what real love was all about."

Bob Harkness stepped to the center of the room. "I'm grateful that each of you is sharing how Mother's love with Roy affected your life. I must admit that I nearly ruined it for all of you by resisting their marriage. Fortunately, our God of love is stronger than anything mortal man can do. I feel extremely blessed to have had a mother who had the compassion and wisdom to inspire all of our lives. We can truly say the world is a better place because Edith Harkness Dutton lived in Rocky Bluff, Montana."

A tiny whimper rose from within the blankets on Angie's lap. The young mother cuddled her new baby to her bosom. Jay looked on proudly. "We all have had so many experiences in which Grandma touched our lives. It was hard to say good-bye to her today, but her memory will always be with us. Every time

I look at little Edith Mae Harkness, I will remember my responsibility to raise my daughter in love and faith. I want her to walk in the footsteps of the greatest woman that Rocky Bluff has ever known—Edith Harkness Dutton."

Love
Remembered

Dedicated to my granddaughter, Jessica Ann Orr,
who was born with spina bifida and hydrocephalus,
and to her older brother, Ryan, and their parents, Philip and Sonya Orr,
who lovingly help Jessica reach her fullest potential.

Chapter 1

"D awn, would you take a look at these ultrasound pictures?" Dr. Fox was unable to mask his concern.

Dawn hurried to the viewing panels and peered over the shoulder of her employer. A faint gasp escaped her lips. "It looks like the spinal cord hasn't closed, and the baby has myelomeningocele. . . . The opening seems to be a little below the axilla, which is going to make it even worse." She fell silent as she continued studying the film. This was more than just malforming cells. This was a human life in the making.

The doctor scowled at the ultrasound pictures and shook his head. "Look at this," he murmured as he traced his finger over the screen. "It appears the right ventricle of the brain is larger than the left. I'm afraid we're going to have a little girl with both spina bifida and hydrocephalus."

Dawn Harkness had worked as an obstetrics nurse in Billings for five years, and she thrived on the thrill of introducing new life to happy parents. She had the unusual position of not only working side by side with the doctor during a woman's pregnancy, but she was called to the hospital when the woman went into labor; then she stayed with her until the newborn had been stabilized and was resting comfortably in either the hospital nursery or in a bassinet near the mother.

Most hospitals and clinics had become impersonal in order to be cost-efficient, and whichever staff member was on duty at the time delivered the babies. However, Dr. Fox was trying to return to more traditional care and encouraged a more personal relationship between his nurses and his patients.

The part Dawn liked most about her job was watching all the hopes and dreams of a young family culminate when she laid the new infant in the mother's arms. She loved to watch them relish in the glow of the miracle of life. Rarely had Dawn faced the heartbreak of the loss of a new baby, but at those dreaded times Dawn's faith in God's love provided her with the strength to comfort the grieving family. When her own words failed her, the Holy Spirit was always there to comfort and guide them.

As she stared at the ultrasound, Dawn suddenly felt overwhelmed with the challenges facing this unborn baby and her family. "The news is going to crush the parents," she sighed. "Who are they?"

Dr. Fox shook his head. "The mother is the young woman who just left my office about a half hour ago. I didn't want to tell her my suspicions until I'd studied the ultrasound in more detail and had a chance to talk with you."

Dawn's shoulders sagged as she took a deep breath. "You mean this is Sarah Brown's baby?" She recalled the shy girl with the frightened hazel eyes. "She doesn't look like she's much over sixteen."

"She's not. According to her records, she just had her sixteenth birthday last month." Dr. Fox shook his head. Even after twenty years in practice, he still became personally involved with each situation, especially the more difficult ones. At times he wished he could take a more clinical approach to the medical challenges he faced, but behind each challenge he always saw the faces of his patients. His calling to medicine included more than healing the physical body; he tried to provide healing for the entire person—body, soul, and spirit.

Dr. Fox motioned Dawn to follow him to his private office. "Sarah refused to give both her parents' names and the name of the father on the information sheet, so I assume she hasn't told them she's pregnant." He handed Dawn the chart as he took his chair behind his desk, while she automatically lowered herself into the one by the window.

"I wish young women, regardless of their personal situation, would see a doctor as soon as they suspect they are pregnant and not wait until they are six months along," Dawn said as she scanned the brief notes.

"Fear and guilt keep a lot of them quiet," Dr. Fox replied, "but in this case I don't think it would have prevented the neural tube defect. Such defects occur during the first weeks of pregnancy. . .long before a woman realizes she's expecting. I was hoping you'd be able to talk with her and get a better handle on the situation. Other social agencies may need to become involved. This is the first time I've seen her, and she appeared almost frightened of me."

"I'll see what I can do," Dawn promised. "I'll call her and see if she can return within a few days so we can discuss her tests. Maybe then we can get an idea of how she feels about the baby and if she has a good support system. With this baby's condition, she'll be ready prey for the abortion-rights activists."

Dr. Fox shook his head. "I'm afraid this may become a politically-charged situation," he sighed. "We'd better prepare her for the pressure she may receive from well-meaning people who are afraid of the challenges of a disabled child."

Immersed in the gravity of the situation, Dawn gazed out the window at the snow-covered trees. She thought of her family in Rocky Bluff and her brother Jay's three beautiful children. Serious birth defects had always been something she had studied from a textbook and learned about in a classroom. She had helped scores of mothers through miscarriages and the loss of premature babies, but never had she had to help them adjust to a lifetime of unlimited challenges.

"I'll try to get ahold of her as soon as possible," Dawn promised, "but I'll make no guarantees. This is going to be extremely difficult for me."

Dr. Fox smiled sympathetically. "There are no guarantees in this world," he said as he rose from behind his desk. He hesitated, then chuckled. "Except for maybe a waiting room full of impatient patients."

As soon as Dawn had a break, she dialed the telephone number on Sarah's chart. She held her breath as it rang several times without a response. *I wonder if she's in school. Maybe I'd better try back after four o'clock.*

Dawn mechanically continued her routine tasks throughout the afternoon as she recorded the weight and blood pressure of pregnant women aglow with the anticipation of the new life growing within them. She could not get her mind off Sarah Brown's baby. *Somehow, it doesn't seem fair,* she mused. *Sarah's baby deserves as much of a normal life as other babies do.*

At four-fifteen, Dawn again dialed the number written on Sarah's chart. After a couple rings, a boy's voice drawled, "Hello-o-o."

"Hello," Dawn greeted warmly. "I'm calling for Sarah Brown."

"She's not here," the voice replied nonchalantly.

"Can you tell me when she might be home?" Dawn persisted.

"I don't know. She usually works until after nine o'clock most nights."

Dawn shrugged her shoulders with frustration. He seemed like a typical ten-year-old brother. "I'll try to catch up with her then," she replied, trying to mask the urgency in her voice. Dawn wanted to be careful not to say who was calling in case Sarah's brother would ask her why someone from a doctor's office was calling.

That evening, as soon as the last patient left the office, Dawn hurried to the Billings Memorial Hospital. She greeted acquaintances and professional colleagues she met in the hallway and joined the short line at the hospital cafeteria. Each one seemed absorbed in their own world, and no one seemed to notice how mechanical their responses were. Dawn selected a simple meat loaf dinner and took a seat by herself at a table by the window. The Christmas lights in the hospital courtyard provided a momentary distraction as she quickly devoured her meal. She had so many unanswered questions, and she was hoping some of the answers lay three floors above.

After returning her cluttered tray to the conveyor belt that led back to the dishwasher, Dawn took the next elevator to the third-floor medical library. She gave a mechanical smile and nod to the reference librarian and went directly to the automated card catalog. She pushed the button to do a keyword search and typed "spina bifida." After printing the call numbers and titles, she walked slowly through the stacks until she located several books on her list.

For the next two hours, Dawn read about the prognosis and treatment of spina bifida and hydrocephalus. Suddenly, her heart began to pound, and her face reddened. *This couldn't have happened in my country. . .in my profession.* But every statement was documented with at least one footnote referring to the original source of the information. *Between 1977 and 1982, American doctors conducted an experiment that proved you can kill disabled babies of poor families and get away with it. Their research was funded by the federal government. Twenty-four babies with spina bifida lost their lives. The experiment was declared a success.*

Dawn hurried to the copier machine, dropped in four quarters, and copied the pages concerning the experiment. She then took the book *The Civil Rights of Handicapped Infants* to the circulation desk and checked it out. *Dr. Fox is right,* she thought as she hurried out the door of the library. *Sarah Brown's baby could become a politically-charged issue, besides a personal tragedy.*

Dawn Harkness arrived at her small two-bedroom apartment at ten minutes past nine. She laid her book on the table, hung her coat in the hall closet, and took the slip of paper containing Sarah Brown's telephone number from her purse. She again dialed the now-familiar numbers. "Hello," a tired woman's voice answered.

"Hello," Dawn replied. "Is Sarah Brown there, please?"

"This is Sarah."

"Hi, Sarah. I'm glad I was finally able to get ahold of you," she said, trying to sound as comforting as possible. "This is Dawn Harkness, Dr. Fox's nurse. We were hoping you'd be able to return to the clinic as soon as possible to discuss the results of today's tests."

A long silence settled over the phone wires. "W–w–was something wrong?" the teenager stammered. "I'm pretty sure I'm pregnant, but why would I need to come back so soon?"

"Yes, Sarah, you're definitely pregnant," Dawn replied, trying to pick her words as carefully as possible, "but you and the baby will need to be monitored closely from now until delivery. Can you come in and see us sometime tomorrow? Maybe as soon as school is over?"

"I have to work late again tomorrow, and I don't want anyone to know that I have an appointment with an obstetrician." Sarah's voice became high and tense. "Please don't let anyone know I'm pregnant," she pleaded, then paused. "Can I come after work Monday instead? I think I can catch a ride with a friend who works a couple blocks away."

"Certainly," Dawn agreed. "Dr. Fox can always work you in at the end of the day. I'm looking forward to seeing you then."

Dawn spent a troubled weekend poring through her book on the civil rights of handicapped children. Late in the afternoon on Sunday, she returned to the medical library and got two more books pertaining to the care and treatment of spina bifida and hydrocephalic children. She stayed up late Sunday night and searched the Internet for the most recent developments in the field. She sought clues as to the psychological adjustment of the mother toward a disabled child. For a loving two-parent family to accept the crushing of their hopes and dreams for their soon-to-be-born child would be hard enough, but how would such news affect a scared unwed sixteen year old?

Promptly at four in the afternoon on Monday, Sarah Brown walked into Dr. Fox's reception area. She was dressed in a tattered sweatshirt from Montana State University and blue jeans, and as hard as she tried, she could no longer hide her bulging stomach. She walked nervously to the reception area. "My name is Sarah Brown, and I'm supposed to meet with Dawn Harkness," she whispered as she glanced over at the two pregnant women in the waiting room.

The receptionist gave a warm smile. "She's expecting you," she replied. "If you'll wait right here, I'll get her."

Within moments, Dawn Harkness appeared in the doorway dressed in a crisp white pantsuit with a stethoscope draped around her neck. Her long blond hair was pulled back with a gold barrette, and she moved with ease and confidence. "Hello, Sarah," she greeted. "Will you come with me? The doctor will be able to see you in just a few minutes."

Instead of taking Sarah into an examining room, Dawn led her to Dr. Fox's private office. The teenager's eyes widened as she noted the plush carpeting, the richly upholstered chairs, and the diplomas in gold frames. "Why don't you make yourself comfortable?" Dawn suggested as she pointed to a chair by the window, then took the one next to it. "I was hoping the doctor would be done with his patients for the day when you arrived, but he had an emergency this morning and has been running late ever since. At least this will give us a chance to become better acquainted."

Sarah stared at the floor while she nodded her head.

Dawn cleared her throat to mask her nervousness. "Sarah, I have a very unique position with Dr. Fox," she explained. "First of all, I'm not only an obstetric nurse, but I'm also a social worker. I not only assist the doctor during office hours, but I occasionally make home visits when there's a nonmedical crisis. I generally stay with the mother at the hospital during the entire labor process until the baby is delivered. We feel consistent medical care makes childbirth much easier for both the mother and the baby."

Sarah sat in silence as she continued staring at the floor. Minutes passed before she finally blurted, "But I'm not married. What are they going to do to me?"

Dawn reached out and took the trembling girl's hand. "No one is going to hurt you. We're here to help you make wise decisions about your future and the future of your child. Have you told anyone yet about your pregnancy?"

Sarah shook her head as she continued staring at the floor. Her face paled as tears built in her eyes.

"Do your parents suspect that you may be pregnant?" Dawn asked.

"I haven't seen my father in eight years. I think he's out on the coast somewhere," Sarah finally murmured.

"And what about your mother?" Dawn persisted.

Sarah shuffled in her seat, then shrugged her shoulders. "I don't know," she stammered. "We don't get along very well. I'd hate to think about what she'll do to me when she finds out." The frightened girl paused; then her voice lowered. "I've thought about running away, but I don't have anywhere to go."

"Would it be helpful if your mother came to the clinic with you and we all discussed it together?" Dawn queried as she watched tears spill from Sarah's soft hazel eyes. She reached for a box of tissues on the doctor's desk and handed it to the crying teenager.

Sarah dabbed her eyes. "She probably wouldn't yell as loud at me if you were there," she whispered, "but how could I get her to come to an obstetrician without her knowing ahead of time that I was pregnant? She'd give me the third degree."

"Just leave that part to me," Dawn promised as the door opened and Dr. Fox entered.

"Hello, Sarah," he greeted as he extended his hand. "I'm sorry you had to wait, but I fell behind in my appointments."

Sarah's hand was moist as she nervously shook the doctor's hand. "Hello, Dr. Fox."

The doctor rolled his chair from behind his desk and placed it under the window next to his patient. He cleared his throat. "Sarah, I need to confirm your suspicions. You are six months pregnant, and the ultrasound suggests that it will probably be a girl."

Sarah sighed. "But why did you bring me here to tell me that? Is this how you normally tell girls they're pregnant—or do you treat unwed mothers differently?"

"No difference," Dr. Fox replied kindly, "but your situation is very different. There is something wrong with the development of your baby." The doctor hesitated. "Do you know what spina bifida is?"

Sarah's eyes widened. "Is something wrong with my baby?" she demanded.

"I don't understand your big words."

Dr. Fox leaned back in his chair and surveyed the troubled girl. "Spina bifida actually means 'open spine,'" he explained. "It occurs when the spinal cord does not form properly during pregnancy. This is not uncommon, since two children out of every thousand are born with spina bifida." He paused, giving Sarah time to assimilate the seriousness of the situation. "Although spina bifida has different forms and varying degrees of effect, most babies born with this condition will need surgery to close the spine soon after birth. Orthopedic surgery is often necessary to correct foot or leg problems, and a shunt from the head to the abdominal cavity is generally needed to drain fluid from the brain. The enlarged head that often results is called hydrocephalus. There can be problems with control of the bladder and bowel functions. Braces or other equipment may be needed for walking—or the child may never be able to walk. Care of these babies can become extremely demanding, but they generally have a cheerful disposition. We will do all we can to help, but this is going to be very difficult for you."

Sarah sat in stunned silence for a few moments. Her lower lip trembled. "What did I do to make this happen? I haven't been doing drugs or drinking or smoking like some of my friends have."

Breaking bad news to patients had always been difficult for Dr. Fox, but the look of terror and bewilderment in Sarah's eyes nearly broke his serious, professional exterior. He reached over and patted Sarah on the shoulder. "No one knows for sure what causes spina bifida, but its cause is beyond the parents' control. Recent studies have shown that one factor that increases the risk of having a spina bifida baby is low folic acid in the mother's system before and during the first few weeks of pregnancy," he explained patiently.

"So what's folic acid?" Sarah asked. "I've never heard of it before."

"Folic acid is a common water-soluble B vitamin that is essential for the functioning of the human body," Dr. Fox continued explaining. "During periods of rapid growth, such as pregnancy and fetal development, the body's requirement for this vitamin increases. The bad thing is that the average American diet does not supply the recommended level of folic acid."

Sarah stared out the window at the darkening street. The Christmas lights were just beginning to come on about the neighborhood. "I don't know what to do or say," she murmured.

"Maybe we should begin by talking this over with your mother," Dawn suggested cautiously. "I'm sure she'll be more supportive than you think during a time of crisis."

Sarah scowled. "Don't bank on it." She shrugged her shoulders and sighed. "But I guess I don't have any other choice."

"Would you mind if I called her right now and asked her to join us?" Dawn persisted.

"I guess it'll be all right," the teen sighed. "She normally tends bar at the DewDrop, but this is her day off. But I'm warning you, she won't be pleasant to deal with."

"What's your mother's name?" Dawn asked.

Sarah shrugged her shoulders. "Doris," she muttered.

Dr. Fox left to help his office staff work through a multitude of insurance questions, while Dawn dialed the number listed on Sarah's chart. She waited nervously. After three rings a sleepy voice uttered a faint hello at the other end of the telephone line.

"Hello, may I speak with Doris Brown, please?" Dawn asked.

"Speaking."

"This is Dr. Fox's office, and your daughter, Sarah, is here with us now," Dawn continued. "We are faced with a serious problem, and we wondered if you could come as soon as possible so we could discuss it with you."

There was a long pause at the other end of the telephone line before a tense voice replied, "Has she been in a car accident? Her friends are always driving recklessly around town."

"No, fortunately she was not involved in an accident," Dawn assured her, "but we do need to see you as soon as possible."

Dawn tried to act calm and in control, but the tone in the mother's voice left her unsettled. "We're located at 2519 Westview Avenue, Suite 35, in the Medical Arts building. How long do you think it will take you to get here?"

"I'll have to change clothes first. It'll probably take me a half hour," Doris Brown replied.

"Thank you, Mrs. Brown. We'll be expecting you," Dawn replied. She ended the conversation and returned the telephone to its cradle, then turned her attention back to the pregnant girl, who was staring blankly out the window. "May I get you a soft drink and a couple of cookies while you wait?"

Sarah nodded, while Dawn tuned a radio to a local station and slipped out the door. Through Dawn's own struggles and trials in growing up, she had learned that there were times when a person needs to be alone. This appeared to be such a time for Sarah. After a few minutes, Dawn returned with refreshments for her patient, and they engaged in small talk as they watched the hands of the clock slowly move to the top of the hour.

They talked about Sarah's school, her job, and friends, anything to ease the tension before Sarah's mother arrived. Dawn was encouraged by the young woman's concern for her friends and her desire to excel in school. Exactly at the top of the hour, Dawn rose. "If you don't mind, I think I better go to the outer office and wait for your mother," she said. "Will you be all right here by yourself?"

"Sure," Sarah replied with a dry smile, "but I warn you—meeting my mother will not be a pleasant experience."

Just as Dawn got to the reception area, a middle-aged woman burst through the door and marched directly toward Dawn. "Why didn't you tell me when you called that Dr. Fox was an obstetrician? You mean that no-good daughter of mine is pregnant?"

"Mrs. Brown, we have an extremely serious situation on our hands, and we were hoping for your full cooperation," Dawn stated firmly. "Please come with me to the doctor's office. Sarah is waiting for us there."

Hearing the outburst, Dr. Fox hurriedly followed the two women into his office. "Hello, Mrs. Brown," he said as he extended his hand in greeting. "I'm Dr. Tyler Fox. We asked you to come to help Sarah with an extremely difficult problem."

"You mean the little wench is pregnant?" she snarled.

Dr. Fox set his jaw, as the veins in his neck protruded. "Yes, the ultrasound showed that Sarah is twenty-five weeks along," he replied firmly, "but to complicate the situation further, it appears the baby is going to have some serious birth defects."

Doris's eyes snapped. "And what kind of defects will that be?"

"Simply put, the baby suffers from neural tube defect." Dr. Fox paused, allowing time for his words to sink in. "She has spina bifida and hydrocephalus."

"That's just a fancy way to say it's a water-head baby. Right?" Doris snarled. "I hope you're planning on performing an abortion right away."

"Right now, an abortion is not a good option. In the last trimester an abortion can be a risk to the mother's health," Dr. Fox replied, while Sarah sat meekly in her chair trembling. "However, there are several types of surgery available today to help these children obtain a better quality of life."

Doris glared at her daughter, then vented more anger at the doctor. "The politicians have been arguing that for years. It's the woman's choice. If you won't perform an abortion, I'll find someone who will."

"Mother," Sarah cried. "I don't want an abortion. I want to keep my baby. We saw pictures of abortions in sex education class, and it's gross—especially late-term abortions."

"So what are you going to do with your monster baby?" Sarah's mother screeched. "You don't even know how to take care of yourself, much less a normal baby."

Sarah cowered back in her chair. "I. . .I. . .I don't know," she whimpered, "but I don't want to kill it."

"You don't expect me to take care of it, do you?" Doris shouted as she jumped to her feet. "Here you were sneaking around behind my back and got yourself pregnant, and now you have the audacity to think I'll help you raise the product of your sin. I don't even want to see you again until you've gotten rid of that baby, one way or another."

Sarah's face blanched as her mother stormed out the door, slamming it behind her. The frightened teen buried her head in her hands and sobbed. "I knew I shouldn't have told her," she murmured. "Now what will I do?"

Dawn knelt beside her and pulled her close. "Things will work out," she tried to assure her. "God has everything under control, even though right now it doesn't seem like it. I have a spare bedroom in my apartment where you can stay until we can get things worked out."

Chapter 2

awn Harkness sat alone in the dim light from her TV. The emotions of the day made sleep elude her. The troubled teenager in the nearby bedroom had finally drifted into a fitful sleep after promising to attend school the next morning, leaving Dawn alone with her thoughts.

What will be best for Sarah and the baby? It's not uncommon for teenage mothers to keep their babies, but that is only recommended when they have a good family support system. The best support we can expect to get from Doris Brown is that she'll box up Sarah's clothes and personal effects. I could pick them up at noon tomorrow. . . . There's a long list of families who want to adopt babies, but few will take a child who is developmentally disabled.

Dawn made herself a cup of hot chocolate. Between sips, she called Sarah's mother, then read a few of her favorite Psalms to relax her mind. Long after midnight she fell exhausted into bed, knowing that her alarm would be ringing promptly at six. She now had to get a teenager to school before she reported to work at nine.

Sarah and Dawn mechanically went through their morning routines; then Dawn dropped Sarah off at the front door of the high school. Arriving at the office, Dawn greeted the receptionist and bookkeeper and quickly reviewed the appointments for the day. Three women were expected to deliver any day now, and she was alerted to be ready for a call to join them at the hospital at any time. When Dr. Fox arrived at the office after a physicians' breakfast meeting, he immediately called Dawn into his private office.

"How's Sarah Brown doing today?" he queried as he took out his stethoscope and hung it around his neck.

"She's doing a lot better this morning, and I was able to convince her to keep going to school," Dawn replied. "I talked with her mother last night, and she was more than happy to box up Sarah's clothes. I'll pick them up during my lunch hour. I have never met anyone as hard and calloused as she is. Sarah tried to warn us, but I never expected her to be this bad."

"So where can this poor girl go? We just can't put her out on the street," Dr. Fox pondered aloud. "Homes for unwed mothers are becoming harder and harder to find since society now encourages the young moms to continue with their education during and after pregnancy."

"I have an extra bedroom. She's more than welcome to stay with me for the next three months," Dawn volunteered, then paused. "Beyond that, we'll have to wait until the baby comes to know how severe her disabilities will be and if Sarah will be able to care for the baby by herself. Sarah's hopes are high, but at this point no one knows what she may be facing."

Dr. Fox paused, his expression doubtful. "I'm sure Medicaid will carry the brunt of the medical costs, but you shouldn't have to bear the financial responsibility of taking care of Sarah for three months. I'll check around and see if I can find any civic or church group that might help in this crisis."

"I really don't mind doing it." Dawn smiled. "But I would gladly accept any outside financial help I could get. Feeding and clothing a teenager could get very expensive."

"I'll see what I can do," the doctor promised as he glanced over his daily schedule. "Right now I have other patients to care for, but I'll get on this as soon as I can find a free moment."

The next week flew by for Dawn as she settled into her role of mothering a pregnant teenager. Sarah continued to work three hours a day after school at the Pizza Parlor, then came home to do her homework. In spite of her personal crisis, Sarah seemed to blossom under the security of knowing others were personally concerned about her plight. Dr. Fox was able to locate three groups that were willing to donate a hundred dollars apiece each month to help Sarah.

❖

Promptly at closing time the following Wednesday, a well-dressed salesperson entered the medical building for a scheduled meeting. The receptionist ushered him into a large conference room at the end of the corridor where he could display the latest medical paraphernalia to hit the market. As soon as they were finished with their last patient of the day, Dr. Fox and his nurse joined the other medical professionals who were examining the display.

A broad grin spread across the sales representative's face as the pair entered the room. "Dawn Harkness, is that you?"

Dawn's face broke into a broad grin. "Ryan Reynolds?" she exclaimed as she gave a quick hug to her old school friend. "I haven't seen you in years. How's life been treating you?"

"It's been going great for me," Ryan replied as he pointed to his display. "As you can see, I'm now a district representative for a major medical supplier."

The physicians and nurses continued examining each of the products, while the old friends renewed their friendship. Dr. Fox held up some samples of nonlatex surgical gloves. "We'd better consider increasing our supply of these. We're going to have an increased demand for them in the near future."

Dawn gave her boss a puzzled look. "Why is that?"

The doctor slipped on one of the gloves and flexed his fingers. "Children with neural tube defects are often allergic to latex," he replied. "With Sarah Brown's baby due in a little over two months, it would be a good idea to have some on hand."

"How soon we forget." Dawn blushed. "That's basic nurses' training 101. I'm glad you reminded me."

As the doctors finished examining the products and placing their orders, Dawn intentionally lingered behind. After writing each order, Ryan looked up to make sure she was still there. As soon as the last doctor left, Ryan hurried over to her. "It's good to see a familiar face. I've been on the road much too long. How about having dinner with me so I can catch up on news from Rocky Bluff?"

"Sounds good to me," Dawn replied, "as long as I'm home by nine."

A look of amusement spread across Ryan's face. "You mean you still have the same curfew you had in high school?" he teased.

"Almost," she laughed. "I have a teenage girl living with me for a few weeks, and she gets off work at nine. She's going through some pretty tough times right now, and I don't want her to spend a lot of time by herself."

"How about if I pick you up in an hour? I'll trust you to pick out the best place to eat." Ryan grinned as he began boxing his supplies.

The old friends bade each other farewell, and Dawn hurried to her car at the far side of the parking lot. Her mind drifted back to her growing-up years in Rocky Bluff, Montana. She remembered how her brother Jay and Ryan had been best friends. They had played on the same football and basketball teams, and they spent a lot of time visiting in each other's homes. Ryan had been several grades ahead of her in school, and he rarely returned to Rocky Bluff once he graduated, so she had completely lost track of him.

Dawn tried to remember the last time she had seen Ryan, but it all seemed so long ago and far away. She drove several blocks over the snowpacked streets before she remembered their last encounter. *Ryan was at Grandma's funeral nearly eight years ago*, she reminded herself. *There were so many people there that I scarcely noticed, but he and his brother did spend a lot of time talking to Jay and Angie and their new baby. I'll never forget that day. People came from all over the state to pay tribute to Grandma and share how she affected their lives. I wish I could become only a fraction of what she was.*

Arriving at her apartment, Dawn left a note for Sarah telling where she would be, in case Sarah got home first. She hurriedly jumped into the shower, then changed into a black pantsuit with gold trim. As she blow-dried her hair, she began to question her motives. *I'm only having dinner with an old high school friend; it's not like I'm going on a formal date or anything. I guess I've been too busy with my career to even think about an evening out. I don't even know if I'll remember how to act.*

Her mind again drifted back to Rocky Bluff, Montana. She had been surrounded by friends and family who had loved and protected her. After school, she would often go to her grandmother's house until her parents got off work at the family hardware store. She had watched the joys and struggles her grandmother, Edith Harkness Dutton, faced as her health began to deteriorate. Yet in spite of poor health, she was able to remarry and help a great many people face a troubled world. Since her grandmother's death, Dawn vowed she would do her best to emulate her grandmother's love and compassion toward those who were overwhelmed with problems.

Just as Dawn finished putting on her makeup, the doorbell rang. Her heart pounded as she hurried to the front door and flung it open. "Ryan, it's good to see you," she greeted cheerfully. "Come in from the cold while I get my coat."

"Better add an extra sweater," Ryan chuckled as he stomped the snow from his boots. "The temperature's dropping fast, and the wind's picking up. The windchill factor may be twenty below before we get back."

"I'm tough," Dawn retorted lightly as she reached for her black suede coat. "I've lived in Montana all my life."

Ryan opened the door, and the pair stepped into the brisk winter air. "Where's the best place to eat?" he asked. "I want this night to be special. It's not often I run into someone from Rocky Bluff."

"People from Rocky Bluff are a unique breed," Dawn agreed. "They all seem to live life with gusto. How about Milton's Steak House on Twenty-ninth Street? We'll celebrate old times."

"Sounds good to me. I'm always hungry for a good filet," Ryan responded as he helped her through the snow.

The Christmas decorations twinkled around them as Ryan drove his late-model car over the slick streets. Dawn admired the strong profile of the man next to her. Memories of him as a fuzzy-faced teen on the basketball floor flashed through her mind. "How long are you going to be in Billings?" she asked as she pulled her coat tighter around herself.

"I'm leaving day after tomorrow," Ryan replied with a shrug of his shoulders. "At first traveling a five-state area was fun, but now it's beginning to get old. One motel room begins to look like another, and one lonely mountain highway looks the same as all the rest."

"I don't know how you cope with living out of a suitcase and driving from one motel to another," Dawn said sympathetically. "A two-week vacation and several extended weekends to visit friends and relatives is about all the traveling I like to do."

"My traveling days may soon be coming to an end," the young businessman said with a note of anticipation. "There are rumors of a corporate restructure. I might be moved to the home office in Chicago. However, city living doesn't excite me, either."

"I can understand that," Dawn replied with a knowing smile. "Anything larger than Billings is too large for me."

Ryan was able to find a parking place close to the entrance of the restaurant. He turned off the ignition and walked around the car to open the door for Dawn. After being independent for several years, she was used to getting out of the car as soon as it stopped, and she had to quickly remind herself of the social graces of dating. So many of her generation had never learned the long-standing traditions of their parents and grandparents, but her family had insisted on proper behavior.

Ryan smiled as he entered the steak house. The people were dressed strictly Montana style. Some were there in long dresses and formal suits and ties, while others wore cowboy hats, boots, and jeans. "I guess we'd be appropriately dressed no matter what we wore," he noted to Dawn as the hostess led them to a corner booth.

Milton's Steak House was busy that night, but Ryan and Dawn were so involved in conversation that they scarcely noticed the tardy arrival of their food. At first conversation revolved around mutual friends and acquaintances back in Rocky Bluff, but gradually attention shifted to events that were more personal.

Ryan studied Dawn's soft blue eyes, which seemed wise beyond their years. "Dawn, you mentioned you had a young girl staying with you. Are you picking up where your grandmother left off? She always seemed to have young people around who needed a little extra love and guidance."

Dawn smiled as she shook her head. "I could never fill my grandmother's shoes," she replied emphatically. "I just accidentally fell into this situation. It's really pathetic. . . . A sixteen-year-old girl came into our office six months pregnant, not realizing how far along she actually was. When Dr. Fox took an ultrasound, he discovered that the spinal column of the child had not closed properly. The baby has spina bifida and hydrocephalus."

"That's a pretty tough pill to swallow," Ryan replied sympathetically. "I know a little about hydrocephalus because one of the products we carry is the shunt they use to drain the fluid from the head to the abdominal cavity. How did the mother take the news?"

Dawn shook her head. "Not good," she replied. She described all that had happened with Sarah and her mother. "She demanded that Sarah have an abortion," Dawn finished. "In fact, she was so angry her daughter had gotten pregnant that she refused to have anything at all to do with her or her handicapped baby."

Ryan shook his head with disgust. "I know the proabortion movement is very strong in Montana, but I don't understand how taking a human life can ever solve any problem."

"I agree with you," Dawn replied, "but unfortunately the mother won't budge from her position, and she won't have anything to do with her daughter until she gets rid of the baby."

"Hence softhearted Dawn took her in?" Ryan teased, trying to lift the tension of the moment.

A smile spread across Dawn's face. "Sarah's a delightful, hardworking girl," she responded. "We've been able to get some welfare and social assistance for her, and she seems to be adjusting to the situation."

"So what's going to happen after the baby is born? Does she plan to keep the baby?" Ryan asked. "It's hard enough for teenage mothers to care for babies under the best of conditions, but caring for a handicapped child would be next to impossible."

"That's a very good question." Dawn hesitated before she replied. "I suppose a lot will depend on the severity of the condition—and of course we won't know that until after the baby is born."

The hours of good food, good conversation, and occasional laughter sped by before Dawn looked at her watch. "I better get home," she said as she took her purse in her hand. "Sarah will be home before I am."

Ryan reached for the bill. "Does she have a key to your apartment?"

"Oh yes. I just like to be there when she gets off work. She needs all the love and security I can give her. I guess I'm a little overprotective, but I'm not used to being a mother," Dawn admitted shyly.

"I'm sure you're being a fine mother," Ryan replied; then a twinkle came into his eyes. "When the baby comes, does that mean you'll be a grandma?"

Dawn gave her childhood friend a playful hit on the shoulder as they walked toward the cashier. It had been a long time since she had sat and just enjoyed the company of another person without feeling she must help them in some way. The laughs they shared had restored her ability to help carry the burdens of the troubled girl for whom she felt responsible.

When Ryan parked his car in front of Dawn's apartment complex, they noted that the lights were already lit in her apartment. "It looks like she beat you home after all," Ryan noted as he turned off the engine.

Dawn's mind raced as she watched him walk around the car. She hated to see the evening end. "Why don't you come in and meet Sarah?" she suggested as he opened the car door for her. "She's a real sweetheart."

Ryan took Dawn's hand as they walked up the sidewalk. Neither one saw the eyes that were peering from behind the drapes. "I'd like that," he replied with a distant look in his eyes. "It's been a long time since I've been around teenagers. I don't get to Running Butte often to see my nieces and nephews, and I really miss them."

"You're kind of late, aren't you?" Sarah giggled as Dawn walked through the door with Ryan close behind. "After all, it is going on nine-thirty."

"Sounds like that's a line you've heard often," Dawn retorted with equal levity.

"About every time I left the house," Sarah replied as she eyed the handsome stranger standing in the entryway.

"Sarah, I'd like you to meet Ryan Reynolds, an old high school friend of mine. Ryan, this is Sarah Brown. She's going to be staying with me for a few months."

Sarah stepped forward and extended her hand. "It's nice to meet you. I'm glad someone was able to get Dawn out of her apartment. She's getting to be a real stay-at-home mom."

"I wish I'd be around longer to help cure that malady," Ryan chuckled. "I guess you'll have to keep her entertained until I'm in town again."

Dawn shook her head with amusement and pleasure, glad to see Sarah so relaxed with a total stranger. "How about you both make yourselves comfortable, and I'll get some cold drinks and make some popcorn?"

"Sounds good to me," Sarah replied, "but I have a lot of homework to do. If you don't mind, I'll just take some juice to my room."

Dawn took a pitcher of orange juice from the refrigerator and poured a glass for Sarah. "Thanks," Sarah replied as she turned to leave. She turned back and snickered. "Don't stay up too late; remember, tomorrow's a workday."

"Wiseacre kid," Dawn smiled as she reached in the cupboard for the popcorn. "I think she's enjoying playing reverse roles."

"No doubt about it," Ryan laughed. "She's a charming young lady. I wish the best for her; she's got a rough road ahead of her."

Ryan and Dawn sat on the couch and watched the evening news, then the late-night talk show. Neither one wanted the evening to end, but both knew it must. Finally Ryan turned to Dawn. "I'll only be in Billings for one more day, so I was wondering if we could have dinner again tomorrow night."

Dawn shook her head. "I wish I could, but I have a Nursing Association meeting tomorrow night. Any other time I would skip it, but I have to give a speech on our experimental program. We have a consistent maternity nurse from early pregnancy through labor, delivery, and postpartum. I'm hoping that with enough publicity for its successes, the practice will spread."

"With your enthusiasm, I'm sure it will," Ryan replied as he stood to leave. "I'll give you a call the next time I'm in town."

Chapter 3

Dawn Harkness gazed sleepily out the windows of the hospital cafeteria. It was midnight, the mother of the latest Billings resident had just fallen asleep, and the father had finally taken his last peek into the hospital nursery and returned home. Dawn wanted one last strong cup of coffee before she braved the slick streets and biting-cold temperatures. Although she was tired, she loved the happy times when she could assist at the birth of a new baby. *Could anyone possibly have a more rewarding job?* she thought. *The doctors get most of the credit and take care of the physical part of childbirth, but I get to personally share the joys and fears with the family.*

A deep voice interrupted her solitude. "You look lost in thought."

Dawn looked up just as a man in a white coat with a stethoscope around his neck set his coffee and donut down and took a chair at the next table facing her. She remembered seeing him in the hospital corridors; they had smiled and nodded when they passed, but they had never been formally introduced. "Just a late night," she sighed. "I'm trying to get my courage up to face the slick streets."

"Lucky you," he replied. "I don't get to sleep until eight in the morning; then all I have is a bed and dresser to call my own."

Dawn surveyed the young blond doctor. His hair was closely cut, and his mustache was well trimmed. His deep blue eyes reflected more depth than his boyish frame implied. "Sounds like you're an intern," she replied warmly.

"You mean it's that obvious?" he joked.

"Anyone who works throughout the night and has only a bed and dresser has got to be an intern," she replied.

The young doctor smiled. "My name's Michael Archer, and I just graduated from the University of Iowa Medical School in August. It took nearly four months to work out the details of my internship and move out here, but I finally made it. Montana's a beautiful state. I just love it here."

"I'll have to agree with the beauty of the state," Dawn replied. "I've lived here all my life, so I kind of take it for granted. I'm Dawn Harkness. Glad to meet you!"

"It's good to finally meet an honest-to-goodness native. I was beginning to think everyone in Montana was an import. Are you involved in any of the winter sports?" Mike continued, scarcely taking a breath.

In a big city, Dawn might have considered the young intern forward, looking for a pickup, but in the relaxed atmosphere of the West, she considered the young man a lonely intern looking for professional companionship. "I tried skiing while I was in college, but since I've come to Billings I've been too busy. How about you?"

Mike grinned, revealing perfectly straight white teeth. Dawn concluded his parents must have had a gigantic orthodontist bill when he was a child. "As you know, interns aren't noted for their abundance of free time, but I have been able to get to Red Lodge a couple of times and rent a snowmobile. There always seemed to be someone experienced around to give me some tips before I managed to kill myself trying the impossible."

"Snowmobiling is something I've never tried, even though it looks like it'd be a lot of fun," Dawn replied; then she broke into a broad smile. "I guess I'm getting so wound up in my work that I'm forgetting there's a world out there."

Mike took another sip of coffee. "I guess that's a professional hazard we face," he replied as he kept his eyes constantly on her face.

Dawn smiled, folded her napkin, and placed it on the table. "Well, I've procrastinated long enough," she said as she rose to leave. "I've got to face the great outdoors sooner or later."

Mike stood as she started to leave. "It was nice visiting with you for a few minutes. It helps break up a lonely intern's long nights."

Dawn smiled to herself. "See you around," she replied as she turned to leave.

The lights were off in her apartment when Dawn returned home. She unlocked the door, turned on the entryway lights, and quietly hung up her coat. Sarah's coat was in the closet, and her schoolbooks were on the end table. She tiptoed down the hallway and opened the young girl's bedroom door. She was curled in a ball beneath a pile of blankets. *Poor thing,* Dawn thought affectionately. *Her size is probably making it uncomfortable to sleep in her customary position. She has come so far in the two weeks she's been with me. I think all she's ever needed was someone to love and care for her. . . . I wonder who the father of the child is. . . . Does he know that she's pregnant? She never talks about anyone special.*

As Dawn prepared for bed, her mind drifted back to the pleasant intern she had just met in the hospital cafeteria. A special quality about him attracted her. She could not decide if it was his warmth of personality, his youthful exuberance, or his need for human contact. From childhood, she had been constantly reminded to never judge anyone by his or her physical appearance. So she tried to push the memory of his intense blue eyes, sandy-blond hair, and handsome features from her consciousness, but they continued to haunt her as she climbed into bed and drifted off to sleep.

The next day was Saturday, and both she and Sarah had the day off. They both slept until ten o'clock that morning. Dawn was just pouring herself a cup of coffee when Sarah stumbled into the kitchen. "Morning," she mumbled. "How were things at the hospital last night?"

"Everything went well," Dawn replied, trying to focus her attention on her job and not on the well-built intern she had met in the hospital cafeteria, even though his dark blue eyes were still haunting her. "The couple has a beautiful baby girl, both mother and daughter are doing well, and the father is floating on cloud nine. That family is optimistic for a great future. I think they're already planning on her becoming the first female president."

"I wish things would go as well for me," Sarah sighed as she reached in the refrigerator for a glass of orange juice. "All I have is an unknown future, and my baby is going to be born with severe birth defects."

Dawn's heart sank. She wished that comforting words could just spew from her mouth, but instead a lump caught in her throat. "None of us knows what lies before us," she replied. "However, we can be thankful that God knows our future and will comfort and sustain us regardless of what happens."

"I wish I had the faith you have," Sarah replied as she sank into the chair across from Dawn. "I didn't even know that Christ cared for me and was concerned about my future until I met you."

"He loves you more than you could ever possibly understand, and He has a plan for you and your baby," Dawn assured her. "He will always be there to take care of you, whether you feel His presence or not."

"But my baby is going to be born with birth defects," Sarah protested. "She doesn't have much of a future, and it's all my fault. If I hadn't gotten pregnant when I did, she wouldn't have to suffer."

Dawn surveyed the troubled teen with bewilderment and concern. "Do you think God is punishing your baby for your sins?"

Sarah stared at the floor and did not speak. She finally shrugged her shoulders. "I don't know," she muttered, "but doesn't that look like what happened?"

"Sarah, God doesn't punish people for someone else's sins. Remember when we first learned of your child's disability, we explained that no one knows what causes spina bifida? Tests show that there's some sort of relationship between the lack of folic acid in a mother's diet early in pregnancy and spina bifida, but nothing yet is proven to directly cause the condition. The best explanation I can give is that it happened because it happened. God is not punishing you."

Gradually the tension began to fade from Sarah's face as she pondered what Dawn had said. "I know you're right," she replied as the corner of her lips began to turn up. "I guess I just need to be reminded from time to time when

I start feeling depressed about my circumstances."

Dawn placed her hand on the young woman's shoulder. "You can be assured that I'll keep reminding you until you quit doubting God's love for you." Dawn stood up and took her coffee cup to the sink. "Since we both have today free, let's go out for breakfast, then go to the mall. I have some Christmas shopping I'd like to finish."

"Sounds great to me," Sarah replied brightly. "I just got paid last night, and I need to do some shopping myself. I want to get a new video game for my brother. He's wanted one for a long time, but after Mom bought groceries and paid the rent, there was never any money left for anything fun."

"A new video store just opened at the far end of the mall. I haven't been in it yet, but maybe they'll have something there he'll like."

"It's worth a try," Sarah replied. Then she paused and wrinkled her forehead. A distant look came into her eyes. "Do you think I ought to get a present for Mom even though she disowned me?"

"It might be a first step toward reconciliation," Dawn replied thoughtfully. "However, don't be surprised or hurt if she doesn't reciprocate. She's going to be a tough egg to crack, but I think eventually she'll come around and accept the situation and forgive you."

Sarah started a smile, but then it quickly faded. "Sometimes I really hope so," she admitted, "but other times I just plain don't care anymore. She's hurt my feelings for so long I think I'm totally numb inside."

Dawn put her arm around her young charge and gave her a quick hug. "If you were totally numb, you wouldn't even think of giving her a gift or wanting a reconciliation. Now hurry and get your clothes on. I'm hungry."

❖

The next few days flew by for both Sarah and Dawn. At six o'clock Wednesday evening, Dawn called Sarah at work at the Pizza Parlor and left a message that another of her patients had gone into labor and she would be at the hospital until the baby was born. She was thankful that Sarah now felt comfortable in her apartment and that she could come in and make herself at home without feeling slighted if Dawn's job kept her away.

When Dawn arrived at the hospital, she found that the expectant mother was surrounded with extended family in the labor room. Her role as primary female supporter was unnecessary until the time of delivery. After visiting with the family and explaining the procedures to the expectant mother, she took her beeper to the hospital cafeteria for a late dinner. *I wish all expectant mothers could have the support this one has, but I guess not everyone can have a mother who's a registered nurse and a compassionate support,* she thought.

As Dawn was enjoying her roast beef and mashed potatoes in quiet solitude, a familiar voice seemed to appear out of nowhere. "Mind if I join you?"

Looking up, she was surprised to see Mike Archer standing at the end of her table. "Sure, have a seat," she invited warmly.

Mike sat down and arranged the dishes from his tray. "Working late again?" he asked.

"I'm waiting for the arrival of another baby," Dawn replied. "The labor room was crowded with family members, and the patient's mother is an RN, so I have an unexpected reprieve for a few minutes."

"I take it you're an OB nurse here at the hospital," he said as he strained to read her name badge.

She glanced down at her badge and blushed. "I guess there are no secrets around here," she laughed. "I'm an OB nurse, but I'm only here when Dr. Fox's patients go into labor."

"That's a unique arrangement," Mike said. "What do you do the rest of the time?"

"I work in his office," Dawn replied as she laid her fork on her plate. "We're trying a different method of patient care. I get to know the pregnant woman personally soon after she learns that she's pregnant. When she's admitted to the hospital, they call me to assist during her labor, and the doctor comes for the actual delivery. The first-time moms seem to especially appreciate having someone they already know at their side when they enter the hospital. Most have never been a patient in a hospital before, and it makes those difficult hours of labor less stressful."

Mike listened to her explanation with intense interest. "That sounds like a good idea, but don't you have a lot of downtime if it's a prolonged labor? It doesn't seem very time- and cost-effective."

"Granted, it's not," Dawn replied, "but a more compassionate labor and delivery is well worth the investment."

"Is this type of maternity care catching on in other places?"

"I'm beginning to hear of similar programs from various parts of the country," Dawn replied with a touch of pride in her voice. "We've written several articles for various medical journals, explaining the benefits from having consistent nursing care from early pregnancy through the postpartum."

The pair soon fell into natural shoptalk concerning the medical practices of the hospital. Neither one realized how fast the time had passed until Dawn's pager beeped. She turned it off and hurriedly gathered her tray. "Sorry," she explained, "but I have to run. I think we're about to have another Billings resident."

Usually Dawn was extremely involved during a delivery, but this time everything went exceptionally well for both the mother and the baby; within an hour the happy family was gathered in the mother's room, and Dawn's services were again no longer needed.

As was her custom after an evening delivery, Dawn stopped at the cafeteria for a cup of coffee before heading home. As she sat staring out the window at the Christmas decorations across the street, she couldn't help wishing that a tall blond intern would appear. She kept trying to push him out of her mind and think about her holiday plans; yet within minutes she caught herself glancing at the doorway, hoping he would appear.

Just when she was about to leave for home, Mike Archer's tall frame did appear in the doorway. She tried to pretend she was intent on gazing out the window when he approached.

"Hi, I was hoping I could catch you before you left," he greeted as he took the chair across the table from Dawn. "Did everything go all right with the delivery?"

"It couldn't have been smoother," she replied, then gave him a teasing grin. "Don't you ever have to work? You seem to be in the cafeteria every time I am."

"I was merely passing through on my way to X-ray," he laughed.

"X-ray's at the other end of the building," Dawn retorted quickly.

"Oh. . .I guess I must have gotten lost," he laughed. "But while I'm here, I actually have a day off Friday, and I was wondering if you could get that day off work as well so we could go snowmobiling at Red Lodge?"

Dawn's face flushed. With all the extra time she had worked in the last couple of months, she knew she had enough hours built up to take a day off, but that only meant she couldn't use work as an excuse. Her mind raced. Was she interested in getting to know the intern well enough to spend an entire day with him doing something she'd never done before? After a long uncomfortable pause she finally replied, "Sure, I think I can arrange the day off. . .that is. . .providing we don't have any unexpected deliveries that day."

"Great, how about if I pick you up around eight Friday morning?" Mike replied with a smile. "Remember to dress warmly. It's usually at least ten degrees colder up there."

"Boy, you sure have gotten cultured in a hurry," Dawn laughed. "You could almost become a Montana climatologist."

Mike shrugged his shoulders. "Occasionally I get to catch the evening news." He reached for Dawn's hand and gave it a quick squeeze. "I think I'd better get back to work before they miss me on the third floor. I'd hate to have my supervisor know I was down here fraternizing with a nurse."

"I thought you were on your way to X-ray," Dawn chided as Mike turned to leave.

❖

Friday dawned bright and crisp. As Mike and Dawn drove toward the lodge that provided rental snowmobiles, the snow glistened around them as if it were a picture postcard. The weather couldn't have been more perfect for a day on the snow. Just as they were renting the snowmobile, two other couples arrived and asked Mike and Dawn if they'd like to join them on the trail. Mike nodded in agreement.

After Mike started the snowmobile, Dawn got on behind him and wrapped her arms around his waist. The roar of the engine prevented conversation, but they both basked in the presence of the other as they followed the leading snowmobiles between the trees into a narrow ravine. Although she had grown up in Montana, Dawn never tired of the wide variety of panorama the state provided. As the sun shifted positions throughout the day, the countryside would continually take on different hues.

At one o'clock the invigorated snowmobilers gathered around a round wooden table in the lodge to enjoy a meal of chili and hot chocolate. One couple said they were from Idaho, and the other was from Washington. Dawn and Mike reveled in their tales of snowmobiling unknown trails, but after half an hour Dawn began to get suspicious that the tales had been growing with each telling.

However, the meal was fun, and they were back on the trail by two o'clock, with less than two and a half hours before dark. Again Dawn marveled at how fast the hours flew by as they explored the mountain trails around Red Lodge. She hadn't enjoyed the great outdoors in the winter this much since she had been in college.

❖

Sarah was up and obviously waiting when Dawn returned that night. "So how was your date with the mysterious intern?" she teased as soon as Dawn walked into the apartment.

"We had a great time," Dawn replied as she took off her boots and hung her coat in the closet. "The weather was perfect."

"Who cares about the weather!" Sarah chided. "How was Mister Tall, Blond, and Handsome?"

Dawn sunk into the deep cushions of the sofa. "He was extremely charming. However, after spending a delightful day with him, I don't feel I know him any better than I did before we left. There was no way we could talk over the roar of the engines."

"Who cares about talking when you've got your arms around a handsome hunk all day long?" Sarah teased.

Dawn tossed a throw pillow at Sarah. She didn't want to admit that she was feeling as giddy as the sixteen year old on the other end of the sofa.

Chapter 4

Sarah Brown skipped her eighth-period class and hurried six blocks to Harrison Middle School. Since she was obviously pregnant, she was certain her teacher wouldn't question her leaving school. Sarah paced back and forth in front of the school, clutching a plastic bag in her hands, waiting for the final bell to ring. The sun was shining, and the snow was beginning to melt, so she didn't mind the wait.

Suddenly a bell sounded within the building, the door burst open, and scores of students flooded out. They came in all shapes and sizes, but she was interested in a four-foot-eleven boy with shoulder-length brown hair, wearing a green tattered parka. Amid all the noise and the giggles, Sarah finally spotted her brother.

"Mark! Mark!" she shouted.

The young boy broke away from his pals and hurried toward his sister. "Hi," he greeted with a sheepish grin. "What are you doing here?"

"I came to give you your Christmas present, Goofball," she replied affectionately as she handed him the plastic bag containing two gift-wrapped packages. "There's one in there for Mom too."

Mark's eyes widened. "You mean after she treated you so terrible and disowned you, you're still going to give her a Christmas present?"

"Since I've been away, I've had a lot of time to think, and Dawn has been a big help to me," Sarah replied. "I'm willing to forgive Mom for the way she treated me before I got pregnant. I can understand why she's so upset about me being pregnant, but I refuse to get rid of my baby." Sarah touched her bulging stomach with both hands. "Even if she's going to have birth defects, she's still a part of me."

Mark shuffled nervously. "Yeah, I agree with you," he replied, trying to sound as grown-up as possible. "I wouldn't want to kill my baby either, but Mom says the baby will just be a drain on society all her life and that there are already too many people on welfare as it is." He waved to some friends passing on the other side of the street, then turned back to his sister. "What are you going to do after the baby is born? Are you going to be able to take care of her yourself? I don't know if anyone will want to adopt a handicapped baby."

Sarah's eyes became distant as a faint tear appeared in the corner of them.

"I really don't know. I try to take each day as it comes. I suppose a lot depends on how severe her condition is."

The brother and sister stood on the corner in silence, each unsure of what to say to the other. When they were living together, they had continually teased and tormented each other, but now things were different, and the minor irritations were forgotten. "I'm going to miss having you home for Christmas," Mark said softly. "What are you going to do? I hope you don't have to work that day."

"Fortunately not," Sarah laughed. "Christmas Day is one of the few days in the entire year that the Pizza Parlor is actually closed. Dawn invited me to go to her mother's in Rocky Bluff. Her father died of a heart attack last February, and this is her mom's first Christmas without him. What are you going to be doing?"

Mark burst out laughing. "Mom's invited her boyfriend over for Christmas. He's a real jerk."

"I didn't know that she had a boyfriend," Sarah replied. "I thought that after Dad left her, she was going to hate all men forever."

"I guess everything changed when she met Wayne in the laundry room of the complex. He's been over almost every night this week," Mark said. "I just stay out of his way."

"It's probably safer that way," Sarah replied as she glanced at her watch. "I better get going. I have to work on my term paper. Call me sometime."

"Sure," he replied. "See ya around."

Sarah headed south across the street, while Mark continued down Third Street. Both were swallowing the huge lump building in their throats. Life was making a radical change, and they were unsure which way it was going to lead them. When they had lived under the same roof, they often ignored each other, but since they had been apart, each was beginning to recognize the value of their family ties.

Sarah walked slowly to Dawn's apartment. This was one of the few days she was not scheduled to work at the Pizza Parlor, and she was looking forward to finishing her term paper on "The Effects of the B Vitamins on Women." Never before had she been anxious to do research on any report, but this topic was different.

When she got to the apartment, she spread her books and notecards on the dining-room table and went to the refrigerator for a soda. Usually the English teachers had assigned report topics, but this time Mrs. Tippet had let the students select their own subject. When Sarah asked for approval on the topic, she did not tell her teacher the real reason that she wanted to write on the B vitamins. She was now obviously pregnant, but Sarah had not told anyone outside the medical community that her baby had spina bifida and that some in the medical profession thought the lack of one of the B vitamins was a contributing factor in this particular birth defect.

The first draft was due in less than a week, and she had only begun to gather her information. The minutes flew by as she read and took notes on the research done on each of the particular vitamins. She intentionally left folic acid to the end. She was afraid once she started on the one that interested her most, she would never work on the others.

Sarah's eyes soon became heavy, and she laid her head on the desk and closed her eyes. Within minutes, she was asleep and didn't hear Dawn return from work until Dawn pulled out a chair across the table from where the note-cards and books were spread.

Sarah raised her head with a start. "Oh, hi," she greeted. "I didn't hear you come in."

"So I noticed," Dawn chuckled. "You were really out of it. That must be a pretty boring paper for you to be that fast asleep."

"Not really," Sarah replied. "Actually, I'm fascinated by my topic, but I've been so tired lately that I can hardly keep my eyes open, even in classes."

Hearing that, Dawn became not only friend and confident, but medical advisor. "Carrying a baby does take a heavy toll on the body," she reminded her. "Sometimes it can feel like all the energy goes to the baby and there's little left for the mother. You're seven months along now. Maybe working and going to school is becoming too hard on you."

"But I have to keep working," Sarah protested. "Otherwise I won't have money for all the little things I need."

Dawn's mind raced. She knew Sarah was right. Financial arrangements had been made to take care of her medical bills, and a local church was paying for her food, but Dawn was more than aware of the costs of cosmetics, clothing, and personal items. "Sarah, we can't let money be the guiding factor. We have to consider your health and the health of the baby first, then trust that God will provide for your daily needs. You have an appointment with Dr. Fox in a couple days. We can discuss your working with him."

The next evening, Dawn attended the women's group of her church. Before the meeting began, the treasurer asked how Sarah was getting along, and Dawn briefly explained the problem of her exhaustion. The treasurer, Jean Merical, didn't have time to respond before the president called the meeting to order. They opened with prayer, read the minutes of the last meeting, had the secretary's report, the treasurer's report, then turned to any unfinished business.

"At the last meeting there was a discussion as to where our local mission offering should go, and we tabled it for a month. However, tonight I was just made aware of a need right here in our own church," Jean Merical explained. "Many of you may already know that Dawn Harkness is caring for a pregnant teenage girl who has been disowned by her family because she refused to have an abortion. This poor girl is still attending school and working in the evenings. It's beginning to take its toll on her. I suggest that we help Sarah Brown with miscellaneous expenses until the baby comes so she will not have to keep working."

A murmur of agreement echoed around the room as each woman nodded her head in unison. The president tapped her gavel. "Would someone like to make that in the form of a motion?" she asked.

"I move that we donate two hundred dollars a month for the next three months to Sarah Brown," a gray-haired woman in the far back said loudly.

She had scarcely closed her mouth when a plump woman in a flowered dress on the other side of the room said, "I second it."

The president smiled and took a deep breath. "It's been moved and seconded to donate two hundred dollars a month to Sarah Brown. All in favor say 'aye.' "

Tears filled Dawn's eyes as a loud unison cry of "aye" filled the room. "Thank you," she murmured. "Sarah will be extremely grateful. This comes as an answer to both our prayers."

"If there is anything else we can do to help, please let us know," the president said kindly as she turned her attention back to Dawn. "Some of us are planning to put together a baby layette for her, so don't be surprised when we turn up at your doorstep."

"I'm certain Sarah will be touched," Dawn replied as her voice began to tremble. "This is a tremendous witness of God's love and forgiveness."

❖

The next two weeks flew by for Dawn and Sarah. Sarah was thankful she could return from school at three-thirty each day and no longer have to go to work at the Pizza Parlor. Fortunately, few babies were scheduled to be born in the month of December, so Dawn's weekends and evenings were full of Christmas parties and programs at the clinic, the hospital, and her church.

Three days before Christmas, Dawn was enjoying a leisurely snack in the hospital cafeteria when Mike appeared beside her table. "I was wondering if you'd ever return," he greeted cheerfully. "I've been wanting to call and see how you were doing, but they've kept me so busy here that by the time I was free you would probably have been in bed. Every time I was close to the cafeteria, I always stopped to see if you were here, but to no avail."

"I just finished my first delivery for this month," Dawn replied as she motioned him to take the chair across the table.

"My thanks to the mother who brought you here," he laughed. He reached across the table and took her hand. "How have you been doing? I've really missed not seeing you since our great snowmobiling adventure."

"I've been doing great," Dawn replied. "This year I've had enough time to enjoy Christmas, and having a teenager around has definitely been an exciting experience. I never know what's going to happen next."

"So how has Sarah been doing? Isn't that baby due pretty soon?" Mike asked.

"She's doing great," Dawn replied. "The baby's due in the first part of February, so we're in the downhill stretch. But going to school and working got to be too much for her."

"You don't think she would have been better off having an abortion? After all, her child is bound to be disabled. Where's the money going to come from to support them?"

"For now, the women of my church are donating enough money to meet Sarah's incidental expenses, so she was able to quit work," Dawn answered. "That was a real answer to prayer. And I'm sure God will provide in the future."

The corner of Mike's lips twitched upward. "Spending so much money and medical resources on a child with severe defects seems like such a waste. You don't actually believe that prayer is anything more than wishful thinking, do you?"

Dawn's face became stern. "As a matter of fact, I do," she replied. "My grandmother was a true prayer warrior, and I saw a great many things happen that I'm sure wouldn't have if she hadn't been praying. Don't ever underestimate the power of God. Each life is precious to Him."

"I guess if prayer gives you some comfort and peace of mind, it's worth something," Mike replied dryly. "As for me. . .I'm so independent and strong enough that I don't need an emotional crutch to get through life."

Dawn shook her head. "I only wish you knew how much you're missing out on," she sighed. "Faith and belief in God give meaning and purpose to life. Without that it would be an 'eat, drink, and be merry for tomorrow we die' lifestyle. Personally, I'd like to think my life was counting for something."

Mike laughed uncomfortably. "I'm a doctor and will heal a lot of people throughout my lifetime. Won't that count for something?"

Dawn hesitated and took a deep breath. "Not much. You can only treat the body; God is the one who heals the body. However, the deeper concern is—who heals the human spirit?"

Mike heaved a sigh of frustration. "This is sure getting to be a pretty heavy discussion. I think the Christmas spirit has really gotten to you," he said as he stood to leave. "I'd love to continue this philosophical discussion, but I've got to get back to work. I hope to see you again before the holidays."

Dawn shook her head. "I doubt it. Sarah and I are leaving for Rocky Bluff the day after tomorrow. If I don't see you before then, have a blessed Christmas."

"Thanks. . .you too. . . Have a nice trip," Mike said as he headed toward the doorway shaking his head.

Dawn immediately disqualified Mike from a deeper friendship and turned her attention to the coming holidays. Regardless of how independent she had become, she always loved returning to Rocky Bluff and the people who had meant so much to her throughout her growing-up years. Her mother thrived on entertaining scores of people for several days at a time, but this was the first Christmas since her father died. She knew he would be sorely missed when the family came together for their Christmas reunion.

Her aunt Jean and uncle Jim always came with their three teenagers. Dawn's brother, Jay, and his Guamanian wife, Angie, would be there with their three little ones; and Angie's mother, Mitzi Quinata, was always included in the Harkness family reunions. Mitzi had retired from teaching in her native island of Guam and had moved to Rocky Bluff to be close to her daughter and grandchildren.

The day before Christmas, Dawn and Sarah packed their car and headed west, then north. The distant mountain peaks seemed to be beckoning them onward. For many miles both women sat lost in their own thoughts. Finally, Dawn broke the silence. "You're extraordinarily quiet. Is something troubling you?"

"Not really," Sarah replied softly. "I was just trying to imagine what next Christmas might be like—and I haven't a clue. I'll be the mother preparing for Christmas instead of having Christmas festivities planned for me."

"This is a major turning point in your life," Dawn replied. "It's just coming to you a few years earlier than most young people, so you'll have to accept it and move on."

"I've accepted the fact that in a couple months I'll never be able to do crazy teenage things again. Now I'm just trying to learn to take each day as it comes, but I'm not doing that very successfully." Sarah watched the snow-covered fields fly by the window of the car for several more miles. Finally, she laughed. "I gave you the reason for my silence. Now, what's yours? Could it be that handsome intern you've been seeing? Whatever happened to him? I haven't heard you talk about him lately."

Dawn glanced at the young woman beside her. Her eyes were young and eager, and yet they held a depth of wisdom that had not been there a few months before. "Boy, you're the insightful one." She paused, wondering how much to confide in a teenager. "To tell you the truth, I haven't thought about him in awhile. Although he was a lot of fun to be around, I discovered we don't share the same values. He sees prayer and faith in God as mere crutches for the weak instead of a source of strength for the believer. That is so sad. Sooner or later, he's going to come upon a situation that's bigger than himself, and he's not going to know where to go for help."

"Three months ago, I would have said you were crazy to let such a well-built hunk get away, but now I'm beginning to see how important it is to have faith in God." Sarah's eyes began to twinkle mischievously. "Dawn, you're not getting any younger. Aren't you concerned about finding a guy and getting married?"

Dawn shook her head and smiled. "Sure, I'd like to get married someday, but if it's not in God's plan, then I'm perfectly happy doing what I'm doing. I love being with the young families as they welcome a new addition into the world. I'm a firm believer that no man at all is better than marrying the wrong man."

Sarah's eyes widened. "I never thought about it like that, but I guess you're right. I think I'm going to have to develop that same philosophy because most guys aren't interested in girls that already have had someone else's baby. . .especially a disabled one."

"Have no fear," Dawn assured her. "The Lord has a plan for your life, and it's going to be fun to see how it develops throughout the coming years."

❖

The pair settled into casual small talk and enjoyed the country music on the radio until Dawn stopped her car in her mother's driveway. They had barely stepped from the car when her mother burst through the front door and immediately immersed her daughter with a warm greeting and embrace. When her mother released her, Dawn said, "Mom, I'd like you to meet Sarah Brown. She's the one who's been living with me for the last few weeks. She's been a real joy to have around."

"Welcome, Sarah," Nancy Harkness said as she extended her hand. "I've heard so many good things about you. I'm glad I finally get to meet you."

"I appreciate you inviting me here for Christmas," Sarah replied. "I wasn't looking forward to spending the holidays by myself."

Nancy put her arm around Sarah's shoulder as they walked up the sidewalk to the front door. "Oh, we'd never permit that. Please consider our home as your own," she said as she opened the front door. Nancy turned her attention back to her daughter. "I hope you don't mind, but I've invited several extras to share Christmas with us."

"The more the merrier," Dawn replied. "Who's coming?"

"Larry Reynolds has been a real jewel, managing the Running Butte store since Jean and Jim moved to Rocky Bluff and took over your dad's store. We just wanted to do something extraspecial for them. They're such a delightful family. Did you know they now have four children?"

"I think I lost track of his family after they had their second one," Dawn replied with a giggle. "They should have a lot of fun with Jay's kids. They've got to be about the same ages."

Nancy smiled as she opened the hall closet and took out two hangers. "It'll be a lot of fun to have so many little ones around for Christmas." She hung up first Sarah's coat, then Dawn's. "Oh, by the way. . .Larry's brother Ryan is here visiting him for the holidays, so I included him in the invitation. I hope that's okay with you?"

Sarah snickered as Dawn winked at her. "Mother, whoever you invite will be fine with me."

Chapter 5

More presents?" six-year-old Edith Harkness squealed as she entered her grandmother's living room on Christmas morning. "There were so many under our tree at home this morning, and now there's even more at Grandma's."

"Well, of course we have presents here for you." Nancy smiled as she gave her granddaughter a hug. "You don't think we'd forget to have a gift for you and everyone else in the family, do you?"

"We brought something special just for you, but I'm not going to tell you what it is," the little girl teased as her dad set a box of gifts under the tree.

Little Edith glanced around the room crowded with family and friends. Her eyes widened. "Aunt Dawn," she exclaimed as she ran over and gave her a hug. "I'm glad you're here because I want to see your face when you open your present. Daddy had a lot of fun picking out your gift."

"I'm sure he did." Dawn laughed as she looked over at her brother, who had a mischievous grin on his face.

"Jay, what kind of a gag gift did you get me this year?" she teased. "I don't think you could possibly top what you did last Christmas."

"I'll never tell," Jay chuckled. "I hope you didn't get me another pair of silk underwear with the Christmas Chipmunks on it. Don't tell anyone, but today was the first time I've ever worn them because I didn't want you to think I was unappreciative."

Dawn's eyes continued to twinkle as she gave her brother a quick hug. "Oh, that was nothing. I found an even better gift this year. Promise me that you'll wear it!"

"We'll see," Jay said as he turned his attention toward his mother, who was taking the snowsuit off his nine-month-old son. "Mom, did you say you invited Larry Reynolds and his family for dinner?"

"They're planning to come about noon," Nancy replied as she sat little Brandon on the floor, then turned her full attention to her own son. "I don't think I've talked to you since I last heard from Libby. She called a couple days ago and said that Ryan was planning to spend Christmas with them, so I asked them to bring him along."

"Great," Jay exclaimed. "I can't remember when I saw him last. I don't even know where he's living now or if he ever got married."

"He's living in Butte and traveling the Northwest selling medical supplies," Dawn replied matter-of-factly, "and, no, he's not married."

Jay's eyes widened, then a twinkle began to brighten them. "Now, how did you know all that if you're living in Billings? Is there something you're not telling your big brother?"

"He came by our clinic a couple weeks ago selling his new line of products," Dawn replied. "We were both surprised to see each other, so he invited me out for dinner. It was fun catching up on old news, but it was no big deal."

"If it was no big deal, why are you blushing?" her brother continued to tease. "Don't you know that I've always been able to read you like a book ever since you were a little kid?"

Dawn shook her head in mock disgust as she knelt on the floor to play with little Brandon. The conversation with her brother was going nowhere fast.

Within a few minutes her aunt Jean, uncle Jim, and their three teenagers noisily filled the living room, and half an hour later the Reynoldses arrived. After greetings had been exchanged, everyone gathered in a circle in the kitchen. Nancy Harkness had been cooking for days, preparing for the gala event, and the table and counters were laden with food.

Since his father's death, Jay had taken over the role of asking the blessing at all the family gatherings. This was their first Christmas that Robert Harkness had not been with them, but everyone treasured the memories they had of him and refused to dwell on their loss. After the prayer, everyone filled their plates and scattered throughout the kitchen and living room, sitting at card tables, the sofa with TV trays, or just balancing their plates on their lap.

Shy Angie immediately found a common bond with even shyer Sarah, and the two spent hours discussing babies and children. The afternoon passed quickly. After Christmas dinner, gifts were exchanged with much fanfare and celebration. All day the room was filled with voices and laughter.

Dawn and Ryan sat across the room from each other, and although all their comments were addressed to the entire group, occasionally their eyes met. The desire to be alone with him rose inexplicably within Dawn. She tried to hide her feelings so she could avoid her brother's teasing, but without success. Jay knew her too well and throughout the afternoon plagued her with knowing looks and winks in Ryan's direction.

Amidst all the gaiety, no one noticed how quiet Sarah had become, until she let out a faint moan and held her stomach.

"Sarah, what's wrong?" Dawn asked as she surveyed the tension lines on the young girl's face.

"I'm just having some stomach pains, and I have a dreadful headache," the teenager murmured, "but I'll be all right."

"Why don't you go lie down in the guest bedroom, and I'll be in and check you. I have to get my blood pressure cuff from the car," Dawn directed as she hurried to the coat closet to retrieve her jacket. A concerned expression crossed the nurse's face as she stepped into the cold December air. *I hadn't noticed until just now, but Sarah's face and hands seem terribly swollen. I hope she's not retaining fluids. We could be in real trouble if she is.*

A few moments later, Dawn was leaning over the pregnant girl and inflating the blood pressure cuff around Sarah's arm. She watched the needle on the dial come down. "Oh, that can't be right," Dawn exclaimed with frustration. "Let me do this again."

Once more Dawn tightened the blood pressure cuff around Sarah's arm and watched the needle descend. "It looks like it's one hundred and eighty over one hundred," she murmured.

A look of sweet innocence spread across Sarah's face as she looked up at Dawn. "Is that bad?"

"It could be very serious," Dawn warned. "I think I'd better take you up to the hospital emergency room and have a doctor check you over."

"Is the baby coming now? It's not due until February."

"I don't think so," the nurse tried to assure her, "but it could be what is known as preeclampsia. It happens when your blood pressure rises late in a pregnancy, while at the same time poisons build up in your body." Dawn reached out her hand to help Sarah to her feet. "Come along, and I'll help you with your coat."

As the pair approached the living room all eyes turned toward them. "You'll have to excuse us," Dawn explained as she opened the closet door. "I need to run Sarah to the emergency room."

Ryan bounded to his feet. "I'll go with you," he exclaimed. "It can be a long lonely wait for both of you."

Dawn gave a dry smile. "That it could be," she replied. "I doubt they have many people working Christmas Day."

Dawn drove the familiar path toward Rocky Bluff Community Hospital with Ryan beside her and Sarah lying in the backseat. Dawn had spent many hours at the hospital while she was growing up. Her grandmother suffered from a severe heart condition for over fifteen years before she passed away and was a patient at the hospital numerous times. Dawn's stepgrandfather, Roy Dutton, had been a patient at the adjacent nursing home for a year before he died. More recently, her father spent a couple of days in the hospital before he passed away.

Dawn stopped the car at the entrance of the emergency room and found an attendant who got a wheelchair and pushed Sarah from the car to an examining room. Just as Dawn had suspected, only a skeleton crew was on duty when they arrived. The head nurse immediately called Dr. Brewer, who arrived within fifteen minutes. Ryan read magazines in the waiting room, while Dawn stayed at Sarah's side and explained the pregnant girl's medical background and symptoms to the doctor. Within minutes, the doctor diagnosed pre-eclampsia and admitted Sarah to the hospital.

Sarah cried softly as they pushed her gurney into a hospital room. Dawn and Ryan stayed with Sarah in her room for several hours, trying to explain the health risks of her condition and trying to reassure her that God loved her and her unborn child, and that He would be with them both during this difficult time. Gradually, Sarah began to relax, and around nine o'clock she fell asleep. Dawn and Ryan tiptoed from the room and headed toward the nearest exit.

The cold winter wind bit at their cheeks as they both wrapped their scarves tighter around their necks. "I'd like to go someplace and get a cup of coffee and a piece of pie, but I don't think any restaurant in Rocky Bluff will be open Christmas night," Ryan said as they walked across the freshly plowed parking lot.

"One of the disadvantages of a small town," Dawn replied lightly. "I bet the restaurants in Billings are doing a booming business tonight."

"How about driving around and looking at the Christmas lights?" Ryan suggested. "The new subdivision on the west end of town used to go all out competing with each other for the best decorations in Rocky Bluff."

Dawn's face brightened. "That sounds like fun," she replied. "I'm glad you called Mother and told her that we would be late—and I'm glad she offered you Jay's old bedroom for the night. I didn't know what to do since it was getting late and your brother needed to get the little ones home to bed."

Ryan became pensive for a moment. "I hope I'm not imposing too much on your mother. She had a hectic day entertaining so many people for Christmas dinner."

"Mom loved every minute of it," Dawn assured him. "She also loves over-night guests. Now that she's rattling around in that big house by herself, she's the first one to offer a bed to anyone who gets snowbound and can't get out of Rocky Bluff for the night."

"But I feel like I'm imposing on both her and you," Ryan continued to protest. "However, Larry offered to come back and get me first thing in the morning, so I'll try not to be too much of an inconvenience."

Dawn laughed. "How many times must I remind you that Mother enjoys having guests," she stated firmly. "She's always opening her home to people who get stranded in Rocky Bluff during snowstorms. She feels like that house is just too big for her to be there by herself."

"I really appreciate the offer," Ryan smiled. "She truly has a great gift of hospitality."

Dawn turned her car west out of the hospital parking lot. All the homes in the area were aglow with Christmas lights. "If there were to be an inconvenience, it would be that Larry would have to come back to Rocky Bluff to get you," she noted as she admired the brilliant lights around her. She hesitated and then said, "I don't want Larry to take time off work to make an extra trip from Running Butte. I can drive you there first thing in the morning, if you'd like."

"Sounds good to me." Ryan smiled as he admired the decorations along the tree-lined streets. "Since I'm going to be in Rocky Bluff tomorrow, I'd like to meet with Pastor Olson, if it's at all possible. I've never officially met him, but we've corresponded several times concerning the statewide Right-to-Life movement. I heard rumors that there's a big project being planned, but I don't know what it is." He paused a moment as his mind returned to the frightened teenager lying in the hospital bed. "Also, I'm sure he'd be extremely interested in Sarah and her dilemma."

Dawn nodded her head. "That sounds like a good idea. If he's available, would you mind if I tagged along? I've always been interested in the Right-to-Life movement, but I've never had time to become actively involved."

Ryan looked over at the attractive blond-haired woman seated beside him. The glow from the streetlights added an extra radiance to her. For many years, he had enjoyed traveling, seeing different places, and meeting hundreds of people, but suddenly he realized how much he had missed having female companionship. "Please do," he encouraged. "Your input could be invaluable."

A faint grin appeared on Dawn's face. "I don't know about that," she replied, "but when I was in college and having serious personal problems, Pastor Olson and his wife Teresa helped me a great deal. In fact, I don't know where I'd be today if it weren't for them. The way I was headed, I'd probably be dead by now."

A look of shock crossed Ryan's face. "I can't imagine sweet, innocent you having been involved in anything that serious," he replied as he remembered the bubbly little sister of his high school best friend. She had always seemed to be at her mother's side helping her. He remembered how at times he and Jay had teased her until she was almost in tears, then would do something extra nice to her and disappear, leaving her totally confused. Life seemed so simple then compared with today.

"You and your entire family have been the strength and model for this entire community for at least three generations," Ryan insisted. "I'll never forget how your grandmother and your dad kept helping and loving Larry, in spite of all the stupid things he did as a teenager. They were the ones who turned *his* life around."

Dawn remained silent as Ryan placed his arm on her shoulder as she propelled her car through the brightly lit new housing subdivision. They marveled at the colorful displays and wondered how much the neighborhood families had expended in order to provide such a brilliant panorama of Christmas lights and decorations.

"I'm afraid that during my older teen years I became more like your brother Larry than my grandmother," Dawn confessed. "To be honest, I became the prodigal daughter in the family."

Ryan shook his head. "That's hard for me to imagine, seeing what you have become today."

The Christmas music on the car radio played softly in the background as Dawn carefully chose her words. Only recently, she had made peace with that time in her life and could now talk about her troubled days freely. "When I went away to college, I wasn't prepared for all the temptations of independent living," she explained softly. "It didn't take long for me to get involved with the wrong crowd and begin drinking heavily and using drugs. To make a long story short, I ended up going through the drug rehab program in Billings, then returning to Rocky Bluff for six months. It was during that time that Pastor Olson and his then-fiancée, Teresa, took me under their wing and directed me down the right path. I was so inspired by their compassion that I wanted to be able to share with others some of the love they shared with me. I then decided to go into nursing. I guess the rest is history."

Ryan patted Dawn's shoulder affectionately. They both realized they were becoming more interested in their conversation and in the presence of the other than in the beauty of their holiday surroundings. "That explains why you were so willing to have Sarah come and live with you when she had no place to go," he said. "I marvel at the inner strength of those who are able to admit their mistakes and completely change so they can lead a productive life from that point onward."

Dawn smiled and shook her head. "It was no great thing I did," she replied softly. "No one has enough inner strength to change their lives. Only God can bring about such a change for those who are willing."

"Spoken like a true woman of faith," Ryan noted with admiration. He remained silent until they approached the end of a street, then glanced at his watch. "It's getting late," he sighed. "I suppose we should be heading back."

Dawn made a wide U-turn at the end of the street. "Mother always stays up and watches the evening news. Maybe we can spend a few minutes with her before she retires. I'm sure she's anxious to learn the details about Sarah's condition."

❖

The next morning, Ryan arose long before Dawn. He found Nancy sitting at the kitchen table reading the morning newspaper while she sipped her coffee. "Good morning," he greeted.

"Good morning, Ryan," she replied, laying the paper beside her plate. "Can I interest you in a cup of coffee while I fix you some breakfast?"

"Coffee will be fine, but don't go to any trouble about breakfast. Cold cereal and milk is my usual fare. I'd like to give Pastor Olson a call and see if he's available to meet with Dawn and me before she takes me back to Running Butte," Ryan explained, while Nancy raised her eyebrows quizzically. The young man smiled to himself and continued. "He and his wife have been active in the Right-to-Life movement, and I'd like to begin coordinating activities with them. I'm often the one who transports materials and information from city to city since I'm on the road anyway for my business."

Nancy reached into the refrigerator for a carton of milk. "I think he's usually in his office by nine every morning," she said, "if you'd like to call him now."

Ryan glanced at his watch, then stepped to the telephone while the older woman set the table for him and Dawn. Pastor Olson answered the telephone on the first ring, and within minutes, he suggested that they meet with him and Teresa at 10:30 that morning.

Ryan turned his attention back to his hostess and the quick breakfast she had set before him. The pair engaged in a lively conversation over the political events in the morning paper, while the young man enjoyed two bowls of cereal, a cup of coffee, and a glass of juice. Nancy would have preferred having the opportunity to fix a large breakfast of bacon, eggs, and hashed brown potatoes, like she was accustomed to when her husband was alive, but she readily understood that many, like her daughter, were light breakfast eaters.

Just as Ryan was taking his last sip of coffee, Dawn entered the kitchen dressed in a red-and-black sweater and jeans. Her blond hair was held back by a matching red band. Ryan beamed.

"Good morning," she greeted with a smile. "I'm sorry I slept so late. I hadn't realized how tired I was until I hit the pillow last night. Has anyone heard from the hospital this morning?"

"The phone hasn't rung," Nancy replied as she poured her daughter a cup of coffee and moved the cereal and milk across the table to her.

Dawn poured the cereal into her bowl. "Hopefully, no news is good news," she said as she reached for the milk. "After I have a quick bite to eat, maybe I should go to the hospital and check on Sarah. Would either of you like to come with me?"

"I'd love to," Ryan replied. "However, I made an appointment for us to meet with Pastor Olson and Teresa at ten-thirty. Maybe I should change the time?"

"That's okay," Dawn assured him. "We may not need to stay at the hospital long. Hopefully they'll dismiss her sometime today." Dawn turned her attention to her mother. "Mom, would you like to come with us? We shouldn't be there long."

Nancy shook her head. She had been noticing the unspoken signals between the two and felt it better to let nature take its course without her presence. "Thanks for asking, but you two run on ahead. You have a lot to get done today."

❧

Twenty minutes later, Dawn and Ryan walked into the hospital and approached the nurses' desk close to Sarah's room. Dawn introduced herself to the nurse on duty and asked about Sarah's condition.

"The doctor just left," the nurse responded matter-of-factly. "Sarah rested comfortably last night, but her blood pressure is still elevated. He wants to keep her here on strict bed rest until he sees signs of improvement. I'm sure she'd like to see you. She's already starting to get bored."

"Thanks for your information," Dawn said, trying to get a smile from the tired nurse. "I think you have my mother's telephone number. Would you call if there's any change in her condition?"

"Yes, we have it on file along with the telephone number of her regular doctor in Billings," the nurse replied politely. "If there's any change, we'll call you right away."

The pair turned and hurried toward the open door a few yards away. Sarah's face broke into a broad smile when she saw Dawn and Ryan in the doorway. "Boy, am I glad to see you," she exclaimed with glee. "I hadn't realized that daytime television was this boring."

"Daytime TV has never been known for it's high intellectual content." Ryan laughed as he took a chair at the side of the bed.

"I'll tell you what," Dawn promised, squeezing the young girl's hand in greeting. "This afternoon I'll go downtown and find you some handicrafts and books to occupy your time. Do you like to do latch hook pillows or embroidery?"

Sarah shrugged her shoulders with resignation. "I'd try anything. The doctor says I'm going to have to stay flat on my back until my blood pressure is down, so I could be here a long while." Not wanting to sound like a whiner, she continued, "There's one good thing—at least my headache went away."

"I'm glad to hear that," Dawn replied sympathetically. "You were feeling pretty low when we brought you in last night."

The three talked and laughed together for half an hour before Dawn looked at her watch. "We're going to have to leave in a few minutes," she said, "but I'll be back late this afternoon or early evening with something for you to do. We have an appointment to meet with Pastor Olson and his wife at ten-thirty. They both have been working in the Right-to-Life movement, and they want to discuss coordinating some of their projects."

Sarah's eyes became sad and distant. "Good for them," she replied. "I wish there were more people out there who could convince people like my mother that my baby has a right to live, even if she'll be disabled."

Chapter 6

Dawn, it's good to see you again," Pastor Olson greeted as Ryan Reynolds and Dawn Harkness stepped into the church study.

"Pastor Olson, this is Ryan Reynolds," said Dawn. "He's an old friend, formerly of Rocky Bluff."

"I'm glad to finally meet you, Ryan," the pastor said as he extended his hand. "I've heard so much about you. I understand you and Jay were close friends in high school," the pastor noted. "How long has it been since you've seen Jay?"

Ryan shrugged his shoulders as he tried to do mental calculations. "I can't remember for sure," he replied, "but it's been several years. I only met Angie a couple of times right after he was discharged from the Air Force. He certainly found a nice wife while he was in Guam."

"Angie is an extremely caring person," Pastor Olson nodded. "And now that her mother has moved to Montana to be close to her grandchildren, it's been a real treat for everyone."

"How does she like Rocky Bluff?" Ryan asked, as he remembered the attractive, middle-aged Guamanian with whom he had shared Christmas. "It's a far cry from Guam."

Pastor Olson smiled. "When Mitzi moved to Rocky Bluff, I questioned whether she would last through the first winter or not. However, she immediately fit right in and dearly loves it now. She and Angie have both been such an asset to the church."

The pastor turned his attention to the young woman beside Ryan. "Dawn, it's good to see you again. Teresa will be here anytime. She's very excited to get to see you, but she had some critical errands she had to run."

Dawn's eyes twinkled. "I can hardly wait to see her again. I've been so busy lately that I haven't been taking the time to write or call those who've meant so much to me over the years."

Just then, footsteps were heard in the hallway, and the door of the church study opened. Teresa Olson entered, flushed from the biting cold outside. "I'm sorry I'm late. There was a fender bender on Main Street, and it slowed traffic for over ten minutes," she said without taking a breath. She looked at Dawn, beamed, and hurried to embrace her. "Dawn, it's great to see you again. We have so much catching up to do."

"I was hoping we could get together sometime during Christmas," Dawn said as she hugged her old friend, "but I was afraid you'd be so involved with Christmas activities that you wouldn't have the time."

"I would always make time for you," Teresa assured her, then turned to Ryan and extended her hand. "Ryan, I'm glad you could come. We've heard a lot about your work with the Right-to-Life movement and are anxious to learn more of what's going on in your area."

Pastor Olson motioned to a green sofa against the wall. "Please make yourselves comfortable. We have a lot to talk about."

Dawn sat on the end of the sofa and scarcely noticed that Ryan was sitting as close to her as possible. He was no longer merely her older brother's high school best friend, but a friend of hers as well. Ryan turned his attention to the pastor. "What are some of the changes you see happening in the Montana Right-to-Life movement?" he queried.

The pastor leaned back in his chair and folded his hands behind his head. "This is quite an exciting time for us," he began with a smile. "We hope to reopen the Billings Crisis Pregnancy Center. It was open for several years but then had to close due to lack of support and poor management. During the time it was closed, the Abortion Rights movement mushroomed in that city. We learned lots from that experience, and we want to reopen the center as soon as possible. The center has a great potential for ministry to unwed mothers. If it's a success, we plan to open another in Great Falls."

"Speaking as one who works with pregnant women every day, I can say a crisis pregnancy center is definitely needed in Billings," Dawn exclaimed with intensity. "What kind of services will it offer?"

"The list is growing every day," the pastor replied. "So far, we plan for the clinic to provide free pregnancy tests, peer counseling on abstinence, abortion alternatives, parenting, and postabortion trauma counseling. Maternity and baby clothes, baby furniture, and other items will be offered free of charge to women in need. Referral services and extended family housing through shepherding homes may also be offered when the need arises. However, they will not hand out contraceptives like some women's clinics do."

As soon as her husband took a breath, Teresa added, "The center will try to encourage young women and provide information for them on what a healthy relationship is so they can work toward a good marriage. Sadly, so many young girls don't know the difference between sex and love."

With each word, Dawn's smile became broader. "I wish one had been opened in Billings a couple of months ago. Sarah could have made good use of it."

Pastor Olson leaned forward in his chair. "Who's Sarah? Is that someone I should know?"

Dawn and Ryan exchanged quick glances. "That's a long story and one of the reasons why we came," Dawn replied. "To start at the beginning. . .a little over a month ago, a sixteen-year-old unwed pregnant girl came into the office where I work. When we took an ultrasound, we found that the baby's spinal column did not close. The baby will be disabled all her life."

Concern spread across Teresa's face as she shook her head sadly. "That's hard enough for a married couple. How is the poor girl going to manage? I hope her family stands behind her."

"A baby with spina bifida is only the beginning of her problems," Dawn explained. "When her mother learned she was pregnant with a child who'd have birth defects, she kicked her daughter out of her house until she got an abortion. Sarah refused to have an abortion and has been living with me for the last few weeks."

Pastor Olson's face remained somber. "How tragic. I hope I'll be able to meet her someday and let her know how proud I am that she was willing to do what was right regardless of the personal pain involved."

"You can." Dawn laughed with a tone of bittersweet sadness in her voice. "I brought her to Rocky Bluff with me for Christmas, but last night she started having problems, and I had to take her to the emergency room. It turned out to be preeclampsia, so Dr. Brewer is going to keep her in the hospital until her blood pressure comes down. She's very upset about being bedridden. It's hard to keep a healthy girl flat on her back."

"Teresa and I will go visit her this afternoon and see what we can do to encourage her," the pastor promised as he glanced at his wife for approval.

"I'm sure she'll appreciate any visitors she can get," Dawn replied. "I just hope she'll be out of the hospital in a couple days, because I have to leave the day after tomorrow to go back to work."

Teresa's compassion for young women in trouble surfaced. "Don't worry about having to leave her behind. If she's not out of the hospital by then, we'll take good care of her," she promised. "Our women's group can adopt her as one of their projects. I'm sure Rebecca Hatfield will be excited to help. Ever since she retired from being high school librarian, she's always looking for ways to stay in contact with young people."

Ryan thought back to his high school days and the librarian who retired to take a two-year assignment to automate a school library on Guam. While she was there, she had a long-distance romance with the Rocky Bluff fire chief, Andy Hatfield, and married him as soon as she returned to the mainland. "I know Sarah would love Rebecca as much as we all did when we were in high school," Ryan said. "She always had a special knack of helping everyone work through their problems."

The four remained in conversation until Teresa glanced at her watch. She looked at her husband, then the couple seated on the green sofa. "It's been great seeing you both, but I imagine everyone's getting hungry. How about joining us for lunch at the Family Fare Restaurant?" she asked.

Ryan and Dawn exchanged questioning looks. Dawn nodded her head while Ryan said, "Dawn was going to drive me back to Larry's home in Running Butte today, but if we get on the road right after lunch, she'll have plenty of time to get there and back before dark."

"Great," Pastor Olson said as he rose to his feet. "We'll meet you both at the Family Fare in fifteen minutes."

❖

That afternoon Dawn and Ryan reveled in their time alone together and admired the snow-covered landscape around them as they drove toward Running Butte. The mountains in the distance looked as if they were ready to be captured on a picture postcard.

"Dawn, it's meant so much to me to get to share Christmas with you," Ryan said as they approached the turnoff to Running Butte. "I'm going to be leaving for Missoula in the morning, and I don't know when I'll be in Billings so we can see each other again." His voice began to crack as he continued. "I'll call you every few days and see how things are going with you and how Sarah is doing. I can only hope and pray for the best for her. She's a mighty brave gal."

Dawn nodded her head as a lump built in her throat. "That she is," she replied. "I just hope I can take her back to Billings with me when I go. This morning she looked so sad lying there in a hospital bed in a strange town."

When the pair arrived at Larry and Libby's home, Libby immediately invited Dawn inside. After a quick cup of coffee and cookies to warm her, Dawn thanked the couple for their kindness and headed toward her car. Ryan walked beside her and unconsciously his hand slipped into hers. "I'm going to miss you," he said as they reached the car. "You're making it very hard for me to go back on the road. I'm beginning to question if I'm really a 'traveling man' after all."

He leaned over and took Dawn's face in his hands. Their eyes met as they simultaneously moved toward each other until their lips touched. Dawn closed her eyes as she melted in the warmth of his kiss.

Tears filled her eyes as she said good-bye. Her well-organized, disciplined life seemed to be coming apart around her.

During the uneventful trip back to Rocky Bluff, Dawn tried to sing along with the local country western radio station, but her mind kept drifting back to her last glimpse of Ryan Reynolds as he stood in front of his brother's home waving at her. Why had she let herself become so busy with her own career that she had lost touch with such an important person from her youth? She promised herself from then on to treasure each friendship as if it were the only one she would ever have.

Upon arriving back in Rocky Bluff, Dawn went immediately to the local discount store. She worked her way through the crowd of after-Christmas bargain hunters and went directly to the craft section. Digging through an array of Christmas crafts that were now half price, she tried to find the most suitable for Sarah. Finally, locating an embroidery kit of baby bibs and a latch hook kit of a kitten that could be made into a pillow, she then went to the front of the store and scoured the shelves for a suitable mystery novel and a magazine of crossword puzzles. She found a brightly colored mylar balloon and joined the long line of postholiday shoppers at the check stand. *I hope Sarah hasn't been too lonely and depressed today while I was gone. I have been gone a lot longer than I expected,* she thought as she greeted the tired checker.

When she entered the young woman's hospital room, Dawn realized that she needn't have worried about Sarah's loneliness. She was confronted by a huge array of flowers and balloons. "Where did these come from?" Dawn exclaimed as she leaned over to hug Sarah who lay on her bed, surrounded by two stuffed animals.

"I've had so much company today I couldn't believe it," Sarah replied brightly. "First, Pastor Olson and Teresa came and brought me the flowers on the nightstand. Then your mom came with your aunt Jean. They were terrific. They brought me the stuffed monkey. They weren't gone more than fifteen minutes when Rebecca Hatfield came with the bouquet of balloons. She said she was the high school librarian when you were in school. Do you remember her?"

Dawn smiled as she pulled a chair close to the bed. "Oh yes, she was one of my favorites," she replied as she examined the cards on two more bouquets. "Who brought you these? I don't recognize any of the names."

"Those were from the kids in the church youth group. Four kids from the church came with balloons and the stuffed lion." Sarah hugged the lion before she continued. "I can't believe how good the people of Rocky Bluff have been to me. And they don't even know me."

Dawn beamed. "There are a pretty wonderful bunch of people here." Dawn became more serious. "Has the doctor stopped to see you since this morning?"

Sarah shook her head. "Not yet," she replied. "I hope he'll let me out of here soon. In spite of how good everyone has been to me, I don't like just lying around."

"I'm glad he hasn't come yet, because I have a couple questions that I'd like to ask him," Dawn said, then handed Sarah the sack from the discount store. "By the way, I brought you some handicrafts to help pass the time. I hope they're activities that you like to do."

Sarah's eyes sparkled as she pulled each item out one at a time. "They're perfect. I definitely won't be able to complain that I'm bored anymore, will I?" she laughed.

"I'm afraid not," Dawn replied as Sarah opened her embroidery kit and began reading through the directions. Every once in awhile, she asked Dawn to help her interpret an unfamiliar stitch.

An hour passed before Dr. Brewer appeared. He greeted the patient and her older friend. Suddenly, a smile spread across his face. "Why, you must be Nancy Harkness's daughter. I think I was the one who brought you into the world."

"That I am," Dawn replied with a smile. "You were the one who took care of all my childhood diseases and dreaded inoculations as well."

"It makes me feel mighty old to see you all grown up now," Dr. Brewer responded with a chuckle. "In fact, this young lady will be one of my last patients, as I'm planning on retiring and moving to Arizona this spring."

The aging doctor read Sarah's chart with great interest. He did a quick exam, then asked her how she was doing.

"I'm doing great," she responded eagerly. "When can I go home?"

The doctor shook his head. "Your blood pressure is down a little, but it's still plenty high, and tests showed that protein was in your urine. I want to keep you here for at least a couple more days."

"But Dawn has to go back to Billings the day after tomorrow, and I don't know what I'll do if I can't go back with her," Sarah protested.

"We'll have to see how you progress tomorrow," the doctor replied reassuringly. "That will give me time to talk with your doctor in Billings to make sure he is aware of what's happened here. At this stage of your pregnancy, it's important you have consistent care."

"If I can go back to Billings with Dawn, I promise I'll take it easy," Sarah begged.

"All I can say is that we'll see what tomorrow brings," the doctor said as he excused himself and left the room.

❖

Two days later Dawn was on her way back to Billings with Sarah at her side. The backseat was full of flowers, balloons, gifts, and stuffed animals. When they reached the outskirts of Rocky Bluff, Sarah rested her head on a pillow against the doorjamb and said, "Thanks for talking the doctor into letting me come home with you. I sure didn't want to stay there any longer."

"It took a lot of talking on my part," Dawn reminded her. "I have to take you to see Dr. Fox as soon as we get to Billings, then make sure you stay in bed. Just because you're feeling better doesn't mean you're out of danger yet."

"But the doctor said my blood pressure was dropping, and the only medicine he prescribed was one baby aspirin a day. I don't understand how that could do any good," Sarah protested. So many strange things were happening to her body that she didn't understand.

"Doctors are limited in the drugs they can give pregnant women. They don't want them to have any adverse effect on the fetus. I know it sounds strange, but a single baby aspirin a day can do wonders in keeping a pregnant woman's blood pressure stabilized," Dawn explained. She drove in silence a few more miles. Her voice then became stern. "The part that concerns me is trying to keep you flat on your back for the next six weeks. Will you promise to follow your doctor's orders?"

"But what about going to school?" Sarah protested. "I've worked so hard to keep my grades up. I can't drop out right before semester tests."

"I'll go to school Monday and talk with your school counselor," Dawn promised. "We'll get something worked out so you can be on the home study program until after the baby is born. I'll start monitoring your schoolwork along with your physical condition. I'm sorry, but this is just something you'll have to force yourself to do, whether you want to or not."

Tears filled Sarah's eyes, then she broke into sobs. For several miles, crying was the only sound within the car. Dawn's stern expression faded. "I know this is a difficult time for you, but with God's help we can get through this together. We'll just have to take it one step at a time."

"But you need to have a life of your own. You should go out with guys and enjoy yourself," Sarah protested. "You can't spend all your time looking after me. I saw the way you and Ryan acted together. . .and are you sure about that intern you went snowmobiling with? Maybe you'll find there's more to him than you thought."

Dawn flushed. Even her mother did not delve into her romantic life, and here was a sixteen year old full of all types of personal questions. *I suppose I shouldn't get too impatient with her,* Dawn scolded herself. *Romance is the center of the high school mentality. I guess I'm becoming too far removed from it to remember what it was really like.*

"Before we went on Christmas vacation, I realized that Mike and I did not share the same values," Dawn reminded Sarah softly. "Therefore, it's not worth pursuing an in-depth relationship with him. I'll still speak to him if we run into each other in the hospital, but nothing more."

"But what about Ryan?" Sarah protested. "I watched the way he looked at you while everyone was opening their Christmas presents at your mother's house. He really likes you."

Dawn blushed. Was their friendship and growing attraction that obvious already?

"Ryan is great to be around, but our jobs will keep us apart." Dawn's eyes became distant and melancholy. "There's no way a friendship can grow when you never get to see each other."

The personal nature of the conversation in the close confines of the car was a rare opportunity for Dawn to try to push through Sarah's hard defenses. "Now that we've discussed my love life, or lack thereof, let's talk about yours. I think it's important for you to let us know who the baby's father is before the child is born."

Sarah wiped her eyes and took a deep breath. "But it's not fair to him," she protested. "I should have known better. We scarcely knew each other."

"He should have known better as well," Dawn reminded her, "but it has happened, and we have to deal with what is, not what should have been."

"But he seemed to be a real nice guy and talked about going to the University of Montana after he graduated this spring. Just because this has ruined my life doesn't mean it should ruin his as well."

"But don't you think he has a right to know that he has fathered a child?" Dawn persisted. "That doesn't mean the two of you have to marry, but he should carry some responsibility for his actions. The consequences of a few minutes of pleasure can cause lifelong repercussions. Guys have to learn that as well as girls. It's never the girl's total responsibility to carry the entire problem alone, although it often turns out that way in reality. We need to help young people learn to share the responsibility, and we can start with you and your baby's father."

Sarah remained silent for many miles as she watched the snow-covered landscape fly past the car windows. Finally, she said, "Where was Ryan going to go after he left his brother's house? It must be interesting to travel to a lot of different cities and meet a lot of different people."

Dawn shook her head with annoyance. She was so hoping that Sarah would share with her who the father was before the baby was born instead of constantly changing the subject. "He's going to Missoula next and plans to be there over a week," she replied, trying to mask her annoyance. "He said he'd call me tomorrow night to see how you're doing."

At the mention of Missoula, Sarah's face blanched as she instinctively reached for her swollen stomach. Dawn caught the movement from the corner of her eye. "What's the matter, Honey? Are you all right?"

Chapter 7

Ryan Reynolds ambled down the long corridor of the Missoula Medical Center. He had just finished his last appointment of the day and was anxious to find a good restaurant and relax.

"Ryan Reynolds," a voice echoed down the hallway.

Ryan turned. A large man stood in a doorway halfway down the corridor. Over his head was a sign that read "Missoula Crisis Center." The face was familiar, but he couldn't remember the man's name. "Yes? I know I should know you, but the name escapes me," he replied.

"I'm Dan Blair," the man reminded him. "I took over the Rocky Bluff Crisis Line after Roy Dutton retired. I married Beth Slater who worked as an assistant in the high school library."

Ryan extended his hand and heartily shook Dan's. "Dan, how could I forget? I've always prided myself in remembering everyone that was a part of that fantastic little community."

"I guess a few extra pounds, a few less hair follicles, and a few more wrinkles can make a difference," Dan laughed. "What have you been doing lately? Since Edith Dutton passed away, we haven't been back to Rocky Bluff to keep up with what is happening."

"I'm traveling the northwestern states selling medical supplies. I plan to be in Missoula until the end of the week before I go on to Spokane," Ryan replied. "I'm based out of Butte, but I rarely get to see my humble condo there."

"Sounds like you could use a good home-cooked meal," Dan chuckled. "Let me call Beth and forewarn her. We'd love to catch up with what's going on in Rocky Bluff."

"Are you sure I won't be intruding? Most wives would complain about having to do extra cooking even with a little forewarning," Ryan protested weakly.

Dan's laughter echoed throughout the hallway. "No problem there. This is my night to cook, and I'm planning on picking up Chinese food on the way home. Do you like Chinese, or would you rather have fried chicken?"

"Chinese is fine with me," Ryan replied.

Ninety minutes later, Ryan was sitting with the Blair family around their kitchen table eating Chinese food. Beth had finished her studies as an elementary teacher at the University of Montana and was now teaching third grade in the neighborhood public school. It was obvious that she loved her job as she described her day with her students. Ten-year-old Edith was a bubbly fifth-grader, while Jeff was a handsome senior at Big Sky High School.

After sharing news about his brother Larry and his family, Ryan then told about Jay Harkness and his family. The Blairs were anxious to hear about their old friends and asked about people that Ryan scarcely remembered. Finally, Beth asked, "While you were in Rocky Bluff did you hear where Dawn Harkness is and what she is doing now? Has she ever married? I heard at one time she was going through drug rehab in Billings, but then I heard she had enrolled in nurses' training. I hope everything worked out for her. She was such a delightful person."

"It's strange that you ask," Ryan grinned. "A couple of months ago I accidentally met her working in a doctors' clinic in Billings. It appears she has been so preoccupied with her career that she hasn't taken the time for socializing."

Dan and Beth exchanged knowing looks before Dan turned his attention back to Ryan and grinned. "Now that you know where she is, are you planning to make a difference in her extracurricular activities?"

Ryan shook his head. A note of sadness was in his eyes. "I'd like to, but I'm on the road most of the time." His eyes became distant as he took a sip of tea. "I'll admit that sometimes the lonely nights in a motel get to be a little depressing. There's going to be an opening in the home office in Chicago, but I don't know if I'd like city life. Since I grew up in a small town, it's hard to imagine myself in the hectic city. Billings would be the largest city I'd be comfortable living in."

"Maybe there will be an opening in a related field," Beth suggested. "Billings is the medical center for a three-state area. Perhaps something will open there."

"It would be nice," Ryan replied. "I know Dawn loves it there, and she's doing fantastic work in the community. She recently opened her home to an unwed teenage mother who is pregnant with a baby who will have spina bifida. This poor girl's mother would not have anything to do with her unless she had an abortion—which Sarah refused to do."

Eighteen-year-old Jeff dropped his fork on his plate with a clang as he shuffled nervously. "You said the girl's name is Sarah? What's her last name? I met a number of girls from that area when we played Billings High School in football."

"Her name's Sarah Brown," Ryan replied matter-of-factly. "She's about five-foot-eight and has long brown hair. Do you know her?"

Jeff turned ashen white, pushed his chair back, and stormed to his room, slamming the door behind him. Beth and Dan exchanged troubled glances.

"I've never seen him act this way before," Beth gasped. "Dan, I think this might need a father's hand."

Dan nodded, excused himself, and disappeared down the hallway, while Ryan, Beth, and little Edith tried to finish their meal as if nothing was wrong. Small talk was difficult as they continued to discuss mutual friends in Rocky Bluff. Finally, Edith finished her dessert and excused herself to go to the family room to watch her favorite television program.

Beth and Ryan were slowly sipping their after-dinner coffee when Dan and Jeff returned to the table, both their faces ashen white. Jeff's eyes remained fixed on the floor. "Beth, Jeff has something to tell you," Dan began seriously.

Beth studied her son's face. *What could he have done that he'd be afraid to tell us?* She had always felt close to her son. As an unwed teenage mother, she had moved to Rocky Bluff, where Edith Harkness Dutton had befriended her and helped her through an extremely difficult time in her life. Edith had encouraged her to continue her education and helped her get a job at the Rocky Bluff High School library. When Jeff's natural father kidnapped him when he was four years old, Edith provided faith in God and encouragement for everyone in the community. After Jeff's father was arrested and sentenced to four years in jail for bringing drugs into Canada, Dan Blair married Beth and adopted little Jeffey. Dan loved the boy as if he were his own child. Through the years, they had been a close family and had always faced the struggles in life together. *Why should this time be any different than other difficult moments?*

Jeff cleared his throat. "Mom," he began as he voice faltered. "There's a good chance that I'm the father of Sarah Brown's baby."

Now Beth's face turned pale. "B–b–but when? Why?"

Jeff hesitated, took a deep breath. "When we were in Billings last June for a football training camp, a bunch of us made friends with some local girls. I really liked Sarah Brown. We had a lot of fun together, and one night after practice I went over to her apartment to hang out and watch TV. Her mother had taken her little brother to a Little League game, and we were there alone."

Beth shook her head. "That was a very unwise decision," she said sadly. "What happened then?"

"We weren't drinking or anything like that," Jeff replied. "That would have been against training rules, but Sarah was so sweet and lovable. I just couldn't keep my hands off her. We just got caught up in the moment."

"But is there any chance that the baby is not yours?" Beth queried. "Could she have been with any other man during that time period?"

Jeff looked down as tears built in his eyes. "N–n–no," he stammered. "I think she was a virgin at the time. I never dreamed that she would get pregnant after just one night."

"It only takes once," Beth sighed. "You probably should have a blood test to confirm paternity, but if it turns out that it's your child, what do you think is the right thing to do under the circumstances?"

"I. . .I. . .I honestly don't know," Jeff stammered. "I don't want to get married yet since I've received that football scholarship to the University of Montana for this coming fall."

"Forced marriages rarely work out," Beth stated solemnly. "Maybe we should go to Billings and sit down with Sarah and Dawn Harkness and talk with them. After all, we all need to be responsible for our own behavior."

Jeff shuffled nervously. "I suppose you're right," he sighed. "I have Martin Luther King Day off from school. Maybe we could drive to Billings then."

Jeff turned his attention to their guest who had remained self-consciously silent throughout the entire conversation. "Ryan, you won't say anything to Dawn before we come, will you?"

Ryan flashed him a reassuring smile. "You have my word. It's an extremely difficult situation, but with God's help I'm sure a solution can be found that will be the best for all concerned."

"I hope so," Jeff sighed. "But what I don't understand is why Sarah didn't get in touch with me. She shouldn't have to deal with this by herself. I know I didn't know her all that well, but if I'm the father of her child, then I should be responsible for her."

"If there's anything I can do to help," Ryan promised, "I'll be glad to do whatever I can."

Jeff's face relaxed. "I appreciate that," he replied.

The conversation about Sarah Brown and her baby ended, and the remainder of the evening the Blairs and Ryan enjoyed their time together, even though a dreadful cloud hung over them. Although he was constantly traveling with his job, Ryan felt that he would be seeing a lot more of these old friends.

❖

The day after returning to Billings, Dawn took Sarah to Dr. Fox for a follow-up examination. After examining the pregnant girl, Dr. Fox studied the papers that had been faxed to him from the Rocky Bluff hospital. He rubbed his chin as he studied the scared face of the pregnant girl. "You're one fortunate young woman," he began. "You've been through an extremely difficult period, and you're not out of the woods. Your blood pressure is still much too high. I'm afraid you'll need to remain flat on your back until the baby is born."

Sarah's chin dropped. "But what about school?" she protested. "It's almost the end of the semester, and I don't want all my hard work to go down the drain."

"Billings High School has a very good home study program," Dr. Fox assured her. "I'm sure Dawn will be able to work something out with the school's counselor and teachers to get your daily assignments. I realize it can be extremely boring to stay flat on your back all day, but for your health and the health of your baby, you have no choice. The next six weeks will pass, although at times it may seem like it will never end."

Sarah hesitated as a look of determination spread across her face. "I'll do the best I can," she promised. "In spite of how hard it gets, I still won't give in to my mother and have an abortion. Late-term abortions are so barbaric."

"You're one brave gal," Dr. Fox replied. "Next week we'll want to take another ultrasound to check the development of the baby. I'm still hoping that you will be able to have a natural birth, but if the head becomes too large, we'll have to schedule you for a cesarean. As for now, take it easy and get a lot of rest."

"Okay. . .I'll be sure and stay down," Sarah promised. "This baby is going to start life with a lot of strikes against her as it is, so I don't want to add anything more to it."

When the doctor had finished, Dawn helped Sarah with her coat, thanked the doctor, and held the door open for her young friend. "I'll be officially back at work tomorrow," she smiled. "I'm glad there weren't any new babies while I was in Rocky Bluff."

"We have several that are trying to hold off and be the first New Year's baby in Montana," Dr. Fox chuckled. "So brace yourself."

❖

Two evenings later while Sarah was trying to do her geometry assignment as she watched television and Dawn was doing laundry, the telephone rang. Dawn hurried to the kitchen and picked up the telephone. "Hello?"

"Hello," the voice greeted in reply. "Is this Dawn Harkness?"

"Yes, it is."

"This is Beth Blair. I don't know if you remember me or not. I used to live in Rocky Bluff. Your grandmother took me under her wing and helped me get my life put together when I was a young unwed mother. I now live in Missoula with my husband and two children."

Dawn's face brightened. "Of course I remember you," she replied. "How have you been?"

"We're all doing fine," Beth replied. "My husband accidentally ran into Ryan Reynolds yesterday, and he brought us up to date on many of our old friends in Rocky Bluff. He told us that you were helping a young pregnant girl named Sarah Brown."

Dawn wrinkled her forehead. "That's right. She's a delightful girl, but she's having more than her share of problems during this pregnancy."

"This may sound like a shocking question," Beth said cautiously, "but has Sarah said who the father of the baby is?"

Dawn hesitated. "No. . .she refuses to tell us. The only thing she has said was that he is from Missoula and plans to attend the University of Montana next year, and she doesn't want to interfere with his future."

Beth took a deep breath. "Th–Th–this is hard for me to say," Beth stammered as she wiped a strand of loose hair from her eyes, "but there is a good chance that my son Jeff is the baby's father."

"Little Jeffey Blair?" Dawn exclaimed with disbelief. "I remember when he was kidnapped when he was four years old, and his picture was posted on milk cartons at school and his poster was all over the state."

"Jeff has grown into a delightful young man, but I never expected anything like this," Beth continued. "He realizes that he has made a serious mistake and would like to take responsibility for what has happened if the child is his. We will be willing to meet with you and Sarah and see what can be done to help."

Dawn could scarcely believe what she was hearing. She never dreamed the father would be someone she knew. However, since Montana was so sparsely populated, coincidences like this seemed to occur with regularity. "We'd love to meet with you. However, Sarah is confined to total bed rest until the baby is born. Would it be possible for you to drive to Billings?"

"Everyone here has a three-day weekend for Martin Luther King Day. Is that a convenient time for you?" Beth queried.

"Our office is closed as well that day," Dawn replied. "Unless we have an unexpected delivery that weekend, it should work out well. If it's all right with you, I'd rather not tell Sarah you are coming until the day of your arrival. I don't want to cause her any more worry than necessary. Her blood pressure has been extremely unstable, and I don't want to do anything that would upset her." Dawn hesitated as she pondered the situation. Finally she continued, "However, I do think it will do her good to not feel she has to carry this burden alone."

"I appreciate all you're doing for her," Beth replied warmly. "After being an unwed mother myself, I can well understand what Sarah is going through. . . being alone and frightened. We'll take care of Jeff's blood test to validate paternity, but by the sound of things, it will be a mere formality."

Dawn's mind raced. What should she tell the possible grandmother of a disabled child? Should she break the news now or leave it to Sarah? Aware of Sarah's reluctance to talk about the complexity of the situation, Dawn took a deep breath and proceeded. "Being young and unmarried is only part of the problem," she explained. "The ultrasound showed that the spinal column has not closed. The baby has spina bifida. . . . We are watching her closely to determine if, and how much, fluid is going to build up around the baby's brain. If the head gets too big, Sarah may have to have a cesarean section, and the baby will need to have a shunt to drain the fluid from the head into the abdomen."

There was a long pause at the other end of the telephone line before Beth responded. "Ryan shared that with us, along with the behavior of the girl's mother," she said as her voice nearly broke. "My heart and prayers really go out to that poor girl. I'm so glad you prepared me. It will help me to help Jeff face his responsibility."

"Thank you for calling," Dawn replied. "Nowadays it seems so rare that young men feel responsible for their mistakes, especially with this set of circumstances. You wouldn't believe how much pressure has been placed on Sarah to have an abortion, especially when people learn that her baby will be disabled."

"You're both doing such a courageous thing. I'm looking forward to meeting with you in a couple of weeks," Beth replied. "In the meantime, we'll keep both you and Sarah in our prayers."

The two women bade each other farewell and returned their telephones into their respective cradles. Beth burst into tears and buried her face in her hands. She had never considered the idea of someday being a grandmother. She was too busy being a wife, mother, and teacher. Now, not only was her son to be a father before he was ready, but that child was going to be disabled. All she could do was cry out to God for strength and guidance to walk the difficult path before her.

After a few moments of sobbing, a sense of peace enveloped her as she realized that just as God sent Edith Harkness Dutton to help her when she needed help, He was now sending Edith's granddaughter Dawn to help Sarah and her baby. *Truly God never gives us more than we can bear without providing a way to escape the pressures of life, if we but trust in Him*, she mused.

Chapter 8

Jeff Blair shuffled nervously on an easy chair in Dawn Harkness's living room, while Sarah Brown reclined on the sofa across the room. "How have you been doing?" he murmured, completely overwhelmed by the enormity of the situation. He was the cause of this girl's swollen abdomen.

"I've been doing okay," Sarah replied shyly. "I'm just getting bored with lying around all day long. I'll be glad when this is over. How have you been doing?"

Sensing the teenagers' discomfort, Dawn turned to Jeff's mother. "Beth, would you like to come to the kitchen and have a cup of coffee? It will be easier for us to reminisce about old times in Rocky Bluff."

"Good idea," replied Beth as she stood to leave.

Jeff breathed a sigh of relief as his mother left the room. As much as he loved her, he knew he had made this mess, and he didn't want to hurt her any more than she already was. "Sarah, I'm sorry for what I've done to you. I didn't mean to hurt you, and now your entire life is changed because of one reckless evening. Will you ever be able to forgive me?"

Tears filled Sarah's eyes as she bit her lip. "It wasn't entirely your fault. I was the one who let it happen. I could have stopped it, but I didn't, and now I have to pay the price." Sarah started to sob. "It's not only me, but my poor baby is going to be deformed," she choked. "I used to think God was punishing me for what I did, but Dawn says that God doesn't punish innocent people that way."

Jeff shrugged his shoulders. "I've never given it much thought," he replied, "but I guess I agree with Dawn. I honestly believe God will forgive us for our sins, but now we have to figure out how to live with the consequences of what we've done."

Sarah gazed silently out the window on the snow-covered yard, while Jeff rubbed his chin as he remained deep in thought. "What do you plan to do after the baby is born?" he finally asked.

Sarah took a deep breath as her eyes settled on the snow-laden tree branches. "I. . .I don't know," she stammered. "I'd like to raise my own baby, but I don't know if I could handle one that is disabled. . . . I suppose it depends on how severe her handicaps are."

Jeff's eyes became intense, and his voice strong. "I hope you plan to finish high school and go on to college," Jeff replied. "It wouldn't be fair if I was able to go to college and you couldn't because of the baby."

"I don't think the baby will be the only thing keeping me from going to college," Sarah explained sadly. "I don't know where I'd get the money. I'll be totally on my own, plus having to pay for child care."

Jeff took a deep breath as he seemed to mature five years in these few difficult moments. His spine became erect against the back of his chair. "I don't want you to feel abandoned and give up on your dreams," he promised. "If you decide to keep the baby, I'll take a part-time job while I'm going to college to help support her."

Little did the teenagers realize that Beth and Dawn were having exactly the same conversation in the kitchen, only at a different level. "What are Sarah's plans after the baby is born?" Beth queried as she set her coffee cup in its saucer. "Knowing the baby will be disabled really complicates the matter for her."

"That it does," Dawn sighed as she nodded her head sadly. "I don't think Sarah fully comprehends how serious the disabilities may be. She still thinks she'll be able to take care of the baby by herself."

Beth shook her head with dismay. "What could happen if she's not able to care for the baby? It's so difficult for disabled children to find adoptive families."

"I honestly don't know," Dawn replied. "I guess we'll have to face that problem when we learn the degree of the baby's disabilities. I have about thirty days of vacation time that I could use to help care for her if we are faced with a prolonged crisis and need more transitional time."

"I'll do what I can to help," Beth promised, "but I probably won't be free to come back to Billings until after school is out for the summer. Of course, we'll have to work something out for Jeff to pay his share of the child's support."

The hours passed swiftly as each one shared their concerns and dreams about the future. By the end of the afternoon, Sarah and Jeff, along with Dawn and Beth, had a better understanding about the problems before them. Although the four had spent little time together before, they were now bound together by their common problem and their faith in God. They realized they would have to trust God to lead them through the uncertain future that lay before them.

After the Blairs returned to Missoula, the next few days passed slowly for Sarah. She lay on the sofa, watched TV, and did handicrafts. Each day the home study coordinator from the school brought her schoolwork and helped her with any problems she was having with the assignments of the day before. At semester time, her grades had gone up except for the incomplete that she received in her cooking class. She took comfort in the fact that she was promised she could complete this class the following semester, when she returned to school after the birth of her baby.

That Friday evening, the telephone rang in Dawn's apartment. Sarah reached over her head for the cordless telephone that was lying on the end table beside the sofa. "Hello," she greeted.

"Hello," a familiar voice replied. "Is this Sarah?"

"Yes," the teenager answered as she tried to remember whose voice it was.

"This is Ryan Reynolds," he explained. "How have you been feeling?"

"Hi, Ryan. It's good to hear from you again. I'm doing great, except I'm bored to death." A mischievous smile spread across her face. "I'm sorry, but Dawn is working at the hospital tonight. I don't know what time she'll be home. I think she has tomorrow off, though. Can I enter your name on her social calendar?"

"Don't tell her I called," Ryan chuckled. "I'll hang around the hospital cafeteria and see if she appears. If not, would you tell her that I'll call her tomorrow?"

"I'll be sure and leave a note for her if I go to bed before she gets home," Sarah promised. "I know she'll be happy to see you again. All work and no play can make Dawn a very dull girl."

The two cheerfully said good-bye to each other. The young mother-to-be sighed. That would probably be the only person she would talk to until Dawn got home that night. She rubbed her stomach as she felt a strong thump. *Will this ever be over?* she asked herself. *I can hardly wait for my doctor's appointment on Wednesday. I don't think I'll be able to take this much longer.*

❖

Dawn Harkness took a cup of coffee and a piece of pie, then paid the cashier. She ambled to her favorite table by the window that overlooked the snow-covered hospital patio. She had just finished assisting at the birth of her forty-seventh baby and was both exhausted and exhilarated at the same time. She never ceased marveling at the miracle of each birth, and yet she was emotionally drained. The mother had been extremely frightened and needed constant reassurance until the crying baby was placed in her arms. Then a relaxed serenity flowed throughout her body as she admired the new life in her arms.

After the mother had fallen asleep, Dawn left her and the newborn under the watchful care of the evening nursing staff. It was time to relax and regroup her thoughts before she returned home to another mother-to-be.

Dawn stared peacefully out the window, lost in thought, when suddenly a shadow fell over her. "May I join you?" a husky voice queried.

Dawn looked up into the blue eyes of intern Mike Archer. She had only seen him a few times since their snowmobiling trip before Christmas and had given him little thought. Although she was uncomfortable with some of his views, he was a welcome relief from the overwhelming loneliness she felt.

"Sure," she said as she motioned to the chair across the table. "I was just getting myself prepared to face the cold winter blast. It looks so calm and peaceful outside, but the weatherman says it's about twenty below zero tonight."

"At least it's warmer than it was last night," Mike laughed.

Dawn studied the young man's tousled hair and bloodshot eyes. "I haven't seen you for quite awhile. Have you been putting in a lot of extra time here at the hospital?"

"I wish I had been working here," Mike said sadly, "but my father had a heart attack the day before Christmas and I had to fly back to Iowa to be with my family."

Dawn's forehead wrinkled. "I'm sorry to hear that," she replied with concern. "How's he doing now? Better, I hope."

Mike admired the concerned blue eyes framed by Dawn's blond hair. "He had a triple bypass, but he's out of the hospital now and doing fairly well," he said, but the tightness remained in his voice. "It's Mother I'm concerned about now. She lost fifteen pounds through the ordeal, and she was already too thin for her height."

Dawn was always searching for words of encouragement in every situation. "Now that your dad's home from the hospital, don't you think it will get better for her?"

"I hope so," Mike replied cautiously. "That is the only reason why I returned to Billings when I did. I'm the only child, and there's no one to take care of them if they are sick at the same time."

"Don't they have friends that could help them out in a crisis?"

"They're surrounded by friends, but it's just not the same." Mike sighed as the burden of responsibility began to overwhelm him. "They pride themselves on being self-sufficient and don't want to accept charity from anyone. I hope they can get along by themselves for awhile longer so I can at least finish my residency. I don't want to be forced to choose between my career and taking care of my parents. I'm afraid I'd have to place them in a nursing home if I continued my career. Neither one would be happy in a care center, but I have my entire life before me."

Dawn shuffled nervously. There was something in his tone that bothered her. *Is he just being selfish about choosing his career over his parents—or is he hard-hearted toward everyone?* Suddenly, she was distracted as she caught sight of a familiar figure coming through the cafeteria door. A smile spread across her tired face as Ryan waved and headed toward her table. "Hello, Ryan. I wasn't expecting you in Billings for several months," she greeted as she reached out to take his hand. "I'd like you to meet Dr. Mike Archer, who is completing his residency here in Billings." She then turned her attention to the young intern across the table from her. "Mike, I'd like you to meet Ryan Reynolds, an old school friend from Rocky Bluff. He's now in the medical supplies business."

Mike Archer rose and extended his hand and smiled. "Rocky Bluff may be a little town, but it sure has produced a good clan of Montanans." He mechanically shook Ryan's hand as he glanced down at the nurse beside him who was beaming at the new arrival. "Ryan, it's nice meeting you. I wish I could stay and get acquainted, but I'm afraid I'll be needed on the third floor. Will you excuse me, please?"

"Certainly," Ryan replied. "It was nice meeting you."

Mike scowled as he hurriedly left the cafeteria. "Did I detect a little jealousy on his part?" Ryan smiled as he took the chair that Mike had just vacated.

Dawn shrugged her shoulders. "If he's at all interested in me, he has a reason to be jealous of you, because I find him a self-centered bore."

"Dawn Harkness, during all the years I've known you, I've never heard you speak negatively about anyone," Ryan teasingly scolded.

"I wish that were true," Dawn sighed. "There's a number of people I speak negatively about; the primary one is Sarah's mother, who won't have anything to do with her daughter when she needs her the most. Mike shares the same viewpoint that we shouldn't bring disabled children into this world to become a drain on society."

"That's such a sad situation," Ryan agreed. "I don't understand how normal people can feel that way. It must be awfully hard on Sarah."

"She's a real trooper, but I don't think she has any concept how handicapped her child might be. I think she's imagining that the worst thing possible is that her child may walk with a limp." A tear glistened in Dawn's eye. "I've seen how serious this problem can be, and sometimes I'm overwhelmed by the 'what-ifs.' "

Ryan studied Dawn's weary face. The circles under her eyes were darker than he had ever seen, and the furrow on her brow had deepened. He reached for her hand. "Dawn, don't feel as if you are the only one who will help Sarah and her baby. I'll do everything I can to help as well."

Dawn took a deep breath and smiled. "But you spend most of your time on the road," she protested.

Ryan grinned. The good news was ready to explode from his lips to replace her burdens. "My company is negotiating with some local contractors to build a medical supply retail outlet here in Billings. They're considering moving me here to manage it."

Dawn's eyes widened as the furrow on her forehead faded. "That's terrific.

When will you know for sure if the deal will go through and you're the one who'll be the manager?"

"I'm meeting with the CEO Tuesday, and I should know within a few days. If I'm the one selected, I'll need to move within a month to begin supervising the construction and hiring personnel."

"Careerwise, this could be one of the biggest breaks in your life," Dawn exclaimed excitedly. "If ever there was a cause for prayer, it is now. Tomorrow I'll call Mom and have her activate her church's prayer chain. They've been in operation ever since Grandma organized it more than twenty-five years ago. They've been upholding Sarah with prayer, and they will just add your name to their list. They've had remarkable answers to their prayers throughout the years."

A silly grin spread across Ryan's face as he reached for Dawn's hand and squeezed it fondly. "This could also be a very big break in my personal life as well, but we'll have to deal with that at a later time."

In spite of the excitement and romance of the moment, fatigue overwhelmed Dawn as she covered her mouth and yawned. "Pardon me," she apologized. "It's not the company; it's my weak body."

"Don't apologize to me," Ryan replied with concern. "I better let you get home and get some sleep. I'll call you again around noon tomorrow."

Ryan walked Dawn to her car in the hospital parking lot as the snow crunched under their feet. When they reached her car, he took Dawn into his arms and pulled her close. Snow flurries floated around them as their eyes met, and slowly their lips joined in a parting kiss.

They both desired a more permanent relationship, but they were afraid to consider it for fear of being disappointed. Finally they said good night, and Dawn drove the sleeping streets of Billings toward her apartment. Thoughts about her evening's work or the pregnant girl waiting for her at home faded as she considered the possibility of Ryan moving to Billings. What would it be like to have his encouraging presence close by all the time?

The rest of the weekend, Ryan and Dawn spent many happy hours together, either walking the mall, watching videos in Dawn's apartment with Sarah, or going to dinner at the Red Lion. On Sunday afternoon they scoured the want ads to check on the availability of apartments. Realizing it was premature to look, they made mental notes of the location and the rent of those listed. There were several that might be possibilities, but would they still be vacant if and when Ryan was ready to move?

When Tuesday finally rolled around, Dawn could not keep her mind off Ryan and his interview with the CEO of his company. Her prayers consisted of simple one-liners as she went about her routine tasks at the medical clinic. Promptly at five o'clock. she was called to the telephone.

"Hello, Dawn," Ryan's welcomed voice greeted her as she answered the telephone. "I didn't want to have to call you at work, but I'm afraid I won't be able to come for dinner tonight. The wheels of the company have invited me out to some overpriced restaurant so they can inspect me under different lights. So far the interview has been going well, and I don't want to blow it now."

Dawn couldn't help but laugh at his vivid description of what must be a tension-filled ordeal. "I'm sure you're impressing the socks off them."

"I hope so," Ryan responded dryly. "Just keep me in your prayers all evening because you know how I hate superficial social situations."

"That I'll do," Dawn assured him. "Please let me know how things turn out."

"I'll call you tomorrow night from Butte. I wish I could stay in town another day, but I have a major sales appointment this Thursday that I don't dare miss," he explained, then laughed. "Would you put my dinner in the freezer, and I'll eat it the next time I'm in Billings?"

"Hopefully, the next time you're in town it will be with a moving van," Dawn joked back. Just then, a pregnant woman approached the window and waited nervously as Dawn finished her telephone conversation. "I'm sorry, but I have to go now. I have someone waiting for me. I'm looking forward to your call tomorrow."

Dawn handed the patient a routine questionnaire, then helped the receptionist close and lock the office. She hurriedly scanned the schedule for the next day and noted that Sarah's appointment was at two o'clock. *After this check-up, hopefully, Sarah's long wait will be over. Dr. Fox will probably schedule a cesarean section for the next day.*

Dawn's emotions were in turmoil during her drive home. Not being able to see Ryan that night, when she had so hoped to hear his cheerful laughter echo throughout her apartment, was devastating. As she put her key in the door, she heard faint sobs from within. She choked back her own emotions as she struggled to meet the emotional needs of her troubled houseguest.

Chapter 9

When Sarah returned from the doctor's office the next day, she threw her coat on a chair and collapsed onto the sofa. "I suppose I should feel elated that my months of waiting will be over tomorrow," she exclaimed, "but truthfully, I'm downright scared."

Dawn Harkness put her arm around the pregnant girl's shoulder. "You have the best obstetrician in Billings along with the prayer support of scores of church people. The Lord hasn't brought you this far to let you down now."

"But what if the baby is so handicapped that I'm not able to take care of her?" Sarah's eyes widened as her voice trembled. "What will I do then? Even worse. . .what if the baby dies? Then my mother probably would be happy."

"No one knows what will happen in the future, but we do know that if we trust in God, He will work everything out according to His great plan," Dawn tried to assure her, her voice becoming firmer. "Every human being has a right to live, regardless of disabilities. Don't let anyone try to convince you otherwise."

This was the first time that Sarah had admitted her concern about losing the baby or the possibility that she might not be able to care for her own child after she was born. *By admitting her fears and limitations, Sarah can finally be helped in making the right decisions concerning the future of her baby,* Dawn thought. *Within a few hours, we will know the severity of the child's handicap. At least I've accumulated several weeks of leave time to help Sarah with the life-changing decisions she will be forced to make.*

Dawn tried to change the subject away from their mutual fears and concerns. "Since you haven't been able to go anyplace in the last six weeks, let's celebrate tonight," Dawn suggested lightly. "You're not supposed to have anything to eat or drink after midnight, but a good steak dinner at six o'clock is just what your nurse orders."

A faint smile spread across Sarah's face as the tension lines relaxed. "I never disobey the orders of my nurse," she laughed dryly.

"Steak it is," Dawn agreed. "After work I'll stop by the mall and pick out a pretty nightgown for you to wear in the hospital. Something cute and lacy always helps lift a new mother's spirits when those postpartum blues set in after the baby arrives." She buttoned her coat and grabbed her purse. "I'd better get back to work. I've got a lot to do before our steak dinner tonight."

When Dawn returned to work at the clinic, Sarah mindlessly watched the afternoon game shows on TV. However, fears and doubts enveloped the young mother-to-be, and she scarcely noticed the winners who were being announced on the screen. She located the literature the doctor had given her on spina bifida and thumbed through it for what seemed like the one hundredth time. She had always pictured her baby being one with limited handicaps, but now she was overwhelmed by the fear that her baby might be one with the severest handicaps. *If my baby needs a shunt, how will I know if it isn't working right? If she never learns to walk, will I be able to lift her in and out of a wheelchair? If she doesn't have bowel and bladder control, will I be able to take care of her personal needs? Maybe I should consider putting the baby up for adoption?. . . If I did that, I might never see her again. I could never give my own child away.*

While Sarah was going through her own personal struggles, Dawn contacted the neonatal specialist, the head pediatric nurse, the hospital social worker, and the hospital chaplain. She alerted the team as to some of the physical, emotional, and family struggles they might face with the birth of Sarah Brown's baby. Up to this time, she felt she had maintained a balance between being both nurse and friend to Sarah, but as the delivery time approached, she felt overwhelmed with emotions. Dawn took a deep breath and returned to work, trying to ignore her inner struggles. Sarah seemed to depend so much on her, and yet she felt so inadequate and too weak to carry such a heavy burden alone. Even her faith in God felt weak at the moment.

Between patients, Dr. Fox noticed Dawn staring out the window, oblivious to her surroundings. He placed a fatherly hand on her shoulder. "Sarah Brown's situation getting you down?"

"I'm afraid so," she sighed. "It's hard to imagine that tomorrow at this time the baby will be here, and we'll be facing an entirely different set of crises."

"We'll have all the specialists available to help us with the baby," the doctor assured her, "but I'm extremely concerned how Sarah will accept the baby. I don't think she fully understands or accepts the enormity of the situation."

"I think it's just now beginning to hit her," Dawn replied. "Until today, her biggest concern was if the baby would be able to learn to walk properly. She has never considered anything more serious. If it is going to be as bad as we suspect, I don't know how she's going to react. She's going to need me more than she ever has throughout her entire pregnancy, but I feel too close to the situation to provide the emotional support she needs." The young nurse hesitated. "I'm afraid I'll react more as a friend than a nurse when it comes time to do my job."

A look of compassion spread across Dr. Fox's face. "I've already considered that," he replied kindly. "I've asked Jane Miller to take your place as nursing assistant so you will be free to devote all your attention to Sarah's emotional state."

"I appreciate that," Dawn replied softly. "You always seem to be one step ahead of me."

The rest of the day, Dawn routinely went about her tasks of taking the blood pressure and weight of each patient and trying to get an overview of how things had been going since their last visit, but her mind was focused elsewhere. *I wish Ryan Reynolds were still in town tonight. He has such a way of making both Sarah and me laugh and forget about our fear. . . . I wonder if he got the job here in Billings. I wish he would call tonight, but he said he would be tied up in meetings until very late.*

At fifteen past five, the last patient left the clinic, and Dawn took her coat from the closet, bade farewell to her coworkers, and hurried toward her car. This was going to be a long night of waiting and wondering. The streetlights cast deep shadows on the midwinter thaw that had turned the snow-packed streets to slush. Dawn gripped the steering wheel tightly as she drove toward her apartment. A feeling of anticipation enveloped her. *Please, God,* she prayed silently. *Give me the wisdom and strength to help Sarah get through these next difficult hours. I feel so weak and inadequate. Our only hope is for Your strength and guidance.*

By the time Dawn arrived home that evening, calm had spread over her. She was determined to make this a night of celebration, not a night of worry. Sarah was dressed in her best maternity blouse and slacks, her long brown hair worked into a French braid. They both were determined that, with the help of God, they would make the best of a bad situation.

The evening passed slowly as the two tried to force themselves to make small talk during their dinner, but their words seemed superficial compared to what was actually on their minds. After the dishes were done, Dawn hurried to a video store and selected two comedy movies that served as a welcome distraction until well after midnight.

❦

The next day, Dawn held Sarah's hand and comforted her throughout the entire surgery. Although it was a routine cesarean section, everyone breathed a sigh of relief when the baby gave its first gasp for air and cried. Tears flowed down Sarah's cheeks as she admired the beautiful face on the enlarged head. The baby's legs dangled limply beneath her body and there was an abnormal hump on her back where the spinal column had not closed properly.

"She's beautiful," the new mother sobbed, "but will she be all right?"

"Her coloring is good," Dr. Fox assured her, "but the pediatricians will have to do more testing on her. They'll need to do surgery to enclose the spinal column and install a shunt in the baby's head to drain the excess fluid."

The pediatric nurses rushed the baby away as Dr. Fox finished closing the incision in Sarah's abdomen. Within minutes, she was wheeled into the recovery room. Slowly she began to relax, and her eyes became heavy.

"You look like you're about ready to fall asleep," Dawn said as she gently pushed a strand of hair from in front of Sarah's face. "I think I'll go to the cafeteria and get something to eat. I'll stop back before I leave the hospital."

"Thanks for staying with me," Sarah murmured as she closed her eyes. "I don't know how I'd have gotten through this without you."

Dawn slipped quietly out the door and down the long corridor. She pushed the button for the elevator and waited. Her shoulders drooped as she relived the vision of the newborn being whisked away by the pediatric nurses. The delivery was finally over, but an uncertain future still lay ahead. A rumble sounded before her, and the elevator door slid open.

"Dawn," a familiar voice greeted. "I was just coming to find you. Is the baby here yet?"

"Oh, hi, Ryan. I was wondering when you were going to get back to Billings," Dawn replied as she stepped into the elevator. "I'm on my way to get a bite to eat. I'll fill you in on the details there."

Ryan wrapped his arm gently around Dawn's shoulder. "I got here just as soon as I could. I didn't want you to have to face another crisis alone." Dawn laid her head against his shoulder. His strength seemed to refresh her.

At the cafeteria line, the pair each selected a salad and the special for the day, although food was the furthest thing from their minds. Dawn led the way to the far table by the window. The February sun glistened down onto the melting snow outside, making it a picture-perfect day, and yet neither one seemed to notice. After settling into their seats, Ryan turned to Dawn. "So how did the delivery go? You look exhausted."

"It was a fairly routine surgery," Dawn explained. "However, due to the extra size of the head, the doctor had to make a larger incision than normal, so it may take Sarah a little longer to heal. There's also a greater chance of infection setting in."

Ryan listened intently. The last few weeks he had found himself caught up in the conflict of standing strong behind his belief in the sanctity of human life under circumstances when others may have chosen an abortion. Sometimes the proabortion crowd presented what could be taken as logical arguments, but he knew in his heart the sanctity of life itself. He took a deep breath before he asked, "And how was the baby?"

Dawn sighed and gave a weak smile. "Her coloring was good, and she was breathing normally when I left," she replied. "She has such a cute little face, but when you see how large the head is, it's enough to make you cry. Her legs just dangle at the end of her body, and her feet are extremely deformed."

Ryan's face sobered. "Is there anything they can do for her?" Ryan queried as he took a sip of his soft drink.

"She'll have to have a shunt placed in her head to drain the excess fluid into the abdominal cavity within forty-eight hours, plus surgery on the back to close the spinal column," Dawn explained matter-of-factly. "It will be several days before we begin to know the extent of her disabilities. Sarah is just beginning to grasp the enormity of the problem."

Ryan noticed that heavy dark circles surrounded Dawn's soft blue eyes. "Do you think that she'll be able to care for the child herself? After all, she's only sixteen. No more than a child herself."

Dawn hesitated, then shook her head. "I honestly don't think it would be a good idea. The child is going to need constant care. But I don't know many women who would take in a foster child who has special needs."

"That sounds so glum," Ryan said. "If it will take such specialized care, the baby will have to be institutionalized from birth."

Dawn set her jaw firmly. The muscles in her neck tightened. "I'll do everything in my power to keep that from happening," she stated. "There is no way a child can receive enough loving care in an institution, regardless of how well trained the staff is. I'll take care of the baby myself before I'll let that happen."

Ryan's eyes widened with amazement. He didn't speak for a few moments while they both ate their meat loaf and mashed potatoes. He had good news to share with her, but it was dwarfed by the severity of the moment. This was not the appropriate time to bring it up. Yet, a question loomed before them. Would the baby make a difference in their future lives?

Finally Dawn laid her fork on her plate and smiled. "I'm sorry. I've been so wrapped up with the new baby, I didn't even ask if you got the job here in Billings."

Ryan reached across the table for her hand. "Yes, I did," he said and smiled. "They want me to find a place to live as soon as possible and begin working with the construction crew, hiring personnel, and ordering supplies. They'd like to have the store operational by the first of March."

"Fantastic," Dawn exclaimed. "That's the first good news I've heard in a long time. I'm really going to enjoy having you in town all the time. You're one of the few people who understands my commitment to help Sarah."

Pushing the events of the last few hours to the background, Dawn and Ryan continued their discussion about the availability of housing in Billings. They knew that both their lives were about to make radical changes, but they were only able to cope with one step at a time. After taking about an hour lunch break, Dawn glanced at her watch. "I think I better get upstairs and check in with the pediatric nurses and Sarah. When she wakes up, I'm sure she'll be full of questions for me. Would you like to come with me?"

"Sure, I'd be delighted," Ryan replied as he began gathering their plates and utensils and stacking them on his tray. "I'm beginning to feel as committed to the welfare of this baby as you are." He placed their tray of dirty dishes on the conveyor belt into the kitchen and reached for Dawn's hand. Together they walked in silence to the elevator. They had only become reacquainted two months before, but it was like they were still two schoolkids back in Rocky Bluff facing an uncertain future.

As they passed the gift shop, Ryan hesitated. "Let's take Sarah up a balloon bouquet. In spite of everything, this is a very exciting day for her."

The pair browsed the store looking for just the right gift. "This is really difficult," Dawn commented. "I want it to express our true feelings, without all the normal new-baby clichés."

Dawn and Ryan finally selected a colorful arrangement of mylar balloons with the words "I love you" tied to a pink teddy bear with little hearts on its feet. "This should make her smile," Ryan noted as he paid the clerk.

Ryan carried the balloons in one hand and held Dawn's hand with the other. When they arrived on the obstetrics floor, they learned that Sarah had been moved into a private room. As Dawn tapped on the door and stuck her head in, Sarah was just hanging up the bedside telephone.

"Hi," Sarah greeted with a smile. "I was afraid you wouldn't find me after they moved me out of the recovery room."

"I know my way around this floor pretty well," Dawn laughed. "May we come in? I brought you a visitor."

"Sure. . .as long as it isn't someone else on the hospital staff." Sarah sighed. "I've never been punched and prodded this much in my entire life."

Ryan stepped around the semiclosed door with the teddy bear in his hand and the balloons floating over his head. "Hi, Sarah. How are you feeling?"

"I'm doing real well," Sarah replied, "but I don't think the anesthetics have worn off yet."

"We brought something to help cheer you," Ryan said as he handed the new mother the teddy bear bouquet.

"Thanks, Ryan. This is really cute," Sarah said as she cradled the bear in her arms. She fondled the bear for a moment, then turned her attention to Dawn. "Have you heard how the baby's doing?"

Dawn stepped closer to the girl's bed and took her hand. "I was just on my way to pediatrics," she replied, "but I wanted to see how you were doing first."

"I guess I'm doing as good as can be expected," Sarah replied. "I just got done talking with Jeff. I told him that the baby had arrived and they were running tests on her. He said to go ahead and put his name on the birth certificate as the father, and he'd be responsible for his share of the child support. I'm going to call her Charity Sue Blair. I picked the name Charity because through her, I met you and scores of other Christians. I learned what Christian love is all about."

Chapter 10

The next day when Dawn returned to the hospital, voices of laughter resounded from behind Sarah's closed door. Dawn tapped lightly and waited.

"Come in," Sarah called.

As Dawn pushed open the door, she tried to hide her surprise at seeing Sarah lying with her bed propped up as high as it would go. Her long hair was pulled back with a ribbon and fresh lipstick was on her smiling face. Doris Brown, Sarah's mother, sat on the far side of the bed, holding her daughter's hand.

"Good morning," Dawn greeted. "I see you're doing much better today."

"Hi, Dawn. I think you met my mother several months ago," Sarah responded brightly.

Doris Brown rose and extended her hand. "It's good to see you again, Dawn. I can't say how much I thank you for what you've done for Sarah and the baby." Tears began to build in the new grandmother's eyes. "When my daughter needed me the most, I turned her out," she confessed. "As the months passed, I felt guiltier and guiltier about the way I treated Sarah, but I was too proud to call her and apologize. I'm truly sorry for all the heartache I've caused. I wish there was some way I could make it up to everyone." Doris reached for a tissue on the nightstand beside the bed.

Dawn put her hand on the weeping grandmother's shoulder. "I'm glad I was able to be there to help. The important thing now is that you and Sarah reconcile. You have a lovely daughter who could have a very bright future, and she needs you."

"I know," Doris replied as she reached for her daughter's hand. "I'm very proud of her and glad that she called to tell me that the baby was born and she was all right. She had the courage to break the stalemate, which I should have done months ago. . .or never created it in the first place."

"Mom, it wasn't all your fault," Sarah replied as tears welled up in her eyes. "I know I hurt you badly when I became pregnant, but I didn't want to choose between you and my baby. Something within me wouldn't let me kill my own flesh and blood, regardless of what her deformity might be."

Doris wiped back a strand of hair that had fallen down in front of her daughter's eyes. "I stopped by the nursery to see the baby on my way to your room. She has the sweetest, most innocent face I have ever seen. I can't imagine depriving her of a chance for life. I'm truly sorry for my behavior. I hope you'll move back home as soon as you get out of the hospital."

Sarah hugged her mother and wept. "But what about little Charity?" she sobbed. "I don't know how severe her disabilities will be or if I'll be able to take care of her myself."

"We'll have to wait to see what the doctors say," Doris assured her. "I'll do whatever I can to help, but I don't have any medical training."

"The hospital social worker will be talking with you in a few days to explore all the options," Dawn tried to assure them. "I'll talk to the doctors after the baby's surgery to get a better idea of her limitations."

"I want to thank both of you," Sarah said as she tried to regain her composure. "The surgery is scheduled for ten o'clock today. I want to be there, but the nurse wanted me to stay in my room and rest and not go down to the neonatal ward."

"I took the day off work so I could be there while the baby is having surgery," Dawn replied. "I'll call you as soon as I receive word from the operating room."

Doris wiped the tears from her eyes with a tissue. The tension faded from her face as she smiled. "Would you mind if I came with you? I've got to get used to the idea that I'm now a grandmother with all the rights and responsibilities that come with it."

"Certainly," Dawn answered as she glanced at her watch. "I'd enjoy the company. I think we'd better go down now so we can talk with the doctors before the surgery begins."

The two women bade good-bye to Sarah and walked toward the elevator together. Dawn's neat, white nurse's uniform was a stark contrast to Doris's untidy shirt and jeans and poorly groomed hair. It was obvious that life had been difficult for Doris as she struggled to raise two children by herself. She had dropped out of high school when she had become pregnant with Sarah, and she was determined that both her children would receive an education and a better lot in life than she had had. When she learned that Sarah had made the same mistake she had as a youth, she was unable to cope with the situation. However, months of guilt-ridden loneliness had softened her attitude toward her daughter. She was now determined to make it up to her daughter, whatever the cost.

"Do you think the baby will be all right?" Doris whispered nervously as they strolled through the long, sterile corridor.

"From all indications, it looks as if she has an excellent chance of survival. Let's just trust the doctors to do whatever is medically best for the baby's well-being," Dawn replied.

Dawn approached the nurses' station, while Doris waited patiently a few feet away. "When is the surgery for Charity Blair scheduled to begin?"

"Are you family?" the head nurse queried.

"I'm Dawn Harkness, the mother's obstetrician's nurse, and this is the baby's grandmother, Doris Brown," she replied.

"Charity has been in surgery for half an hour already," the nurse explained as she came from behind her desk and motioned to a sign halfway down the hallway. "Would you care to wait in the waiting room off the surgical ward? I'm sure the surgeon will want to talk with you as soon as it's over."

"Thank you." Dawn smiled as she turned to follow her down the hallway.

"I'll let you know as soon as we have word from the operating room," the nurse promised.

The minutes ticked by slowly as the two women waited. Every so often, the nurse would stop by the waiting room and report how the surgery was progressing.

"Dawn, I told Sarah she could come home as soon as the baby was born, but what about the baby? I'll have to keep working two jobs just to keep my two children in school. Neither Sarah nor I know how to take care of a disabled child. But it would break Sarah's heart if we had to put little Charity in an institution."

"I've been considering all the possibilities for some time," Dawn replied. "Whatever her condition, the baby will need specialized care for several months. I have a lot of personal and holiday leave days that I haven't used yet. Maybe I could bring Charity home with me for awhile. This would give Sarah a chance to go back to school and get her feet on the ground again. You both could come by and see the baby every day, if you'd like."

Doris breathed a sigh of relief. "Thank you," she whispered. "You've taken a load off my mind. Have you told Sarah this yet?"

Dawn shook her head. "No. She's having trouble accepting the severity of the problem. I thought I'd wait until we had a specific prognosis before I discussed it with her."

Two hours later, a tall, gray-haired doctor appeared in the doorway of the waiting room, still dressed in surgical green, followed by the head nurse of the neonatal ward and Dr. Mike Archer. "Miss Harkness. . .Mrs. Brown," the doctor began as both women rose to their feet. "I'm Dr. Harris. I'd like you to meet Dr. Archer, who assisted me with the surgery on Charity Blair."

Dawn's face flushed. The person who did not feel it was necessary to spend a great deal of medical resources on a child with severe birth defects had been the assistant on little Charity. "We've met," Dawn murmured, as Mike's eyes seemed to burrow into her soul.

"He's a fine young surgeon. I'm sure he'll go far." Dr. Harris smiled, then motioned to the sofa. "Let's all be seated. We have a lot to talk about."

"Is the baby all right?" Doris blurted, unable to contain her worry any longer.

"She came through quite well," Dr. Harris assured her. "We inserted a shunt into her head that will continually drain the excess fluid into the abdominal cavity. We also closed the opening in the spine. Unfortunately, the deformity was higher than we expected, so we do not think she'll have feeling or movement from breast level on down. However, the baby's reflexes on her upper extremities seem to be normal. We'll want to keep her in our neonatal unit for three to four weeks to make sure she has stabilized and is eating on her own."

The doctor went on to explain more of the medical details of the surgery. Dawn clearly understood, but a glazed stare remained on Doris's face. When he had finished, the doctor looked at both women and said, "Are there any other questions I can help you with?"

"Is the baby going to be all right, in spite of all her problems?" Doris asked hesitantly, completely overwhelmed with all the medical terms.

"As of right now her prognosis is very good," the doctor assured her. "Of course, the next forty-eight hours will be critical."

"Thank goodness," Doris sighed. "I've been so worried about her. When can I see the baby?"

"You can see her right now, if you'd like," Dr. Harris replied kindly. "However, we have to keep the baby in a clean environment until we're positive she's out of danger."

Dr. Harris bade the women good-bye and excused himself, while the head nurse led Doris down the hall toward the neonatal intensive care unit. Dawn rose and found herself face to face with the man who claimed he saw little future for children with severe birth defects.

"Dawn, I know I hurt you when I said what I did about children with disabilities. That was extremely unprofessional of me. If nothing else, I should have remembered our medical oath to 'do no harm.' After working on the baby, I realized the possibilities the child will have, instead of only her disabilities. Maybe you did have a partial answer to your prayers after all. I am truly sorry for my behavior. Will you be able to forgive me? We could go back to where we were when we went snowmobiling near Red Lodge."

Dawn's lower lip trembled. Mike would never be half the man that Ryan was. "Yes, I will forgive you," she assured him, "but I think our relationship should be a purely professional one."

"But I have so little free time; I'd like nothing better than to spend those few hours with you," Mike persisted. "You're not interested in someone else, are you?"

"Yes, as a matter of fact, I am seeing someone," Dawn stated firmly. "I've known him ever since we were kids in Rocky Bluff. He's now in the process of relocating to Billings."

A faint smile curled Mike's lips. "That must be the fellow you were with in the hospital cafeteria sometime back. He's a fine, wholesome-looking young man, but he appeared to be a little boring for you. He looks like the type who'd like nothing more out of life than a whole houseful of little kids and an obedient wife."

"He is an outstanding person, and I am very fond of him," Dawn retorted sharply.

A spark of anger appeared in the intern's eyes. "I'm sorry to hear that," Mike mumbled. "I guess I should say that I wish you the very best, but if you ever change your mind, you'll know where to find me."

"I'm sure I won't change my mind," Dawn said dryly. "If you'll excuse me, I'd like to catch up with Doris and see the baby."

I'm glad he wasn't the baby's primary surgeon because I doubt that during the surgery he suddenly realized the baby's potential, she thought sarcastically as she hurried down the hospital corridor. *I certainly hope he wasn't just using that as a ploy to get me to help him fill his free hours.*

When Dawn approached the neonatal nursery, she found Doris peering through the glass with tears in her eyes. On the other side of the window was a bassinet containing a sleeping infant with a beautiful face. The tiny upturned nose was identical to Sarah's. A bandage covered the right side of her elongated head, while tubes extended from her little arms and feet. The baby's legs curled motionless at the end of her body.

Dawn put her arm around Doris, who turned and laid her head on Dawn's shoulder. "She's such a beautiful baby," the new grandmother sobbed. "Yet it's not fair. Charity will have so many obstacles to overcome in her life. Why did God let this happen? And to think I was the one who didn't think this child had a right to live because of her deformities."

"It's hard to understand why God allows trials into our lives," Dawn replied gently. "However, through little Charity's life I'm sure that many will come to realize the preciousness of human life. God has given us a very special gift to treasure."

Doris took a tissue from her purse and dried her eyes. Gradually her sobbing ceased. "I haven't thought much about God since I was little and my grandmother took me to Sunday school with her, but looking at this priceless little one, I can somehow feel God's loving hand enveloping and protecting her. I want to pick her up and snuggle her close to me."

"I'm sure they'll let you hold her in a few days," Dawn assured her. "Shall we go back and tell Sarah what a beautiful child she has and that the doctor's prognosis for her is extremely good?"

Doris's face brightened. "I can hardly wait. It took the bravery of my daughter to teach me how precious human life actually is. Now I can understand why some people take such a strong stand against abortion."

"Sometimes it takes a tragedy to wake us up to the great power and wonder of God," Dawn replied as the pair hurried through the busy hospital's corridors. The young nurse noticed how the worry and tension lines seemed to be fading from the new grandmother's face. Even in her wildest imagination, she could not have dreamed that Sarah's hardened mother would ever forgive Sarah, much less become her greatest supporter and a champion of the right for every child to have the best quality of life possible.

As Dawn pushed open the door to Sarah's room, familiar laughter greeted them. Her face brightened. "Ryan, I'm glad you could make it. I wasn't expecting you this soon."

Ryan took her hand. "I wanted to be here earlier, but I got detained at the construction site. Then just as I was leaving, one of the workers drove up and told me that his brother was moving to Arizona and had a town house that he'd like to rent to someone he could trust. He wanted to take me right over before his brother left town and turned the place over to a realtor to rent for him. I couldn't pass up such an offer and jumped in this guy's car almost before I knew his name."

"Did you like the place?" Dawn asked.

"It was perfect," Ryan replied. A twinkle appeared in his eyes. "It's less than two miles from your apartment, and I can take possession within three weeks."

"Great. I can hardly wait to see it," Dawn said, then turned her attention to the young mother who was propped up on the hospital bed. "You're looking well," she said as she took Sarah's hand.

"I feel a lot better than yesterday," Sarah assured them. "I've been impatient for you to get back and let me know how Charity came through the surgery. I was so glad Ryan came to keep me company, and then the aide brought in those gorgeous flowers." She pointed to a new spray of flowers on the nightstand.

"They're beautiful," Dawn noted. "Who are they from?"

Sarah beamed. "Jeff. He wrote on the note that he was glad the baby had finally arrived, and he would do all he could to help with her and to be a part of her life." She hesitated and stared at the flowers. "Someday he'll make someone a fine husband, but neither one of us is ready for marriage now."

"I'm sure of that," Dawn agreed softly.

Sarah turned her attention toward her mother. "How's Charity?" she asked. Her eyes became serious and intense. "Did she come through the surgery okay?"

"She came through her surgery fine," Doris assured her as she took her hand. "She's a beautiful little girl with your little upturned nose. The doctor says her prognosis is very good."

"But will she ever be able to walk?" Sarah asked eagerly.

"She's paralyzed from the breast line down," Dawn explained. "But the doctor assured us that she has normal reflexes in her upper extremities. I hope that they got the shunt in the head before the excess fluid caused too much pressure on the brain. It's too early to tell, but the chances are good that she will have near normal intelligence."

Sarah's face became serious as she looked at the friend who had opened her home to her three months before. "I don't know how to care for a normal baby, much less one that is paralyzed. What am I going to do?"

"The baby will be in the hospital for about three weeks and then I have several weeks of personal leave that I can take. I can care for her myself at home," Dawn assured her. "By then Charity will be older, and we can make a better decision how to best help her. You can come by every evening after school, and I'll teach you how to take care of her."

Sarah smiled at Dawn, then looked quizzically at Ryan before she spoke. "But what about Ryan? I think something special is developing between the two of you, and I don't want my problems to come between you. You need time to be alone together and date, just like everyone else does."

"Wild horses couldn't keep us apart, much less a tiny newborn," Ryan chuckled. "You're just being a hopeless romantic. Little Charity helped draw us together even before she was born, so I can't imagine how she could possibly separate us later." Ryan reached for Dawn's hand. "If God wants us together, He'll make it possible for us. Otherwise, all would be for naught anyway."

Chapter 11

Five days later, a warm February breeze greeted Sarah as the nursing assistant wheeled her from the hospital's main entrance to Dawn's waiting car. As she slid onto the front seat, she felt the stitches in her stomach tighten. "This seems so weird," she said as she held her stomach and looked backward. "It's like I'm leaving part of myself behind."

"In a sense you are," Dawn assured her as she opened the backseat door of her sedan for the young mother. "A part of your body and soul is still up there in the neonatal unit. However, someone will make sure you get to come back and see Charity every day."

Sarah slid into the backseat, while her mother got in the front door. Doris turned halfway around so she could see her daughter. "Sarah, are you sure you feel up to moving your things home now? I don't want you to get overtired."

"Yes, Mom, I do," Sarah exclaimed emphatically. "As much as I've enjoyed living with Dawn, I've dreamed of coming back home for the last three months. If you want me home, I'm ready to move right now."

"Don't worry about a thing," Dawn assured her. "You can just rest on your bed and direct your mother and me while we pack. I picked up some empty boxes at the grocery store this morning, so we can move you to your mother's home whenever you like."

"Thanks, Dawn. You think of everything," she stammered, unable to find the words to express her gratitude. "I don't know how I'll ever be able to repay you for all you've done."

"The biggest repayment I could ever get would be to see you finish high school, receive training for a good job, and continue walking with the Lord," Dawn replied as she turned out of the hospital parking lot onto a busy street.

Upon arriving at Dawn's apartment, Sarah stretched out on her bed, while Dawn began taking clothes from the closet and dresser, and Doris folded them and placed them in the suitcase and extra boxes. "My, you have such lovely things," Doris noted as she held up a sweater made of virgin wool.

"Mom, you wouldn't believe how good the people in Dawn's church have been to me. Many of the younger women donated their used maternity clothes to me along with some nice stuff that I can wear after delivery. They taught me what Christian love and charity was all about," Sarah said as she leaned back against the headboard of the bed. "That's why I wanted to name my baby Charity."

Doris's face became long as her chin dropped, and her eyes became downcast. "They must all think I'm a terrible mother for turning her daughter out when she needed her the most."

"Mother, they are a very forgiving church," Sarah replied softly. "I told them how much I had hurt you by getting pregnant in the first place. I'm sure they'll all want to meet you. They are the most loving bunch of people I've ever met in my life. I hope you and Mark will come to church with me and see for yourselves."

Doris took a deep breath, sat on the edge of the bed beside her daughter, and took Sarah's hand. "You know, Honey. . .I haven't been to church since my grandmother died when I was ten years old. In fact, I'd completely turned my back on God when I married your father against my family's wishes." Doris paused as both their eyes filled with tears. "During these last few months without you, guilt began to overwhelm me. I needed help from someone beyond myself. I began to wonder if maybe there's a lot more to what Grandma tried to teach me about love and forgiveness. I think that it's about time we start attending church as a family. I'd like to thank them personally for helping you during a time when I failed miserably. I need to find that inner strength you seem to have found."

With that, mother and daughter collapsed into each other's arms, as tears of refreshment and healing flowed freely. Years of misunderstandings and anger melted away, and a new sense of hope for the future emerged. They were both anxious to get Sarah moved back home.

❦

The next day at work, time passed quickly for Dawn as several women visited the obstetrician for the first time. She recorded their medical history, took their vital statistics, and discussed basic prenatal care with each of them. After the last patient had left, Dawn approached Dr. Fox as he was making notes on his last chart. "Could I talk to you for a few moments?"

"Sure, come in and have a seat," he said as he motioned to a chair in front of the window. "I was wanting to talk to you about Sarah Brown and her baby. Do you think she'll be able to take care of the baby?"

Dawn smiled. "That was exactly what I wanted to talk to you about. After hearing of the severity of the baby's disabilities, Sarah lost her determination to take care of the baby by herself. Since I have more than thirty days of vacation time built up, I was wondering if I could take my leave as soon as the baby is released from the hospital. This will give me an opportunity to teach Sarah how to care for her baby and search for a more permanent home for Charity."

Dr. Fox leaned back in his chair and linked his fingers behind his head. "I think we could work that out. I'm sure there's a retired nurse who'd be able to cover for you. I'll get to work on that first thing tomorrow."

"Thank you," Dawn replied. "The pediatrician believes the baby can be dismissed from the hospital in three to four weeks. I'll let you know as soon as I have the exact date."

"Dawn, your work with Sarah raised some critical medical and social issues that I brought before our state medical association. They decided to form a committee to address the needs of children with disabilities, and they made me the chair. For the last few weeks, we've been writing a grant that would provide group homes for special-needs infants and children. Our goal is to work as closely as possible with the parents and train them to care for their own child, even if it's only for a limited time, instead of totally institutionalizing the child."

"That sounds like exactly what Sarah needs," Dawn replied excitedly. "Someday she might be an excellent parent, but she has a lot of hurdles to cross before that time. When will you know if you get the grant?"

"They should let us know by the end of May if the funding is available. Then we'll need to find a location and the personnel to oversee the project. Hopefully, we could be operational before fall."

"I hope the home works out," Dawn replied with a touch of dejection in her voice. "However, there's no way it could be operational soon enough for little Charity Blair."

That evening, Dawn went home to an empty apartment. After more than three months with a teenage houseguest, the silence seemed almost deafening. She hurriedly made herself a plate of spaghetti, tidied the kitchen, then collapsed into her favorite chair in the living room. The idea of a group home for disabled children that actually worked with and trained the parents fascinated her. *I've known so many parents who have wanted to do more for their disabled child, but that child's needs had to be weighed against the needs of other children in the family and job responsibilities. Such a group home could be an ideal situation for many different families in a variety of circumstances.*

Dawn reached for the remote and turned on the television to her favorite news show. She smiled to herself when she realized that it had been three months since she had had sole control of the remote. She had never spent much time in front of the screen and generally only kept it on for company, so when Sarah lived with her, Dawn had been more than willing to let her make the selections.

Just before Dawn retired, the telephone rang. She reached over and took the cordless telephone from the end table. "Hello."

"Hi, Dawn. I hope you haven't gone to bed yet."

"Ryan. I was just sitting here relaxing. I'm glad you called. It seems so strange to come home to an empty apartment without schoolbooks cluttering the coffee table."

"I wanted to call earlier, but I just got back to the motel. There seems to be no end of decisions to make and details to take care of when starting a new business."

"I'm sure working twelve-hour days must be getting very tiresome," Dawn agreed sympathetically.

"It is," Ryan sighed, "but hopefully, the long days will come to an end soon and we can spend more time together. I just wanted to tell you that I was going to go back to Butte this weekend and pack my apartment. My new landlord said I could store my things in his garage until he has moved out of the condo. I figured I might as well save myself some rent money. I was wondering if you'd be able to have dinner with me Thursday night before I leave."

"Sure, I'd love to," Dawn replied without hesitation. "I could be ready about seven."

The pair visited for the next few minutes about Sarah Brown and the condition of her baby. Dawn detailed how she was planning to change her guest room into a temporary nursery. She then went on to tell about the grant Dr. Fox had been working on that would provide a group home for disabled infants and children.

"That sounds like a great idea," Ryan exclaimed. "I'm sure Pastor Olson in Rocky Bluff will be anxious to hear about it. He's been so active with the Right-to-Life movement in Montana, and this seems to go hand in hand with their goals. He may know some parents to refer to the program."

"As soon as I know if they are awarded the grant, I'll let him know right away," Dawn promised. "Maybe some sort of referral service can be developed between the two groups."

Dawn could not hold back a yawn in the middle of a sentence, and Ryan picked up the cue. "I'm sorry to have called so late. I'm looking forward to seeing you Thursday. I better let you get a good night's sleep."

❖

Two weeks after Sarah was dismissed from the hospital, she and her mother went to the high school to visit the guidance counselor. Sarah was able to get her assignments for the three weeks she had missed and promised to have them all completed within the next two weeks.

Walking down the hallway and seeing her old friends troubled Sarah. When they got to the school parking lot, Sarah turned to her mother. "It seemed so strange to see all the kids wandering around in the hall. . . . I felt so different. . . . I can still go to class and talk to everyone, but it won't be the same. Now I have the baby to think about. No one will want to date a sixteen year old who's already a mother."

"Granted, this has forced you to grow up in a hurry, but I'm confident that you're up to the challenges," Doris assured her as she reached into her purse for the car keys. "Not many girls could have withstood the pressures that you have and still be eager to complete her education and get on with her life."

"But little Charity's future will always be my primary concern." Sarah sighed as she slid into the passenger's seat. "She's so sweet and innocent."

"I'm so proud that you feel strongly about your responsibility to Charity," Doris replied. "Not many girls in the same circumstances would feel the same way."

Doris turned the car out of the school parking lot and onto the busy street. She glanced at the long, forlorn expression on her daughter's face. "Would you like to stop at the hospital and see the baby before we go home?"

"I'd love to," Sarah murmured. "I hope she's out of the incubator and strong enough so that they'll let me hold her."

The neonatal nurse greeted them with a smile. "Sarah, your baby's breathing has improved so we've taken the oxygen off. This morning we began introducing her to a bottle. Would you like to try and feed her?"

"Certainly." Sarah beamed as she looked over at her mother. They followed the nurse down a narrow aisle lined with bassinets. Many of the babies could be held in the palm of one's hand. Tubes were going into and out of their little bodies. Some were lustily crying, while others lay limply in their beds. In the far corner was the largest baby of the group. Charity Blair now weighed a hefty eight pounds six ounces.

The nurse reached into a nearby cabinet and handed a gown to each of them. "I'd like to have you both slip one of these on before you hold the baby."

Sarah nervously put on the gown. "I don't know how to hold her," she said. "What if I accidentally bump the shunt in her head?"

"It's not much different than holding a baby who doesn't suffer from neural tube defects," the nurse assured them. "I'll give you some tips to follow. These babies need to be held and loved the same as healthy babies."

The nurse leaned over and gently picked up the baby, gently supporting the infant's head with her arm. She then reached into a container nearby and took out a four-ounce bottle half filled with a creamy substance. "We have a mother's room you can use. Just follow me."

For the next two hours, Sarah and her mother took turns holding and cuddling little Charity. After the baby drank an ounce from the bottle, she began to fuss. The nurse immediately arrived. "She probably needs to be burped," she explained. "It will be a little tricky at the beginning because you'll want to be careful not to pat the part of the back where the surgery was performed. This, of course, will heal in time, but she'll always have an abnormal hump there." She reached for the infant in Sarah's arms. "Here. . .I'll show you."

Sarah promptly lifted the baby toward the nurse. "I knew it might be difficult, but I never realized there would be so many different things to watch for when I cared for a baby with spina bifida."

"You'll learn," the nurse assured her kindly. "Every time you come, I'll help you."

Sarah continued to cuddle her baby until she fell asleep. The nurse gently put little Charity back in her bassinet, while Sarah and her mother removed their hospital gowns, thanked the nurse, and left the neonatal unit. As they walked down the now-familiar corridor, Doris turned to her daughter. "It's getting late, and Mark won't be getting home until after basketball practice. How would you like to stop at the hospital cafeteria and get something to eat before we go home?"

"It may not be the Ritz, but it beats cooking." Sarah laughed.

Sarah and her mother made their selection from the cafeteria line. Doris paid the cashier, while Sarah wandered ahead to look for a place to sit. Sitting by herself at a table by the window was Dawn Harkness. Dawn looked up and motioned to the pair to join her. Sarah immediately obeyed and took the chair next to the window, leaving the outside one for her mother.

After the two were seated, Dawn asked, "How was the baby today?"

"She's beautiful," Sarah responded proudly. "I got to hold and feed her for the first time."

"That's great." Dawn smiled. Her delight matched the young mother's. "I didn't know she was able to eat on her own yet."

"The nurse said she took her first bottle yesterday," Sarah replied; then her eyes became sad and distant. "I didn't know how to burp her because of her back surgery. There's just so much that I need to learn. I'm glad you're going to take Charity home with you when she's released from the hospital, but what's going to happen when you have to return to work? I don't know if I'll be able to care for her myself, and I certainly don't want her placed in an institution."

"We'll have to take it one day at a time," Dawn assured her. "God has a special plan for little Charity, and we must have faith in His love."

❖

The next three weeks passed quickly for Dawn Harkness. She worked full-time and assisted with the delivery of three babies; in addition, every day she visited baby Charity in the neonatal unit of the hospital. Clare Thompson had agreed to fill in for Dawn while she was on leave from the doctor's office. For a week, Clare shadowed Dawn and quickly learned the office routines.

On Friday evening Dawn was busy putting the final touches on her temporary nursery when the telephone rang. She hurried down the hall to answer it. "Hello," she greeted as she took the cordless telephone and sank onto the sofa.

"Hi, Beautiful," a cheerful voice greeted. "It's all set. I can move in tomorrow."

Dawn chuckled as she recognized the husky voice. "Ryan, it sounds like you had a good day. You mean the painters finally finished the condo?"

"The last pail of paint was carried out this afternoon so I can take possession in the morning. No more motel rooms for me."

"I've moved enough in my life, and I know it's not a lot of fun," Dawn laughed. "Would you like some help?"

"Why do you think I called?" he teased. "That condo is going to need a female touch, so I thought I'd have it done right from the very beginning. Afterwards I'll treat you to a steak dinner at the Longhorn."

"That sounds like a deal," Dawn agreed. "It may be the last time I'll be able to go out for quite awhile. If all goes as planned, I'll be bringing little Charity home from the hospital on Monday."

"I'm not going to let a helpless little baby come between us," Ryan scolded good-naturedly. "I'll have to start bringing in Chinese food to your apartment and ordering out for pizzas. Where there's a will, there will always be a way."

"Ryan, I appreciate your understanding. Sometimes I don't fully understand my concern for Charity myself, but it's such an intense urge that I can't walk away from it."

"I know," Ryan answered softly. "I can't turn my back on innocent babies, either. That's why the Right-to-Life movement has become so important to me."

Chapter 12

Each day after eighth period, Sarah immediately caught the city bus to the downtown hospital. As soon as she got to the neonatal unit, she went directly to the nurses' station. Her question was always the same: "How has little Charity been today?"

The response was usually the same: How much food she was able to take from a bottle, how many grams of weight she had gained, or how long she was alert that day. After being briefed on the health of her baby, Sarah would put on a hospital gown, take Charity to a mother's room, and rock her. She comfortably gave the baby a bottle when she was hungry, but when it was time to change Charity's diapers, Sarah would immediately call a nurse.

After asking for assistance every day for over a week, the head nurse finally asked, "Sarah, you're so good at caring for your baby and seem to be learning very quickly how to work with her disabilities; yet you seem afraid to change her diapers. Is there something bothering you about changing her?"

Tears filled Sarah's eyes. "Charity's so normal down to her waist, but then nothing looks right from the waist down. Her little legs are dislocated and twisted. I can tell that she can't feel anything there, and I'm afraid I won't get her clean enough or dry enough and she'll get some kind of sores. Most babies would cry if they had a diaper rash, but Charity wouldn't know the difference, and it could get really bad before anyone would know."

The pediatric nurse placed her hand gently on the young mother's shoulder. "Sarah, you are wise beyond your years. That is one of the biggest problems with babies with neural tube defects. I'm glad you've learned that while the baby is still in the hospital. It will save you many problems later on."

Sarah blushed. "The last few weeks that I was pregnant I was on complete bed rest, so I had a lot of time to read. It seemed like I read all kinds of things, but mostly I read about babies with special needs." She hesitated and bit her lip. "I finally accepted the fact that I might not be able to care for my baby for a long time. I'm glad that Dawn Harkness has agreed to take care of Charity for at least a month after she gets out of the hospital, but then I don't know what I'll do. I don't want to have to put Charity in an institution."

"I know Social Services is looking for a suitable foster home for your daughter," the nurse explained gently, "but foster homes are hard to find."

"Yes. . .especially for special needs children," Sarah added dryly.

Exactly three weeks after Charity was born, Sarah accompanied Dawn to the hospital to bring the baby home to Dawn's apartment. Church friends had loaned Dawn a car seat, a bassinet, and an assortment of other baby items.

Sarah covered the baby's face against the brisk March wind that was blowing across the hospital parking lot. "I can't believe Charity's finally leaving the hospital," the young mother said. "Hopefully, she won't have to go back for a long time."

"She'll probably see a lot of hospitals in her lifetime," Dawn assured her as she opened the back door of her car. "We know the doctors are hoping to do corrective surgery on her feet when she gets a little older, and probably there will be other corrective surgeries after that."

Sarah fumbled with the car seat and finally got Charity positioned and strapped into place. "I never realized it was so difficult to put a baby in a car seat," she noted as she backed out of the rear seat and closed the door. "I've watched other mothers do this, and it looked so easy. I feel so clumsy at it. I think it's going to be a long time before I'm ready to become a full-time mom."

"You're doing the right thing, under the circumstances," Dawn said as she slid behind the wheel of her car. "You're realistic about your limitations, and you're getting an education so you can make the best home possible for your baby and yourself someday."

"There's nothing I'd like better," Sarah replied as she looked over her shoulder at the sleeping infant. "I really don't want her put in an institution."

That evening while Dawn was considering what to fix herself for dinner, the telephone rang. "Hello," she greeted as she picked up the receiver.

"Hi, Sweetheart. I just wanted to check to see how the new mother's doing," Ryan answered cheerfully.

"I'm doing great. Little Charity has been sleeping ever since we got her home. I suppose that means I'll be up a lot in the middle of the night."

"Possibly," Ryan chuckled in agreement. "To save you some work, why don't I pick up some fried chicken and bring it over? It would save you having to take time to fix something for yourself."

"You must be clairvoyant," Dawn teased. "I was just opening the refrigerator door to figure out what to eat when the phone rang. Of course, it's always a lot more fun to have someone to eat with."

"I'll be there in forty-five minutes," Ryan promised, then bade her good-bye.

True to his word, an hour later, Ryan had spread the chicken, coleslaw, and French fries around Dawn's kitchen table, and they both were enjoying the levity of the moment. They almost forgot they were no longer alone when suddenly a stormy cry was heard from the bedroom. "I guess we're not the only ones who are hungry," Dawn laughed as she hurried to the bedroom.

Charity quieted as soon as she was cuddled against Dawn's warm chest, but she kept puckering her little lips. "Ryan, would you mind holding her while I fix a bottle?" Dawn asked as she handed the baby to her friend.

"I'd love to." Ryan reached for the infant as the smile widened on his face. An immediate bonding was made as the young bachelor gazed into the baby's soft blue eyes. Charity's body relaxed even more, but her lips kept twitching.

After Dawn checked the bottle's temperature, Ryan reached out his hand. "Would you mind if I feed her?"

"Sure, but you might be more comfortable in the rocking chair."

While Ryan fed the baby, Dawn began tidying the kitchen and preparing more bottles for the next day. Before long, Charity was asleep in his arms with a contented expression on her face. Ryan kept rocking and admiring the child. "Dawn," he called quietly, "have you ever noticed what a beautiful face she has?"

"That was the first thing I noticed about her when she was born," Dawn answered as she wiped off the countertop. "Hopefully, she'll grow into her head in a few years. Right now it looks so disproportionate to the rest of her body."

Ryan kept admiring the precious child in his arms. "It's a good thing they were able to get the shunt in right away so the pressure wouldn't keep building up in her skull. At least we can have hope that her cognitive learning center hasn't been damaged."

"And when her hair comes in, it will hide the lump under the skin of her head where the shunt is," Dawn added as the infant slept in Ryan's arms.

Those words were scarcely out of her mouth when Charity gave a pained scream. "What's wrong?" Ryan panicked. "She was sleeping so peacefully. You don't think her shunt blocked up, do you?"

Dawn gently touched the skin over the shunt. "It's still soft and collapsible, so I don't think it's the shunt. Did you remember to burp her when she finished eating?"

Ryan's face reddened. "Oops," he said as he lifted the baby to his shoulder and began to pat her on the back. "I was so concerned about her disabilities that I forgot the obvious."

"That's one of the disadvantages that people with disabilities face every day," Dawn replied as she made herself comfortable on the sofa. "Too many people focus on the disability instead of the normalcy and strengths of the person."

Ryan continued rocking, and within a few moments Charity was again peacefully asleep in his arms. He gently walked her into the bedroom and laid her in her bassinet. When he returned, Dawn was sitting on the edge of the sofa with her legs curled beneath her. The soft light from the lamp added an innocent sweetness to her face.

Ryan sat beside her and took her hand. "I'm so glad my company had me relocate to Billings to manage their new store. Just seeing you sitting there and feeling the warmth of your home makes me certain that my days of travel are over. I'm ready to settle down and establish roots."

Dawn blushed as he squeezed her hand, while he put his other arm around her shoulders. "I don't know how you stood motel life for as long as you did," she stammered.

Ryan pulled her closer against his chest. "It wasn't too bad of a life. That is, until I became reacquainted with you. Then all the peaceful memories and family life of Rocky Bluff flooded over me. Dawn, you don't have to answer me right now." Ryan paused as their eyes locked and reached into each other's soul. "Dawn, would you consider making this a permanent relationship? Would you marry me? I have never met anyone that I could ever love as much as I love you, and I want to spend the rest of my life with you."

Dawn gulped. For one of the first times in her life, words seemed to escape her.

Finally she blurted, "Ryan, I do love you. It. . .it's just that there's so much going on now. Your new job is just getting off the ground. I have an extremely demanding nursing career. . .and now there is my commitment to little Charity. I just don't know what to say."

Ryan brushed back a lock of hair that had fallen in front of Dawn's eyes. "You don't have to say anything right now. All I ask is that you give it some thought and prayer. If our marriage is supposed to happen, God will work out the details in His own good time and in His own way. If it isn't His will that we marry, we would be miserable together."

Ryan's lips moved toward hers. "Ryan," she whispered, "you're so right."

❦

Every evening, Sarah came to see her daughter. Oftentimes her mother accompanied her, and occasionally her younger brother Mark. A new warmth and closeness had developed with their family that had never been there before. Not only had they developed a deeper relationship with each other, but also they had begun to attend church as a family and were developing a deeper relationship with God.

One evening, when both Doris and Sarah were there to see the baby, Ryan arrived. He always stopped by Dawn's place after work, but tonight he was two hours early. Sarah was rocking her baby in Dawn's padded rocker and only half listening to the conversation when she heard Ryan say, "I have all my employees in place now except for someone to answer the telephone and work the front desk from four to six in the afternoons. I have an excellent young woman who can only work until four because she has small, school-age children, and she doesn't want to leave them at home alone after school."

Doris nodded her head. "I can't say that I blame her," she agreed. "I remember what a problem it was for me to work, knowing that Sarah was at home taking care of Mark after school."

Sarah's attention suddenly shifted from the infant in her arms to those seated around her. Her eyes brightened. "Ryan, what does the job consist of?"

"Mainly answering the telephone, basic word processing, and ringing up the merchandise once a salesperson has made a sale," Ryan explained. He paused and surveyed the young mother in the rocking chair. "Sarah, would you like to have the job? It pays a little more than minimum wage to start, then goes up every six months after that."

"Sure," the teenager blurted without hesitation. "I've finally gotten my schoolwork caught up, and I know Mom is having trouble meeting the expenses for all of us. Mark just took a paper route last week, so it's only fair that I do my part as well."

"Great," Ryan exclaimed. "You can come to the store at four o'clock Monday to fill out the paperwork, and you can start right away."

Sarah could scarcely contain her delight. "Thanks, Ryan. I'll work my hardest for you. You and Dawn have been so good to me, and I owe you both so much. I don't know what I'd have done if I'd never met either of you."

❖

A week later Sarah came bounding into Dawn's apartment. Even before she had time to pick up the baby, she announced, "Jeff called me this afternoon, and he and his family are planning to come to Billings for Easter. They all want to meet Charity. Isn't that exciting?"

Dawn hurried in from the kitchen and gave the excited girl a hug. "That's tremendous. When are they going to get here?"

"They're going to drive all day Friday and get here about seven that night. They're planning to stay with some of his mom's friends for the weekend and leave early Monday morning," Sarah exclaimed. She hurried to the bassinet and picked up her daughter. "Charity, Daddy's going to come see you. Isn't that nice?"

All day Friday Dawn went about her routine with a vague sense of apprehension. How should she face such a difficult situation? She was glad that both the kids had admitted their mistake in having brought a child into the world long before they were ready for marriage and parenthood. For the sake of little Charity, she had to be glad that both her natural parents were taking such an interest in her, although neither one would be ready to care for the child for several years. . .but what should their relationship be until that time?

Promptly at eight o'clock Friday night, Dawn's doorbell rang. When she opened it, there stood Sarah with Jeff and his entire family. "Welcome," Dawn greeted as she motioned them to enter. "Do come in. How was your trip from Missoula?"

"Pretty uneventful," Dan chuckled. "Except that we let Jeff drive, and we got here a little before we should have."

Dawn gave Jeff a sympathetic look. "I understand how that can happen. I sometimes have trouble keeping my speed down as well when I'm coming across the wide open spaces of Montana." She then nodded at the others. "Please take off your coats and have a seat."

Sarah rushed into the bedroom and picked up her sleeping child. She proudly carried her into the living room. Everyone commented on Charity's beautiful eyes, her cute turned-up nose, and her sweet little face. However, everyone was uncomfortable to ask about her disabilities. Finally, Sarah put their discomfort to rest when she began telling about Charity's medical problems. She pointed to the location of the shunt and explained how it worked and how to recognize signs when it might become plugged and not draining properly. She showed them the baby's twisted feet and told how the doctors wanted to do surgery on them when Charity was older. Sarah then went on to explain how both hips were out of joint and how they did surgery on the baby's back to close the spinal column the day after she was born.

Everyone listened to Sarah with amazement. They had never been close to a child with a neural tube defect, and now it had happened to someone that was part of their flesh and blood. The Blair family shuffled nervously until Beth responded.

"Sarah, she's a beautiful baby," Beth said kindly. "I'm impressed with how much you've learned about her disabilities. You're doing an excellent job under the circumstances. May I hold her?"

"Sure," Sarah responded as she handed the baby to her other grandmother. "I've become really interested in disabilities since I had Charity, and I'm thinking of eventually going to college and majoring in occupational therapy. I'd like to help people with special needs reach their fullest potential."

Jeff sat quietly with a serious expression on his face. "She's really cute," he whispered hesitantly. "It's hard for me to get used to being a daddy, but I think she does have my eyes. . . . Regardless of what happens, I want her to grow up knowing who her natural father is and that he truly loves her."

Jeff slowly arose and walked to his mother's side. "Mom," he said timidly, "may I hold my daughter? It's totally amazing how fragile life can be." Tears filled his eyes as he awkwardly took his child and returned to his seat at the end of the sofa. The others maintained a lively conversation about Charity's daily routine, while Jeff could not take his eyes off her little face.

The Blairs stayed at Dawn's apartment until well after ten o'clock. Dawn was amazed how Charity's parents did not seem like regular teenagers. They both carried an air of wisdom and strength brought about by having to live with the serious consequences of their mistakes.

❖

Saturday afternoon, Dawn's doorbell rang. When she answered it, there stood Jeff and Sarah, giggling like the couple of teenagers they were. "We've been at the mall most of the day, but Jeff wanted to spend the rest of the time with our daughter. Would you mind?" Sarah said breezily.

Dawn smiled at the intensity of their request. She was pleased they would voluntarily give up a night on the town to spend it with their daughter. "Of course not," she replied. "Do come in. In fact, tonight let's see if Ryan could pick up a couple of movies on his way home from work, and we'll order out for pizza. I know the time Jeff has here in Billings is pretty precious to both of you."

Sarah entered the apartment, tossed her coat over the back of a chair, and went straight to the bassinet. Charity was just waking, and it was obvious she was hungry. Sarah cradled the baby in one arm while she took an already filled bottle from the refrigerator and put it in a pan of water on the stove. Jeff shyly followed behind.

"Sarah, you do that like you've done it for years," Jeff said with amazement as he watched her every movement.

She tested the warmth of the formula on her wrist, then put the nipple in the baby's mouth. "I've got this end down fine," she laughed. "It's the other end I'm not so good at taking care of."

Chapter 13

As the time for her to return to work drew closer, Dawn became increasingly perplexed. Social Services had been unable to locate foster parents that were willing to take in a disabled child. The longer she had taken care of Charity, the more attached to her she had become. A week before she was scheduled to return to work, she bundled the baby against the late April breeze and went to the clinic just as Dr. Fox was seeing his last patient of the day.

He motioned her to wait in his personal office until he was through. As she relaxed in those familiar surroundings with the infant lying beside her, a sense of ambivalence swept over her. Her love for her job was conflicting with the new love that was developing toward little Charity. Finally, Dr. Fox returned to his office and immediately took the baby in his arms.

"It looks like she's thriving under your care," he said as he admired the infant in his arms.

Dawn beamed as if she were the biological mother. "Under the circumstances, she's doing quite well," she replied. Without indulging in small talk, Dawn got right to the objective of her visit. "The reason why I stopped by is that I'm scheduled to return to work Monday, and Social Services does not have a place for Charity except in the state institution. She's doing so well that I cannot bear the thought of her being institutionalized."

Dr. Fox shook his head. "Neither can I," he agreed. "Maybe we could come up with another solution. There's an excellent chance that we will get the grant to establish a home for handicapped infants. We should know for sure within six weeks. Is there any way possible you could hold on until we hear on the grant?"

Dawn hesitated. She had examined that question from every angle, but nothing had come to mind. Slowly, the corner of her lips began to turn up. "Maybe Mother could come and stay with me for a few weeks and take care of Charity while I'm at work. She's always been good with kids, and she's been looking for ways to volunteer her services since Dad died. I'll give her a call this evening."

Dr. Fox returned the sleeping child to her infant seat. "That's a good idea. If your mother's willing to come, it would buy us more time. After all our hard work in applying for this grant, I'd hate to have Charity miss its benefits."

The doctor and his nurse continued discussing the details of the proposed home; then the conversation turned to the current patients and when each of their babies was due. Dawn was anxious to be back working with them, if only she could find a solution for Charity.

When she returned home, Dawn immediately dialed her mother. Nancy answered the telephone on the third ring. "Hello, Dawn. It's so nice that you called. How's that little one doing for you?"

"Charity's doing great," Dawn replied as she cradled the baby in her arms. "She's already sleeping at least six hours straight every night."

Nancy could not hide her motherly pride. "I'm so proud of what you're doing for her. Few people would give up all their vacation time to take care of a special-needs child. Have they found a permanent home for her yet?"

"That's the reason why I'm calling," Dawn said as she took a deep breath. "They haven't been able to find a home for her yet, but there is a possibility of one becoming available in six weeks."

"So what are they planning to do with Charity until that time?"

"Mom. . .I was wondering if you'd like to come to Billings and stay with me for a few weeks and take care of Charity while I'm at work."

Nancy paused. Her mind raced through her daily routines and any up-coming social events. "I'd never have thought of that before, but I don't know any reason why I can't," she replied. "Your brother can watch the house and take care of the lawn while I'm gone. My mothering skills may be a little rusty, but I'm sure they'll come back in a hurry."

"Mom, I really appreciate this. You're a true champion. When do you think you'd be able to come?"

"How about if I drive down Sunday afternoon after church? I'll let all my friends know I'm going to be gone and where to reach me if necessary."

They finished their conversation and bade each other good-bye. Dawn nearly sang as she hung up the telephone after talking with her mother. She was going to have the best of all worlds. Extra time with her mother, a chance to go back to the job she loved, and more time to find a permanent caregiver for Charity.

That evening when Sarah stopped to see her daughter, she was not her normal bubbly self, even after hearing the good news that Dawn's mother was going to come and help care for Charity. Sarah's usually well-groomed hair was dirty and in disarray, and there were dark bags under her eyes. She only spoke when she was spoken to, and her eyes were misty as she silently rocked her baby.

"Sarah, what is wrong?" Dawn said kindly as she took a seat on the end of the sofa next to the rocking chair.

"Nothing…really," the young mother muttered.

"It's written all over your face," Dawn persisted. "Did you have a bad day at school?"

Sarah shook her head. "No, school was okay," she said as she continued staring blankly into space.

The furrow deepened on Dawn's forehead. "How long have you been feeling this low?"

"I don't know," she answered dryly. "Each day is getting worse, but nothing particular has happened. I'm just not with the program anymore, and I don't care about anything but Charity."

"Sarah, have you been sleeping well at night?"

"I don't know. . .not really. . . . I've been getting up a lot and watching TV until one or two in the morning," she slowly admitted.

"How long has this been going on?" Dawn persisted.

Sarah shrugged her shoulders. "I don't know. . .probably about three weeks. I was able to hide it for a long time, but I think that whatever it is, it's finally getting the better of me."

Dawn's concern continued to mount. "Have you ever heard of postpartum depression?"

Sarah shook her head. "No. What is it?"

"After having a baby, most new mothers think that they'll be able to get back to their prepregnancy state right away, but that doesn't always happen," Dawn explained as she studied Sarah's dejected face and demeanor. "Your hormones might be having trouble adjusting to no longer preparing for a baby. I think you'd better see Dr. Fox as soon as possible. Would you come to the office right after school tomorrow and talk to him about this?"

"But what about my job?" Sarah protested.

"I'll let Ryan know you'll be a little late," Dawn promised. "In fact, I'll pick you up and drive you to work myself. It's most important that you see a doctor as soon as possible."

Knowing that there may be a biological reason for why she was feeling so sad helped ease Sarah's pain a little. She was becoming afraid she was going to lose her mind with the sadness of Charity's condition and the guilt she felt for having gotten pregnant out of wedlock. Now she saw a faint ray of hope that the midnight of her soul would end and that this was not a permanent condition. She thanked Dawn for her concern and returned the baby to her bassinet.

Sarah had scarcely left Dawn's apartment when Ryan arrived. It was becoming almost a routine that he stopped to see Dawn on his way home each evening. He would often bring food with him or else Dawn would have dinner ready for them to eat. This particular evening, Dawn had a meat loaf and baked potatoes in the oven when he arrived. Ryan helped her put the finishing touches on their evening meal. As they sat down to eat, he noted the tired bags under his sweetheart's eyes. "Honey, you look extremely tired. Have you been getting enough sleep?"

"I just finished giving Sarah the third degree about her emotional state, and now you're doing the same to me," Dawn laughed. She took a deep breath and sighed. "Actually, I've just had a busy day."

"Sorry to intrude," Ryan replied as he laid his fork on the side of his plate and gave her his full attention. "I'm just concerned about you. You mean so much to me, and I hate to see you wearing down."

"I'll be fine," Dawn assured him. "We haven't been able to find a permanent home for Charity yet, and I have to go back to work next Monday, so I went to talk with Dr. Fox today."

"Did he have any suggestions?" Ryan queried. "We're getting down to hour zero."

"He said it looked pretty good that the grant to start a home for infants and children with special needs will be approved," she explained. "However, they won't know for another six weeks."

"Oh. . .that could present a problem. Did he have any suggestions on what to do with Charity until they know for sure if they got the grant?" Ryan asked.

Just then, soft cries came from the bassinet. Ryan rose to get the baby. Immediately, the child was comforted and relaxed in his arms with a faint smile on her face. Ryan returned to his chair at the kitchen table with Charity cradled in his arms.

"Thanks," Dawn said, then returned to the subject at hand. "I called Mother, and she said she would come and stay with me for a few weeks and take care of Charity while I'm at work. I think it will be good for all of us."

"I hope so, but after you've worked all day and often spent nights helping with deliveries, don't you think it might be too hard on you to come home and take care of a baby?" Ryan said as he snuggled the baby against his broad chest.

Dawn could not help smiling at the warming picture of love and security Ryan created as he gently held the infant. "I love taking care of her," she replied. "Besides, there are a lot of single moms who work all day, then come home and take care of a family."

"I realize that," Ryan agreed, "but it's still a lot of hard work and a difficult position to be in."

Dawn shrugged her shoulders, then turned the attention away from herself. "Right now I'm more concerned about Sarah."

Ryan wrinkled his forehead. "What's going on with her?"

"I think she's suffering from postpartum depression," Dawn replied, shaking her head sadly. "I insisted that she see Dr. Fox right after school tomorrow, and I told her I'd talk to you about her being late to work. I hope you'll be able to find someone to fill in for her until she gets there."

Little Charity began to fuss in Ryan's arms. Dawn immediately got up, went to the refrigerator, and took out a bottle. She put it in a pan of water, then stood by the stove while the bottle warmed.

Ryan shook his head. "There may be more problems with her job than just being late to work tomorrow," he said with a sigh of worry. "It's being rumored that a national chain is trying to buy out our company, which means we could all be out of a job."

Dawn's face blanched. "But how can they sell out now?" she protested as she handed the warm bottle to Ryan. "Your company just invested several million dollars in building the store here in Billings."

"It's hard to understand what goes on in corporate boardrooms," Ryan said as he gently put the bottle in the baby's mouth. "My guess is that they overextended themselves when they opened this store. I should know more about what's going on sometime next week."

Ryan finished feeding the baby, laid her back in the bassinet, then helped Dawn load the dishwasher. An air of uncertainty and apprehension hung over them. Just when they had finally considered marriage, Ryan might be losing his job. The complexities of the day overwhelmed Dawn as she tried to hold back her tears.

Ryan took her in his arms as she burst into tears and laid her head on his shoulder. He stroked her hair as he held her tight. "It will all work out for the best," he tried to assure her. "You're just tired. Things will look brighter tomorrow. God hasn't brought us this far just to abandon us now. We'll have to trust Him as we wait for the answers to our prayers."

❀

Late Sunday afternoon, Nancy Harkness parked her car in the parking lot of her daughter's apartment complex. She looked forward to the next few weeks with Dawn. Her son, Jay, his wife, and three children lived in Rocky Bluff and she was able to see each of them every few days, but Nancy missed not getting to spend the same amount of time with her grown daughter. Through all the good times and bad times of their lives, the Harknesses were an extremely close family.

Nancy took one of her suitcases from the trunk and headed for Dawn's apartment. As soon as she rang the doorbell, she was greeted by a warm hug. "Mother, I'm so glad you could come. I don't know what we'd have done without you."

"Dawn, I'm so glad you invited me to come. I'm just looking forward to us having quality time together," Nancy replied as she picked up her suitcase and stepped into the apartment. "You've been under such a strain ever since you invited Sarah to come and live with you, and you deserve a break. So many good things have been happening, but you're just too tired to recognize them."

Dawn took her mother's coat and hung it in the closet. "Sit down and rest, Mom. I'll bring your other things in later. How was your drive?"

"It was pretty uneventful," Nancy replied, "except there was a lot of road construction, and I had to wait for several lead cars to guide us through."

"That's typical," Dawn laughed. "As soon as the snow is gone in Montana, the road crews appear out of nowhere."

For the next couple of hours, Dawn brought her mother up to date as to the baby's condition, habits, and favorite things. After listening patiently, Nancy began to laugh. "Relax. Don't forget I have had just a little experience with babies. After all, both of mine turned out mighty fine. I'm sure Charity and I will have no problems together."

Dawn began to giggle. That laughter was just the medicine she needed. "I'm sorry, Mom. I guess I've just gotten too emotionally involved with this entire situation."

Nancy nodded her head. "Yes, you probably have," she agreed, "but that's a sign of your concern and that you're doing a mighty fine job with Charity. Just please let others help carry the load with you. You can't continue carrying it by yourself without breaking."

"Thanks, Mom. You're right as always."

Just then, the doorbell rang, and Dawn hurried to answer it. "Ryan, I'm glad you were able to come," she exclaimed as he gave her a quick kiss. "Mother just got here."

Ryan laid his coat on the back of a chair, went across the room, and shook Nancy's hand. Dawn went to the kitchen to make coffee, while Nancy brought Ryan up to date on the people and events in Rocky Bluff. He was especially interested in Pastor Olson and his continued work with the Right-to-Life movement. Their plans of reopening a pregnancy crisis center in Billings had built a strong bond between them.

Dawn returned with the coffee, then joined them in the living room. Ryan smiled and winked at her, then turned to her mother. "Besides getting a Rocky Bluff update, Dawn and I have something we'd like to discuss with you."

Nancy raised her eyebrows, looked at her daughter, and smiled. "Hmm. . . this sounds serious."

"It is," Ryan laughed. "I would seriously like to marry your daughter because I seriously love her."

Nancy beamed as she reached over and squeezed Ryan's hand. "I'm so happy for both of you. It's about time you both found someone and settled down. When are you thinking about tying the knot?"

Dawn's chin dropped. "That's part of the problem," she replied. "There's a good chance that a national chain is going to buy out Ryan's company and bring in their own employees from wherever. We can't plan anything until he has a job that he can depend upon."

Nancy took another sip of coffee. "I'm sure you won't have any trouble finding work here in Billings. It's such a big place you won't know which job to choose."

"I wish it were that easy," Ryan sighed. "Too many people from the West Coast have been moving into this part of the state and taking the good jobs. I'll have to have a job that pays enough to support a family. Neither one of us is getting any younger."

"Speak for yourself," Dawn laughed. "I may not be getting any younger, but I'm definitely not getting any older."

Just then, a loud wail was heard from the bedroom, and Dawn automatically jumped to her feet. "Sit down and rest," Nancy ordered kindly. "Now it's my turn to take care of the baby. I haven't had a chance to hold one for several months."

Moments later, Nancy returned with the baby in her arms. She was carrying her abnormally far away from her own body. "Charity's soaking wet," she laughed. "Where do you keep the diapers?"

"Just a moment, and I'll get one for you," Dawn replied as she hurried into the spare bedroom. She located a fresh diaper, a clean, pink sleeper, and a dry receiving blanket and brought them back to the living room. Nancy automatically began unwrapping the baby and taking off her wet clothes. She could not hold back her gasp when she saw the twisted feet and legs.

"Oh, the poor dear," she cried. "You warned me about how bad her disabilities were, but I didn't fully understand until I saw it for myself. No wonder you feel so committed to help her."

"I know," Dawn said, almost in a whisper. "Regardless of what their little bodies are like, you can always feel the spirit and love of God with each new child that enters this world. . . . I guess that's why I became an obstetrics nurse."

Chapter 14

Friday evening, Dawn and Ryan relaxed over dinner at the Long Branch Supper Club. This was the first time they had been able to go out to dinner alone since little Charity was born two and a half months before. Since Dawn's mother had come to Billings to help with the baby, Dawn was able to return to work at the clinic and to occasionally have some free time alone with her best friend and sweetheart.

After dessert, Ryan reached into his pocket and took out a small, square box. He took her left hand, while he flipped open the box. "Dawn, I know we won't be able to set a date for awhile, but I'd like you to have this and tell the world that we're in love and plan to be married."

Dawn's eyes widened. A broad smile spread across her face. "Ryan, it's beautiful," she gasped as she marveled at the three-quarter-karat diamond. "But you shouldn't have."

Ryan slipped the ring onto her third finger. "I only wish it could have been twice as big. I want the world to know how much I love you."

"But you spent so much on me," Dawn protested. "What if you lose your job in the company buyout?"

"Dawn, you're always trying to be too practical," Ryan teased as he put his arm around her shoulder and pulled her against him. "I've been saving for this for a long time, and I decided that you needed at least one luxury in your life. You've done so much for others; it's time someone did something extraspecial for you."

Tears gleamed in her eyes. "Thank you," she murmured. "I'll cherish this forever."

"And I promise to cherish you," Ryan replied as his eyes melted into her soul. "As soon as I know what is going to happen with my job, we can go ahead and set a wedding date."

"I. . .I. . .I don't know what to say," Dawn stammered, "except. . .I love you."

"That's all I need to hear to make my life complete," Ryan said lightly. He then took a sip of his coffee and scowled. "This has gotten cold," he laughed. "I wonder if that's a sign that we should go? I'm anxious to let your mother know that we're one step closer."

Dawn laughed as she folded her napkin and placed it beside her plate.

"Mother will be thrilled. She was concerned that I'd go through life an old maid, and she insists that being single will become more difficult the older I get."

"We'll just have to let her know that her worries are over," Ryan teased.

Dawn became serious as she pulled his hands next to her mouth and kissed his knuckles. "I've always told her that marrying the wrong man is worse than not marrying at all," she replied, "but now I'm positive that I will be marrying the right man. . .the one that God intended for me to spend my life with."

Ryan wrapped his arm around his fiancée as he helped her rise to her feet. Holding hands, they stepped into the warm spring air. Their spirits matched the singing birds in the nearby trees as they strolled across the parking lot. They both had waited so long for these moments. Although the future was uncertain, there was one thing that they could be certain about—their love for each other.

When they returned to Dawn's apartment, the excitement of the moment was tempered by the harshness of reality. Nancy was sitting in the rocking chair trying to console the baby, but Charity's painful cries persisted.

"This has been going on ever since you left," Nancy explained as Dawn reached for the baby. "I tried to feed her, change her, and do all the normal things one would do to comfort a little one, but nothing seems to work. She acts like she's in pain, but I can't tell where. She's not pulling on her ear or anything."

Dawn gently rocked the infant in her arms, while the crying persisted. She lightly touched the skin over the shunt. A frown covered her face. "I don't like this," she said. "It's not soft and flexible like it should be. I think we better telephone the hospital and check with the pediatrician who's on call this evening."

Cradling the baby in her arm, Dawn dialed the hospital telephone number. After a brief conversation, she turned back to Ryan and her mother. "They think we should bring her up to the hospital right away, and the doctor will meet us in the emergency room."

Dawn hurried to the bedroom for the diaper bag and an extra blanket. Her nervousness was contagious to the others.

"Would you like me to drive for you?" Ryan asked as he held the front door opened for Dawn and her mother.

"I'd appreciate that," she replied, reaching into her purse for her car keys.

When they arrived at the emergency room, the nurses took Charity immediately to an examining room. The minutes ticked by as the pediatrician examined the baby and ran a battery of tests. Finally, the doctor looked at Dawn and said, "I'm afraid her shunt has become blocked and fluid is building up around the brain. That's causing her a great deal of pain." The doctor tried to comfort the distraught child, but to no avail. "Although it's getting late, there's no reason for this child to suffer the way she is. I'll get a surgical team together right away, and we'll replace the shunt."

While the hospital personnel prepared Charity for surgery, Dawn called Sarah. She carefully explained the pending surgery, which caused Sarah to burst into tears. "I'll be right there," she sobbed. "I don't want anything to happen to my baby."

"Sarah. . .calm down. . . . Everything's going to be all right," Dawn tried to assure her. "This is a very common surgery for children with hydrocephalus. We're just glad that we spotted it as soon as we did."

There was a long silence on the other end of the line. "Sarah?. . .Sarah?. . . Sarah, are you all right?"

"Yes, I'm fine," the young mother gasped. "Charity was abnormally fussy when I was there after work, but I thought she was just tired or something. If it was up to me, I probably wouldn't have taken her to the hospital, and she might have died."

"Honey, it's all right," Dawn continued to assure her. "Charity is in God's hands, and He knew the best time to bring her to the hospital for treatment. If you'd feel better, meet us in the surgical waiting room. The nurses will let us know how the surgery is progressing."

Gradually, Sarah calmed, said good-bye to Dawn, and hung up the telephone. Within twenty minutes, she and her mother joined Dawn, Ryan, and Nancy in the surgical waiting room.

"How's she doing?" Sarah asked even before she greeted anyone.

Dawn put her arm around Sarah's shoulder. "The surgical team has just arrived, and they have given Charity the anesthesia. They're not expecting any problems with the shunt replacement. However, they'll want to monitor the baby for at least twenty-four hours afterwards."

"I'm glad to hear that," Sarah sighed as she sank onto the edge of the sofa. "I was so worried."

Dawn took the seat beside the young mother. "How have you been? I've been real concerned about your depression," she said.

"I'm doing a lot better," Sarah admitted. "The doctor prescribed some medicine, and he made arrangements for me to see a Christian counselor. I don't think I could have handled this at all if Charity's shunt would have blocked a month ago. But I hate to think that I have to depend on mind-altering drugs."

A look of concern covered Dawn's face. They had discussed this several times, but the meaning had not seemed to influence the young mother. "Sarah, taking an antidepressant is nothing to be ashamed of," Dawn persisted.

"Postpartum depression is biologically caused; it's not a character disorder."

Sarah's eyes became distant as she shrugged her shoulders.

"You wouldn't hesitate taking an antibiotic if you had an infection, would you?" Dawn persisted.

"Well. . .no," Sarah muttered, then hesitated. "I know you're right. I guess it's just going to take time for me to get used to all the changes in my life this past year."

The topic of conversation changed to each of their summer plans. Knowing that her job working with Ryan would probably be short-lived, Sarah was already looking for a full-time summer job. She told how she was hoping to work with the YMCA day camp. She was interested in majoring in occupational therapy when she went to college and thought this was a good way to get experience with children.

Doris explained that she was hoping to take a week off work and visit her parents in Indiana, while Nancy said that she'd like to visit Disney World with her son Jay and his family. Ryan and Dawn exchanged knowing looks. Their greatest desire was to marry, but nothing could be decided until his job situation was settled. Time passed faster than they expected, and suddenly, the doctor was standing in the doorway.

"The baby is a tough fighter," the doctor explained with a smile, "and the surgery went well."

"Thank you," Sarah whispered. "When can I see her?"

"You can look in through the glass," the doctor said, "but she'll probably be sleeping until morning. Get some sleep tonight and check back with us tomorrow. If she's stabilized, we'll let you take her home."

"Thank you, Doctor," Dawn said as she shook his hand. Each of the others in the party followed suit and shook the doctor's hand as they thanked him. As they left for their respective homes, each wondered how many other such crises Charity might have to face throughout her lifetime.

❧

During the next two weeks, Charity became more alert than ever. She began reaching for toys that were held before her. She would turn her head toward a familiar voice and smile. Sarah was thrilled at each new developmental stage her daughter entered. With each passing day, Dawn could see more and more of a change in Sarah, who was again laughing and enjoying life.

A couple weeks later, Sarah hurried to Dawn's apartment after work. As soon as Dawn invited her in, Sarah blurted, "Guess what? This was my last day working with Ryan. The new owners came in and gave all of us a termination notice and two weeks of pay."

"You sure don't seem very upset about losing your job." Dawn smiled.

"I'm not," Sarah exclaimed, "because I just got a notice yesterday that I got the summer job I wanted with the YMCA day camp. In addition. . .best of all. . .Jeff got a job at the same place. He's going to come to Billings for the summer, stay with his parents' friends, and save money for college and help with Charity's expenses."

Dawn gave Sarah a congratulatory hug. "That's great. I knew things would eventually work out for the best for you."

Sarah hurried to the bassinet and picked up her daughter who was beginning to whimper for her evening feeding. "Did you hear the good news?" she giggled. "Mommy's got a good job for the summer, and your daddy's going to be able to see you more often this summer."

Dawn warmed a bottle and handed it to Sarah, who was aglow with pride and happiness. By 8:00 P.M., Charity was changed and ready for bed. Sarah gave her one last kiss, laid her in her bed, said good-bye to Dawn and Nancy, and left. Both women marveled at the change in Sarah in the last few weeks.

Shortly after Sarah left, the doorbell rang. "That must be Ryan," Dawn said to her mother as she hurried to the door. "I wonder how he fared with the company layoff."

Dawn opened the door and greeted Ryan with a kiss. "Do you still have a job?" Dawn queried as she noted the serious look on his face.

"They're bringing their own crew in tomorrow, so they gave everyone their dismissal papers today along with two weeks' pay," Ryan said as he entered the living room and flashed a faint smile at Nancy. "However, they'd like me to stay on and work for two more weeks to make sure there's a smooth transition, then I'll be let go."

"Do you have any idea what you're going to do after that?" Dawn asked as she led him by the hand to the sofa.

"I've been watching the want ads in the paper lately, but nothing has looked very appealing. I'm planning to register at Job Service tomorrow and see what's available through them," Ryan explained as he sat down and pulled Dawn close. "I want to be selective about a job, because I want it to be able to support a wife and family."

"I'm sure God will provide an even better job for you," Nancy reminded him. "We'll just have to make it a concerted prayer effort. Maybe we can have the prayer chains in your church and mine in Rocky Bluff pray for a suitable job for you."

"I'll take any prayers on my behalf I can get," Ryan chuckled.

The next couple of hours, they discussed the possibilities of different jobs in Billings, yet nothing seemed to match Ryan's needs and skills. The evening ended on a discouraging note for them. Just when they were becoming eager to marry, the practicality of it was becoming more and more remote.

❀

The next day, after the last patient left the clinic, Dr. Fox called Dawn into his office. "Would you mind staying after work for a few minutes? There's something I'd like to discuss with you."

Dawn took the chair by the window, glad to have a few minutes to get off her feet and rest. "No problem," she replied. "Mother is so good with little Charity that I don't have to be concerned about her care. I just don't know what I'll do when Mom has to return to Rocky Bluff."

Dr. Fox took the stethoscope from around his neck and sat down in his overstuffed chair behind his desk. "That is part of what I wanted to discuss with you," he said as he took a large white envelope from beneath a pile of papers. "We just received word that our committee from the Montana Medical Association was awarded the grant to establish a group home for infants and children with birth defects."

"How exciting!" Dawn exclaimed. "When will you be able to begin working on it? Will it be available soon enough to help little Charity?"

"We can start right away," Dr. Fox replied, "and the interesting part is that Dr. Richard Brewer from Rocky Bluff is retiring and moving to Arizona—and he's willing to donate his building for a group home. Since you grew up in Rocky Bluff, do you know him and the location of the building?"

Dawn gasped as her eyes widened. "Dr. Brewer has been our family physician for four generations. He took care of my grandmother during her heart attack and last days, then my father's final illness, and now he's taking care of my brother's children."

"I've heard that he's been very committed to his patients throughout the years and is highly respected in the community," Dr. Fox noted. "What do you know about the building he's in? Is it in good condition?"

Dawn tried to visualize the building she had dreaded going to for her childhood immunizations. She remembered how Dr. Brewer was always there during every family crisis. It was hard for her to imagine that one of the icons of Rocky Bluff would no longer be there.

"His clinic is a nice brick building on the edge of town with maybe ten thousand square feet of overall floor space," Dawn assured him. "It was built sometime in the sixties, and I think it's been remodeled a time or two since then."

"It's nice that it's at the edge of town," Dr. Fox noted with increasing interest. "Do you think it'd take much work to convert it into a group home?"

"Probably not," Dawn replied as she tried to visualize the interior of Dr.

Brewer's office. "The waiting room is about the ideal size for a living room, the nurse's station could easily be made into a kitchen, and each of the examining rooms could be made into bedrooms."

Dr. Fox locked his fingers behind his head and rested his head against his palms. He leaned back in his chair and smiled. "So far it sounds perfect. I'd like to go to Rocky Bluff and see it."

"I'm sure you'll like the building. You'll be impressed with the community," Dawn said with pride. "A smaller town with a family atmosphere would probably be a better place to pilot such a project as opposed to one of Montana's larger cities."

"You do have a point there," Dr. Fox agreed, "but how are the medical services there? That will be one of the key requirements of such a home."

Dawn nodded her head and smiled. "That shouldn't be a problem," she assured him. "There are several doctors in Rocky Bluff and an excellent community hospital. They also make good use of the medevac helicopter services from the Great Falls hospitals. I think they can transport a patient in a little over half an hour."

"Hmm," the doctor said as he gazed out the window deep in thought. "You make this more interesting with every sentence. I'd like to drive over there this weekend in my van. Would you and your mother like to bring little Charity and ride along? I could really use your input."

"I'll talk to Mother," Dawn promised, "but I'm sure it can be arranged."

"Good," Dr. Fox exclaimed. "I'll check to see if the rest of the committee can join us. Then as soon as we get the location selected, we can begin looking for a director."

Dawn grimaced. "That could be a problem. It may be difficult to find someone with such specialized skills who would move to a small town."

"That's true," Dr. Fox agreed. "We'll just have to see what happens. Sometimes people are anxious to move into a small town to get away from the problems of city life. I'm looking forward to the trip this weekend. Thanks for your help with this project."

Dawn rose to leave. A look of concern spread across her face as she remembered that she and Ryan had had plans for the weekend. However, she was sure he'd understand the necessity of the trip.

As if he were reading her mind, Dr. Fox called to her, "Dawn, I don't want to completely deprive you of your weekend. Isn't Ryan Reynolds also from Rocky Bluff?"

Dawn turned and smiled. "Oh yes. He and my brother were best friends in high school."

"Why don't you ask him to come with us? There'll be plenty of room in the van, and I could use another point of view when we look at the building."

"I'll talk to him tonight and give you a call," Dawn replied with a smile. "There's a nice motel close to the clinic. I could make reservations for you and the committee, if you'd like."

Chapter 15

That Saturday, while Nancy Harkness cared for little Charity in her home, Dr. Fox, Dawn Harkness, and Ryan Reynolds, along with three other doctors from the Group Home Grant Committee, met with Dr. Brewer at his clinic. After an hour of inspecting and discussing the potential of each corner of the building, Dr. Fox turned to the aging physician as he led the small band back to the clinic's waiting room. "Dr. Brewer, you have a lovely facility here. I'm sure you hate to leave it."

The elderly doctor beamed. "It has served both me and the community well," he replied proudly. "However, now it's time to move on. I've bought a nice condominium in Arizona, and three young doctors have built a beautiful new clinic beside the hospital. Rocky Bluff and the entire medical profession have been extremely good to me, and I'd just like to leave something as a legacy. A group home such as you've proposed seems to be something that will serve the entire state for years to come."

"We appreciate your generosity," Dr. Pierce said as each one found a seat in the waiting room. "I think I can safely speak for everyone on the committee that we're more than willing to take you up on your generous offer. When do you plan to vacate your building?"

"I plan to be out by the first of June," Dr. Brewer explained. "I've already started selling and giving away a lot of my equipment. I'll sign the papers right away, and you're welcome to begin remodeling the next day, if you'd like."

"After all the months of planning, then waiting, things are happening almost too quickly." Dr. Fox sighed as he looked over at the other doctors on the committee. "If we only had a director, I'd say let's go ahead and begin work immediately, but I'm afraid to move forward until we have someone who'd be able to take full responsibility for the project. We're all too involved with our practices to devote as much time as will be needed to develop this."

Everyone nodded in agreement.

"We've discussed the qualifications of a director before, but I'm afraid we're asking too much to expect to find someone with all the skills that we'd like," Dr. Pierce said cautiously.

"If we want to remain true to our original goal of having a home environment, we should try to look for a husband/wife combination," Dr. Jannings said as he pushed his glasses onto his forehead. "That is definitely going to limit our field of candidates."

Dr. Fox shrugged his shoulders with frustration. "But we also need someone with nursing or a related field of training—plus someone with strong managerial skills who relates well, not only with the medical professionals, but the community at large. . . . And, of course, it'd be most helpful if they could drop everything and begin work in Rocky Bluff right away."

Dr. Brewer chuckled with sympathy at the doctors' dilemma. "That means you'll need someone who's already familiar with the community so they can hire and supervise the contractors who will be doing the remodeling."

Suddenly, the group grew quiet. In one accord they looked first at Dawn, then at Ryan. "The only problem is," laughed Dr. Brewer, "they're not a married couple."

"I could take care of that in a hurry." Ryan laughed as he squeezed Dawn's hand.

Suddenly, the levity stopped, and the doctors' faces became serious. "Would it be possible that the two of you might be interested in directing the group home?" Dr. Pierce asked. "You'd both be perfect for the job."

Ryan and Dawn turned to each other with quizzical eyes, but before they could answer, Dr. Fox protested, "But you're suggesting taking the best nurse in Billings away from me."

"That's a sacrifice worth making for the cause," Dr. Pierce retorted with a smile. "If Dawn's willing to take the job, I'd be willing to help you find another nurse."

Dawn looked at Ryan, and they both smiled and nodded. Through the last several months, they had become so attuned to each other's thoughts and feelings that they were nearly positive of what the other was thinking. "I'd like nothing better than to return to Rocky Bluff," Dawn replied. "I could stay in Billings long enough to help train a replacement, then live with Mother until the home is ready."

Dr. Fox's face became serious. "Dawn, I'd hate to lose you as a nurse," he began, "but most of all, I want you to do what you feel will work out best for you." He then turned his attention to the man sitting next to her, holding her hand. "Ryan, how do you feel about the project?"

"It sounds perfect," he exclaimed excitedly. "I only have one week left with my company, then I'm free to do whatever. I could probably do a lot of the remodeling myself and save quite a bit of money."

Dr. Pierce rubbed his chin. "Hmm. . .sounds like everything is falling into place pretty well. I suggest we meet next Saturday in Billings to finalize the arrangements after we've all had time to do our legal homework."

The group agreed on a place and location, bade each other good-bye, and went their separate ways. As the doctors strolled toward the parking lot, Ryan turned to Dawn. "Let's walk over to the restaurant across the street and have a soft drink and a dish of ice cream. We have a lot of planning to do."

The pair walked across the street hand in hand. At last, they could begin to set a date and plan their wedding. For the next hour, Dawn and Ryan relaxed over their ice cream as they planned their future lives together. All their hopes and dreams were finally becoming a reality.

"Let's call Pastor Olson and invite him and Teresa to dinner after church Sunday. We can ask him to marry us the last week in August," Ryan suggested.

"Are you sure we can get everything done in three months?" Dawn questioned. "You know if we get married here in Rocky Bluff, by the time we invite all our relatives and close friends we'll end up inviting half the town," she laughed.

"I think we can have a large wedding and still keep it simple," Ryan replied as he reached for her hand. "I know your mother will be in her glory planning a wedding."

Dawn laughed at the thought of her mother, the queen of weddings, calling on all her friends to help her with the plans. "Ever since Mother helped plan my grandmother's wedding when Grandma was sixty-seven, the wedding bug bit. Now she and Rebecca Hatfield are chairwomen of the social committee at the church and work with all the newlyweds' families in making their special day even more memorable. They've earned quite a reputation around Rocky Bluff for their organizational talents."

"Well, let's give them the challenge of their lives," Ryan laughed, "and propose the wedding of the century."

Sunday morning, Nancy accompanied Dawn, Ryan, and little Charity to church. After the service, the parishioners gathered around Dawn and Nancy. They all seemed excited to learn about the proposed children's group home being planned for Rocky Bluff and Dawn and Ryan's upcoming marriage. Many were unaware of the tremendous needs of children born with disabilities. Some of the people remembered when Sarah Brown was in the hospital in Rocky Bluff the past Christmas. After they met little Charity, many were anxious to volunteer their time helping at the home. Several retired carpenters volunteered to help Ryan remodel the clinic.

At dinner, Ryan, Dawn, and the Olsons engaged in an animated conversation about the Montana Right-to-Life movement and Pastor Olson's work in that area. Finally, Ryan said, "You know, Pastor, I've always been active in the antiabortion movement, but I always had a judgmental attitude toward those who sought an abortion," he confessed. He paused as he looked at Dawn, who was listening with adoring eyes. "However, after I met Sarah Brown and saw what she went through to preserve the life of a child who was known to have birth defects, I was really convicted about my judgmental attitude. . . . If I'm ever going to make a vocal statement against abortion, I should be willing to help expectant mothers who refuse to destroy the human life growing within them. . . . Helping with this group home is my way of working for the Right-to-Life movement. I want to show the world that these children's lives are worth saving, even if they do have certain physical or mental limitations."

"How nobly put," Pastor Olson said. "If there's ever anything I can do to help with the project, please let me know."

"Well, there is one thing," Ryan replied with a grin.

"What's that?" Pastor Olson asked as he surveyed the smiling faces of the pair across the table.

"Dawn and I would like to marry the last weekend in August. Would you and the church be available at that time?"

Pastor Olson reached into his coat pocket and pulled out his daily planner. He flipped a few pages and said, "It looks like that date is free. What time would you like to schedule the wedding, and do you want to reserve the fellowship hall for a reception?"

Ryan looked at Dawn. "How about two-thirty in the afternoon?" Dawn replied; then a silly grin spread across her face. "Of course, we'd have to have a reception in the fellowship hall with all the trimmings. I'm sure Mother would never accept anything less."

The old friends continued making plans for the upcoming wedding. As the conversation evolved, they all became increasingly excited, not only about the wedding, but also about the possible group home. Before Teresa had married Pastor Olson, she had been instrumental in founding a battered women's shelter in Rocky Bluff and knew many of the challenges in establishing such a project.

"Dawn, I'm so proud of how you took Sarah Brown under your wing in her time of need," Teresa said as they were finishing their desserts. "She was a teenager in trouble, but you didn't give up on her."

"I'm just glad you didn't give up on me when I was the troubled teenager and got involved in drugs. It's really scary where I might be today if you hadn't intervened," Dawn replied as she reached across the table and patted Teresa's hand. "I guess helping Sarah is my way of passing on the compassionate love that you showed to me."

"I guess it's the each-one-help-one philosophy that holds our society together," Teresa replied with a smile.

Three hours later, Dr. Fox was driving his van back to Billings with Dawn,

Ryan, Nancy, and baby Charity, as the sun set behind the western mountains. Their spirits were high at the weekend's surprising turn of events. Without realizing it, Nancy began humming her favorite hymn, and within moments, everyone picked up the tune and began singing along with her. By unselfishly doing what they felt was right, good was going to triumph over the bad.

❖

A week later, Dawn was relaxing in her apartment watching television when the telephone rang. She reached for the telephone at the end of the sofa. "Hello."

"Hello, Dawn. This is Mike Archer. How have you been doing? I haven't seen you for several weeks."

"Hello, Mike. It's good to hear from you again. I've been extra busy with my work and taking care of little Charity."

"I was hoping we could get together for a couple hours. I've really missed seeing you."

"I'm sorry, Mike, but I don't think it would be appropriate. Ryan and I have announced our engagement and plan to be married the end of August."

There was a long silence on the telephone line before Mike said dejectedly, "Congratulations. I wish you the very best. . . . However, I have something very important I need to discuss with you. You're the only one in Billings I know who can help me."

"Wow. . .that sounds serious," Dawn replied, not knowing whether she was being manipulated or if he did have a real need. After all, he didn't know many people in Billings since his work schedule was so heavy.

"I'm afraid it is," Mike said. "I've been extremely concerned about my father's health for some time, but I just received a call that my mother had a stroke and is in critical condition. I've always been close to my father, but Mother provided the stability in my life. I don't know what I'll do if I lose her. I'm going to be flying back to Iowa in the morning."

Dawn hesitated. Little Charity was asleep in the bedroom, and her mother was sitting in the recliner reading a mystery novel. "I don't think Mother would object to keeping an eye on the baby while I'm gone. I could meet you in the hospital dining room in twenty minutes."

An audible sigh of relief echoed over the telephone lines. "Thanks, Dawn. I promise I won't impose on you again."

For over an hour Dawn listened to Mike's concern about his mother and the void that he felt in his life just thinking about what life might be like without her. For the first time in his life, his strong-willed self-sufficiency failed him. He now wanted to know more about Dawn's faith in God and the power of prayer.

Dawn was more than eager to share the gospel of Christ's love and sacrifice with him. She knew firsthand how Christ could change a person's life and give meaning and direction in a seemingly hopeless situation. Mike's entire countenance changed as he began to understand the good news that Dawn was sharing with him. She encouraged him to begin reading the Gospels to better understand what she was telling him, then she wrote an address and a couple of telephone numbers on a sheet of paper.

"Mike, I understand that you're required to work long hours at the hospital, but every Christian needs to be networked with other Christians. Here's the address of my church and pastor. I'm sure you'll find them extremely helpful."

Mike gave a faint smile. "You know. . .I haven't been to church since I was in junior high school. The church folk I know, though, seem to have a much better understanding of life without a college education than I have with a doctor's degree."

"There are just some things we can't learn from a book—unless it's from the Holy Bible," Dawn replied. "Recognizing that there's a power higher than yourself will make you a much better doctor when you realize that a doctor can treat the human body, but only God can heal it."

"Dawn, you've taught me so much," Mike said softly. "Just watching your persistence in maintaining the value of a severely disabled child taught me that there had to be more to human life than just a combination of cells. From now on, I'm going to take an entirely different approach to my profession. I just want to thank you for all you've done for me, and if I do not see you again, I'd like to wish you the very best in your upcoming marriage."

Tears filled Dawn's eyes as she left the hospital. If Dr. Mike Archer had not become acquainted with the innocent life of a severely disabled child, he might have continued relying only on his own skills and not realized the source of all true healing. She again saw another example that, eventually, all things do work together for good for those who turn to God for hope and guidance.

❖

On Monday Dawn anxiously awaited Sarah's daily after-school visit. When the young mother arrived, she immediately picked up her daughter and took her to the rocking chair. Dawn took the end of the sofa next to her. "Sarah, I have great news for you," she began excitedly. "Ryan and I have agreed to become directors of the group home for children with disabilities."

"Fantastic!" Sarah exclaimed. "So you'll be able to take care of Charity until I finish my education and hopefully Jeff and I marry."

"If we can get all the legal and medical details worked out, that's how it looks right now," Dawn replied.

Sarah's eyes continued to shine as she snuggled her baby next to her breast.

"I'll get to keep seeing my baby almost every day until I'm ready to take full custody of her."

Dawn hesitated. "Well, not exactly," she said cautiously. "Dr. Brewer donated his medical building in Rocky Bluff to be used for the group home, and Ryan will begin remodeling it in June. We plan to be married the end of August and have the home operational by the beginning of September."

Sarah's chin dropped as tears filled her eyes. "That's not fair," she sobbed. "If you move to Rocky Bluff, I won't be able to see Charity very often."

"I never thought of it in those terms," Dawn sympathized, "but I guess you're right. However, there is a community college in Rocky Bluff; maybe you could take some of your college work there."

Sarah remained quiet as she cuddled her baby and continued to rock her vigorously. She looked down on the infant's face and whispered. "I'll do whatever's best for you—but I don't want to have to part with you."

Sarah handed the baby to Dawn and started to sob again. "I don't know if I'm strong enough to see that Charity gets the best care regardless of my own desires."

"Sarah, you're stronger than you realize," Dawn comforted. "I'll let you know every new development Charity makes, and if things work out, someday you'll be able to care for the child yourself."

"I know," Sarah replied, as she tried to choke back her sobs. "My head knows that this is the best thing to happen to Charity, but my heart can hardly bear it."

"You've become a strong, compassionate young woman. Only time and faith in God will help ease the pain," Dawn continued softly. "In the meantime, we'll have to continue taking each day as it comes. Will you be my maid of honor at my wedding? We will always be bound together by our mutual love for little Charity and the value of all human life."

Chapter 16

August thirtieth was a day of flurry and activities. Rebecca Hatfield had spent the last two months helping Nancy Harkness plan decorations and refreshments for the big day. They reserved a block of rooms at the nearest hotel for out-of-town wedding guests. The rehearsal dinner the night before had been a smashing success, and now the big moment was about to begin. Dawn Harkness was to become the bride of Ryan Reynolds.

Dawn waited in the side room of the church sanctuary with her brother, Jay, who was about to escort her down the aisle. A lifetime of memories and faces flashed before her. Through a crack in an open door, she saw Jeff Blair holding his daughter, Charity. Jeff's parents, Dan and Beth, were beside him. Dawn's thoughts drifted back to the days when she was a little girl and Beth an unwed teenage mother. She remembered how the entire community rallied to Beth's support when her toddler was kidnapped by his natural father and taken out of the country. Dawn remembered how her beloved grandmother, Edith, had helped Beth through her difficult times and had been instrumental in introducing her to Dan Blair, who had taken over the management of the Rocky Bluff Crisis Center from her second husband, Roy Dutton. Dan later married Beth and adopted her son Jeffery as his own.

Dawn spotted Rebecca and Andy Hatfield sitting near the aisle. She remembered how Rebecca had followed her grandmother's example and had found love and marriage during her later years. Dawn smiled as she remembered having Rebecca help her with her high school research projects as the school librarian. When Rebecca retired, she took a school librarian's position on Guam where she met Mitzi Quinata. Because of Rebecca's love for Guam, Jay requested an Air Force assignment at Andersen Air Force Base, Guam. Soon after arriving on Guam, Jay met and fell in love with Mitzi's daughter, Angie.

Dawn's mind drifted to the pastor's study, where her soon-to-be husband was waiting. She remembered how Ryan had played with Jay in elementary school and how the two had become inseparable sports heroes in high school. She knew Ryan's brother Larry was waiting with him as his brother's best man. Her grandmother had been instrumental in helping Larry get through a difficult period in his life.

The organ began to play a joyful prelude. Dawn pictured her friend, Teresa

Olson, on the organ bench. She remembered when she first came to Rocky Bluff to start the Spouse Abuse Center. Teresa had been Dawn's stabilizing factor during her time in drug rehabilitation; then she remembered how excited she had been when she learned that Teresa was going to wed the new pastor in town, Bryan Olson.

Dawn continued to scan the more than four hundred people who had gathered to celebrate her marriage to Ryan Reynolds. Seated in the church audience were people that Dawn had known and loved all her life. Dave Wood and his new wife, Louise, were there; Dave had been her attorney when she had been arrested as a rebellious teenager involved with drugs. Dave had convinced the court to order her to drug rehabilitation rather than jail. Then there was Stuart Leonard and his wife, Joy. Stuart was the county attorney for Little Big Horn County. He had handled all of the legal problems that arose when little Jeffey Blair had been kidnapped by his natural father and taken to Canada. Next was Rocky Bluff's retired chief of police, Phil Mooney, and his wife, Jessica, two of the most respected elders in the community. Seated beside them was Rocky Bluff's current chief of police, Scott Packwood, and his wife, Kim. Phil and Scott were lifelong friends and partners on the Rocky Bluff police force for many years. Dawn remembered how hard they had worked to try and find the cause of the fire that destroyed her father's hardware store, only to have to call in the state's arson investigator to learn it was caused by electrical problems.

Tears filled her eyes as the people's love and support throughout the years overwhelmed her. Truly, Rocky Bluff was a special place of love and healing.

Suddenly, a warm hand touched her shoulder. "Dawn, are you ready?"

The tearful bride looked up into her mother's eyes, then pulled her close. "Yes, Mother. I'm ready to return to Rocky Bluff."

Love
Abounds

Chapter 1

Sarah Brown dropped the letter onto her desk as her tearful eyes drifted listlessly toward the window toward the administration building of Rocky Bluff Community College. The grass was a brittle brown, while the leaves lay in piles against the surrounding structures. Generally, there would have been at least one major snowfall in central Montana before Thanksgiving, but this had been an exceptionally warm autumn, and the strongest leaves were still clinging tenaciously to the trees. Her term paper was due the following week, she had a group presentation consisting of a debate before the entire class on their selected topic, plus final exams were two weeks away.

Why does this have to happen to me now? She groaned with frustration as a lump built in her throat. *In spite of how hard I've worked, it looks as if I'll have to drop out of school and work two jobs until I can save enough money to finish. My financial aid for next semester is only going to be enough to cover my tuition and books, and not nearly enough to cover my room and board. As much as I hate to do it, I suppose I'd better go talk to my advisor tomorrow and let him know that I won't be back for spring semester.*

A shrill ring interrupted Sarah's worries. She reached for the telephone on the corner of her desk. "Hello."

"Hello, Sarah," a cheerful baritone voice greeted. "I thought you were going to meet with our debate team at the library at two o'clock." A slight tease resonated in his voice. "We can't function here without you."

Sarah glanced at the clock over her roommate's dresser and gasped. "Oh no, I forgot all about it. I'll get my notes and be right over."

"Great. We'll be waiting for you in the corner study room on the main floor."

Sarah nearly ran the entire way across campus to the library. When she breathlessly arrived five minutes later, three of her classmates were already clustered around a rectangular table, engaged in heavy debate.

"Glad you could join us," Ryder Long scolded jovially as he pulled out the chair next to him for her. "We're in the process of deciding who will take the affirmative position in support of the United States' involvement in the building of the International Space Station and who will argue against it. So far, we have two in favor of the project and one uncommitted. How do you stand?"

Sarah took her seat and glanced around the table at her classmates. As much as she liked each one of them, she would much rather work on a project independently. Although collaboration was considered an extremely effective educational tool, Sarah often felt as if they were designing an elephant by committee instead of planning a usable presentation. However, in spite of her misgiving, she immediately joined into the group dynamics. "I've been doing a lot of research over the Internet about the ISS, and from what I've learned, I think our country would be much farther ahead spending our tax money on social services instead of more hardware toys for the scientists," she stated firmly.

"Spoken like a true liberal," Ryder teased.

Sarah's face reddened as she tried to maintain her composure. "My viewpoint has nothing to do with my politics," she retorted sharply. "But it has a lot to do with my own personal experiences. I don't like to see some people have extra while others starve and can't pay their bills."

Marcella Cross's eyes widened, and an expression of concern spread across her face. "How are you in more pain than the rest of us?" she queried sarcastically. "Aren't we all in this college struggle together?"

Sarah studied her friend's innocent face and trendy clothing. Sarah rarely shared her background with her classmates, because most would not understand the hurtful, complex events that had brought her to Rocky Bluff to attend college. Knowing that she could only tell part of the story, Sarah took a deep breath and replied, "For one thing, I just learned that my financial aid for next semester won't be enough to cover my room and board, so I'll have to drop out of school until I can save enough money to finish. If more money were available for education, I'd be able to graduate this spring with everyone else."

A shocked look spread across each of her classmates' faces. She knew that those who were able to live at home with their parents had little understanding of the pressures of those who had to pay for their own room and board.

"Surely there's some way you can stay in school," Ryder responded sympathetically. "I'd hate to think that you got within five months of graduation, then weren't able to finish your associate's degree. You're one of the hardest workers in our class."

Sarah fixed her eyes. "Don't worry. . . I'll be back," she promised. "I have a better motivator to complete my degree and get a good paying job than most students." Before anyone could question her further, Sarah immediately changed the subject. "Now back to the space station question. . . How are we going to proceed with our debate? It looks like whoever is undecided will need to argue against the U.S. involvement in the International Space Station with me. He or she can supply the objective facts, and I'll supply the passion."

Everyone nodded in agreement. "That settles the easy part," Ryder shrugged. "Now for the hard part—how can we obtain enough documentation to substantiate our individual viewpoints?"

The other team members looked at each other with blank stares and shrugged their shoulders as Sarah shuffled through her papers. "I found a fantastic Webquest on the Internet that was put together by a high school principal in Brazil and a high school media specialist in Iowa. It contains links to all kinds of Internet sites pertaining to the International Space Station, and it's organized by how each group with a vested interest in the space station views the need for this project."

❖

As Sarah spoke, Ryder studied Sarah's delicate features and strong determination. There was something mysteriously different about her. She was not only highly intelligent and highly motivated, but the intensity in her eyes portrayed an aura of mystery that none of her peers possessed. "At least one person has done her homework," he said with a smile as the others glanced ashamedly at the floor. "Could you tell us the Internet address so we can all take a look at it?"

"Just a second," Sarah muttered as the others took out their pencils and waited, while she shuffled through her notebook. "Here it is," she replied after a long pause.

"Has anyone else done any research on the topic?" Ryder asked as his eyes went from Marcella to Josh. "We can't expect Sarah to do all the work." Both shook their heads as their faces flushed with embarrassment.

This collaborative group project was developing the same way that most of the other groups that Sarah had been involved with had gone. The faces were different, but the roles people played were always the same. First, there was the self-appointed leader—in this case, it was Ryder. The leader's position was generally not based on ability, but on personal assertiveness. Generally, the leader did not have to work so hard as the others because he had the talent of motivating others. There often seemed to be at least one person who was either too busy or too lazy to carry his share of the assignment, offset by one overachiever who was willing to do the majority of the work in order to receive the highest grade possible. Sarah smiled to herself as she realized that she was once again playing the role of the overachiever. She often wished that she would not become so emotionally involved in her studies, but she seemed not to be able to control herself. She occasionally laughed about this trait's being an obsessive-compulsive disorder.

Ryder leaned back in his chair. "Sarah has already done her homework," he declared as he maintained his role of group leader. "Can everyone meet here tomorrow at four o'clock to begin putting this thing together? Time is beginning to run out on us."

"Fine by me," Marcella agreed, knowing that she had a date with one of the football players and would probably not be home until late.

"I think I can make it," Josh nodded.

Sarah's eyes drifted from person to person, as her spirits dropped. "I hate being a spoilsport," she said softly, sensing their potential disapproval, "but I have a commitment every day at four. Could we meet a little earlier?"

Josh Richardson shook his head, while he gave a frustrated sigh. "I don't get off work at the student union until three, but you could start without me. I could probably be here by three-fifteen at the latest."

Everyone looked at Ryder for his approval. "Then let's meet at three, and Josh can join us as soon as he can," he said authoritatively. The others nodded with agreement without noticing the pained expression spreading across Sarah's face. One by one, the foursome put on their coats, gathered their books, said farewell, and left.

Sarah's sense of isolation followed her outside where a sharp northerly wind ruffled her light-brown hair. *I wonder how long it will take me to save enough money to come back to college,* she mused as she walked the two blocks to the nearest bus stop as she had done nearly every day at this time since she'd been in Rocky Bluff. She had the schedule of the shuttle between the small campus and the downtown memorized—every half hour until six o'clock and once an hour between six and midnight.

God has brought me this far; why would He let me down now? She tried to convince herself, but the familiar saying merely mocked her frustration.

Sarah heard footsteps behind her and decided to ignore them until a familiar voice said, "May I give you a lift?" Ryder matched strides with her. "There's no reason to freeze waiting for the shuttle when I'm going through town myself."

Sarah shuddered in the cold as she shook her head. The offer was tempting, but she'd been able to keep her double life a secret from her classmates for over eighteen months, and she still felt she wasn't ready to explain her daily visits to the Little Lambs Children's Center. She had a great deal of respect for Ryder, and she didn't want her past to come between their casual friendship. Nearly three years before, Sarah had vowed that she would never again become interested in men. However, since she entered college, she was beginning to find it more and more difficult to keep that vow.

After a few moments of contemplation, Sarah turned her attention back to Ryder. "Thanks for the offer," she responded graciously, "but I don't want to be an inconvenience. The bus should be along within five minutes."

❦

Ryder's shoulders slumped. He had met Sarah during freshman orientation and was immediately impressed with her enthusiasm toward learning. Yet, an aura of painful mystery seemed always to surround her, and he was not able to find a way to break through her aloof exterior. "Whenever you need a ride and the bus is late, just give me a call," he said as he placed his arm on her shoulder. "In the meantime, I'll see you tomorrow at three. Don't work too hard on the project tonight. Make the others do their share."

"Don't worry about that," Sarah smiled as she sat down on the edge of the bench at the bus stop. She watched as Ryder strolled confidently toward the parking lot. His thick jet-black hair fell smoothly to his shoulders characteristic of many of the Native Americans in the area. Sarah had often seen Ryder Long in church, plus he had been in several of her classes during the last two semesters. She was impressed with his work ethic and drive for success. He never seemed to be lacking for friends and was the first one to greet a new student and welcome him to the campus. *If I had come to college strictly to meet guys, Ryder would be one of the first I'd check out,* Sarah sighed, *but I have to accept the fact that my life will never follow a traditional pattern of education, job, marriage, then a family.*

Just then, the shuttle pulled to a stop, and the door slid open. Sarah showed the driver her pass and took a seat near the front. She blankly watched the rows of ranch-style homes fly past the window. Until she received the letter about her student aid, she thought she had her future well planned, but now fears and uncertainties enveloped her. What would the future hold for her and her daughter if she had to drop out of college?

Twenty minutes later, Sarah stepped from the city shuttle and walked the two blocks to Little Lambs Children's Center. The building was once the center for most of the medical care in Rocky Bluff, but when Dr. Brewer retired nearly three years before, the building was converted to a foster home for children with severe birth defects. Sarah still marveled at the seemingly miraculous series of events that led Dawn Harkness Reynolds and her husband, Ryan, to become directors of the home. They both sacrificed well-paying careers to return to Rocky Bluff to care for helpless, needy babies.

Dawn had been a successful obstetrics nurse in Billings when she became reacquainted with Ryan Reynolds, an old schoolmate from Rocky Bluff. Their common heritage added fuel to their smoldering romance. Shortly before they were married, the opportunity to return to their hometown to help establish the Little Lambs Children's Center presented itself, and neither one could resist. Both had been active in the Right-to-Life movement and felt a deep desire to help both mothers and their disabled children. In the last three years, the home had cared for over thirty babies and had trained ten of the mothers to care for their own child so that they could accept full custodial care. Sarah longed for the day that she, too, would be able to take her child home with her.

Upon arriving at the center, Sarah rang the bell and waited. Within a few minutes, a tall blond cradling an infant in her arms opened the door. "Sarah," Dawn Reynolds greeted. "It's good to see you again. Do come in."

Sarah stepped inside and stomped the dust from her shoes. "Charity is still napping," Dawn explained, "but help yourself to a soda in the lounge and join me in the playroom. One of the assistants is sick today so I'm having to cover for her."

Sarah hung her coat on the rack in the lounge and decided against a soft drink. She tiptoed into the small room next door containing four toddler beds. She bent over the one in the far corner and admired the sleeping child. An angelic expression covered the little girl's face. Sarah smiled as she noted how the child's hair was now almost long enough to conceal the shunt that drained the excess fluid from her head to reduce the pressure on her brain. Sarah longed to cuddle Charity in her arms but did not want to interrupt such a peaceful sleep. Instead, Sarah joined Dawn in the playroom.

Dawn motioned Sarah to take the chair beside her as she continued rocking the infant in her arms. "How was your day?" Dawn asked with a smile.

"Not good," Sarah sighed. "I received some bad news in the mail. . . . I'm afraid I'll have to drop out of school next semester."

Dawn's forehead wrinkled as her mouth dropped. She knew how hard Sarah had worked and how far she had come in a short time. "What happened?" she queried.

"I got a notice that they will be cutting my financial aid, and it will barely be enough to cover my tuition and books," Sarah replied sadly. "Until I finish my training, there is no way I can make enough at a part-time job to pay for my room and board. Tomorrow I'm going to have to tell my advisor that I'm dropping out."

Dawn hesitated. There had to be a way for Sarah to obtain enough money to pay for her room and board for just one more semester. She remembered how four years ago her church in Billings had rallied to help Sarah as an unwed mother who had been disowned by her family. Because of their love and encouragement, Sarah felt the guilt of what she had done and soon accepted Christ's love and forgiveness. In spite of their youth, both Sarah and Jeff Blair, the father, accepted the responsibility for their child born with severe spina bifida and were determined to do whatever was necessary to see that she lived as productive a life as possible.

"I hate to see you drop out," Dawn replied. "Let's give it a few more days and see what might turn up. What is the last possible day you can let them know if you will be returning for spring semester?"

Sarah shrugged her shoulders. "We have to register for classes December eleventh; then we have Christmas vacation from the fifteenth to the third of January. There are so few good paying jobs here in Rocky Bluff, that I'll probably have to go job hunting in Billings during vacation time."

"If you move back to Billings, you won't be able to see Charity every day, and you'll postpone your biggest goal of all—that of being a self-supporting, custodial parent," Dawn reminded her.

❖

Sarah continued rocking silently. Her eyes studied the designs in the tile. She knew how true Dawn's words were, but could she muster enough faith to believe that somewhere out there, God had a solution to her problem? Suddenly, her thoughts were interrupted by a familiar cry from the adjoining room, "Want up. Want up."

Sarah hurried to her daughter's bedside. Charity's face brightened as her mother leaned over to pick her up. The child's legs hung limply from her torso. The opening of the spinal column that was closed soon after her birth was just below her armpit, and Charity had no feeling or movement below that level.

"Hi, Mommy," she greeted. "Want dolly."

Sarah smiled as she hugged her daughter and leaned over to fetch the Raggedy Ann doll in the corner of the bed. She had purchased the stuffed doll at the local discount store and had given it to Charity for her second birthday. Since that time, Charity and Raggedy Ann had been inseparable, and Sarah had taken pride in selecting a toy that would meet her daughter's need to cuddle. Little by little, Sarah was learning how to care for her daughter, and her goal was to have total custody of Charity by the child's fifth birthday. At that time, she hoped to have completed her associate's degree as a computer technician and obtained a well-paying job.

Sarah carried her daughter into the playroom and took Charity's favorite storybook from the shelf. Returning to the rocking chair beside Dawn, Sarah quietly read the all-too-familiar tale to her daughter. After completing the book, the young mother picked up a plastic game board and began pointing to each of the primary colors and saying its name slowly. Charity was quick to imitate her mother's sounds and was beginning to make the association between the color and its name.

After at least fifteen minutes of providing undivided attention to her daughter, Sarah turned to the director of the center. "Dawn, it's amazing how many words she's learned. I may be prejudiced, but Charity seems to be smarter than any of the other kids here."

Dawn smiled at the young mother's innocent pride. They had been monitoring the child's language development to help determine if there had been any brain damage from the hydrocephalus, but so far, Charity's language skills were average for her age group. "The specialists have been extremely pleased with her development," Dawn assured her. "Tomorrow her occupational therapist will be here at two o'clock. Would you be able to come a little early and be here when she works with Charity? She'll be able to answer more of your questions about her development."

Sarah took a deep breath. "I promised my study group I'd meet with them at three o'clock tomorrow to work on a boring debate about the International Space Station. I don't know what to do. I've got to get a good grade in my political science class, but I also want to be a good mother to Charity."

Dawn patted Sarah on the arm. "Don't put a guilt trip on yourself," she reminded her. "If you don't see the therapist tomorrow, she'll be here again next week. Maybe she'll have even more details for you then."

Sarah nodded her head. "I know," she sighed, "but I'd really like to talk with her as soon as possible. I'll make some phone calls tonight and see what I can do."

Dawn laid the child she was holding on the play mat, excused herself, and went to the kitchen to check the progress of the evening meal. Sarah laid Charity on the mat on the opposite corner. In the center of the mat was an assortment of toddler toys. The two children began scooting toward the toys, pulling with their arms and dragging their limp legs behind them. Sarah watched with amazement. Even though neither one had feeling nor movement below the waist, they both were learning to adapt to their limitations and overcome them.

Sarah's eyes widened as she glanced at her watch. She hurried to the kitchen door and caught Dawn's attention while she was checking the day's shopping list. "Time got away from me again," she said with a smile. "I'm going to have to run so I can catch the five o'clock shuttle back to the campus. I'll see you tomorrow."

"Bye now," Dawn shouted as Sarah hurried out the door.

Chapter 2

S arah Brown thumbed through the student directory. Her hands trembled. She hated to ask a favor of a man, but he had offered her a ride any time she needed one, and this time her desire to meet with the occupational therapist outweighed her embarrassment about asking for a favor. There it was on page ten. Ryder Long: 259-8157. She took a deep breath, then dialed the numbers.

"Hello."

"Hello. Is Ryder Long available, please?" Sarah asked, her voice trembling.

"This is he."

"Hello, Ryder. This is Sarah Brown. I hate to bother you, but I have a favor to ask of you."

Ryder stretched out his long legs, muted the TV, and leaned back on the sofa. "Hi, Sarah. I'm glad you called. I was getting kind of bored tonight and needed someone to talk to."

Sarah hesitated; she wanted to hang up, but the face of her daughter flashed before her. "Ryder, earlier today you mentioned that if I ever needed a ride to give you a call. . . . Well, I do have a need for a ride. . .that is. . .if it wouldn't be too inconvenient for you."

"Nothing for you would be too inconvenient," Ryder laughed. "When can I come and get you?"

"Are you busy between two-thirty and three o'clock tomorrow afternoon?" Sarah asked hesitantly. "I have an appointment at two o'clock downtown, but if I wait for the shuttle, I might not make it back for our group meeting at three."

Ryder smiled. This was the first time Sarah had spoken to him about anything that wasn't related to their class work. He hoped that maybe this would be the time he could get past her mysterious exterior. "That's no problem at all," he assured her. "I have to come through downtown on my way to the campus anyway. Where would you like me to meet you?"

Sarah knew the moment of truth had come. She'd at least have to tell a portion of her secret. Fortunately, Ryder seemed to be the type who would accept her just the way she was, without prying into her background. "I'll be at the Little Lambs Children's Center. Do you know where that is?"

Ryder wrinkled his forehead. "I've lived in Rocky Bluff all my life, but I've never heard of Little Lambs. Where is it?"

"In the 600 block of Dodge Street. . .where Dr. Brewer's office used to be. They remodeled the building after he retired three years ago."

"I spent a lot of unhappy hours in that office," Ryder chuckled, remembering all his childhood diseases and injuries. "So they changed it into a day care center, huh?"

Sarah gulped. "Not exactly. . . . It's a foster home for children who are born with spina bifida and other such birth defects."

"Sounds interesting. . . Are you working there part-time or something?"

"Well. . .er. . .not exactly. . . . It's more like volunteer work."

Ryder could not miss the hesitation in her voice. "Sorry, I didn't mean to sound like I was prying. I think that's a noble project to be connected with. Maybe I should do some community service there as well."

Sarah's fingers tightened around the phone as her face blanched. "Yeah. . . . You'll have to give them a call sometime. . . . See you tomorrow."

"I'll be there at ten of three tomorrow," Ryder promised. "In the meantime, I have a lot of research to do on the space station. It wouldn't be fair if you had to do all the work."

Sarah said good-bye, hung up the phone, and buried her head in her hands. She wanted to become an advocate for children with disabilities, but she knew that if she did, she would be forced to tell her long-held secret. Deciding to continue masking her heartache and pain, Sarah took her coat from the hook behind the door and headed toward the computer lab in the next building. There she could immerse herself in the development of a detailed spreadsheet, while she pushed her fears to the far crevices of her mind.

Most of the other students owned their own computers, but Sarah felt fortunate just to receive financial aid to cover her tuition and room and board and could only dream of the day when she would own her own computer. Ever since she had returned to high school after the birth of little Charity, Sarah had become fascinated with hardware and systems components of computers. While most of the girls seemed interested only in word processing and simple graphics, Sarah sat side by side with the computer nerds learning about the computer's inner components and how to install programs, networks, and all the peripheral devices.

Now, just when she was one semester from completing the course, the government was cutting back on her financial aid. She was determined not to worry about it until after she took her last test of the semester, but in spite of her best efforts, her fears continued to haunt her. If she had to drop out of college, she wanted to make sure her grades would be good enough so that when she returned she could pick up exactly where she left off. What troubled her most was the realization of how fast technology was changing, and if she had to interrupt her education for just six months, she would be put several years behind.

While Sarah was peering into a monitor in the back of the lab, her troubles began to fade. The challenge of figuring out how to manipulate the numbers with a simple click of a mouse served as a needed distraction to make the hours fly. Sarah's reputation as one of the more knowledgeable students in the field spread rapidly. Every time she was in the computer lab, she was usually interrupted several times by questions from other students. She thrived on keeping her personal relationships on an academic and polite level, but occasionally she felt the walls begin to crumble. Whenever she was with Ryder Long, she found it harder and harder to maintain her aloof, intellectual façade.

❖

At 2:45 P.M. the next day, Ryder Long stopped his green sports car in front of the large, brick, one-story building on Dodge Street. His curiosity was further piqued by the sign:

> Little Lambs Children's Center
> Montana Home and Education Center
>   for Children with Birth Defects
> Directors: Ryan Reynolds and Dawn Reynolds

Could the director be the same Ryan Reynolds who was my sports idol in grade school? Ryder wondered. *It's hard to imagine a high school jock specializing in handicapped children instead of becoming a coach somewhere, but the chance of someone else with that name turning up in Rocky Bluff seems remote.*

As Ryder sat immersed in thought, Sarah emerged from the front entrance and hurried toward the waiting car. "Hi, Ryder. I hope I didn't keep you waiting," she greeted as she opened the passenger door and joined her classmate.

"You're right on time," the young man assured her as he started the engine. "I was a couple of minutes early."

Sarah shuffled nervously. This was the closest she wanted anyone in school to come to her secret. "I sure appreciate your giving me a ride. If there's ever a favor I can do for you, just let me know."

"The next time my hard drive crashes, you'll be the first one I'll call," Ryder laughed. He then paused as a serious expression spread across his face. "While I was waiting, I noticed on the sign that Ryan Reynolds was one of the directors. Do you happen to know where he went to high school? Was it here in Rocky Bluff?"

"Yes, he grew up here, and like most of the others, he left soon after graduation to get an education," Sarah explained cautiously, wondering where the conversation was heading. "When I first met him, he was selling medical supplies."

Ryder turned onto the street toward the campus and drove in silence for a few blocks. "That's interesting," he replied thoughtfully. "I wonder what got him interested in disabled children. . . . I remember him as one of the best athletes in high school and wouldn't have been at all surprised if he had ended up coaching a university football team."

"People do change," Sarah replied, thinking more of her own situation than Ryan's. "All I know is that he'd been involved in the Montana Right-to-Life movement for some time, and when he married Dawn Harkness, they returned to Rocky Bluff and helped start Little Lambs."

Ryder couldn't hold back his fond memories and began laughing. "Don't tell me he married the daughter of the man who used to run the hardware store? She was some beauty. I think she was even the homecoming queen one year. Every boy in the third grade had a crush on her when she was in high school."

Little by little, Sarah relaxed. Maybe Ryder could be someone she could trust after all. Campus life had become extremely lonely for her as she tried to keep the most important part of her life a secret. "Dawn is still beautiful," Sarah replied, "only now in a much different way. I don't know where I'd be without her."

"I'd like to meet her again sometime," Ryder said as he turned through the main gate of the campus. "I'm always fascinated with the different paths the people of Rocky Bluff take; yet, they always seem to maintain an allegiance to this little town."

Ryder found a parking spot in the second row from the main entrance to the library. They sprang from the car and rushed into the library toward the study room on the main floor. Marcella was already waiting, her fingers tapping the table with impatience.

"Sorry we're late," Ryder gasped, as he took off his coat and threw it on the chair next to him. "I hope you haven't been waiting long."

"I got out early from my last class," she explained, "so I came directly to the library. I have to meet my folks at four-thirty, so I hope we can finish this project in a hurry."

Just then, Josh rushed into the library study room. Everyone nodded and muttered greetings to each other. Ryder took out his notebook in his typical authoritarian manner. "Here's a list of Internet sites that I found on the International Space Station. I starred the ones that support the U.S.

involvement and wrote a brief summary on each site. I could take everyone's lists to the copier so all of us have the same sources."

"Good idea," Josh agreed, reaching into his backpack for his notes.

Sarah handed Ryder three pages of detailed notes, while Marcella's were a half page long. Ryder frowned as he perused her abbreviated list.

"Sorry," she shrugged. "I was extra busy last night and didn't have much time to work on this."

Ryder rolled his eyes and headed to the copier machine. During the next forty-five minutes, the group busily summarized and discussed their main points. When they were finally satisfied that they were organized enough to conduct a reasonable debate before their class, the foursome said good-bye to each other and went their separate ways.

The cold November wind whipped through Sarah's long brown hair as she walked slowly toward her dormitory. An aura of sadness enveloped her. She had trouble imagining that she only had a few more weeks left at Rocky Bluff Community College before she would be working again full-time. Her job would not be in her dreamed profession, but probably at another fast-food restaurant. The thought of Ryder's laughing eyes and shining dark hair should have made her smile, but instead it sunk her deeper into depression. *Just when I think I've met someone I can trust, it looks like I'm going to have to drop out of school and probably not see him again,* she mused as she kicked a pile of leaves on the sidewalk. *Oh, well. . .it's probably better to stop a relationship before it even gets started. It would only lead to more heartache, anyway. . . . Besides, who would want a friend who is the single parent of a disabled child? I might as well accept the harsh, cruel facts and go see my advisor tomorrow to let him know I'm dropping out of school.*

❖

The next day, Sarah Brown was done with classes by noon and made an appointment to see her advisor, Jay Harkness, at two o'clock. Mr. Harkness was not only Sarah's college advisor, but she had taken at least two computer classes a semester from him. One of the many things that had attracted her to Rocky Bluff Community College was the fact that Dawn Reynolds's brother was head of the department in which she wanted to major. The more she had studied under him, the more impressed she had become, not only with his intellectual background, but also with his concern for the future of each of his students.

Sarah remembered how proudly Dawn had told her about what a good college instructor her brother was. He had received his bachelor's degree from Montana Tech, then obtained his master's degree and most of his computer training while he was in the Air Force stationed on Guam. Since returning to

Montana, he went to as many workshops and training sessions as possible in order to stay on the cutting edge of a fast-changing industry. All this had made him one of the most well-respected professors on campus.

Promptly at two o'clock, Sarah timidly approached Mr. Harkness's office. When she reached the open door, the prematurely graying professor looked up from his computer screen and smiled. "Come in, Sarah, and have a chair. It's good to see you again."

Sarah smiled as she took the chair beside her advisor's desk. "Thanks for seeing me on such short notice," she whispered as she clutched her purse nervously in her lap.

"That's what I'm here for," Jay assured her as he studied the deep furrows in her forehead. "You look troubled. Is there something I can do to help?"

Sarah hesitated and took a deep breath. "I'm afraid I'm not going to be able to come back to school next semester," she replied sadly as a lump began to grow in her throat.

Jay's eyes widened with disapproval. "Why is that?" he queried. "You've been on the dean's list every semester you've been here, and you only have one semester until you receive your degree."

"I know," she replied as she gazed at the floor. "I hate the thought of dropping out when the end is almost in sight, but I don't have any other alternative. I just learned that my financial aid is being cut, and it will only be enough to cover my tuition and books for next semester, and not my room and board. The only option I can come up with is to drop out of school, return to Billings where I could live with my mother, and save enough money so I can finish school later."

Jay shook his head. "I'd hate to see that happen. There has to be a way for you to earn your room and board for five months here in Rocky Bluff."

Sarah sat in silence as a smile gradually spread across Jay's face. He reached for the telephone. "I have an idea. It's a long shot, but maybe something can be worked out so that you can remain in school."

Sarah watched her advisor with puzzlement as he checked the phone book, then dialed.

❖

"Hello, Pastor," Jay greeted as Pastor Olson answered his office phone in the church. "This is Jay Harkness. I hope I didn't catch you at a bad time."

"I was just working on Sunday's sermon. What can I do for you?"

"I have a student who will need room and board for next semester, and I was wondering if they have found anyone to stay with Rebecca Hatfield yet," Jay asked, as he remembered the health care needs of a friend and coworker of his grandmother's.

Rebecca had been the librarian of Rocky Bluff High School while Jay and Dawn Harkness were students. When she retired, she went to Guam for two years to help automate a school library there at the same time that Jay was there on a military assignment to Andersen Air Force Base on the northern tip of the island. Having someone from his hometown there helped ease his homesickness during his first months of duty. Before Rebecca returned to Montana, she introduced Jay to one of her students, Angie Quinata. When Jay was discharged from the service, the two were married and established their first home in Rocky Bluff. Angie quickly fell in love with Montana, in spite of the drastic change of climate from her tropical homeland, and invited her mother to move to Rocky Bluff when she retired from teaching.

Like Jay's grandmother, Edith Harkness Dutton, Rebecca also had found love and fulfillment in a late-in-life marriage. Upon returning to Rocky Bluff, Rebecca married retired Fire Chief Andy Hatfield, and the couple spent ten happy years together volunteering for all types of community and church activities. However, the last few months of Andy's life had been extremely difficult for the aging couple. Rebecca was beginning to exhibit symptoms of the first stages of Alzheimer's disease. Andy had lovingly cared for her and had seen that she had the best medical care possible. And since the Hatfields did not have a family, Andy had arranged for attorney David Wood to be responsible for Rebecca's affairs if something should happen to him.

Then three weeks ago, the entire community mourned the loss of one of their leading citizens, Andy Hatfield. He had suffered a heart attack while mowing his lawn. Friends and church members rallied to Rebecca's support, offering to help her maintain as independent a lifestyle as possible for as long she was capable. Social services arranged for daily home health care, and different women from her church took turns spending the night with Rebecca until permanent arrangements could be made.

Pastor Olson was assisting in the search for a permanent, live-in caregiver, but to no avail. He had never thought of the possibility of using a college student. He leaned back in his study chair as he pondered Jay's suggestion. "That's a good idea. I'll have to contact Dave Wood to find out what the status is of Rebecca's home health care needs. Who is the student?"

"Sarah Brown is looking for a situation where she could work for her room and board," Jay explained. "I thought that possibly some arrangements could be worked out between the two of them."

"Umm. . .interesting thought," Pastor Olson replied. "I'll give Dave Wood a call and get back to you as soon as I know something."

The phone conversation ended, and Jay turned back to Sarah who was listening with amazement. She had never met the Hatfields but had heard many prayer requests for them when she was in church. "Obviously, I don't know the details, but would you be interested in staying with Rebecca Hatfield and helping her with minor household chores in the evening in exchange for your room and board? Home health care services will help during the daytime, but she needs someone to be with her at night."

Sarah smiled as she breathed a sigh of relief. "I'd be willing to do whatever is necessary in order to finish school."

"Good. . .I'll give you a call as soon as I learn something," Jay replied. "Don't give up hope. I'm sure we can get something worked out for you."

Sarah's return walk across campus was brisker, and her steps lighter than they had been in days. God had helped her through many difficult situations, and now her faith was again being restored that He was still directing her life through extremely difficult circumstances.

Chapter 3

Political Science 101 was the liveliest it had been all semester as four students emotionally debated their views concerning the United States involvement in the International Space Station Project. Sarah Brown led the way in strongly defending the position to spend the billions of dollars now used on the ISS on human services; although Josh supported her, he contributed very little and only seemed to be there to boost her morale. Ryder Long tried to persuade the class that the space station was necessary for national security and scientific research, as Marcella Cross looked on with little to add.

Although Ryder's arguments were strong, Sarah's passion for the need to use the funding for social programs convinced both the majority of the students and the instructor that Congress should use tax money for human welfare and not research on the International Space Station in which there were no guarantees of success. Wasn't the care of a single human life much more important than all the specialized space research in the world?

When the final bell rang, the instructor handed evaluation sheets to each member of the debate team. Sarah beamed as she saw an "A" at the top of the page. Her hard work had paid off once again. Walking down the hallway, she scanned the points she received in each of the categories on the teacher's rubric. All of them were either the maximum number of points or one point away.

"Great job," Ryder said as he matched strides with her. "You almost had me convinced, but I didn't want to change positions midstream and get marked down for it."

Sarah looked up and laughed. "Thanks," she replied. "You weren't so bad yourself."

A blast of cold air greeted the pair as Ryder opened the door for Sarah. Both instinctively pulled their coats tightly around their necks. "To celebrate your hard-earned 'A,' how would you like to join me at the Black Angus for an early dinner, then catch a movie at The Capri?"

Sarah's mind raced. *Should I accept his offer for dinner? I decided a long while ago that I'd never have a serious relationship with anyone. . .but a casual dinner with Ryder couldn't possibly lead to anything. . . . Anyway, at this point, who knows if I'll be able to stay in Rocky Bluff much longer. The situation with Mrs. Hatfield could fall through, so I might as well enjoy it.*

"Penny for your thoughts," Ryder teased in order to break the tension her silence was building between them. "Don't look so perplexed. I'm not inviting you to travel on the space station with me."

Sarah turned her attention back to the young man beside her. "Sure, it sounds like fun. After all the time spent working on the project, I need to get out of the dormitory and the library for awhile."

"Great! What time would be best for you?" Ryder asked. "Will you be going to the Little Lambs Center later this afternoon?"

"I usually go between four and five every afternoon," Sarah replied. "The only times I've missed have been when I've been sick."

"How about if I pick you up there so you don't have to take the shuttle back to the campus?" Ryder suggested.

Although she was a little shaken by the thought that Ryder might learn the details of her secret, Sarah relaxed and replied, "I'd appreciate the ride. The shuttle is often extremely cold this time of year."

After Ryder nodded and smiled with agreement, Sarah returned their conversation to their political science class as they walked toward her dormitory. She had gained a small degree of confidence in taking a partial step toward disclosing her long-held secret, but her class work was a much more comfortable topic for her. When they arrived at the entrance of the women's dorm, they said a quick good-bye, and from behind the glass doorway, Sarah watched Ryder jog to the parking lot.

Back in her room, Sarah tried to recall everything she knew about Ryder. Other than the fact that he was a good student, well liked by both faculty and students, president of the college's Native Americans' Club, and attended church regularly, she realized how little she actually knew about him.

Since the birth of her child, Sarah had not dated anyone. She cringed at the thought of being alone with a man for more than a few isolated moments. *No,* she told herself. *This is not a date. It's merely dinner with a classmate. It won't be any different from having dinner with one of the girls in the dorm.*

❖

Promptly at four o'clock, Sarah rang the doorbell at the Little Lambs Children's Center. Nancy, one of the day workers, answered the door. "Hello, Sarah," she greeted. "Do come in. Charity just got up from her nap and is in the playroom. She's been asking for you."

Sarah hung her coat on a hook by the door and hurried to the playroom. She spotted her daughter lying on the mat playing with Raggedy Ann. "Hi, Mommy," Charity squealed as she held out her arms.

Sarah knelt and picked up her daughter. Holding her close, she kissed her on the forehead. "Hello, Sweetheart. How are you today?"

"I fine," Charity replied, displaying her new set of baby teeth.

Sarah beamed as she carried her daughter to a nearby rocking chair. Each day, Charity was adding several new words and short sentences to her vocabulary. Never missing a chance to help increase her daughter's vocabulary, Sarah pointed to the different parts of her body and encouraged her to call them by name.

Within minutes, Dawn entered the playroom and took the rocking chair next to Sarah. The director of the center was rarely seen without one child or another in her arms. "Hi, how's it going?" she greeted.

"Great," Sarah replied. "I'm amazed at how fast Charity's learning to talk. She even knows her colors and the parts of her body."

"Everyone's delighted with her development," Dawn assured her. "Her first wheelchair should be here within a few days, and then you'll see a big change in her as she gains control of more and more of her environment."

"I was hoping to be able to take care of Charity by myself as soon as I finished my education and had a good job, but since there's been such a cutback in my financial aid, it looks like my full custody will be delayed," Sarah noted, unable to mask her discouragement.

Dawn did not want to mention that she had spoken with her brother, Jay Harkness, the day before and that several people were working on the possibility of Sarah's assisting Rebecca Hatfield in exchange for her room and board. "I'm sure something will turn up between now and the first of the year. I don't want you to give up hope so easily."

Sarah tried to mask her pessimism. *I've been disappointed so many times before that I don't want to get my hopes up, then be hurt again.*

Dawn quickly changed the subject. "Jeff Blair called this afternoon to check on Charity," she explained brightly. "He sounded very upbeat. He plans to come to Rocky Bluff during Thanksgiving break to spend some time with her."

Sarah smiled. Even though their lives had gone in different directions, she was pleased that Jeff was taking an active interest in his daughter's life. She and Jeff had become intimate during one reckless summer while they were in high school. Jeff had been in Billings for a high school football camp, and she had become attracted to him and had let her guard down. When she could no longer hide the possibility that she was pregnant, Sarah made an appointment to see an obstetrician.

After having an ultrasound during her sixth month, Sarah learned that she was not only pregnant, but that her child had spina bifida. At that moment, her life began to collapse. Her mother had insisted that she have an abortion and would have nothing to do with her until she did. Fortunately, Dawn Harkness, the obstetrician's nurse, provided a home for her until the baby was born. A sense of guilt had enveloped the pregnant teen as she tried to bear total responsibility for the unwanted pregnancy. However, under a strange set of circumstances, when the network of Rocky Bluff friendships shared their mutual joys and concerns, Jeff learned Sarah's secret. Refusing to let her carry the total responsibility for their mistake, Jeff stepped forward and helped with the financial support of little Charity.

"Great, I'm glad he can come," Sarah replied to Dawn after a moment of reflection. "I'd like to see him again myself and fill him in on Charity's latest accomplishments. . . . I wonder if he'll want to see me again. It's been such a long time since we've been together, since I've been in Billings during college breaks the last few times he's been in Rocky Bluff."

The child in Dawn's arms began to fuss, so the director diverted her attention from Sarah and began to speak softly to the baby and pat her on the back. When the little girl finally quit crying, Dawn continued, "Jeff asked if you'd still be in town the week over Thanksgiving vacation. The only time he's able to come is during college breaks, and that's usually when you're also on break and go to Billings to see your family. I gave him your number in the dormitory, and he said he'd give you a call before he came."

"Thanks," Sarah replied, her voice barely above a whisper. "Although our lives have gone in different directions, there will always be a bond between us. . .namely, little Charity."

Sarah continued playing with her daughter, but in her mind, she began to compare Jeff with Ryder. Of course, their outward appearance was extremely different, but she was now more concerned with inner beauty and character. She had watched Jeff mature from a self-centered high school jock into a compassionate, caring Christian college student. She knew what had made Jeff what he was today, but she had no clue about Ryder's background.

Suddenly, Sarah's thoughts were interrupted with the request, "Floor. . . floor."

She smiled at her daughter. "Charity, do you want to play on the mat?"

"Yes," the child replied as she leaned forward in her mother's arms grinning from ear to ear. Even though Charity was not able to move about like normal children her age, she was extremely adept at letting everyone know where she wanted to go and what she wanted to do.

Sarah laid her daughter on her stomach on the mat, then went to the toy box and found a small foam ball. Sitting five feet from her, Sarah rolled the ball.

Charity grabbed the ball and smiled proudly. "Catch," she squealed as she threw it in the general direction of her mother. This game continued

·for several minutes until Ryan Reynolds, the codirector of the center and Dawn's husband, appeared. "Sarah, there's a young man at the door asking for you."

Sarah glanced at her watch and blushed. "We were having so much fun I forgot the time." She leaned over and gave her daughter a hug and kiss. "Bye, bye. Mommy's got to go now," she said. "I'll come see you tomorrow."

"I'll finish the game," Ryan laughed as he knelt on the mat and reached for the foam ball. "It will be much easier for you to make an exit without her tears if I distract her."

"Thanks, Ryan," Sarah replied as she hurried from the playroom. "I appreciate it."

Sarah grabbed her coat from the hook in the lounge, slipped her arms through the sleeves, and stepped into the late November air where Ryder was waiting.

"Hi," she greeted brightly. "I'm sorry to keep you waiting."

Ryder took her arm and escorted her to his car. "I didn't think you saw me pull up, so I thought I'd better ring the bell. I hope you didn't mind."

"I should have been watching for you, but I got so involved with what I was doing that I forgot the time," Sarah explained as she slid into the passenger seat of his green sports car.

Ryder closed the door behind her, then hurried around and slipped behind the wheel. "I admire your dedication in volunteering to help with the disabled children, especially when you don't have any personal connection with any of them."

Sarah gulped. She felt she had to be honest, but she had never before shared her secret with any of her college classmates. A multitude of questions flashed before her. *What will his reaction be? Will he ever want to see me again? Could he also have a hidden secret in his background?*

Lights began to brighten the streets as dusk settled over the community of Rocky Bluff, Montana. For the next few blocks, they drove in silence enjoying the fading sunset. Finally, Sarah developed enough courage to break the silence. "To tell you the truth," Sarah began. "I have a personal interest at Little Lambs. I'll explain it over dinner."

Ryder's dark eyes sparkled as he surveyed the attractive passenger beside him through his rearview mirror. "I thought there had to be more to the story than what met the eye," he replied, "and I'm looking forward to hearing all about it. In the meantime. . .was that Ryan Reynolds who answered the door?"

"Yes, it was," Sarah replied, thankful for the change in subject. "Did he recognize you?"

Ryder shook his head. "Oh no, I was just a little kid when he was in high school. In fact, if his name hadn't been on the plaque outside, I probably wouldn't have recognized him at all."

"Ryan does most of the administrative work, plus maintains the building, and also helps with the children whenever needed. He's so good with them, and they all love him," Sarah explained. "It wouldn't surprise me if Dawn and Ryan would be starting a family of their own soon."

Ryder turned into the parking lot of the Black Angus Steak House, parked his car, then escorted Sarah into the restaurant. As if sensing their need for privacy, a friendly hostess led them to a back booth. Within minutes, a waitress brought them two glasses of iced water and took their order. While they were waiting for their food, Ryder looked sympathetically into Sarah's deep hazel eyes. "Would you like to share what your personal interest is in Little Lambs now? I can tell it means an awful lot to you."

Sarah took a deep breath. She knew that sooner or later she would have to tell her story, so it might as well be now. Besides, what difference would it make. She wasn't even sure she'd be in Rocky Bluff after semester break. "I haven't even told this to my roommate, Vanessa," she began hesitantly as she studied Ryder's face for any expression of rejection. "The reason I spend so much time at Little Lambs Children's Center is that one of the children in the home is my own."

Ryder's eyes widened, and his face flushed. "I'm sorry. I didn't mean to pry into your personal life."

"That's okay," Sarah assured him. "I feel I can trust you. I made a very stupid mistake when I was in high school. Even though I know God has forgiven me, many people have suffered because of it, especially little Charity."

Ryder paused a moment for Sarah to collect her thoughts. "Since she's at Little Lambs, does that mean she's disabled?"

"I'm afraid so," she explained. "She was born with a severe case of spina bifida and hydrocephalus. Some people encouraged me to have an abortion, but I just couldn't go through with it. . . . Every time I see how sweetly Charity is developing, I'm so glad that I didn't. She is the most precious thing in the world to me."

"I'm glad you didn't give in to the pressure," Ryder assured her. "I've never understood how people could use abortion as a form of birth control."

Sarah shook her head. "If Dawn hadn't come into my life at that time, I don't know what I would have done. She provided both physical and emotional support during a very difficult time. When she and Ryan married and started Little Lambs, Charity was their first resident. I've been going to the center every day, not only to spend time with my daughter, but also to learn how to care for disabled children. As soon as I finish school and get a well-paying job, I want to raise her myself," Sarah explained. That's why I was so upset when I didn't get enough financial assistance to finish my associate's degree this spring."

"I'm sure something will work out for you," Ryder tried to assure her. Then, as if sensing she had shared as much as she was comfortable with at that time, he changed the subject. "I'm extremely fortunate that all my college expenses are paid by a grant from my Indian reservation. Sometimes I feel a little guilty when I see how other students have to work plus take out huge student loans just to get through college while I have all my expenses paid."

"You're extremely fortunate," Sarah noted as the waitress served their plates of filet mignon. "What are you majoring in?"

"I'm taking basic general education classes here at Rocky Bluff, but I plan to transfer to the University of Iowa and enroll in their Physician's Assistant program. I heard they have one of the best in the country. When I complete my education, I plan to return to the reservation where my grandparents live and help my own people. They have a fantastic medical clinic at the reservation near Running Butte, but it seems that they're always short of medical services. Dawn Reynolds's aunt founded the clinic nearly twenty years ago."

"I've heard of Running Butte, but I don't know too much about it," Sarah replied with interest. "I think Ryan Reynolds also has a brother who lives there."

"You're getting to know the local history well," Ryder laughed. "His brother Larry runs Harkness Hardware Two, and his wife, Libby, is a paralegal for the tribal attorney. I see him in the store almost every time I go back. They're a real nice family and have done a lot to help improve the standard of living for those on the reservation."

The young couple enjoyed a few bites of their filets, baked potatoes, and vegetables in silence. Both relaxed in the openness of their conversation. As their eyes accidentally met, they both smiled. "This is excellent," Sarah exclaimed. "I'm afraid I'm going to put on five pounds from this meal alone."

"If you do, you'll burn it off tomorrow, as hardworking as you are," Ryder teased.

Sarah blushed and responded with a grin. Ryder continued, "If I remember right, Larry Reynolds went through some pretty difficult years while he was in his late teens. I don't know all the details, but the Harknesses were instrumental in helping him get straightened out. I think they also named one of their children Charity."

"That's interesting," Sarah replied. "I picked the name Charity because she was a source of so much love. Because of her, I learned the love of my family, friends, a church community, and most importantly, I learned about the love Jesus Christ has for me."

Ryder reached for Sarah's hand. "That's such an inspiring story. You shouldn't be ashamed of what you've been through. You should use it to encourage high school kids about the dangers of what can happen through careless decisions. They need to be reminded whatever problems they may face, Jesus is sufficient to meet their needs."

Sarah paused, glad to hear his words of faith and also challenged by them. Her eyes settled on a distant mural. "I never thought of it in those terms. . . . Maybe I shouldn't hide the lessons I've learned the hard way but instead turn the painful situation into a teaching tool. I'll have to give it some thought and prayer."

Ryder and Sarah finished their meal, paid the cashier, and drove to the Capri Theater where a two-year-old comedy was playing. They realized they could rent similar movies at the video rental store, but nothing could compare to the wide screen, the smell of popcorn, and being surrounded by friends and neighbors.

The evening ended all too soon. As Ryder walked Sarah to the front entrance of her dormitory, he asked, "When you were in Sunday school as a child, did you ever learn the song, 'This Little Light of Mine, I'm Going to Let It Shine'?"

Sarah had only attended Sunday school a few times as a child, but when she was there, that had been her favorite song. "Are you trying to tell me that I'm hiding my light under a bushel basket?" she replied lightheartedly as the truth of the words seared deeply into her soul.

Ryder put his arm around her and pulled her close. "What do you think?" he asked seriously.

Chapter 4

Large flakes of snow slowly drifted to the ground as Sarah strolled across the campus of Rocky Bluff Community College the week before Thanksgiving. The beauty of the first snowfall of the season escaped her as her mind bounced from her fear that she would have to return to Billings at the end of the semester to look for a job, to her sense of relief at still being accepted by a classmate after sharing her secret about Charity. Suddenly, her thoughts returned to her surroundings as a voice behind her shouted, "Sarah, wait up."

Sarah turned. "Hi, Ryder," she greeted as his tall dark form ran to catch up with her. "I missed you in political science class today."

"I had a flat tire on the way to school, and by the time I got it changed, the class was over," Ryder said. "When I explained the situation to our instructor, she was kind enough to give me the notes of her lecture, but I wish I'd been a part of the class discussion. I always enjoy a good heated debate."

Sarah giggled as the two slowly walked toward her dormitory. "It was rather boring today," she confided. "Josh got on his liberal soapbox again, and no one else got a chance to say much. Fortunately, after a few minutes of his monologue, the instructor redirected the conversation. We began discussing the fallacy of the Iowa Straw Poll and how Iowa has caucuses instead of primaries during each presidential election year."

"How boring," Ryder said with mock disgust. "I'm glad I wasn't there." He then glanced at his watch. "It's almost four. Are you planning to go to Little Lambs this afternoon?"

"I wouldn't miss it for anything," Sarah assured him. "I wanted to drop my books off in my room, then head for the shuttle stop."

"Would you like a ride? I'm going right by there."

Sarah smiled, pleasantly surprised that Ryder seemed more interested in her than ever. "Sure, it's a lot better than sitting on the bench collecting snow," she chuckled. "Would you mind waiting in the lobby? I'll hurry to my room, leave my books, and get the toy I just bought for Charity."

❖

Ryder Long stood at the window of the women's dormitory lobby, while Sarah hurried down the hallway to her room. Since he was hoping to someday become a physician's assistant and possibly specialize in pediatrics, his interest in the Little Lambs Children's Home intensified. A fresh idea flashed through his mind. He loved working with children and seeing their excited smiles when he had brought momentary joy into their lives. Also, knowing the competition in the medical field, he was always interested in projects that would give him practical experience with children and would add strength to his résumé. *I wonder if they use volunteers at Little Lambs to help with the children. I wonder how I can become involved without appearing like I'm only doing it to impress Sarah.*

Hearing footsteps behind him, Ryder turned and watched Sarah hurrying down the hall toward him; her purse was slung over her left shoulder while she grasped a small sack in her right hand. Her bright smile always lifted his spirits. "Ready?" he asked as she approached.

"Sure am," Sarah replied as Ryder held the door open for her. "The older Charity gets the stronger the bond is becoming between us. I can hardly wait until I'm able to care for her myself."

Ryder took Sarah's hand as they walked toward the parking lot. The snow was getting heavier with each passing minute. "You've talked so much about Charity since you first told me about her that I'd love to meet her. Do you think that might be possible sometime?"

Sarah beamed. "How about today? She's learning how to talk, and it's so much fun hearing her try to use the new words she's learned."

When the pair arrived at Little Lambs, they found Charity playing in the ball pit. She loved lying in the pile of balls and throwing them in all directions. "Mommy," she squealed, holding her arms out to be picked up as Sarah and Ryder entered the playroom.

Sarah picked up her daughter and carried her to the sofa with Ryder following close behind. "How are you today?" Sarah asked, giving her daughter a big hug.

"I fine," Charity replied with a grin.

"This is Ryder," Sarah said as she motioned to her friend beside her. "Can you say 'Hi' to Ryder?"

"Hi, Ryder," Charity cooed as he reached out to squeeze her hand. Instead, Charity raised her chubby arms toward him. "Hold, hold."

Sarah and Ryder exchanged pleased glances as she handed her daughter to his waiting arms.

Charity grinned at him and began to rub his cheeks. "Pretty, pretty," she cooed. Her infectious warmth immediately won Ryder's heart as he began to play finger games and sound games with her. An hour and a half passed before they realized the time.

"I'd better get out of here before I miss the last shuttle of the evening,"

Sarah gasped as she glanced at her watch.

"Don't worry about it," Ryder assured her. "I'll give you a ride back to the campus."

At last the pair said good-bye to little Charity and handed her to Dawn Reynolds who had just entered the playroom to start preparing the children for the evening meal. Sarah's heart nearly broke as she heard Charity cry out, "Mommy, no go. Mommy, no go."

Knowing what had to be done, Sarah blew her daughter a kiss from across the room, put on her coat, and stepped into the early darkness. About two inches of snow had accumulated while they were inside. Ryder opened the passenger door for her, walked around the car, slid behind the wheel, and started the engine. He then took his snow scraper from under his seat and began sweeping the snow from the car.

As Ryder worked, Sarah watched with fondness. Here was a man who was strong and masculine, and yet exhibited such gentleness while playing with Charity and the other children. *With his charisma with small children, he'll be excellent working in pediatrics,* she thought. *In spite of being extremely intense and serious, Ryder has a mysterious inner spark that seems to calm the children while it brings excitement into their play.*

When the engine was warm and they were on their way, Ryder turned south toward the college. They rode in silence for a few moments before he spoke. "Sarah, I feel sorry for you and Charity and all those other precious children. It just doesn't seem fair that some are born with such terrible birth defects. I'd like to do whatever I possibly can to help."

Sarah flushed with frustration. "I'm not interested in people's sympathy, and neither are the children," she protested. "Those children are like any others, except they need a little more understanding and assistance because of their disabilities."

Now it was Ryder's turn to grow red. "I. . .I know," he stammered, "but I can't help but feel sorry for them. Their twisted bodies are so pathetic; it just makes my heart ache to see them."

Sarah rode in silence the remainder of the way to the campus. *Just when I thought I'd found a friend who would understand me and my intense love for Charity, I'm disappointed again,* she thought. *Ryder is too wrapped up with the disability to see the intensity of the human spirit within.*

Upon arriving at the campus, Sarah gave a polite "thank you" and hurried in to her dormitory, hoping to clear her frustrations about being the object of pity instead of understanding. Upon opening her door, she spotted a note in her roommate's familiar scrawled handwriting taped to her telephone. "Call Teresa Olson" with a phone number.

I wonder why our minister's wife would be calling me, she asked herself as she removed her coat and hung it in the closet. Sarah picked up the phone and punched the appropriate buttons. "Hello, this is Mrs. Olson," a gentle voice answered the ringing telephone.

"This is Sarah Brown. I just returned from Little Lambs and found a note to call you."

"Hello, Sarah," Teresa replied. "How have you been doing? You generally leave church so quickly that I rarely get a chance to visit with you."

"I've been pretty busy lately getting ready for final exams. I have several major papers that are due within two weeks."

"Most college students are swamped this time of year," Teresa acknowledged, then took a deep breath, indicating that she was ready to get to the real purpose of her call.

"I understand that you might be interested in finding a place where you could work for your room and board while you finish your education."

"That's true," Sarah sighed. "I'm only going to be able to receive enough financial aid next semester to pay for my tuition and books, but not enough to pay for my housing and food. I don't want to drop out of school, but so far I don't have any other options."

"If things can be worked out, we may have a solution for you," Teresa continued confidently. "Rebecca Hatfield needs someone to fix her breakfast and evening meal, make sure she takes her medications on time, and stay with her at night. We are arranging for her to have home services with her during the day, but if we can't find anyone to stay with her in the evenings, she'll have to be cared for in a nursing home. We'd like to postpone that as long as possible."

Sarah gasped as her eyes widened. She was willing to try almost anything in order to finish her education, and this situation seemed almost tailor-made for her. "My advisor, Jay Harkness, told me a little about her problems. I remember her husband's bringing her to church every Sunday, but he always took her home right after the service so I never got to actually meet her."

"She once had a very sweet personality," Teresa explained sadly, "but Alzheimer's disease is taking a real toll on her, and she is becoming extremely unpredictable and needs closer supervision. Would you like to go over and meet her and decide if you would want to take the job?"

"Sure," Sarah replied without hesitation. "When would be a good time?"

"How about Saturday afternoon at two-thirty?"

"That's fine with me."

"I'll pick you up at the dormitory and take you to Rebecca's house. After meeting with her and looking over the situation, if you're still interested, I could take you to see David Wood. He's the attorney who is trustee over her legal and financial care. Some of your responsibilities will include getting Rebecca up in the morning, helping her bathe and dress, and making sure she takes her medicine and has a good breakfast," Teresa Olson explained. "In the evening you'll need to see that she eats supper and later help her prepare for bed. One of the most important things is to watch her for safety issues. She has been known to wander out at night and to leave the burners lit after she was done cooking."

Sarah nodded as she listened intently. The more Teresa talked the more interested she became in the challenge of helping Rebecca Hatfield.

"Too often young people would not have the patience or understanding to work with Alzheimer's patients," the pastor's wife noted, "but you have a special compassion and understanding for the disabled. I'm certain you'd be a great caregiver for Rebecca."

Sarah remembered her emotions toward Ryder's sympathetic comments less than an hour before. Disabled people need understanding, not sympathy. She was determined not to slip into that mode of thinking herself.

❖

As soon as Sarah finished classes the next afternoon, she hurried to the computer lab where she could have Internet access. She immediately did a search for the Alzheimer Association's web page. She sat with her eyes glued to the screen, following as many links as possible that helped her learn about the disabling disease. Before beginning her research, Sarah was only aware of the short-term memory loss and was not aware of the disturbance in behavior and appearance that could also be observed. She learned that she needed to be prepared to face agitation, irritability, quarrelsomeness, and Rebecca's diminishing ability to dress appropriately.

All night, Sarah tossed and turned in her bed. She began to question whether she was up to the challenge. She prayed for wisdom to make the right decisions and strength to face whatever the future would hold. By morning, Sarah was exhausted, but she felt a peace that whatever happened, God was in control of the situation.

At two-thirty the next afternoon, Sarah waited at the front door of the dormitory for Teresa Olson. As soon as she recognized Teresa in her blue van when it pulled to the curb, Sarah hurried to the vehicle.

"Hi, Sarah," the pastor's wife greeted, as she opened the van door and motioned for the coed to join her. "It's good to see you again. When I talked with Rebecca this morning, she was looking forward to meeting you, but don't be surprised if she doesn't remember anything about that conversation this afternoon."

"During the last two days, I've done a lot of reading about Alzheimer's,"

Sarah responded. "I hope this arrangement will work out. Helping Rebecca could be an answer to both our prayers."

Teresa explained more of the responsibilities that caring for a person with Alzheimer's would involve as she drove through the snow-packed streets of Rocky Bluff. When Teresa stopped her vehicle in the Hatfields' driveway, Sarah said, "It's a lovely home. I can understand how one person could become very lonely in such a large home. Maintaining it must be overwhelming to Rebecca."

Both women exchanged glances and smiled as they saw a hand holding back the front curtains and a set of intense gray eyes watching them.

"It looks like Rebecca remembered and could scarcely wait for us to arrive," Teresa laughed.

Rebecca threw open the door before Teresa had a chance to ring the bell. "Mrs. Olson, please come in," she greeted. "I'm glad you could visit me."

"It's good to see you again," Teresa greeted as she gave Rebecca a quick hug. "I'd like you to meet Sarah Brown," she continued as she motioned to Sarah.

Sarah stepped forward and shook the frail woman's hand. "Rebecca, it's nice to meet you. You have such a lovely home."

"Are you the one who's going to live with me?" Rebecca queried.

Sarah smiled. "I hope so."

"Then follow me, and I'll show you your bedroom," the older woman said, not wanting to waste any time with formalities. "I hope you'll be able to stay with me, because I don't want to have to go to a nursing home."

Sarah's heart melted as she saw the desperate look in Rebecca's soft eyes. "I'll see what I can do to help you," Sarah promised. "Maybe together we can help each other and solve both our problems."

Rebecca took Sarah's hand as she led her down the hallway. "I've always liked helping other people," she exclaimed, "but lately, I'm having trouble even taking care of myself. The only thing I can do to help you is to offer you a place to stay."

"This is a lovely room," Sarah said as Rebecca proudly opened the door to the bedroom. Sarah's eyes immediately fell on the handmade bedspread. "Did you crochet the bedspread? It's beautiful."

"I did that a long time ago," Rebecca replied proudly. "I don't think I'd be able to do it today. Do you crochet?"

Sarah shook her head. "I've never taken the time, but maybe you could teach me a few basic stitches."

❖

Teresa smiled as she watched a rapport build between the coed and the fragile, older woman. This was exactly what she had wanted to see. In order for the proposed arrangement to work, Sarah's most important task was to gain the love and respect of Rebecca so that she could work with her in such a way as to minimize the older woman's confusion and agitation level.

❖

Before the afternoon was over, Sarah agreed to move into one of Rebecca's spare bedrooms on January 3, the day before classes were to begin following Christmas vacation. Sarah could scarcely contain her relief. "Rebecca seemed so sweet," she said, as Teresa backed the blue van out of the driveway. "Since I didn't know her well before, it was hard for me to tell that she had any memory problems at all."

"For the short term, Rebecca is often able to mask her disability if she concentrates hard enough," Teresa explained, "but as you spend more time with her, you'll recognize that her recall is still fairly acute, but her problem-solving abilities have become extremely limited. Her judgment in taking care of herself can no longer be trusted. She often forgets her medicines, or fails to bathe or dress herself properly."

Sarah's eyes sparkled, and the corners of her mouth continued to rise. "This is truly an answer to my prayers. Besides being able to help Rebecca, I'll be able to stay in college and visit Charity regularly," she exclaimed. "Since you'll be going right by Little Lambs, would you mind dropping me off there? I can hardly wait to tell Dawn Reynolds the good news."

"No problem," Teresa replied. "She and her brother have been working hard trying to find a way for you to be able to stay in school."

Just as Teresa had predicted, Dawn was overjoyed to learn of the arrangement with Rebecca Hatfield. After listening to Sarah's excited explanation, she too had news to share. "Sarah, Jeff Blair called this morning. He's planning on spending Thanksgiving vacation in Rocky Bluff so he can have some time with Charity. He asked if you were planning to stay in town or go to Billings during the break. He sounded as though he wants to spend some time with you as well."

Sarah's eyes brightened even more. "I was thinking about taking the bus to Billings for Thanksgiving, but I haven't seen Jeff since last summer. I could easily be persuaded to stay in the dormitory."

"I don't mean to pry," Dawn said cautiously, "but I was wondering about your relationship with Ryder. I was getting the impression something serious was developing between the two of you."

Sarah shook her head. "I don't think I'm going to continue seeing him," she replied. "He's a nice guy and everything, but ever since he learned about little Charity, I feel that he looks on us as objects of pity. I told him that I wanted understanding instead of sympathy."

"I appreciate how you feel," Dawn replied, "but some people have trouble expressing the difference between sympathy and empathy." The former nurse paused while she comforted the fussing child in her arms before continuing. "Ryder seems to be developing quite an interest in disabled children. He stopped by early this morning and signed up on our volunteer list."

Sarah's eyes widened. "Really? When is he going to help?"

"We have trouble getting volunteers on Sunday afternoons because most people want to be with their families," Dawn replied, "but since he's single, he's more than willing to spend Sundays with the children."

Sarah looked down, her face flushed. "That was thoughtful of him," she replied softly. "Maybe I did misread his intentions and jumped to the wrong conclusion."

Dawn put her hand on Sarah's shoulder. "Don't blame yourself," she said. "There's nothing to prevent you from still being friends without having a romantic involvement."

Sarah hung her head. "I think I owe Ryder an apology for being so short with him about not wanting his sympathy. However, I would also like to spend time with Jeff while he's here." Sarah paused, then her silence turned to laughter. "I've spent nearly three years thinking I'd never have a date again in my life, and now I'm having a chance to possibly see two different guys."

"The Lord works in mysterious ways," Dawn reminded her. "I think it's time you accept your past and see yourself as an attractive young woman who possesses a wealth of gifts and talents to offer to the world. Just because you made a mistake when you were sixteen years old doesn't mean you are branded for life. You have asked God for forgiveness, and He has forgiven you. Now it's time for you to forgive yourself and go on with your life."

Chapter 5

"Lord, on this Thanksgiving Day we'd like to thank You for this bountiful feast and for all the many blessings You have provided for us," Ryan Reynolds prayed. He lifted his eyes and glanced around the table at the toddlers in their specially designed high chairs and the parents who sat beside them. His heart became overwhelmed with gratitude. "Thank You, God, for these precious children for whom You have given us the privilege of caring and for their parents who have loved them through the difficult moments along with the good times. May we continue to walk in Your love and mercy throughout our remaining days on earth. In Jesus' Name. Amen."

Four long tables laden with all types of festive foods had been pushed together in the playroom of Little Lambs Children's Center. All but two of the children had family members to help celebrate Thanksgiving together. Dawn Reynolds's mother, Nancy Harkness, had worked for two weeks preparing food for the first annual Little Lambs Family Thanksgiving Dinner. The children giggled with delight at the extra attention they were receiving. Dawn and Ryan basked in the interest the parents were showing their children, and Nancy Harkness enjoyed the opportunity to be of service to such an important ministry.

Little Charity Blair sat in a form-fitted high chair between Sarah Brown and Jeff Blair. As the turkey, dressing, and all the side dishes were passed, Sarah prepared a small plate for Charity before she filled her own plate. She was careful to either mash the food or cut it into extremely small pieces. Sarah helped Charity guide the spoon toward her mouth and ignored it when the three year old used her fingers instead. Jeff watched Charity try to feed herself, then compared her with the children of similar age. Although the others were messy and alternated between using their fingers and a spoon or fork, they ate independently. Jeff leaned behind Charity's chair and whispered to Sarah, "I thought Charity had average intelligence. Why isn't she able to feed herself like the others?"

"She is normal." Sarah smiled. "But she is what they call 'orally defensive.' She has trouble accepting different textures and tastes in food. Even brushing her teeth can sometimes be a real nightmare."

Jeff's face flushed. "I didn't know that," he whispered. "I wish I could spend more time with her and learn more about the various challenges she faces."

"I know you're doing the best you can," Sarah tried to assure him. "Charity is getting the best care possible, but right now it's important that you and I complete our education and find good jobs so that we can take on more responsibility for her care."

Jeff nodded in agreement and turned his attention back to the turkey drumstick on his plate. "I have a year and a half before I complete my degree in physical education. When I finish, I hope there will be a job for me close to Rocky Bluff. I never realized how much being a father would mean to me when she was first born. I have to admit, the older I get the more Charity tugs on my heartstrings."

The day passed swiftly for the happy gathering. At two o'clock, the children were taken to the sleeping rooms and put down for their afternoon naps. While they slept, the parents gathered in the playroom. They all helped clear the table. While the women loaded the dishwasher and straightened the kitchen, the men took down the folding tables and rearranged the chairs.

After the work was completed, Dawn motioned for everyone to place their chairs in a circle and said, "We all come from a variety of backgrounds, but we share a common interest—the love of a child with spina bifida. Most of us have read a great deal about the disability but feel isolated in the personal struggles that we face trying to do what's best for our child. Now might be a good time to share the joys, challenges, and heartaches you've faced as parents of children with disabilities."

Everyone nodded with agreement and looked nervously around the room to see who would have the courage to speak first. Much to Sarah's surprise, Jeff began sharing his feelings of guilt concerning the pregnancy and the child's disability and the decisions he faced as a single father trying to do what was right for his daughter and her mother, and most importantly, before God.

Jeff's honest confession helped others obtain the courage to share many of their deepest fears concerning their child. They no longer felt isolated in their struggles. A bond of friendship developed among them, and they soon were exchanging addresses, telephone numbers, and E-mail addresses.

When the little ones began waking, they were brought out to the families in the playroom. The activities shifted from being adult-centered to child-centered as, one by one, the parents started playing with their own child. When Charity awoke, Jeff and Sarah sat on the floor and stacked blocks with her until they toppled to the floor. Each time they fell, Charity would laugh with an infectious giggle that caused the others to follow suit. Before they realized it, the sun had set, and it was time to feed the children a light evening meal, have an hour of quiet, and put them to bed.

After the children were in their beds, the parents bade each other farewell and promised to try to get together at Christmastime. As Jeff and Sarah stepped into the crisp late fall air, they looked at each other, unable to say good-bye after a nearly perfect day. "How about taking in the late show at the theater tonight?" Jeff asked. "When I drove through town this morning, I noticed there's a good comedy playing tonight at the Capri. Would you be interested in seeing it with me?"

"Sounds like fun," Sarah replied as her heart began to race and her face flushed.

Jeff instinctively took her arm and led Sarah to the car on the pretext of keeping her from slipping on the ice. But a new sense of warmth and protection spread over him. He had dated several different girls at the University of Montana. Although they were exciting and nice looking, he never felt so comfortable with any other girl as he did at that moment with Sarah. As they shared laughs throughout the movie, Jeff was sure he wanted to see more of the mother of his child, but he, like Sarah, was committed to completing his education above all else.

When the movie was over, the pair stood to leave. As they waited for the lines to clear, Sarah gasped, "I've never laughed so much in my life. If there wasn't a funny line on the screen, you were whispering something hilarious in my ear."

"They say laughter is the best medicine," Jeff replied lightly and hesitated briefly before continuing. "And from what I've seen, you've been working much too hard and haven't taken enough time to just relax and enjoy life."

Sarah squeezed Jeff's hand as the line began to move. "You have excellent insight into my mind and soul. I feel better tonight than I have in a long time."

The pair exchanged puns, jokes, and silly stories as they drove across town. When they arrived at the parking lot, Jeff escorted Sarah to her dormitory. "It's been a memorable day," he said as he took her hand in his. "I'd like to spend as much time as possible with both you and Charity while I'm in Rocky Bluff. What do you think of the idea of taking her to the mall tomorrow to look at the Christmas decorations? She seems fascinated by bright, flashing lights. I'm not comfortable having total care of her, but you seem to be ready to step in as full-time caregiver."

"I wish that were true," Sarah sighed, "but I still have a lot to learn." She hesitated. She had longed for a chance to do more things with her daughter, but without a car of her own, she had been unable to even consider it. It would be nice to have their daughter to themselves. "We could talk to Dawn about taking Charity to the mall. The malls are crowded the day after Thanksgiving, but we could go early in the day and avoid the rush."

"Why don't I pick you up at ten-thirty, and we can go to Little Lambs together," Jeff suggested. "If we can't take Charity out, then we could stay there and play with her. If you'd agree, I'd take you to lunch during her nap time."

"Sounds good to me," Sarah replied, then tried to muffle a yawn. "I'm looking forward to tomorrow, but right now I think it's time to get some shut-eye."

That night Sarah tossed in her bed. Images of the laughter she had had throughout the day with Jeff kept bouncing against the serious concern and compassion she felt when she was with Ryder. In many ways, they were alike. Both men were strong Christians who attended church regularly. They both loved their families and took their education seriously. However, in other ways they were very different from each other. Ryder was quieter and more serious around people, while Jeff was outgoing and gregarious. Ryder immediately struck a rapport with the children with disabilities, while Jeff appeared to be a little awkward with the other children at Little Lambs.

It's ironic, Sarah thought, *for more than three years I refused to be attracted to men, but now I find myself attracted to two at the same time.*

Sarah's roommate, Vanessa White, had gone home for the holidays, so Sarah enjoyed the luxury of sleeping later in the morning without interruption. At nine o'clock, the loud ringing of her telephone awakened her. Sarah stumbled to the desk under the window. "Hello," she murmured.

"Hello, Sarah. Did I awaken you?" a familiar voice asked as the coed slumped into the chair at the desk.

"Oh, hi, Mom," Sarah replied as she stretched and became more alert. "I guess I did oversleep a little this morning."

"You probably needed the rest," Doris Brown replied in her soft motherly tone. "I'm sure you've been spending too much time hovering over books and computers and not getting enough sleep."

"I have been doing a lot of studying lately," Sarah admitted, "but I think my immediate problem was that I stayed out too late last night with Jeff Blair."

"So Jeff's in Rocky Bluff for the Thanksgiving holidays?" her mother teased. "I wondered why you postponed your visit home."

The mother-daughter relationship between Sarah and Doris had not always been close. Four years ago, upon learning that her daughter was pregnant, Doris had insisted that she get an abortion, and when Sarah refused, Doris disowned her during the most difficult time in her life.

Yet through that troubled time, Sarah learned about the love and forgiveness of Jesus Christ. Doris Brown was so moved by the change in her daughter and the birth of her first grandchild that she reconciled and accepted the same Christian love and forgiveness that Sarah had embraced. From that time forward, the family warmth and understanding far exceeded what either one ever thought possible.

"Mother, don't get the wrong idea," Sarah responded lightly. "I stayed behind because I was out of money and couldn't afford a bus ticket. I really wanted to see you and Mark."

Doris shook her head. "Why didn't you tell me? I would have sent money for a ticket," she scolded.

"Mom, you work hard for what you have and don't have that much to spare," Sarah protested with a lump building in her throat, "and besides, I want to be able to make it on my own."

Doris smiled to herself as she recalled the stubborn self-reliance that had always seemed a part of her daughter's personality, even before she became pregnant with Charity. "I'm very proud of all you've accomplished," she assured her daughter, "but your brother and I would both like to see you. Besides, he's taking driver's education and needs to get some practice time on the road. We were wondering if it would be okay if we came to Rocky Bluff Sunday to see you and Charity?"

Sarah's eyes brightened. "Of course it's okay. I'd love to have you come," she exclaimed. "I have some good news for you, but I'll wait until you get here to tell you."

Doris Brown snickered with affection for her daughter. "You know how I hate secrets. Do I have to wait two days before I find out?"

"I'm afraid you'll have to because I'm good at keeping secrets," Sarah teased. "I'm looking forward to seeing you. What time do you expect to arrive?"

Doris hesitated, while she did some mental calculations. "If we get an early start, we should be there by ten o'clock; then we can go to church with you before we see little Charity. From the last pictures you sent, it looks like she's really grown."

"You won't believe it when you see her," Sarah announced proudly. "She's learning to talk and is becoming extremely expressive. She loves being around people."

"I can hardly wait. I'll be at your dorm around ten on Sunday. We can go to brunch after church, then to see Charity."

"Sounds great to me," Sarah responded excitedly. "Good-bye for now. I love you."

"I love you too. See you Sunday."

As Sarah showered and dressed, she basked in the blessings of the last few days. She had obtained a job, working for her room and board so she would not have to drop out of college; she had found a friend in Ryder Long who she felt accepted her in spite of her troubled background; Jeff had come to Rocky

Bluff to see Charity and ended up spending a lot of time with her; and now her mother and brother were coming to see her.

Sarah hummed her favorite hymn as she hurriedly slipped into a pair of black slacks and a multicolored sweater. She blow-dried her hair, then styled it with her curling iron. She had just finished putting on the final touches of her makeup when she received a call from the receptionist in the dormitory lobby saying that she had a guest waiting for her.

Her face carried an extra glow as she grabbed her coat and hurried to the lobby. Jeff Blair greeted her with a warm hello and a quick hug. "You look happy today. You must have had a good night's rest."

"Just the opposite," Sarah confessed as Jeff opened the door of the dormitory and they stepped into the brisk November air. "I was so wound up from all the laughs we had that I had trouble falling asleep. I didn't wake up until nine o'clock when my mother called."

Through the years, Jeff had developed a special fondness for his baby's grandmother. The last time he had seen Doris Brown was at Dawn and Ryan Reynolds's wedding two and a half years ago. When Charity was born, Doris had been extremely rude to him, but gradually she was able to forgive him and was able to carry on a pleasant conversation with him at the wedding. "That was nice of her to call. I assume she wanted to wish you a Happy Thanksgiving since you weren't at home yesterday."

"It's even better than that," Sarah exclaimed as they trudged across the frozen parking lot. "She and my brother are coming to Rocky Bluff Sunday. Mark is taking driver's education and needs more practice behind the wheel, so she's going to let him drive the entire way. They're really excited about seeing Charity again."

Jeff opened the car door for Sarah, walked around, and slid behind the wheel. "I'm glad that things are finally working out for your family," he said as he turned the key in the ignition. "Since your mother left her job at the lounge and got one in that fancy restaurant, she seems to be a lot happier."

"She's a totally different woman than she was three years ago," Sarah replied. "She's now the mother that I had always wished I had."

"There have been so many blessings that came out of Charity's birth," Jeff noted as he reached for her hand while he stopped at a traffic light. "Three years ago the future looked extremely bleak for all of us. . .and now look at it."

Jeff's positive attitude had been one of the main traits that had attracted Sarah to him before her pregnancy. She had always felt overwhelmed with life's problems, and Jeff had a special way of helping lift her gloom and making her laugh.

When the pair arrived at Little Lambs, Dawn was pleased that Charity would have a chance to go to the mall with her parents. "The more contact children have with the outside world the better their minds are stimulated," the former nurse explained. "She's already eaten breakfast, and you can feed her in the food court when she gets hungry. However, try to get her back before two o'clock. She's used to having a two-hour nap, and I'm sure she'll be getting cranky by then."

Sarah and Jeff looked at each other and laughed knowingly. "You can trust us to get her back as soon as she begins to get tired," Sarah replied.

For the next couple of hours, Sarah and Jeff took turns pushing Charity's wheelchair up one side of the mall and down the other. Occasionally, they would let go of the wheelchair, and Charity would try to control it herself by pushing on the wheels. Little by little, she gained confidence in her newfound independence. The child's eyes sparkled as she kept saying, "Pretty. . .pretty," whenever bright lights and decorations caught her attention. When they arrived in front of a toy store, Charity tried to turn her wheelchair into the doorway by herself. "Wanna see," she exclaimed as she gave an extra hard push on the wheels.

Jeff and Sarah exchanged glances and laughed. Sarah instinctively took the handles and pushed the chair into the store. They walked slowly up and down the aisle and often stopped to let Charity handle the toys that caught her attention. When she finished looking at each toy, Jeff would return it to its spot on the shelf and go on to another one. When she spotted a miniature chord organ, she reached her arm out. "Wanna see. Wanna see."

Jeff took the little organ from the shelf, turned it on, and set it on Charity's lap. The child laughed with glee as she struck each key one by one. One minute passed, then two, three, and five, while Charity kept experimenting with each of the sounds on the keyboard. "Shall we put the organ back and look at some of the other toys?" Jeff asked as he reached for the organ.

Charity wrapped her arms firmly around the organ. "No. Mine."

Jeff and Sarah could not contain their amusement. "I think we just bought an organ," Jeff chuckled, then turned his attention back to his daughter. "Charity, would you like to buy the organ and take it home with you?"

The little girl grinned. "Want organ."

Jeff reached for an organ that was still in its original container. "Charity, we have to put the organ you have back on the shelf and take this box with the organ to the lady in the front so we can pay for it."

Charity studied the box, making sure that the picture of the organ on the cover was exactly the same as the one in her arms. She reluctantly handed it to her father and reached for the one in his hands. Charity clung tightly to the box, while Sarah pushed the wheelchair through the crowded aisles toward the checkout, and Jeff followed close behind with an enormous smile on his face. Finally, he was able to give Charity something that he knew she'd really like.

With extra coaxing, Charity released the treasured box long enough for the clerk to scan the bar code; then Jeff immediately returned it to her waiting arms. As soon as Jeff finished paying for the organ, Charity squealed, "Wanna go home. Wanna go home."

Sarah leaned over the wheelchair. "Don't you want to look in some of the other stores?"

"No," Charity insisted. "Wanna go home now."

The young couple looked at each other, shrugged their shoulders, and said in unison, "I guess that settles that."

Sarah put Charity's coat on her, and they headed for the car. Their first outing to the mall was a success, only much shorter than they had hoped.

When they arrived at Little Lambs, Charity insisted on opening the box as soon as she got inside the door. She kept the organ beside her when she ate a light lunch. At nap time, Charity took it to bed with her. Amused by the intensity of the child's attraction to the organ, Dawn compromised with her and let her take it to bed with her as long as the power was off.

"Looks like we have a budding musician on our hands," Dawn chuckled as she returned to the playroom after putting Charity down for her nap. "Since she'll never be able to walk, music may become a vital outlet for her."

The three continued sharing their experiences with Charity at the mall until there was a loud wail from one of the sleeping rooms, and Dawn's responsibility took her to the anxious child.

When they were alone, Jeff turned to Sarah. "While she's sleeping, how about you and I go back to the mall and see the things we didn't get to see when we had Charity? We can make the food court our first stop."

"Sounds great to me," Sarah agreed. The couple said good-bye to Dawn and hurried to the lounge for their coats.

Sarah and Jeff spent the remainder of the afternoon wandering through the variety of stores in the mall. They laughed and joked as if they didn't have a care in the world. When they noticed the lights in the parking lot come on, Jeff said, "Hamburgers are great for lunch, but now it's time for real food. How about dinner at the Black Angus Steak House? I have to leave first thing in the morning to return to Missoula and won't be able to see you or Charity until my next trip."

Sarah readily agreed. This would be a perfect ending for a nearly perfect day. The evening seemed to fly by as the couple laughed and joked together throughout their entire meal. However, in the midst of the gaiety, Sarah couldn't help comparing the evening with the last time she had dinner at the

Black Angus with Ryder Long. Both were very special, yet so different. She and Ryder had discussed their pasts, their dreams of the future, and their class work; while she and Jeff knew each other's past, they did not share their class work, but he saw humor and joy in the simplest things of life. Sarah was thankful that they were both simply friends and she would not be forced to choose between the two men.

Chapter 6

Sarah glanced nervously out her dorm window, anxiously awaiting the arrival of her family. She had not seen her mother and brother since she returned to college after summer vacation. During her summer break, she had worked full-time at the same Pizza Parlor in Billings where she had worked during her high school days. However, this time she was the shift supervisor and found herself overseeing high school students like herself just four years before. During her rare free moments, she marveled at the change in thinking and motivation that had occurred in the high school subculture during the last few years. The young workers displayed a level of disrespect for authority that she would never have imagined when she had been in their position.

Meanwhile, the Brown family had the best summer together they had ever had. Her mother had given up her job at the DewDrop several months before and had found a better one as hostess at Milton's Steak House. She no longer wearily fell into bed each night after her shift was over. Plus, she no longer had to count pennies after she paid her rent. Doris Brown was happier than she had been since childhood. Not only was she now attending church regularly, but she had also become active in their women's group and had an entirely new set of friends.

Sarah's brother, Mark, had matured from an awkward adolescent to a vibrant teenager. This past summer he had found a part-time job at the nearby convenience store and was saving his money for his own car. Sarah smiled with amusement as she imagined her mother having to ride all the way to Rocky Bluff with Mark driving so that he could meet his behind-the-wheel requirement for his driver's license.

During the fall, Sarah found her mother's letters and phone calls extremely encouraging. They always seemed to arrive at just the right time when she felt tempted to give up and go home. At the same time, the E-mails from her brother kept her entertained and in touch with what she considered the less serious things of life.

Sarah squinted her eyes as a blue Ford turned into the parking lot. Hoping it was her mother's, she watched as the car parked in the nearly empty lot; a young teen stepped from behind the wheel, and a middle-aged woman got

386

out of the passenger seat. Leaving her coat behind, Sarah ran outside into the biting cold to meet her family.

After greeting each with a hug, Sarah led her mother and brother into the holiday-quiet dormitory. Mark glanced around the huge lobby with awe. *So this is how college students live,* he mused. *I wonder if I'll ever be able to go to college. . . . If Sarah can do it, surely I can do it as well.*

Sarah proudly pointed out the TV room, the group study room, and the laundry room as they headed down the long hallway toward her room. "This is it," she exclaimed as she threw open the door to her room. "It doesn't always look this way," she laughed. "I spent most of yesterday afternoon cleaning it, and my roommate took a lot of her stuff home for Thanksgiving."

"It's very nice, Dear," Doris replied as she slowly looked around the small dormitory room. "You've certainly added a homey touch. . .and to think you did it with a lot of ingenuity and little money. I hope you won't have to drop out of school because they cut your financial assistance. You've accomplished so much in the last couple of years."

Sarah beamed, unable to contain her good news. "Mom, I didn't want to tell you until you got here," she exclaimed, "but God answered my prayers in a most unbelievable way. . . . I probably won't have to drop out after all."

"Well, what happened?" Doris urged as she sat on the corner of the bed. "You know I can't stand suspense."

"I think I told you that Dawn's brother is my academic advisor," Sarah began excitedly. "After I explained my situation to him, he talked with our pastor, and they were able to arrange for me to work for my room and board for a widow who is in the early stages of Alzheimer's."

"I'm pleased that you're willing to take on such a challenge in order to get your education," Doris said as she put her arm around her daughter. "I just hope it's not too demanding on you."

"I know it's a big step," Sarah replied, "but Rebecca Hatfield is so sweet, and I have a lot of support from the church. They don't want her to have to go into a care center until it's absolutely necessary."

Mark began to laugh his typical little-brother chuckle. "What do you know about old people?" he teased.

Sarah returned a phony glare. "I can always learn," she retorted. "I didn't know anything about babies until three years ago, and it won't be long before I'll be able to have permanent custody of Charity."

"We've all learned a lot about basic Christian compassion these last few years," their mother inserted as if trying to alleviate the sibling teasing. "I'm sure you'll be an excellent caregiver for Rebecca." Doris glanced at her watch. "Doesn't your church start at ten-thirty?"

Sarah flushed as she hurried to the closet for her coat. "It sure does, and it takes a good ten minutes to get there. Mom, do you mind if I drive? I know a few shortcuts."

Mark scowled as Doris handed the car keys to her daughter.

❖

Following church and a Sunday buffet at the Black Angus Steak House, the Brown family hurried to the Little Lambs Children's Center. Doris could scarcely contain her excitement at seeing her granddaughter again. She had brought Sarah to college September first and had seen Charity at that time, but she had not seen her since.

"I hope we don't interrupt their nap time," Doris said as Sarah parked the car in front of the Children's Center.

Sarah glanced at the clock on the dash. "They usually start waking up about this time," she replied. "We can wait in the lobby or play with the other children in the playroom until Charity wakes up."

Sarah rang the doorbell to the Children's Center, and within seconds, Dawn answered and greeted Doris and Mark with a warm handshake. "I'm glad you could come." She smiled. "Please come in."

"Dawn, it's good to see you again," Doris replied. "How have you been doing?"

"Keeping busy," Dawn laughed, "and you?"

"I guess I can truthfully say exactly the same thing," Doris retorted in jest before she asked seriously, "How has little Charity been doing?"

"Just wonderful." Dawn beamed. "She's becoming quite independent since she's learned to get around by herself in a wheelchair."

Dawn showed Doris and Mark where to hang their coats in the lobby. "Is Charity awake yet?" Doris asked eagerly as she listened for her granddaughter's familiar voice.

"She was one of the first ones to wake up today," the nurse/director replied. "She's with one of the volunteers in the playroom now."

The Browns hurried toward the playroom, then stopped in the doorway when they spotted Charity across the room. She was happily building with blocks on the tray on her wheelchair with a dark-haired young man. They both seemed to be enjoying themselves so much that no one wanted to interrupt their fun. Finally, the young girl looked up. "Mom. . .my," she squealed as she began wheeling herself across the floor toward them.

Instead of rushing toward her daughter, Sarah knelt down with outstretched arms. Charity pushed the wheels as hard as she could to get to her mother. "Wow," Mark gasped. "Look at her go."

As soon as she had gotten across the room, Sarah proudly lifted her from her wheelchair and hugged her. "That was great, Charity," she exclaimed. "You're really getting good with your new set of wheels."

"I'm playing with Ryder," Charity exclaimed as she pointed to the young man who had been building blocks with her.

Ryder strolled across the room and smiled at Sarah. "Hi, Sarah. It's good to see you again. Is this your family?"

Sarah paused as she admired his dark eyes and quiet spirit. "Ryder, I'd like you to meet my mother, Doris Brown, and my brother, Mark.

"Mother, this is Ryder Long. He's in several of my classes, and we've worked on several group projects together."

"It's nice to meet you," Doris said as she extended her hand. "Charity seems to be enjoying your company. Do you volunteer here often?"

"I've started coming every Sunday afternoon," Ryder replied as he patted Charity's outstretched hand. "Most of the volunteers need to be with their own families on weekends, and that is the only time that I have free."

"Ryder plans to go on to the University of Iowa and become a physician's assistant," Sarah explained as she continued hugging Charity close to her bosom.

Suddenly a child's voice was heard from the bedroom.

"It sounds like someone else is ready to get up from their nap," Ryder chuckled. "Would you please excuse me?"

As Ryder left the room, all the attention turned to the girl in Sarah's arms. "Hi, Charity," Doris cooed as she reached for her hand. "How are you today?"

"I fine," Charity said in her most grown-up manner.

"I'm your grandma," Doris continued as Charity returned a mildly confused look. "I'm your mommy's mommy."

With those words, Charity began to relax as a smile spread across her face.

"Would you let me hold you?" Doris asked as she stretched out her arms.

Immediately, Charity's smile became broader as she leaned toward her grandmother. Doris took the child with delight and carried her to one of the rocking chairs in the corner. When they were both comfortable, Doris began playing the same finger games she had once played with her own children. When those became tiresome, she pondered the next thing she could do in order to bond with her only granddaughter. Eyeing the books on the shelf beside her, Doris said, "Charity, would you like Grandma to read you a story?"

Charity nodded her head. "Story. . .story," she exclaimed excitedly as she pointed to the books beside them.

For the next half hour, Doris and Charity were oblivious to anyone else in the room as they read one story after another. Mark finally became bored and wandered into the lobby where there was a college football game on the television. Not wanting to interrupt her mother's precious moments with her granddaughter, Sarah went to help Ryder get the other children who were beginning to awaken from their naps.

"Your mother seems extremely proud of her granddaughter," Ryder whispered to Sarah as they picked up children in adjoining beds. "It's hard to imagine that she was once so hostile about having a disabled grandchild."

"It's been a miracle beyond my wildest imagination," Sarah replied softly. "Our entire family has completely changed, and it's just wonderful. I have so much to be thankful for this Thanksgiving."

Sarah and Ryder continued changing diapers, carrying children to the playroom, and getting them interested in various activities. When everyone appeared content, Ryder quietly slipped into the lobby where Mark was engrossed in the football game. "Who's winning?" he asked as he joined the youth on the sofa.

"Texas, right now," Mark replied, "but Oklahoma is getting ready to score again."

The afternoon flew by as the Brown family enjoyed Charity and the other children and Mark found a fellow football enthusiast in Ryder. At five o'clock, the staff began assembling the children into the large dining room for the evening meal. Sarah, her mother, and brother said their farewells and stepped into the brisk late-fall air. Only a faint glow illumined the western sky.

"I hate to see today end," Doris sighed, "but Mark has school tomorrow, and we have almost a four-hour drive ahead of us. If you'd like, we could drop you at your dormitory on the way out of town."

"Thanks, Mom," Sarah replied as she gave her a quick hug, "but I think I'll stay and help with supper. Ryder said he'd give me a lift back to campus."

"Hmm. . .this sounds serious," Mark taunted. "I suppose next thing you're going to tell us is that there are going to be wedding bells."

Sarah returned a teasing scowl. "Mark, he's just a friend. Someday you'll learn that men and women can just be friends without being romantically involved."

"Yeah, sure, Sis," Mark replied as he gave Sarah a good-bye hug. "I'll check with you at Christmastime and see how your love life is going."

Sarah gave her mother a parting hug, then stood in the yard of Little Lambs Children's Center waving as they drove away. Tears filled her eyes. The day had gone so well; it was hard to part, knowing that it would be nearly another month before she would see them again.

Suddenly the trembling coed felt a light hand on her shoulder. "It's sometimes hard to say good-bye, isn't it?" Ryder said softly.

"It sure is," Sarah replied. She brushed away her tear, took a deep breath, and continued, "I suppose I should go in and help Dawn feed the children since she's short of help this weekend."

Ryder nodded with agreement. The pair returned to the kitchen and began washing little fingers as one by one the children finished eating. When she got back to Charity, she noticed her eyes were glazed, and she was nonresponsive. Her breathing was labored, and her lips were turning blue. Her left arm started convulsing.

"Dawn," Sarah shouted, "what's wrong with her?"

Dawn ran to their side. She made sure Charity did not have any food in her mouth, and she peered into the child's eyes. "I don't like the looks of this," she exclaimed as Ryan joined her. "I think we'd better call an ambulance and get her to the hospital."

The next few hours were a blur for the frightened young mother. An ambulance arrived within minutes and quickly whisked Charity away. While Dawn rode in the ambulance with Charity, Ryder and Sarah followed in his green sports car. She whispered a string of prayers under her breath, and Ryder reached for her hand to comfort her. When they arrived at the hospital, Sarah jumped from the car as Ryder stopped a few yards from the parked ambulance. She ran behind the gurney into the emergency room. Dawn was beside the child, making sure the oxygen mask stayed on her face.

The lab technician drew blood from Charity's arm to run tests, and within minutes, a doctor was talking to the frightened mother. "Sarah, it looks like your daughter had a grand mal seizure. At this time, we don't know what caused it, but it's common for children with neural tube damage to have seizures. I would like to medevac her to Great Falls where they can do more testing and she can have a CAT scan. Would you be willing to sign the necessary medical release papers?"

"Of course," Sarah replied mechanically. "Anything to make sure she gets the best care possible." Although a medical team, plus Dawn and Ryder surrounded her, Sarah felt totally alone. None of them could fully understand the fear she felt behind her brave mask. The only one who could possibly share the intensity of her feelings would be the father of her child, and he was many miles away.

While waiting for the medical helicopter to arrive from Great Falls, Sarah slipped out and found a pay phone near the lobby. She reached into her purse and took out an address book. She flipped to the Bs and dialed the Missoula number. Her hand trembled while she waited for a response on the other end of the line. Finally, a familiar voice said, "Hello."

"Hello, Jeff," Sarah gasped, almost in tears. "Something awful happened. They think little Charity had a grand mal seizure. They rushed her to the hospital in Rocky Bluff, but the doctor wants to medevac her to the hospital in Great Falls for more testing."

There was a long silence on the other end of the line before there was a response. "What happened? She was so happy Friday when I left," Jeff protested.

"They don't know," Sarah replied, trying to choke back her tears. "It all happened so fast. . . . I'm going to ride with Dawn to Great Falls. We'll probably get there a couple of hours behind Charity. The doctor said they'd probably have most of the testing done by the time we get there."

There was a long silence again before Jeff spoke. "I should be at the hospital as well. If I leave right away, I can be in Great Falls in three and a half hours. I'll meet you there."

"Thanks," Sarah replied, then said good-bye, grateful that he was planning to meet them.

When Sarah returned to the emergency room, she found Dawn looking for her. "Sarah, we may need to spend the night in Great Falls. Would you like to stop by your dorm room and grab a change of clothes and a toothbrush? I'll need to stop by Little Lambs and get a few things myself. I want to be sure and take a car seat along. I hope we'll be able to bring Charity home with us tomorrow."

The possibility of bringing her daughter home the next day helped ease Sarah's fears. She said a speedy farewell to Ryder and asked him to explain the situation to her instructors and to notify her dorm supervisor that she was called out of town for a family emergency. At this point, she no longer cared about her long-kept secret. Her only concern was for the health and safety of her beautiful daughter.

❖

Sarah was thankful she was with a nurse during the long ride to Great Falls. Dawn was able to explain some of the causes and treatments of seizures and how people learned to live very normal lives in spite of the inconvenience. When they arrived at the hospital, Charity had just finished having the CAT scan, and the doctor was waiting for them. A nurse led them into a small conference room where several people were gathered around a long table. "They're meeting concerning Charity's condition," she said as she pushed open the door.

Sarah and Dawn had just introduced themselves and took chairs across from the doctor when the same nurse reappeared in the doorway. "The father is here and would like to be a part of the discussion. Should I show him in?"

Dr. Williams turned to Sarah who smiled and nodded. "By all means," the doctor instructed.

Jeff Blair entered the room. His eyes were heavy, and tension lines wrinkled his forehead. The doctor rose, shook the young man's hand, and introduced himself as Dr. Williams. Jeff then greeted Dawn, gave Sarah a hug, and took the chair beside her.

"I'm glad you could all be here," Dr. Williams began in a businesslike fashion. "I know this is an extremely difficult time for you, but fortunately, I have encouraging news for you. The CAT scan did not show any abnormalities, and Charity is now resting normally. We'd like to keep her overnight for observation, but if all goes well, you'll be able to take her home in the morning."

"Thank you," Sarah murmured as she squeezed Jeff's hand.

"What's her prognosis?" Dawn inquired as she studied the doctor's face for any clue. "Will she need medication to control seizures?"

Dr. Williams leaned back in his chair. "At this point there's no way to know," he replied. "She could have another seizure in ten minutes, or she may never have another one. I could prescribe medication now, but at the present, I think we'd be better off waiting to see if she has any more seizures before we make a final decision. I'll notify your doctor in Rocky Bluff as to my findings. I'll be making rounds about nine o'clock tomorrow, and if all is well, I'll dismiss her at that time."

Dawn breathed a heavy sigh of relief. "Thank you very much," she said. "We appreciate all you've done for us."

The doctor shook hands with each of them as he left the conference room. When he was gone, Sarah turned to Dawn. "Do you think it would be possible to see Charity? She looked so terrible the last time I saw her. I need to see her just to alleviate my own fears."

"I'll see what I can do," Dawn replied. "Follow me, and I'll ask the nurse in charge."

Within a few minutes, the three were gathered around the bed where little Charity slept. "She has the face of an angel," Jeff whispered.

"I know," Sarah replied. "She's been through so much in her short lifetime, and yet she's always such a happy child."

After everyone was comforted knowing that Charity was all right, the threesome tiptoed from the room. "I'll call and try to get a motel room across the street for us," Dawn said. "Jeff, would you like me to reserve one for you as well? It's been a long day, and I'm sure we're all exhausted."

"I'd appreciate that," he replied wearily. "I don't want to leave Great Falls until I'm certain she's going to be all right."

Chapter 7

Without taking time for breakfast, Sarah and Dawn showered, dressed, and hurried into the pediatrics ward of the Great Falls hospital. "Good morning, sleepyheads," a familiar voice greeted as the two women stepped off the elevator and found themselves face-to-face with Jeff Blair. "Are you going my way?" he teased as he reached for Sarah's hand.

"I think we have a mutual concern just down the hallway," Sarah retorted lightly. "Do you know if she had any further problems last night?"

Jeff's eyes twinkled as he said, "The nurse said that she slept like a baby, so I assume that's a good sign."

"I hope so," Sarah responded seriously, "because I'm looking forward to taking her home this morning."

"I wish I could go back with her," Jeff said with a distant look in his eye, "but I have a couple of term papers due next week, and I haven't started my research. I'll need to get back to the university as soon as I know Charity is going to be all right."

As the couple continued discussing their child, Dawn hurried to the nurses' station. "Good morning," she greeted the middle-aged woman studying a patient's chart. "I'm Dawn Reynolds. I currently have custodial care of Charity Blair and was wondering how she is doing."

Without looking up, the nurse responded dryly, "Charity had an unremarkable night with no indication of any further seizures. The doctor will make his rounds before nine o'clock. I assume he will dismiss her today."

"Thank goodness," Sarah injected as she joined Dawn at the counter. "May we see Charity now?"

"Certainly," the ward nurse replied, finally giving the hospital visitors her undivided attention. "The last time I was in there she was awake and playing with toys from the playroom."

The three hurried down the hall to room number 605. Sarah pushed open the door as a broad smile spread across Charity's face. "Mommy," she squealed as she stretched out her arms to be picked up from the crib.

Sarah hugged her daughter; then Charity made it a game to reach for Dawn and giggled. After Dawn hugged her, Charity reached for Jeff, and after a hug from him, she reached for Sarah again. After the three of them had each hugged her four times, they tried to interest her in another game but were interrupted when the doctor walked into the room followed by the head nurse.

"It looks like she's not lacking in attention," Dr. Williams chuckled.

"Who can resist those baby blue eyes?" Jeff replied.

Dr. Williams took the child from her father and laid her in the crib. He did a quick exam and muttered several observations which the nurse quietly recorded on the chart. "She doesn't seem to have any recurring symptoms of the seizure she had yesterday. I'll go ahead and discharge her without prescribing any medication, but if she shows any similar symptoms, be sure and get her to the hospital as soon as possible."

"Thank you so much for all you've done," Dawn said as the doctor turned to leave. "I'll keep an extra close eye on her for any symptoms that closely resemble another seizure."

The nurse helped them gather the patient's few belongings, then carried Charity down the elevator to the lobby with Dawn, Sarah, and Jeff close behind. "I'll wait here with her, if you'd like to go and get the car," she suggested as Dawn reached into her purse for her car keys and headed toward the front door.

Within a few minutes, Dawn and Sarah had thanked the nurse, buckled Charity in her car seat, bade good-bye to Jeff, and turned onto the main thoroughfare toward Rocky Bluff. "Are you as hungry as I am?" Dawn asked her younger friend.

"With all the excitement about bringing little Charity home, I completely forgot about breakfast. I guess I am pretty hungry."

"There's a fast-food drive-thru ahead. It won't be a gourmet meal, but it should hold us over until we get back to Rocky Bluff," Dawn replied as she slowed her car and turned it into the next drive.

❖

"Hey, Sarah, wait up," Ryder shouted as the political science class filed into the hallway and began to scatter in different directions.

Sarah turned at the sound of the familiar greeting as Ryder worked his way through the crowd of students. "You weren't in class yesterday, and I was worried about Charity. How is she?"

"She appears fine. Her CAT scan didn't show any problems, and she didn't have any more symptoms of a seizure so we brought her home yesterday. I'm going to Little Lambs now. Would you like to join me?"

"I'd love to," Ryder replied. "I've been so concerned about her that I even called Teresa Olson and asked her to start the church prayer chain."

Sarah smiled. "Their prayers must have been what did it, because in no time at all, she was back to her same giggly self."

The harsh December wind whipped against their faces as they stepped into the parking lot. They wrapped their scarves tightly around their necks and reached for their gloves in their pockets. "I'm parked at the far north end of the lot. Would you like to wait inside while I bring the car around?" Ryder suggested. "There's no need for both of us to freeze."

"Nah, I'm tough," Sarah laughed as they hurried across the parking lot together. The wind prevented conversation, but Sarah's mind continued to race. *Ryder is always thoughtful and concerned about others. The majority of the other guys in my classes seem self-absorbed and interested only in material possessions and recreation, but Ryder is different. He'll make a good physician's assistant and a good husband to some lucky woman.*

❖

After the pair was settled in the warmth of Ryder's sports car and they had left the college parking lot, Sarah said, "What did you do in class yesterday? I hated to miss it. It was the first class I missed all semester, but I didn't have much of a choice. Some things just naturally take priority."

"Not much," Ryder replied as he smiled. He admired the vibrant glow in Sarah's cheeks caused by the biting cold. "We just reviewed for our test tomorrow."

"Oh, dear. I forgot all about it," Sarah gasped. "I really need to get a good grade on that test. Did you happen to take good notes?"

"You, worry?" Ryder teased. "Are you afraid you'll get an A minus instead of an A?" Noticing the panic in her eyes, he quickly changed his tone. "I took the best notes I could," he tried to assure her. "I didn't think I'd need them today so I left them home. After we leave Little Lambs, would you like to get a bite to eat at the Black Angus, then come to my house so we can study for the test together? That is. . .if my little brother will leave us alone. He has a knack of turning up everyplace he's not welcome."

"I appreciate your offer. I dislike group projects intensely, but I seem to remember stuff so much better when I work with just one person, and we can question each other back and forth without interruption," Sarah replied as her smile broadened. "I understand about little brothers. Only recently has Mark begun to show human characteristics."

That afternoon flew by as Sarah played with Charity and Ryder played with several of the other children, helping them with their cognitive learning skills. Seeing Charity laughing and back to normal helped Sarah forget her dread of the upcoming test.

When it was the children's supper time, Sarah and Ryder hugged the children good-bye, retrieved their coats, and slipped into the dark, cold winter air. During the month of December in Montana, it was dark by four-thirty in the afternoon, and city lights were ablaze when people got off work. The Christmas lights lit the city streets as they approached the Black Angus, while Christmas carols echoed from the car radio. If it weren't for the nagging fear of the upcoming exam, Sarah would have claimed that the entire world was perfect.

For nearly an hour, the two students shared their mutual concerns about college and their future. Both were concerned that they would not get an A in all their classes. Ryder was extremely concerned about getting admitted to the University of Iowa, and Sarah wanted to prove to herself that she could get good grades and become a role model for her daughter. As they cruised slowly down the street where Rebecca Hatfield lived, the surrounding houses were aglow with blinking lights, while Rebecca's stood dark and sterile with only a single dim light and the reflection from the TV flickering through the window.

"It's kind of sad, isn't it?" Ryder noted. "The bleakness in her home seems to reflect the bleakness that is consuming her once vibrant life."

"I hope I'll be able to bring a little joy into her life when I move in," Sarah replied wistfully.

Glancing to his side, Ryder admired the attractive young woman beside him. He was inspired by the inner strength with which she faced the problems in her life and yet had the compassion and concern to reach out to the needs of others. "When do you plan to move in?"

"I'd like to move my stuff right after I finish my last test at the end of the term, then leave for Billings the same day," Sarah replied, "but I have a lot of details yet to work through."

"Do you have anyone to help you?"

"I've been so busy with Charity's problems that I haven't given it any consideration." A teasing twinkle entered Sarah's eyes. "Does that mean you're volunteering for the job?"

"You are extremely perceptive, Miss Brown," Ryder snickered back. "As soon as tests are over, your time is my time. In fact, if you need a ride to Billings, I'd be glad to give you a lift. I have an aunt living there whom I haven't seen in a couple of years. I'm sure I could spend the night with her before heading back."

"Yeah. . .sure," she readily agreed. "I never turn down help." Sarah was amazed at the kindness the people in Rocky Bluff had shown her since her daughter moved into Little Lambs Children's Center. Even before she enrolled in the community college, she had attended church every time she was in town, and the congregation immediately embraced her with Christian love and understanding without judging her for her sinful past.

For the remainder of the evening, the pair discussed the details of Sarah's move, from Ryder's borrowing a pickup to where to obtain enough boxes to pack her personal items. After their plans were completed, Sarah finally said, "It's been a good evening, but I'm becoming extremely weary. Would you mind taking me home?"

"I'm sorry," Ryder replied as he glanced at his watch and pointed his car toward the campus. "I hadn't realized it was so late."

A relaxed peace settled upon them as he retraced his familiar path through the well-lit streets of Rocky Bluff. With Charity out of immediate danger, Sarah reminded herself of her ambivalent feelings toward developing a serious relationship with a man. Any man.

When the young couple arrived at the parking lot outside the women's dormitory, Ryder parked the car and escorted Sarah through the cold and blustery air. He wrapped his arm protectively around her and pulled her close to himself as she shuddered in the briskness of a December evening in Montana. When they reached the front door, Sarah looked up into his warm dark eyes to thank him for the delightful evening. As their eyes met, they locked. Slowly and silently, Ryder moved his lips toward hers, and instinctively, Sarah pressed her lips against his.

After maintaining their embrace for several moments, Sarah pulled away. "Thank you for a lovely evening." She smiled. "I'll see you in class tomorrow."

"This evening was special for me. Would you mind if I join you tomorrow when you visit Charity?" Ryder asked.

"Please do," Sarah smiled as she disappeared behind the glass door of her dormitory.

When Sarah returned to her dorm room, she was anxious to obtain a few quiet moments to bask in the tenderness of the last few moments. However, her roommate, Vanessa, was eager to tell everyone about the date she just had with the quarterback of the football team.

"I had the greatest time tonight," Vanessa exclaimed. "Doug and I went to the Bobcat Grill for dinner and dancing. Several of his teammates showed up and asked me to dance as well. . . . I never had it so good. . .and to top it all off, I saw several of the cheerleaders there with nerdy guys. I'm sure they were green with jealousy."

"Sounds like fun," Sarah replied, trying to sound polite as her mind kept drifting back to the closeness she felt toward Ryder as compared with the stability and sense of history she shared with Jeff. Suddenly, the ringing of the telephone rudely interrupted their discussion.

"Hello," Sarah greeted as she brushed her long brown hair behind her ear.

"Hello. . . Is this Sarah?"

"Yes it is," she replied, trying to recognize the familiar voice.

"This is Beth Blair, Jeff's mother," a trembling voice replied. "I have some bad news for you."

Sarah's eyes widened. "What happened?"

"Jeff had an accident on his way back from Great Falls," the anxious mother explained, trying to maintain a calm exterior. "His car slid off the road when he hit a patch of ice coming down Rodger's Pass. I suppose it could have been a lot worse. Fortunately the car was stopped by a tree before he slid all the way to the bottom."

"Oh no," Sarah gasped. "Was he hurt?"

Beth explained the seriousness of Jeff's injuries. The young woman already had enough on her mind with her concern for little Charity and the intensity with which she took on her college studies. It was nearing final exam week, and Sarah would need to focus all her attention on her finals and not Jeff's injuries.

"Jeff has four broken ribs, cracks to several disks in his back, and bruises all over his body. He was fortunate that his neck was not broken. He'll be in the hospital for some time, then will require physical therapy for several more months after that."

Sarah's mind raced as she imagined the father of her child lying in a hospital bed racked with pain. There had to be something she could do to help. "Beth, I want to come to Missoula to be with him," she exclaimed, "but I don't have the money, and I have several tests and term papers due before the fourteenth."

"That's okay, Dear," Beth tried to calm her. "Jeff will understand your concern, but truthfully, there's little you can do to help, except pray. He's in a lot of pain and needs to rest quietly to let his body heal itself. Some of the medicines he's taking make him sleep a lot, but I'll let him know of your concern when he wakes up."

"Beth, thank you for calling. If there's anything I can do, please let me know." Sarah took a deep breath and tried to sound brave, even though the lilt in her voice betrayed her weak confidence. "I'll notify the church prayer chain and ask them to pray for Jeff."

"I'll keep you updated on his progress," Beth promised. "Just leave Jeff in the hands of God and the doctors and focus on your schoolwork. You have a lot of things on your mind right now, and I don't want your grades to suffer."

"I'll do my best," Sarah assured her as she bade her farewell, hung up the telephone, and flopped across her bed.

Sarah lay quietly for several minutes with her face buried in her pillow. As if unable to withstand the silence, Vanessa sat on the corner of Sarah's bed and put her hand on Sarah's shoulder.

❖

Sarah was different from the other girls she knew. Sarah rarely talked about her past, but Vanessa gathered that she had been through much heartache that made her what she was today. Vanessa admired the inner strength and security of her roommate that seemed to come from her faith in Christ and the people in her church. She wanted to someday have the same peace that Sarah had, but right now, she was enjoying the fun she was having with her college friends. Vanessa did not want to take the time away from her friends to discover the source of Sarah's inner strength.

But now, when she needed a source of wisdom to comfort her roommate, Vanessa only felt an inner emptiness.

"I'm so sorry," Vanessa said, trying to comfort her roommate, but her voice trembled with lack of confidence. "There seems to be a lot of stuff swirling around in your head right now. Would you like to talk about it?"

"Maybe later," Sarah replied as she rolled over and forced a smile at her roommate. "Right now I just need a little time to pray and get my thoughts sorted out. Every time it looks like things are finally falling into place, something else happens."

Vanessa squeezed her roommate's hand. "I understand. I'll go down to the lounge to study for awhile so you can be by yourself."

"Thanks," Sarah murmured as Vanessa slipped quietly out the door.

❖

The glow of the magical evening with Ryder faded into a faint memory. Sarah stared at the ceiling as she tried to remember each moment that she had had with Jeff. She remembered the reckless summer nearly four years ago when they had let down their guard and several weeks later when she discovered she was pregnant. She thought of the months he stood by her after she learned the baby would be born with birth defects. She admired his faithfulness of paying child support for the care of Charity at Little Lambs and the frequent visits he made to Rocky Bluff to visit her. She thought of the tenderness Jeff displayed when he held his daughter in his arms. She remembered the fun they had during the Thanksgiving Dinner at Little Lambs and the next day when they took their daughter to the mall to see the Christmas decorations. The thought of Jeff's strong, muscular body lying bruised and broken in a hospital bed in Missoula brought tears to her eyes. *I suppose his football days are over. If so, will he lose his football scholarship and have to drop out of college? Will he still be able to walk when he gets out of the hospital?*

Sarah tried praying, but she felt her prayers of desperation were not even reaching the ceiling of her dorm room. She tried reading comforting words from Scripture, but her favorite passages did not contain their normal encouragement. She turned the radio on to a Christian music station, but the music could not cut through her pain. Feeling herself sinking deeper and deeper into despair, Sarah did what she often did when the pressures of life became overwhelming. She reached for the telephone and dialed Dawn Reynolds.

Chapter 8

Through a fog of pain, Jeff Blair stared at the ceiling tile in his hospital room. His neck brace felt like a vise, and his chest was encompassed in a modified body cast. He tried to remember the events of the last few hours, but drugs had dimmed his memory. "Jeff, how are you feeling?" a familiar voice queried.

The injured football player tried to turn his head to answer his mother, but the pain intensified. "Mom, I've never hurt this bad in my life. I can scarcely move. What happened?"

"Your car slid off Rodger's Pass and hit a tree," Beth replied as she brushed a lock of hair from his sweaty brow. "Even though you feel miserable right now, you're a mighty lucky man."

Jeff's weak voice became panicky. "Am I going to be all right?"

Beth took a deep breath as tears gathered in her eyes. "You have four broken ribs, cracks to several disks, and several torn ligaments," she explained. "You'll need to be in physical therapy for several months, but the doctors think there's a good chance you'll make a total recovery."

Jeff's already pale face whitened even more as he gulped. "You mean there's a chance I might not be able to walk again."

Beth patted his hand. "There are people all over the country praying for your recovery. We must trust that God will work a miracle on your behalf."

Jeff looked away and closed his eyes, trying not to let his mother see the tears that threatened to spill. Jeff and his mother had always been close, and he knew that she could sense his need for quiet, to let him work through his emotions. Jeff's first five years had been extremely difficult, and his mother had done everything she could to protect him from the harshness in life. Even after she had married Dan Blair, that same pattern persisted; but now there was nothing she could do but pray and encourage others to storm heaven with their prayers for Jeff.

❖

When Beth Slater was a teenager in Rocky Bluff, she had learned to depend on the Lord for both the minor and the most complicated issues of life. She had been a struggling single mother trying to care for her baby, Jeffey, when Dawn Reynolds's grandmother, Edith Harkness Dutton, took her under her wing. Edith not only provided motherly advice on how to care for a baby, but she also led Beth into an understanding and acceptance of the Christian faith. Edith had encouraged Beth to finish her high school education and become a financially self-supporting and capable, nurturing mother.

Edith had been Beth's stabilizing force during those traumatic days when little Jeffey's natural father had kidnapped him and taken him to Canada. Jeffey's return under the most difficult and unlikely circumstances had fully convinced her of the power of prayer. But now, as she sat vigil at her son's bedside, she again threw herself on the mercy of Christ for help.

❖

While his mother was struggling to maintain optimism and faith during a difficult situation, Jeff slowly slipped into periods of self-examination and questioning. *If I'm not able to play football, I'll lose my football scholarship and have to increase my hours at the Pizza Parlor. But, if I can't stand for long periods at a time, I won't be able to make pizzas. . . . If I started delivering pizzas, I wouldn't be able to earn enough to pay both tuition and child support.*

Little Charity's innocent face flashed before him. Whatever the cost, he had to keep going, on her account. Her birth was totally unplanned and unintended. However, from the beginning it was obvious that God had a reason for her young life. Already, in the three short years of her life, she had been a witness of personal strength and determination.

During the first summer that he knew Sarah, he saw her only as a silly, shallow teenager. But through the years, he had watched her change into a mature young woman striving hard to receive an education so that she could not only financially support her daughter, but also be able to care for the multitude of medical needs that Charity had.

The squeaking of the hospital door interrupted Jeff's moments of contemplation. "How are you doing?" a nurse inquired as she approached his bed.

Jeff tried to turn his head that was still constrained in a neck brace. He grimaced as pain engulfed his entire body. "I feel miserable," he moaned. "I hurt all over."

"This will help take the intensity of the pain away," the nurse replied as she held up a needle that appeared to be two feet long.

"At this point I'll accept about anything," Jeff retorted, trying to make a feeble attempt at humor to mask his pain and depression.

After the shot, Jeff was asleep within minutes, and his mother slipped quietly from the hospital room. The hours at her son's bedside were taking a heavy toll on her body, and every muscle seemed to cry out for sleep.

❖

For the next few hours, Jeff drifted in and out of consciousness. Several times he was aware of his father's presence but only mumbled a brief greeting before going back to sleep. He was never fully awake until the young assistant from the food service noisily set a tray on his table and loudly announced, "Good morning, Mr. Blair. Your breakfast is here."

Jeff opened his eyes and faked a weak smile. "Thank you," he murmured as he surveyed the tray of toast, cereal, fruit, and coffee. He ate slowly as his chest muscles seemed to shudder with each swallow. *At least there's less pain than yesterday, so I assume that's progress,* he told himself.

For the next two hours, Jeff's time was filled with doctor visits, nursing assistants taking care of his personal needs, and a mild workout with the physical therapist. When he was finally alone, he again drifted back into his state of self-absorption and reflection. *Will my injuries keep me from marrying?* He thought about his growing feelings toward Sarah. *What would it be like spending my entire lifetime with Sarah? If I would marry her, would it be because I truly love her or would it be because of my sense of duty for having fathered her child?*

The more Jeff's mind dwelled on Sarah's sweet smile and bubbly personality, the more he began to convince himself that he truly loved her. *If I would marry Sarah, would we have another disabled child?* he pondered. *It's generally thought that spina bifida is caused by the lack of folic acid in the mother's system during early pregnancy, but no one is one hundred percent sure of that fact. What if I am a carrier of a gene that causes birth defects? I don't know anything about my natural father's medical history. Maybe I shouldn't even think about marriage until I am certain it wouldn't happen again.*

Jeff stared at the ceiling without moving, while he considered the complexity of his relationship with Sarah Brown. He became more determined than ever that he had to find his natural father before he could consider a serious relationship with her or any other woman.

While Jeff was trapped in his intense soul-searching, his mother entered the room. "How are you doing today, Dear?" Beth said as she leaned over and kissed her son on the forehead.

"I'm feeling a lot better today," he replied dryly. "However, I've been doing a lot of thinking." Jeff studied his mother's face, trying to figure out how to explain his dilemma without hurting the two people who had done so much for him. He took a deep breath, but even that slight motion caused pain.

"Mom," he began cautiously. "You know how much I love you and Dad. I wouldn't do anything in the world that would hurt you." Jeff hesitated, trying to search for the right words, while Beth waited patiently. "I've been doing a lot of thinking about little Charity. She's such a precious child, but I'm concerned about what caused her neural tube deficiency. What if I'm carrying a defective gene that I could pass on to other children? I'm not sure that I should ever consider marriage if that is the case."

Beth took her son's hand and stroked his forehead. "Jeff, no one knows for sure what causes each individual birth defect. Right now it's more important that you concentrate on getting well. You can research the possible causes of spina bifida when you get out of the hospital."

"Mother, you don't understand," he persisted. "I need to know my natural father's medical history before I even consider any kind of relationship with a woman. I don't want to be accused of leading a girl on, then dropping her just when it appears that we might become serious. Sarah doesn't deserve any more pain in her life."

"In this case, I don't agree with you," Beth replied kindly. "If a young woman truly loves a person, she'll accept him, regardless of what his medical history may be. . . . However, I understand why you feel the way you do. . . . Is there anything I can do to help?"

Jeff squeezed his mother's hand. She had stood by him every moment in his life, and now she was again willing to uphold him. "Mom, what do you know about my natural father? Do you know where I might locate him?"

Beth gulped, and her face blanched. "Truthfully, I know very little about him and haven't heard anything about him since he went to jail in Canada after he kidnapped you when you were four years old. His name is Mickey Kilmer. He grew up in Elders Point, Montana. After he learned I was pregnant with his child, he joined the Marines. However, his military career didn't last long, and he received a bad-conduct discharge for wrongful use and possession of a controlled substance."

"Do you know what happened to him after he left the Marines?" Jeff queried.

Beth shook her head. "I completely lost track of Mickey until he turned up in Rocky Bluff in a black Porsche and took you from the day care."

"I faintly remember that," Jeff replied. "I was really impressed with his fancy car, but I couldn't understand why he didn't take me back to you when I started crying. I think I cried nonstop for three days."

"There was a massive search for you, and your picture as a missing child even ended up on milk cartons in all the states of the Northwest and in Canada. Several weeks later, the Royal Canadian Mounted Police arrested Mickey for possession of two kilos of cocaine and an illegal handgun, and who knows what else. I think he was sentenced to ten years in prison, but he could have gotten out in four to five for good behavior. I'm not sure."

Jeff shook his head with disgust. "He must have been some wild dude."

The furrows on Beth's forehead deepened as she tried to remain calm. "Knowing that your natural father was in jail for drugs, are you certain you want to locate him? You may not like what you find."

"Because of his more antisocial behavior, it makes it even more imperative that I find him," Jeff stated firmly. "That means it's even more likely that I might have a genetic defect in my background. Maybe he has a serious mental illness or something. I could be a genetic time bomb waiting to explode."

"Jeff, I think you're having too much time on your hands to think," Beth scolded good-naturedly. "You're letting your imagination get the better of you."

Jeff remained silent for a few minutes, frustrated at his mother's response. "Mother, I don't think you understand how important this is to me," he said quietly. "If I'm ever to marry, I have to know my medical background."

Beth shook her head. "Like I said before, I'll do whatever I can to help you find your natural father," she repeated. "However, there's not much more I can tell you. . . . When Dan and I were married, an attorney in Rocky Bluff named Stuart Leonard made arrangements through a Canadian attorney to have your natural father sign papers surrendering all custody rights to you. As soon as the paperwork was completed, Dan was able to legally adopt you, and he raised you as if you were his natural-born son."

Jeff's eyes filled with tears. "It's hard to imagine what my life would have been like if Dan Blair hadn't adopted me. He's been the best father imaginable."

"I have to admit my entire life changed when Dan Blair entered my life," Beth replied. "Edith Harkness Dutton helped me get my life together, then Dan accepted me with all my warts and blemishes, and he readily accepted you as if you were his own son."

"He made me feel so special at your wedding, the way he included me," Jeff replied with his customary twinkle reappearing in his eyes. "It took me a long time to figure out that not all kids got to be a part of their parents' wedding."

Jeff and his mother continued discussing their early years alone together for another hour. With each passing sentence, Jeff became more and more determined to find Mickey Kilmer. Their conversation ended when the cafeteria assistant delivered the noon meal, and Beth excused herself to have lunch in the hospital cafeteria.

As Jeff ate his meat loaf and vegetables, his mind drifted back to his daughter, Charity, and her mother. How he wanted to pursue a mature romance with Sarah Brown, but until he knew the truth of his background, he was afraid to do so. Ironically, just as he was thinking about her, the phone beside his bed rang. Painfully, he reached to answer it.

"Hello."

"Hello. . .is that you, Jeff?"

The pain of stretching his sore muscles faded as he recognized the voice of the very person he was thinking about. "Yes. Is this Sarah?"

"Yes it is," she replied cautiously. "I wanted to check on how you were doing, so I called your house to talk with your mother, but no one answered. I thought she would probably be at the hospital with you and would answer the phone. This is a thrill to actually hear your voice."

"Mom's down in the cafeteria eating right now, and I'm just lying here indulging in this fantastic hospital food," Jeff chuckled weakly.

"So how are you doing? I was stunned to learn of your accident."

"I'm feeling a lot better than I did a couple of days ago," Jeff admitted, "but I still have a long way to go. I'll have to have physical therapy for several months, and right now I don't know if I'll ever be able to walk normally again."

"What. . .what. . .will you do if you can't walk? Will you still be able to go to school? What will happen to your football scholarship?" Sarah stammered.

Jeff wanted to share his inner fears and frustrations, but he didn't want to let her know how much she meant to him. That was. . .not until he knew the truth about his background; then he would be able to bare his soul to her. "The buildings are all handicapped accessible, but financing my education could become a real challenge," he replied with fake confidence. "I'm sure something will work out. Mom says a lot of people are praying for me."

The two talked for several minutes, but Jeff's responses became shorter and more abrupt as he struggled between wanting to share openly with Sarah and being afraid he would lose his determination to find his father's medical records.

Sarah detected a distance and coolness in his voice that she had never heard before. Her first instinct was to feel hurt; then she tried to rationalize. *I've never heard him sound so aloof and disinterested before, even when we talked about Charity. He must be in a lot of pain.*

"Are you getting too tired to talk?" Sarah queried.

"Not especially."

"Oh," Sarah responded weakly. "Your voice was becoming weak."

Jeff hesitated. "I was just looking at my lunch and thinking how cold it was becoming."

Sarah's voice cracked. "I'd better let you get back to your lunch. I'll keep you in my prayers."

"Thanks," he murmured as he hung up the phone.

Tears welled up in Jeff's eyes. It had been so difficult not to tell Sarah how frightened he was of the future and the fear that engulfed him that he might not be able to keep up his child support payments. If only he knew that he could not pass any birth defects or serious illnesses on to his future children, he would let Sarah know how much he loved her.

❦

Sarah and Ryder had just finished their last test of the semester and hurried across campus to the women's dormitory. The halls were a flurry of students, their parents, and boyfriends carrying boxes from each of the rooms. Sarah pushed her key into the keyhole. Her roommate's possessions were stacked on one side of the room, and hers on the other.

"With this mess, I don't even know where to begin," Sarah sighed.

"One box at a time," Ryder chuckled. "Just make sure you keep the suitcases you're going to take with you to Billings separate. That would cause all kinds of frustrations going through Christmas break without the things you need."

For the next half hour, Sarah and Ryder carried all Sarah's earthly belongings to Ryder's borrowed pickup truck. When Sarah's half of the room was empty, they each picked up the suitcases that she was planning to take home with her, locked the door, and left the key at the front desk.

"We'll have to hurry and unload," Ryder exclaimed as he slid behind the wheel of the truck. "I told my friend I'd be done by two o'clock so he could move his girlfriend's stuff."

"It shouldn't take us too long," Sarah replied. "Teresa Olson said she would be waiting for us at Rebecca Hatfield's. She offered to help us unload so we can leave for Billings as soon as possible."

Ryder turned the borrowed truck out of the college parking lot and onto a main street as Sarah took one long look at the dormitory. Even though she would be attending classes for one more semester, she would no longer be living on campus. Her life seemed to be always in a state of change.

"How has Rebecca been doing lately?" Ryder queried, unable to imagine what it would be like living with and caring for someone with Alzheimer's.

"Teresa said she has her good days and her bad days but that the bad days are becoming more and more frequent. I just hope I'm up to the challenge."

"I'm sure you will be," Ryder assured her. "You seem to have a real knack for taking care of the sick and disabled. Sometimes I wonder why you don't train for a medical career instead of computers."

Sarah thought a moment. "I've seriously considered it," she replied. "However, I get too emotionally involved with those I try to help. I don't think I'd be able to maintain the professional distance necessary to make objective decisions for patients."

Chapter 9

Jeff Blair rose from the wheelchair, took his walker, and stepped into the cold December air. After more than three weeks of lying in a hospital bed and going through hours of grueling physical therapy, he was now ready to go home. For days, his family had hoped and prayed that Jeff would be able to be home for Christmas; and now their prayers were finally answered when the doctor signed his release form on the twenty-fourth of December. In spite of the hours the family had spent at the hospital sitting by Jeff's bedside, they had found time to put up the Christmas decorations, and gifts were piled high beneath the tree. An aura of praise, anticipation, and thanksgiving filled the house.

Jeff finally had accepted the fact that with intense physical therapy, he would probably be able to walk again on his own but would never have the agility that he once had. However, now he was so excited to be going home that he did not consider his long-range plans. His father helped him into the backseat of the car, then folded his walker and placed it in the trunk. Jeff's little sister, Edith, greeted him excitedly, while their mother smiled proudly at her offspring from the front seat.

As soon as Jeff arrived home, instead of going directly to the refrigerator, which was his custom, he went to the computer in the office. "Gee, it's good to see you again," he chuckled as he patted the monitor.

"You're just as weird as you ever were," Edith teased as she followed her brother into the office, as if not wanting to admit how excited she was to have her older brother home again.

"Pardon me, little sis," Jeff said as he sat down and booted up the computer, "but I have some serious research to do."

"What kind of research is it?" Edith persisted. "You haven't started back to school yet, and your teachers have all given you an extension on your course work. Usually your research consists of the contents of the refrigerator."

"I just want to use the people finder on the Internet. Now, why don't you go play. . .and on your way you might bring me back a can of pop."

"You haven't changed a bit," the thirteen year old retorted lightly as she left the room, ignoring his request for a soft drink.

As soon as his sister was gone, Jeff located a people finder on the

Internet and typed in Mickey Kilmer. Much to his surprise, three different addresses appeared on the screen—one in Albany, Georgia, one in Portland, Maine, and one in Spokane, Washington. He copied the three addresses onto his hard drive, then printed them out. Two of the addresses provided E-mail addresses.

Jeff then wrote the same message to the Mickey Kilmer in Georgia and the one in Maine.

> *Dear Mickey:*
> *I am trying to locate the Mickey Kilmer who was born in Elders Point, Montana, approximately forty years ago. Could you be that person?*
>
> *Jeff Blair*
> *Missoula, Montana*

The entire process took Jeff a little over fifteen minutes. After shutting down the computer, Jeff took his walker and inched his way toward the kitchen. He was thankful to be home and as independent as he was but extremely frustrated that he could not move faster.

Beth Blair was standing in front of the open refrigerator when Jeff entered. "You have that 'I need a can of pop' look on your face," she chuckled as she reached into the refrigerator.

"Thanks, Mom," Jeff replied as he took a chair at the kitchen table. "You always could read my mind."

"That comes with being a mother," she laughed as she gave him a quick hug. "Since it's your first night home, I'll give you a choice for what we'll have. But if I know you, you'll probably select spaghetti."

Jeff's eyes sparkled as he responded to his mother's squeeze. "That's exactly right," he agreed; then his expression became serious. "Who did you say was the attorney who handled my adoption?"

"Stuart Leonard," Beth replied, unable to hide her puzzlement. "He should be getting close to retirement age by now. I don't know if he's still in Rocky Bluff or not."

Jeff took a sip of his soft drink, then set the can on the table beside him. "I think I'll call Dawn Reynolds and see if she knows anything about him. Besides, I want to check to see how Charity is doing. I haven't heard anything for a couple of weeks." Jeff took a worn slip of paper from his wallet and reached for the cordless phone on the wall beside him.

In a few moments, the director of Little Lambs Children's Center was answering the phone with a cheery "Merry Christmas."

"Hello, Dawn, this is Jeff Blair," the young man greeted. "I just wanted to call and wish you a Merry Christmas and to see how Charity is doing. Has she had any more seizures?"

"Charity is doing remarkably well," Dawn assured him. "And there have not been any more seizures. I hope the one she had last Thanksgiving was an isolated event. The only bad thing is that since Sarah went home to Billings a few days ago, she seems so sad. Every so often she'll say, 'When's Mommy coming? When's Mommy coming?'"

"I wish I were there to hold her," Jeff sighed, "but I'm glad she's doing better and that Sarah has a chance to go back to Billings. She's been working much too hard—she needed a vacation." Every time he heard Sarah's name, a corner of his soul seemed to jump for joy.

"How are you doing?" Dawn queried. "I know it's been a long haul for you."

Jeff took a deep breath. He had a reputation of always being jovial and on top of the world, able to mask his inner fears and doubts. However, after three weeks of intense self-examination, he was no longer able to live behind his superficial mask. "They finally let me out of the hospital this afternoon," Jeff explained, "but I'm not getting around too well. I'm afraid I'm going to be in physical therapy for a long while, and I don't have any assurances that I'll ever be able to run again."

"I'm sorry to hear that," Dawn replied in a tone expressing her deep compassion for another's suffering. "I'll be remembering you in my prayers," she assured him. "If there's anything else I can do for you, please feel free to ask."

Jeff hesitated. "Well. . .er. . .there is one thing."

"What's that?" Dawn queried.

"Do you know if there is still an attorney in town by the name of Stuart Leonard?"

"Yes, I see him at church quite often," Dawn replied. "He's semiretired now, and I think he only takes Social Security cases. Why do you ask?"

"Mother says that he was the one who handled my adoption and was able to get my natural father to give up all parental rights so Dan could adopt me. I want to find my natural father so that I can learn more about my medical background."

Dawn hesitated. "Jeff, are you afraid there might be genetic complications that were aggravated by your injury?"

"Oh no, it has nothing to do with my own health," he replied hastily. "I just want to make sure that I'm not carrying any gene that would lead to serious birth defects or mental illness. How do I know that Charity's spina bifida wasn't caused by a gene I was carrying?"

"Jeff, no one knows the exact cause of spina bifida, so right now all we can do is accept the fact it happened and help Charity live life to its fullest potential," Dawn insisted.

"But what if I'm carrying a bad gene? I shouldn't have any more children," Jeff persisted. "In fact, I really shouldn't even consider marriage. And if I can't consider marriage, I shouldn't show much interest in girls because they might mistake my kindness for something more serious; then they will only be hurt."

Jeff's words tumbled out one on top of another, while Dawn listened patiently. "Is there one girl in particular that you're afraid of hurting?"

Sarah's intense hazel eyes and innocent face flashed before him. He had already caused her enough pain in her life; he could not think of causing any more. "Dawn, to be honest with you, I'm beginning to see Sarah in a totally different light. She's no longer that silly teenager working in a pizza parlor in Billings, but she is one of the most intelligent, compassionate women I've ever met. I don't want to even consider a serious relationship with her until I know for sure that I'm not carrying a bad gene."

Dawn hesitated, as she again searched for the right words of comfort. "Jeff, no child enters this world without God's planning. As sad as it is to see little Charity's deformities, you have already seen all the joy she has brought to so many people's lives. You cannot live a life of fear and deny yourself love because of what might, or might not, happen. Life can't exist on 'what-ifs' but on faith and trust in God."

Jeff paused. He knew Dawn was right; he was letting his fear get the better of him. However, before he could respond, Dawn continued, "Jeff, whenever I'm feeling discouraged, I always go back to the Bible in Proverbs 3:5–6. 'Trust in the Lord with all thine heart; and lean not unto thine own understanding. In all thy ways acknowledge Him, and He shall direct thy paths.'"

"Dawn, to tell you the truth, I have done a lot of soul-searching while I was lying in the hospital. Things that used to seem so important no longer seem important at all, and the things I've always taken for granted are now extremely precious to me. I've always loved my family, but now I realize how lacking my love toward them has been," Jeff confessed.

Dawn's thoughts turned back to the time she struggled through her own period of soul-searching. She remembered her early years of college when she became more interested in partying and having a good time than she was in studying. Her social drinking had led to problem drinking, then to marijuana use, and finally to experimentation with cocaine. After being arrested at a party, along with several of her college friends, Dawn had spent several weeks in the Rimrock Rehabilitation Center in Billings. During that period, she too did a lot of soul-searching, then returned to a right relationship with her family and, most importantly, with her God.

"Jeff, I've been through many struggles similar to what you are going through," Dawn reminded him. "If there's ever anything I can do or if you just need someone to listen, remember that I'm always available. If necessary, call me collect, even if it's in the middle of the night."

Dawn seemed to be the first person who understood the inner struggles he was going through. To him, everyone else listened politely, but their eyes betrayed their lack of understanding. Jeff relaxed as he continued to confide in her. "There is one thing that would help me," he said meekly. "After Christmas would you try to contact Stuart Leonard and ask him if he would be able to contact the Canadian officials and help me locate Mickey Kilmer? Also, would you ask him what his fee would be? I hope I can afford him. Now that I can't stand for long periods of time, I'm going to have to give up my current part-time job and find another."

"I'll be happy to try to contact Stuart," Dawn replied, "but I may have to wait until after the first of the year. A lot of the professionals in town are taking extended vacations over the holidays."

Finally finding someone who he thought understood his plight, Jeff's spirits began to lift. He did not want to have to break off his friendship with Sarah, at least not until he knew the truth of his background. However, relieved that Dawn was going to help with his search, Jeff gained the confidence to call Sarah in Billings to reassure her of their friendship and wish her a Merry Christmas.

❖

At three o'clock on January 2, Doris Brown stopped their family car in front of Rebecca Hatfield's home. "This is it," she said as tears began to build in her eyes. "We had a great vacation together, and it's hard to say good-bye, but you have to get on with your life."

Sarah leaned over and hugged her mother. "Thanks for everything you've done for me. I just hope I can live up to everyone's expectations. I've never been around anyone with Alzheimer's before."

"I'm certain you'll do just fine," her mother assured her. "Just make sure you get enough rest and eat properly. You'll need all the strength you can get."

Sarah gave her mother another hurried hug as she smiled at her familiar admonition to be sure and take care of herself. Sarah then got out of the car, reclaimed her suitcases from the trunk, took a deep breath, and walked up the front sidewalk. Although Teresa Olson had given her a front-door key to Rebecca's home, Sarah felt it wiser not to startle Rebecca by using it and rang the doorbell instead.

A short matronly woman whom Sarah did not know opened the door.

"Hello," she greeted, "may I help you?"

Sarah gulped. Whoever this person was, she didn't know anything about her coming. "Hello," she responded. "I'm Sarah Brown. I'm going to be living with Rebecca for the next few months."

"I'm sorry. I should have recognized you," the woman replied kindly. "Do come in. They told me you were coming late this afternoon, but I wasn't expecting you so soon. My name is Ellen Booth, and I'm only here on weekends."

Ellen helped Sarah carry her suitcases to her bedroom. "Rebecca's been sleeping for over an hour, so I'm expecting her to wake up any time. She's been having a few more problems lately, and the doctor has changed her medication."

"What's been wrong?" Sarah asked as she laid her suitcase on the bed, then followed the home health care worker back to the living room. "Is there anything different I should do for her than what I was told before Christmas?"

Ellen took a seat on the sofa and motioned Sarah to join her. "The only thing I can suggest is to be prepared for more of the unexpected. Her moods seem to be vacillating a lot more from happy and complacent to angry and cantankerous. She does not adapt well to anything out of the routine." Ellen gave a dry smile. "For example, never sit in her recliner. It takes her several hours to calm down from even the simplest disruption in the routine. She likes to put together simple jig-saw puzzles but is easily frustrated when they do not fit. I try to give her a lot of clues as to where each piece might belong."

"Does she remember that I'm going to be staying here?" Sarah queried.

"I've told her several times today that you'd be coming, but I'm not sure she fully understands. I'll stay a little later than normal so she gets used to your presence," Ellen promised. "Teresa Olson said she'd be here in the morning before you have to go to class so Rebecca won't have to be by herself.

"A dietician plans her meals, allowing for certain flexibility. She stops by each week to check on the grocery needs and does the shopping," Ellen explained. "Those records are kept on the inside cupboard door over the dishwasher. An emergency call list is posted beside the telephone."

"Every possible need seems to be mapped out with extreme detail and forethought," Sarah noted, trying not to sound overwhelmed by her new job.

"Rebecca has contributed a lot to this community," Ellen replied, "and this is the least the people of Rocky Bluff could do to show their appreciation. In a lot of communities, she would have been in a nursing home six months ago. Rebecca is terrified to go to a nursing home, so everyone is doing their best to keep her home as long as possible."

"How much longer do they think she'll be able to stay in her own home?" Sarah asked.

Ellen shook her head sadly. "I personally think that if she can make it until June, we'll be extremely fortunate."

Suddenly, they heard shuffling in the hallway. "Rebecca," Ellen called out. "We're in the living room. Would you like to come and join us?"

The older woman entered the living room and took her favorite recliner. A pillow crease still left an indention on her wrinkled cheek. "Who are you?" she asked sharply as she noticed Sarah sitting on the end of the sofa.

"I'm Sarah Brown," she began softly as she smiled and extended her hand. "I'm a student at the community college. I'm going to be staying with you for a few months and helping with some of your chores."

Rebecca took the young girl's hand and smiled. "I like having company, especially at night. Do you like to cook spaghetti? That's my favorite food."

"That's a coincidence," Sarah replied as she took the chair beside Rebecca. "That's my favorite food as well."

"What other foods do you like?" Sarah asked, trying to make small talk with her.

"Spaghetti is the only food I like," Rebecca replied dryly.

"You must eat other foods besides spaghetti," Sarah responded, unsure how to handle her first unclear conversation with Rebecca.

"People try to make me eat other stuff, but I won't do it regardless of what they say. You won't try to make me eat weird stuff, will you?"

Realizing that the first few hours they were together would be critical to their relationship, Sarah tried to think of something they could do together without being confrontational. Remembering one of the details that Ellen had just told her, Sarah said, "I understand that you like to put together jig-saw puzzles. Would you like me to set up the card table so we can work on one together?"

Rebecca's eyes brightened. "I'd love to. I'll show you where the card table is, and I'll get my favorite puzzle. It has a really pretty mountain scene on it."

Ellen finished cleaning the kitchen and stayed in the background, while Sarah began building a relationship with Rebecca. She made a light supper of grilled cheese sandwiches and soup.

When Rebecca looked at her plate, she said, "Where's my spaghetti? I won't eat anything but spaghetti."

Sarah took a deep breath. "Let's close our eyes and pretend the toast is one large piece of spaghetti and the cheese is the sauce."

"That's silly," Rebecca retorted.

"Try it and see if they don't taste the same," Sarah replied as she closed her eyes and took a bite of her toast.

Much to Sarah's surprise, Rebecca copied her actions, then said, "You're right. It does taste like spaghetti."

From that point on, Rebecca ate her meal without complaint, while Sarah and Ellen exchanged knowing glances.

After the three women had eaten and the kitchen was tidied, Ellen turned to Sarah. "It looks like you have a handle on everything now, so I think I'll take this time to slip out. If you have any questions, just call me. My number is over the telephone."

Sarah stood to walk her to the door, while Rebecca followed slowly behind them. "Good-bye, Ellen," Rebecca said. "Thanks for coming. I think I'll ask Sarah to spend the night with me to keep me company."

Ellen and Sarah exchanged knowing looks and smiled. "You're on your own now," Ellen said. "I'm sure you'll do a good job."

"Thanks," Sarah replied. "Just be sure and keep us in your prayers."

Chapter 10

Jeff Blair slid out from behind the wheel of his newly purchased, ten-year-old Ford and leaned against the car as he opened the back door. He removed his walker and breathed a sigh of relief to be able to bear his weight with his arms. He had just completed his first week back in class after his accident and was beginning to understand the reason for the federal law requiring all buildings to be handicap accessible.

Jeff hurried inside his home and went immediately to the office. He had so much schoolwork he needed to do. The mental struggle of starting a new semester while he was finishing projects and exams from the last semester was extremely challenging, but he was determined to make it. He had just become comfortable behind the computer when the phone rang.

"Hello."

"Hello. Is this Jeff?"

"Yes, it is."

"Hi, Jeff, this is Dawn Reynolds," the director of Little Lambs Children's Center replied. "Neither Sarah nor I had heard from you since before Christmas, and we were wondering how you were doing."

"Physically I'm doing better, but I still need the walker for anything more than four steps," he replied. "Mentally I'm bushed. There's so much work to get done, and so little time to do it in. I just hope I get all my course work made up before my extension runs out. I don't want to have to repeat any classes." The tone in Jeff's voice left no doubt as to the academic stress he was under.

"I wanted to bring you up-to-date on Charity's progress," Dawn continued. "She had one mild seizure earlier this week, but after it was over, she was able to sleep it off and had no signs of side effects or physical damage."

Jeff's chin dropped as his forehead wrinkled. "Since she had a second one, will she have to go on seizure medication?" he asked, wishing he could be more involved in the day-to-day care of his child.

"Not at this time," Dawn replied. "Outside of those two bad episodes, Charity is doing remarkably well. We have a little computer at the center where the children can play storybooks on CD-ROM, and they can interact with the story using the mouse. She just loves it and has trouble sharing it with the others."

Jeff smiled at the thought of his daughter's using a computer, and he remembered how at Thanksgiving time Charity would let go of the miniature organ scarcely long enough for the clerk to scan the price. "Like I've said before," he laughed, "we have a budding genius on our hands."

"No doubt in my mind." Dawn laughed, then lowered her voice. "I do have some bad news for you," she began. "Stuart Leonard is going to be away in Arizona until the first of April, so I won't be able to see if he can trace Mickey Kilmer. I know how much finding him means to you, but it looks like we're dead-ended for a few months."

Jeff's eyes lowered as his mind wandered. "I still have a couple more things I could do," he finally murmured. "According to the people finder on the Internet, there is a Mickey Kilmer living in Spokane, but it only gives a post office box for an address. I called directory assistance for a telephone number and was told that his number was unpublished. My next step would be to go to Spokane and try to find him, but I won't be able to do that until I'm a little more steady on my twos."

Fortunately, Jeff couldn't see Dawn shaking her head on the other end of the telephone line. "That might be like finding a needle in a haystack. Spokane is a pretty large city for that," she reminded him. "What is your other option?"

"I could make a trip to Elders Point and ask around town and see if any of his family or old friends have heard from him recently," Jeff replied. "The problem with that action is that, even though it's still in Montana, Elders Point is nearly six hundred miles away. I won't be able to go there until summer vacation."

"It looks like either way it will be awhile before you'll have an answer to your search." Dawn scolded teasingly as she continued, "I hope you're not intentionally going to withdraw from the female species until you find your natural father."

Jeff laughed, trying to mask his frustrations. "Nothing like that. Believe it or not, I've actually been too busy for any kind of social life. How has Sarah been doing lately?"

For a few moments, Dawn was lost for words. She would like to see the pair eventually marry and provide a stable home for their daughter, but a marriage to the wrong person, or when either one was not ready, would be totally devastating. "Taking care of someone with Alzheimer's has been extremely challenging for her, but she's doing an excellent job. Why don't you call her direct?" Then she gave him Sarah's number.

Jeff hurriedly scribbled the number on a piece of scrap paper lying on the desk. He continued his conversation with Dawn for a few more minutes, then bade her good-bye and hung up the phone. *Maybe I should give Sarah a call. I really do miss her, and it will probably be a long while before I know my full medical background,* he tried to justify to himself. *Surely, a simple phone call couldn't be construed as leading her on. Before I give her a call, I'd better get me a can of pop from the refrigerator; it could be a long conversation.*

Jeff took a chair at the kitchen table where he opened his soft drink. Just as he took his first sip, his mother burst through the front door with more exuberance than he had seen in her in a long time. "Jeff, I have some great news," she exclaimed as she threw her coat over a kitchen chair and took the seat next to him. "I talked to your physical therapist today, and there is a new treatment that might help your injuries. They're not equipped to do it in Missoula yet, but they already have the equipment and training in a hospital in Spokane. She said she could arrange for you to go there within a month, but you'd have to stay there for over a week. If this treatment helps you, then they would have an even stronger argument to help convince the hospital board to purchase it for this hospital. I promised her that I'd talk with you this evening."

"Of course. . .I'll try anything," Jeff replied cheerfully. "However, I won't be able to go until after I've finished my work from last semester. I should be done in another week."

"Why don't you call her and set up a time?" Beth suggested.

Jeff reached for the kitchen phone and dialed the hospital number. After being switched between three different stations in the hospital, he finally was connected to the physical therapy department. The receptionist promptly informed him that the therapist was with a patient, but she would take his name and number and get back to him as soon as she was free. Jeff hung up the phone dejectedly. That meant he had to keep the telephone line open for the therapist's call and would not be able to call Sarah.

❀

"Wait up, Sarah," Ryder Long shouted as he sprinted across campus to catch up with her. "I haven't had a chance to talk with you since you came back from Christmas break."

"Sorry about that," Sarah replied. "I've been super busy keeping up with my class work, taking care of little Charity, and now Rebecca. I didn't realize taking care of someone with Alzheimer's would be so taxing."

"Do you have some time to tell me about it?" Ryder queried as he studied the dark circles under her eyes. "I'd love to buy you a soft drink or cup of coffee in the Commons."

The thought of having a few minutes to relax with a friend was extremely inviting. She was beginning to discover that in the midst of her caregiving to others, she was neglecting to care for her own emotional needs. "Sure, I'd love to," she replied. "I have another hour before I catch the shuttle downtown to see Charity."

The two hurried to the Commons in the next building to get out of the biting wind. Ryder purchased two soft drinks, and the pair found a booth in the far back corner.

Ryder studied Sarah's drawn face. "Is something bothering you? You haven't been the same for several days."

Tears welled up in her eyes. "It's like walking on eggshells when I'm with Rebecca Hatfield," Sarah confessed. "Everything that happens is my fault."

Ryder reached across the table and patted her on the hand. "I know it must be difficult."

"Just last night, Rebecca couldn't find her slippers, and she was certain that I had stolen them," Sarah explained as she wiped a tear from her eye. "I found them an hour later under her bed, but by that time she'd forgotten all about her outrage or even her desire for her slippers."

"It must be extremely hard to be wrongly accused of something and not be able to explain reality so that she can understand it," Ryder said, as he searched for words of comfort. "It must be kind of like when Jesus was falsely accused of all kinds of things, but He said nothing."

Sarah's eyes brightened. "I never thought of it in that manner. . .but what I feel is only like a grain of sand compared to what Christ must have felt."

"I certainly understand why you feel like you're walking on eggshells," Ryder said, trying to reaffirm his understanding of her internal conflict.

Sarah took a deep breath. "When something happens one time, it brings her great pleasure, and the next time she becomes angry with me and everything around her," she sighed. "I never know how she's going to react. One minute she's smiling and happy, and the next she's shouting and extremely cantankerous. It takes a lot of patience not to react and take her criticism personally. Sometimes I question my own wisdom in how I handle certain situations."

"I'm certain you're doing an excellent job," Ryder tried to assure her. "I'm sure one of the hardest parts of the job is not having the confirmation and assurance from anyone that you have done the right thing."

Sarah's eyes became misty again. "You said exactly what I've been feeling, except I've been unable to put my feelings into words. I appreciate your listening to my frustrations. I don't seem to have time to talk with anyone lately."

Ryder reached over and took the young woman's hand. "With the heavy burden you are carrying, you need someone objective to confide in on a regular basis. How about meeting here at the same time every day after class and just unloading on me for a few minutes? It would probably do you a world of good."

Sarah smiled. "I usually have a half hour between my last class and when

I catch the shuttle. It would be nice having someone my own age to talk with for awhile. I'm either listening to lectures, talking kid talk with Charity, or trying to keep Rebecca connected with the day-to-day world the rest of the time."

As the days passed, Sarah found herself more and more looking forward to the short meetings with Ryder. Those few minutes together helped her gain a different perspective on the complexities of her life. But a faint gnawing seemed to be always with her as well. She was beginning to miss Jeff's sense of humor.

❖

Knowing there was a chance for a different type of therapy, one that might possibly improve his condition, Jeff increased his hours of study even more. As soon as he completed all his work from the previous semester, he would be able to go to Spokane for a few days for treatment. Perhaps while he was there, he might find some leads as to the Mickey Kilmer who lived in that city.

The day before Jeff's therapy was to begin, Dan Blair drove his son to the Spokane Medical Center. During the two-and-a-half-hour drive between Missoula and Spokane, Jeff and Dan had the most intense father-son talk they had ever had.

"I hope you're not offended by my trying to find my biological father," Jeff began, after they had left the outskirts of the city.

"Of course not," Dan replied as he glanced at his handsome son beside him. "It's very natural for a child to want to know as much about his past as possible. Finding your biological father will never erase the years of enjoyment we have had together."

A smile spread across Jeff's face. "Thanks, Dad," he replied. "You'll never know how much I've grown to love and respect you."

"The feeling is totally mutual," Dan replied. "In some ways I kind of feel sorry for Mickey Kilmer. He could have had those parenting joys himself, but he chose to walk away from one of the greatest experiences of life—that of being a father."

After sharing several special father-son memories, the pair fell into a relaxed silence. Jeff tried to think of ways he might be able to locate Mickey Kilmer. *If he owned property, would I be able to find information at the county courthouse? Would I be able to get his address from a car registration? Would I be able to get an address from a credit report?* The more Jeff tried to think of ways to locate Mickey, the more concerned he became that some of his ideas were in violation of a person's right to privacy and he might never find his natural father.

Dan and Jeff checked into the motel across the street from the hospital, then went to dinner in a nearby restaurant. As soon as Jeff completed his series of therapy sessions, Dan planned to return to Spokane and drive Jeff home. Dan wished he could stay with his son longer, but the winter months were his busiest season at the Missoula Crisis Center, and he felt he had no other option.

By the second day of his therapy, Jeff was becoming extremely discouraged. His muscles did not seem to do what was expected of them, and some of the movements were extremely painful. Just when he was beginning to question the wisdom of taking time from his college studies, a voice echoed over the speaker system, "Paging Mickey Kilmer. . . Would Mickey Kilmer please report to the conference room?"

Jeff turned to his therapist. "Janet, does a Mickey Kilmer work for this hospital?"

"I think he's one of the maintenance men," the therapist replied. "Do you know him?"

Jeff nodded as his mind began to race. "I'm not sure. I've been trying to locate a Mickey Kilmer who used to live in Montana, but it could just be a coincidence. I found two others over the Internet, but neither one was the one I was trying to find. Is there some way I could meet this Mickey?"

Janet thought a moment, then went to her desk and dialed a number. "Hello, Adam. This is Janet up in Physical Therapy. I have a patient here who would like to meet Mickey Kilmer. Do you think you could arrange it?"

"I don't see a problem with that," the head of maintenance replied. "Mickey gets off work at three o'clock and has to stop here to check out. I'll ask him to wait until your patient gets here."

"Thanks. I appreciate your help," Janet replied, hung up the phone, and relayed the message to Jeff.

With the hope of finally meeting the Mickey Kilmer of Spokane, Jeff was able to ignore his pain while his muscles became energized. *Will this be the end of my search, or will I be disappointed once again?* he wondered. *My biological father working in this hospital is just too much of a coincidence.*

Ten minutes before three o'clock, Jeff entered the maintenance area of the hospital. He spoke to the head of the department, who pointed him in the direction of the lounge and assured him that he'd have Mickey stop before he went home. Jeff took a chair at a table where he could see everyone who came and left. He closely examined every man who could possibly be in his forties. No one seemed to match the physical description that his mother had given him.

Five minutes passed. . .then ten. . .fifteen, then twenty. Just when Jeff was getting ready to leave, a dark-haired man with graying temples approached him. "Hello, my name is Mickey Kilmer," he said as he extended his calloused hand. "I understand you were waiting to meet me."

Jeff stood and took the stranger's hand. He was amazed at how much he physically resembled the older man. "I was trying to locate the Mickey Kilmer who used to live in Elders Point, Montana, more than twenty years ago. Could you possibly be he?"

The man's face reddened, and the veins protruded from his neck. "What do you want him for?" he snapped.

Jeff gulped. "When he was a teenager, he dated Beth Slater, and she later had a child."

"So what business is that of yours?" Mickey retorted.

"I am that child," Jeff replied meekly. "I'm in need of my medical history and was hoping to find some answers."

Mickey's hardened face twitched. "Sit down," he ordered. "I'll give you my basic medical history, and that is all. I don't want anyone digging into my personal past. In fact, I'll contact my doctor and have him mail you the entire file. Would that be enough to make you happy?" he added sarcastically.

In spite of Mickey's gruffness, Jeff beamed. "I'd appreciate that very much. There is a young woman I'm interested in marrying and having a family with, but I'm afraid to make any commitment until I'm certain I'm not the carrier of any genetic disorders."

At his words, Jeff studied the inner turmoil that reflected in his father's eyes. He wondered what he must have felt like having to sign over all rights to his son to another man. As hard as it was for him to make child support payments while he was in high school, Jeff was grateful that he had continued to maintain contact with his daughter. Charity had brought so much joy and meaning into his life during the past three years.

Finally, Mickey broke the silence. "As far as I know, I'm genetically normal. I've just done some stupid things in my life." He again hesitated, as if trying to make sense of what was happening to him. Then Mickey softened, and his shoulders relaxed. "Jeff, do you remember going to Canada when you were four years old?"

"That was one of my earliest memories," Jeff replied, trying to recall the scene. "I loved that black sports car. I was so excited to get a chance to ride in it, but I didn't understand why I couldn't go back to my momma when it started to get dark."

"Taking you that day was one of the dumbest things I've ever done," Mickey confessed. "You could never understand what it's like to father a child and want to be a part of his life on the one hand and yet, at the same time, not want to assume the full responsibility of being a parent."

The wall between father and son was beginning to crumble, as Jeff understood the reason for the rejection by his biological father. "I identify with the situation more than you can imagine," Jeff replied. "During my senior year in high school, I, too, fathered a child. Sadly, our little Charity was born with severe spina bifida and hydrocephalus. I accepted paternity and have paid child support ever since. However, now that I'm finding myself falling in love with Charity's mother, I'm afraid to marry her for fear I was the cause of Charity's birth defects and any other children I might have would be affected."

Mickey put his hand on Jeff's shoulder. "You were much more of a man than I ever was under similar circumstances," he said. "I want to ask you just one question—would you still marry this girl if it could be proven that the birth defects without a shadow of a doubt came from the mother's side?"

Without hesitating, Jeff replied, "Of course I would. We would seek medical advice and trust God to direct our path as to family planning, adoption, or remaining childless. Aside from Charity, I mean."

"I think you answered your own question," Mickey replied wisely. "Go ahead and date that girl. She'll be a mighty lucky woman to get you. In the meantime, I'll mail you my medical records." Mickey's eyes became distant. "Maybe we should get better acquainted. I think we have a lot to learn from each other."

Chapter 11

S arah, why do you keep stealing my things?" Rebecca screamed. "I don't like living with a thief. I want you to leave immediately."

Sarah gulped. "Rebecca what are you looking for?" she asked calmly.

"I'm looking for my red afghan. It's my favorite one, and it's not on my bed. You should go to jail for this," Rebecca retorted as she reached to grab Sarah's arm.

Sarah tried to remain calm, as her heart raced wildly. "I just finished washing the afghan. It's in the dryer now," she explained as she hurried to the basement, hoping the dryer had finished its cycle. She threw open the door, snatched the red afghan, and rushed upstairs.

"My afghan. My afghan," Rebecca cried as she clutched it to her bosom. "I knew I would find it."

Sarah shrugged her shoulders. After two months of following a rigid routine of caring for Rebecca while watching her slow yet steady decline, Sarah was able to find strength and encouragement from her faith in God and from her fellow Christians. As the external circumstances became more and more glum, Sarah's inner spirit grew vibrant. Even the people close to her began to notice the difference.

One morning on her way to class, a familiar voice called out to her; Sarah turned and found herself face-to-face with Vanessa. "Sarah, how's it going? I haven't seen you in a long time," her former roommate exclaimed as she gave Sarah a quick hug.

"I've been keeping busy helping Rebecca, so I don't get out very often," Sarah replied as she studied the deep circles under Vanessa's eyes. "How are things going with you?"

Vanessa shook her head as they trudged toward Briar Hall. "I wish I could say 'great,' but that would be the farthest from the truth. . . . I don't want to bore you with the gloomy details."

"Of course I want to know the details," Sarah retorted. "I'm just sorry we haven't had so much time to spend together as when we shared the same dormitory room."

"Things have been pretty bad lately," Vanessa sighed, unable to hide her dejection.

Sarah was accustomed to Vanessa's mood swings, but this time it appeared more serious. "We've got to get together and talk, just like we used to," Sarah insisted. "Rebecca is generally in bed by eight-thirty. Why don't you come over then, and I'll make popcorn for the two of us?"

Vanessa beamed. "I'd like that," she replied. "You're one of the few people whom I feel comfortable talking with. We've been through a lot of rough times together."

With that, the two women bade each other good-bye and hurried to their separate classes. While waiting for her instructor to arrive, Sarah thought about the conversation that she just had. *Vanessa has often poured out her troubles to me,* she thought, *but I usually didn't pay much attention. At the time, it all seemed so trivial. Vanessa usually didn't take life too seriously, but this morning she appeared almost panicky. I wonder what's going on.*

After class, Sarah met Ryder in the Commons for their usual half hour of relaxation. "You never would have believed what happened last night with Rebecca," Sarah said softly.

"I'm almost afraid to ask," Ryder said cautiously.

"She screamed at me about stealing her red afghan and ordered me to leave. When I brought it up from the dryer, she said she knew all along that she would find it."

Ryder couldn't help but smile with sympathy for Sarah's frustrations. "I don't know how long you're going to be able care for Rebecca. It sounds like she's soon going to need more specialized care."

"I just take one day at a time," Sarah said before turning the conversation to her former roommate. "Ryder," she began as she admired his dark eyes and shining black hair. "Have you seen Vanessa much this semester?"

"Not really," he replied as he set his coffee cup into its saucer. "But I have heard that she was pretty upset when her boyfriend broke up with her. I have one class with her, and from what I can tell, she's starting to let her grades drop. She's also talking about going to the University of Iowa next year, but if she lets her GPA fall, she won't be able to transfer her credits. Why do you ask?"

"I've been so wrapped up in my own problems that I haven't kept in close contact with her," Sarah explained. "However, I ran into her between classes, and she sounded as if she was sinking into deep depression. I hadn't heard about her last breakup, but she's going to come over to Rebecca's tonight so we can talk."

Ryder wrinkled his forehead. "Good luck," he replied. "Those kinds of discussions can get pretty heavy at times."

"I know," Sarah sighed. "I'll need your prayer support."

"You can be assured of that," Ryder replied.

❀

That evening, while Sarah helped prepare Rebecca for bed, her mind kept drifting back to the days when she lived in the dormitory. She had been extremely careful not to let anyone know her secret of having a disabled child at Little Lambs, and yet there had been such a change that came about in her life after she turned to God for help and opened up to those around her. In retrospect, she felt she had missed many opportunities to share the love and forgiveness of Jesus Christ that were available to all who believed. She was determined that if she had such an opportunity this evening with Vanessa she would not let it pass by again.

Promptly at eight-thirty, Vanessa rang the doorbell at Rebecca Hatfield's home. Sarah immediately answered the door and led her to the living room. Vanessa flopped onto the sofa. "Sarah, I don't know how you do it!" she exclaimed. "You've had ten times more problems in your life, and yet you always seem so in control and at peace. How do you do it? My life is falling apart; my boyfriend, Doug, left me for one of the cheerleaders, and I have nothing left to look forward to."

The moment Sarah had been praying for was upon her. She was now able to share the faith and peace she had found in Jesus Christ. The two young women talked until eleven. Never before had they shared their innermost thoughts and fears. Not only did Vanessa tell of her broken romance but also of the emptiness and lack of purpose she felt. She admitted that she'd been hiding this void under a mask of parties and good times, but when her boyfriend left her, all the parties seemed pointless, and there was nothing there to sustain her.

Sarah shared the source of her strength through her many trials and tribulations of life. She told about her pregnancy, being disowned by her mother, and, in the process, coming to know a love that never failed. She talked openly and freely about her relationship with Jesus. The more Vanessa heard, the more convinced she became that she wanted to learn more about the Savior who had helped Sarah through the difficult periods in her life.

"Vanessa, I don't know how I could possibly get through a hectic week without attending church and hearing Pastor Olson proclaim the gospel of Jesus Christ," Sarah stated firmly. "I'd like to share that source of strength with you. Would you like to come this Sunday?"

Much to Sarah's surprise, Vanessa replied, "I'd love to go, but I don't like to go someplace like that by myself."

"I wish I could go with you," Sarah smiled. "But I'm so busy getting Rebecca ready that I'm afraid I won't be able to help you. Give me until tomorrow, and I'll find someone to give you a ride and introduce you to those around you," she promised confidently.

After nearly two and a half hours of intense conversation and soul-searching, Vanessa yawned. "Thanks for spending your entire evening with me. I feel so exhilarated. . .like I'm on the verge of an entirely new life. I'd better let you get some rest. We both have classes tomorrow."

Sarah rose to escort her friend to the door. "I'm so glad you came over. I'll call you tomorrow evening and finalize our plans for Sunday."

❖

The next day Sarah could scarcely wait for her few moments of relaxation in the Commons with Ryder. As soon as they were seated in their favorite booth, she exclaimed, "Ryder, a very exciting thing happened last night. I was able to talk about spiritual things with Vanessa for the first time ever. She showed a lot of interest in the gospel and wants to attend church Sunday, if she doesn't have to go alone. Do you know anyone who might be willing to take her?"

Ryder smiled and reached for Sarah's hand. "If you wouldn't mind, I could give Vanessa a ride to church and introduce her to some of the others. I'm sure she'll feel right at home."

Sarah giggled. "Why would I mind?" she asked. "I was just getting ready to ask you to take Vanessa."

"Sarah, you mean so much to me that I don't want to do anything that would cause you to be uncomfortable," Ryder explained. "I feel honored that you would consider having me give your old roommate a ride. Try to save us a seat close to you and Rebecca, so we can all be together."

That evening, after Rebecca was in bed and the house was quiet, Sarah contemplated the events of the night before. She was excited about Vanessa's wanting to know more about the Christian faith and wanting to attend church, but even though she tried to convince herself that Ryder's taking Vanessa to church didn't matter, Sarah knew it did. *Why am I letting this bother me so much? she scolded herself. I have no long-term commitment to Ryder. Anyway, he'll be leaving in a few months for the University of Iowa.*

❖

After a week of intense physical therapy, Jeff was able to put away his walker and walk confidently with a cane. The evening before he was to leave Spokane, he agreed to meet Mickey Kilmer for dinner. The young man was ecstatic when Mickey promised to bring copies of as many of his medical records as he could. His search was now over, and he could become more serious with Sarah. It should have given him a sense of fulfillment, but something still seemed to be lacking. As evening approached, he realized that he wanted to continue his relationship with Mickey. More importantly, Jeff wanted to be sure that his biological father knew about the saving power of Jesus Christ.

Having a couple of hours to spare, Jeff stopped at the hospital gift shop and browsed through the books. There in the far back of the rack was a New Testament. Jeff admired its large, easy-to-read print and colorful cover. He held it in his hand while he continued browsing. Two rows lower was the book *How to Accept the Love and Forgiveness of Jesus Christ.*

This'll be perfect, Jeff thought. *I know what I believe, but I often have trouble articulating my faith. These books say it so much better than I ever could.* He took his selections to the cashier and laid a twenty-dollar bill on the counter. The money seemed like such a small sacrifice to help introduce his natural father to the faith that he'd taken for granted all his life.

That evening the dinner conversation between the two men was more relaxed than either thought possible. Mickey openly shared the details of his struggle with drugs, his time in prison, and the months he had spent in rehabilitation as if this was the first time anyone had been concerned enough about him to listen.

"After I got out of prison, I was fortunate to get a job in the maintenance department of the Spokane Medical Clinic," Mickey explained. "It gave me a reason to stay drug and alcohol free these last few years." He then hesitated as a pained expression crossed his face. "In spite of all my determination and victories in overcoming my troubled background, I still feel an emptiness and lack of purpose."

Jeff was hoping for this opening. "Mickey, there's something that can fill that emptiness," he began. "The answer is in these books," he said as he took out the books he had purchased in the hospital gift shop. "These tell about the love and forgiveness in Christ so much better than I ever could. I don't know where I would be today without the strength of Jesus Christ, and I'm certain He'll fill the same need for you."

Mickey looked at him skeptically. "I've tried everything else except religion, and none of them seemed to work, so I might as well give it a try."

"This is more than just religion," Jeff protested, "I'm talking about a personal relationship with Jesus Christ and a belief that He has the power to forgive us our sins and give us eternal life."

Mickey thought for a moment, as if not completely understanding the difference between the two, but not wanting to go any deeper into the subject. Finally, he shrugged his shoulders, "Okay, I'll check it out for a few weeks. I don't have anything to lose."

"You'll never regret it," Jeff replied.

Mickey shrugged his shoulders. "By the way, did you watch this last Super Bowl game? Wasn't that a real barn burner?"

Picking up the cue, Jeff whispered a silent prayer for Mickey's spiritual quest and enjoyed their relaxed conversation for the remainder of the evening. Before they parted, the two men exchanged telephone numbers and addresses and promised to keep in contact.

Jeff's spirits were high when he returned to his motel room. His reason for keeping his distance from Sarah was now gone. He felt free to pursue a deeper relationship with her and see where it led. He took a scrap of paper from his wallet and dialed the number scribbled on it. He waited a few moments as he listened to the phone ring on the other end. Just when he was ready to hang up, a familiar voice entered the line.

"Hello. Rebecca Hatfield's residence. Sarah Brown speaking."

"Hello, Sarah. This is Jeff. It's been a long time since I've talked with you," the young man began. "I've been extremely busy trying to catch up on my schoolwork; then I've spent the last few days in Spokane having physical therapy. I just wanted to let you know how much I've missed you."

"I wondered how you were doing," Sarah replied, sounding surprised by the unexpected telephone call. "I was beginning to wonder if I'd done something to upset you."

Jeff's heart sank. He hadn't meant to hurt her. "Of course you didn't upset me. I would have let you know if you had. I'm the kind who'd rather talk things out than hold grudges," he assured her. "There was a reason for my preoccupation that I'd like to explain to you."

Sarah wrinkled her forehead. "You don't have to explain," she replied. "We both have busy lives right now and a lot to accomplish in a short amount of time."

"Sarah, it's more than that," Jeff persisted. "I won't be able to come to Rocky Bluff until spring break at the end of March, but I just want you to know how much I'm looking forward to seeing you then."

Sarah smiled. "I'm looking forward to seeing you too. Charity has often asked about you. She still talks about the time we took her to the mall over Thanksgiving."

"Memories of that day in the mall were what kept me going through those painful hours in the hospital," Jeff replied. "How is she doing? I imagine she's grown a lot since then."

Sarah shook her head. "Physically, she's not growing as much as we'd like, and she's well below normal for her age, but intellectually she seems to be well above average."

When the two finished discussing their daughter, the conversation changed to some of the frustrations involved in caring for someone with Alzheimer's. While Ryder was extremely intense and analytical about the problems that surrounded her, Sarah found Jeff's sense of humor and optimistic approach a welcome relief to the tension she bore.

After nearly an hour on the phone, Sarah reminded him, "We're running a pretty big phone bill, and I haven't heard Rebecca for some while. I'd better check to make sure she is okay."

"It's been great talking with you," Jeff replied. "From now on I promise to call at least every three days and to e-mail you every day."

Sarah's spirits soared as she returned the phone to its cradle. Their relationship was now lifted to an even higher pitch.

❂

On Sunday morning Sarah helped Rebecca to her customary pew on the front left side of the church. Before the organist began, Vanessa slipped into the pew beside Sarah followed closely by Ryder. They all nodded in greeting just as the organist began the prelude. During the service, Sarah kept watching Vanessa from the corner of her eye. At times, she thought she saw tears glistening in the corners of her eyes, and other times, when Pastor Olson talked about the love of God, Vanessa seemed to beam. There was no doubt in Sarah's mind that her former roommate was being touched by the entire worship experience.

Following the service, members and guests gathered for a time of fellowship in the multipurpose room next to the sanctuary. While Sarah helped Rebecca with her refreshments and found a comfortable seat in the corner so that they could enjoy watching the crowd, Ryder took Vanessa by the arm and introduced her to many in the assembly.

Sarah watched the happiness that radiated from Vanessa. She was not certain if it was the afterglow of a moving sermon, the warmth of the congregation. . .or. . .could it possibly be the attention she was receiving from Ryder.

"Hello, Stranger," Teresa Olson, the pastor's wife, greeted as she took the chair next to Sarah. "I haven't talked with you in some time. How has it been going?"

"Really well, thank you," Sarah answered mechanically, but her eyes divulged the frustrations she was trying to mask.

"I have something I'd like to discuss with you in private. Would you mind joining me in the kitchen?" Teresa asked as she stood and motioned Sarah to follow. "Mrs. Fargo will be here to keep an eye on Rebecca for you."

Sarah and Teresa made themselves comfortable on a couple of stools in the far corner of the kitchen, away from the women who were serving the refreshments. "Now tell me the truth," Teresa stated firmly. "I realize that Rebecca is becoming more and more temperamental and unpredictable; is it beginning to bother you?"

Sarah gulped as tears built in her eyes. "How did you know? Is it that obvious?"

Teresa put her arms around Sarah. "I'm afraid so. Those dark bags under your eyes speak volumes."

"But. . .but. . .I don't want people to think I can't do my job," Sarah protested. "I really love Rebecca. Usually she's sweet to be around, but more and more, she's getting angry at little things and saying extremely demeaning things to me. I know she can't control everything she does, but that doesn't take away the sting."

"Sarah, you have a good understanding of what's going on, but unfortunately there will come a day when Rebecca will no longer be able to stay in her own home," Teresa reminded her. "Maybe that day is quickly approaching."

"But if I lose my job, I won't be able to stay in school," Sarah blurted as her world seemed to come crashing in around her.

Teresa squeezed her hand. "Don't worry; we're not going to put you out in the street. Since there's a waiting list to get into the local care center, it would probably be wise if we put Rebecca's name on the waiting list now, so she'll be sure to have a place to go when her problems become too complex to be handled at home."

"I don't know what to say," Sarah responded as she took a tissue from her purse and dried her eyes.

"You don't have to say anything right now," Teresa tried to comfort her. "I just want you to remember you're not alone. The women that stay with her in the daytime face the same frustrations you do. If Rebecca ends up going to the care center before the semester is over, you can stay in the guest room in the parsonage for a few weeks."

"Thanks. I appreciate your understanding," Sarah replied, then glanced at her watch, "but now I suppose I'd better get Rebecca home so I can fix lunch for her. If she gets off schedule, she can become extremely confused."

That afternoon, while Rebecca was taking her afternoon nap, Sarah took out her computer applications textbook and began studying. There rarely seemed to be a break to lighten the intensity of her cycle—study. . . work. . .and visit her daughter. After she had read only five pages, the telephone rang.

"Hello, Rebecca Hatfield's residence," she greeted.

"Hello, Sarah," Jeff replied. "I was just sitting here getting bored with my studies and wondering what you were doing."

Sarah giggled. "I'm doing the same thing—just sitting here getting bored with my studies."

"I wish I were there to help enjoy your boredom," Jeff replied, "but I'll have to wait three more weeks. How has little Charity been?"

"She's doing great," Sarah replied, "but she's definitely developing an extremely strong will. Yesterday, she had to spend ten minutes in "time out" for scratching one of the other children for playing with the same ball she wanted to play with."

"I guess it's all part of learning to get along with others," Jeff replied with a chuckle.

For the next fifteen minutes, the pair discussed the antics of their daughter as if they were a normal married couple, instead of two college students trying to make the best of the consequences of the sins of their youth.

When they finally ended their conversation and Sarah hung up the phone, a feeling of hope and optimism overtook her. After her talk with Teresa and hearing Jeff's concern for Charity, Sarah began considering the possibilities of what might happen to herself when Rebecca went to the nursing home. Life might have been difficult at times, but there always seemed to be someone who stepped in to help her carry her burdens.

Chapter 12

Sarah hurried to the booth she and Ryder usually shared in the Commons after class each day. She was anxious to learn of Vanessa's reaction to the church service and hoped that she would be interested in attending on a regular basis. Had Ryder been able to help her understand the basis of faith in Jesus Christ? When Sarah arrived, she found Ryder already in the booth with a soft drink waiting for her.

"Hi," he greeted jovially. "What took you so long?"

Sarah glanced at her watch and smiled. She was actually five minutes earlier than normal. "I just can't run as fast as I used to," she retorted as she slipped into the booth across from her classmate. "I could hardly wait to see you. Vanessa looked as if she was extremely moved during the worship service. What did she say afterwards?"

"I took her out to lunch, and we had a very interesting conversation," Ryder explained, unable to hide his excitement. "To make a long story short, she ended up saying that she did believe in Jesus Christ as her Savior and was interested in learning more. I told her about the class for new believers, and she seemed eager to attend it."

"I'm not surprised," Sarah replied. "Even when Vanessa appeared to be only interested in superficial things, underneath there was a sensitive longing waiting to be tapped. I'm sure she'll take on her spiritual quest with the same intensity she does the rest of life."

Ryder studied the deep creases on Sarah's forehead. "How have things been going with Rebecca?" he queried.

Sarah shook her head. "Each day is worse than the day before. Some days I'm beginning to question my own sanity. After listening to Rebecca talk, I require a good reality check."

"I know it's tough," Ryder replied, "but it will all be over in a few weeks."

"That's the only thing that keeps me going," Sarah sighed, then took a deep breath as if to refresh her entire being.

The pair continued sharing news of their church, their class work, activities at Little Lambs; however, Ryder appeared more distracted than normal. Finally, he reached across the table and took Sarah's hand. "You have so many pressures on you at this time that I've hesitated to add to them," he began, "but

I have some good news and some bad news to tell you."

Sarah set her can of soda on the table and leaned forward. "Give the good news first. I need some cheering up."

"I got a part-time job as an assistant in the pediatrics ward at the hospital," he explained. "They heard about my work at Little Lambs and approached me about providing entertainment for the sick children a couple of hours every afternoon. It sounds like it would be a lot of fun and would also be good experience for me."

Sarah smiled and reached across the table and took his hand. "Congratulations. When do you begin?"

"That's the bad news. I start tomorrow, and we won't be able to meet anymore after classes," Ryder replied. "I've enjoyed our times together, and I'm going to miss our regular, heart-to-heart talks. They've been the highlight of my day."

"I will too," Sarah admitted, trying to hide her disappointment. "I don't know how I could have survived the last few weeks if it hadn't been for these few minutes we've had together each day."

"Don't worry. I'm not abandoning you," Ryder assured her as he squeezed her hand. "I'll try to call you every night and see how your day went. It's not as good as face-to-face, but it beats trying to go it alone like you did when you first moved in with Rebecca."

"I'd appreciate that," she replied, realizing that with Jeff's calling long distance every other evening, there could potentially be a time conflict. She was grateful that Rebecca had call-waiting on her telephone.

As the two finished their drinks, Ryder glanced at his watch. "We'd better get moving if you're going to get to Little Lambs by three o'clock. There's no shuttle today, but I'll run and get my car and pick you up at the south entryway."

"Thanks," Sarah replied. "I forgot all about the schedule change. You always seem to be available when I need help."

❧

When Sarah arrived at Little Lambs, Charity was just waking from her nap. She hugged her daughter close to her bosom, then carried her into the playroom. This time Charity was anxious to play on the floor with a little boy about her own age, giving Sarah a chance to talk with Dawn. For the last several days, Charity had monopolized all of Sarah's time while she was at Little Lambs so she had little time for even minor discussions with anyone else.

"How has Rebecca been lately?" Dawn queried. "When I saw her in church Sunday, she didn't look well."

Sarah shook her head. "She's due for a physical next week, but her temperament is becoming extremely difficult to deal with. She's doing more and more shouting and is starting to take swings at me when she doesn't get her way."

"That sounds serious," Dawn replied as the furrow in her forehead deepened. "Have you told anyone yet about this behavior?"

Sarah took a deep breath. Although she knew Rebecca's change of behavior was caused by the natural progression of the disease, somehow she was afraid that people would think that she couldn't do her job properly. After all, she had learned to care for extremely disabled children; why couldn't she also care for mentally disabled elderly people? "I talked to Teresa after church Sunday, and she thought they needed to get Rebecca's name on the waiting list of the care center," she explained cautiously. "However, what I'm concerned about is that she'll have to go to the nursing home before I'm finished with college, and I won't have a job, nor a place to stay."

"I don't think you'll have to worry about that," Dawn assured her. "We have a small room in the back that is being used for storage right now. If push comes to shove, we can clean that out for you, and you can earn your room and board by taking care of the children several hours each day. We've found ourselves short of staff in the evenings when we're trying to get the children to bed."

Sarah relaxed. She now had two offers for housing. "That seems like an ideal backup plan," she replied. "That will give me more time to learn to care for disabled children, and at the same time, I can send out résumés and begin looking for a full-time job."

Just then, a unified cry erupted from the floor as Charity and her playmate each tried to claim possession of the same toy bear at the same time. Sarah grabbed Raggedy Ann and offered it to Charity who immediately claimed it and forgot about the stuffed toy they were fussing over. The rest of the time with Charity flew by, and before she realized it, the time had come to hug her daughter good-bye and go care for Rebecca. Each time she found it harder and harder to leave her daughter, but if she was to accomplish her final goal, she had to make the sacrifice.

❖

Jeff Blair clenched the steering wheel as his car made the hairpin turns over Rodger's Pass. It had been more than four months since his fateful accident, but as he approached the site, it became more and more difficult for him not to turn around in terror and return to Missoula. His hands were sweating, and his breathing increased. He prayed for strength to overcome his fears and focused his mind on little Charity and Sarah. He realized that if he did not overcome his anxiety of driving mountain passes he would always be separated from the woman he was growing to love.

Once he had passed the exact location of the accident, a sense of relief overwhelmed him. He breathed a big sigh and smiled at himself in the rearview mirror. He had faced one of the biggest fears in his life and, with God's help, had overcome it. Jeff now felt the courage to take on any other challenge that might present itself.

Upon arriving in Rocky Bluff, Jeff went directly to Little Lambs and rang the doorbell. "Jeff, it's good to see you again," Dawn greeted as she motioned him to enter. "How have you been doing?"

Jeff entered the hallway and laid his cane against the wall while he removed his coat. "It was a long, difficult trip," he admitted, "but I finally made it."

Dawn studied the young man's face. He looked as if he'd aged five years since she had last seen him in the hospital in Great Falls after Charity's seizure at the end of November. "Charity is still sleeping," she began. "Why don't you come into the family lounge with me? We have a lot of catching up to do."

Jeff hung his coat on the rack, took a spot on the end of the sofa, and laid the cane beside him. After sitting in the same position for nearly four hours during the drive, the muscles in his back and legs were beginning to throb, but he tried to keep his face from reflecting his pain. "How has Charity been?" he asked as Dawn took a seat in the chair beside him.

"She's been doing remarkably well," Dawn assured him. "You'll be surprised by how much she's grown since the last time you saw her."

"Sarah mentioned over the phone that she's had more seizures since the bad one in November. How serious have they been?" Jeff queried.

Dawn smiled as she tried to choose the right words to explain Charity's condition. "Of course, no seizure is good for the body, but from what we can tell, they have all been minor, and there have not been any lasting effects. So far, the doctor hasn't prescribed any seizure medication."

"That takes a load off my mind," Jeff sighed. "Seizures can be really scary for me."

Dawn eyed the cane beside the young man. "How have you been doing?" she asked with concern. "Have you been mending well from the accident?"

Jeff thought back through the months of agony and physical therapy. At times, he wasn't sure if he'd ever walk again, but his strong determination had carried him over the difficult spots. "I'm getting along fairly well," he replied. "I'm not ready to run the Boston Marathon, by any means, but I've come a long way. I've had to accept the fact that my football career is over, and I'm changing my major from physical education to business administration."

"I'm sure you'll have a good future in whatever you choose to do," Dawn assured him. "Are you still having a lot of trouble getting around?"

"Sometimes," Jeff admitted, knowing there was no way he could hide the depth of his problem from the trained nurse. "When it's icy out, or if I'm extremely tired, I still need the walker. However, I feel very self-conscious when I have the walker. Everyone assumes that walkers are for old people, and they seem shocked seeing a former jock shuffling along with one."

"I'm sure, if there are stares, they're in sympathy and not shock," Dawn replied, then felt it wiser to change the subject. "I'm sorry I haven't been able to get ahold of Stuart Leonard yet to help you locate your birth father."

Before Jeff could respond, the doorbell rang, and Dawn hurried to answer it. Upon hearing Sarah's voice, Jeff picked up his cane and ambled to the hallway to greet her. Oblivious to the director standing in the corner, they gave each other a fond embrace and a short kiss.

Sarah was shocked to see how much weight Jeff had lost, but she tried her best to mask it. "How was your trip?" she asked as Jeff took her hand and led her to the sofa in the lounge, while Dawn quietly slipped away to the playroom so the two could be alone.

Jeff shook his head. "It was extremely long and tiresome," he replied. "If I didn't know that you and Charity were on the other side of the mountain, I don't think I could have made it."

"Flattery will get you everywhere," Sarah giggled. "I have to admit that it's good seeing you again. It seems like it was a lifetime ago since we last saw each other."

"To me, it seems like ten lifetimes," Jeff replied just as a familiar cry came from the children's bedroom.

Sarah hurried to get her daughter, while Jeff shuffled slowly behind, bearing part of his weight on his cane. By the time Jeff had gotten to the bedroom door, Sarah was already returning with her daughter in her arms. Charity's eyes brightened. "Daddy," she squealed as she reached out for her father to take her.

Suddenly, the truth of his injuries bore down on him. He would not be able to carry his daughter and walk with his cane at the same time. Sensing what was going through Jeff's head, Sarah said, "Charity, let's go to the playroom; then Daddy will hold you."

When Jeff was seated comfortably in one of the rocking chairs, Sarah placed their daughter on his lap. He tried not to grimace with pain as she wiggled against his tender muscles. "Hi, Daddy," she said as she held tightly to his hand. "I missed you."

"I missed you too, Muffin," he replied. "You've gotten so big and so pretty since I last saw you."

"Play on the floor, play on the floor," she pled as a pained expression crossed Jeff's face.

Sarah quickly said, "Daddy hurts too much to get on the floor. I'll get you your favorite storybook, and Daddy can read to you."

After Jeff finished reading the story to his daughter, Sarah put her in her wheelchair and slid the tray into place. With Charity in her chair, Jeff was able to help her color and play with her toys on the tray. When they tired of the toys, Jeff tried to teach her to sing "Jesus Loves Me."

Charity quickly learned the words and tune to the song. When Jeff sang, "Little Ones to Him belong; they are weak, but He is strong," his eyes met Sarah's. "After playing super jock for so many years, after my accident I once again learned what it felt like to be weak and know that Jesus is the only one who is strong."

Time passed swiftly as the three tried to accept Jeff's new limitations and discover ways to modify the simple routines they were accustomed to. At a quarter to five, Sarah reluctantly said, "I hate to leave, but I have to fix dinner for Rebecca."

"It's nearly time for the children to begin getting ready for dinner," Jeff noted. "I still need to get a motel room for the evening so I'd better be going as well. Would you mind if I came over to Rebecca's later this evening to see you?"

Sarah smiled as she took their child from Jeff's lap, hugged her, then placed her on the mat in the center of the room where Dawn was playing with two other children. The pair walked slowly to the lounge to get their coats. "I'd love to have you come this evening," Sarah said. "Rebecca is usually in bed by eight-thirty. I could fix us some treats, and we can catch up on the last few months. So much has happened since we've last been together."

❁

As Sarah went about her nightly routine of feeding Rebecca and preparing her for bed, her mind drifted back to the short time she had with Jeff that afternoon. Even though most of their attention was centered on Charity, there were times that personal glances intensified her need to find answers to unasked questions. Jeff had obviously changed. Even though his sense of humor was still intact, there was a seriousness about him that she had not seen before. She could hardly wait for him to arrive later that evening.

❁

Likewise, Jeff could hardly wait to spend time alone with Sarah. He drove to the Round Rock Motel and checked in, then crossed the street to the Green House Family Restaurant. He noticed something different about Sarah. She appeared tired and worn, yet, at the same time, excited to see him. In just a few hours, he would be able to share some of the innermost thoughts with her that had been building for the last four months.

Promptly at eight-thirty, Jeff rang the doorbell to Rebecca Hatfield's home. He waited for what seemed an eternity before Sarah appeared. "I'm sorry it took so long," she greeted as she motioned Jeff to enter. "I was busy making a special dessert for you, and my hands were all messy."

Jeff leaned over and gave her a quick kiss. "You shouldn't have gone to any extra trouble. Just having time to be alone together is enough to make me happy."

In spite of Jeff's mild protests to Sarah's extra work, he thoroughly enjoyed the apple crisp and whipped cream she set before him. As they exchanged the details of the difficulties they each had faced during the last few months, the bond between them intensified. After they finished their first cup of coffee, Jeff took Sarah's hand. "I'm sorry I stayed so aloof for several months, but I had a lot of things going on in my mind that I had to work out before I felt I could pursue our relationship."

Sarah wrinkled her forehead in anticipation of what he had to say. She felt certain that, whatever the reason for his distance, she could easily forgive him.

"Sarah," he began softly, "as I lay in the hospital, staring at the blank ceiling hour after hour, all I could think about was you. I knew that what we did years ago was wrong, and I wondered if I might have been the cause of Charity's birth defects. Perhaps I carried some defective genes. I didn't want to become close to anybody until I knew my medical history."

"Did you ever find your natural father?" Sarah asked, as she thought about her own father whom she had seen only twice since she was three. A few years ago, she learned of his death from AIDS.

"I met him in Spokane while I was there for therapy," Jeff began. "He gave me full access to his medical records, and there was nothing remarkable about them, just normal illnesses. Since I now know that I'm not carrying some sort of bad gene, I feel free to pursue a normal male/female relationship and enter the dating arena. However, you're the only one whom I've ever held a deep fondness for."

Sarah held Jeff's hand and gazed into his soft green eyes. "I can understand why you might worry about carrying a bad gene since you didn't know your natural father, but don't you realize that I've lain awake nights worrying about the same thing? That I was the reason for Charity's problems."

Jeff had never before questioned Sarah about her father. He had always assumed it was something that was too painful for her to discuss and did not want to intrude into her private thoughts, until now. "What happened to your father? Do you know anything about his medical history?"

Sarah took a deep breath. "My parents divorced when I was small, and I never really knew my father. Mother never spoke kindly of him and was not sure of his medical background, so when Charity was born with a birth defect I often wondered if I was carrying a bad gene. Dawn tried to convince me that no one knows what causes spina bifida, but doctors are suspicious that it's the lack of folic acid in the mother's body. Either way, I felt that I was either carrying a bad gene or something was lacking in my body to cause the defect, so I vowed I would never marry. I did not want another child to suffer the things Charity has suffered."

"But God has a purpose for Charity," Jeff persisted. "She was not a horrible accident." Jeff paused. The two sat in silence for several minutes before he continued, "We both suffered needlessly by blaming ourselves for Charity's birth defects. If we would have trusted God's wisdom and accepted the path He set before us, we could have spared ourselves so much heartache. . . . Sarah, you mean so much to me. I hope our lives will grow in the same direction so that someday we might become one."

Chapter 13

Sarah Brown perused the bulletin board outside the college placement service office. It had been a long, uphill struggle, but she was now within two months of graduation. She had already accepted the fact that there were few jobs in her field in Rocky Bluff and that she'd have to consider some of the bigger cities of Montana. She thought about returning to Billings, so her mother could help her with Charity. However, if she had little Charity with her in Billings, Jeff would not be able to be an active part of her life. Suddenly, a poster caught her eye.

JOB FAIR
All Careers
Memorial Union Building
University of Montana Campus
Missoula, Montana
May 5th
9:00 A.M. – 3:00 P.M.

I sure would like to go to that, Sarah pondered. *I've always liked Missoula, and it's growing so fast that I'm sure there are plenty of job opportunities. If I raise Charity in Missoula, she'll at least have a chance to know her father. But it's not likely that I'd be able to get enough money for the bus and a motel room. Even if I did get a job there, I wouldn't have the money to move there and support myself until I got my first paycheck.*

In spite of her doubts, Sarah jotted the date of the job fair on a scrap of paper in her notebook and hurried on to class. All during the period, while the instructor droned on and occasionally paused to ask the students questions, Sarah could not keep her mind off the possibility of getting a job in Missoula. She tried to convince herself that her interest in Missoula was strictly for Charity's benefit, but deep inside, she knew that she too would like to be close to Jeff Blair.

While Sarah was walking across campus to the bus stop, Ryder's familiar voice shouted, "Hey, Sarah. Wait up."

Sarah turned and waited for Ryder Long to catch up with her. It had been nearly two months since their daily meetings in the Commons had stopped when he took the part-time job at the hospital. They had shared greetings before and after classes, and he did call occasionally in the evenings, but not every night as he'd promised. And she had noticed that he had been bringing Vanessa to church nearly every Sunday. It seemed as if their lives were taking them in different directions.

"Hi, Ryder," she greeted as he caught up with her. "How have you been doing?"

"I've been awfully busy," he replied as they continued walking toward the bus stop. "I've been putting in a lot more hours at the hospital, and I'm trying to get all As this semester."

"As shouldn't be too hard for you to get," Sarah teased.

"Ha! If you only knew how hard I have to work to get them," he joked back, then became serious. "It's paying off though. I just got word that I was accepted into the University of Iowa for next fall. I'm really excited about going," he paused and took a deep breath before continuing. "Vanessa White was also accepted there. I don't know if you've heard or not, but we have started going steady, and things seem to be developing very quickly between the two of us."

Even though Sarah had been extremely fond of Ryder, she'd never felt anything more than friendship for him. He had been there to give her strength and encouragement during some extremely difficult times. They had shared a lot of laughs and good times, but he had always treated her more like a sister than a girlfriend. Yet, her heart dropped a little to have her suspicions confirmed. She thought she saw sparks between Ryder and Vanessa while they were in church. Little things, like how their eyes met or holding hands under the hymnal, betrayed that theirs was not just a casual relationship.

"I'm so happy for you," Sarah said, trying to act pleased. "You make a handsome couple and have a lot in common. I wish you the best."

"Thanks, and I hope things work out for you," Ryder replied. "You've been a true friend and a model student."

Just then, the shuttle to downtown arrived, and Sarah said good-bye as she stepped on board. Strange emotions enveloped her as the familiar houses flew past the window. *Surely I'm not jealous*, she scolded herself. *Maybe I'll always have a soft spot in my heart for Ryder, because outside of Jeff, he's the only guy who has ever paid any attention to me.*

Charity was already up from her afternoon nap when Sarah arrived. As soon as she saw her mother enter the playroom, she immediately rolled her wheelchair across the room to meet her. "Hi, Mommy," she squealed.

"Hi, Sweetheart," her mother replied. "What are you doing?"

"We're playing with clay," the little girl announced. "See. . .I made a snake."

"That's a nice snake," Sarah replied. "Can you make some baby snakes to go with it?"

"Sure," Charity replied as she turned her interest back to the clay on the tray of her wheelchair.

Just then, Ryan and Dawn entered the room, each carrying a child. "Hi, Sarah. It's good to see you again," Ryan greeted as he and Dawn each took a rocking chair. "How have you been doing?"

Sarah sank into a chair beside Dawn. "I'm needing to start my job search, but I don't know what to do. There aren't many jobs in my field here in Rocky Bluff, yet it's so complicated trying to apply for jobs in other towns."

"I know how that is," Ryan agreed. "I've been there myself. It's tough, but it can be done."

"There's a job fair in Missoula May fifth," Sarah explained. "I'd really like to go, but I don't have money for a bus ticket or a motel room."

Dawn and Ryan exchanged glances as if they were both thinking the same thing. "We have a medical seminar in Missoula the fourth and fifth. We could give you a ride," Dawn suggested. "I think several of the church campus ministries have guest rooms for student use. I could check around and see if one is available that weekend."

Sarah beamed. "Really? I can hardly believe it could be that easy."

"Don't worry," Dawn replied. "Applying for jobs and attending job fairs is hard work. It can almost be a full-time job in and of itself."

❖

Jeff Blair tapped on the door of his college advisor's office. It was two days before preregistration for fall semester, and Jeff had finally accepted the fact that he was not going to be able to major in physical education. His minor was in business administration, so now was the time to make an official change.

"Come in," the gray-haired professor shouted. "It's open."

Jeff timidly opened the door, his cane in hand. "Good day, Sir."

"Have a seat young man," Dr. Westcott commanded. "What can I do to help?"

"I think I need to change my major," Jeff began cautiously. "I don't think I'll ever be as physically fit as I was before my car accident."

Dr. Westcott's expression softened. "I'm sorry to hear that," he replied, "but if you have to make a change, it's better to do it before you take any more credits that won't count toward graduation."

"That's what I figured," Jeff sighed. "That's why I need help in changing my major before I preregister for fall classes."

Dr. Wescott reached for the current college catalog, then into the file beside his desk for Jeff's grade sheets. "What were you considering majoring in?" he asked.

"I was considering business administration," Jeff replied, "since that had been my minor, and I already have had a couple of introductory classes."

"Sounds like a wise decision," Dr. Wescott replied. "Many students start out majoring in physical education, then change to majors not based on physical ability that will diminish in a few short years." The professor then spent the next fifteen minutes explaining which classes Jeff would need to complete a business major.

The more Dr. Wescott explained, the more excited Jeff became. "I've always liked math," he responded. "I should have picked this as a major early on, instead of wasting my time with physical education."

"A lot of students have to try several different majors before they find one that suits them," the professor encouraged. "In fact, it's best to get as much training in a given field before you get close to graduation. Just yesterday, I had a local realtor contact me about arranging for a paid intern program. Would you be interested in checking into it?"

Jeff beamed. "That would be perfect," he exclaimed. "Since I can't stand on my feet for a long period of time, I've had to give up my job at the Pizza Parlor. I was going to have to look for another job anyway."

Dr. Westcott picked up the phone, and within minutes, he had arranged for Jeff to interview with the Big Sky Realtors the following day. Jeff thanked his advisor for his help and left his office, the happiest he'd been since he'd found his natural father and learned that he wasn't a carrier of genetic defects.

❀

On May fifth, dressed in a conservative plaid suit with a pale blue blouse, Sarah walked nervously into the Memorial Union Building at the University of Montana, carrying a folder filled with professional résumés. The room was full of rows and rows of booths with banners hanging over them, naming their particular business. Sarah walked slowly through the crowd of eager students, trying to locate those companies that were interested in hiring computer technicians.

After she had located ten such businesses at the fair, Sarah approached a young woman behind a table. "Hello," she greeted as she extended her right hand. "My name is Sarah Brown. I'll be receiving an associate's degree in computer technology from Rocky Bluff Community College. I'm seeking a computer technician position."

"You came to the right place," the businesswoman smiled, seeming genuinely interested in Sarah's background. Do you have copy of your résumé with you?"

Sarah handed the résumé to the woman who glanced over it, then motioned her to have a chair. After a brief conversation, the older woman gave

Sarah a copy of the job description and her business card and promised to be in touch.

At first, Sarah was encouraged, but as she listened to the conversations around her, she began to wonder how many others received the same treatment. Trying to mask her feeling of desperation, Sarah talked with every business that was looking for a computer technician. When she exhaustedly left the campus at the end of the afternoon, she mused, *I did the best I could in trying to obtain a job; now I've got to relax and let God direct my path. He knows just the right place for me.*

Sarah walked slowly across the street to the restaurant where Jeff had agreed to meet her after the job fair. He was sitting in the window watching, when he saw her approach. He limped out the door toward her. "Hi, Sarah. Did you have any luck?" he greeted as he put his arm around her and guided her into the restaurant.

"I hope so," she sighed. "I gave it my best shot. Several businesses seemed interested, but I won't know for several weeks. A few said they wanted to check my references, then get back to me."

"That's a good sign," Jeff exclaimed as he led the way to a corner booth. "Just think, in a couple of months, you could be working in Missoula, and we could see each other nearly every day."

"I hope so," Sarah replied as the waitress brought them their menus.

After they placed their order, Jeff took Sarah's hand, "I have more good news," he said. "I've changed my major to business administration and have just accepted a position as a paid intern at Big Sky Realtors. In spite of my physical problems, I can now get back on track with a good career possibility."

Sarah's spirits soared as she thought of having Jeff close by to talk and laugh with every day. He was the one person who always seemed to understand the joys and frustrations that she felt, regardless of what was happening in his own life. She prayed that her desire for a job in Missoula, where she could be closer to the man she was growing to love, would not be in vain.

❖

The next day on her return trip to Rocky Bluff with Ryan and Dawn, Sarah was anxious to share her response and hopes from the job fair and Jeff's good fortune in finding a job. "I want to get excited about the possibilities before me," Sarah explained, "but there are still so many loose ends that would have to work out in order for me to get a job and move to Missoula. I don't know where I could get the money to move and live on until I get my first paycheck."

"Don't give up hope," Ryan reminded her. "If you get a job, I'll go with you to the credit union and co-sign a short-term loan for you. You have a lot of friends in Rocky Bluff who are anxious to help you. You'll be surprised who'll come to your assistance."

Sarah's eyes widened. "I've never had a loan before," she exclaimed, then relaxed and giggled. "I guess that will be my first step into the adult world."

"It happens to the best of us," Dawn teased before she became serious. "The important thing is to make your payments on time and establish a good credit rating."

"That's what worries me," Sarah replied. "I saw how hard my mother had to work to pay the rent, buy the food, and get all the bills paid each week. Now that I'm faced with the same challenges, I have a better appreciation for all she's done for me."

The day after Sarah returned to Rocky Bluff, she had trouble focusing on her classes. She was now within three weeks of graduation, and it was becoming harder and harder to concentrate on her studies. During class time, she often caught herself staring out the window, imagining herself with little Charity in her own apartment in Missoula. She began to wonder how difficult it would be to find adequate day care for a disabled child, but she tried not to dwell on that obstacle until she had total custody of her daughter.

When Sarah returned to Rebecca's home that evening, Teresa Olson greeted her, while Rebecca sat on the sofa, crying softly. "Come join us," Teresa called as Sarah unlocked the front door and hung her coat in the hall closet. "We have something to discuss with you."

A puzzled look covered Sarah's face, while she took a seat on the sofa beside Rebecca. "What's happening?"

"I just received word that there is an opening at the care center, and Rebecca can move in tomorrow," Teresa explained. "Rebecca is just getting used to the idea of having to leave her home. After dinner tonight, I was going to help her decide what she'd like to take with her."

Sarah faced the news with mixed emotions. Since Rebecca's personality was beginning to change and she was now taking swings at caregivers who did not do what she wanted them to do, Sarah knew the care center was the only solution. Yet, Rebecca loved her home. It seemed her last link to her former life, and it was now being taken away from her.

Sarah fixed dinner for Teresa and Rebecca, while Teresa tried explaining some of the activities and services of the care center. One minute Rebecca seemed accepting of the idea, and the next minute she would say, "That's nice, but I'm not going."

During dinner, Teresa tried to keep the conversation on the happy times in Rebecca's life: the years she was high school librarian in Rocky Bluff, the time she spent as librarian on Guam, and the years she was married to Andy Hatfield. Rebecca smiled with delight as she recalled those happy days. Yet the closer the stories got to the present, the less Rebecca was able to relate to the situation.

After they had finished eating, Sarah began clearing the table, while Teresa accompanied Rebecca into her bedroom and began going through Rebecca's things. Teresa helped Rebecca fill two suitcases, then helped her select her favorite pictures to take with her. At times Rebecca did not appear to understand why she was putting her favorite things in a suitcase, but Teresa tried to help her use her best judgment in the selections.

When the two suitcases and a cardboard box were full, Teresa helped Rebecca prepare for bed.

It was the last night she would be sleeping in her own home.

❀

Sarah was wiping the counter when Teresa returned to the kitchen and took two coffee mugs from the cupboard. "Sarah, can I get a cup of coffee for you?"

"Sure," Sarah replied, trying to mask her unsettledness. "I was just finishing up."

Teresa filled both mugs, set them on the kitchen table, and motioned Sarah to take the chair beside her. "I'm certain you have a lot of questions about what is happening to Rebecca and how it will affect you."

Sarah grimaced. "You're right; I do," she replied cautiously. "I'm within three weeks of graduation. I'll not only need a place to stay, but I'll need cash to pay my living expenses. Dawn has offered me assistance if Rebecca went to a nursing home, but we haven't discussed it in detail yet."

"While you were in class today, I had a long discussion with Dawn and Ryan as to how best to help you make a transition into the workday world," Teresa explained. "Rebecca's house will have to be put on the market, and it may take several weeks before it is sold. In the meantime, we thought it would be better if you kept on living here, both for security and to keep up the appearance of the house."

"Thank you," Sarah replied. "I really appreciate everything people are doing to help me. I don't know what I'd have done without that help."

"The important thing is that when you are on your feet, you turn around and help others in need," Teresa reminded her. She then took another sip of her coffee. "In the meantime, Sarah, Dawn agreed to pay you for four hours of work each day for at least a month. Do you think you could keep up with your schoolwork and work that much?"

Sarah's eyes became misty. "Like I said when I took this job caring for Rebecca, I'll do whatever is necessary to be able to finish college, get a job, and obtain full custody of my daughter."

Chapter 14

Sarah hung her coat in the closet of Rebecca's home, laid her books on the end table, and collapsed onto the sofa. It seemed strange returning to an empty house. Spending five hours a day on campus, then another four hours working at the Little Lambs Children's Center was exhausting but worth the effort. It had been two weeks since Rebecca had moved to the care center, and Sarah had just ten days until her graduation. Her mother and younger brother were going to drive from Billings for the ceremony, and Jeff was planning to come from Missoula. From that point on, the future was a misty fog. However, tonight she was too tired to worry about anything.

Just then, the telephone rang. Sarah mustered all the lagging energy she could and went to the kitchen and picked up the phone. "Hello," she greeted as she sank into a kitchen chair.

"Hello. Is Sarah Brown available, please?"

"This is she," Sarah replied, wondering who would be calling using such a businesslike tone.

"This is Eric Johnson from Quality Computers in Missoula. I met you at the job fair a couple of weeks ago and have since checked your references. If you're still available, I would like to offer you the position of computer technician at Quality Computers. Would you be interested?"

Sarah gasped. She remembered having talked with him but felt she had little chance of getting the position. She had noticed a long line of applicants approach their booth since Quality Computers was one of the largest computer stores in Missoula and offered the best salary package. "Yes. . .sure," she stammered.

"When will you be able to start?" Eric asked. "I realize that you'll need some time to relocate."

Sarah's heart raced. She'd waited for this moment for three years. But now that it was here, she was unsure of what to say. "I graduate a week from Saturday," she began hesitatingly. "I could start any time after that."

"You'll need some time to apartment hunt and get settled," the store manager noted. "Would you be able to start work on Monday, June fifth?"

"Sure," Sarah readily agreed. "What time would you like me there?"

"We open at nine o'clock. If you would come to my office then, we could begin filling out the paperwork," Eric said. "In the meantime, if there's anything we can do to help you relocate, please let us know."

A few minutes before, Sarah had felt totally exhausted, but now her adrenalin was pumping, and she could scarcely control her excitement. "Thank you, thank you very much," she exclaimed. "I'll be there bright and early on the fifth of June."

As soon as she hung up, Sarah immediately dialed Jeff's home. Jeff seemed to be even more excited about Sarah's job offer than she was. "Not only did you get hired by the best computer store in Missoula," he exclaimed, "but Quality Computers is only two blocks from Big Sky Realtors where I'll be working."

"I can hardly believe it," Sarah replied. "I only have a couple of weeks to get things worked out. I don't know where to begin."

"God will direct you, the same way as He's done so many times before," Jeff tried to comfort her. "I'll start looking around for an apartment for you that'll be close to your work. The first of June is a good time to apartment hunt, since a lot of college students will be moving out and heading home for the summer."

"Thanks," Sarah replied. "Tomorrow when I'm in the computer lab, I'll go to the *Missoulian*'s web site and check their classified section for rentals as well.

"Someday I'd like to have my own house," Sarah continued, "but now I'd be happy with a simple one-bedroom furnished apartment."

Jeff smiled as he gazed out the windows to the distant mountains. "Someday I'd like to have a large house on acreage with horses. However, it would have to be on a main road and close enough to a city so that I could commute to work every day."

The young couple continued talking for almost an hour, both shared their hopes and dreams for their future. After knowing each other for nearly four years, their lives were now headed in the same direction. When Sarah finally hung up the telephone, she realized that it was much too late to call Dawn and Ryan and tell them the good news. With an early morning class, she wondered if she would be able to contain her excitement until she could talk with them when she went to work late in the afternoon.

Sarah could scarcely sleep that night as her mind continued to race in anticipation of her good fortune. She was up early, walked the three blocks to the bus stop, and arrived on campus as soon as the computer lab opened. She immediately went to the *Missoulian*'s web page and printed out a list of ten possible apartments. She then went to an online street atlas and located them on the Missoula city map. Three of them were within walking distance to Quality Computers. All of this was done before she went to her first class.

Sarah eagerly told her entire political science class about her exciting job offer. "Congratulations," Ryder said as the others nodded in agreement. "I knew you could do it."

As soon as classes were over, Sarah hurried to the bus stop. The warm spring breeze invigorated her. As she waited, she began to do her mental calculations. From the prices she saw in the Missoula newspaper, she got the general idea of the amount she'd need for a deposit and first month's rent on an apartment. She estimated the amount of money she'd need for groceries and incidentals until she received her first paycheck. She remembered making a personal budget as an assignment in her Life Skills class in high school, but now she was doing it for real. She smiled to herself—she liked being a grownup.

Fortunately, Ryan was at Little Lambs when Sarah arrived, and she could share her good news with him and Dawn at the same time. When Sarah had finished, Ryan said, "You have a fairly realistic idea about the amount of money you'll need for your move. We're not real busy now so I can take you to the credit union and see if we can set you up with a short-term loan."

"Thanks. I won't let you down," Sarah promised as she reached for her coat. "I'll make sure I make my payments on time every month."

After returning to the Children's Center, Sarah could scarcely keep her mind on what needed to be done. She kept imagining what it would be like having Charity with her all the time. While all the children were playing, Dawn suggested, "Why don't you use the phone in the lounge and call your mother. I know she'll be anxious to hear your good news."

It didn't take much encouragement for Sarah to hurry and dial the familiar number. Knowing this was her day off work, Sarah waited impatiently until her mother answered. "Hello, Mom," she nearly shouted as soon as she heard her mother's voice. "I got a job in Missoula. It's at Quality Computers, and I start June fifth."

"Congratulations," Doris Brown replied, "but please slow down. You're so excited I can scarcely understand you. When are you planning to move?"

"I'm so busy with classes that I won't be able to go over until after graduation," Sarah explained. "Ryan Reynolds co-signed a loan for me so I could have enough money to get an apartment."

"Since Mark and I were planning to come for your graduation, maybe we could leave for Missoula right afterwards and help you go apartment hunting," Doris suggested. "I have several vacation days I haven't used, and we could make this into a nice family vacation. It might be the last one we'll be able to have together."

Sarah was bursting with joy at her mother's obvious pride. How different their relationship had become from what it had been five years earlier. "That sounds like a lot of fun," she exclaimed. "Jeff was planning to come for my graduation. Maybe between the two cars, I can get all my stuff to Missoula, and I won't have to rent a trailer or pickup."

"I'm so proud of you, Sarah," Doris Brown exclaimed. "You've worked extremely hard to get yourself out of a bad situation, and I'm sure you'll be able to handle whatever challenge befalls you."

❀

On June fifth Sarah awoke early in her furnished apartment in Missoula. Jeff had been able to convince a landlord to hold the cute little place until Sarah and her mother were able to come to Missoula to check it out. It was a basic, one-bedroom apartment, perfect for a single, working woman. Sarah planned where she would put Charity's bed, toys, and all her adaptive equipment. She scanned the morning newspaper for a possible day care for her daughter. She noticed one connected with the University that specialized in disabled children. The only problem was, she did not have a car to drive the five miles there.

At eight-thirty, Sarah locked the door to her apartment and walked the four blocks to her new job. On the one hand, she could scarcely contain her excitement, but on the other, a sense of nervousness enveloped her. She questioned if she was up to the challenge.

Upon arriving at Quality Computers, Sarah went directly to Eric Johnson's office. "Welcome to Quality Computers," the manager greeted as he extended his right hand. "We're privileged to have someone with your qualifications join our business."

Sarah blushed as she murmured, "Thank you."

"The first thing we have to do is take care of the boring paperwork," the manager stated. "The bad part is that most of it we can't do on computer but have to use old-fashioned pen and paper."

Sarah filled in forms and read insurance agreements for nearly an hour. When she was finished, Eric led her to the repair room in the back, introduced her to her coworkers, and showed her where the various parts and diagnostic tools were kept. The store manager finally showed Sarah where her workstation would be and already had a computer there for her to repair.

Within a half hour, Sarah had her first computer passing all the diagnostic tests, much to the amazement of the other technicians. For lunch, while the others went to a nearby restaurant, Sarah ate a simple peanut butter sandwich, apple, and chips in the employee lounge. She was so eager to get back to her next assignment that she returned to work twenty minutes early.

Sarah scarcely noticed the time until ten minutes past five when she heard Jeff Blair's voice in the front, asking for her. She immediately cleared her work area and joined him. "Would you like to stop for dinner on the way home?" he asked as he held the front door open for her, his cane in his right hand. "There's a real cute place just down the block."

"I'd enjoy that," Sarah replied. "I am pretty tired."

Throughout their meal, the couple centered their discussion on the air pollution in Missoula and how irritating it can become for those with breathing problems. "I don't understand why Missoula has so much smog compared to other Montana cities," Sarah queried. "Isn't this supposed to be Big Sky Country?"

"We've been plagued with air-quality problems as long as I can remember," Jeff replied. "When the air conditions are right, the smog gets trapped in the valley and isn't able to rise above the bordering mountain peaks. That's why as soon as I can afford it, I want to move out of town, away from the smog."

Through their meal, the couple kept their discussion on local Missoula issues. However, over dessert, their conversation became more personal. Jeff reached across the table and took her hand. "Sarah, we've come through so much together," he began, "and through it all, I've come to realize how much I love you." Jeff paused as he gazed lovingly into her eyes. "I would like to spend the rest of my life with you. Will you marry me?"

Tears welled in Sarah's eyes. She had long hoped that someday she and Jeff would marry, but she wanted to make sure he wanted her because of a mature love and not merely because he was the father of her child. Now she was sure Jeff loved her, in spite of what happened in the past. "Of course, I'll marry you," Sarah cried. "I've loved you for so long, but there always seemed to be a huge mountain separating us."

"You've crossed that mountain, both literally and figuratively," Jeff reminded her. "Now all we need to do is work out the details."

"First of all, we need to have Charity here with us, instead of in Rocky Bluff," Sarah stated firmly. "I'll need to find a good day care for her before I can get her."

"I called the University Day Care today, and there will be an opening for a disabled child the first of July," Jeff said. "They also said they had a special van they use to pick up handicapped children. Would you like to stop by there tomorrow after work and talk with them?"

Sarah beamed. Jeff was acting more and more like a father with each passing day. "Of course," she replied. "What I like best about that particular day care is that it's where students majoring in special education are trained. Charity would have the best experience possible there—excited young teachers, experienced supervisors, and cutting-edge technology to help her be her best."

❁

As soon as Sarah was done with work on the Friday before the long Fourth of July weekend, she hurried home and began packing a small suitcase. Early in the morning, she and Jeff were going to leave for Rocky Bluff to bring Charity back with them. She had just received her first paycheck, paid her rent, and written out a check for her loan to the Rocky Bluff Credit Union.

After dinner, she and Jeff went to the mall to get a few remaining items they needed for their daughter. The young couple strolled through the expensive children's stores.

"Isn't this adorable?" Sarah cooed as she took a pink lace dress from the rack.

Jeff nodded in agreement and instinctively reached for the price tag and laughed. "I think it will be a long time before we'll be able to dress Charity in that."

Sarah shrugged her shoulders and sighed. "The best we can do right now are thrift-store specials, but I've seen some pretty cute things there. It's just fun to dream."

After they wearied of walking the mall, Jeff and Sarah decided to stop at the food court before returning home. While they sipped their soft drinks, Jeff said softly, "I still have an entire year before I graduate. I don't think I can stand to wait until then to get married."

Sarah looked deep into his eyes. "I don't want to wait a year myself. I know money will be tight, but with the salary from your part-time job and my salary, if we live frugally, I'm sure we can make it. Besides, it would be so much better if both of us shared in Charity's care."

Jeff beamed as he squeezed her hand. "Since we both feel the same way, shall we announce our engagement to the world?" he asked.

"I'd like to shout it so the entire world can hear," Sarah exclaimed excitedly. "Since we'll be in Rocky Bluff tomorrow, I'd like Dawn and Ryan to be the first to know."

"I can hardly wait to tell them," Jeff said, then paused as his eyes sparkled. "While we're in Rocky Bluff, why don't we ask Pastor Olson if he'll marry us over my Christmas break?"

Sarah could scarcely believe this was happening to her. Truly, her cup was overflowing with happiness.

As soon as Dawn learned the young couple's plans, she could scarcely contain her excitement. "I know you won't be able to afford a large wedding," Dawn said, "but there'll be many in our church who would like to attend. I'm certain Teresa, Mother, and I can help you arrange an extremely nice wedding on a tight budget."

"But you've already done so much for us," Sarah protested weakly. "I can't expect you to do all that as well."

Dawn gave a teasing smirk. "Surely you won't deny us an opportunity to plan another celebration?" she said.

"If you put it in those terms, we'll just turn our wedding plans over to your willing hands," Sarah laughed. "In the meantime, we'll begin contacting our family and friends."

❖

"Hello, Mickey," Jeff greeted as his birth father answered the telephone. "This is Jeff. I have some exciting news for you."

Mickey could scarcely believe his ears. It had been several weeks since he'd heard from his son, and he was becoming concerned that perhaps Jeff did not want to be a part of his life after all. "Hi, Jeff," he replied. "What's going on?"

"Remember how I told you that the reason I wanted to know my medical background was because I was interested in someday getting married and having a family?" Jeff responded.

"How could I ever forget?" Mickey teased. "Who is the lucky girl?"

Jeff's voice became serious. "Her name is Sarah Brown. She's the mother of my daughter, Charity. Sarah got a job here in Missoula, and last weekend we drove to Rocky Bluff and brought our daughter back with us. We plan to be married over Christmas break."

"Congratulations, Jeff. I'm extremely proud of you. . .not only for what you've done but whom you introduced me to."

Jeff was perplexed. He knew that while he was in Spokane he hadn't introduced Mickey to anyone, not even his father, Dan Blair. "Whom did I introduce you to?"

"You gave me a Bible and introduced me to Jesus Christ," Mickey explained. "I didn't realize it at the time, but that was the very thing I'd been looking for my entire life."

"I. . .I. . .I don't know what to say," Jeff stammered. "I'm so happy for you. I can hardly wait to tell my mom and dad. They'll be delighted."

Mickey became silent. He thought of all the wild, wicked things he had done in his life. His years in jail did not remove his guilt, but the Good News brought to him by his own son whom he'd given up for adoption had provided him with a peace he'd never known before. "I have a lot of restitution to make for all my misdeeds, especially for those I've harmed. Do you think your mother would be willing to see me so that I can ask her forgiveness for all the pain I caused in her life?"

"I'm certain my parents will grant you their forgiveness," Jeff replied. "Would you like to come to Missoula?"

"I'd like that very much," Mickey replied. "I'll have to check my work schedule, but I think I might be able to come the Labor Day weekend. Do you think that would be a good time?"

"Of course, I'll have to check with my parents, but I don't think they have anything planned. I'll call you back this weekend and let you know."

Mickey hesitated, then asked weakly, "If I do come, would it be possible to meet my granddaughter?"

Chapter 15

On December 28, Sarah stood in a side room in the back of the Rocky Bluff Community Church, listening to the prelude music for her wedding. So much had happened since she had stood in the same room more than three and a half years before, waiting for Dawn Harkness to walk down the aisle to become Dawn Reynolds.

Charity was sitting in her wheelchair, dressed in a fancy new pink dress, holding a basket of rose petals in her lap. Dawn, who was the matron of honor, was busy straightening her husband's tie. In just a few minutes, Ryan would escort Sarah down the aisle where she was to become the bride of Jeff Blair.

Jeff's parents, Beth and Dan Blair, had just been ushered into the sanctuary, followed closely by his younger sister, Edith. Although the church had been completely remodeled, this church was the same one the Blairs had been married in many years before. At that moment, all of Sarah's life seemed to come together in a sense of fulfillment and joy.

Sarah's mother was beaming as she sat on the front row. Her tall, sixteen-year-old son, Mark, was beside her. During Mark's many visits to Rocky Bluff Community College, he had decided that he too would like to attend RBCC as well. Sarah had been the first person in their family to go to college, but as he watched what his sister had accomplished, he figured "if she can do it, so can I."

In the far back of the church, a distinguished-looking man sat by himself, smiling with joy. This was the first time Mickey Kilmer had been back in Rocky Bluff since he had kidnapped his son, Jeffey, away from the boy's unwed mother. If any person had made a dramatic change in his life, it was Mickey. Since becoming a Christian, Mickey had asked forgiveness from Beth and Dan for the heartache he had caused them. He was now sitting in the same church at the same time as the police officers and attorneys who worked the case against him. All were there as redeemed sinners celebrating the marriage and miracles in the lives of Sarah Brown, Jeff Blair, and little Charity.

Sarah spotted Jay and Angie Harkness sitting near the front of the church with their three children and her mother, Mitzi Quinata. As her college instructor and advisor, Jay had helped her over many difficult periods of discouragement and frustration. He was obviously aglow with the satisfaction of seeing another student of his make a success of her life.

Nancy Harkness, Jay and Dawn's mother, had just completed the final details for the gala reception that was to follow. Even though her steps were beginning to slow, Nancy was the first one that people in Rocky Bluff called upon whenever there was a social event that needed expert planning. Sarah had always admired the many talents of the matriarch of the community.

Ryder Long and Vanessa White were sitting in the middle of the church holding hands. A bright diamond ring adorned Vanessa's hand. Both had returned from the University of Iowa to spend Christmas with their families. Neither one wanted to miss the wedding of their college friend and dreamed of the day they too would be saying their vows at the altar.

Teresa Olson had brought Rebecca Hatfield from the nursing home. Rebecca was dressed in a new dress and smiled sweetly to everyone, but her eyes were blank with confusion. However, when she saw Sarah walk down the aisle, a flicker of connection entered her eyes. Somewhere, under the worn-out body and mind, the spirit of Rebecca Hatfield was as strong and loving as ever.

Sarah's eyes blended into Jeff's as she walked down the aisle on Ryan Reynolds's arm. Whether they had had a child out of wedlock or not, Sarah was certain their love was so strong that they still would be marrying each other. As they spoke their wedding vows, Sarah and Jeff's eyes did not leave each other's until they closed them in prayer. Truly, this marriage was founded on the love and forgiveness of Jesus Christ.

When Pastor Olson raised his hand to give the traditional wedding blessing, he added something personal for the unique situation.

"Rocky Bluff is not only a place; it is a state of mind," he reminded them. "Rocky Bluff is not only a town in Montana, but it can be anyplace where people still share the love of Jesus Christ with those around them. The ideals of Rocky Bluff are based on a loving community, and I pray that we all might take them with us wherever our individual paths may lead. Let us all be assured that those who know and believe in Jesus Christ will someday be together again in a place far better than our mountain home of Rocky Bluff, Montana."

A Letter to Our Readers

Dear Readers:

In order that we might better contribute to your reading enjoyment, we would appreciate you taking a few minutes to respond to the following questions. When completed, please return to the following: Fiction Editor, Barbour Publishing, Inc., P.O. Box 719, Uhrichsville, OH 44683.

1. Did you enjoy reading *Montana Skies?*
   - ❑ Very much. I would like to see more books like this.
   - ❑ Moderately—I would have enjoyed it more if _____

   _____

   _____

2. What influenced your decision to purchase this book?
   (Check those that apply.)
   - ❑ Cover
   - ❑ Back cover copy
   - ❑ Title
   - ❑ Price
   - ❑ Friends
   - ❑ Publicity
   - ❑ Other

3. Which story was your favorite?
   - ❑ *Healing Love*
   - ❑ *Love Remembered*
   - ❑ *Compassionate Love*
   - ❑ *Love Abounds*

4. Please check your age range:
   - ❑ Under 18
   - ❑ 18–24
   - ❑ 25–34
   - ❑ 35–45
   - ❑ 46–55
   - ❑ Over 55

5. How many hours per week do you read? _____

Name _____

Occupation _____

Address _____

City _____ State _____ Zip _____

If you enjoyed

MONTANA SKIES

then read:

Wisconsin Blessings

Three Romances Renew One Family's Faith
by Becky Melby and Cathy Wienke

Beauty for Ashes

Garments of Praise

Far Above Rubies
